THE PLANET OF MORTAL WORSHIP

To Duane

Best Wishes

&

God Bless!

[signature]

Matthew 5. 7

want

Best of wishes

God Bless.

Matthew 5:

THE PLANET OF MORTAL WORSHIP

DONALD I. TEMPLEMAN

iUniverse, Inc.
New York Lincoln Shanghai

THE PLANET OF MORTAL WORSHIP

iUniverse, Inc.

For information address:
iUniverse, Inc.
2021 Pine Lake Road, Suite 100
Lincoln, NE 68512
www.iuniverse.com

ISBN: 0-595-32512-2 (pbk)
ISBN: 0-595-66617-5 (cloth)

Printed in the United States of America

For Aunt Johnnie who taught me to read.
To Pamela Jean for cookies under the door.
And for Willow Virginia Templeman who lovingly provided everything else!

"I will seek that which was lost, and bring again that which was driven away, and will bind up that which was broken, and will strengthen that which was sick: but I will destroy the fat and the strong; I will feed them with judgment."

—Ezekiel 34:16

Contents

▼

POST PORTENT

I.

It was another comfortable summer evening. The window shutters sat open, beckoning the gentle caress of the night's cool winds whose serenity rustled the leaves of the trees in the north yard. Occasionally, the voices of a young family taking an evening stroll along the outer paths would murmur in the distance. And Goss, the neighbor's pet, could be heard fussing and chasing pesky critters into the brush along the base of the front porch.

It was peaceful. It was quiet. It was home.

Yet Crilen had never felt so anxiously displaced as he sat amidst the familiar clutter of his private study.

His notes and graphs were spread across his desk in the same disarray they had always been. The red pen was uncapped. The blue and yellow pens were capped. Pages one, three and seven were clipped together. Pages five and six were emphatically crossed out. Pages two, four and eight through fifteen were dog-eared for further scrutiny. And page sixteen sat under his hand with a half sentence, uncompleted. The elemental variance matrices on pyrogenic combustion were rated in order of their probabilities. He remembered performing and recording each and every calibration himself. But still, there loomed an inexplicable and disquieting sense of temporal distance between him and his work.

He glanced at his half-empty juice glass, and then touched it with the tip of his finger. The condensation broke and streamed down its sides, bleeding a wet ring onto a scribbled note. The message, now smeared, was not in his own handwriting. In fact, it was another cryptic hypothesis from his former partner, Dr. Quinson, clipped to a letter of resignation from the project. Crilen's expression grew wry as he read:

Dr. Crilen:

I have valued our professional relationship over the past two years and yield to your preeminent expertise in the field of PYROGENICS. However I now feel that your progression into the experimentation with living sub-jects has reached a stage at which I can no longer include myself as a will-ing participant. The acceleration of your advances has been impressive and ambitious. But my personal convictions, as you know, seriously ques-tion whether our accomplishments have circumvented our wisdom and prudence with respect to the consequential scope and impact of our work. I must, therefore, resign from the PYROGENIC Project, effective immediately. This, in no way, is meant to reflect upon you or your profes-sional standing as a bio-genetic explorer. This is more a matter of personal choice for myself, my career, and my family. I wish you all the best and I hope that we can remain friends and colleagues.

Sincerely,

Dr. Limpton Quinson ZPZU

"So paranoid," Crilen reflected. "His caution will save his tenure. But no one will ever remember any of his work. A life's work should stand for more than a pile of published articles and an engraved retirement plate on your shingle."

His eyes drifted, lured away by the movements of the motion picture loop of him and Aami frolicking in the Cape Beach surf on their third wedding anniversary. It still remained inadequately preserved in its five-by-seven cardboard frame. A crumpled grey note he had scratched out over a year ago, to have the photo enlarged and properly mounted, remained folded next to it. He just hadn't found the time in all these…"Months?" he hesitated.

Months?

He was beset by a cold draft of unsettling remorse which left him momentarily ill-at-ease with the tranquility of his house, his life, everything around him. It was all so normal, yet so horribly unsynchronized with the tempo of his equilibrium. It was like a spring day in the middle of winter. A succulent fruit pruned from the heart of an infertile desert. A warm memory, temporally displaced in a cold and present vacuum of reality.

But all at once, the eeriness which pimpled his flesh for no accountable reason gradually dimmed back into obscurity. Before he could even begin to interpret the shadows of his fears, his haunted anxieties re-submerged themselves into the walls and the furniture around him like the hastened departure of a translucent apparition.

"She's right upstairs. Listen," he whispered to the stillness. "I can hear her pacing back and forth, jabbering away to her sister on the com-call, I'll bet. And she's rummaging around…probably prepping a site for some domestic chore that requires 'both of us' to finish it. So what am I worried about?"

On his terminal monitor, the seventh page of the athletics news was on display with the picture of a bloodied, muddied and despondent hometown combatant slumped to his knees in utter and inconsolable defeat. The caption beneath it read simply: "Maybe Next Year," a cruel and nearly satirical trivialization of the woeful abjection pictured above it.

"We were so close that year," Crilen reflected quietly. "This year," he corrected himself with a blink and a frown.

Crilen remembered watching the matches with his younger brother, Jerad, as they heartily consumed volumes of heavily spiced, deep-fried snacks in ritualistic defiance of their good health. And he remembered conversing intermittently over the matter of some new girl his brother had begun to pursue across campus, at the peril of both his studies and his sanity. The brief exchange, during which Jerad lamented the dubious veracity of this female and her ridicule of the sincerity of his own affections toward her, reminded Crilen of how wonderful it was to be married after all, and be done, for all time, with the aches and mysteries of untethered courtships.

"If he's not careful, she'll graduate with honors while he'll wind up having to retake the whole semester." Crilen chuckled. "I should know."

But then, a cold nauseating draft of imminent tragedy swept through his mood again. It was like the murmur of a forgotten line from an old play at its most poignant turn. A distant, faint, and mired hieroglyphic, obscured by the fresh traffic of ideas and experiences which had weathered away the relevance of its former urgency.

He tried to believe that everything was fine, but he couldn't escape the manic sensation that it shouldn't be…or wouldn't be.

And where was Jerad now?

"School…I guess." He strained his memory. "I guess? I should know."

Crilen snorted in puzzlement as he kneaded his thumb and fingers deeply into his furrowed brow. It was as if some black chasm of time separated him from his immediate past and his memories were riddled with holes censoring the random, commonplace details of everyday existence. It was as if…yesterday or even an hour ago had happened…decades past.

The mounting sensation of displacement became unbearable. He pushed forward out of his high-backed desk chair and purposefully rose to his feet. He rubbed the sides of his face with his hand, questioning whether he was even real to himself. He felt a light brush of stubble around his chin and over his upper lip. The contours of his nose and forehead felt very familiar. Only the hairline, or perhaps it was the hair length, made him uncertain of everything else.

He needed a mirror.

Crilen whirled around, scouring the walls of his study. A few pictures of people and places, whose origins or identities momentarily eluded him, hung coated with a thin film of dust. Shelved books on chemistry, anatomy and biology lined the walls as well. Some, he recognized. Others, he could only vaguely recollect.

He wandered out into the living room where he felt his bare feet adhering clammily to the cool tiles. He looked down and faintly remembered the plaid shorts he was wearing. He found himself tracing the muscles of his legs into the protrusion of his knees. They appeared perfectly normal…except for the hair. He touched his chest and stomach lightly, and honestly couldn't discern whether they were less firm than they should have been or if he had simply lost the measurements in his bewildered imagination.

None of the living room furniture was particularly familiar, yet it was distinctly familiar in his wife's taste. Ivory walls, ivory draperies, ivory sofas, ivory chairs and ivory carpeting, lightly accentuated by either thin pin lines or confettied flecks of charcoal and noire. And, at the center, bleeding color into this decoratively arranged portrait, was an ancient vase of bright scarlet and gold mounted on an ivory tea table. It was all so refined and beautiful to him. Or maybe it was just that it reminded him so fondly of her manner.

Having nearly forgotten his initial reason for coming to the room, he turned and was frozen by his reflection in a giant mirror above the mantle.

It was him after all. The dark, inset eyes. The bobbed nose. The black brows. The rounded cheeks. And the drooping mouth that could alter from disgust to warmth to fury in an instant.

"Fury?" he wondered aloud.

Had this face really known such a violent and hate-filled emotion? Blazing, savage, monstrous anger? Yes, yes, of course. But at this juncture? Married to Aami? Living in this home? Working in the profession that he loved so much? Fury felt like such a grand centerpiece to the puzzle of his life, yet it had no place here. Not now. Not today. And not yesterday…or the day or month before.

When, then?

"Narcissist!" intervened a playful female voice from just above. "I'm sure that you've been totally faithful darling, but I'm still horribly jealous of the time you give to yourself. I swear I'm going to kill that man in the mirror if he doesn't stop looking at you that way! You're mine, do you understand me?"

Crilen gazed up the staircase and was shaken by the radiant, elegance of his wife, Aami, as she leaned tauntingly over the balustrade. She wore only one of his white lab shirts which flowered loosely about her lean diminutive figure like a puffed smock; a single button at her navel was all that withheld her delicate form from totally bared disrobement. Her dark, playful eyes held the mischief of an immortal child who saw the world as a wondrous park of amusement and life as an expedition of joy. Her smile was, to him, the warm caress of a morning's sunrise upon his cool ocean. Her voice was the song which set his world to a grand symphony of emotional bliss.

Yet still, he could not fathom why his stomach felt like it would plummet into the well of his bowels. She was so beautiful and he wanted to feel so happy, but something vague and unfocused in his memory wouldn't allow it.

"Hey. What's wrong with you?" Aami tilted her head curiously, running the tips of her fingers briskly through her neatly cropped black hair.

Crilen tried to absorb every curve and line which defined her lithesome figure. This vision of her had become a magical and enchanting moment he prayed to relive for the rest of his life. But in another instant, as she moved again, he dreaded there would be little time left for anything.

Aami curiously followed the path of his eyes back to her body. She looked down at herself and held up the open collar of the lab shirt, innocently unveiling more of her smooth, alluring flesh than she was conscious of.

"Oh! You're worried about the shirt?" Aami mocked him. "It's all right. It's already dirty. In fact, it stinks of you."

She held the collar up to her nose and deeply inhaled. "But then a woman has to take what she can get when her man is so disgustingly preoccupied all the time."

Her shining brown eyes longingly pierced his heart. Gradually, they became as serious as she would allow without tears welling in the bottom of their lids. Observing this, Crilen's concerns over time fell mute as he was drawn wholly into the reality of the present: This confounding, seductive scene and the enveloping love he had always had for his wife.

"I didn't mean to hurt you." Crilen fumbled over the context of his words.

"Hurt?" Aami sounded mildly confused. "I wouldn't say hurt. Maybe, neglected or ignored or forgotten…"

"I'd never forget you!" he stepped toward the stairwell. "Never."

She observed him strangely again. "Honey, are you all right? I mean, you're making me feel like I'm dying, all of a sudden."

"I'm not sure." Crilen tried to focus his thoughts.

"Not sure of what?" Aami asked. "Not sure that I'm not dying?"

"No." Crilen looked up to her. "That's not what I meant."

He froze momentarily, groping to gather up his thoughts as they wafted randomly from his grasp like a swirl of autumn leaves.

"Oh, damn, Lenny." Aami skipped down two steps and took her husband by the hand. She appeared to intuitively understand what was troubling him.

"Sit." she commanded in her girlish imitation of a matron.

Crilen felt her gentle hand glide soothingly across the tensed muscles in his back as she gracefully settled her body next to his on the stairs. Her fingers lightly caressed the nape of his neck. He again, found himself wishing he could remain feeling just so, forever.

"It was a miscarriage, darling. That's all," she spoke to him tenderly. "I was never in any danger. And I'm all right now. In fact, I've never felt better, really. And its certainly no one's fault. Certainly not yours."

"I know." Crilen felt the sad memories of their lost child return. "I know these things happen. I just wish…"

"What, Len?" she spoke into his ear. "That you could make life perfect? That you could make things so that you or I would never ever feel any pain? That we would never suffer any loss?"

"Why not?" Crilen turned his head and regretfully stared into her eyes.

"Because that's not real life, Lenny." She slipped her hand onto his cheek. "Because tragedy is part of life, and no one can get through life avoiding it. Instead, we have to find the strength, the wisdom…and the faith to deal with it when it comes. That's how we make it. That's how we survive it."

"I never want to lose you…" the words choked in Crilen's throat, and he heard the word "again" echo in his mind. "Again" as if he already had lost her.

She gazed at him with love and fondness. So much care for him, in her hour of distress, he marveled. Just as her eyes moistened, she defensively infused them with playful mischief.

Abruptly, Aami rose to her feet and purposefully kicked him in the back of his head.

"You're too damn serious for me tonight," She cursed with mock disdain. "You'd better stay down here and play by yourself after all, 'Mr. Narcissist, in love with myself, serious all the time, scientist bastard'!"

"Hey!" Crilen stumbled down a step.

Aami pranced gleefully up the staircase laughing loudly, as the oversized shirt rolled behind her like a giant cape. A blissful smile swept over Crilen's face as he righted himself and hurriedly charged after her, two stairs at a time.

As he reached the upstairs hallway, he saw her sprinting down the corridor toward the bedroom. For an instant, he stopped and marveled at how she always appeared to be moving at such a frenetic pace, yet never seemed to arrive anywhere very quickly.

He raced after her, making up most of the distance between them almost immediately. He could hear Aami starting to giggle between her short, excited breaths.

As he closed to within a step of her, he envisioned yanking his shirt from her naked body and twirling her to the floor. He found the thought quite provocative in fact, but just as he reached forward, Aami stopped in her tracks and ducked down onto her haunches.

Crilen found his legs suddenly cut from beneath him by her crouched figure. He was abruptly flung head over heels, slamming loudly, upside down, against the bedroom door.

"Damnit!" Crilen cursed, his entire body lying twisted over his neck and shoulders.

Aami sprung to her feet and laughed, pointing and teasing at him.

"Hah!" Aami taunted breathlessly. "What a louse! Just like that lousy team of yours! Why don't you just go back downstairs and watch them lose some more! You deserve each other you loser!"

"I can't." Crilen groaned as he rolled over onto his side. "They were eliminated last night. They're out of it."

"Hah!" Aami scoffed without sympathy. "I could have told you that would happen months ago. They're terrible! They always are!"

"They had a good team this year." Crilen winced and tried to shake loose the cobwebs.

"Then why did they lose again if they were so good?" She dug at his pride with the brash simplicity of a five-year old.

"Because…" Crilen started to answer.

"Because they were lousy, that's why!" she cut him off. "But they always dupe you into watching them anyway. Our lousy team, and Crilen, their only stupid lousy fan. If you'd stop watching and sold your season passes, they could shut down the entire clumsy operation and make the world a better place! One without pitiful losing teams and the lousy pitiful fools stupid enough to patronize them!"

"All right, that's it!" Crilen jumped to his feet and glared at her with a devilish grin.

"No!" Aami shrieked and backpedaled, laughing hysterically. She knew exactly what it meant when the lines in his brow deepened and he smiled, baring his teeth like a ravenous predator.

She turned belatedly and attempted to sprint away from him again. Before she could finish two steps, she found her feet no longer touching the carpet and her body slung over his shoulder like a loose garment sack.

"Let me go." She tried to speak with a calm foreboding threat in her voice.

Crilen snorted, then snickered under his breath.

"Don't laugh at me!" she feigned outrage.

"Who's laughing?" Crilen smacked her on the hind cheek as he hauled her into the moonlit bedroom. "I must be the only husband on the planet who has to take his fleeing wife like a back-alley molester."

"You love molesting," she spoke lowly, running her nails down his back.

Crilen unceremoniously dumped her onto the bed and immediately pinned her wrists with his hands. "You love molesting." He smiled his evil smile and pressed his chest against hers.

"Careful, doctor. You don't want to ruin your shirt," she warned him.

"To hell with the shirt." His nostrils flared as he yanked open the garment, popping the single button across the room until it caromed against the bedroom window, then rang loudly off the side of an empty brass pitcher sitting on the dresser. The pitcher's prolonged ringing intruded upon their intimate silence with a vibrating "clang" that sounded much like a cow bell dropped carelessly into the middle of a piano recital. The sound lingered just long enough to cause both of them to chuckle as they met each other's eyes once more.

"And so refined a molester you are." She giggled, freeing her arms and draping them around his neck. "I will 'cherish' this most 'fabled' moment in our marriage for the rest of my life!"

With another smile, she pulled him close and kissed him with the exaggerated, guileless suction of a poorly trained stage actress.

As he lifted his head and looked down at her, she was laughing again, her bare shoulders framing the radiant sincerity in her glowing smile. Yet, Crilen was, again, unsteadied by the chilled, discomforting inertia he had felt in his study.

The honeyed smell of Aami's flesh was so pleasantly familiar as it filled his nostrils. The caress of her slender arms about his neck; her smooth legs about his waist; her soothing voice all around him; her sweet breath intermingled with his own, all felt distantly out of harmony with who he was.

"What is it?" she whispered, pulling him close again.

Crilen felt as if he were fading from a dream. A tragic dream whose course he could not divert.

"I love you." his voice shivered.

"I know." She shook her head thoughtfully.

"You were the only woman who ever cared enough to find out who I was," he continued.

"'Were'?" she lifted an eyebrow. "Aren't I still here?"

"Yes," Crilen corrected himself. "Yes, of course you are."

"Lenny, I knew who you were the moment I met you." She smirked and looked away. "You weren't that complicated. You were just alone."

"I love you for who you are and who you've made me." Crilen recaptured her eyes. "I love you more than life."

"Don't be so serious," she scolded mildly as she touched his cheek.

Crilen wanted to comply, but found himself more enamored with her command for calm than the desire to actually do so. When he sensed her disapproval, however, he pretended to lighten the air.

"So what about me?" He smiled.

"Yes?" She arched her eyebrows, feigning cluelessness.

"Yes?" He mimicked her.

"What?" She remained in character.

"Do you love me?" He fell serious again.

"Oh Len, must you ask?" She became nearly vexed.

"I need to hear it." He seemed drained by her reluctance.

Aami sighed deeply, like an interrogant being forced, once more, to profess a plain and obvious truth. Her eyes melted into naked feminine innocence and she warmly avowed to him in a quiet, assuring voice: "I love hearing you reach into the mysteries of life with a question, then answering it with a dozen more. I love watching you stride, dauntlessly, through the struggles of this life. I love hearing you laugh when something puzzles you. I love hearing you sigh when something disappoints you. I love feeling you breathe when everything is still. I can only love you more than I did yesterday, and tomorrow more than today. And Lenny, that's how it will always be."

With this, his passion brushed aside the looming doubts which haunted and muddled his troubled conscience. Aami's hands found their way to his belt and undid the hooks of his trousers as if they were her own.

His mouth came to rest upon her lips and he kissed her beyond the passion of their wedding night; full of love, eternal devotion and promise.

"Oh, I've needed you," he thought to himself. "How could I have survived all these years…"

Crilen caught himself again. "Years?" he murmured under his breath. Aami continued beneath him, unnoticing.

He was inside of her before he was cognizant of it, their muscles ebbing and merging together as if one mind, one flesh conducted their deepest movements. He was amazed by the fluent and harmonious rhythm of the impassioned duet their bodies reprised with no forethought. Still, a fragment of his mind was suspended in removed observance, as if he were divided from his consciousness, a third party to the physical proceedings.

Suddenly, he felt a flash of uncomfortable heat mount from within.

Perspiration burst across his forehead and raced down the sides of his face to his chin. His chest and back became saturated with dampness as he felt Aami's nails traverse the crevices behind his shoulders, carving tributary impressions into his muscular flesh.

"I love you so much." Aami whispered.

Crilen's heart plummeted. Enveloping horror violently abducted the center of his emotions. An unnatural heat, a damned and cursed familiar heat, smoldered from beneath his skin. The blood in his veins burned like acid or molten metal. Hastily he sought to pull himself from the love-making and save Aami's life. But before the thought was completed, the heat quickly flourished into an open fire.

"No!!" Crilen howled as the flames roared over the surfaces of his body.

Aami's soft moans erupted into horrid, unrecognizable screams of searing agony. Screams that begged the mercy of some unfathomable inhuman betrayal.

Crilen winced and quivered, nauseated by the sickening smell of her sizzling flesh as her cries died away into the sound of a collapsing stone wall. The entire chateau exploded into a black and golden tower of smoke and fire, and he felt himself rocketed skyward, propelled, not by the conflagration below, but by the fires that continued to rage outward through his pores from the blood in his own veins.

As his fiery form hurtled into the distance, he desperately groped through the biological flames which engulfed him for any sign of Aami's life that might be rescued. But as his mind finally cleared itself to the present, he became remorsefully certain she was gone. Dead. Incinerated along with all matters pertaining to the insignificant hopes and happiness of his ephemeral humanity.

II.

Crilen awoke in a smoldering trench melted deeply into the iron sand of the craggy asteroid surface. He was face down in a pool of hot liquid metal. A human in such a pool of water might have drowned, but the physical laws of his mortality had been mutated over a decade ago by his own ambitious experiments. He did not require breath, therefore he could not be drowned. And, in the soundless void of space, even his anguished shouts went unheard, except within his own tortured mind.

He glanced outward and observed the orbiting procession of giant rocks trapped in the asteroid belt. The mental fog dispersed. Gradually his recollections discovered themselves intact. Everything was, again, as it should be, much to his dismay.

He hauled himself slowly to his feet, as the hot molten muck dripped from his limbs like a thick black paste. "That so horribly vivid.

"I used to…carry on conversations with her, knowing full well she wasn't there anymore." He fought to contain his sorrow. "And my memories of what she'd say would always answer. I'd ramble to myself for hours that way…all alone…laughing myself to tears or crying myself to sleep! I'd hear the ring of her bracelets amidst the rustle of fall leaves, or the cadence of her steps along a busy walkway. Sometimes I'd feel her fingers tickling the back of my shoulders but find that it was only my flesh begging to feel her touch me again. If I closed my eyes, I'd see her standing just in front of me. In a gentle breeze, I'd smell the remnants of her fragrance everywhere…in places she'd never even been.

"But that was so long ago. Fifteen years. I thought I'd come to terms with it. But if so, why did the memory come back with such physical clarity? Why does it feel as if I lost her only a moment ago? Why do the old wounds sting, as fresh and deep as their first hour?"

Crilen swallowed hard and tried to recess the gory graphic memory of Aami's death, but the more he struggled to submerge it, the more vivid and nauseating the charred, contorted mask of her dying face became.

He gritted his teeth and tried snarling the image away.

"Quinson." Crilen murmured, working his jaw. "That smarmy fat little insignificant man. He probably snickered over our graves. After all, he was right! I was a reckless fool. My work was too dangerous and I knew it. But the louder he warned me, the more determined I was to prove him wrong…even if he wasn't! It was so damned important to me at the time, and it cost me her life…our life!"

A violent rage swelled through him. His eyes roiled into hot crimson coals. His fists ignited into billowing torches of golden fire. Then, without warning, a powerful burst of flames roared skyward from his hands and shattered a craggy spire fifty meters overhead.

Unfortunately, the expulsion of rage failed to diminish the clarity of the images etched in his memory: Aami, smiling contented and secure. Then dead, seconds later, roasted and disfigured against his own fiery flesh.

Exasperated by the vivid horror, Crilen dropped to his knees and clutched at his temples.

"I can't continue like this!" he begged his sanity.

"You needn't," said another voice inside of his head.

He turned and looked up toward the pulverized spire he had destroyed. There, grinning with a malevolent serenity, was a being like none he had ever seen.

Its head was adorned with the antlers of a twelve-point stag and a thick tuft of brown hair curled over its wrinkled forehead. Its eyes were deep, moist black pools, reflecting the field of stars all around them, including the yellow flame flickering from the top of Crilen's grey scalp. Its torso was like the thin, grey, gnarled trunk of a withered sapling, Its legs were like the hind quarters of a four-legged hoofed animal, and its long skinny arms resembled twisted wiry antennae with six multi-jointed needles at each end forming fingers.

"Who are you?" Crilen frowned with more annoyance than surprise.

"Not a friend, I assure you." It smiled its toothy carnivorous grin. "I'm long done with samaritanism. A kind hand nurtures a specious and poisonous fruit. I've simply come to deal."

"Deal?" Crilen relented from the torment of his dream. "With me?"

"No other." It chuckled, gesturing to the emptiness all around them.

"And why would I trust you?" Crilen asked.

"Trust?" It smiled the evil grin again. "Oh, there's nothing to trust out here. If I took you for fool enough to trust anything I'd say, I wouldn't bother with you at all. There'll be no promise in this deal for you. Just a plain and cut exchange of services. Nothing other."

"Service?" Crilen questioned.

"Your work is known." It tipped its antlers in mock tribute. "Violent. Thorough. Honorable. Convicted. A teacher to sentient life. A rueful judge. A merciless executioner. And foremost, a penitent and humble servant to the God of the Universe. For me, you'll perform quite well, I'm certain."

"So you say." Crilen's eyes flickered red.

"So I've seen." It mused over Crilen's distrust.

"Seen where?"

"Wherever."

"That's no answer."

"Isn't it?"

"Not for my service."

"For your servitude, it will suffice."

"I'll judge that."

"And you'll judge it so."

"So as to be of no service to you!"

"So as to be of service to yourself."

"How?" Crilen questioned.

It smiled broadly and stroked its pointed chin. "So you are prepared to deal?"

"Not until I know what I'm dealing with."

"The Devil." It smirked and thumped an antler. "Horn of head. Talons at my fingertips. Deceit pervading every duplicitous word flung from my cankered throat. Who else could I be but the black prince of blighted spirits and tormented souls? The lord of the lost, king of the living dead?"

"You're not the Devil." Crilen spoke with even toned impatience. "There's an ache in your thoughts; a lack of glee in your discontent. Being a miserable monstrosity doesn't seat you as the prince of evil things. In fact, my planet's embodiment of evil is actually symbolized by the most beautiful temptress: Loving eyes; skin, soft and warm; hair, a flowing, shimmering mane of silk. I quote: 'At first turn she's a dainty princess. But intimately, she becomes a lioness of sensuality and manipulation. She's what every foolish man desires and what every foolish woman wishes to become. She's the rotten fruit on the tree of death veiled by a honeyed, alluring fragrance that promises sweet and instantaneous gratification to short-sighted sentient libidos. She's the best of humanity devoid of soul or substance. A decorative and vacant orifice making waste of all material which entereth therein. And in the end, her followers travel no road to hell, but their hollow and wasted existences simply disperse into fathomless oblivion. For it is so written that those who live for lies and falsehoods ne'er live at all. Rather, their lives in shadow, simply evaporate against the fortified surfaces of undeniable truth!'"

It gave Crilen a curious sidelong glance, tilting its antlers as a deer might while observing some newfound oddity. It smiled in acknowledgment. "I'm to understand you've given the notion of deviltry some thought?"

Crilen offered a perturbed nod.

"Then did you ever consider that truth is only perception and that happiness, by any means, is all that anyone could ever ask for?"

"In the absence of God, yes," Crilen answered. "But I believe in a living God and a single truth we needn't merely perceive."

"And that makes you happy?" It questioned.

"I'm content." Crilen frowned.

"But is that enough?"

"Sir?"

"I mean," It hunched over and pouted, "for all you claim to know, are you happy...'Lenny'?"

"Wh...What?" Crilen stammered.

"You don't follow?" It drew back, feigning exaggerated disbelief.

"No." Crilen answered softly. "You said my name. I mean...her name for me."

"Yes?" It made nothing of it.

"How...where did you hear that?" Crilen grew uneasy. "I haven't been called that..."

"...since you killed your wife." It finished. "I know. I just thought familiarity might..."

"Familiarity?" Crilen snapped. "Are you some kind of mind-reader?"

"More of a historian, really." It picked its sharp teeth with a pointed finger. "Personal history. Everyone wears their past in their face, their gait, their skin, the food they eat, the turns in their sleep and every other way imaginable. I could see her name on your lips. And your name in the curve of your ears. Your loss is stenciled into every cell of your body. Like a lost little boy at a market bazaar, every way about you screams 'Mommy', or rather 'Aami' in this case! Boo hoo."

"That's enough!" Crilen seethed

"Still so sensitive after all of these years, Lenny?" It shook its head. "Wounds never heal if you pick the scabs! And if you eat the scabs, they'll make you sick!"

Crilen's lips folded bitterly.

"I knew a space traveler," It continued, "who actually kept the putrefied remains of its mate in the bunk above his own bed. Oh, he became familiar to the smell. And, on particularly lonely sojourns, he would even climb up top and..."

"Stop!" Crilen cut him off.

"A tad necrophilic, you must admit, yet a sentimental journey not entirely unlike your own." It continued.

Crilen's fists ignited, and, in an instant, he unleashed a rain of fiery spheres in Its direction. When the brightness of the onslaught finally dissipated, he saw the rocky ledge melted away and the creature was nowhere to be found.

"Damn him!" Crilen cursed.

He suddenly sensed footfalls crunching rapidly from behind. His hands ignited again; he spun around poised to defend himself.

"Hold!" It froze in its tracks, then fanned smoke from its tall antlers. "That was very close up there!"

"Not close enough," Crilen simmered, dousing the flames of his hands.

Without warning, Crilen smashed a closed fist into It's snouted nose, toppling it clumsily to the ground.

"I should have shown more restraint." Crilen's was more than prepared for a fight. But instead, a smile simply curled along the sides of its mouth; a gleam of irony flickered in its eye.

"You should have shown more restraint some time ago, I think." It said as it rolled back to its feet.

"What do you mean?" Crilen asked.

"I mean its obvious that you loved your wife far too much," It answered matter of factly, brushing metallic dust from its arms and legs. "It will see you undone. Mark me."

"I'm undone already," Crilen lamented without emotion in his tone. "The moment she died I was undone."

"But you're a champion of the cosmos." It leaned forward. "The sword hand of God, meting out justice throughout the universe. How can you be undone?"

"The work I do now...is not for me." Crilen met It's eyes. "Because there's nothing I can do for me. You asked me if I'm happy. Well...I was. In my limited, ignorant mortal simplicity, I was very happy. I was a success. I guess that means I was the envy of my peers. And yes, I was very much in love with a selfless angel who could salve pain with a glance and a smile. And even more amazing was that she was in love with me. But she's gone now...dead. And while I'm content, I don't count on ever being that happy again. I've seen too much of this universe. I know too much."

"And you don't know the half of it," It communicated in a rueful tone.

"No?" Crilen paused for a moment. He clenched his fists tightly and craned his neck skyward. It was as if he beckoned the dispersion of Aami's essence to return to him from every star in the universe.

"A great woman teaches a man to feel," he began. "To smile and to love in his heart. She makes him more than he could have ever been on his own. Her touch is the plumed caress of an angel. Her voice is the melodic song of heaven. Her thoughts become forever the garden adorning his interpretations of the world. And when she dies, it's nothing less than the cruelest mutilation of the survivor. A phantom pain of the soul that lingers into infinity. There aren't proper words to describe it. 'Loss' is pitifully inadequate. An oversimplification of what happens to the living soul when it's violently rendered parcel to what it was."

Crilen wedged his thumb into his temple as he thought.

"I could never stay angry at her. She could insult the root of my manhood at one turn, but then smile or touch me and simply cause the entire matter to evaporate. And she had an ability to make me feel so lonely. I thrive in my solitude, but when she'd walk away and leave me in silence, it would sap the life from every living thing around me…and deride my innocence with scathing guilt. I'd feel so abandoned. Like a frightened child, I'd suddenly fear that she would never come back. I'd become horrified at the thought that I might have carelessly killed everything about us that I loved."

"Well you finally managed to do that." It snorted coldly. "You're probably much the better for it."

Crilen's eyes narrowed and flushed to a hot, surly crimson.

"Your problem is that you took that little siren to heart." It started to lecture. "She tenderized your spine with honey-glazed feminine propaganda. And you probably broke your back trying to please her, to little or no avail. And for what?"

"She was my conscience!" Crilen seethed. "She was my…"

"She was a female!" It interrupted waggling a forefinger. "Nothing more, unless you were foolish enough to allow her to be. Mark me: Never ignore what a female says. There may often be something of use in it. But never take everything that a female says to heart, for she herself will abandon most of it shortly after it has been uttered. And you will find yourself the caretaker of an orphaned ideal."

It crossed its wiry arms over its chest and held its shoulders with its needle-point fingers. It shook its head nervously as if a chill shivered through its body.

"I've seen so many good males drowned in the undertow of female duplicity." It spoke with truculent disdain. "Would that they all were as reputable as whores, I say! At least a whore is honest. A whore does her business, collects her wage and settles her affairs in neat order. Most females, false as they are, extract thrice the toll for a fraction of the pleasure and leave the doting male in irreparable disarray. Females are the zig and the zag. The yin and the yang. The backside of the truth and the front end of the lie. They don't play by the rules because rules constrict and expose their hollow plots. So they cheat and cry and whine and pout and blame. And, in the end, laugh behind your back for believing any of it."

"Sounds more like envy to me," Crilen accused.

"Envy?" Its snouted mouth hung open and its eyes bulged. "The only virtue a male may envy of the female condition is their inherent lack of the necessity for accountability. If a female goes wrong, certainly some male, somewhere, at some point in her life is more responsible for it than she. If the female lies, steals, adulterates or even murders, society will assure you that some domineering, serpentine, male influence brought her to it. And that she, otherwise, would have flowered into a bloom of innocence and splendor commensurate with her goodly feminine nature.

"Of course females have it easier in another regard, if only during the spring of their lives. That is, a female, an attractive female, mind you, can be forgiven all of her other failings so long as she remains alluring or sensual in some manner. Her intellect can be blighted by ignorance and immaturity. Her domestic crafts needn't stray far from her ability to primp and pose in front of her own embellished reflection. Even the chill of her passionless consortium can be fictionalized into a warm illusion, so long as she remains an enviable decoration in the trophy case of her…lessor. But tragically, let her beauty weather or waver, let her posture slump or her radiance dim or her posterior sag wide and soft, or her ankles fatten or her veins spew varicose or her voice crack to a shrill, monotonous harangue, and no measure of character or substance will forgive her those horrible transgressions. She becomes a dull and dented ornament, no longer worthy of display upon the mantle. She requires overhaul, or, more often, replacement. And, with this reality, any measure of false esteem she might have mustered crumbles into an apprehensive self-conscious neurosis. Ultimately, in the absence of beauty lost or never attained, she flounders through the vacuum of her existence resenting not having been born male. After all, a fulfilled male builds his life around his work, his ideals and his principles. But a female, fulfilled, is only capable of building her life around…a male."

"You're boring me," Crilen responded. "That kind of misogyny is always born from love unfulfilled."

"Au contraire, mon frere." It shook its head. "I fulfilled my love all to well! And paid cruelly for the delusion."

An odd silence ensued.

"How?" Crilen finally asked.

"Almost as you did." It met his eyes with empathic irony.

Crilen could only offer an expression of puzzlement.

It continued: "The first mistake a male usually makes…and he allows it to derail his pursuit of all matters of greater import…is to penitently embrace the masculine theology that heaven lies between the hallowed walls of a female's thighs and that nothing will ever supersede his ejaculatory ecstasy therein. For, as it is said, 'no man may serve two masters for he will hate the one, and love the other, or else he will hold to the one and despise the other.' When a male chooses to hold to his female, he inevitably comes to despise no less than God for her pleasure.

"I never elevated Aami above God!"

"Didn't you?" It's even-toned accusation hung starkly between them.

Crilen fell silent to reflect. "More than God?" he thought to himself.

Then, suddenly, he was home again.

He was inside of her before he was cognizant of it, their muscles ebbing and merging together as if one mind, one flesh, conducted their deepest movements. He was amazed by the fluent and harmonious rhythm of the impassioned duet their bodies reprised with no forethought. But despite the power of their consuming intimacy, a fragment of his mind suspended him in removed observance as if he were separate from his consciousness, a third party to the physical proceedings.

Abruptly, he felt a flash of uncomfortable heat emerge from within.

"No!" he cried out loud.

Aami continued quietly, as if he had said nothing.

Perspiration burst across his forehead and raced down the sides of his face to his chin. His chest and back became damp as he felt Aami's nails traversing the crevices behind his shoulders, raking tributary pathways into his muscular flesh.

"I love you so much," Aami whispered.

"Not again." Crilen pleaded.

Enveloping horror violently abducted the center of his emotions. An unnatural heat, a damned and cursed familiar heat smoldered from beneath his flesh. The blood in his veins burned like acid or molten metal. He violently tried to pull himself from the love making and save Aami's life. But before his thoughts oriented themselves, the heat quickly ignited into an open fire.

"No!!" Crilen howled as the scorching flames roared across his skin.

Aami's soft moans erupted into horrid, unrecognizable screams of searing agony. Screams that begged the mercy of some unfathomable inhuman betrayal.

Crilen winced and quivered, nauseated by the sickening smell of her sizzling flesh as her shattering cries soon died away into the sound of a collapsing stone wall. The entire chateau exploded into a black and golden swell of smoke and fire, and he felt himself rocketed skyward, propelled not by the conflagration below, but by the fires that continued to rage out of every pore from the blood in his own veins.

As his fiery form hurtled into the distance, he desperately groped through the biological flames which engulfed him for any sign of Aami's life that might be rescued.

He opened his eyes and found his clenching fingers ablaze, melted deep into a deformed stalagmite. Eyes glazed with disbelief and hyperventilating with despair, Crilen slumped to his knees and fought back his tears.

"Now you tell me." It crouched next to him and tickled his ear with It's snout. "More than God?"

"What…was…that?" Crilen seethed.

"What was what?" It tilted its antlers and feigned an expression of innocence.

Crilen sneered angrily, as his eyes blazed bright scarlet, "What did you do to me? How did you force me to relive that memory?"

"Memory?" It lifted its brows mischievously. "It wasn't a memory. It was very real."

"Impossible." Crilen's eyes narrowed.

"Possible, Lenny." It mocked him. "As possible as I'm talking in your skull in the soundless void of outer space, you just made love to your wife for the second time in nearly an hour."

"A trick…" Crilen charged.

"A trick?" It taunted with a toothy, wolf-like smile. "You saw her! Those deep, moist, brown eyes pouring life into your barren soul. You felt her! Those sweating bulbous breasts heaving passionately against your bosom."

Crilen put his hand to his chest without realizing it.

"It was her…in the flesh!" It cajoled.

"How?" Crilen demanded. "Dimensional transportation? Time…"

"Ah, ah, ah." It admonished with a wave of its six-jointed finger. "If I told you that, there wouldn't be much balance to our deal, would there?"

"That depends." Crilen frowned. "On whether you're a fake."

"A fake?". It shook its head. "A trick. How did so spirited a girl as your wife ever come to love so dark a skeptic?"

"I wasn't a skeptic then," Crilen answered. "Wisdom made me skeptical. Experience has made me tired of the endless pretenses put on by, everyone. I've learned that if you always assume the worst about someone, you'll find yourself closer to the truth and further from being deceived."

"How disturbingly true". It concurred with little expression. "But I assure you that this has nothing to do with deceit. The bargain is a clean and simple one. Today I offer you the return of your wife, just as you've seen her this past hour. Her life, her love preserved."

"In exchange for?" Crilen folded his arms and arched an eyebrow.

It bowed it's head in reflection. "In exchange for the return of my world."

"And what world would that be?" Crilen was perplexed. "I don't recognize your..species. And how do I know that restoring your world wouldn't cause more problems for this galaxy than its demise. I hate to sound callous, but the destruction of your world might have been a good thing."

"The ultimate skeptic." It chuckled. "Regarding my appearance, you see me as your mind interprets me. A corporeal interpretation of my spirit. In truth, you and I have very little in common as biological life forms. Gas and flesh coexist, but they rarely socialize. That's the best explanation I can offer you. As for my world, you see it now all around us!"

"There's nothing but dead asteroids all around us." Crilen observed.

"Yes." It sounded slightly remorseful. "My world…as it came to be. As with all asteroid belts, these giant chunks of rock circle-dance about its sun to the music of planetary physics. As you well know, belts of asteroids are comprised of material which contain matter insufficient for planetary formation…"

"Or debris left over from a destroyed planet." Crilen completed the sentence.

"Yes." It continued. "My destroyed world fell prey to the latter."

Crilen observed how the subtleties in its expressions became more pronounced. Where once he was uncertain of its cynical, dark disposition, the traces of regret which trickled out gradually formed a portrait.

"They destroyed themselves," It lamented. "They destroyed everything."

"Where are the others?" Crilen asked.

"There are none," It confirmed with somber reflection "I am all there is."

"You're speaking in abstractions," Crilen noted with annoyance.

"Indeed." It responded with a measure of humility. "My apologies. Let me be more direct: In every planet's history, there are critical moments in time where the actions of one individual literally set the course of an entire galaxy for hundreds of millennia. One such moment occurred here. The fate of one solitary female altered the destiny of the entire planetary system. Had she survived, who knows what glory the denizens of this planet might have experienced. Unfortunately, her premature demise led to this: a field of orbiting debris.

"Like all sentient species, once we found the need for civilization, or a society if you will, we required a body of irrefutable laws that would hold our world together," It continued. "Laws that everyone would be required to adhere to. And those laws could not just be tied to a democracy; a democracy changes its direction nearly as often as the wind. But rather a bedrock foundation of laws and values that would require everyone's obedience for the long-term good of the all. It was about this time that God was alleged to have held council with the warlords of our planet's different factions. He demanded they should never again raise arms against each other. And that they would work tirelessly to draft a moral code of ethics which would endure for all time.

"They obeyed. They obeyed very well. They scribed every letter of God's Word so that the world would be bound to Heaven, ensuring temporal peace, love and freedom as well as everlasting life eternal. The people would remain forever impregnable to the assaults of secular reason and logic. This world became a paradise for a time. But somewhere along the way, doctrine fell prey to...ritual."

"Ritual?" Crilen frowned.

"Yes." It shook it's head sadly. "Ritual.

"You see, all sentient life forms have the capacity to understand their relationship with things which extend beyond the physical form. Everyone could conceive of spiritual matters. The problem was that not everyone was predisposed to do so, even though they had the capability. It was much easier to live in the pragmatists' realm of facts and figures and flesh and stone and water and air and food and sex, than to tie down so remote an abstraction as the will of God. So to combat this spiritual myopia, a secular institution was devised to bridge the gap between the abstractions of Heaven and the realities of mortal life. At first, this institution was painfully obtuse in its treatment of those who deviated from the doctrine. The result was a savage age of tribunals, infidel persecutions and massive executions of those who failed to conform.

"But as the taste for the blood of non-believers grew foul and the persecutors found themselves convicted by their hypocrisy, it was decided that a newer, cleaner mechanism was required so that people could get on with their lives without the institution policing their every indiscretion. So a mechanism was employed by the church whereby anyone who wished to gain access to God could do so by mouthing words, performing tasks and outwardly sustaining a penitential facade. And if anyone transgressed at any time against the doctrine, the transgression could be wiped clean with a mere promise not to do so again, and the payment of a sanction. There would be no limit on forgiveness for the individual who was always repentant, therefore eliminating any need for persecutions. The person would simply admit to their failure or crime, pledge their rededication, pay a fine and go on their way. Little did I or any of us realize, that we had sown bulbs which would choke off the roots which held our society together.

"Gradually, God became more and more obscured by the doctrines of mortals. Gradually, mortals became discontented with the moral impositions of their peers. God receded into the shadows. Secularism took center stage.

"Allow me to illustrate."

III.

Crilen watched as streams of incandescent midnight scrolled down from all sides of the universe like a sprawling spill of paint, slowly, but inexorably draping over the horizons. Within the lines of the forming sky, a white and distant star swelled into a dull and yellow moon. Another speck of light spun itself into a shadowy orange lunar twin, forty-five degrees to the west of it.

The jagged and creviced asteroid spires swirled into smooth, cylindrical blonde buildings with mushroomed turret heads set against the darkened backdrop. Beneath his feet, the iron grey sand scattered into the mortar of a mahogany brick surface that gradually widened into a winding avenue at the center of a town.

He heard a noise followed by an angry voice and laughter billowed from inside a lamp-lit doorway nearby.

"Where is this?" he frowned at the alien surroundings. "The sky…the constellations…the moons…

He paused and turned around looking up and down the street then, to the doorways, the windows, and, finally, the rooftops.

His alien host was gone.

A violent, muffled crash interrupted the flow of his thoughts. There was a cry of horror followed by another round of taunting, mischievous laughter from the lamp-lit doorway.

Crilen moved toward the disturbance.

He carefully creaked open the door and found his view obscured by the backs of large men who were fervently cheering the escalation of some violent altercation. The expansive bar room was filled with a thick aromatic smoke which forced his eyelids to flicker involuntarily, and there were the sounds of shattering bottles and clinking glasses accompanied by the odors of alcohol consumption en masse.

There was another loud crash followed closely by a deep groan and the whimpering of a young woman. The crowd burst into another cheer. As the patrons once more raised their fists and steins triumphantly, Crilen wedged and pried his way forward until he reached the center of the throng.

At the heart of the densely clouded mayhem were two men bound to one another at the wrists by a short iron chain. One of the men was young, tall, and bony, clad in tight dark navy leather from the neck down. His damp yellow hair shagged messily over his face, making him appear a mad, emaciated barbarian who had just grappled for sparse morsels of food on a dirty dungeon floor. He staggered wearily over his kneeling opponent attempting, awkwardly, to summon any pride his blatant inebriation would allow. All told, he did not appear to be much of a warrior, but then his opposition scarcely warranted as much.

The other man appeared to have been, at some point, a well groomed gentleman of middle age. Though now, his thinning grey scalp, his manicured white beard and his buttoned down dress shirt were lathered with his own dark blood. There was nothing of his face which identified him other than its wet crimson coat and a fresh wound or two swelling about his eyes and forehead.

"Your turn." The younger man pulled on the chain, jerking the older man up onto his buckling legs.

"No, stop!" cried out a desperate woman's voice.

Crilen looked across the floor and found at chest level, the source of the intermittent sorrow which had faintly whined its shudders under the boisterous currents of savage zeal. She was small and slight, clad in a bright pink and navy blue striped leather mini-dress. Her hair was short, dyed an unnatural green, and curled into a succession of bangs swirled around her forehead and cheeks. The make-up on her cloud white face formed a smudged mask of contorted anguish as she wept without restraint. And, though she had tried to dress in accord with all the renegades in attendance, her reactions to the vicious brutality bore out that her bred inclinations were more delicately aligned with the elder gentleman's sensibilities.

The middle-aged man flailed a futile lunge toward the younger man, but fell forward into near unconsciousness.

"You missed," the young man calmly acknowledged, jerking his opponent back on to his feet with a tug of the chain.

The audience growled low sadistic laughter as they beckoned him to continue the assault.

"You can always quit," the young man taunted.

The elder man's mouth moved, but nothing audible came out. Slowly, he worked his swollen jaws, pursed his shredded lips and managed to eject a huge ball of bloody phlegm directly into the younger man's face.

The onlookers cursed and jibed disparagingly at this contumacious gesture. A few of them began a chant which grew louder and louder until everyone was stomping and yelling in unison: "Durn! Durn! Durn! Durn! Durn! Durn! Durn! Durn! Durn! Durn!"

The younger man's pale features momentarily flared with hate-filled rage, but he coaxed himself behind a thin veil of conceit as he absorbed the cheers of his roaring compatriots. He closed up his insecure rage into a sharp fist, and reached back toward the floor with all of his scrawny, tightly muscled might and fired a crisp, overhand bludgeon into the older man's pulped, swelling face.

For an instant, the impact appeared to have broken the elder gentleman's neck; his head twisted and dangled unnaturally about his shoulders like a wilted flower drooping over its broken stem. Oozed clots of blood from the older man's face ejected several meters into the crowd and bar area. The screaming woman, now reduced to raw hysterics, collapsed to her knees as if she had taken a mortal stab to the abdomen. The older man, still profusely bleeding, slumped backward at the end of the chain, gravely still.

Crilen had idly witnessed all he could stand. He stepped forward as part of the crowd took notice of him for the first time. He appeared ready to take on the entire gathering, if that's what it took, but another figure pushed to the center.

"This is done." The broad backed, stocky intercedent spoke to Durn. "You win."

The crowd moaned it's disapproval.

"He hasn't quit, Rabbel!" Durn complained.

"He can't quit, Durn." Rabbel frowned.

"What? Because he's unconscious?" Durn answered with frustration.

"He's dead, you idiot!" yelled a back-row observer.

The bar room broke into sporadic cackles.

Durn smiled, in spite of the insult.

"He won't quit." Rabbel knelt down to inspect the battered older man. "And, frankly, I think he'd like it if you did kill him. Unfortunately, that would bring us more trouble than either of you are worth. Now give me the combination."

"It's not done." Durn raised his chin, shifting from side to side with uneasy defiance.

Rabbel stood up and authoritatively leaned his imposing bulk toward the younger man. Rabbel was shorter than Durn by nearly half a meter; he was shorter than all of the men who now fell into an anxious silence. But he exuded a commanding presence with his militant posture and his pitch black, weather-worn face. His foreboding stare rolled through the room like a dark storm cloud draping a pall of impending disaster over the evening's festivities.

"I can show everyone in this bar how to skin a dumb scraggly animal with a broken bottle neck, or you can give me the combination to this goddamned chain in the next two seconds." Rabbel gnashed the whispered threat through his teeth.

Durn's eyes darted around the room. His rousing support of only moments ago had vanished into a sullen hush. The only sound he could hear now was the creaking of the floor, the rattling of an awning across the street and the sniffling of the young woman with the green hair who stared mournfully into the bloodied swollen face of his fallen victim.

Nervously, Durn tried to reconfigure his spindly challenge into a logical acquiescence.

"Sure." Durn nodded with an unbalanced smirk. "101865."

Rabbel knelt down and punched the combination into the electronic lock. As the iron shackle fell from his scraped wrist, the gentleman groaned, spit up blood and tried to speak.

"My dauther…" he rasped and gurgled between broken teeth as his eyes bulged bright white behind his thick red mask. "My dau…"

"Go home." Rabbel interrupted as he stood. "Your daughter doesn't need you. And you don't need us. We'll take good care of her. You have my word."

"Your…wurr?" The gentleman rolled to his knees and spit up blood again.

"That's all you've got, old man." Rabbel gazed down at him sternly. "You can do what you want with it. But don't do it here anymore. And remember: If you tell anyone where we are, we'll find you and kill everyone you know."

Rabbel gestured toward two men, who quickly sat down their drinks and took up the older gentleman by his arms.

"Take him home," Rabbel ordered. "And call him a doctor."

"Da-do!" the young girl called after them as they dragged the man out the front door.

Rabbel shot her an angry scowl and she quickly looked down and away. She hopped back onto her bar stool and fumbled nervously for the warm drink she had almost forgotten.

The murmur of casual and subdued conversations slowly resumed as the patrons returned to their private circles. Imperceptibly, a quartet of musicians filtered soft instrumentation back into the scene, sounding most like a medieval ensemble of string, horn and drums.

Crilen observed the thin and sweaty Durn swagger over to his emerald-coifed prize, smiling through long yellow teeth. She ignored him at first. But Durn reached down behind her, firmly clutching her taut buttocks with both hands. Then he leaned over and whispered into her ear.

"I love you." He wheezed and smiled as the smell of smoke and alcohol on his breath polluted her nostrils. "I hope this proves it."

"You stink." She sniffed back her tears and offered only a brash and haughty rejection.

A dangerous rage once more, skittered across Durn's gnarled, bony face. He was very poor at concealing emotion, but the girl didn't seem to care much what he thought. With scant acknowledgment of his presence, she pressed down the curls surrounding her face with her fingertips, then she took her warm glass and swallowed the rest of its contents in one very unfeminine gulp.

"I mean it." she turned up the short pointed nose on her bright white face. "Clean yourself!"

Durn looked around the room to see who could see him being rebuffed, but they all looked away before he could spot any of them.

"All right." He manufactured an odd imbalanced grin. "I'll be back, my tight little tooty."

He shoved his hand between her legs, causing her to jump and tense up. Then he turned away, smiled at everyone who would look and swaggered toward the staircase.

Crilen watched Durn disappear, then he looked back toward Rabbel who was now immersed in conversation with two other men and a tall lanky female.

No one was paying Crilen much attention, which struck him as odd since no one else was bald, grey-skinned or had pointed ears besides himself. "It must be providing me with cover," he concluded. The only thing which anyone may have considered conspicuous was that he was the only person standing without a stein or a glass.

So he turned toward the bar area again and watched a couple next to the young woman with the emerald hair tab out with a loud and hearty farewell. An empty seat was left open. Crilen concluded the time had come for him to interact. He discreetly maneuvered himself through the crowd and up to the bar until he stood, respectfully, behind the young woman.

"Excuse me," Crilen addressed her politely.

She turned and looked him up and down through deadened, remorseless eye slits. The distress she had so openly and painfully displayed minutes before appeared to have receded as she mechanically sipped from another glass of dark blue alcohol. In her eyes she appeared to be pining for the death of her soul. There were strange hesitations in her confidence.

She attempted to eye him with a poorly contrived disdain. Then, all at once, she wearied of the facade, and decided to shelve her attitude until Durn showed up again.

"What?" she still answered coldly.

"Do you mind if I sit?" Crilen asked.

"Just don't grab my ass, will you?" she smirked as she jostled her drink in her fingers. "It's getting sore, you know? It's getting old, too."

"I'm sorry to hear that." Crilen eased onto his chair.

It was then he caught a glimpse of himself in the mirror behind the bar. He recognized the contours of his face, but everything else had changed. His head was full of dark hair, his ears were rounded at the tips and his skin was tinted the same deep ebony color as Rabbel's. His burgundy sweater had been replaced by a brown leather coverall which resembled the dress of at least half a dozen other people in the room. Altogether, he was very surprised and relieved to find that he actually looked quite common among the patrons.

"Um, I'm sorry, but I'm new here…" Crilen began.

"Reza!" She leaned over and kissed him on the cheek.

"Excuse me?" Crilen glanced around the bar.

"My name." She tilted her head curiously. "I'm Reza!"

"Oh." Crilen regathered himself. "I'm Len."

"Pleased to meet you, Len." She brightened to an eerie gregariousness. "I didn't mean to act like a bitch, you know? I mean, here you are, new in town, right? And you walk into this place and there's this big mad fight going on and I'm screeching like a harpy with a hot iron up my ass and you're probably asking yourself 'What the fuck is wrong with these people?' Am I right?"

"Uh…something like that." Crilen tried again to measure her.

"Well," she continued on, "It's just that I'm having one of the most 'burn me at the stake' days of my life…do you want a drink? And, um, I just don't have my shit together at all tonight, you know? I mean, I know you're a man and you probably don't have any idea what I'm talking about, but there are some days when it seems like everything you're running away from is chasing after you and the only thing that can save you is, like, totally in doubt, you understand what I'm saying? I mean, who the fuck thought that my fucking father would come here tonight? Nineteen twinmoons, and he hasn't given a dead foreskin what I do, then tonight…excuse me, could you get him a drink? What are you having?"

"Whatever you're having." Crilen filled in.

"No. This is a girl's drink." Reza shook her head. "Get him something manly! You know. Something with an erection! And put it on Durn's tab. This guy's new in town! Then tonight, my father shows up like fucking holier than thou patriarch of the fucking nine tribes and says he's going to haul my ass home like I'm five twinmoons old! I mean, what the fuck, you know? I mean, I love the old bastard but…Da-do, get the fuck out of here before you get your ass kicked! Which of course happens! So then its all my fault, right? Holy running shitpiles, can you believe it?"

"Sure." Crilen answered as he watched the bartender pinch up a tiny squirming eel, drop it into a stein of brown liquor and slide it toward him.

"You do?" Reza's mouth hung open as if he had betrayed her deepest convictions. "Well how do you take Da-do's side when you don't even know the creepy whore sore? Especially after I buy you a drink! What is that?"

"You ordered it." Crilen sighed as he watched the eel twist and glide through the liquor in his glass.

"I think you're supposed to drink it before it dies." She sounded reasonably certain.

"He seems to be doing well enough." Crilen observed. "I'll wait."

Unexpectedly, Reza crossed her spiked-heel ankle boots up onto Crilen's lap as she slouched down in her chair. She suddenly appeared very intrigued with his take on matters.

"So why are you on my father's side?" She eyed him suspiciously as she leaned forward, pulled a small pipe from her rolled sock and lit it with a match.

"No revelation, really." Crilen offered. "You're his daughter. It looks like he tried to raise you well…"

"Looks like?" she interrupted. "Then what in fuck's butthole am I doing here?"

"Slumming, I'd say." Crilen answered, suppressing a smile. "All the leather hide, alcohol and foul language in the world couldn't make you fit here. You wreak prim and proper whether you want to or not."

"Oh really." She blew smoke from her nose and narrowed her eyes. "Then explain to me how prim and proper me, as you say, wound up here, hmm? Oh, but you've read my mind, right? You know that my father is a grandstanding, hypocritical, lawbooking sphincter, right? A man who only cared about how things looked instead of how they were! When I had problems…real problems…he'd always say 'Put on a happy face, darling. It doesn't look good to frown up that pretty face.' Yeah. Put on a happy fucking face when I was thinking about suicide. Put on a happy fucking face after he ran my mother away and divorced her for some flood sale hooker! Put on a happy fucking face when my brothers and their buddies raped me at Da-do's fucking doily-dick dinner party! 'We'll smooth this out,' he said to me. 'Now go do your homework!' That's right, Reza, put on a happy fucking face even though life feels like you've got a rusty pole shoved up your ass! And then that crotch-rot chewing, varicose vein has the gall to show up here, embarrass the fuck out of me and get six liters of piss beat out of himself! And for what?"

"Well…" Crilen started.

Reza reached across Crilen and grabbed his stein. She slurped his drink loudly then smiled as she sucked the eel through her teeth.

"I'm listening." She smiled at him, then worked the heels of her boots into his midsection. "Wow! You're strong! How 'bout kicking the stink out of Durn for me when he comes back? That's a lot of kicking! I mean, I like him. He's weird. But he thinks he loves me and it's getting rude. Like he fucking really even knows what love is! Stupid pus pimple really thinks he impressed me kicking the shit out of my father. Like I'm supposed to love him for that? Is he out of his fucking still-born larvae? I mean I like him. But I love Da-do, you know? Can't stand him. Definitely can't live with him. But I love him! Is that crazy?"

"No." Crilen took her ankles and pulled her heels out of his stomach.

"Oh! Was I hurting you?" Reza asked. "I'm sorry. I do this to Rabbel and he never says anything."

"So what does Rabbel do here?" Crilen tried to reel in the conversation.

Reza smiled and rolled her eyes around as if he had rummaged into the most provocative little secret. She took another drag from her pipe and narrowed her eyes with sudden and focused lucidity.

"Uhhh…well…" she started with a smirk. "Rabbel Mennis is into everything, really. Politics mostly. Not the elected kind. But the kind that really makes things happen, you know? I don't mean moron terrorist shit either. At least I don't think so. I mean more like social awareness things. Real world things. Things that don't have to do with religion or fake moral shit. You know: Freedom, that kind of thing."

"And all these people work for him?" Crilen asked.

"For him, with him, because of him mostly." She blew a stream of smoke into the air. "He knows his shit. God, does he ever. Now him, I love. But it figures, he's taken. All the good ones are. Are you seeing anybody? Back home, I mean?"

"No." Crilen picked up his drink. "Not for some time."

"Hmh." Her brows danced into her curled bangs as she gulped from her own glass. "Relationships are awful, really. Always getting swept up into who someone else wants you to be. I don't think you can ever really find yourself in a relation-ship. I mean, who you are, you know? I'd love to be alone for awhile. A good while. But then, where do you get sex from? Strangers? God, I'd rather have a bad relationship than fuck a good stranger. Strangers are…very weird…like ghosts. You see them, you even fuck them, but you can't feel them, you know? I guess that's why I keep falling into relationships. Even with fart gas like Durn! I mean he's skinny, he's ugly, he's stupid, hung like a thunderhorse, but has no clue which end of the stick he's on! Did I leave out stupid? God! Why doesn't Rabbel dump that PJ bitch? I'd be on him in two seconds! And I'd make him so fucking happy!"

"Is that her, over there?" Crilen nodded toward the dark angular woman next to Rabbel.

"I don't think so." Reza sipped her drink. "Not even close, actually. Leesla would rather chew the cheese with her girl, Hesh, than get poked in the peghole by a guy. Know what I mean?"

"Uh…right." Crilen filed away the names. "But who is PJ?"

"I'm not sure." Reza suddenly became careful. "I mean, I really shouldn't say. I mean, you're really neat and all, but it's Rabbel's business. And this is all I have right now, you know?"

Suddenly, Reza arched her back and tensed up. She rolled her eyes and started to frown.

"Guess who?" came a voice from behind her as a pair of hands worked their way around her posterior to her outer thighs.

"Oh gee, how many guesses do I get?" She shook her head with annoyance. "Someone who treats my ass like it belongs at the petting zoo?"

"Nope." Durn's stubbled face appeared over her shoulder. "Someone who knows your ass belongs to me."

Durn smiled his toothy yellow smile as he worked his hands up to Reza's breasts and pushed them together. Reza's brows gnarled with dismay, but she closed her eyes opened her mouth and kissed him deeply as she held his scruffy, pointed chin in her tiny hand.

Crilen felt a twinge of sadness for the girl, but he turned in his chair, took up his glass and decided to survey the premises.

Leesla and the other two men who had been speaking to Rabbel still stood together in serious conversation, but Rabbel had suddenly disappeared. Crilen noticed symbols on the arms of their tunics: an outline of a spired dome structure with a large dagger impaled through its roof. As he scrutinized the crowd he found many more of these symbols on tunics, cloaks and tattooed flesh. He scoured the walls and found postings bearing still more of the markings, accompanied by smaller printed literature which he could not make out from his chair.

"Hey!" A voice interrupted his train of thought. It was Durn. "Do you have a reservation?"

"Sorry." Crilen sized him up. "I don't follow."

"You're sitting next to my woman," Durn taunted arrogantly. "So I assume you must have a reservation. Otherwise, I'd check your bags and get the fuck out of here if I was you!"

Crilen rolled his eyes and looked away momentarily. He instinctively expected to feel the warmth of his fire smolder in the palms of his hands, but he didn't. He looked up, assessed the scrawny bully and suddenly found his arms very badly wanting to render Durn in a way that would have made Reza's horribly beaten father look fit for a formal dinner dance.

"Durn, don't!" Reza jumped out of her chair and came between them.

"How many asses do I have to kick for you, bitch?" Durn grabbed her and pushed her against the bar. "Or maybe I should just kick your ass instead?"

Durn raised a fist toward Reza. But Crilen snatched Durn's wrist firmly. Durn snapped a glare toward Crilen that fell between shock and insanity. Crilen clutched Durn by the back of the neck and bluntly smashed his forehead against the edge of the bar. Durn's limp body bounced back into Crilen's arms. He hoisted the gangly man into his vacant chair and propped him up, slumping against the bar before anyone other than Reza even noticed.

"When he wakes up, tell him he won again." Crilen looked at Reza who was visibly shaken. "He gets the seat, he gets the girl."

"You…you didn't have to do that." Her voice shook. "He wasn't going to hit me. He never does. He's really sweet. He's just a little fucked up sometimes, you know?"

"Well, then, I guess we three have very bad chemistry." Crilen shook his head and sighed.

Reza frowned, turned away and tenderly administered to Durn. Crilen watched her ask the barkeeper for a towel, then he dismissed the pair and decided to take a walk.

IV.

Maybe it was paranoia, but Crilen felt certain he was being watched. Despite the physiological cover It had provided for him, he sensed it was only a matter of time before someone found him to be out of place through his movements or responses. And since this was not just any tavern, but a meeting place for those with some socio-political agenda, he dreaded becoming the object of an impromptu persecution.

Which led him back to the disconcerting discovery that his fire powers had been dealt away in the exchange for his false identity. In an emergency, he would not be able to burn his way through or fly his way out. He would have to rely on his fists, and perhaps a skull-butt or two.

"Of course, its conceivable that I can't really be hurt here." he thought to himself. "After all, this has all been orchestrated by my host."

But then he recounted the moments with Aami. The smells, the warmth, the joy, the horror. "All very real" It had said. Which meant that here, death could be as real a sensation as anything else.

Crilen kept his back to the walls as he moved along the perimeter of the room. He scanned several faces for Rabbel but did not find the stocky, muscular leader anywhere. He did, momentarily, focus in on Leesla, the tall female who now looked less serious than she had appeared earlier. She presently seemed most concerned with the seduction of another young lady as they laughed and drank and petted one another intermittently.

Meanwhile, the music quietly grew lasciviously aggressive in tempo as the powerful rhythms of the percussionist took the lead on several compelling selections. A number of couples set aside their drinks and danced provocatively intimate duets through the tides of passionate arrangements.

Crilen glanced back at Reza for an instant and caught her staring at him from across the crowded room. She smiled nervously, then shifted her attentions back to Durn as she went on about drowning him in her run-on banter while he single-mindedly pawed her bare thighs.

"Got one, brother?" A man with long hair and a thick beard briskly walked by and pushed a sheet of paper into Crilen's chest.

"No," he answered to the man's back as he moved on quickly.

Crilen examined the document. The domed symbol with the dagger impaled through its roof, was stamped as the heading. Surprisingly, or perhaps not, the rest of the document was in a language he readily understood.

"Hmh."

Crilen read:

> Today there is greater despondency and dissonance amongst the religious theocrats than our government would dare let anyone know. The self-anointed people of God are becoming people like us...people who want answers to their problems, not prayers that go unheard. They want freedom, not repression. They want love, not guilt. They want to live as best they can, instead of dying for a world they will

never see. The self-anointed people of God love their children as we do. The self-anointed people of God love their lovers as we do. The self-anointed people of God love their families as we do.

But these so-called people of God can't understand why God won't let them love unconditionally. Why something that feels wonderful is called a perversion. Why suffering needlessly is considered a virtue. And they can't understand why there must be barriers to true happiness. They can't understand why their natures lure them into hypocrisy so that "God" can condemn them for their nature. They've heard about God's meeting with the nine chieftains…over two thousand twin-moons ago. And how the laws and commandments of that meeting at the Temple were to ensure the grace of God for everyone on this planet for millennia to follow. They've heard about the legendary Aschen~exol miracle supposedly witnessed by thousands.

But has anyone seen God lately? Have there been any updates from God's king-dom? Or have we been left to fend for ourselves in a problematic world filled with a myriad of ills and complexities unheard of during the time of the chieftains. The self-anointed people of God are beginning to wonder: What did the nine chieftains know of the future? What did they know of you and I and our world today? It was a different world that they lived in then. A world devoid of the societal dynamics we wrestle with here and now.

So the self-anointed people of God are coming to realize that like the child who leaves home and must find his or her own way, we must find our own way and leave God and his nine chieftains and the Lord's Summit at the Temple and all of the old legends in the past. There are two kinds of people left on this planet. Those who believe as we do, and those who are afraid to admit to themselves that they believe as we do. Our job is to lift up the truth in their hearts, and unshackle the oppression of the religious legacy for a free and greater society! We will fight for this. We will die for this. Peace, Love and Freedom!

—PJ

"Ready to join?" a familiar voice spoke into his ear.

Startled, Crilen jumped back and looked into his face.

The man was ghost white, with tall brown hair that curved upward like a pair of shaggy horns. He had a long sloping nose that mirrored the slope of his chin, and he bore a pernicious, thin lipped smile which was all too recently familiar.

"You!" Crilen recognized It behind it's humanoid disguise.

It offered its hand. "So good to see you again!"

"What are you doing here?" Crilen frowned.

"Well, it is my world." It offered a wry smile. "I can shimmy around the old digs every now and again, can't I?"

Crilen opened his mouth when It whirled around and expertly plucked a drink from the tray of a passing barmaid.

The perturbed barmaid halted carefully, then turned to glare admonishingly at the two of them.

"Durn." Crilen gestured toward the bar. "We're on Durn's tab."

The barmaid eyed them suspiciously, then, with a wary nod, continued on her way, weaving briskly through the sea of bodies.

"This is a happening place!" It eyed the barmaid's figure as she disappeared into the crowd. "Very relaxed. Very quaint. And the root of all our troubles."

"How so?" Crilen asked.

"You read the notice, didn't you?" It pinched the paper away. "This is the epi-center of the end of civilization. Right here, amongst these wretched souls."

"Because they disdain the popular government?" Crilen offered.

"Don't be ridiculous." It turned up its nose. "Governments mean absolutely nothing. They're the flavor of the decade, or maybe the century if they're lucky! Whatever ideal keeps people's bellies fullest or their hopes the highest is 'le gouv-ernement de jour'. Lots of food and lots of promises, that's the key. The less food you have, the better the promises must be. If you have enough food, the people won't even notice when you've stopped promising anything. Warm and fed, just like swaddled children. Who needs to think when you're warm and fed? Hah! Government is the most irrelevant contrivance imaginable."

"I don't need another lecture." Crilen interrupted.

"But of course you do." It snorted. "You're not much of a sleuth, are you? 'Let's see, I'll spend the first half-hour talking to the vacuum-brained trollop, whining at the bar.'"

"She's a decent girl." Crilen found himself defending Reza. "Just a bit trou-bled."

"And you didn't even get to the good part." It taunted him.

"She gave me a couple of names." Crilen continued. "Pointed out a few of the main characters."

"Like...?"

"Durn."

"A yellow mongrel blessed with all the good sense of a hairy genital."

"Leesla."

"A very, very pernicious woman's woman."

"Rabbel."

It arched an eyebrow and smiled "Finally, a keeper. You're one out of three."

"PJ."

"Where?" It turned around suddenly, its levitous mood shattered all at once.

Crilen observed as It fretfully scoured the barroom. It appeared as though PJ would be a keeper as well.

"She's not here." Crilen spoke after a pause. "At least, I haven't met her yet if she is."

It tried to regain its composure, but the effect was already obvious.

"So who is she?" Crilen asked.

It turned on him with a cold and rueful scowl.

"You'll see." It pushed the paper back into Crilen's chest. "You'll try to save this world. You'll try to save your wife. You'll try to rescue all the misbegotten living souls from themselves...and you'll see."

It set down its glass, turned and forced its way through the dense congregation of bodies until it reached the door. As It reached for the handle, the door pulled open from the outside and four hooded, cloaked figures filtered in. It glanced at them with an odd smirk of recognition, then exited into the night. Several patrons trailed off their conversations and fixed their attention upon the arrivals.

"Rabbel!" called the lead figure. The familiar cadence caused Crilen's heart to leap in his chest. "Rabbel, where the hell are you?"

The woman threw back her hood and tossed her hands through her straight, dark mane which was tied off in a pony tail. As her face became visible, Crilen crumpled the notice tightly into his fist.

Her smooth snowy complexion struck him unusual and her bright scarlet lips were a brash divergence from her other features, but the arch in the dark brows, the dance of mischief in the large brown eyes, and the distinctive grace and elegance in her posture were disquietingly unmistakable.

Crilen knew his woman was Aami, his long deceased wife.

V.

"Rabbel!" she called out again. The crowd muttered and searched along with her.

Her clothing made no pretense she was anything other than a visitor. No leather. No rebellious symbols. No rough hewn edges to mar her stately femininity. She covered herself in a black leotard which clung neatly to every curve of her lean and delicate figure. The densely woven fabric appeared to magically refract the light around her like the disorienting incandescence of a swirling black hole. An oversized, jeweled bracelet hung loosely from her left wrist, glittering sharp reflections with her slightest movements. Her shoes were shimmering black slippers, cushioned to quiet her footfalls. She moved through the center of the crowd, as light and soundless as a domestic feline, gliding stealthily upon the coarse, wooden floorboards making nary a sound. She poised herself at the center of the room with the litheness of a classically schooled ballerina adapting to the role of a mirthful gamine.

An odd stillness ensued. The mesmerized mob waited anxiously for her next word.

"All right then!" she challenged the silence. "Someone get me something to drink while we wait!"

The other three cloaked figures moved toward the bar in dutiful servitude.

"Take mine!" called an inebriated voice.

"Sorry." She turned and winked at him. "I wouldn't dream of breaking up a matched set!"

The fat, thistle-faced patron wobbled as his mouth hung open with a quizzical look.

"You and your cup!" She smiled winsomely. "A cup…and a saucer!"

The crowd broke into a frivolous giggle. The fat drunkard looked at his tankard, then felt the air beneath it.

"What saucer?" he droned cluelessly.

All at once, the bawdy gathering exploded into loud laughter. Meanwhile, she berated the patron's dullardry with a sarcastic roll of her eyes. She gracefully sauntered through the parting crowd toward the corner stage from which the ensemble had taken an intermission. She popped up onto a stool and gazed out over the array of smiling faces with the genuine warmth and freshness of a young teacher on her first day of class.

"Well, people." She leaned over and smirked at them, mimicking a good girl up to no good. "While we wait on Mr. Rabbel…and my drink," she lifted her chin toward the bar and drew attention to her companions who were having difficulty gaining the barkeeper's attention. "I have a little story to tell you all."

Anticipatory cackling dotted the throng.

"Now quiet," she mockingly admonished them. "This is serious business!"

They quieted just a tad. There were still smatterings of irrepressible giggles and snickers.

"Oh finally!" She smiled as her drink arrived from just off stage.

She sipped very lightly, but acted out as if she were quenching a ravenous thirst.

"Thank God!" she shook her head and clutched her glass. "This is a terrible story I have to relate to you."

"Yeah!" several individuals encouraged, hoping for something lewd.

"No, really." She pretended to frown. "This happened just a few kilometers up the road, I swear.

"You see, this lady storms into her cathedral the morning after Solemnday and yells for the Churchlord. I won't use any names because you might know these people. Anyway, she's screaming and cursing and blaspheming like you wouldn't believe. Of course she doesn't care that she's cursing in a cathedral. After all, its not Solemnday anymore, so what does it matter? So anyway, the Churchlord comes out of his office dressed in regal robes and what have you and greets the angry woman, who's kicking at the altar she's so bloody pissed off. The Churchlord tries to calm her down, but she won't have any of it. She's cursing him and his ancestry in all manner of filthy language. Well, finally the Churchlord calms her down to the point where she can speak rationally, and he asks her what this is all about. She looks at him and she snarls, 'My daughter came home from choir practice yesterday, and she said that after practice, you took her into your study, told her to sit on your lap and you put your hand down the front of her blouse and fondled her!'

"Well, the Churchlord gasps with horror. 'Oh, my god' he says. 'How could she tell such a horrible lie? Madame, I give you my word before God almighty that I never did such a thing to your daughter. It would be sacrilegious to defile a sweet girl in such a manner!' Well, the woman is still furious. But she's known the Churchlord for over twenty twinmoons, so she looks at the Churchlord and she says, 'Perhaps you're right. She's only ten and at a strange age where children tend to tell stories. Please forgive me my lord.' And the Churchlord says, 'Yes, I forgive you. We'll speak no more of it.' And the woman leaves.

"Well two weeks pass. And the lady shows up again in hysterics. She's jumping up and down, cursing and swearing again and yanking tapestries from the wall. The Churchlord comes running out of his study and begs the woman to stop. He says 'Madame, this is a holy place, you cannot do this!' And she spits at his feet and screams at him, 'My daughter says that yesterday you took her into your study and removed her blouse and began kissing and licking her all over!' The Churchlord jumps back and holds up his hands. 'Madame', he says, 'I believe in the virginal sanctity of all women before marriage, let alone a girl so young and precious as your daughter. I am incapable of such a crime! I beg you, madame, seek counsel for your daughter for I am innocent of this filthy charge.' The woman shakes her head and drops to her knees and begs the Churchlord's forgiveness. 'I do not know what I'm going to do with her. She has never told such horrible lies as this before!'

"The Churchlord lifted the woman to her feet and held her with fatherly tenderness. 'I will pray for her, madame. And you must also' he said. Heartbroken, the woman walks out of the cathedral wondering what she'll do about her daughter. Well, a month passes, and the Churchlord is in his study when suddenly he smells something burning. He goes running out into the sanctuary and sees the pulpit has been set afire! He turns to call the safety department when he sees the angry woman standing in the pews with a torch in her hand. The Churchlord looks at her and asks 'My god, madame, what have you done?' She hurls the torch at him and begins screaming and cursing every measure of his personal anatomy. The Churchlord is so angry at what she's done, he curses back at her, and says 'Madame, I have told you I have not touched your daughter and am incapable of such a blasphemous act of utter vulgarity. Your daughter needs help!'

"Well the woman will have none of it this time. She's taken her daughter to counselors and psychologists and no one believes the girl is lying. So the mother who is seething with anger, says: 'My daughter returned to choir practice last week, and she said that you took her into your study, removed her trousers and panties and took her from behind until she bled! And this time a doctor has confirmed it!' The Churchlord is beside himself. He does not understand why this girl has lied about him. So finally he yells to the woman, 'Bring her! Bring her here now and I will put an end to this nonsense!' Well, the woman says that her daughter is outside and is afraid to enter the cathedral anymore. So the Churchlord says, 'Fine! Then I will go out and we will confront her.'

"So the woman and the Churchlord step out of the smoking sanctuary and out onto the front steps of the cathedral. 'Where is she?' the Churchlord bellows with indignation. The mother reaches behind the front door where the girl is hiding and guides her out by the hand. The girl has short orange hair, freckles, and wears a white blouse with short little green trousers. 'My God!' the Churchlord yells at the girl. 'My God!' he yells as he clenched his fists. 'Oh my lord,' the woman said as he surged into a fit. 'Please don't be too severe with her! I see by your revelation that this has to be a mistake!' But the Churchlord drops to his knees, shaking his fists like he's nearly gone insane. 'My God!' he yells at the mother. 'I had thought she was a little boy!'"

The bar crowd, which had restrained its fervor to this point, collapsed into wild hilarity. Women fell into men and men fell into each other as if all their strings of self control had been cut loose.

The young woman (Aami, Crilen had already decided), shrugged meekly and tossed up her hands as though she were merely lost in dumbfounded commiseration with the poor Churchlord, himself.

"Fucking rancid!" yelled a man sloshing a raised stein in tribute.

"Fucking true, too!" Leesla grinned a broad, devilish, white-toothed grin as she stroked the back of the other tall female.

"I think we all agree that 'fucking' Churchlords are the problem." The young woman on stage raised her glass.

"Fucking hypocrites, to be precise," came a deep, stern voice from just off stage.

It was Rabbel. He offered her his hand to lead her from the stage.

"Oh, look at this everyone." She drew back from him, playfully defiant. "Rabbel Mennis finally shows his face and I'm supposed to just jilt the lot of you like that!" She snapped her fingers.

The patrons laughed again, though with a tinge of cautious reserve.

"Well, I'm not done yet!" She crossed her legs and haughtily lifted her gaze away from Rabbel to the crowd.

The women in the audience hooted and applauded.

"PJ!" Rabbel sounded serious. "Business?"

She paused for a moment and eyed him again. She tried to muster a look of momentary disrespect, but fell just short. Still, she turned away from him and continued on.

"Two women are walking home from cathedral Solemnday afternoon."

There was loud applause and cheers, mostly from the females in the audience.

"The first woman," she continued, "says to the second, 'I'm tired of all those lecherous married men ogling us all the time. It's totally disgusting.' The second woman says, 'Oh pay them no mind. They're just looking. There's no harm in it.' 'Well', the first woman says, 'I'll bet you that if you offered them sex, half the married men at our cathedral would go to bed with you without a conscience.' The second woman laughs and says, 'Half! How can you be so cynical?' 'Because,' the first woman smiles, 'I've slept with three-quarters of them already!' 'Three-quarters!' the second woman exclaims. 'But you said half just a moment ago!' 'Oh yes, darling,' the first woman said. 'But I was talking about you, not me!'"

Another swell of laughter ensued, followed by loud applause, hooting and whistling.

PJ/Aami slid from her stool, curtsied for the audience, then daintily offered her hand to Rabbel, who, with some impatience, carefully guided her from the stage.

"PJ." Crilen muttered to himself. "So this is PJ. What in the world is going on here?"

As Rabbel led PJ from the stage area, the ensemble filed back to their places and started a very low and poignant melody.

"You're late," Rabbel scolded PJ privately.

"Oh, Rabbel." She smiled and tweaked him on the cheek. "How can you possibly be late in a place that stays open all night? You don't even have chronometers on the walls."

"You own a chronis." Rabbel pointed to her wrist.

"And so do you." Some authority crept into her playfulness. "We've got all evening, Rabbel Mennis. Besides, you know how hard it is for me to get away. By itinerary, I'm supposed to be 300 kilometers north of here. I did the best I could. Now don't be cross!"

Rabbel sighed as she draped her arms around his thickly muscled neck and swayed back and forth.

"Sorry." He shook his head. "There's just a lot that needs to be done in the next few days and you're not always available."

"I know," she concurred. "I hate it. I thought of dancing with you like this all week. But bloody 'business' kept getting in the way."

"Well, before we get carried away..." Rabbel started.

"No. This first," she whispered, pulling herself closer, kissing him with deep affection on the lips.

Crilen found himself bristling as the kiss seemed to go on forever.

"What's wrong, friend?" A burly, bearded drinker nudged him out of his prolonged stare. "Never seen a pauper and a princess kiss before?"

"What does he have over her?" Crilen poorly masked his annoyance.

"Anything she wants," the bearded man responded and slapped Crilen on the back. "Any thing she wants."

Rabbel finally appeared to relent as PJ restfully closed her eyes and laid her head on his shoulder as they danced slowly. Crilen watched as Rabbel's large hands climbed gingerly up the crevice of her back until they found a comfortable place to hold her. Crilen found himself circling the pair from a discreet distance, trying to read their faces, their movements, anything that would indicate how intimate they had become.

PJ continued to move with Rabbel, as Aami long ago, had moved with Crilen. His fondest recollection of her touch had become nearly as torturous as the conjured lovemaking had been. There was a joy which accompanied these memories, but they always led him to a precipice of sorrow. So he tried, with difficulty, to convince himself that none of what he was seeing was real, even though he had been told that it was.

Finally, and mercifully, the song ended. PJ opened her eyes with the smile of a child who had just awakened from a wonderful dream. She kissed Rabbel again and tried to hold him, only this time his vacillations permitted him to pry himself away.

"We really have to talk," he spoke firmly.

PJ folded her arms and scowled her rebellion.

"Whenever you're ready." Rabbel turned and disappeared back into the crowd.

The ensemble started into another slow-tempo melody. PJ, left by herself, quickly became surrounded by couples dancing affectionately, nose to nose, bosom to bosom.

The thistle faced drunkard staggered up to her and offered himself for the second dance. She smiled kindly to him, but smartly backed away.

"You look like you could use a dance partner." another voice offered.

She turned and looked up into Crilen's broad smile. She assessed him quickly and concluded that he would do. She grasped his hand as Crilen gently took her by the waist, and then they met each other's eyes.

"Aami?" Crilen whispered to her.

"Excuse me?" PJ regarded him oddly.

"Oh, I'm sorry." Crilen saw no hint of recognition in her face.

"Do you know me from somewhere?" she asked.

"Um, well actually, you remind me a bit of a woman I used to know," Crilen offered.

"Really?" She sounded suspicious.

"But I'm not from around here," he qualified.

"Well neither am I. Where are you from?" she probed.

"I'm sorry. It doesn't matter." Crilen retrenched. "I know you're not her."

"And how do you know that?" she suddenly seized control of the exchange.

"Because." The words crumbled apart in his mouth. "Because she's dead," he finally managed.

"Oh." PJ was momentarily disarmed. "I'm so sorry."

"You needn't be." Crilen smiled reflectively. "It's been a long while. Too long for me to be acting this way."

"It's never too long if you loved her." PJ smiled. "I hope that if something ever happens to me, there'll be a man somewhere who's heart will be broken, and he'll still have my name on his lips years afterward, whenever he dances with another woman."

Crilen could only sigh as he turned her slowly.

"I know it's selfish." She smiled with a bit of humility. "But isn't it romantic?"

"Yes," he replied in a whisper. "Yes, it certainly is."

"So you were married?" PJ asked.

"Yes," he answered, marveling at her insight.

"I could tell." she smiled again. "A man doesn't miss a girlfriend or a lover like he misses his wife. 'One flesh', I was always taught about married people. Married people who are in love, that is. It's like cutting a single person in half when they're separated. Even lovers don't have that."

"You're right." Crilen felt a slight chill.

"She died suddenly?" PJ continued.

"Yes."

"I could see that, too." She sounded like an adolescent solving a puzzle. "You didn't have time to say good-bye. You just looked up and she was gone."

"Something like that." He grimaced.

"Well, she was lucky." PJ sighed like Aami.

"How so?"

"Lucky that she had such a fine man to love her so much." She sounded very serious. "I'm sure she died happy."

Crilen was besieged by a surge of emotion he wasn't prepared for. He struggled to redirect the conversation.

"So you say you're not from around here?"

"No." She was strangely concise all of a sudden.

"But it seems as though you're familiar with this place," he observed. "And it with you, for that matter."

"Oh, I visit from time to time," she answered vaguely. "My beau is here. And the company is so down to earth."

"Unlike home?"

"Not at all like home," she answered with a tinge of rue.

"So why not stay…get married," Crilen continued.

"Oh." she sighed again, "I've got obligations. A lot of responsibilities that just won't allow it right now."

"That doesn't sound very romantic," he accused.

"Well we all can't be romantics, Mr…".

"Crilen." He looked into her eyes, hoping the name would mean something to her. "Or you can call me Len."

"That's different." She chuckled at his name. "Well, Mr. Len, sometimes our responsibilities get in the way of our romances. And then we have to choose. That's why you and your wife were so lucky, I guess."

The tune slowly faded out and the patrons gave light and uncharacteristically civilized applause.

"Well." she suddenly dropped her hands to her sides. "I guess I'd better tend to some of those obligations now."

Crilen felt a pang of emptiness as her hands slipped away and he relinquished her waist.

"Well I guess I should let you tend to it, Miss…?" Crilen feigned ignorance.

"PJ." She smiled at him.

"Which stands for?"

"Are you sure you're not with the government?" PJ frowned playfully.

"If I were, I'd know what PJ stood for, wouldn't I?" Crilen smiled.

"Well, it's just PJ around here." She extended her delicate hand "Nice meeting you, Lenny. Be seeing you."

Crilen took her hand and kissed the back of it with a gentleman's grace he had nearly forgotten. She even smelled like Aami.

"You certainly aren't from around here, are you?" PJ chuckled and withdrew.

She pirouetted and glided away smiling and waving like a celebrity to the adoring crowd. In another moment, she disappeared from sight to attend to her "obligations" with Rabbel Mennis.

Meanwhile, the name "Lenny" echoed in Crilen's mind, indistinguishable from his memories of Aami uttering those same syllables. He found himself short of breath, his heart throbbing heavily in his chest. This time, it had not been a memory. It had been something very real. Something remarkably, painfully, present. Something he had just held in his arms.

He staggered for a moment, then finally charged for the exit to seize a gulp of fresh air and regather control of his wits.

VI.

"Are we enjoying the play, good sir?" It greeted Crilen on the dark street.

"You!" Crilen snarled.

"Now, now! Not to worry!" It assured him. "You're not you and she's not her. This is my world. My tragedy. Always remember that."

"Then why in hell does that woman look and sound and…smell like my wife?" Crilen pounded his fist against the side of the stone building.

"Smell?" It giggled. "Good grief. You widowers are certainly a sorry lot!"

"Answer me!" Crilen thundered.

"Because that's how you interpret her," It replied simply. "It's no more complex than that."

"Unless you're playing some game!" Crilen accused.

"Oh, haven't we been through that?" It yawned mockingly. "Games are for fun. Are you having fun, Lenny?"

Crilen's eyes narrowed. His jaw muscles tightened.

"Neither am I," It continued. "Your wispy woebegone sentiments won't serve you here. Lose sight of what you must do and no one will survive."

Crilen obstinately fixed his eyes straight ahead.

"Oh dear lord!" It grew annoyed. "If this were sport, I'd hand you a water bucket and ladle. If this were theatre, I'd hand you a pushbroom. Green-haired girls and bar fights? It's going to take you forever to figure out what's really going on here."

"Then do tell." Crilen sneered.

"I can't." It looked serious again. "Or rather, I shan't. But let me toss you another hint whilst you stew in the broth of your stupor."

With a gesture of It's taloned fingers, the stone wall of the building spiraled open like a thick liquid, revealing two figures in a private office. They carried on unaware of their invisible audience.

"We've got a problem," Rabbel spoke forebodingly.

PJ merely smiled, tossed back her ponytail and wiggled her dangling feet over the top of the cushioned chair she had contorted herself onto.

"Are you listening to me?" Rabbel raised his voice.

"Of course I am, darling." She sighed, flipping her slippers to the edges of her feet with her toes. "I always listen to what you say. I just don't always understand what you mean."

Her wiggling feet stung Rabbel's raw nerves. She wasn't listening and didn't even care enough to hide her indifference.

In a smoldering fit, he stalked angrily toward her, snatched up both of her ankles with one hand and squeezed them together until her restless feet were still.

"Let go of me!" PJ hissed after a brief and fruitless struggle.

"Are you going to listen?" Rabbel pulled on her ankles.

"I was listening!" PJ tried to wiggle free.

"No. You weren't listening." Rabbel shook her feet as he scolded her. "You were humoring me with that condescending classist air of yours."

"Rabbel, you're hurting me." She ignored his comments. "You're bruising my ankles."

"Oh, well now, we can't have that!" Rabbel scoffed.

"Well it wouldn't be very easy to explain, now would it?" PJ grew flustered.

"I thought you said he doesn't look at you anymore." Rabbel loosened his grip just a tad.

"I said we don't love each other anymore." She raised her voice. "That doesn't mean he doesn't look. In fact, it means he can look and take without caring how I feel one way or another, if you really must know. It's actually very convenient for him! Are you happy?"

Rabbel's expression softened apologetically. He let her ankles loose and turned away.

"Oh, now look who's being condescending!" PJ spun around and righted herself on the chair. "My husband is my problem. I can handle him."

"You don't have to." Rabbel turned and faced her, distress diluting his resolve. "He doesn't love you and I do. So why don't you just get the hell out of there and come stay with me?"

"I can't."

"You won't." Rabbel raised his voice.

"Rabbel, we've been through all of this!" She rose and stepped gingerly toward him. "I want to be with you. You know I do! I risk everything just to get away to see you when I can. But you know that coming here to stay would ruin everything we've been working for. And there are so many people depending on us, we can't afford to be selfish, can we?"

"No," Rabbel conceded, as she gently took him by the hand. "No, we can't."

"Well, don't be so gloomy about it." She smiled cheerfully. "It won't be like this forever. And, when its over, I can come here and we can live together."

"And you'll tend bar?" He smiled.

"What is this fantasy you have about me tending the bar?" She wrinkled her nose and chuckled. "Isn't it enough that I'm going to be serving you? Do you want me serving the whole world?"

"Who better?" He caressed her ribs with his fingertips.

"Well, I've had enough of being all things to all people." She turned just a tad serious. "All I want is you, your home, your friends…"

"…my children," Rabbel added.

PJ strolled her fingers up the front his chest until her soft hands slipped delicately behind his neck. She kissed him passionately and shivered in his arms.

"Okay." Rabbel bowed his head in resignation. "I'm sorry if I hurt you. And I'm sorry for being irrational."

"It's all right." she rubbed his neck. "I think that's part of the lure, really. That, and those eyes."

Rabbel reached up and framed her face with his giant hand. She really was the feminine portrait he had dreamed of possessing his entire life. Intellect, polish and tenderness rolled into one courageous soul.

"Well, I can see where this is going," he spoke softly. "But first, there really is a problem and we have to talk about it."

"Now?" she pouted.

"Yes. Right now."

PJ abruptly dropped her arms to her sides and pirouetted to attention. To a former military man like Rabbel, it was almost laughable watching this soft, slender creature attempt to emulate a soldier's resolve. He nearly lost his concentration again, but retrieved it enough to refrain from laughing.

"The memorandum." He spoke firmly to her profile.

"Yes, what about it?" She remained stiffened to as formal a posture as possible.

"It wasn't what I wanted." He spoke sternly, but still tried to spare her feelings.

"Is that all?" PJ broke rank and smiled again, gesturing with relief. "Well, I'm sorry. I know it wasn't exactly what we discussed. But sweetheart, you've got to realize that we can't hit people over the head with a club if we want them on our side. We have to take them by the hand and guide them…"

"It wasn't what we talked about." Rabbel cut her off. "At all!"

"Look," PJ began cheerfully. "I understand that you want to smash the religious hierarchy right in the chops with the back end of a shovel. There's nothing I'd rather do myself. But people have invested a lot in their faith and you just can't ask them to drop it like a rotten candy unless you show them where they're going."

"They're going nowhere. That's the problem," Rabbel answered. "Anywhere is better than where we are right now. They have to believe that the only way for them to swim to the surface is to untie themselves from the bottom of the lake!"

"But they have to know what lies at the surface, don't they?"

"Not if they're drowning," Rabbel stated flatly. "When you're drowning, you don't care about what might be waiting for you up top. All you know is that you want to live!"

PJ placed her hands on her hips and huffed. Clearly, this revisited debate was going nowhere.

"Fine," she relented. "Next time, I'll let you run it through the strainer to your heart's content. I'm very sorry. Hopefully, I haven't done too much damage."

"You haven't done any damage." Rabbel folded his arms. "I changed it."

"You what?" PJ's mouth dropped open.

"I changed it," Rabbel stated with emphasis. "I gave it some bite, some rage, some fire. No compromise."

"Well I hope you took my name off." PJ became annoyed.

"I couldn't." Rabbel stammered a confession. "These things have to come from you. People need validation from the north and that's what you represent! I told you that!"

"Rabbel!" PJ shouted. "How could you? You put words in my mouth? I'm perfectly capable of speaking my own mind, thank you! And I don't need an editor or advisor to tell me what to think! Damn you!"

"Peej, I tried to reach you for three days. You were on the road and surrounded by your husband's entourage. There was no way to get in touch with you."

"Well," PJ paced across the room, "well, then there shouldn't have been any memo. Not from me!"

"I told you what I wanted. You went ahead and wrote what you felt like writing," Rabbel retorted. "We can't just sit on our hands when you're 'indisposed'."

"What next?" Her voice grew louder. "Back to terrorism and street murders and all the things that put a price on your head? All the things that made people shy away?"

"No." Rabbel sounded nearly contrite. "I promised you no more of that. But you've also got to realize that even if we don't go looking for violence, violence may come looking for us."

PJ stopped and stared at the floor. She tapped her foot against the hard wood with the rhythm of a metronome: taut and steady. She folded her lips and worked her jaws. Her thumbs rubbed tightly against the sides of her closed fists.

"Rabbel," her voice quivered, "are you using me?"

"What?" Rabbel nearly gasped at the accusation.

"I need to know." Her voice shook even more. "Because if you are, then…then I might as well be dead."

"Honey…"

"If you are using me, and all of this is some ruse that I've fallen into to suit your own agenda, then I might as well be dead. I'm giving up everything I have and everything I am to be with you and there's no going back. When all of this comes to a head, I won't have anywhere else to go or anyone else to turn to. I'll be jumping off a steep cliff with the enemy hard on my heels, do you understand? And if I don't have you there to break my fall…then I'm dead. I'm dead…or worse if I'm caught!"

"Peej," Rabbel tried to soothe her with his voice, "we both want the same thing…"

"Do we?" PJ interrupted. "Are you certain?"

"I'm positive." Rabbel answered, rubbing her shoulder. "We want our freedom. But there's got to be a price paid for that."

"Your price is war." she sniffed. "Bloodshed. And I've told you that's not acceptable."

"So when they find us and have us executed because we wouldn't fight them with anything but words, then what?"

PJ held her palm to her forehead and swayed as if she were going to pass out. Rabbel tried to steady her, but she jerked away and searched for her cloak.

"I have to go," she said despondently.

"You just got here!"

"You wanted to talk business and we've talked business. Now I have to go!"

"You don't have to go!"

"I have a busy day tomorrow, Rabbel." She snatched up her cloak from the sofa. "And I don't want to carry it on, hungover and smelling of smoke after spending the night with a mercenary who doesn't care what happens to me…or the rest of the world, for that matter!"

PJ marched toward the door. Rabbel cut her off and blocked her exit with his giant forearm.

"I love you, Peej." His voice shook. "I love you and I won't let any of this come between us."

She eyed him with a cold royal stare which was tempered by a recessed measure of sadness and uncertainty.

"Good night, Mr. Mennis," she spoke in a whisper. "I have to go."

Rabbel found his trough of words exhausted. He could make her stay. He could force her to stay, but that she always came to him willingly was the heart of his joy in her company. For all of his physical strength and command, it was still she who possessed the power to simply walk away and leave him feeling very empty and very alone.

Slowly, he lifted his arm from the door, and she scurried through the crack like a reluctant pet freed from its cage.

PJ motioned to her attendants from across the room. They mechanically broke off their conversations, set down their drinks and followed her out of the tavern without delay.

A portion of the crowd turned toward Rabbel as he hung in his office doorway bearing a foul dark mask of perturbation. Then, before anyone could look away, he thunderously slammed his door to all of them.

Outside, Crilen and It watched as a cloaked PJ and her attendants hurried out of the tavern and into a waiting vehicle.

The long sleek vehicle hummed quietly, its stealthy black surface camouflaged against the backdrop of the dark night. It most resembled a sleek shining missile balanced upon a pair of massive treaded wheels with a band of dark reflective glass lining the passenger level. Four retractable legs silently folded into its belly as the concussive ignition of a jet engine pierced the light evening din. In another instant, the vehicle rocketed past them, bolted over a distant hill and blurred into the village on the first turn.

"Never got to drive one of those." It admired the vehicle's trail, as it stroked its pointed chin.

"He's betraying her," Crilen concluded, as the jet engine's echo faded into the horizon. "She's in over her head and now she can't go back."

"She's in league with the devil." It leaned against his shoulder and spoke into his ear. "And that's not even the half of it. Lives are at stake. Generations of lives. Billions of fragile, deluded, little lives. Keep that in mind before you cast her as some benign little ingénue from across the grassy meadow!"

"Trust me." Crilen snapped. "I'm not a fool."

"The only man who is no fool is the man who loves no woman," It recited. "He's a fool. You're a fool."

The eerie, embittered words trailed off into a mild breeze. Crilen felt it's hand lift from his shoulder.

"You…" he whirled around to confront It, but found himself alone on the lamplit curb.

VII.

To the east, the yellow moon had set hours ago. The lingering orange moon followed reluctantly, descending into the black distant hills which guarded the outskirts of town. From the west came the faint luminescence of sunrise painted dimly across the fading tide of starry night. Meanwhile, the chaotic sounds of late evening relented to an eerie stillness as the voiceless stirrings of early morning dragged and squeaked and bumped and coughed its mirthless preparations for yet another indistinguishable day of living.

Crilen rested upon an empty bench a block away from the tavern as he watched the people of the night scatter away before the people of the morning should see them in daylight.

He then wandered for an indeterminate amount of time, losing his way along the narrow, winding streets. Each time he looked behind him, the scenery was altered from that which he had just passed. Each time he circled a block, it became a new block at every bend. At some point, he even looked to the skies for direction or guidance, but the constellations were partnered to the conspiracy, rearranging themselves with every glance. Finally he conceded to what could only be It's new course of deception and he focused on the one thing…the one person, which remained a constant in his thoughts.

"PJ." he whispered to himself, recalling her delicate touch, her grace, her wise and whimsical voice reading his complexity like a children's storybook.

"Aami." He sighed and pushed his fingers into his forehead.

"This is not my wife," he reasoned again. "Yet I see her as my wife, It said. Why would I do that? Why would I do that here?"

"The center of a revolution. To what end?" He thumbed his chin and followed a swirling trail of paper taken up by a subtle morning breeze. "And what is she doing with Rabbel and all the rest of these malcontents? And what in the name of God am I supposed to do about her, or them…or any of it?"

As Crilen yawned and wiped the drowsiness from his eyes, the shape of an obese, yet nattily accoutered man materialized, crossing the street two blocks away. By the hitches in his gait, Crilen surmised him to be older as he laboriously tottered through the intersection and disappeared into a row of distant doorways.

Then Crilen noticed a second man, to his right, hastening across the street with a lumpy hat scrunched over his forehead. This man also appeared to be middle aged, though he was as thin as the first man had been fat.

Crilen followed the second man's path. And, it appeared as though he were headed toward the same doorway as the first.

"Sorry, but this does feel like a bloody game," Crilen muttered to himself.

He decided to shadow the second man at a discreet distance.

It was difficult to pursue the thin man's hurried gait; Crilen found himself wishing he had followed the heavier man instead. It was far from easy to remain both quick and quiet on the concrete walks. As they neared the doorways, a strong aroma of fried meat and baked bread charmed his senses.

The second man turned into a doorway, pulled open the door and hastened inside. He was heartily met with the sounds of familiar greetings all around.

Crilen stopped just short of the entrance and suddenly felt someone bump him from behind.

Crilen spun around defensively, tensed for a physical confrontation. When he looked up for an adversary, however, he saw only the top of a thinning scalp. He looked down and gazed into the face of a very perturbed third man whose passage he had apparently obstructed.

Crilen stepped aside and apologized. The short man smirked, murmured some inaudible wisecrack and made his way inside. As before, this man was also greeted warmly by those inside. Soon thereafter, boisterous laughter was accompanied by the clatter of dishes and eating utensils.

Crilen meandered to the front picture window to see if he could manage a glimpse of the layout inside. He noted several tables, though only one was occupied. Against the far wall was a counter behind which a cook and waitress hustled carefully around one another as if one's touch might shatter the performance of the other.

On a side wall was a large, flat, sixty centimeter monitor which appeared to be reviewing a succession of events from the day before. There were men and women delivering speeches from podiums before cameras and crowds. Then followed studio disseminators breathlessly slanting for the masses all that they had already seen. Finally, there were grim images from the remnants of a battle scene; bloody dismembered corpses amid shrapnel-pitted ruins littered a city street.

"So, you coming in, are you?" The short dark waitress appeared at the door.

"Um…" was all a startled Crilen could manage.

"Come on." She winked, wiping her hands on her apron. "Cook ain't much to look at but it's gourmet in here, trust me."

"I, uh…"

"Yeah, sure." She grinned admonishingly. "Out drinking all night. I can see it. But no one cares about that. So long as you find the lavatory when you need to."

"That shouldn't be a problem," Crilen said, straight-faced.

"Then come eat!" The waitress threw up her hands and stepped back inside.

The matter appeared to be settled right then and there. Crilen inspected the streets one last time. It remained quiet as dawn glowed faintly between the buildings. He smiled to himself, shook his head and stepped into the diner.

As he entered, noises, barely audible from the outside, became sharply amplified. The monitor volume was raised so the cook could hear the broadcast above the sizzling meat on the grill and the loud conversation at the center table.

And the center table was very noisy, as the verbal jousting between the three combatants escalated. The third man Crilen had nearly run into cackled and snickered, filling every break in the exchange. The thin man in the rumpled hat appeared strained and distressed as though making himself heard were a matter of life or death. Meanwhile, the largest and most vociferous of the three appeared relaxed as he arrogantly reclined in his oversized chair and smiled his enjoyment at being able to parry away any philosophical challenge with minimal exertion.

The large man's demeanor was much like that of a criminal boss partaking in condescending debate with underlings whom he could gesture silent at his indulgence. As long as the sparring played to the gratification of his ego, he would revel in it. Should he become the least bit annoyed or (God forbid) threatened, he would command immediate cessation of the proceedings and declare himself the victor.

For the time being, the debate raged on.

"Join 'em!" The waitress whisked by, balancing two oversized dishes which she skillfully settled in front of the larger man.

"I'd prefer..." Crilen began.

"Hey, Yolo!" The woman's sharp voice cut through the men's discourse.

The three men suddenly stopped and looked up.

"This gentleman's gonna bite a hole in your fat ass, Yolo!" She winked.

The large man laughed loudly and slammed his hand on the table. The other two only smiled cautiously.

"In case you don't know him, and of course you're supposed to," she gestured toward the table, "this is Master Yolo Pigue. You know...Yolo Media Enterprises?"

"Of...course." Crilen feigned recognition.

"And these two kissers of the derriere are Mr. Nil and Mr. Pont."

"Pleased to meet you." Crilen nodded. "I'm sorry to..."

"Sit and learn!" Yolo bellowed as a clump of food fell from the side of his wide mouth.

Without another word, Crilen pulled out a chair and sat at the table. Then, as if there had been no interruption at all, the conversation seamlessly resumed.

"So you're saying that you don't believe in the Covenant of the Nine." Mr. Pont hastened to a conclusion.

Yolo raised his bushy brows as he continued to expertly vivisect his meal. His copious jowls pumped like machinery, processing ground mounds of food into a giant roll at the top of his neck. Then, he inhaled, swallowed, and it all appeared to slide into storage vessels which began at the top of his wide throat and tapered into pouches of flesh which jiggled above his shoulder blades. He paused to draw a labored breath. Then, without missing a beat, filled his jowls anew and resumed the smelting of sustenance-to-mass all over again.

"Yolo?" Mr. Nil repeated.

Yolo paused abruptly, in mid-chew, as if the interruption to speak would upset the entire balance of his day. With an air of inconvenienced concession, he withdrew his utensils, tongued the food in his mouth behind his gapped and crooked teeth, and began to lecture them all straight on.

"It's not a matter of belief." Yolo said disdainfully. "Belief has nothing to do with it. Certainly, what I believe serves no purpose in this business. The minute I believe that my personal beliefs count for anything in the public eye, my integrity as a journalist is lost. It's not my beliefs that matter, you see. It's the public's beliefs that matter. Manipulation of their flaccid, conflicting beliefs is the marrow of popular journalism. Public beliefs, I can shape, mold, fuel or defecate upon. Whatever sells, dear boys. If someone doesn't like the way I see or say something and it still sells, then I've done my job. If everyone loves what I say and it sells, then that's what matters. It has nothing to do with right or wrong or truth. You'll find those virtues tightly scrawled in fine print upon every unread leaflet fluttering against the gutter. Too much depth! No one has time for that sort of academic rubbish!

"I, on the other hand, and quite successfully, mind you, feast concisely upon the symbiotic organism comprised of public interest, public subjects, and, most importantly, my conveyance twixt the two. That's journalism, understand? I see what I see and I tell what I see and I play the public psyche like a two-note horn. If I'm despised for my castigation of an icon, so be it. If I'm revered for my stroking of a repugnant pastime which creates a warm and fuzzy feeling in everyone's belly and my infamy, thereby, thrives upon it, then that's all that matters."

"And what about morality?" Crilen entered the conversation.

Yolo chuckled as he assembled another mass of food from his jowls and swallowed it whole. He continued his carving and dicing as a maestro would resume conduction of a symphony.

"Morality?" Yolo scoffed. "What in God's world is morality, I ask you? The Deliverer says that morality lies rooted in the church Addendums which are no less than the liberalized bastardized interpretations of the scribblings of warlords who died two thousand twinmoons ago. Don't do this, don't do that, sing these songs on Solemnday, lead a chaste and repressive life and when you die…good luck! The Break says that scripture is rubbish, that everyone is 'morally' obligated to free themselves from the church and must do whatever is rational and pragmatic for society. Then you have the starving thief who says its 'moral' for him to rob and steal. The unhappily married man who best loves his prostitute at the brothel. The policer who commits random murder to protect us from us. And, last but far from least, is the Accommodant who believes that morality blows in the direction of the latest popularity poll."

"Amen!" The cook laughed out loud as he clanged his metal spatula against the grill. "My thoughts exactly!"

"Why just yesterday," Yolo continued between chews, "in the same speech, our elected buffoon described the church as the continuing 'foundation of our moral fiber.' Then, not five minutes later he still proclaimed that we must all 'embrace the free choices of our fellows for an open and dynamic society.' I'm certain his auditory convictions must be little more than the amalgamation of a random backstage sampling of fan mail. He's a fine fence sitter, mind you, but he has no clue how impeccably stupid he sounds to thinking intelligent people. Though come to think of it, since thinking, intelligent people don't comprise the majority of the electorate, he may yet be wiser than all of us."

Yolo leaned back and smiled to himself as he dabbed away the spillage of consumption from his lips with a large cloth napkin.

Mr. Nil smiled and looked about to see if all were in agreement with Yolo.

"Then you're saying you don't have any morals?" Crilen masked his annoyance behind a permeable veil of respect.

There fell a momentary quiet. It was suddenly silent as if the entire diner were emptied save the sizzle of the grill and the drone of the monitor on the wall.

The waitress dropped something that sounded like a glass or a cup and everyone snapped out of their momentary trance.

"Now just a minute!" Mr. Nil belatedly jumped to Yolo's defense.

Yolo cut him off with a raised hand, calmly prepared to defend himself.

"Young sir, do you have a name?" Yolo rallied behind the pleasantry.

"Len," Crilen answered, poised.

"Well, Len," Yolo resumed dicing and carving his meal, "I believe that the conversation was about journalism, not my personal take on issues one way or the other."

"Then you're saying that a journalist should have no morals," Crilen corrected himself.

Yolo could not help but wince and frown. He stabbed a bloody stack of meat, bread and melon with his skewer. He gestured with it, as if he would have liked to have added Crilen's head as the bottom piece.

"Why of course a journalist should have morals," Yolo answered tersely. "Integrity, I believe, is the proper term. A journalist must, above all other things, have integrity. Otherwise, he simply becomes the teller of fibs and fairy tales."

"He becomes a liar," Crilen interjected.

"Precisely!" Yolo lauded with a wave of his skewer.

"Well then, what comprises this integrity?" Crilen asked.

"Hmmmh." Yolo paused and smiled as he ground and chewed until he could fill his jowls once more.

"His heart!" Mr. Nil filled the pause.

Yolo slammed his fist on the table causing everyone, including Crilen, to jump in their seats. He sneered at Mr. Nil, calling him "an idiot" without uttering a syllable. After a prolonged glare, Yolo withdrew from the silent chastisement, pushed his food down the silo of his giant throat and spoke again.

"His heart," Yolo scoffed. "No journalist can write with his heart! He becomes no less than a sopping driveller of poetry and sonnets when he even attempts any such thing. A whiner, a complainer, a sentimental sniveler that no one can respect and fewer care to hear from. No, no! Never the heart. A critical organ, no question. But useless as a tool to any scribe worth the snot in his rag.

"The FACTS!" Yolo bellowed emphatically. "The facts are the very mortar which holds journalistic integrity together. If you don't have the facts of the matter, then you don't have anything of use to your public. You must take something important to them that is absolutely undeniably factual and hold it hostage. Then you jade it, slant it, torture it, mutilate it, canonize it, cremate it, castrate it, murder and resurrect it, sauté and finally consume it right before their eyes, when you're certain they'll sup with you! Do whatever it takes to hold your audience. Whatever it takes to make you their oracle, their soothsayer, the conduit of their fortunes!"

"I see." Crilen settled back.

"Well, good. I'd thought you were blind." Yolo snorted and reclined in his chair again.

Everyone else offered a half-hearted laugh; they wished the topic closed.

Crilen smiled as well and gestured for the waitress to come over.

"Decided to eat?" She smiled to him.

"Yes." Crilen returned the smile. "I'll have one-fourth of what he's having. Easy on the oil and the blood."

Yolo glanced up from his plate and concealed his ire behind a polite, congenial smile.

Crilen nodded in kind, but posed another question. "You said that facts have everything to do with journalistic integrity."

Mr. Pont and Mr. Nil grimaced at the resumption of the conversation.

"Yes." Yolo slurped and chewed.

"But you said before that truth has nothing to do with it."

"Quite right." Yolo swallowed another mass.

"Explain." Crilen's brow furrowed.

Yolo looked wisely at Mr. Nil. Mr. Nil grinned and nodded back with no cognizance of why he was doing so.

"Because," Yolo cleared his throat with a grotesque rake of pasted dross, "You don't necessarily need to tell the truth about the facts. Indeed, one rarely should. Any toddler with a bare wall and crayon can do that. You become little more than a note pad or an audio recorder when you dim-wittedly lay out the truth plain and simple. It's speculation, innuendo and the specter of doubt that make journalism. It's churning the facts into curdles of uncertainty that feeds the public's anxiety. And an anxious public needs ME! They become the conflagration clamoring for the petrol, and I control all the taps at the fueling station!"

Crilen leaned forward on his elbow. For him the discussion was only beginning.

"So how can you have fact and integrity without the truth?" Crilen tried to contain his enthusiasm for an imminent turn in the war of words.

Yolo merely raised his hand and gestured toward the monitor. Crilen turned and saw nothing extraordinary. He looked back at Yolo and the large man's gaze remained fixed upon the screen. Relieved, Mr. Nil and Mr. Pont likewise disengaged from the discussion altogether.

Crilen sat with his mouth left open, begging for someone to hear him put Yolo to task. But the audience had summarily dismissed him as if, right or wrong, nothing he could say would ever matter.

"Here you go!" whispered the waitress as she slid Crilen's plate in front of him.

She turned away, but Crilen touched her on the sleeve and motioned her back.

"What is that?" Crilen pointed toward the screen.

"Oh. Baloni's Walk," she answered with a frown.

"Baloni's what?" he responded.

"Baloni's WALK," she emphasized with a bit of annoyance. "'Walk' as in I should walk away from you, ya' heathen."

"Heathen?"

"Shhhhh." Mr. Pont admonished them.

"Sorry!" The waitress fanned her cloth back at him.

"What makes me a heathen?" Crilen lowered his voice.

"Well it's one thing to be a rebel." She shook her head. "But its a whole 'nother matter to be totally ignorant of the ways of the church."

"I'm sorry, my family didn't practice." Crilen created an explanation.

"Well, shame on them. But it's never too late." She winked, patted him on the shoulder and walked away.

Crilen looked back up at the monitor and tried to examine the scene more closely.

There were scores of people, black-faced and white-faced, draped in plain, soggy clothing, trudging wearily through what appeared to be a vast field of green mud. As they marched onward, mired ankle-deep in stringy emerald filth, they sang reverently in polyphonic unison. And though the words were unclear, the sentiment was one of dauntless sacrifice in the name something holy.

"Bloody nonsense there," Yolo scoffed as he resumed his eating.

Mr. Pont snapped around and raised up in his chair, rankled.

"Nonsense?" Mr. Pont's voice shook with uncertainty. "Why it's…it's not!"

"But of course it is, dear man. Now sit down." Yolo chuckled through his stuffed cheeks. "It's utterly pathetic and you know it. Men and women slogging through a swamp of animal excrement singing praise be to God! God should give them the good sense to climb out of the feces!"

"But it's beautiful!" Mr. Pont challenged. "And it's tradition!"

"Well, I can't argue with a tradition." Yolo wiped his face. "Especially with those bent on practicing it no matter how foolish. But beautiful? Come, you can't be serious, poor fellow."

"I'm damn serious." Mr. Pont craned his neck and twisted his mouth.

"I know you are." Yolo sighed. "More's the pity. But tell me, oh pious fellow, why you sit here with us if splendor and salvation awaits you squishing about in the manure?"

"Well I…"

"I'll tell you why." Yolo cut him off. "It's because you sense that these people are making fools of themselves, so, of course, you'd rather not. Yet you're afraid, even in my company, to admit it. You'd rather throw your lot in with a religious charade, than trust the whisper of your wits which tell you it's ridiculous. It's easier to conform to an absurdity than to stand apart in good sense. You'd gorge yourself on poison if a room full of people told you they were doing the same. And all for the one true living God: social acceptance. Now of course, the benefit is that you'll never be challenged or shunt. And the masses will always consider you a good fellow for your complicity with their translucent farces! Yes, you're the kind of man who prays with one eye open to see if everyone else's eyes are closed. And if your God should ever grant you the peace of mind to quell the nagging of what little individuality you possess, the world will be a perfect place, indeed."

"You don't understand!" Mr. Pont stood up and threw down his napkin.

"No, I'm afraid it's you who don't understand." Yolo calmly continued dicing and cutting again. "And that's what makes it such utter nonsense. You and people like you will go slogging about in the feces simply because someone tells you that you should. And you'll do it without having any idea as to the why or the wherefore so long as there's plenty of company to condone the ignorance of it all. That's a pity and that's a shame. And I'm sorry for you and everyone like you. People could do so much better. But what can be said? That's mortal worship, isn't it? 'The core of our moral fiber,' as our dear Accommodant would say!"

"The only reason I'm not there is because you asked me to be HERE!" Mr. Pont shook with anger.

"Oh, really?" Yolo chuckled. "Then do hurry along. Don't scare yourself into Hell on my account. Or better still, perhaps I can arrange a simulation for you in the lavatory."

Mr. Nil snickered out loud. Crilen paused from his meal to observe what would happen next.

"I have a better idea, pig man!" Mr. Pont shouted. "Why don't you just fire me!

Mr. Pont stormed toward the door in a fit of anger. He stumbled into two chairs on his way out and seemed indecisive about whether to straighten them before he departed. Finally, he just left them askew and stalked out into street.

"I won't fire you because you're too rich a source of amusement, dear boy." Yolo said after Mr. Pont left. "And most entertaining when you're 'damn serious'."

"'Pig man', sir?" Mr. Nil questioned.

"Oh, come." Yolo set down his utensils and patted his lips with a new napkin. "I've been impugned with greater imagination than that. If I fire Mr. Pont now, I'd be afraid I'd be doing him a favor. So no, I'll wait until there's some advantage to his dismissal. Perhaps, when the populace is less inclined to be stroked by the cowardice of his condescending views."

"He works for you?" Crilen pursued the obvious.

"If you can call it working," Yolo smiled broadly. "Actually, his daily columns run contrary to everything I stand for, but he provides a feeble, opposing viewpoint which only helps to validate my own. It's kind of like picking the general for your enemy's army to assure a resounding victory."

"And Mr. Nil?" Crilen gestured.

"Mr. Nil produces a satellite program and has his own column. I, of course, ghost write for both. But it gives the public the impression that I'm not pulling all the strings."

"Shouldn't that be a secret?" Crilen sounded surprised.

"If you mean should I be concerned about revealing these things to you, not at all." Yolo shook his head, "Unless you have a billion coin and own thirty broadcast satellites, I don't think it matters much what I tell you. I am the media of this planet. As others have learned the hard way, cross me and when I'm done with you, I'll have angry mobs in every city looking to rend you limb from limb. And all because, in the back of their shallow little minds, they'll dignify some vague rumor we've planted that you said or did something which threatens civilization as we know it."

"Oh, how sweet, you big baby," the waitress said as she cleared some of the dishes.

"There she is!" Mr. Nil pointed to the monitor.

Crilen turned and saw the same throng of worshippers trudging across the filthy tableau. Only now, at the front, was a woman in a shining golden robe flanked by two other figures in wine-colored robes. Their heads were adorned with jeweled crowns while oversized giant necklaces of gems and stones hung from their shoulders. Their faces remained obscured by sheer silken veils.

"There's the queen hag!" shouted Yolo. "Shepherdess of mortal fears! If she told them to crawl on their hands and knees on hot coals, they'd do it. I stand corrected, Mr. Len. My influence is nominal compared to that! The day I can get people to gleefully stroll through manure, is the day I go to Heaven. And I don't believe in Heaven, mind you, so suffice it to say it would come as quite a shock!"

"Who is she?" Crilen asked.

Yolo and Mr. Nil gave Crilen an odd look.

"A heathen," the waitress interjected.

"Quite a heathen indeed." Yolo regarded him oddly. "Grow up floating in the middle of the ocean, did you?"

"Be nice." The waitress shook her rag.

"Well, that's Deliveress Jen," Yolo informed him. "Queen Mother of the Holy Cathedral. If anyone wants to get to God, they have to go through her."

"And the...walk?" Crilen asked.

"Baloni's Walk," Yolo stated.

"I heard that, but what does this all mean?" Crilen asked.

"Well, look at me." Yolo smiled to Mr. Nil and the waitress. "I'm about to give my first Solemnday lesson. This must be a holy day!"

"Yolo!" The waitress threatened to pop him with her rag.

"Oh, very well." Yolo leaned back and smiled. "Some would call it religion. But for our purposes let's refer to it as legend. Over two thousand twinmoons ago, God supposedly instructed the chieftains of the warring nine tribes to meet at the Temple of Chry to settle their disputes once and for all. God allegedly told them that if all nine did not agree to meet, then the wars, which were decimating the world economy as well as hundreds of thousands of lives, would continue until the world was destroyed. Well, Baloni, then chieftain of the Manucus tribe, had the furthest journey to Chry. He'd traveled four days on his mount with only one night's rest to make the conference. As fate would have it, on the fifth and last day of his journey, Baloni's mount keeled over and died. Without it, there was no way he could make the conference in time, meaning that the wars would continue and the great Summit with God would never come to pass.

"As is told through scripture, had Baloni not made the conference, God presumably would have used the wars to destroy the world. So, Baloni's mount died and he had no transportation to carry him other than his own two legs. Thus, in typically heroic Text-fashion, Baloni did the unthinkable for any sane man who valued his life. He knew that the road was a thirty-kilometer journey, but he also knew that if he cut through the marshes and farmlands, it would only be seven. So he took up his bill blade and started out on foot. During the first four kilometers of his journey, Baloni is said to have been assailed by all manner of beasts and ghouls trying to deter him. He fearlessly fought them off until he came to the Chry farmlands. Well, the farmlands were flooded with rains and fertilized in mounds of animal feces, but he could see the torchlit tower of the temple in the distance. So he walked the last three kilometers through the muck and arrived at the conference, much the worst for wear and stench, with only a minute and a half to spare. Needless to say, the rest, for better or for worse, is history. The Chieftains allegedly met with God. The Chieftains subsequently chose the first Deliverer of the church, supposedly God's chosen, and God's law was administered, hence forth, through modern day."

"Oh, well told, Yolo." The waitress clapped. "You should have been a Churchlord!"

"My mother would have been delighted." Yolo raised his eyebrows. "But my father would have unfleshed my hide. He raised a son to see after the family fortune, not to dabble in mysticism and folklore."

"Tell him about the Aschen~exol," the waitress entreated Yolo to continue.

Yolo winced as his lips pursed with disdain.

"Oh, such delusional rubbish." Yolo rolled his eyes.

"You know the story, don't you?" The waitress smiled.

"Only that the last Chieftain, whose name escapes me, in reward for his pious purity, was alleged to have been drawn up into Heaven by God himself." Yolo recounted contemptuously. "As with most of the ancient vagaries of the Text, the event was said to have been witnessed by thousands who happened to be attending some Chry Temple festival. It was a miracle, or so they say. A miracle without a shred of historical evidence that it ever took place. How convenient for the ancient scribes of dubious legend."

"But that's what a miracle is!" the waitress scolded.

"A pity," Yolo snorted.

"So you don't believe any of it?" Crilen asked as he reflected upon the Text stories.

"Well, history chronicles that the nine Chieftains certainly did meet." Yolo frowned. "And a Deliverer was certainly chosen several twinmoons later. But as for the attendance of God at the Temple of Chry, we have only their word for it. The Lord wasn't kind enough to leave a group photograph or a lock of hair for secular posterity. And as for any chieftain being drawn into Heaven, all of the chieftains scattered into destitute obscurity with nary a trace. One could fashion any tall tale as to their final disposition. In fact, the Text does exactly that. So for the last two thousand twinmoons, we're left with only our faith, or lack thereof, the divine lineage of the Deliverers, and, of course, our popularly elected government headed by the Accommodant."

"So the answer is no," Crilen concluded.

"You're rather presumptuous for a heathen, Mr. Len." Yolo poked a large cigar between his thick lips and lit it.

"I'm just trying to learn, sir." Crilen held the large man's eyes.

"Then, so you shall." Yolo released a large cloud of red smoke. "I believe that the only thing we can ever be certain of in this life is that we will live and we will die. How much pleasure one gleans from this life in between is up to the individual. The world offers a myriad of experiences and pleasures. The more one partakes, the more one lives life to its fullest. But I also believe that the most important thing in many people's lives is to be able to sleep with both eyes shut. Most beings can't fathom the absolute death of body and soul, so they need to be assured that there is a preordained master plan in which they may partake through fear or through faith. A plan that will ultimately allow them to find bliss in…eternity, if you will. Alas, they cling to their religion or personal fairy tales as a means of proving that which cannot be disproved. And they live their lives trying to fulfill the requirements of their convoluted philosophy so that they may qualify for this eternal life.

"Now I admit that this line of thinking has its enchanting qualities, but I'm a pragmatist. I can't imagine that I'll ever wield as much power in Heaven as I do right this moment. In fact I can imagine God saying: 'Yolo, you've got to give it all back now and sit down next to the shoeshine boy whom you never offered gratuities.' And I'd wager the food wouldn't be very good either. You never read about God eating a bloody thing. I fear they may eat nothing in eternity. Hardly my accounting of bliss, I assure you. Heaven? No, thank you, I'll pass."

"Well, it sounds to me that even you've incorporated God into your matrix." Crilen pointed out.

Yolo frowned momentarily. He released another cloud of red smoke from his cigar. Gradually, he hoisted his massive bulk from his chair and smiled.

"Mr. Len, you should resume sparring with people at your own level. You're a smart lad, I'll grant you, but a bit out of your depth. Read up a bit more on historical events and perhaps we'll chat again. It has been interesting."

Mr. Nil hurried to the door and held it open. Yolo slowly plodded toward the exit.

"See ya tomorrow, Yolo!" the waitress called after him.

"Of course you will." He waved without turning around.

Mr. Nil smiled as his wealthy employer tottered ponderously into the street. He winked at the waitress and the cook and darted out after the broad shadow of Yolo Pigue.

VIII.

Crilen watched his plate shrink into a tiny dot along with all that remained of his meal. The table disintegrated into the floorboards. Finally, the floorboards themselves dissolved into grey metallic sand.

He gazed skyward and found the ceiling had opened into a deep, enveloping starfield. He noticed that the walls had reverted to the craggy surfaces of the asteroid where it had all begun.

Strangely, he could still hear and smell the frying of meat on the diner grill. He turned and saw the cook, spatula in hand, bearing a familiar and mischievous smile.

"Can I get you anything else?" It doffed its chef's toque.

Crilen stood up and felt a sharp pain on his rear end. He felt beneath him and learned that his chair had been transformed back into a jagged iron stalagmite.

"A warning would have been nice." Crilen rubbed his backside.

"Hmm." It looked over. "Rather abrupt, wasn't it? Though it might have been worse."

Crilen sighed and frowned.

"So is it coming into focus for you?" It tossed its toque onto the grill. The grill collapsed into sand particles. Then It's antlers sprouted from its bare scalp once more.

"Somewhat." Crilen dusted himself off. "Though the scenario is not an uncommon one. We have a religious order with an agnostic following. We have an atheist rebellion whose intent is fractured and unfocused. We have a political leader, the Accommodant, who's apparently trying to please everyone. We have a media baron looking to exploit the entire mess for the sake of his own egocentric empire. And then there's PJ…whom I haven't really figured out at all yet."

"Well that's an improvement." It evaluated him. "Earlier, you wasted so much time with the green haired slut-de jeur, that I expected you to tell me that the dumpy little waitress was matriarch of the galaxy."

"Everyone matters." Crilen frowned.

"Oh no! Here we go again!" It scoffed.

"That's right." Crilen cut him off. "These scenarios are your doing. I suspect that everything means something…and everyone."

"Then you disappoint me." It's mood became surly. "Tragically, some people are just filler…water between the rocks. They're only the shells of living beings who never claimed their souls. They're the pencil drawings of the great painter. Poorly defined. Hollow. Stock. Of course, they laugh when they're tickled and they wail when they're pinched. But all told, they're little more than background noise for we who compose the symphonies of life. Six of one will get you a half-dozen of the other, et cetera."

"I'm supposed to assume she's just some stupid little…"

"Oh no, I never said stupid." It reprimanded him with a forefinger. "The most foolhardy assumption a man can ever make about a woman is that she is stupid. Oh, the net summation of her emotional dementia wrapped loosely about her muddled extrapolations will make her seem as much. And any deluded male who relies wholly upon a female mask of consistency should just as soon quench his thirst on the venom of adders. But for a man to presume that any woman is altogether lacking intelligence is to impale himself on the stake of any such claim.

"Females know full well how men, in their swaggering impertinence, can be goaded, like the blindest vermin, into so vain a presumption. Thus, they play up the role of the ingénue, the innocent, the naïf, and if need be, the utter dupe…so long as it suits their ends. If she covets money, you may have her. If she lusts for sex, you shall have her. If she yearns for pain, she'll fan your sadistic fires. And if your love is what she wants most…God help you!

"But be most certain that whatever the circumstance, if ever the overconfident male should turn his back on his 'stupid' woman, she will certainly deal to him, with cunning precision, a mortal blow so deadly and swift he'll never even feel it. He'll simply die, a dazed, buffoon, gurgling away his final breaths in the excrement of his empty, masculine conceit.

"Now, I'm certain this rambling emerald imp is actually very bright, despite herself." It sighed. "But I submit to you that in the grand scheme of worldly ideals, she still does not matter. Her ilk is of a woefully common breed."

Crilen's face hardened. "Everyone matters."

Their eyes locked for a moment until It smiled and shook its head.

"Suit yourself." It gestured. "But you won't have forever to sort through the rubble looking to save every dead soul. Play for the pawns and you'll lose the Queen."

"But do the pawns serve the Queen, or does the Queen serve the pawns?" Crilen grew annoyed.

"Once you lose the Queen, all of the pawns fall shortly thereafter." It replied. "Lose a pawn for the Queen's sake…and no one even remembers or cares when it fell."

"In a game," Crilen responded.

"And everywhere else," It concluded. "But of course, I leave it to you. If your wife's return balances against millions of generic lumps of pulsating flesh, that's your affair. But in the meantime, allow me to continue your initiation lest you forget what I've shown you already."

A faint rumbling came from the distance followed by the subtle jar of a small tremor. The sand at Crilen's feet rippled until the mounting vibration caused the dust to dance upon the tops of his boots. The rocky asteroid spires started to crack and crumble as small rocks began to break loose, tumbling freely into the opening crevices. At last, with the force of a massive geological explosion, a giant fission ripped across the asteroid terrain until a narrow canyon, roughly an eighth of a kilometer in width, was formed.

Crilen ignited himself into a bright yellow flame, burst several feet into the air and cautiously hovered over the violent transformation. He was reasonably certain this was only the beginning of another scene change, but he still considered it prudent to observe the evolution from a discreet vantage point.

He tried to look down into the chasm which yawned across the asteroid surface, but he could only discern a faint light through the thickness of the dust and sand collapsing into its mouth. Then he noticed the dim light was gradually beginning to rise and intensify.

With explosive suddenness, a huge golden steeple emerged through the clouded eruption and raged skyward like a missile, the size of a tall building. The large, white, cylindrical construct ascended briskly, up past Crilen until it's mammoth silhouette eclipsed the starry sky. Eight smaller steeples arose, short equal distances from the first. Initially, it seemed as if a tiny affluent village were forming right before his eyes, but then the outlines of stone walls and iron gates became visible. Gradually, the steeples were linked by emerging brick pathways of glistening gold, teeming courtyards of richly colored foliage and sparkling skywalks comprised of ornate crystal.

Amidst the shock waves, Crilen noted that the landscape's horizon now extended farther into the distance. The asteroid was gone again. He had, indeed, returned to It's planet's surface.

He glided up toward the tallest steeple and observed that its ivory walls were entirely covered by series upon series of swirled carvings. Carvings arranged in such a fashion as to reveal some ancient, cataclysmic social movement, miraculous and epic in its magnitude.

Holy wars were depicted with kings, queens, Deliverers, Accommodants, martyrs, and the masses all playing out their assigned roles within the winding tautological pathway of history. Chronicles of zealous violence, glorious heroism, improbable betrayals, hideous deaths and eternal damnations and redemptions, were meticulously, brilliantly etched into the smooth ivory stone.

At the base of the primary tower sprawled a wide and daunting staircase, several stories in height. At the top of the staircase rose an enormous marble statue of a crowned, robed figure holding a giant book in one hand and a flickering, burning torch in the other.

As the rumbling finally subsided, Crilen decided it was safe to take a closer look. He slowly descended toward the statue until he alighted at the base of it. He was immediately taken aback by the enormity of it and the opulent, expansive cathedral laid before him.

The swirling marble statue stood nearly twenty meters in height. The towering, partially robed, muscular figure was weathered by the centuries, yet remained imposing. The thickly bearded face bore the authoritative scowl of one man charged with the rearing of all the world's children. In many ways, he had been. This was the legendary first Deliverer, chosen by the original Chieftains: Bius the Binder.

The inscription upon the pedestal read: "Bius I, Binder of the Tribes, Deliverer of God." And then inscribed beneath those words, the CDR:

> **COMPLICITY** *to the law, to the Deliverer, to the Cathedral, the Deliverancy Lineage and the legacy of Addendums.*
>
> **DUTY** *to the giver of life and to the people of the planet.*
>
> **REVERENCE** *for the miracle of life, for the wisdom of the Nine, and for the legacy of the Deliverers.*

—BIUS

Crilen recognized the name "Manucus" engraved onto the crown which sat upon the statue's head. Several other names, eight to be exact, formed a circle around the rim of the crown symbolizing the unification of the nine tribes. Carved onto the cover of the book it held was the domed symbol of the Temple of Chry.

The torch's stem bore the names of Baloni and the other eight Chieftains who sowed peace through their summit with God. Its flame flickered and danced toward the heavens in fiery tribute to the hallowed faith nurtured within the monolithic cathedral walls. Crilen knew little of this alien religion, but this reverent sight stirred his soul.

At his feet was a mosaic mural which extended concentrically toward the basilica stairs. It appeared to be a grand depiction of an ancient miracle. At the center was one of the chieftains, illuminated by fiery power and golden light, being drawn up into Heaven with thousands of onlookers reaching up to his sandaled feet. Outlining the illuminated crown of the figure was the phrase: Aschen~exol. The artistic detail was striking. The centuries-old hues still held their brilliance. The meaning, however, appeared more mythical or symbolic than literal or historic.

Crilen extinguished his own flame and looked toward the opening of the Bius Basilica. Despite the visual grandeur of this edifice, the smell emanating from the large entrance was quite foul. He looked around and noticed greenish-brown tracks of muck trailing from the doors all the way down the giant staircases. It did not take long for him to deduce the odor's origin: Baloni's Walk.

From just outside he could also hear the rich polyphonic harmonies he had heard from the monitor in the diner. Now they were far more powerful and resonant as the voices of thousands reverberated through the corridors of the basilica's central chamber. Crilen walked through the open doors and fully expected to find himself submerged in a sea of faithful parishioners. But while the voices grew stronger still, there was no one yet in sight.

He found himself at the entrance of a giant sky-lighted atrium where there were more statues, two or three stories in height…huge, elaborate marble sculptures of men and women in robes, standing either tall and resolute or perched regally upon densely ornate thrones worthy of the greatest monarchist rulers in the galaxy. All were crowned Deliverers, the dates of their reigns chiseled into the bases beneath their feet.

Some of the statues' marble swirled more black than white. Others swirled more white than green. A few of the figures held mammoth texts. Many more displayed staffs of gold and jewels. A few of the enshrined Deliverers gazed piously skyward. Others brandished sabers toward an enemy unseen. Most bore immortal frowns of stern admonishment cast downward upon any laymen who might happen by. Crilen shook his head.

The earlier sculptures also displayed the words "Complicity, Duty and Reverence" artistically integrated into the ornate decor. However, later statues bore only the abbreviation "C.D.R." with diminishing emphasis.

What remained consistent, ancient or modern, was that all of the statues were embedded with an array of glistening stones and gems. And every Deliverer's headdress grew in height as the tall cylindrical ornament bore the names of all of its previous bearers.

To Crilen, the towering corridor housing these gargantuan figures appeared to extend far beyond the capacity of the main hall he had observed from the outside. After some time, Crilen hoped he had finally reached the end of it, but as he turned to his left, he found himself staring down another long sky-lighted corridor filled with more of the same.

"Hall of the gods," Crilen exclaimed. In all his travels through the universe, he had never seen so dense a collection of mammoth tributes to living beings.

"Isn't there anything about the Lord's Summit?" Crilen heard a child's voice echo. He turned and watched a father and son gazing up at the great statues as they walked toward him.

"The Lord's Summit is in the Scripture," the father answered mildly.

"And what about the Chieftains?" the boy asked. "They saw God...spoke to him. Shouldn't there be a painting or statues of them?"

"This is the Bius Basilica, son." The man spoke with reverence. "Bius was the first Deliverer to bring God's word to our ancestors. And all of these Deliverers continued his great work, bringing goodness to all of us, guiding us toward better lives, teaching us how to get to Heaven. There's no greater work that's ever been done on this planet than the work of these people."

The boy grimaced as if he wanted to understand his father's words and accept them, but something was missing.

"But what about God and the Summit?" the boy finally repeated.

"Shhh." The father smiled warmly, petted his son on the head and moved them along.

Crilen glared thoughtfully up and down the tall corridor of statues once more.

"Yes," he muttered to himself, "what about God?"

Crilen hastened down the second corridor at a much quicker pace than he had the first. Even the grandeur of these immaculate tributes grew redundant, lined up one alongside another. He had not come here to assess dedications to the entombed, but rather he had been drawn by the hearts and souls of the living who sang their praises to God.

As he finally neared the central chamber, the voices grew stronger in their rich, ethereal quality. Voices which sounded as though they could beckon the very light of Heaven to descend upon the earth and illuminate every living soul.

Unfortunately, the mounting spiritual sensation produced by the songs was tempered by the pungent stench of animal manure which intensified with every step.

He turned the corner of the second long corridor and found himself engulfed by a sea of parishioners, their filthy clothing still damp from Baloni's Walk.

The faces were white and black; male and female; older, younger, and all ages in between. They stood some forty to fifty rows deep, surrounding the triangular altar in the center of the ground floor. The hall itself resembled a cavernous medieval arena, decorated in dark square copperstones, triforiums, stained glass, figurines and golden religious ornaments which rained from the twenty-meter crystal chandelier at the center of the skylight roof down the walls to the base of the marble floor.

The shoes, boots and hemlines of everyone's clothing was thickly caked with greenish brown filth. Drying speckles of manure dotted the rest of their bodies up to their chests. And it wasn't hard to discern who had fallen during the short but hallowed pilgrimage. They were the ones with smeared cheeks, matted hair and fingers encrusted with dried dung. Still, few seemed disparaged by their appearance. In fact, the ritual appeared to have cleansed them of all their secular burdens.

At the altar stood the four robed figures Crilen had seen on the diner monitor. Somehow, they had managed to keep themselves much cleaner than the parishioners. With the exception of their muddied hems, they appeared before everyone as regal and dignified, unsullied royalty.

The three figures in wine robes stood at opposing corners of the platform. Short lines of parishioners formed on the altar stairs in front of them. One at a time, each person would kneel before the robed administrator and have something from a brass urn smeared down the bridge their noses. The parishioner would then stand, nod in penitent gratitude, and descend the stairs, resuming the song of the chorus.

Deliveress Jen, cloaked in a robe of shimmering golden sequins layered like the plumage of a great bird, stood poised behind a podium at the center of the altar. Balanced upon her head was the tiered headdress Crilen had already seen sculpted on most of the statues. Hers was by far the tallest, nearly two meters in height. How she managed to balance it steadily and remain a portrait of absolute authority and competence was no minor miracle. That she managed, somehow, to appear even a bit graceful as she presided over the huge throng was a testament to her well-engrained austerity.

Crilen looked about the grand hall once more and observed that most of the parish had already received their smears. And it did not take much deduction for him to conclude what the smear was. It was also brownish-green in hue and matched the dried consistency of the filth staining everyone's clothing.

He looked back up to the altar and saw the lines of people on the stairs had dwindled to only a few. Deliveress Jen slowly extricated herself from beneath the tall, cumbersome headdress. He could see from a distance that her hair was neatly cropped, though the scarf still concealed her features. His curiosity about this religious leader intensified.

"Maybe its time to get my smear." He maneuvered through the large crowd, down the aisles of pews toward the altar. The song sounded as though it were peaking toward a climax. As he arrived at the base of the altar stairs, he saw that the last parishioners were receiving their smears. He hurried up the stairs toward an older man standing in a wine-colored robe. Another deep, pungent odor assaulted his senses.

At first, he thought it was a smell emanating from the urn of runny manure sitting at the edge of the altar, but then he looked up and saw Deliveress Jen circling the platform with a smoking censer suspended by thin chains. Her scarf was finally down around her neck and pushed away from her face. From a side view, however, he still could only discern that she seemed remarkably young for one charged with so powerful a position.

His concentration was broken as the cool finger of the older man in the robe poked the center of his forehead and pushed down the bridge of his nose, leaving a smelly moist trail that ended just above his lip. His first inclination was to wipe it away immediately, but the old man smiled to him and gestured. Crilen remembered to bow penitently as the others had done before him.

Crilen lifted his head and was about to turn to leave when he felt the stinging smoke from the censer in his eyes. The Deliveress was now directly behind the man in the wine robe. Crilen blinked several times to clear his blurring vision; he could only vaguely make out the golden figure of the Deliveress moving directly in front of him. His eyes cleared for just a moment, and he gasped at what he saw.

At first he thought it was Aami. Even her hair was identical this time. But when he gathered his wits enough to remember where he was, he was shocked even more by the discovery that Deliveress Jen was also the woman he had danced with at the rebel tavern.

Deliveress Jen was PJ!

IX.

As he stood frozen on the stairs of the altar, Crilen thought perhaps this was a trick of his imagination. Or, maybe, another perception of a woman who might appear as his deceased wife in this strange alien world.

But as she continued to circle the altar, PJ suddenly caught sight of Crilen. Her eyes flashed and darted with sudden apprehension. Her mouth fell open, forgetting its last words. She clumsily swung the smoking censer into the backside of one of the robed men and the man nearly jumped into the crowd from the sting of hot metal.

Deliveress Jen fought to quickly recover herself and resumed her procession around the altar. Meanwhile, Crilen felt himself being guided down the stairs by an attendant, though he watched her carefully as she glanced sideways at him once more.

A deep, heavy bell rang loudly, vibrating throughout the central chamber. It jarred PJ back into her dutiful composure. She recollected her mask of authority and serenity and refocused on her ritual tasks. She handed the censer to an attendant as the lights fell low over the huge gathering until she stood alone at the podium under a single shadowy spotlight. She began to speak.

As Crilen backed into the crowd he tried to concentrate on her words. He recognized her voice, though now it was monotonous and regimented in tone. Then he realized she was speaking in an entirely different language. He looked around the darkened hall and watched the faces of the parishioners. Some were chanting independently with their eyes closed; others were fixated upon her every word, nodding blankly as they tried to understand. But there were many, in dim light, who appeared to suddenly disengage from the embrace of anything spiritual altogether. They folded their arms in respite or yawned with wearied disinterest. Or they quietly whispered and giggled like children to pass the time away. There were very few who seemed to really care or understand what their religious leader had to say.

Crilen found his own attentions drawn back to the altar, but he, too, was guilty of hearing very little. Instead, his mind raced through extrapolations that could balance a mischievous PJ holding court upon the dingy tavern stage, with Deliveress Jen, presiding over the religious faithful from atop the Bius Basilica altar. It was a maddening visual paradox. And he had not even begun to weigh how their identical resemblance to his Aami figured into the equation.

"These are the words of our Lord God," the Deliveress switched languages. "May His will be carried through each of us today and always."

"THE LORD'S GLORY!" thundered the parish in one voice. In unison, everyone took their seat.

Crilen did likewise.

"On the way back to the Cathedral this morning," the Deliveress spoke, "I heard a man speaking to his wife. He looked at all of us returning from Baloni's Walk and he said to her 'Those people smell like Hell.' And she replied to him 'And they look worse than they smell, and I feel sorry for them.'"

Low laughter traveled through the audience.

"Well, I suppose," PJ continued, "that if I were this woman, standing on a corner with my husband, witnessing a throng of people passing by, covered in manure, and I had no clue why these people looked as they did and smelled as they did and knew only that I wanted no part of it, I am certain that we are exactly what Hell would look and smell like to me. Dirty, smelly and tired. It can't get any worse if you think with your eyes and reason through your nose and bind up your spirit only in the things other people care about. But to me, as I stand before you, I can only say that it smells like Heaven in here. And it looks like Heaven. From those fertilized fields two kilometers away…to the stairs of the

Cathedral…to the hall of the Deliverers…to this very room. Because, without the courage and determination of Baloni to reach the Temple of Chry, there would have been no Lord's Summit. And without the Lord's Summit there would be no Heaven. And without Heaven there's only one place left for all of us!

"Baloni arrived at the Temple in much the same condition as you and I arrived here this morning. He was tired. He looked terrible. And to anyone who didn't realize the importance of his arrival, he smelled like Hell. In fact, according to the Text, we are told that Baloni had traveled through all obstacles of Hell to get to the Temple of Chry. But to the other eight Chieftains who awaited his arrival and feared that the destruction of every life on the planet was nigh, he smelled like hope. He smelled like salvation. He smelled like Heaven…because he made it!

"I submit to you that if Baloni had been vain, if Baloni had been lax in his duty to this world, if when his mount died, he had decided, as many of us do when we go to work or to cathedral or to somewhere else where people are depending on us to be on time, that he was simply going to be late that day. If he had walked the thirty kilometers to the Temple and avoided the forest of shadows, avoided the field of manure, and walked into the Temple smelling like a flower on a spring day, to the other Chieftains who had arrived on time and seen a wrathful God pronounce damnation upon this planet, Baloni would have smelled like Hell. He would have been to them the herald of destruction, the herald of death for the world. But fortunately for all of us, Baloni wasn't worried about what he 'might' look like. Baloni wasn't worried about how he might smell. Baloni was only concerned with what he had promised. What had been agreed upon. And he didn't care what it took for him to make good his word. And, in so doing, Baloni opened the gates to Heaven so that all of us may see God. And this is why we honor him as we do on this day. Lord's Glory."

"Lord's Glory!" The parish thundered in unison, rallying together from the varied divisions of their attention.

Everyone rose to their feet.

The Deliveress started to sing, reverting back to the old language very few could understand. Still, the parishioners joined in and the rich harmony of all of their voices was very beautiful. The precise words were not certain, but the intent of the polyphonic resonance again sounded to soar towards Heaven.

Crilen tried to make his way back toward the altar. He wanted, or perhaps needed, to see PJ's face one more time, but as he came within a few rows of the altar stairs, he was intercepted by two very large attendants who locked his arms to theirs and held him fast.

Crilen instinctively increased the temperature of his body to loosen their grip, but they seemed impervious to the heat and tightened their hold.

Crilen finally resigned himself to desperately trying to focus on the Deliveress's face from where he stood, but the more he tried to concentrate, the more distorted all of the images became. He felt drugged as he watched her golden robe appear to melt and roll until her body resembled a golden rod suspended in mid-air. The singing slowly faded into an echo from a recessed cavern. The altar spotlight appeared to expand into the blinding luminescence of a white star.

Crilen did not want to close his eyes because he was certain he would lose touch with the Deliveress, the basilica and everything else. But it became clear that he would lose his sight if he did not.

He closed his eyes tightly, but could still sense the blinding light through his eyelids. He fought to cover his face with his hands, but his arms were still tightly bound. He even tried to kick at his captors but felt no ground beneath his feet. When his heel did strike something, it did not feel humanoid at all.

Crilen finally yelled as loud as he could for his freedom. His arms remained bound, but he felt the intense light begin to dissipate. He slumped down, his feet dangling beneath him, and tried to flicker his eyes open.

"Hel-loooo," called a familiar voice to him. "Are we having a religious experience up there?"

Crilen managed to squint his eyes to slits. He could make out a blurry figure standing beneath him. He snapped his head to and fro to finally look upon his captors who had felt so incredibly strong. What he found instead, was that his arms were bound into the iron face of an asteroid wall. He looked down again and saw his feet dangling in the air.

Secure in the knowledge that no one could be injured, Crilen increased his body temperature and melted himself free. Slightly fatigued, he slid down the wall face until he landed wearily, slumped directly in front of It.

"It's people like you that give church a bad name," It facetiously chastised. "Charging the altar? Really. You got your smear of shit just like everyone else. But no, you had to make a scene. At least, at your trial, you could have pleaded that you were possessed. Then they'd have institutionalized you. But I'm certain you'd have tried to tell them how smart you are, in which case they'd have tried you for attempted assassination of the Deliveress, punishable by public execution."

"Deliveress," Crilen sneered. "What the hell is going on? That was PJ!"

"Deliveress Panla Jen." It chuckled.

"But PJ hates the church!" Crilen responded.

"Oh, I think hate is too strong a word," It countered. "Displeased would be a better term."

"But she's the Deliveress!" Crilen exclaimed.

"Quite correct. And much more." It became just a little serious.

"But I don't understand!" Crilen became vexed. "How can she be PJ to the rebellion and Deliveress Jen to everyone else?"

"Maybe she just wants to be all things to all people," It smirked, "doesn't want to hurt anyone's feelings. I've known women like that. Haven't you?"

"I think this is a little more complicated than that!" Crilen shouted.

"So it is," It responded gravely.

Crilen paced toward the edge of the asteroid. He looked out into the stellar void as if he simply wanted to fly off into the cosmos and away from the sea of questions that drowned his better judgment. He was certain of an imminent danger. But much worse, he was certain he was being drawn into a deep emotional entanglement that might demolish years of reconciliation with his past.

A world he could rescue. But his soul?

"Why does she have to mimic my wife?" Crilen whispered through his teeth.

"I've already answered that." It shook its antlers. "And now its time for you to provide me with an answer."

"You want me to kill her?" Crilen asked meekly.

"If you must. I don't know," It replied.

"You want me to save her?" Crilen asked.

"I can't tell you what to do." It looked away. "At one point, I considered both."

"Then how am I supposed to know…" Crilen started.

"Do what you do, Crilen." It addressed him seriously. "Do what you've been doing for fifteen years. I can't tell you who should die and who should live. All I can tell you is that I want you to save my world. Keep my world from dying…this time. Do that for me, and I swear that the life you've lost…the life you covet…will be yours once again."

"How am I supposed to do something you couldn't?" Crilen asked. "You know everyone. You know everything that's going on. If you couldn't do it…"

"Knowledge is often far flung from wisdom." It interrupted. "And I fear that I may have been a large piece of the problem, perhaps the largest. I've seen your work. And while I don't agree with your ideals, I'm certain that my methodology won't do. Indeed, I'm parcel to the sum that begot our destruction. And no matter how you rearrange the components, they add up to the same vile solution.

"My only hope is that by introducing you into my planetary mix, you will dilute the terminal state of my world's plight...and save it."

"You can't alter PJ's appearance?" Crilen looked down and away.

"Only you can," It answered him, straight on.

"Then I don't know what good I can do you if I'm swooning like some love-struck adolescent." Crilen conceded.

"You can't fare worse than I."

Crilen looked up at It. He again detected its deep, morosely concealed regret and, now, it's desperation.

"All right." Crilen accepted.

It showed little surprise and offered less in the way of gratitude.

"Very good. Your starting point will be at the office of the Accommodant. He's going to offer you a job and you're going to take it."

"And from there?" Crilen lifted an eyebrow.

"From there, it will all become apparent to you. You'll either succeed or fail."

"My power?" Crilen asked.

"It will be Real Time from now on, Lenny." It grimaced. "Aside from your native disguise, you are who you are. Your power is at your discretion. I don't expect you to declare yourself God or anything like that. I know you hate false deities."

"I would use a stronger word than hate." Crilen's jaw tightened.

"So would I."

"Will I see you there?" Crilen asked.

"You mean, will I be holding your hand anymore?" It's mood lightened a tad. "I'm afraid not. For one thing, again, this will be Real Time. I can't be myself and this self at the same time. To be this self, I'd have to extract myself from Real Time. And while I wasn't able to save my world, my removal from events as they unfold would hasten the planet's demise. Besides, as I said before, I can't counsel you any further because my answers won't really do anyone any good. For better or worse, your own answers will have to suffice. That's why you're here."

"So who will you be...in Real Time. Crilen wondered.

"You'd be surprised." It chuckled. "But I can't tell you that, lest you focus too intently upon me and not enough upon the job at hand. Needless to say, I'll be around, and, if you're still curious when this is over, I'll be more than happy to tell you, then."

Crilen sighed heavily, then looked up at the stars one last time.

"We've both lost everything already." It placed its spindly talons on his shoulder. "Think of all that could be gained."

Crilen shook his head and wrinkled his brow, more in thought than about anything that It had said. He stepped back and braced himself.

"I'm ready," he declared.

With a motion, It beckoned all of the lead asteroids in the belt to halt while the others hastily came rushing upon them, causing a series of violent asteroid collisions all around them.

Crilen knelt down and shielded himself in a ball of intense heat as the stars disappeared behind the assemblage of black asteroid mass.

The giant rocks continued to cluster one upon another as they orbited the binary solar center. The planet was miraculously reforming itself. And, at the heart of this cosmic recreation, Crilen wondered how he would fair once Real Time began.

REAL TIME

I.

"Rights!" The Accommodant jabbed his forefinger into the long black meeting room table. "We have to protect everyone's rights, no matter what the cost!"

The Accommodant's staff, seated along the table, offered tepid concurrence through vague nods and tenuous smiles.

"I...agree sir." a young woman's voice pushed through the mendacious accord which fouled the air in the room. "But it has been expressed by many, including the Deliveress, that teaching children about the Nine Chieftains and the origins of the Deliverancy is, at the least, more a matter of teaching fundamental history than it is a matter of keeping religion in or out of our schools."

The Accommodant paused and stared at the woman for a moment. He garnished his response with a politically condescending smile: "I understand the concerns of those people. And, certainly, I understand and respect the position of the Deliveress. But our history has shown that when you combine the interests of religious institutions with those of the government, the individual rights of citizens invariably become a casualty. We cannot have a free society if we are going to elevate one set of philosophical beliefs above another. Certainly, it's not the government's role to endorse one set of beliefs, forsaking all other alternative viewpoints."

"But sir," the woman spoke carefully, "when we fail to support a set of beliefs, does that not place us in opposition to those beliefs?"

"Allabel, you sound like my wife." The Accommodant chuckled.

Nervous laughter followed as chiding glances were exchanged all around the table.

"I agree that it often appears as though the government is performing a high wire act in trying to maintain a position of neutrality on such matters," the Accommodant continued. "But neutral we must remain. In order to serve the needs of ALL of the people, we must not only walk the wire, but must unerringly avoid tipping the balance toward one side or another. That is the promise we have made to ensure that every living being receives equal protection and representation under the law."

"So you don't believe that by omitting any teaching of the foundations of our religion in schools, you are, in effect, showing government support for the anti-religious Break movement?" Allabel queried.

"Well, it's not like we're advocating anti-religion," the Accommodant asserted firmly. "It's not like we're telling children to go out and join the Break. Break literature is no more acceptable in our schools than teaching the Text."

"Except that at the core of the Break is the abolishment of religion." Allabel fought her agitation. "So, we're making ourselves the Break's greatest ally. I mean, how does our position really differ from their own? Every child on the planet knows the name of Rabbel Mennis because he's in the media almost every day. Every child is exposed to the Break's dogma because its part of our daily current events. Even the entertainment community has skewed the values it espouses toward the Break and away from the Church! We certainly can't understate their impact on enabling deviant youth behaviors. By contrast, fewer and fewer young people are familiar with the Deliveress…"

"I think every child knows who the Deliveress is." The Accommodant smiled.

"Yes, but very few have any idea what she's talking about," Allabel continued, "because she's a religious figure and nothing about religion can be discussed in the schools!"

"Forgive me if I'm wrong," the Accommodant, becoming mildly annoyed, "but when we were children, didn't we learn all about the Chieftains, the Deliverers and the Text at cathedral? Isn't there an entire day in the middle of every week set aside for religious institutions to have the undivided attention of everyone on the planet? I wish I had the average churchlord's Solemnday audience on a weekly basis instead of having everything I say cut and spliced through the media."

"With all due respect, sir," Allabel held up her hands, "as you can appreciate, the media is also part of the problem. The media isn't exactly selling morality. And it certainly isn't selling anything that has to do with Deliverance. It's selling the people what they want and what they want is more ballgames, sexually explicit dramas and vulgar pop concerts to go to on a Solemnday afternoon. To me, that leans toward the Break."

"I give the people of this planet a little more credit than that," the Accommodant declared.

"What about the polls that reveal that while most people claim to still support the Cathedral in principal," Allabel rattled her papers, "Solemnday mass attendance around the world is fifty percent of what it was half a century ago. Fewer young people are applying to the seminaries. Deviant and criminal behaviors are rising exponentially…"

"Listen," the Accommodant cut in, "I'm willing to concede that we may be going through a mild social adjustment period. But I can point to at least ten other instances over the course of our history where, at some point, there were concerns over some sort of moral collapse. I can also point to just as many instances where people felt equally threatened by the imposition of overreaching religious influences from the Bius Basilica.

"Your concerns are appreciated. But I'm not going to change the law of the land, tip the scales of freedom out of balance with its democratic foundation, and compromise everything that my office stands for. If people want religion, they're free to go to any of the thousands of cathedrals towering over every third street corner. But if you're asking that I autocratically impose government-sanctioned religious teachings in our schools, I cannot, in good conscience, allow it!"

"Yes, sir," Allabel grudgingly acquiesced. She loudly stacked her papers and peevishly fell back in her chair.

"The strange thing," the Accommodant continued, "is that the Deliveress herself hasn't voiced this degree of urgency. Perhaps those of us who are so worried about religious stability should follow her lead."

"Here, here." droned several voices from around the table.

"Nonetheless," the Accommodant concluded with a politician's off-tempo smile, "I appreciate us all coming together like this. It's important for me to hear what all of you have to say."

"Even if you don't really give a fuck," Allabel whispered.

"Excuse me?" The Accommodant lifted his chin.

"Thank you." Allabel smiled. "As always, it was a pleasure to be able to openly express our concerns."

"You're welcome, all of you." The Accommodant stood. "Now, if you'll excuse me, I have someone waiting for me in my outer office."

The members of the Accommodant's staff all stood respectfully, in their places until the elected leader of the world departed, then there fell a collective sigh followed by murmurs of genuine concern.

"Have you ever heard of a bad career move?"

Allabel turned and looked up into the stone white face of Obseq, a part-time suitor and full-time rival.

"Have you ever heard of the truth?" Allabel frowned. "He could stand to hear it some time."

"Yeah, but it doesn't mean much when you're trying to get ahead." He smiled and rubbed her shoulder.

"Ahead?" Allabel pulled away. "Ahead of what? Ahead of where?"

"Ahead of unemployment for one thing." Obseq reached out to her.

"That's the last thing I'm worried about," Allabel spewed. "You aren't as smart as you think you are. I'm just worried about the whole world going to shit."

"My, my." Obseq chuckled. "Are we just a bit tense here, or what? I get the distinct feeling someone's not getting any."

A vein in the middle of Allabel's forehead suddenly became pronounced. Her dove white skin fell grey, shaded by a stormy cloud of inner-conflict.

"I'm getting plenty," Allabel sneered. "In fact, I think I've had just about enough."

Allabel spun hard about and stalked out of the conference room.

Obseq stood, his mouth agape, as the room trickled empty around him.

II.

Crilen had not felt the anxiety of a job interview since he had been an adolescent. That marked the last time he had wanted any job more than it had wanted him.

He had applied to be a ballboy for his favorite professional sport club...he and about forty other boys his age. He won the job when the interviewer accidentally dropped a ball into a mud puddle. Before it bounced even twice, Crilen had dove onto the ball, rolled through the mud and wiped the ball clean with the inside of his shirt. He was never quite certain whether it had been a veiled test by the interviewer or if his anxiety had simply caused him to make an utter fool of himself. But the net result, in either case, was that he won the job and was allowed to retrieve and clean balls, with a towel, all season long.

From that point on, however, jobs pursued him. That is, they pursued his academic brilliance and his peerless ambition. Whenever he resigned from a position, he was assured of at least a week of begging and bidding from his former employer. And, once his scientific skills were set out on the open market, he was always courted enthusiastically.

Of course all of this changed on that one fateful evening in the arms of his wife, Aami. Since then, there had been plenty of work, but little that paid. And even fewer jobs that, persons alien or otherwise, earnestly wanted done. Yet he did them anyway, in the service of his conscience, if not the God of all things. This heroic vocation had become the most soul quenching and satisfying he had ever conceived possible: Liberating billions of lives through fire and verse, from their dictators, monarchs, false gods, and, most often, themselves.

Still, despite his impressive cosmic résumé, all he could think of as he waited for the Accommodant was when he should, once more, dive into the mud.

That, and the imperial, albeit antiseptic, dignity of the large office in which he sat. Daylight shone through white sheers covering the tall windows leading to a brightly pasteled garden area. A large multi-colored flag hung from a short staff protruding from its wall mount. And a pair of greenish blue plants or small trees, he could not ascertain which, stood attentively, framing the doorway and windows.

Across the walls, encircling the room, was a sprawling painted mural depicting the enactment of some historical legislative debate which appeared to rage across the chronicle of time. In fact, two well-dressed statesmen were coming to blows just above the Accommodant's high-backed leather chair and polished wooden desk. Light years from home, he observed that this depiction of political strife could have been taken from any time, any place, on any sentient world.

The desk itself was as pristine and stark as everything else in the room. It was as if it had been preserved as part of a sterile tourists' exhibit, rather than a place in which the most powerful man on the planet conducted the world's affairs. There was an assortment of ornate paper weights carved from rare stones, a glistening brass pen set and a hand carved wooden picture frame which certainly displayed some garishly impersonal family photo staged for public viewing. There was no nick, scratch or vague imperfection that even remotely implied that anything of relevance or importance had ever taken place here. The entire setting was perfectly accommodating.

Suddenly, he heard the approach of brisk footsteps from the hallway. The door behind him swung open and Accommodant Tem's congenial presence filled the room.

He was tall, distinguished and grey haired, but youthful in his demeanor. He extended a well-rehearsed handshake to Crilen which was firm and impressive.

The man's expression appeared warm and affable. And behind the affability glowed a powerful, assertive confidence. The one thing Crilen could not read as the Accommodant dropped into his chair and leaned forward, was whether, behind the mask of warm stately benevolence, this man could be trusted.

"I apologize for being late." Accommodant Tem smiled.

"I hadn't noticed the time," Crilen responded truthfully.

"Have they gotten you anything to eat?"

"I'd eaten," Crilen responded.

"Drink?"

"I'm fine, thank you."

"Very good." The Accommodant clasped his hands together and shifted to a serious tone. "There will be times in this job, more often than not, where there won't be any amenities for you. You'll go hungry many a night while dignitaries are gorging themselves on dinner and drink. So, no one should have to tell you to look after your personal needs before you come to work. Once you're working, the only personal needs you will be concerned with are those of your subject, understand?"

"Yes sir," Crilen sensed he had just rolled through the mud puddle.

"Do you have any idea how important my wife is?" the Accommodant continued.

"I'm sure she's very important to you." Crilen answered.

"That's not what I meant." The Accommodant frowned. "Of course she's very important to me. But do you have any idea how important she is to this planet?"

Crilen suddenly had the impression that there was something he did not know which he needed to know. Something obvious to any commoner. Something that, being ignorant of, might make him sound alien if not totally foolish. For a moment, he pondered a confession, but opted to muddle through.

"I'm sure she represents a great deal to the people of this planet," Crilen hedged.

"Mr. Len, you have a gift for understatement." The Accommodant smiled. "My wife represents as much to the people of this planet as my office does. More, in the eyes of many. If anything happened to her, I'm convinced that the entire political structure of our world would be unleveled. Not to mention the great personal loss it would mean to myself, of course. Now, my own security is very important. But I don't have any concerns there. Unfortunately, I can't say the same for hers.

"Recently, one of my wife's personal security people was found to have ties to the Break. This woman was caught transmitting messages to the southern continent where the Break leader, Rabbel Mennis, has a stronghold. She had been hand-picked by my wife and had full access to her, myself and every corner of the Accommodant Mansion. Now it's probable that she may have simply been a spy, but it's alarming to consider what acts of terrorism might have been done by this person, considering the free run she was given. In fact, we've had security people sweeping the entire building for the past twenty-six hours looking for bombs, poisons, time-released toxins and even unfriendly micro-organisms. The possibilities are endless when you consider that she had a room four doors from ours and lived here for almost three full twinmoons."

"That is alarming." Crilen commented.

"Needless to say, my wife was crushed when she received the news. She considered this woman to be a friend. They and her attendants even held prayer together before going to bed. That's how close they were or so she thought."

"Prayers can be trusted, but people need to be watched," Crilen responded.

"My wife would probably agree with you." The Accommodant smiled. "Me? I try not to trust prayer, people or anything else but my instincts. In my position, that's all there is.

"But let's get to the point." The Accommodant withdrew from the philosophy. "My wife travels extensively and makes a continual stream of public appearances. There's no way around it. So she needs the best protection the planet has to offer. Now I could send her out with an armed detail everywhere she goes, and I'd love to. But unfortunately, image is also a large part of our business. If she has to travel under heavily-armed security, I think the people would get the feeling that we're under siege."

"Are we?" Crilen asked respectfully.

"I'm working on that." The Accommodant met his eyes. "But the main thing is, we can't give the people that impression even if we are. So security has to continue to be discreet."

"Have there been any threats?" Crilen asked.

"A few." The Accommodant answered matter-of-factly. "But nothing out of the ordinary. Mostly angry rhetoric from fringe rebels who don't even have any connection to anything going on in the southern continent other than what they read in the media. What actually scares me is the threats we haven't received. If your enemy wants to scare you, he threatens you. If your enemy wants to kill you, he says nothing at all. He just comes. I don't know how much rebel literature you've seen, but it's pretty hostile. And I can't believe that my wife isn't high on someone's hit list."

"Sir," Crilen cut in, "I know you said that your own security isn't a problem, but don't you think you're as big a target, if not bigger?"

"Well, Mr. Len, you might think so." The Accommodant leaned back in his chair and looked away. "But I'm a realist. Politicians come and go. They could kill me tonight, and, by dawn, there'd be another person in a dark suit sitting in this chair doing and saying basically the same things. To the average pedestrian, I can present myself as an original. But to political factions who understand how the world works, I'm a far cry from being irreplaceable. But my wife...she means so much. And I'm not sure it has a whole lot to do with her position. She's just one of those people you either love with all your heart or loathe beyond contempt."

Crilen remained silent as he tried to compose a portrait of the Accommodant's wife. A first-lady. A queen. And something which extended even beyond that. He wondered how It could have left so prominent a figure out of his earlier indoctrinations.

"You come highly recommended." The Accommodant looked down and leafed through what appeared to be a résumé folder. "In fact, if you hadn't been a Regent's assistant, I might consider you to be downright dangerous. What made you quit the Urban Police and go work for a Regent? It couldn't have been the pay."

"God." Crilen spoke after a brief hesitation.

"God?" The Accommodant lifted his brows. "How so?"

"After...twinmoons of trying to make a difference on the streets," Crilen manufactured his motivation, "I found that I wasn't making the difference in people's lives that I thought I could. I guess I was worn down. The job had a means but there didn't seem to be an end in sight. So I quit and decided to get into something more spiritually rewarding."

"Like working for a Regent?" The Accommodant spoke with skepticism.

"Yes," Crilen answered firmly. "It put my life back into focus really. Helped me start believing in people again. Everyone isn't intrinsically bad. They're just lacking knowledge, wisdom or guidance in most cases."

"So why did you leave?" the Accommodant asked with a raised eyebrow.

"The pay." Crilen offered a wry smile.

The Accommodant's face broke into a wide grin.

"A God-fearing man with a sense of pragmatism." He laughed. "I think my wife's going to love you. Only I hope not too much."

Crilen smiled uneasily, noting an edge to the remark.

"Well," The Accommodant stood up. "Internal Security says you're fine. And you seem okay to me. But now you have to pass the real test. If the missus doesn't like you, you're still just another dusty folder headed for the cellar cabinets."

The Accommodant punched a button on a console at the corner of his desk.

"Could you find Mrs. Tem and ask her to come to my office, please?"

"Yes sir," a monotone voice answered.

The Accommodant leaned back in his chair and pressed the tips of his fingers together. His easy mannerisms relaxed the stately air of the room.

"So, Mr. Len, you're not married?" he asked calmly.

"I'm sure that's in my file, sir," Crilen answered smartly.

"Yes, you're right." The Accommodant shut Crilen's file. "Let me rephrase. I meant to ask: Why aren't you married?"

"I guess I never found the time or maybe the right woman." Crilen fabricated.

"You're a young man, Mr. Len." The Accommodant looked out the window. "There's always time. And as for the right woman. Trust me. There's always a right woman for the right occasion. Don't be so picky. You're cheating yourself."

"So I've been told, sir." Crilen spoke earnestly. "I guess I'm just an idealist. I'd like to believe that there's that one woman out there who'll be everything I could ever pray for."

"Well, I don't think you pray for women." The Accommodant smiled and rubbed his chin. "I think you go look for them. Impress the hell out of them. Then lure them back to your house."

"And introduce them to Mother?" Crilen raised an eyebrow.

The Accommodant laughed out loud.

"More like introduce them to your limo driver in the morning." He chuckled to himself. "Preferably before dawn."

"Ah." Crilen managed a polite smile.

"Believe me, position has its privileges." The Accommodant winked. "If you're in this job long enough, I'm willing to bet you'll meet more than a few women who'll…answer your prayers."

"I'd be…" Crilen started.

"Sweetheart!" The Accommodant bounced up from his seat and looked over Crilen's chair toward the doorway. "I have someone here I hope you're going to like."

"Well I should hope you wouldn't introduce me to someone I wouldn't like," a startlingly familiar voice answered.

Crilen rose to his feet. He turned around to greet the Accommodant's wife. When he saw her face, he nearly fell over the arms of the chair.

"Mr. Len," the Accommodant spoke proudly, "I'd like you to meet my wife, Deliveress Panla Jen Tem!"

III.

The Southern Continent.

The room was black and bottomless, but it smelled a sharp, foul, pungent stench of dead rotted meat, dried feces and rank urine. Thin wires which suspended her, pinching cruelly into her tiny wrists and her bare ankles, reminded her to remain still, but not too tense and not too limp either, lest the pain which burned through her arms and legs excruciated beyond her pleasure.

She struggled weakly against the coarse, ill-fitting blindfold knotted tightly across the bridge of her nose. It was so horribly uncomfortable that it caused the muscles between her thighs to tingle. An occasional draft, sometimes cool, but more often hot and damp, breathed over her naked, goose-pimpling flesh. She found the utter helplessness of her plight, deliciously, preciously rapturous.

"Oh! Fucking god, fuck me!" Reza whispered breathlessly against her racing heart. "Please just fucking kill me! Drop me on a jagged fucking stake, sweet god!"

Suddenly, there was movement in the room. She could not hear it, but she could smell it. The original sickening odors rearranged themselves. They shifted with the currents of someone moving toward her. A new vile stink filled her nostrils. A heavy, sweating musk so rancid, her stomach started to push down through her colon with anticipation.

"Y...you wreak like a shit-sucking derelict, you rotten clit licker." she spoke in a quivering chuckle.

Without warning, a gritty hand pinched her taut buttocks and she flinched, accidentally causing the wires to pinch into her wrists and ankles again. Reza squealed for an instant, but fought to regain control before the metal wires severed an artery or a tendon.

The large crusty paw brushed and scratched its vulgar intrusion to the crevice of her anus, then crawled like a hairy vermin between her legs. "Let...let...let me down," she whispered meekly under her breath. "Uh! Huh! Please!"

Instead, a sharp, unexpected pain pierced the ball of her foot and exited between her toes.

Reza let loose with a curdling scream that melted into maniacally indistinguishable sobs that mimicked laughter.

Another long needle impaled her other foot, and again she screamed until her throat sounded raw. Then another needle entered the flesh of her inner thigh and exited a few centimeters below her pelvis. As she felt the blood begin to seep along the surface of her skin, Reza wildly hyperventilated until she orgasmed uncontrollably.

The large filthy paw clutched her by her throat and choked her. She tried to breathe, but nearly swallowed her own tongue.

Through the fugue of suffocation, Reza wondered what her father would think of her now. His virgin princess, hatefully degraded. His glowing angel, viciously defiled. And all those whining suitors who wanted to play her shining prince; the fools who regaled her winsome virtues as though she were a gilded queen. She would love to see them see her thus. Then they would understand.

As the giant hand tightened down on her windpipe, Reza became horribly afraid. Afraid of the answers to her endless scroll of questions about life. But mostly, afraid that in the next hour or so, this torture would finally end.

IV.

"She wants what we want!" Rabbel bellowed.

"You think so?" Leesla shot back.

"I know so." Rabbel leaned his compact muscular bulk forward. "She's risking everything."

"No, Rabbel. We're risking everything!" Leesla raised her voice. "This tavern. The printing press downstairs. Our small cache of weapons. It's all we have! She, on the other hand, can go running back to her husband with tears in her eyes and get a political pardon while the rest of us get summarily executed by the government's military! Yes, she'll be the object of public ridicule for a while. And she'll have to give up her precious Deliveress title. But in the end she'll go to sleep on a pile of soft pillows under quilted bedsheets while our burned carcasses will be rotting in an open lot somewhere. And then one day, maybe ten twinmoons from now, she'll write a book about us…"

"That's enough!" Rabbel seethed through his teeth.

"Oh, I'm sorry." Leesla's face became a black mask of disdain. "I forgot how much in love you're supposed to be. Maybe when she's selling the rest of us out, she'll put you on a leash and lead you back up north for a little back-door clemency. Her thanks for an educational cross-cultural fling!"

With an imperceptible quickness, Rabbel snatched the tall woman by the hair and pinned her head against the desk.

"If anyone's going to mess things up around here, it's you!" Rabbel growled angrily. "I'm doing my job and PJ's doing hers. But all I see from you is someone who's trying to undermine all our hard work with jealous, paranoid innuendoes!

If you don't believe in what we're doing here, you're welcome to get out. You may think you're irreplaceable, but with two words I can get anybody in the Break to drop you into a deep dark hole no one would ever find."

"Rabbel, alright." Leesla's voice softened.

Rabbel released his hold. Leesla unfolded herself upright and worked her jaw until it felt loosened. The respect returned to her eyes. In Rabbel's she found smoldering contrition.

"Sorry," Rabbel said in a whisper.

"At least I know you still have it in you." Leesla frowned.

"Still?" Rabbel looked surprised.

"Everyone saw Miss Priss storm out of here the other night." Leesla sneered. "Right after she put you in your place. I'm not here to tell you how to run your personal business, but some of us are afraid that the entire Break is riding on your sex life! When she first started coming around, we thought it was a coup and she seemed sincere. But once it got personal between the two of you, it just hasn't seemed right."

"To you?" Rabbel accused.

"Not just to me," Leesla replied. "We see her on the media saying one thing, then she comes down here and says something else, and then scurries off to be alone with you. It just seems like the whole damned movement's become incidental to you and her getting together."

"Well, you're wrong." Rabbel's jaw reset. "If you must know, my argument with PJ was about the fact that things aren't moving fast enough. She's treating time like a luxury, and I told her that it's not. That and she's got to make a choice. I'm not going to let her straddle the fence much longer."

"Did you slam *her* head against the desk?" Leesla raised a hand up on her hip.

Rabbel dropped his arms to his side.

"I didn't think so," Leesla answered herself. "In fact, you looked like she'd slammed you around a little bit before she left. Did she?"

"You don't have any idea what you're talking about." Rabbel took a deep breath and looked away.

"Maybe not. But one thing I do know is that it takes two to be in love. And that woman doesn't love you. She likes you okay. Thinks it's...fun to hang out with the lowlifes. But when she stomped out of here the other night, the pain was in your eyes, not hers. I'd remember that the next time she does something you don't like. The next time she puts that little hand on your chest and tells you to trust her with your life or our lives, for that matter."

Rabbel strolled to the far side of the room and paused. He looked up and smiled at Leesla. "You want me to break it off?" He raised his brows. "Have her killed the next time she comes walking through that door?"

"You're asking the wrong woman. You know what I think." Leesla folded her arms and leaned her back against the wall.

"Well I can't, even if I wanted to." Rabbel's eyes narrowed. "You know who she is and the repercussions would be disastrous."

"No one says you have to." Leesla craned her neck forward. "If you love her, that's your thing. All I'm saying is, just like you want her to stop straddling the fence, you've got to make up your mind: If it comes down to a choice between everything we've been working for over the last several twinmoons or your loves-truck infatuation with a flighty, fickle Deliveress who has no idea what we're really fighting for, you've got to choose."

"It won't come to that." Rabbel stood firm.

"You better hope it doesn't." Leesla straightened herself. "Because there are a helluva lot of people out there who have broken their backs for you. Given up their families for you. Made themselves outlaws for you. And all because they believe that there's a better world to be had. A better world that needs to be fought for. A better world that you promised them! A world without scriptures and texts telling us there's only one way to live! A world without Churchlords and Regents…and Deliverers! It'd be a goddamned shame if they wind up dead and forgotten some day just because your penis got hard one time too many."

Leesla paused for a moment to see if Rabbel wanted to make a case of it, but he stood still, staring into space. She took his repose as her cue to relinquish him to his thoughts as she quietly slipped from his office.

V.

The Accommodant's Mansion.

Crilen and Panla held each other's gazes with stunned stares that neither could conceal.

Her blue-trimmed, sun gold dress, which stopped just above the knee, was stylishly conservative, as would befit the first lady of the world. Her hair was black and cropped short, like Aami's. And her face was a fluid compromise between PJ's vivacious mischief and the ethereal piety of Deliveress Jen. All three women bore an intellectual innocence which unerringly merged them as one and the same. Crilen was transfixed.

"The two of you know each other?" The Accommodant broke through their trance.

N...y...oh...es!" Crilen and Panla answered simultaneously, appearing much like two guilty, nervous children who had failed to corroborate their stories with one another.

"Well." The Accommodant stepped slowly around the desk and folded his arms. "Which is it?"

"I...I...I.." Panla stammered.

"I recognized the first lady from the media," Crilen intervened. "I had no idea she'd be so stunning in person."

The Accommodant regarded the compliment with some suspicion.

"Oh, darling." Panla relaxed into sociable grace. "I could swear I met this gentleman at the ball last month.

"Didn't we dance?" She turned to Crilen.

"I don't believe so, Queen Mother." Crilen took her hand and bowed respectfully. "I'd remember if I had danced, recently, with a lady. But alas, over the past several months, I've frequented only a tavern or two where certainly no woman of any repute could be found."

Panla blinked twice, smiled tactfully, and then daintily withdrew her fingers.

"You don't have to address her as the Queen Mother here, Mr. Len." The Accommodant smiled, patting Crilen on the shoulder. "Only when she's in the scarf and robes. Around here, it's Mrs. Tem."

"Or Panla, if you like," she added.

"You bear a lot titles, Mrs. Tem." Crilen addressed her formally. "I'll try to distinguish them all as best I can."

"I'm certain you'll get the knack of it, Mr. Len." Panla folded her arms. "If you're around me long enough, I'm sure you'll develop a talent for ubiquity."

"You seem to be the expert." Crilen smiled and nodded.

"Mr. Len is already quite ubiquitous in is own right." The Accommodant leaned against his desk.

"I'm sure." Panla glared discreetly in Crilen's direction.

"He was an Urban Policer in the south for several twinmoons," the Accommodant continued, "then decided to become a Regent's assistant out east."

"Really?" Panla paced toward the far window and turned. "Which Regent might that have been?"

"Regent Falzly," Crilen answered without hesitation.

"Good old Pil Falzly?" She smiled brightly. "The Midnight Messiah they call him out east! I haven't spoken to him in months! Is he well?"

"Very," Crilen answered stiffly.

DONALD I. TEMPLEMAN 91

"I had heard he had lost some of his fire since the fall." Panla expressed concern.

"Then you didn't hear his sermon two weeks ago, Mrs. Tem. It was so rousing that the mobile medics couldn't handle all the runs to and from the cathedral that evening. God held him up and spoke through him as never before. I was nearly overcome with emotion myself. His fall left him bruised, but his gift for preaching the Text remains unrivaled."

"That's wonderful to hear." Panla smiled affectionately. "I'll have to give him a call and see how he's doing. And then I can also find out what kind of...assistant you were."

"I was adequate," Crilen said without expression.

"He was fantastic!" The Accommodant fingered the file on his desk. "The best assistant the Regent ever had in forty twinmoons! 'A meticulous planner, an eye for detail, and ran security like a well-oiled machine!' Plus, his service record in the south was exemplary. Considering how bad things can get down there, it's remarkable Mr. Len never crossed the lines."

"You mean you never killed anyone?" Panla looked Crilen in the eye.

"I had to kill several." Crilen looked away. "Crossing the lines in policer work simply means that I never broke any rules."

"And how do you feel about killing, Mr. Len?" she addressed him sternly.

"The Lord says that taking another life under any circumstance is a sin." Crilen looked up and met her eyes. "However, to protect the innocent and the righteous, I'm willing to take the life of the unrighteous, by the grace of God."

"Interesting." Panla stepped closer as if to inspect him. "And by God's grace you are willing to kill wantonly?"

"There's nothing I do wantonly, Queen Mother. I pray that the Lord will grant me wisdom and guidance as I act in His name. And that if I should fail, He will forgive me."

"Well that's all well and good, Mr. Len." Her face became gravely serious. "However, you should remember that you cannot receive forgiveness without penance. And you cannot do penance outside of the cathedral. You won't find any salvation on your own. You must find salvation as you cleave to your parish and your churchlord, or you shall not find it at all."

"And, in their absence, I will live to the letter of the Text and cleave to your divinity, Queen Mother."

Panla looked over to her husband, who continued to lean against the desk with his arms folded and his mouth sealed. She looked up into Crilen's chiseled features, which had hardened into a dark mask of black stone. Her mind was ablaze with questions. But for now, she would have to withdraw.

"He'll do." She turned away.

The Accommodant popped off of the desk and grabbed Crilen's hand offering congratulations.

"My office is one floor down and three doors from the lift," Panla said as she whisked out of the doorway. "I'll expect you there in four minutes to go over my itinerary."

In another instant, Panla was gone except for the fading cadence of her heels marching down the corridor.

"I don't know exactly what you said at the end." The Accommodant held his hand and patted him on the back. "But I know that look in her eye. She likes you and I'm glad. I think the two of you are going to be a perfect match!"

Crilen smiled and nodded to the Accommodant, but his thoughts were fixed on Panla, and the unsettling void she had left in the room.

VI.

"He's really a good boy!" the woman on the monitor cajoled.

"Of course he is." Yolo Pigue leaned back in his wide swivel chair and a cloud of red smoke billowed forth from his nostrils. "Any young gentleman is likely to go off on a murderous tangent of rape and butchery at some point, my dear. And finding one's girlfriend…"

"Fiancée," the woman corrected.

"Yes, fiancée." Yolo chuckled, "…in copulatory ecstasy with one's own father is quite a hideous way to learn that the bliss of your impending nuptials may be in jeopardy. Still, he might have asked his father, before decapitating the old lecher, if this was to be an ongoing arrangement or rather an isolated inventory of the young lady's dowry."

"Mr. Pigue!" the woman was aghast.

"Oh, come now, my dear woman." Yolo set down his smoldering cigar. "Certainly there is nothing I can say at this juncture to appall you any more than your son already has. Your husband is headless, your daughter-in-law-to-be was raped, gutted and hided like auction house livestock, and now your son sits in prison pondering whether it might have been better to have politely asked the girl for a refund on the engagement necklace."

"He's all I have left!" the woman cried into her handkerchief.

"A pity," Yolo snorted uncaringly.

"Mr. Pigue, please!" the woman begged. "I've managed to strike a bargain with the judicial office. If I pay twelve million coin and move to another province they will dismiss the charges and we can start all over again. But if this becomes a media event, there won't be anywhere we can go that we won't be recognized and tormented by this...this accident!"

"Well, my dear lady," Yolo shifted his weight, "that's all well and good. But I would think that your son's next girlfriend/calf-in-waiting would be entitled to knowledge of his previous...misfortunes. And, for that matter, a great many more people would find it compelling that a duo-life prison term can be purchased away for the tidy sum of...twelve million, was it?"

"Mr. Pigue," the woman pleaded, "we just want to get on with our lives! Public exposure would make that absolutely impossible. We couldn't live anywhere in peace without being branded by scandal! Death threats! Rallies on our front lawn! Railed from city to city! Is that fair to us?"

"Madame, you'll find that I'm not very fanatical about what's fair and what's not," Yolo lectured. "The only thing I care about is what's news. Fairness begets fair-ness which becomes synonymous with mediocrity. And, when the news becomes mediocre, people turn to alternate sources to fill the dead catacombs of their consciences. At such instances, my relevance becomes shrunken and flaccid, which is, of course, totally unacceptable.

"I am the disseminator of history. The conduit through which the past, present, and future shall be interpreted. And every occurrence, deemed an event, beckons the media to record it one way or the other. And if I do not do it my way, then someone else will do it theirs, regardless of what's fair to the subject, mind you. The purpose of the media is to intrigue and mold public opinion. That, and, of course, sell space for advertising to pay for all the frills. So I'm afraid this all flows contrary to what you're proposing."

The woman's face folded into a mask of sorrow. Her shoulders slumped and she began to sob.

"Fortunately for you," Yolo raked the back of his throat and chewed upon the residue, "your son's story is actually old news."

The woman's watery eyes peered up from behind her clutched handkerchief.

"Old...news?" she sniffed.

"In a manner of speaking." Yolo smiled. "You see, we've been gorging the public lust for murders of passion for the past several months. Lovers killing lovers. Lovers killing lover's lovers. Husbands killing wives. Wives killing daughters over husbands. Sons killing husbands over mothers. Serial killers killing in varied assortments of serials. Virtually, a new killer every other day. Gruesome, macabre, senseless tales of love, betrayal, incest, insanity...whatever sells, dear woman. But I believe the world, at this juncture, has satiated its capacity for this particular entree. One more multiple slaying, more or less, just won't gratify the palate as it will, say, a twinmoon from now. Hence, I see little to be gained by reconstituting a tired plot."

"Then you're saying...that you won't..." the woman whimpered hopefully.

"All I'm saying, madame," Yolo lectured with agitation, "is that your son has missed his media flight. If he's going to get anywhere now, he'll have to walk because we won't be carrying him."

"Oh, thank you, thank you, thank you!" the woman's face lit up with elation.

"No thanks is in order." Yolo suppressed a yawn. "This is a business decision. In the meantime, I do hope you instruct your boy in the virtues of behaviors more befitting that of a man. I know its a daunting task for a woman, but if he thinks the betrayal of a fiancée is a capital offense, I would hate to see his reaction when his future wife of some twinmoons does him considerably worse...and mark me, she shall! In the meantime, do say hello to your new neighbors! Good day!"

"Um..."

Yolo punched a button on his console and the woman's confused expression evaporated from his monitor.

He flipped on the intercom and called to the outer office:

"Mr. Nil! Please make note of the following: Until the next twinmoon, we will be tilting our turrets toward the volatile, socio-religious strife which appears to be dividing our dull-witted majority. What's morally right? What's morally wrong? That sort of tautological drivel. The manner of topic which always piques the indignation of the holy, the depraved and every intellectual derelict who strains thinly 'twixt the two.

"I'm sure the public, like babies clamoring for a rattle, would prefer to see us torture some dull reticent sports hero with his self-absorbed reticence. Or anoint another dim, oversexed trollop as the next tabloid goddess of the entertainment world. And of course, we shall at some future date, but now is a time for the atrophied intellects of the masses to have their go at something meaty. If nothing else, it will provide a splendid opportunity for all of us to show all of them how stupid they really are.

"Gather up all the composite information you can on the players. That is, Accommodant Tem, queen hag Tem, Rabbel Mennis and any supporting cast members who may capture the public's fancy. We'll meet in two hours to discuss our stratagem. In the meantime, if you need me for anything, I'll be down the block a tad. It's time for my mid-morning cream roll!"

"Yes sir!" answered an attentive voice over the intercom.

Yolo hoisted himself to his feet and looked out over the city from his fortieth story window. He smiled over the vast scope of his influence, flatulated loudly, then laboriously tottered out of his office door.

VII.

"Who in the hell are you supposed to be?" The veins in Panla's slender neck writhed.

"I'm your new security man," Crilen responded evenly.

"Security?" Panla's voice rose another octave. "More like my husband's spy!"

"Hardly," Crilen answered.

"Then, certainly, a media mongrel!" she accused.

"No."

Panla thought for a moment. Her expression suddenly became fearful.

"An...an assassin?" She squared her shoulders and lifted her chin.

"No." He tried to steady her with his voice.

"All right." Panla recovered herself neatly. "Then tell me who you are and who you work for this instant!"

"I am your new security man, Mrs. Tem," Crilen answered in earnest. "I work for you."

"Oh, really." Her eyes narrowed as she folded her arms. "Then I suppose you were working for me that night at the tavern? And then, 450 kilometers north, at the Cathedral the next morning, you just...happened by, to receive your Baloni's blessing in the course of your employment? No, I don't think so, Mr. Len, or whoever you're supposed to be. I may be a busy woman, but I know damn well when I'm being stalked. And your kind of stalking, whatever the motive, is more likely to get me and/or a lot of other people killed."

"Not if I can help it," Crilen answered.

"Not if you...?" Panla gasped. "Do you have any idea what you're flirting with?"

"Do you?"

Panla shot him a look that was part indignation and part uncertainty.

"Indeed I do," she answered softly and looked away.

"Well, let's see," Crilen started, "you're a revolutionary benefactor of some kind. Under cloak and cover you endear yourself to the anti-religious left and make love to the Break leader, Rabbel Mennis..."

"Excuse me! You don't know that!" Panla's body stiffened.

"Careful. You shouldn't lie unless you know what I know." Crilen met her eyes. "You may know that you've been stalked, but you don't know where or when."

A sudden cloud of guilt paled Panla's radiant dignity. She quietly took her seat, then asked with her eyes for him to continue.

"You're also the Queen Mother of the religious right. Rather paradoxical, wouldn't you say? Curator of the faith, yet co-conspirator of the unfaithful. Which side of the fence do you fall on in your dreams, I wonder?"

"There is no fence." Panla became annoyed.

"Oh, certainly, there is!" Crilen leaned forward, planting his palms onto her desk. "Only there's a third side. The side behind which lies a politician. Or should I say, the side upon which the politician roosts between the other two. He can't decide which side to choose so he becomes a fence-sitter. Meanwhile, his loving wife has taken up with both factions. Other than for the shear sake of madness, the one thing I can't seem to figure out is the why. Why the layers of deception? Why play one hand against the other? Why put yourself in such a precarious position when it could cost you your life? I mean, there has to be a better way to accomplish whatever it is you're up to."

Panla slowly rose to her feet. She stared off into nothing as if she were processing Crilen's assessment, laying his words down alongside her own convictions.

"No, Mr. Len," she finally spoke in a whisper, "there isn't another way."

In her abject repose, Crilen suddenly saw his wife again. Her vulnerable sensitivity covered over by a complex shield of strength and wisdom. He walked over to her and carefully placed his hands on her shoulders.

She flinched, but then reached up and touched his fingers.

"So," she sighed under the repression of a sob, "are you going to turn me in?"

"To whom?" Crilen spoke into her ear.

"Whomever it is that sent you, I guess." she sniffed.

"Did it ever occur to you that Rabbel may have sent me?" Crilen offered.

"Now who's being deceptive?" she chuckled wearily. "Rabbel and I don't work that way. He would have told me. Besides, at the tavern, you were the one who was asking all of the questions. Rabbel sending you doesn't add up. I'm certain of that. Now won't you please stop playing this dangerous game and tell me the truth?"

"I can't."

"Then I'll have to tell my husband that you're a spy." She turned and confronted him.

"And you'll have to explain to him how you know I'm a spy." Crilen clutched her shoulders firmly. "That could be a problem, couldn't it?"

"Maybe." She frowned and jerked herself away. "And maybe he knows all about me already."

"You can't expect me to believe that." Crilen shook his head. "When you saw me in his office, you nearly fainted. Him knowing all about you is the last thing you want."

"I could have exposed you without telling him about the tavern." Panla backed away.

"How so?"

"Regent Falzly."

"What about him?" Crilen gestured.

"HER." Panla lifted her chin and looked down her nose. "SHE has been dead for three twinmoons. And she virtually never spoke in public, let alone gave sermons."

Crilen was momentarily stunned. Lying through that part of their conversation had been awkward. Now he knew why.

"So why didn't your husband…?"

"My husband doesn't pay heed to detail where the Cathedral is concerned." Panla leaned against her desk. "He leaves those matters to me. He doesn't give a damn about Regents or scriptural interpretations or even myself unless it affects his political standing."

"Strange. Your husband said that you're very important to him," Crilen felt the need to interject.

Panla released another heavy sigh. She paced to and from her desk.

"Well I'm not." she suppressed her anger. "Trust me, I'm a thorn in his side. He personally disagrees with everything I believe in. But publicly, he's afraid that I carry so much weight that he's not sure which of us the majority would take sides with if we split. I think I know, but that's not the direction I want to take. Not just yet anyway."

There it was again, Crilen thought. Aami, formulating, calculating. Mustering her inner strength. But keeping all of her pain and fear inside until she was prepared to discuss it conclusively. Much like the miscarriage.

"Mrs. Tem." Crilen tried to break through. "Panla. Will you tell me what this is all about? Tell me what it is you're trying to do? I know you have no reason to trust me. But clearly, I'm neither working for your husband, Rabbel Mennis or the media. I'm working for you. And I want to help."

"Everybody's a liar." She tried to smile as she wrestled with her composure. "Everyone's got their little secrets, their little plans. And everyone gets caught, eventually. I guess this serves me right."

"I'm not here to hurt you," he tried to reassure her.

Panla did not move. Her eyes moistened as they remained fixed upon the dilemma inside of her head. Up to this point she had not been forced to confide in anyone. Now she felt suddenly trapped...cornered by a complete stranger. A man she could not read who knew far too much already.

She collapsed into her chair, rubbed her fingers up the sides of her face and through her short black hair. She looked up at him with the odd smile of a convict, prepared to confess all of her crimes. This, too, was an expression he had seen before...on the face of his wife.

"Well, I guess I shouldn't bore you with the biographical data," she said with another sigh. "I'm sure I've been researched quite thoroughly."

"Actually I haven't," Crilen conceded. "This assignment came up rather suddenly. I don't know much about you or anyone else other than what I've been able to pull together in the last couple of days."

"Hmh." she smiled. "This assignment. At least you've admitted that you've been assigned."

"So I have." He gestured openly. "But for all I really know about you or any of what's going on, I might as well be...from another planet."

"Wouldn't that be something." She met his eyes. "An alien from another planet come cross the galaxy just to be...assigned to me. Well we both know you're far too good a dancer for all of that, don't we, Mr. Len?"

Crilen's brows lifted.

"Well," Panla started as she leaned back in her chair, "now that you've pieced together what I do and where I do it, you'd like to know why. Isn't that what you said?"

"Yes," he answered bluntly.

"Well, take a seat." She motioned to one of the white upholstered chairs in her plush office.

As the tension in the room appeared to subside, Crilen allowed himself to take in a little of the decor. Stark, but brilliant patterns of black splashed across the eggshell walls, carpeting and furniture. It was much like their old living room; his old living room, back home, years ago.

"So how did I come to this, you're wondering?" Panla pitched her fingertips together. "How did I wind up on both sides of the fence, as you say? Well, I guess I've always been a sociological hybrid of sorts. You see, my father was a Cathedral

Regent. And my mother was a third generation district governor. Father wanted me to study the Text and become a Churchlord, but Mother wanted me to carry on the family's political mantle. I wish they'd found the time to birth a sibling. It would have made things so much less complicated. But as the only child, I learned to become 'ubiquitous' at a very early age. To please both of my parents I diligently studied both the theological and political sciences throughout my academic life. It would have been nice to study music or dance or something fun, at some point. But there never seemed to be any time for it.

"Shortly after I graduated from school, my mother died suddenly. It was very sad, but we were really never very close. And I know this may sound horrible, but there was actually some sense of relief in that I felt I could finally bury the burden of mother's half of the family legacy. I mean, I loved the Cathedral and I hated politics! But surprisingly, even after I became a Cathedral Regent, the boys from mother's social register kept calling. I finally wound up marrying one of them just to keep the others out of my hair. Not that I didn't care for him, mind you. But I loved the Cathedral more than anything else. So I figured that if I got marriage out of the way, I wouldn't be dogged by the social pressures of courtships anymore. Unfortunately, my husband became bored with being a lawbooker and he decided to jump into the political arena himself. Believe me, if I'd had any inkling that he would ever do such a thing, I'd have married a derelict before I'd have married an aspiring politician! But before I knew it, I found myself swept back into my mother's ugly little world again.

"I'm certain that it was this interval that ruined our marriage. I began to see him as someone I never knew, all of his campaigning and lying and manipulation to get ahead. It made me sick. And it helped me understand why my mother and father were never close. The world of politics is the most sordid, ungenuine cesspool of mendacity God ever put on this planet. The truth means nothing in politics. Winning is everything. Still, when his career seemed to have plateaued and he became established in the political community, we almost became happy again. But then I was nominated and confirmed the new Deliveress. It was a dream come true for me. But it made my husband miserable. He literally took to the streets and the back alleys with scandal nipping at his heels. He was tortured by jealousy. And he was going to do whatever it took to surpass me, or bring both of us crashing down.

Then, one day, by sheer luck, he rolled out of the gutter and into the political jackpot. Drunk, wired on pills and facing a bevy of sex and racketeering indictments, he gave one of the greatest political speeches the world had ever seen at the Accommodant's retirement gala. The media loved it. So his Union packaged and sold him to the entire planet as 'the future of our world'. 'It's time for a change' was his tired unimaginative slogan. Unfortunately, the voters gobbled it up like the latest fashion. Before I'd been the Deliveress for more than two twinmoons, I became the wife of the next Accommodant as well. Hence, all things to all people, once again."

"That's fascinating." Crilen shifted in his chair. "But what does that have to do with your role in the Break? You said you love the Cathedral and that this title you're holding was a dream come true."

"Yes." Panla sat back and rubbed her temples. "Yes, I did say that. But I was speaking in the past tense. I loved the Cathedral. There's a huge difference, you see."

"You don't believe in God anymore?"

"No, you're wrong." She raised a finger. "I love God. I love Him more than I ever have in my life! And I love the Word of God. But I do hate the Cathedral and everything it's become!"

"How do you separate the two?" Crilen wondered.

"I don't." Her eyes became sharply focused. "The Cathedral does!

"Let's take Baloni's walk as an example!" Her voice became agitated. "A great, great historical event documented in the Text! It happened, no question about it! Without Baloni, the world is dead to God! Period. But look what we've done to it. Somewhere, down the line, a Deliverer said that everyone must walk through a field of manure every twinmoon and have manure smeared all over their faces or they are living outside the laws of God. Outside of God's church! Where does that come from, I ask you? Is it scriptural? Is it a commandment from Heaven that every living soul on the planet reenact Baloni's walk each and every twinmoon? No, it's not! And those who have fallen away from the church will tell you its absolutely ridiculous, and they'd be right. It is ridiculous! But the reenactment of Baloni's walk has been written into the doctrines of the Cathedral. And, therefore, as Deliveress, I must not only enforce the custom, but appear to embrace it with every fiber of my being."

"Then why don't you, as Deliveress, change the doctrine?" Crilen questioned.

"Because deletions of Addendums are viewed as heretical, undoing that which was sanctified as holy! There's no way around it! And besides, that's only one example of what I'm talking about.

"Another example: Our Churchlords are forced to take a vow of celibacy before they're assigned to a parish. If they break the vow, they're not only removed from their positions, but they are branded and excommunicated from the Cathedral altogether."

"But you're married." Crilen noted.

"Yes," Panla stamped her finger onto the desk, "but only after I became a Regent. Once you become a Regent, you're no longer directly involved in the affairs of parishioners, and, therefore, are allowed to have a family of your own. Convenient, isn't it?"

"What kind of rule is that?" he asked.

"A secular rule, Mr. Len." She shook her head. "A damned bloody, stupidly flawed, ill-conceived secular rule. The kind of rule mortals make for other mortals. It's not scriptural, it's not part of the Text. It's not part of the Chieftains conference with God! It's just made up by men. So what do we have now? Sexually repressed Churchlords, bunkered down in an increasingly licentious and reprobate world, attempting to counsel on subjects about which they literally know nothing!

"Not to mention the social deviants drawn into service to the church by the celibate Churchlord lifestyle. We've become overrun with sexually perverted predators passing themselves off as Churchlords, and everyone knows it. It's become a sick joke!"

"I think I heard you tell one." Crilen referred to PJ's tale at Rabbel's tavern.

Panla carried on very seriously.

"They use the rectory as a means to climb straight into the rectums of our children!" She shook her head mournfully. "I get three to four inquests a month from around the world, citing sexual improprieties committed by our Churchlords! And, if we can't put a quiet lid on the scandal, we lose a whole community's following. Most normal young adults do not want to give up the opportunity to wed, so we systematically drive away the best candidates who could be our brightest leaders. Nowhere in the Text does it say that a Churchlord can't also be a husband, wife, father or mother. But the Addendums say they can't and so it's law!"

"But can't the literal interpretations of the Texts override any Addendums?"

"It could and it should, except that the Addendums forbid it!"

"So what makes the Addendums so strong, so irrefutable?" Crilen asked.

"History." Panla sighed. "Tradition, and, I found, a poor interpretation of the Text, made centuries ago. Bius the Binder, our first Deliverer, claimed that the Chieftains empowered the Deliverers to rule the world in their stead. And whatever a Deliverer should bind on this planet should be bound in Heaven. But again, as I refer to the literal Text itself, no such commandment was ever made by God. And no such thing was written by any of the nine Chieftains. And, even if it were, certainly God never meant for any mortal to override God's own will!

"What I've actually learned from the Cathedral library is that the Chieftains didn't even choose a Deliverer until twenty twinmoons after the Lord's Summit at the Chry Temple. The Chieftains scribed the Text. And the Chieftains were the ones who brought God's word to the people. But in order to continue their work, they needed to create a person who could serve as a unified authority after they'd passed on. They chose Bius as that person. Unfortunately, the legacy of the Deliverers went on to form its own monarchy and its own religion. They constructed a wrought-iron gate between God and His mortal subjects and forged, for themselves, the key. They've tried to legislate morality through fear of men and secular laws, when morality must rely wholly upon love, faith, grace and the embrace of God's promises. The Deliverancy has evolved religion so far from our original scripture, that now, people either maim their souls trying to live up to the secular standard, or fall away completely, rejecting anything remotely connected to the church, the Text or our structured religion.

"Even the CDR was an invention of Deliverer Addendum. Complicity? Duty? Reverence? What's happened to the Love, Grace, Forgiveness and Redemption the Chieftains scribed from their conference with God? Religion isn't a job, it's a faith!"

Panla's face was awash with exasperation.

"And now we have this world God never intended for His children," she lamented, "We're losing our way to Him and with it, our place in His universe. And now I see the secular forces of mortality rallying for an ideological war that will hurl us irretrievably off course as living souls. Parents will pass their malignant ignorance on to their children. Generations will be lost forever!

"I must find a way to cut through the mortal Church addendums and get us back to the Word before it's too late! If I can make the Text plain to the world, show them that they don't need a 'holy' Churchlord or Regent or Deliverer for their prayers to be heard. Show them that you don't get to Heaven by the things that you do and rituals you perform and the people to whom you pay homage, but through love and obedience to God himself, which can only be read on your heart!"

Crilen was moved by her impassioned plea, but he was less enthused by her method.

"And for this you need a rebellion?" he questioned. "A 'Break' from your own church?"

"It stopped being my church centuries before I was born," she spoke sadly. "And, yes, I need a rebellion. A movement that shows the world that the church as it stands, does not serve us.

"Like a lot of people, when I was growing up, I had questions. Millions of questions. From how we get to Heaven, to if God is so good, why must there be pain and suffering in the world? And my grandfather would always say, 'The Deliverer and the Churchlord are good people, but if you become confused or disheartened, always refer to the Text. Any mortal can lead others astray without even meaning to. But God's word will always be true.' Now, of course, my grandfather wasn't a rebel. He very much supported the religious structure, even though he knew there were flaws. He felt that without a firm institution, the people would scatter in all directions. Still, I don't think he ever envisioned the world coming apart like it is now...so much selfishness, so much hatred. Such utter confusion. I shudder to think what God makes of us all."

"Panla," Crilen spoke quietly, "correct me if I'm wrong, but isn't the Break an entirely anti-religious movement?"

"Yes, it is." She sat back and looked away.

"Then why are you supporting it?" His brow furrowed. "I would think that some sort of reform would be better than a full blown revolt."

"I agree, Mr. Len." She frowned. "But have you ever sat in a room full of religious scholars and attempted to arrive at any reasonable conclusions you could act upon? As PJ, I tried for twinmoons to pull revisionist factions together for that very purpose, but they were all so fractured and fragmented in their reasoning. To them, every letter of every word in the Text was open to interpretation. They couldn't agree on anything. They couldn't even agree on how to pronounce the names of the nine Tribes. It was a hopeless quagmire!

"At least Rabbel and his people are in accord, and they have purpose. Their movement marks a historical watershed we may not see again for a millennium. For the first time in our history, we have a movement that's larger than a handful of radicals shouting in the wilderness. They actually have the strength in numbers and the will to bring the church to its knees."

"But if Rabbel Mennis and the Break have their way, there won't be any religion at all. No God. No Text. No anything." Crilen reasoned.

"Not, if things are done properly." Panla's eyes lit up. "Not if I'm able to take hold of the rudder of this huge movement and steer it in a logical direction that makes sense.

"The average person doesn't embrace extremes. No one feels safe at the end of a spectrum, so they always eventually look for a compromising middle ground. The church is one extreme, the Break is another. But people are no more willing to accept that the Deliveress is a mortal descendent of God than they'll accept that there's no God at all. Yes, the Break is irrational, illogical and depraved. But at this point in time, it has the strength to topple the church. And I have the strength and rationale to topple the Break into the gully right behind it."

"Do you?" Crilen wondered.

"Oh, yes!" Panla started to beam. "Their amoral, empty, hedonistic ideals are flimsy at best. Full of holes. I mean there's definitely some surface appeal, but there are so many historical precedents where movements like this flamed out from the sheer lack of a solid foundation. And as a result, people always came rushing back to the church. Only this time…"

"Only this time they'll come rushing back to you," Crilen concluded in an accusatory tone.

Panla paused for a moment. He could see she wanted to be angry, but the anger relented to an inner peace.

"Well." Her eyes softened. "It seems you've underestimated me, Mr. Len. I don't want anyone rushing back to me. In fact, I have serious doubts that I'll even survive to see it through. All I want…all I've ever wanted…is to see the souls of as many beings as possible saved to see the glory of Heaven. Saved instead of wasted.

"Our lives are gifts. Miraculous gifts from God almighty. But there's so much short-sighted earthly waste. All of the pain and sadness in the world, so easily cured. But we look to the ground for our answers instead of to the transcendent beauty of Heaven. We want a Deliverer or a Churchlord to cure our ills. Or a drink or a drug or another person's body. How can we ask such imperfections to perfect us?"

Crilen looked at her and could feel remnants of his wife's essence ringing true chords in his soul. Panla sat before him, a martyr in waiting. A martyr for so great a cause, that her sacrifice could even be withstood by those who loved her. Withstood and accepted with joy by anyone who could understand. Anyone, perhaps, but himself.

"Panla." Crilen swallowed. "Queen Mother. I have seen war and death. More than my share. And on occasion, I've seen soldiers call the fire of their comrades down upon themselves to destroy the surrounding enemy. You're risking everything."

"Everything I have in this world." She smiled.

"There has to be another way." Crilen became somber.

"If you think of one, let me know." Panla stood. "But in the meanwhile, if the government crushes the rebellion, then we're condemned to remain trapped in this death-spiral of spiritual decay. We'll become a world of repressed laymen and impotent agnostics, feasting on our own excrement. Dead to God. Dead to salvation."

"So," Crilen sounded resigned, "where do we go from here?"

Panla straightened herself and appeared somewhat relieved. "Today, Mrs. Tem is scheduled to visit Saint Baloni's Medical for the Terminally Ill. Then we leave for the north central region where I'm scheduled to attend a luncheon in my honor and give a speech. Afterward, in the early evening, Deliveress Jen is scheduled to appear on a live interview program for satellite. And then..."

Panla seemed hesitant even though she had already confided everything.

"Then," she continued, "PJ has a meeting with Rabbel Mennis."

"PJ." Crilen shook his head.

"An alter ego I actually cooked up as a child," she reflected. "PJ was the girl who wasn't confined or restricted by her parent's position in society. I fancied her a happy orphan, if there is such a thing. She could dance and curse and stay out all night and make her own friends. She could do whatever, wherever, whenever and no one would really care."

"And how does God see PJ?" Crilen asked.

"PJ's not a bad girl, Mr. Len." she smiled. "She simply serves God without sweating over excommunication and Holy Inquisitions. Unlike the person I've had to be my entire life, PJ is free. Really, really free."

"Is she?" Crilen wondered aloud.

Panla's eyes flickered for a moment. She dismissed his query, stood up and extended her hand.

"Welcome aboard, Mr. Len." She smiled. "I'll try not to make your job of protecting me too stressful."

"To ubiquity." Crilen held her fingers gently.

"To ubiquity." Panla chuckled, and held his probing eyes.

VIII.

A narrow rusted transport vehicle bounced and rumbled through the rocky southern badlands known as the Thanaton Desert.

"Are we fucking there yet?" Reza whined as she rested her head on Durn's stomach, painting her nails.

"I wish I was fucking here." Durn's fingers crept up her leg and under her skirt.

"Ugh!" Reza pushed his hand away. "This bumpy dick ride is giving me the rims!"

"If you ask that one more time, you'll be 'there yet' off the next bumpy cliff, little bitch," Leesla growled as she looked out over the passing rocky reddish landscape.

"Now that wasn't nice." Durn smiled a toothy yellow smile as he played in Reza's green locks.

"My name is not 'little bitch'!" Reza piped up.

"Oh, I'm sorry." Leesla spat. "I meant to say, little cunt!"

"Oh, look who's talking!" Reza sat up. "Stinky gashed, fucking dyke-sucking clit-sniffer! Scratch the dried spunk out of that rat's nest hair sometime!"

Leesla uncoiled like a giant cat and snatched Reza out of Durn's lap. She pried the nail polish out of Reza's tiny hand and doused her with it as Reza struggled weakly.

"Well, don't get that shit on me!" Durn rolled over, checking his dark leather pants.

"That's enough!" Rabbel bellowed from the front of the vehicle.

Leesla looked over at Rabbel, then drove her sharp knee into Reza's stomach and tossed the smaller woman to the floor like a sack of rubbish.

Durn suddenly jumped to his feet. Leesla crouched into a tensed ready position with her pointed elbows raised and her fists tightly clenched.

"I said that's it!" Rabbel raised his voice to a baritone growl.

"Just checkin' on the lady." Durn held up his hands and smiled, his eyes dancing between Leesla and Rabbel. "Just checkin' on the lady."

"Leesla." Rabbel called. "Sit."

Leesla's eyes remained fixed on Durn as she watched him tentatively move toward Reza. She cautiously lowered her slender, muscular arms, and backed toward her seat like a rankled panther, poised to pounce at the first flicker of aggression.

"No," Rabbel commanded. "Up here with me."

Leesla took one last glance at Reza curled into a fetal position, trying to catch her breath with green nail polish spattered across her greying features. She turned away and eased into a front seat next to Rabbel Mennis.

"You alright, princess?" Durn knelt down to check on Reza.

Reza sobbed as she struggled to catch her breath.

Durn stroked her legs, then slid his hands up under skirt again.

"No!" Reza jumped up, crying. "Is everything a reason to stick your scratchy paws up my bloody sphincter, you pin-dicked fucking pet molester?"

"I...I...I..." Durn tried to think of some other way to comfort her.

Reza turned over on her side, vomited and passed out with her open eyes rolled back in her head.

"Baby?" Durn reached for her breasts.

Up front, Rabbel fixed his eyes on the craggy crimson terrain in front of them, while the driver navigated the transport around boulder after giant boulder.

"Why don't we take it up?" Leesla asked. "The little bitch is right. This is taking forever."

"PJ says the government's all over the southern continent with aerial sensors." Rabbel grimaced. "As long as we're rolling, we look like every other commuter on the ground. We take to the skies, and we might as well broadcast to the media about everything we're doing."

"PJ," Leesla spoke disdainfully. "So where is our sweet benefactor this morning?"

"Busy," Rabbel answered curtly.

"Of course," Leesla sneered. "While we go stick our heads into this incinerator, she kicks back with a glass of wine, spilling our secrets into the Accommodant's bed!"

"We've been through this!" Rabbel snapped.

"No, Rabbel," Leesla seethed. "We're going through 'this', right now...today!"

"I told you before, you don't have to stay." Rabbel fixed his eyes to the front window of the vehicle.

"Just like that?" Leesla's clipped enunciations became more pronounced. "Just hop off the hayride and go home?"

"If you like," Rabbel answered with mild exasperation.

"Rabbel," Leesla sat up and leaned forward. "Reza doesn't have to stay. She can call up her father this afternoon, and he'd send a limousine to carry her twisted little perverted pussy home to daddy's mansion. He'd give her a nice bath, wash the green gunk out of her hair and then introduce her to some poor unsuspecting young man with a bright future. And poof! She'd become just another cute little wealthy housewife, with the skeletons in her closet scuttled away in her selective little memories!

"Durn doesn't have to stay. He can go back to police work in some small province that doesn't review psychological profiles. He can go back to strong-arming little people, cowering behind his badge and selling his 'duty' to the highest bidders!

"Even you don't HAVE to stay. If you packed it all in right now, PJ could get you clemency. You could probably go back to the military or work the Accommodant's security or even go into business for yourself with a big payoff. You have plenty of options!

"But me?" Leesla poked her thumb into her chest "I HAVE to stay. I have to! This isn't mercenary work for me. This isn't for kicks! This is my life, we're talking about. I don't have a family to go back to. We disowned each other a long time ago. I got discharged from the military because of my so-called immoral sexual behaviors. I don't even have a neighborhood to go back to. Not a neighborhood where its legal to live the way I want to live...in the open! There isn't a place on this planet where I'm free, really free! Even here, in the south, I have to sneak around in the dark if I want to be with a beautiful woman like Hesh. Is that fair?

"And what about our right to raise a kid in the kind of household we want to raise it in? A household without God and the goddamned Deliverancy trying to jam some cock into our life. I want to be the one to decide what's right for me and mine. I don't want some religious leader and his or her mythology dictating an outline for my happiness to me. I want to live and I want to live free. I want to live, but I would rather die than be told by someone who doesn't fucking know me how my life should be lived. Rabbel, I have to stay. More than anyone else, I have to!"

Rabbel rolled his eyes toward the tall woman.

For a moment, Leesla wondered whether she had, again, zealously overstepped her place. She watched his hands. He was so very quick and deadly with those hands. But instead of movement, she heard a light snicker through his nose as a smile crept across his thick dark face.

"'Jam some cock' into your life?" He raised an eyebrow.

Leesla blinked for a moment, then shook her head.

"Well, you know what I meant." she answered with embarrassment. "Nothing personal. I just hate those damn things."

"I know." Rabbel sighed. "I know. And you have the right to hate...or love anything that you want. We all do. That's why I have to stay, too."

Leesla settled back in her chair and sighed. "Why can't I find a woman like you?"

"You mean: short, muscular, and hairy?" Rabbel smiled. "I think they're all chasing men like me."

Leesla let out a loud laugh that stirred Reza and Durn. The tall woman leaned over and gently kissed Rabbel on the cheek.

IX.

"How do I look?" Panla checked herself in the luxury transport mirror one last time.

"Lovely," Crilen thought to himself.

She flicked and feathered her dark bangs, then dabbed away an imaginary shine from the tip of her nose which she had already dutifully dulled minutes before. She pursed her plum-red lips, then stretched them wide to detect imperfections. Finally, she lifted her chin turning to and fro, making certain the faint coloring in her cheeks balanced symmetrically with the shadow of her eyelids.

With an abrupt sigh, she folded away the mirror into a pocket next to her seat. She turned and tilted her head in a hauntingly familiar manner which caused the hair on Crilen's neck to tingle.

"Well?" Panla addressed him with Aami's sarcastic impatience.

Crilen shook himself from his momentary trance, trying vainly, to recall It's warning.

"You look fine." Crilen sat on his emotions.

"Fine?" Panla chuckled. "Just 'fine?'"

"Very nice." Crilen frowned rigidly.

"Hmh." Panla shook her head and smiled. "You really know how to instill confidence in a lady, don't you, dear?"

The transport came to a smooth and gradual stop. Through the cream-colored metallic hull and smoked glass swelled a vibration of muffled noises that enveloped the entire vehicle. The side door to the rear cabin slid open, and, all at once, the glaring lights and crisp noises of the outside world came roaring in around them.

Panla took up her brown leather satchel and popped out of the transport behind Linnfeld, her lead attendant. They were out and away before Crilen could even gather his bearings. After a stunned pause, he followed after them. As he emerged, he found himself further alarmed by the dense, disorienting bedlam which had come crushing down upon them all.

There appeared to be hundreds of media and pedestrians leaning in on Panla and her small entourage as they tried to maneuver their way into St. Baloni's entrance. An endless barrage of fragmented questions and comments were being lobbed from all directions. Many desperately benign. Others as malevolent and intrusive as poisonous spears. In any case, the queries and jeers, alike, were confounding by their scope, their depth or their lack thereof:

"The fucking Cathedral's dead, you fucking bitch!"

"We love you, Panla!"

"Is it true you and your husband aren't sleeping together?"

"Are you going to meet with the leaders of the Break?"

"Heal my leg, Queen Mother! Heal my leg!"

"Are the Scriptures a lie?"

"I'll bring you Rabbel Mennis's head!"

"Is that a new dress?"

"Stop the Break!"

"Will you reverse your stance on IVC research?"

"Are you resigning the Deliverancy?"

"Suck this, whore!"

"Are you getting psychiatric help?"

"God bless you, Queen Mother!"

"Does the Accommodant have a mistress?"

"Join the Break, Panla!"

"Why are you here today?"

"Did the Accommodant ever hit you, Mrs. Tem?"

"Marry me, Panla Jen! Marry me!"

Panla clutched Linnfeld's coattail as they funneled toward the front staircase, but everything jammed to a halt. Several policers held back the fervent crowd, but pedestrians and media still managed to clog the entrance way in their frenetic, myopic pursuit of their famed quarry.

Crilen's hands and neck grew hot at the sight of Panla's momentary distress. An overprotective rage nearly consumed him. The thought of scorching a flamed path through the sea of unyielding bodies appealed to his darker sensibilities, but he swallowed hard, grimaced and fell back upon a subtler resolution.

With careful discretion, Crilen reached out and lightly touched a woman holding a directional microphone. The stinging heat caused her to jump backward. Then he reached into the swarm of bodies and touched another man who had been cursing and swearing. With a loud wail, he too leapt backward into the swaying crowd.

Crilen pushed past the rear attendant and held his arm out between the pressing mass and Panla Jen. He emitted a scarcely perceptible wave of pyrogenic heat which forced everyone to involuntarily loosen their positions. At that instant, Linnfeld found a sliver of yield in the swarm of bodies and quickly hastened Panla up the staircase and into the front entrance.

Crilen, looking neither right or left, trotted up the stairs behind them.

His first instinct was to see if Panla had been unsettled by the wild jostling outside. But as he searched down the main corridor, he saw she had already set a brisk pace which her attendants struggled to maintain.

Crilen hurried along, impressed by how difficult it was to keep up with her. Her strides were strong, purposeful and remarkably routine in their cadence.

Such was the fortitude with which the first lady and Queen Mother of the world managed her days.

"Are you all right?" Crilen hustled to come alongside of her.

"What are you talking about?" Panla answered without breaking stride.

"Well, that was a little rough out there," Crilen spoke with sympathy.

"For who?" she sounded mildly annoyed.

"For…you I thought." Crilen tried to read her as she moved along.

"Oh, come now, Mr. Len." She chuckled. "I've been pushed around much worse during a Solemnday Mass."

"Well, not just that," Crilen added. "What about the questions? Some of it was pretty rude…"

"And crude, I imagine." Panla waved her hand. "To be honest, I learned a long time ago not to hear a word of it. It's all so haplessly random, no sane person could begin to make head or tail of it. I was actually concentrating on my itinerary."

"Then you weren't worried?"

"About what?" She became short. "I've heard everything out there a million times before. There's nothing new."

"Then you did hear," Crilen countered.

"Some of it." She shook her head. "But it's all such babble! If those people care so much about the world they live in, they'd tend more carefully to their own affairs rather than build their mornings around shouting at me. Some people act as if I'm the center of the universe, as if tearing away strips of my mortal flesh will somehow bring divine purpose into their own lives. It's all so ridiculous!

"Now let's drop it now, shall we?" She briefly made eye contact.

Her perturbation bordered on aloofness. Crilen had witnessed dozens of disenchanted monarchs fall contemptuous of their subjects before. Here, he sensed something else. Something, he prayed, that was not contrived by his feelings for her.

"Good morning, Mrs. Tem." An older man appeared from an adjoining hallway.

"Good morning, Mr. Crouss." She extended her hand.

Crouss appeared hesitant as he held Panla's fingers awkwardly, pursing his lips.

"I'm here as the wife of the Accommodant." Panla smiled. "A simple handshake will suffice."

Crouss returned a smile of relief and shook her hand.

"It does get confusing." He straightened himself up.

"For me as well, sometimes, Mr. Crouss," Panla assured him. "Allow me to introduce my first attendant, Mr. Linnfeld, and my security lead, Mr. Len."

"Linnfeld and Len." Crouss chuckled nervously. "I'll try to keep those names straight. Welcome to Saint Baloni Medical for the Terminally Ill."

"The pleasure is ours." Panla nodded.

"Well, I've assembled our staff in the courtyard." Crouss gestured. "If you please, they've all been looking forward to…"

"Mr. Crouss," Panla interrupted. "I'd very much like to meet with the staff here. The work they do is quite remarkable. However, I'd first like to take a tour of the patient ward. After all, the patients are why all of us are here."

Crouss appeared momentarily flustered.

"I apologize, Mrs. Tem." he began. "As you said, since you are here on behalf of the Accommodant's office, I assumed that you might not wish to be bothered…"

"Mr. Crouss," Panla became authoritatively short again, "I am the wife of the Accommodant, by the will of the people. However, I am the Deliveress by the will of God. Though I cherish the people's will with all of my heart, the will of God always comes first."

"But," Crouss tried weakly to persuade her, "we've set aside some residents for you to meet after…."

"I know, Mr. Crouss," Panla answered with firm politeness, "but I'm not interested in 'set asides.' I'm interested in everyone else."

"Yes Mrs…Queen Mother." Crouss became exasperated by his own confusion. "This way."

Effectively derailed, Crouss turned and led the group toward the patient ward.

"Was that fair?" Crilen whispered aside to her. "It does get confusing."

Panla marched on, appearing as though she had not heard a word he had said.

Crilen glanced at Linnfeld; the short pudgy man was also locked into an official demeanor. The two female attendants were, likewise, locked in their professional modes.

The group approached a large metal door at the end of a stark, white antiseptic hallway. Crouss spoke into a voice decoder lock, and the door slowly sunk into a narrow seam in the floor.

The odors of medicines, cleaners and bodily eliminations quickly filled the air. And there were row upon row of beds filled with frail, eroded sculptures of waning lives faded in their twilight. Souls awaiting whatever comes next, after a lifetime in flesh and blood.

Panla gazed over the large area with pensive reserve.

Crouss, Linnfeld and the other attendants appeared restless to move on.

Crilen felt some measure of pity for this sickly gathering. Though, certainly, in his travels, he had seen much worse…in war.

"Straight to Hell!" a raspy, shaking, male voice chuckled from across the ward. "Straight to Hell! That's where I'm going!"

Panla looked up and searched across the large room.

"Over here!" the dusty voice yelled ruefully. "Come pull my pants up!"

Panla scanned to her right until she found a dark skeletal figure waving from a chair by the window.

Crilen could sense what was coming next.

Crouss quietly signaled to a pair of nurses to quell the man's disturbance, but Panla held up her hand and everyone froze in their tracks.

"I'll tend to him." Panla regarded the man with acute interest and started toward him.

Crouss grimaced silently to himself as his hands flopped at his side.

Linnfeld folded his arms and took the occasion to browbeat his subordinate attendants.

Crilen, however, followed closely behind her.

Panla halted abruptly and spun about.

"Mr. Len," she addressed him coldly, "I believe I said that *I* would tend to him?"

"Yes, Mrs. Tem." he answered in a tone she was doggedly growing accustomed to. "And I am tending to you."

"Well, that's all well and good," she met his eyes with a stark scowl, "but you'll do so from over there."

"As your security man," Crilen replied evenly, "it would be remiss for me to attempt to perform my duties from across the room. And I believe the Accommodant would expect no less from the protector of his wife."

"My husb…!" Panla raised her voice, then caught herself as she glanced over at Crouss and her attendants.

"What my husband wants," she restarted in a whisper, "would surprise you, Mr. Len."

Crilen noted she had suddenly become exceedingly flustered.

She caught him reading her, and turned quickly away.

"Very well," she acquiesced. "but I don't want to know that you're there."

"As you wish."

Panla resumed her course toward the old man in the chair.

The old man's flesh was a wrinkled leathery blackish grey. His hair was thinning, white and swirled wildly about his dried spotted scalp. His eyes were yellowed orbs, sunken deep into their red-rimmed sockets. His limbs were gnarled and twisted with affliction, and his hands and feet were covered with pinkened sores.

"Could you pull up my pants?" the old man turned slightly, revealing that his trousers had not been pulled up all the way.

Crilen moved forward. Again, Panla held up her hand and froze him where he stood.

She leaned over the old man and reached around his waist.

"You're going to have to help me." She spoke into his ear.

The old man gripped the arms of his chair. With all the strain he could muster, he hoisted his frail shaking body roughly a centimeter over his seat. Panla saw the old man's clothing was stained, but she grabbed hold of them without hesitation. In another instant, Panla quickly tugged the rear of the old man's trousers and covered his bare posterior. The old man fell back into his chair with a ragged groan of gracious relief.

"Thank you." The old man sighed, settling back. "Thank you so much. The fucking idiots here don't know how to dress people, you know? I may not be able to dress myself, but at least I know how! Fucking idiots!"

Panla could not suppress a smile.

Meanwhile the old man's eyes inspected her, from head to toe. "Rough morning?"

"Excuse me?" Panla's smile wilted.

"You look like you had a rough morning," the old man clarified. "You look a lot neater on satellite."

"Oh." Panla subconsciously pushed her fingers through her hair.

"But what the hell?" He chuckled through his rotting crooked teeth. "You're just stopping through to visit a bunch of dying, worthless fucks. Who gives a shit, right?"

"Well..." Panla started to blush.

"Ah, don't mind me," The old man gestured. "I didn't say I didn't think you looked beautiful. I just said you look like you had a rough morning, that's all."

"Why...thank you." Panla presumed there was a compliment in there someplace.

"Who's he?" The old man looked up at Crilen.

"Oh," Panla smiled again, "just security."

"Security, huh?" The old man squinted. "Looks like he thinks he's some kind of bad ass. 'Course, those are the ones that usually ain't.'"

"He's fine," Panla responded.

"Yeah, well look here, bad ass," the old man raised his voice, "this is the Queen Mother you're watching after! I may not look like nothin', but you let something happen to this one and I'll come after you! May not get there fast, but I'll get there! You can bet your bad ass on that!"

Crilen remained outwardly impassive, though inwardly he was amused.

Panla, meanwhile, knelt down before the old man and took his twisted fingers into her hand.

"Tell me," the old man spoke softly, "you're a fine young lady. Why'd you marry that sorry husband of yours? Lying, scamming, backstabbing con artist! You could do a hell of a lot better than that bastard. Why?"

Panla smiled again and looked down at his festering hand. "You don't know him like I do," she whispered.

"Yeah, I'll bet," he groused. "That's fine. You don't have to tell me. I'm just a dying piece of shit in a medical. I can't help you anyway. But no woman who's the Queen Mother could be happy married to a man who don't stand for nothin'. I know that much!"

There was a short pause. Panla lifted her head up and perkily smiled at the old man as if she hadn't heard him.

"So why do you think you're going to Hell?" she said starting a clean slate.

"Hmh." The old man leaned to one side and held her eyes. "Why not?"

Panla frowned. Her expression demanded an answer.

"Look, don't take this personally," he shook her hand, "but I hate the god-damned church! Everything about it. I hate the goddamned music. I hate the stupid fuckin' costumes. I hate the suck-on-my-wallet commercial holidays! I hate the shiny shitty-ass décor. I hate the hypocrisy of all the so-called holy people who show up to pretend to pray every Solemnday. I hate the queer-ass Churchlords and their 'divine' rights. And sometimes, I think I even hate God for making the shit up and giving me the brains to see through all the bullshit! I mean, at least he could have made me one of those ignorant fuckers who just follow along!"

Panla folded her lips.

"I don't mean to be disrespectful." The old man's eyes apologized like a repentant child's.

Panla raised an eyebrow.

"I've always been this way." he continued with reflection. "Anything that ever smelled like religion…I ran from it. Oh, I ran like the wind! Nobody was gonna' make a pious fool out of me! Instead, I ran after life. Like a starving man in the desert, chasing every oasis on the next horizon…I ran after life. I saw the world as one big picture show, and I didn't want to miss a frame. Didn't want to miss one thing I felt I was entitled to see or do. I traveled the world! Must have gotten high or drunk in every town on the planet at least twice. Got rich. Got married. Got divorced. Got kids. Got poor. Got rich again. Got married again. Got more kids. Got more divorced. Got sick. Got old. Fuck!"

The old man's voice trailed off into a whimper. He slumped and reached up to cover his face.

Panla put her hand on his shoulder and tried to comfort him.

"My first wife?" he sniffled. "Churchlord's daughter. She was a saint. 'Course, I took her virginity on the second date. God, I was so proud of that! Got her pregnant a few months later. That pissed me off, but I think I was proud of that, too. Anything that seemed to make her a little dirtier, a little less holy. A little more like me. It was like a triumph, bringing her down!

"I beat her. Brought strange women home in the middle of the night…and fucked 'em right in front of her and the kids. And they'd cry and I'd either just laugh or go berserk and beat the hell out of everyone. One Solemnday morning, I must have beat her half way up the street for taking my kids to cathedral. But she went anyway. My god, that woman was a saint!

"I blew all our money! Then I blamed her for it, and I split! Disappeared. Knocked around for a few twinmoons 'til this other business deal came through. Then I was on top again. Clubs! Vacations! A little notoriety in a nice circle of upscales! And women! Those were great days! And then I met the finest piece of feminine flesh God ever made. A trophy! First time I think I ever had someone I really wanted to keep. She was half my age, but I was rich. So we got married. I built me another family. One I really liked this time. And I'll be damned, she was the one who fucked around on me! I gave that bitch everything and she still…I laugh about it now, but…"

The old man paused and tilted his head back. His voice cracked.

"Only time I've ever went to cathedral was for weddings or funerals. And, usually, I was either high, or thinking about getting high. I even missed my mother's funeral. I couldn't find…

"Shit!" the old man's mouth quivered.

"I never gave anything to anybody. Told myself charity was just a fucking scam! I owned people but I never loved anybody, not even my goddamn kids. I lied to relatives. Stole from friends. Fucked their daughters and wives. Used up my body. Made myself sick. Cursed God…"

"Mrs. Tem," Crouss whispered.

Crilen placed his hand in the middle of Crouss's chest and motioned for him to refrain.

"And now I'm sick…dying." The old man began to sob. "I can't dress myself. Can't even wipe my own ass. And now I'm going to Hell!"

Panla stood and embraced the old man as he sobbed on her shoulder.

"It's never too late," she whispered to him. "It's never too late to ask forgiveness."

The old man hung his head and suddenly tried to push her away.

"Bitch, you can't absolve me!" he cried angrily. "You're just a fucking person! Just like me and everybody else!"

Passionately, Panla knelt down and clutched his sickly hand again.

"You're right," she spoke urgently in a hushed voice, "there's nothing divine about me. I'm just a person, but you don't need me! All you need is to apply your soul to God. Ask Him for your absolution. And, if He can read the truth in your heart, your soul may yet see Heaven."

The old man leaned back in his chair and looked down at her with an aching gratitude. He quivered as the hope in his heart wrestled mightily with the anguish in his soul. For the first time, he heard a truth which resonated with his aching conscience.

"Thank you, Queen Mother," he said in a barely audible voice. "Thank you for not bullshitting me."

Panla stood and straightened the hem of her dress.

"You're welcome," she said softly. "Lord's Glory."

The old man met her eyes and nodded.

"Mrs. Tem…" Crouss tried to intervene once more.

"I think this patient needs a gown," she strongly suggested.

Crouss froze in his tracks.

Panla turned and slowly walked to the center of the ward, ignoring anyone who might have tried to deter her. She stopped and looked out over the gathering with hope and confidence in her eyes.

"I know that these appear to be your darkest hours on this planet," she said in an audible tone that filled the entire room. "But I submit to you, that there isn't one of us living and breathing today who won't someday face the inevitable end of our lives. You may be asking yourselves 'Why me?' as if your fate has never befallen another living soul. But the test you now face has been the same for every soul on this planet for the last two thousand twinmoons. And lest we die suddenly and without time for preparation, every male and female will someday reach the precipice upon which you find yourselves.

"Of course its natural to reflect upon what we did with our lives or failed to do. Who we'll miss and who shall miss us. The wrongs that we did and the good that we tried to do. How we fell short of God's expectations and commandments. How disobedient we often chose to be. How unworthy, even at our best, we all are, of His grace. But there's nothing any of us can do about the past. It's gone...over with. But what we can affect...what we must affect...is the future. Not the future of this world, but the future of our souls and their bond with God in Heaven. Our lives here are finite, minuscule, a mere flicker in the grand scheme of eternity. But our immortal souls are the treasure we must guard from sin and corruption. Our immortal souls are the gift from God which we must offer back to Him...pure, naked, clean and devoted to His unconditional love for all of us. I ask you to pray today. Not to the church or the Deliverancy or any edifice of this world. I ask you to pray to God that He may save your immortal souls and guide you to His kingdom in Heaven."

Panla, closed her eyelids and sang. Her unaccompanied voice carried with it an airy resonance that transcended all the physical paradigms of life. The song's rhythm was archaic, but she abandoned the ancient language and sang in a contemporary dialect which lent enriched clarity and beauty to its meaning. The overall effect was as if the long, linear path of sentient history was being conjoined into a miraculously singular moment in space and time.

Crilen could sense every living soul being caressed by the single hand of God. Not just the souls in the room. Not just the souls on the planet. But every penitent, vital soul...past present and future...convergent upon God's glistening throne. He closed his eyes for an instant and imagined himself home again, standing on a hillside overlooking the temple of his ancestors. He could feel his father and his mother, and his grandparents and their parents all descendent in spiritual unison upon his heart. And he felt assurance from the creator of the universe warm his restless conscience. He considered that if ever the intonation of a solitary mortal voice could guide souls to their salvation, he was hearing it at that moment. The experience brought an amazing, immeasurable comfort he wanted to bask and revel in, but he flickered his eyes open and found himself still in the ward, still amongst the living, after all.

There were some patients who appeared either too feeble or too afflicted to fully comprehend. And there were a few who frowned defiantly, as if the Deliveress were no more than a brazen door-to-door saleswoman, heaping prattle upon their private misery. But for most, it was as if a cleansing tide of spiritual inertia were washing through every crevice of their wounds, dissolving strife, dismay and confusion, and clearing a pathway of certainty to God's eternal peace.

When Panla's song concluded silence fell. Then, an old woman cried, "God bless you, Queen Mother! Praise God our Lord!"

Others followed suit with praise for Panla Jen's visit.

Panla bowed graciously and turned to Mr. Crouss. "I'll see your staff now." She spoke almost apologetically.

Crouss smiled nervously and mopped his brow as he tried to recompose himself. It was difficult to tell whether he, too, had been moved by Panla's message to the ward, or whether he was merely flustered by the rearrangement of his morning's schedule.

X.

"I got the distinct impression you had a problem with our meeting today." The Accommodant filled two glasses with dark brown liquor and handed one to Allabel.

"I didn't mean to be disrespectful." Allabel lowered her eyes and took the triangular glass.

"Sure you did." The Accommodant smiled. "You couldn't help it. It's because you care."

"And you don't?" Allabel's mouth fell open.

"Of course I do." The Accommodant walked slowly to the bed and sat down. "The difference is, you care about what you think people should have. I care about what the people think the people should have."

"Well, sometimes, maybe the people don't know what's best for them," Allabel gestured "Maybe they have to rely on their leaders to lead them."

"A one-term electoral strategy if ever I heard one." The Accommodant motioned for her to sit next to him.

"Oh, I know," she whined with resignation and eased herself onto his lap. "It just seems all wrong. Backwards. Leaders should lead. Followers should follow…"

"Shhh." the Accommodant held a forefinger up to his lips. "Maybe in a dictatorship or monarchy or theocracy. But this is a democracy we're talking about. The Accommodant's role in a democracy is to ensure that the will of the people is accommodated."

"What about the welfare of the people?" Allabel countered.

"The welfare of the people belongs in the people's hands." he answered, massaging the young woman's outer thigh. "Our highest principle in a free society is that the majority are empowered with the freedom to choose their own destiny."

"Even if it's wrong?" She sipped from her glass.

"Wrong?" The Accommodant chuckled. "You sound like my wife."

"No I don't!" She playfully stuck out her tongue. "I haven't been to cathedral in twinmoons, and my Text is sitting up under one of my plants so it can get more moonlight. I just think that there are some things that are clearly right and some things that are clearly wrong, that's all."

"Like what?" He smirked and lifted his eyebrows.

"Oh, I know that look." She laughed. "That's the look that says 'Let Allabel run off on a tangent and then I'll squash her entire philosophy when I see a convenient place to jump in.'"

"No, no." The Accommodant smiled and drained his glass. "You started it. I want to hear this. Like what?"

"Well," Allabel sighed as she tried to assemble her argument, "like murder."

"Murder's good." He leaned over and plucked the liquor bottle from the silver tray.

"No, murder is not good!" She finished her drink and handed him her glass. "Murder is as bad as it gets. Murder is wrong, wrong, wrong, wrong, wrong!"

"Says who?" The Accommodant refilled her glass.

"Says everybody!" Allabel exclaimed.

"Then what's the problem?" The Accommodant sipped his drink.

"There is no problem!" Allabel became flustered. "I'm just saying that murder is an example of something that is absolutely wrong."

"You'll get no argument from me." He smiled and leaned back on the bed.

"Klin!" her shoulders slumped. "Are you following what I'm saying?"

"Murder's wrong." The Accommodant smirked.

"Right!" She poked his stomach. "But that's just one example of something that is absolutely wrong."

"Fine. Where's this going?"

"Lying!" Allabel spoke with emphasis. "Lying is something that's absolutely positively wrong."

"Under any circumstance?" He sat up on his elbows.

"Absolutely!" She nodded her head.

"What if it's in someone's best interest to lie?"

"No, its wrong!" She was emphatic.

"What if the lie is just…a temporary lie until everyone concerned can…handle the truth?"

"Still wrong!" She confidently sipped her drink.

"What if not lying would cause someone to commit murder?" The Accommodant sipped again.

Allabel's face went blank for a moment, then she glared at him with an admonishing frown. "I hate you!" she stood up and paced to the other side of the room.

"Okay, I'm sorry." The Accommodant sat up.

"What I'm trying to say is that I'm no fan of the Church." Allabel became serious. "I think it's become repressive, outdated and wholly rooted in tired superstitions and foolish legends. But there's also some basic things in there that people need. We can't just throw those things away. I mean, the Text isn't gospel, but we could do a helluva lot worse than keeping some of it as part of our society's structure."

"Maybe we'll get those things you're worried about from somewhere else." He stood up and approached her. "Maybe the people will give it to themselves."

"And what if they don't?" She felt his hand touch her shoulder. "What if future generations of children grow up without any direction, aimless."

"They'll find their way." He breathed onto her neck. "It's not like all the cathedrals will be locking their doors to the public. People will simply carry on as they always have, but with choices."

"And without the government's blessing." She reached back and ran her fingers between his legs.

"If that's the will of the people," he whispered and slowly unhooked the back of her dress.

"And what if the Break is the will of the people?" she turned and let her dress fall away.

"Then we'll see." He set down his glass and kissed her.

"Wait!" She placed her fingers on his chin.

The Accommodant rolled his eyes and shook his head.

"No, I'm serious about this!" Allabel pleaded.

"So am I." His voice became firm. "I've got a confirmation hearing I have to chair in an hour."

"The judicial confirmation?"

"Right." He glided his fingers up the side of her ribcage.

"That guy's been a crusader against the Cathedral for decades." Allabel gulped her drink. "Do you really think you'll get him on the high court?"

"The time is right." the Accommodant smiled. "It'd be a popular move! And besides that, he's got some great anecdotes of personal tragedy. He could be a mass murderer and get confirmed by the time he gets through talking about his family. Plus, according to the media polls, he's as hot as judicial candidates get. People are tired of the same old stodgy conservatives. It's time for the wind to blow in another direction."

"The wind." Allabel sighed. "Is that all you care about?"

"Oh look, my wife is home," he teased her as he ran his hand over the curve of her buttocks.

"Shut up!" She laughed out loud again and accidentally spilled her drink onto the floor.

"Nice move." He took her glass.

"You're the one making all the moves." She wiped her hand on his shirt.

"And you're the one who's wasting our time." He sounded mildly annoyed.

"Why? Just because I have a point?"

"No, because you're missing the big picture," the Accommodant lectured. "You really don't have any idea what burdens organized religion places on this society."

"Burdens?"

"Listen." The Accommodant held up one finger. "Tell me what you think of fornication?"

"What?"

"You know. Fornication: sex between two unmarried people."

"I don't know." Allabel shrugged and twirled her hair. "As long as it's not rape or something…"

"That's not what the Text says." He reached out to caress her bare shoulder. "According to the Text, two people can't have sex unless they're married to each other."

"Well that's ridiculous!" Allabel chuckled half-heartedly.

"I agree." He slid the back of his hand across her bosom. "But the Cathedral says anyone who is a fornicator is wrong. No exceptions!"

"Well I guess that just proves that the Texts are outdated, like I said." She fumbled with the buttons of his tunic.

"Same goes for adultery." he leaned forward and rubbed his nose next to hers. "No matter how lonely or miserable or empty your marriage is, you're stuck there for life…unless you commit murder!"

"Oh god!" Allabel laughed out loud.

"And then that presents a whole other set of problems, doesn't it?" He guided his lips down to the top of her shoulder.

"Where is she now?" The young woman ran her fingers through his grey hair.

"Way the far fuck away from here." He reached around her waist and moved them toward the bed.

"So...ow!"

"Sorry."

"Why did the two of you get married in the first place?" she asked breathlessly.

"I had a thing for spoiled little ice princesses." He slipped his hand beneath her undergarment. "And she was the grand prize. Unfortunately, it turned out that she hadn't developed much of an appetite or imagination in matters of passion. That's what happens when you marry God first and your husband as an afterthought."

"How does she feel about your position?" Allabel began unbuttoning his pants.

"This one?" he snickered

"No, silly, your position on the Cathedral."

"Hmh. I never assumed that she wouldn't disagree. But it's not me she needs to worry about. I'm just here to accommodate the will of the people. If their will is to limit the Cathedral's influence...oh! that's it!...then I've got to do what I've got to do."

"Doesn't it bother you that the Break is a violent, terrorist organization?" Allabel paused.

"One man's terrorist is another man's patriot," he recited. "Their methods may be crude, but to a lot of people, Rabbel Mennis is fighting their battle for them. Maybe he's fighting our battle."

"'Our' battle, hmm?" She slid her hands down the front of his chest.

"Sure." The Accommodant breathed. "Imagine what the...Deliveress would say if she saw us now."

"Let's not think about it."

"Let's not talk about it."

They laughed as they kissed.

"So is this fornication? Adultery? Sin? Or what?" Allabel wrapped her lean leg over the Accommodant's shoulder.

"Mmmh!" He let loose a low groan. "All of the above, darlin'. All of the above, I'm pretty sure."

XI.

"Dead?" Yolo bellowed into the monitor as he choked on his cigar smoke. "Finx Melder and Preppi Deyz are both dead? Proptz, I'm running low on my pressure medicine! I know its late evening there, but it's mid-afternoon here and I was having a decent day. Do tell me your call from the wee hours of the northeast is only some dreadful miscarriage of humor."

"Sorry, dear Yolo, but it seems as though we lost control of the situation." The woman's pointed pale features looked drawn and remorseful.

"Lost control?" Yolo coughed up a hearty roll of phlegm. "You and your pack of scurrilous predators chase the world's most popular, though not talented, actor to a fiery death and you call that a 'loss of control'? I'd hate to see what you could've accomplished had you simply set out to commit murder to begin with!"

"Murder?" Proptz recoiled.

"Well, we can't very well call it anything else, can we?" Yolo smeared the spittle from his mouth. "The man certainly wouldn't have driven he and his date through a wrought iron barricade, over a steep rocky embankment and headlong into a combustible fuel tank without a fair measure of prodding, don't you agree?"

"I...guess." Proptz lowered her eyes. "But Finx had just started dating that sportsgirl! He knew we needed a story!"

"Yes. Clearly, by this courtship, he harkened the knell of death," Yolo deadpanned.

"Yolo, don't pretend with me!" The woman grew annoyed. "Your celebrity division offered millions in bounty for the first images of Finx and Preppi together!"

"And we'll pay millions more for footage of the coup de theatre, assuming your minions were competent enough to get any."

"Oh there's plenty of that!" Proptz suddenly brightened. "A good fifteen minutes worth before the policers showed up! I got the impact of his sport sedan hitting the fuel tank and the full explosion myself! And we found both bodies jettisoned some 200 meters from the epicenter. Horribly burned and dismembered, mind you. Too bad we didn't have time to look for limbs! But Loblo said he actually got some gurgling out of Preppi just before she expired. I haven't seen everyone's complete footage yet, but when we splice it all together its going to be spectacular stuff. Not to mention lucrative!"

"Did any of you try to put out the fire?" Yolo doused his cigar.

"We're journalists, not firefighters, Yolo!" She was taken aback.

"What about first aid?" Yolo lifted his heavy brows. "Did anyone try to administer any aid to the victims?"

"Um...no." Proptz became concerned. "No, I don't think so. But who had the proper equip...?"

"Good." Yolo interrupted her. "The last thing we need is some kind of Samaritan malpractice suit on top of everything else."

Proptz settled back and appeared to relax. "So we're in the clear?"

"Hardly." Yolo grumbled. "Now tell me how you 'lost control' of this soon-to-be infamous evening.

"Well," Proptz started like a school child sweating out a confession to the principal, "it all started with a call I got from Loblo. He'd begun to stake out Preppi's neighborhood and paid the grocer near her home to contact him if he got wind of anything. Well the grocer called Loblo and told him that Preppi was planning to make dinner for Finx at her parents' bungalow by the creek. Loblo had no problem finding her parents' address in the directory."

"Melder is unlisted. Preppi is unlisted. So Preppi plans a dinner at her parents and tells the world." Yolo shook his head. "Cunning prey, these athletes."

"Anyway," Proptz continued, "Loblo calls me and then assembles his air and road squads. By the time Melder gets to Preppi's parents' house mid-evening, the place is swarming with hidden cameras and microphones. Loblo's air reconnaissance tracked Melder as soon as his sedan hit a main drag. It was a sweet set-up! But the one problem was that Loblo's people get trigger happy. They could have gotten everything from pre-dinner cocktails to second-story footage of them rolling around in the loft all night. But someone had to pounce Melder with a camera light as soon as he got out of his vehicle. Melder ran into the house covering his face, grabbed Preppi from inside and peeled out of her parents' yard like a wild man!"

"Wild man." Yolo mumbled. "Let's hope the authorities find he was spinning on some of those pills he liked. That may be useful down the road."

"Well, Loblo's a high speed expert," Proptz continued. "Melder wailed through traffic but never came close to losing them. Meantime, Loblo's on the com to me and tells me to get my people to this small inn about five kilometers away. At first, I thought he was joshing me, trying to throw me off the scent. But then I figured, why would he call me to begin with? So my people and I get to the inn and sure enough, there comes Melder's vehicle creeping into the inn parking stalls with his lights off. Apparently, Loblo let Melder think they'd given us the slip.

"Well as soon Melder and Preppi hit the inn lobby, we nailed them, kissing no less! Probably the last kiss! Melder punches one of my people and Preppi just starts crying. Then they run back out to Melder's sedan and there's Loblo's squad sitting right there, hovercraft lights blazing, cameras rolling! It was a masterpiece! Well, Melder and Preppi hop back into their vehicle and take off again, only now, both of our squads are hot on their trail. Melder's blowing traffic signals, cutting through yards, careening though walkways and we're still right on them. I swear, Yolo, it was all so exciting I nearly came!"

"Lovely," Yolo sighed.

"Well," Proptz swallowed her embarrassment, "Loblo actually suggested that it was getting dangerous and called back his road squad. So I told him his air people should take the lead. Loblo knew his stuff, because, not thirty seconds later, a passenger jumbo cut Melder off. He swerved and smashed through that metal barricade! From the top of the hill we watched them fly over the ravine, bounce off the rocks and right into that fuel tank! Then, BOOM! Sunrise at midnight! We all fanned out and surrounded the scene. We knew we wouldn't have much time before the authorities got there. But what a night, Yolo! What a fucking night!!"

"Fucking night, indeed." Yolo leaned back in his large chair. "Be sure you repeat this story to no one."

"What?" Proptz dropped her jaw.

"That is unless you want your murder trial to supersede everything you've just told me as the biggest story since that housekeeper's young daughter filed harassment charges against the Accommodant," Yolo answered.

"My murder trial?" The woman looked sick.

"I'm afraid so, my dear, though you may plead down to Negligent Proximate Cause, if you're lucky." Yolo continued. "The problem is, by your own admission, you herded these poor, tawdry simpletons to their doom. Public outcry for some semblance of justice over the death of their favorite actor and his dizzy little companion will undoubtedly be enormous. No judge, prosecutor or defense lawyer in their right mind will do anything other than conspire to expediently hang you and/or good Loblo from the nearest light post. You'll be lucky if you're able to hear the testimonies against you over the hammering together of the gallows outside the justice hall.

"And, no, I won't be there to help you. Even I'm not fool enough to try to defend the media's right to hunt, hound and barbecue its subjects. In fact, I'll be trumpeting the need for media reforms, all the while selling your trial's air time like it's going out of style. Of course, once you're convicted, no one will really care whether there's any reform or not. They'll have you. And then I'll be able to get on about my business as if nothing had ever happened."

"Oh, shit, Yolo." Proptz smacked her hand against her forehead.

"Oh, dear, you haven't come again, have you?" Yolo chuckled.

"What the hell are we supposed to do now?" She seemed on the verge of tears.

"Well, the problem is, you've gone and found the story of the twinmoon," he smiled broadly, "but you've set yourself right in the heart of it. Right now this whole mess is like a prize-winning photograph, only with the photographer's thumb sitting in the middle."

"What do I do?"

"First, gather up your jackals and collect all their footage. Then bag and tag it all for some time next twinmoon!" Yolo drummed his fingers.

"Next twinmoon?" Proptz was stunned.

"Unless you want it to be the backbone of your own indictment, I suggest you do so." he continued. "The moment is all wrong for your work to pay dividends. It will have to sit and mature like a sound investment. Today, that footage will only fuel the public's idiotic need to express outrage and indignation at the horror of their loss. A twinmoon from now, the mourning will be long past and they'll giddily lap up the garish gore you've recorded like the bloodlusting parasites they really are.

"Second, and I know this will be a stretch, make every member of your bureau dispense with their devil's fangs for a week or two and put on the garb of angels!"

"Sir?" Proptz was totally puzzled.

"Perhaps if we can make enough of an overbearing schmaltz festival of the funerals, we may evaporate most of our...excuse me...your blame into turbid obscurity.

"By sunrise, I want cameras, hundreds of cameras, capturing every imbecilic expression of melancholic devotion for Finx Melder and Dippy, that sportsgirl. I want to see the ratty homemade signs and the blubbering bovine housewives with rivers of snot gushing from their portly snouts. I want your jackal journalists perched upon every street corner, transformed into weeping, sentimental, teary-eyed poets, romancing this inane tragedy well beyond the intelligent boundaries of sound reason and good taste.

"I want flowers and cards and letters, ankle deep. Pay the hordes of homeless and destitute to hand carry them just for effect. I want interviews with loved ones of the deceased. Whining, whimpering loved ones! And childhood photos of Melder and what's-her-name with baby food smeared all over their slobbering little faces. I want the charitable causes their agents forced them to patronize trumpeted as if they lived for little else. I want images of the grief-stricken parents keeling over on their front stoops and the nosy know-nothing neighbors shaking their heads in nosy disbelief. Show the footage of the burnt-out fuel tank and melted sedan until the overexposure makes everyone think its a painting on their wall. And be sure to raise a zillion questions to exponentially dilute the media's singular guilt in this matter! This is the only way to both save your scrawny, opportunistic hide and fatten my bottom line in the process.

"Hopefully, after a week or two of seemingly endless streams of warbling tribute songs and preposterous eulogies and insipid retrospectives and tedious introspectives, the public will no more care whether the poor buggers died of manic narcissism, or if I, myself, had gunned that monosyllabic drug addict and his busty little brute down in broad daylight!

"Muddy the facts. Blur the blame. Spread the culpability over, nice and thin. Replay the interviews of anyone who knows nothing and pay away everyone who seems to know something. Pound the whole sorry mess into everyone's skull until their urine smells like the inside of Melder's coffin! Then, finally, make this entire matter scream into oblivion like a screeching holiday fireworks display: Loud, brilliant and indigestibly forgettable!"

"And the authorities?" Proptz blinked.

"The authorities won't care if the public doesn't care." Yolo smiled. "Why should they make an enemy out of a perfectly good friend if there's no public sentiment to be gained? They won't ask much and we'll tell them even less, and the whole thing will eventually dry up and blow away."

"Won't the families pursue it?"

"The 'it' the families will pursue will be the royalty rights to their 'loved ones' estates."

"How can you be sure?"

"If ever you wish to predict behavior," Yolo smiled, "track the two purest inertias in the world: Lust and Lucre. Those are the only true living gods."

"Well, damn." Proptz sighed and folded her arms. "Looks like I won't be getting any sleep this week."

"You're still young. Another pill-popping binge won't kill you." Yolo half-snickered. "Think of those chunky-legged housewives trying to trample you under their hooves when they find out that you've done away with the object of their wet dreams. A few days of journalistic prestidigitation can't possibly be worse than that."

"You're right." Proptz hung her head.

"And besides, a twinmoon from now you'll be basking that pale stick of a body of yours in new found riches...when you cash in your annuity!"

"Yeah, yeah." She shook her head. "Talk to me in a twinmoon."

"Would that that were possible," Yolo chided. "Unfortunately, you're my eastern bureau chief. So I suppose I'll hear from you sooner."

"Are you sure you don't want to oversee this yourself?" Proptz asked.

"You're quite capable, my dear." Yolo lit another cigar. "Besides, I have a bigger beast to broil."

"Do tell." Proptz raised an eyebrow.

"Well, outside the hollow realm of entertainment and celebrity, there's a game being played called Real Life." Yolo loosed red smoke from his nostrils. "And the stakes of this game are the tangible hopes, fears and dreams of the entire populace of this planet. The players who run the board are few but powerful, to be sure. One of those players is on her way here to do an interview in a few hours."

"Deliveress Panla Jen?" Proptz was certain.

"Panla Jen Tem." Yolo confirmed.

"Now her, I'd like to expose."

"I'm sure you would." Yolo snorted. "However, the government would certainly make you and anyone who looks like you disappear off the face of the planet if you even tried...using your methods."

"But your methods, on the other hand...?"

"My methods aren't designed to expose, you see." Yolo admired his cigar. "Rather they are designed to allow the subject to expose themselves."

"Sounds complicated." Proptz was impressed. "Too bad. I'm not a complicated girl."

"I know, Proptz." Yolo released a gargantuan yawn. "Good day!"

Yolo clicked off his monitor and arose as his wheezing leather chair gasped for breath.

XII.

The blackened walls of the underground cavern were scorched by a raw, raking, shriek of blind torment. It's shrill and haunting echo danced eerily into the darkness, leaving behind the spattered stain of ruthless torture in the ears of any listener. An odd, unnerving silence then followed.

For a prolonged interval, the dense silence relented only to the occasional moaning of the wind rushing quietly along the cool, rocky subterranean surfaces. A distant drop of water pierced a puddle somewhere nearby. Another soundless moment held sway for an eternity of seconds.

Finally, a shattering scream of blind anguish ripped through the air, once more. The scream of an animal begging for death.

A jolting explosion blasted through the curdling yelps, and a low murmur of anxious voices followed, under its chilling echo.

"Fucking spunk me!" Reza marveled.

"Whenever you want." Durn's long yellow teeth formed a crooked grin.

"It'll work." Leesla's almond eyes brightened.

"It'll do, Juds." Rabbel tucked away his smoking hand weapon as he knelt down and inspected the smoldering headless contortion of bone and flesh still bubbling its way into the ground.

"It'll do?'" Juds, a pale, thin, dark haired man walked up to Rabbel. "It'll do?"

The man turned away and nodded nervously into the distance. He turned again and met Rabbel's stern scowl with agitated perturbation. "Rabbel, what the fuck do I look like, huh?" Juds raised his finger. "A fucking lab student? A fucking pimple faced masturbator playing with a toy store chem set?"

"I masturbate." Reza fingered her pelvis and flicked her tongue.

"But you got me!" Durn smiled and reached toward her.

"Exactly." Reza turned up her nose and pushed his hands away with her elbows.

"Juds," Rabbel addressed the thin man, "it's fine."

"Fine?" Juds' pitted jaws dropped. "I've got drug gangs, militias and city governments begging me for exclusives to this sadistic delight and all you can say to me is that it's fine? Let's see, stop me if I missed something! Did we not just watch some staggering homeless wretch metamorphasize from a cringing unbathed assemblage of flesh and booze into a caustic liter of bubbling gelatin?"

"I can scream like that." Reza winked at Juds.

"Shut...up!" Leesla raised a fist.

"Look," Rabbel held up his hands, "I'm not questioning you. I'm just trying to think through how we can use this to our best advantage."

"En masse." Leesla sneered through her teeth.

"Sounds like a winner to me." Durn smiled as he leaned back against the cavern wall.

"You take a ninety liter drum of this paste," Juds held up a small capsule, "detonate it outside a cathedral on a bright sunny Solemnday morning and you could shovel the remains of a whole town into one funeral casket made for a five-twin-moon-old child."

"Economical, too." Durn grinned.

"Gross!" Reza giggled.

"It's supposed to be." Leesla spat into the sizzling remnants of the deteriorated corpse. "You can't expect to convince these religious types with mere words. They've got an answer for everything. We need to fight them on our terms, see if they'll really embrace their enemy. Draw them into a bloody war! Show them that we…and the free world mean business!"

"Leesla's right." Rabbel's dark face was solemn. "We've got to show the government how we feel, being oppressed by the influence of the church's doctrines and edicts. Frankly, it feels a lot like this homeless man must've felt. Powerless, helpless and without any voice in how things should be. What did God ever do for him?"

"What did we ever do for him?" Juds snickered. "Hey, look, I'm on your side. I believe in the same burn-the-Text bullshit you guys believe in. What? I'm gonna' wait 'til I get married again before I get laid? Consenting adults, that's what I say. Some broad wants to roll around with me with no promises, she takes her chances. Shit, I'm happier now than I ever was chained up in matrimony! Crazy wives, whining brats! At least now, when I get pissed off, I can walk the fuck out without some judicator garnishing my fucking paycheck. 'Hasta la vista, ya' dumb snatch! That's the way I like it!"

"Snatch?" Anger flashed across Leesla's features.

"No offense," Juds smirked cautiously.

"None taken." Reza smiled and winked back at him.

"Excuse me," Juds rubbed his chin and eyed Reza, "maybe it's just me, but I'm getting one helluva horny vibe here. When we're done with this little transaction, you wanna…?"

"She's taken." Durn stared with a threat in his eyes.

"Yeah?" Juds watched Reza fondle the edge of her skirt. "Well the pastry's startin' to glaze and you ain't the baker."

"We need to figure out a delivery system that takes out the intended targets." Rabbel held up one of the small capsules. "I won't be responsible for killing innocents, especially children. They're the ones we're doing this for, so that they can have the chances we didn't: To grow up in a totally free society without a 'god' hanging over their heads."

"Beautiful, sentiment Rabbel." Juds folded his arms impatiently. "But my kids are already fucked up. My ex and her little girlfriend have my son taking fairy lessons while my daughter hates boys and wants to be king stud of her school's male slamball team! I see the little shits only about four times a twinmoon and its still supposed to be all my fault somehow. Blame God, alcohol or the dim bar lights that made me forget to wear protection, its all the same to me now. So what's it gonna' be? En masse or one pan fried torso at a time?"

"If we can come up with a loose metal casing for these capsules," Durn plucked one from a nearby table, "I'm sure I can rig a weapon that can shoot far and straight."

"Careful with that!" Juds warned. "That capsule cracks open and spills paste on your finger, you'll be begging your boss to blow your brains out. The paste is part nerve agent and part bio-molecular corrosive with an airborne life span of about three minutes. Once it hits flesh, it seeks and consumes organic elements in seconds. By the time it's done with the subject, there's nothing left but a mucous puddle of inert elements and cloth fragments. One capsule pretty much consumes the average-sized male.

"And, no, the shit don't wash off with soap and water!" Juds smiled at the end of his sales pitch.

"You said other groups were interested?" Rabbel rubbed his chin. "Like who?"

"Like, my list of clientele is confidential, Rabbel. Okay?" Juds shook his head. "They wouldn't want me spilling their name to you any more than you might want me to spill your name to say…the office of the Accommodant."

"I hear you." Rabbel nodded.

"Let me just put it this way." Juds smiled a crooked smile. "The only contingent I haven't heard from on this deal is the Cathedral. And if I call in and check my messages…well ya' never know. They got a lotta' cash in those heavenly coffers."

"It's the only way they get to 'Heaven'." Leesla turned up her mouth.

"Sucks, doesn't it?" Juds chuckled nervously. "I mean, some rich guy who could give a shit about sports, buying his way into front row seats at a ballgame is bad enough. But God has a fucking price? What next?"

"My da gave his cathedral six million coin for Bius Charities last twinmoon." Reza chimed in, oddly serious. "Got his big wrinkly sphincter on the media getting a wreath from the hairy nostriled Regent. I'm sure he'll be eating his little teenage mistress in Heaven after that fine donation!"

"He'll be gummin' her." Durn crept up behind Reza again. "Last time I saw him, he didn't have too many teeth left."

Reza grimaced and stiffened as Durn rubbed his hands over her buttocks and thighs.

"Oh yeah!" Juds observed. "She's lovin' that!"

Durn's eyes suddenly flashed wild. "Mister, you…!"

"Okay!" Rabbel raised his voice.

Durn's unshaven face twitched with rage as he savagely stared at Juds. Softly, Reza reached for Durn's hand and pulled him back to her. She rubbed his bony shoulders with her fingers to settle him. And, slowly, his mad gaze melted into a flimsy mask of flushed arrogance.

"Huh." Juds regarded the pair. "I think I get it."

"We'll take them," Rabbel decided.

"What's that?" Juds looked back at Rabbel.

"I said, we'll take them," Rabbel repeated. "Everything you've got."

"Well…well, great." Juds ran his fingers through his hair and looked relieved. "Great. Uh, let's transfer the funds."

"Fine by me. Leesla." Rabbel motioned to the tall dark woman.

She approached Juds slowly, making sharp eye contact with the smaller man. She made him nervous, but there was also something perniciously sensual in her movements that appealed to him. She reached into her jacket and pulled out a small electronic box the shape of a remote control. She pressed a button and two small metal prongs popped out of the top like a pair of antennae. Juds held her eyes as he reached into his back pocket and pulled out a similar device. He held his up to hers and they pressed the two together until they clicked and made a whirring sound.

"My second favorite kind of transaction." He winked at her.

"You're not my type," Leesla answered in a clipped cadence as she glared down at him.

Juds rolled his eyes and sighed. "Well, I can see I'm not gonna' get laid on this business trip." Juds maintained the eye contact. "Rabbel, what's with these broads you're traveling with? I heard you were a lot more fun than this."

The two devices beeped, signaling the end of the transaction. Leesla rudely jerked the devices apart, causing Juds to momentarily stumble backward. The tall woman stalked back to her place along the cavern wall and rigidly stood at attention.

"There's a time and a place for fun." Rabbel gazed at the capsules on the table. "Work isn't fun. Winning is fun. And when I win this, you'll be invited to the biggest bash the old tavern's ever seen."

"Hotter broads than this, I hope." Juds extended his hand to Rabbel.

"The best." Rabbel clasped his palm. "But for now, I need you to outline some options for an optimum way to deliver these capsules. Hand weapons at close range won't always be practical. For every one of these I shoot, I don't want a man caught and taken into custody. We need sniping capability. Something that'll leave people wondering where the hell these things came from while our people are putting kilometers between themselves and the whole scene."

"Sniping." Juds smirked. "No more hand to hand? You guys really are planning to move up in the world. Got your targets all picked out?"

"Not yet, but I've got some ideas." Rabbel projected visions in his voice.

"Not the Accommodant, I hope." Juds held up a finger. "You ever listen to that guy? He's on our side. He won't come out and say it, but he is! He doesn't give a flaming fuck what anybody does. Live and let live. Just listen to him! Poor bastard's married to that pedantic little bitch and she winds up driving him over to our side. Ain't marriage a beautiful thing?"

"It's supposed to be," Rabbel answered dryly. "Ask your churchlord why it always turns sour."

"Y'know," Juds paused and furrowed his brow, "why don't you kill the Deliveress? Cut the head right off the dragon...pop! Right between those big pearl earrings. You could come back in an hour and scoop out all the jewelry."

"Yes." Leesla lifted her brows. "Why don't you?"

"We can't." Rabbel's face became suddenly tense. "It'd be like killing the leader of your enemy's government. Without a leader, there's no one left to negotiate terms, no one to capitulate. It can't be her."

"You know, I see her on the media," Juds continued, "and all I can think of is oral sex. I'm mean, what would it be like to get oral sex from a broad wearin' expensive jewelry like that? But then again, I bet someone like her doesn't even go for that kind of thing. Straight, textbook biology and a peck on the cheek, I bet. No wonder the Accommodant's screwin' everything that moves. His wife sure doesn't. Move that is. That tight sleek body going to waste! Boy, the things I could teach her! Y'know Rabbel, before your guys pop her, maybe we could offer her a choice. She sucks us off and we let her live as our sex slave. She might even get to liking the idea under all that repressed dogma. Why don't...."

"I said, NOT HER!" Rabbel shouted, his voice thundering through the caverns.

Reza and Durn were jolted from their conversation. Even Leesla was shaken by the bellowing pronouncement.

"Yeah...right, Rabbel." Juds looked into his snarled black face and held up his hands. "No sweat. Just shootin' the breeze, right?"

Rabbel glanced around at the foursome in the cave. One by one, they all lowered their eyes and busied themselves with...anything.

Rabbel walked away to collect himself.

XIII.

Strips of glaring sunlight rippled over the tops of her bright yellow pumps, rolled up the cross of her smooth, slender calves, danced over the sparkling golden buttons of her woolen dress, and illuminated the fine hairs at the nape of Panla's neck. Crilen found himself enamored once more, by the visage of this refined lady who bore a confounding resemblance to his long-deceased wife.

He could still hear the engine of the limousine humming quietly toward its destination as the setting sun strobed her figure. And he occasionally noticed the muffled voices of Linnfeld and his subordinate attendants calibrating the remainder of her day in the limousine's center cabin. But very little could distract his fixation from this mesmerizing, personal interlude.

Panla appeared as still and restful as a tired toddler while she sat, nestled snugly against the plush cabin walls to capture a moment's peace. At times, it was as if she weren't even breathing, frozen upon the canvas of some elegantly painted portrait. But intermittently, she would release an indolent breath or a delicate swallow. Her brows would wrinkle and soften. Finally, she would adjust her head against the velour cushions and lay motionless once again.

Crilen recalled the memories of past, early mornings when he would delay a moment simply to marvel at his wife's slumber before ambling off to another fifteen-hour day in his laboratory. As he recorded Panla's every movement, he concluded that any dissimilarities between her and Aami were, at the moment, perceptibly immaterial.

"You're staring." she said with her eyes still closed.

"What?" Crilen was jolted from his trance.

Panla stretched her arms, worked her neck and arched her back as she suppressed a pronounced yawn.

"I said, you're staring." She half-smiled and opened her eyes.

"I'm sorry." Crilen nodded and wished the limousine's rear cabin had room enough for him to stand and pace.

"It's your wife, isn't it?" Panla was certain. "Do I really look so much like her?"

"'So much' is an understatement." Crilen seemed embarrassed. "You look exactly like her."

"Well, we do seem to have a comparable taste in men." A bit of the mischievous PJ slipped out of her.

"I've seen your taste in men," Crilen attempted to lighten his mood, "and before she met me, I'm afraid her dating patterns were similar."

"Similar?" Panla swung her legs up to rest them along her seat. "In what way?"

"Well, in prep school, she was serious with the class president," he reflected, "but when she got to the university, she switched to some hardened, rebellious athlete all the other girls wanted."

"And then she finally fell for a quiet, surly, thoughtful man who showed her the meaning of love," Panla teased him.

Her insight made him uncomfortable.

"Something like that," he said after a pause.

"Oh, don't be coy, Mr. Len," she continued, playfully. "I may yet do so myself. I deserve a good turn at romance."

As with Aami, he wasn't sure if she were only teasing him.

"I...I never did get it, really." Crilen tried to ignore the flirtation. "She was bright and popular and came from a family that was fairly well-to-do. Meanwhile, I was working three jobs to get myself through school. She knew everyone. I knew almost no one. She dressed with sophistication while I dressed with patches mostly. It took all the nerve I had just to approach her and ask her out. And then I was even more terrified after she said yes. 'What am I supposed to do now?', I thought. But she made it so easy for me. When I spoke, she'd always listen and smile. And when she spoke, the rhythm of her voice was like poetry on the wind. She was so kind and friendly and nothing like the snob I thought she'd be."

"If you thought she was a snob, why did you ask her out to begin with?" Panla chuckled.

"Because I knew she was a snob," Crilen shook his head, "and I knew she'd say no."

"And they say females don't make any sense." Panla raised an eyebrow.

"Oh, it made perfect sense." Crilen smiled. "I'd ask her out. She'd offer some condescending rejection. And then I could spend the rest of eternity telling all of my friends what a stuck up bitch she was. Only she said yes, and, somehow, I wound up with a wife instead."

"Funny how that works." Panla smiled at him.

"Funny." He shook his head in reflection.

"So how did she die?" Panla asked in a tender voice.

"A fire," he spoke concisely.

"What kind of...?"

"A fire." Crilen walled up the incident. "One that I still feel responsible for."

"I'm sorry." Panla folded her lips. "Very sorry, indeed."

"She couldn't sing, though," Crilen shifted.

"I beg your pardon?" Panla tilted her head.

"My wife," he clarified, "she couldn't sing. Couldn't carry a note if her life depended on it. Not even in the shower where the acoustics could make a wounded animal sound operatic."

"But you, on the other hand," he shook his head in adoring disbelief, "your singing in the patient ward was one of the most beautiful things I've ever heard."

"Really, Mr. Len, you don't flatter your tastes." She was modest. "I'm always much happier hiding my voice behind the Cathedral choir. It took a great many hours of training just to make my voice bearable. Though I admit that I do enjoy soloing for a smaller audience. Captive, if you will."

"Captivated would be more like it," he assured her. "And what you did for that elderly man…"

"Oh, you mean pulling up his pants?" Her face brightened. "That wasn't anything. I did mission work for a twinmoon in a flooded farm province in the south. Pulling up the soiled pants of the elderly and the crippled was the least of it. Besides, its times like those, when God lays something like that before you, that you must try your humility. No one expects the Deliveress to humble herself before someone of such low estate, yet the Text teaches us that this is exactly what we must do. I can't imagine what God would make of me on the day I decide I mustn't dirty my hands to help someone."

"And what you said…" Crilen recalled.

"I didn't say much," she said. "All I really did was listen. That's what most people need. Just someone who's willing to take the time to listen and understand."

"But what you said about absolution…"

"You heard that?" She looked at him suspiciously. "I thought I told you to stand away."

"I've always had acute listening skills." Crilen winked. "It's been useful in my line of work."

"Your 'line of work'?" her eyes narrowed. "You mean spy work, don't you?"

"I'm no spy," he tried once again to assure her.

"Oh, that's right!" She rubbed her forehead. "You've been 'assigned' to me. Only I'm not allowed to know the why or the wherefore."

"You wouldn't believe me if I told you." He raised his brows. "But I swear to you, you're in the best of hands."

"How comforting." Panla raised an eyebrow.

"Anyway, you told the old man that you were only a person." Crilen reined in the topic. "That there could be no absolution through you, but only through God."

"You should forget you heard that." she became short.

"Why?"

"Because that's contrary to the Addendums of the Cathedral." She sounded stressed.

"So?"

"So, the Deliverer of the Cathedral is supposed to be a mortal, infallible descendent of God. She can't go around spewing dogma that's contrary to Cathedral doctrine, can she?"

"If she's right," Crilen concluded.

"No, not even if she's right," Panla lectured. "I have to be very careful. If Cathedral officials got wind of what I told that man about absolution, it would be grounds for my excommunication!"

"They should see you with long hair in a refracting leotard," Crilen referred to PJ.

The comment appeared only to add to Panla's mounting tension. "That would be something, wouldn't it?" Panla grimaced and rubbed her temples.

"Or in bed with Rabbel Mennis," Crilen added.

Panla's head popped up from between her fingers. The expression on her face fell somewhere between outrage, hurt and contrition. Then she managed to erase it all away with a blunter countenance of anger.

"Mr. Len, I assume you're speaking figuratively!" she hissed with authority, just above a whisper.

"You tell me." Crilen met her eyes with a poker stare.

"This is the second time you've hurled that accusation at me." Panla raised her voice.

"And the second time you haven't given me a straight answer," Crilen shot back at her. "Or doesn't it count when PJ sleeps around?"

"I'm going to have Linnfeld throw you off this transport." Panla reached for the intercom button. "You're fired!"

"Given a choice, I think Linnfeld would prefer to throw himself off the transport." Crilen folded his muscular arms. "And, though I'm working for you, only your husband has the authority to fire me."

Panla's nostrils flared as the tired circles under her eyes became more pronounced. She withdrew her finger from the intercom button, but swung herself upright to face her accuser.

"I hope you thought better of your wife than you do of me," she began. "I am married to the Accommodant of this planet. I am the Deliveress of the Cathedral of this planet. But above all else, I am a servant to God Almighty. God, who unequivocally condemns fornication, infidelity and anything of the like. No, I don't love my husband anymore. I'm not sure if I ever did. Yes, he sleeps with other women. And he's much more discreet about whether the media knows, than whether or not I happen to run into an occasional half-naked concubine bouncing in and out of his little playroom. But I am loyal to God and to the vows I made to Him when I married. Things between my husband and I are certainly not as I would like them to be, but I will not use that as an excuse to break my bond with Heaven!"

"So how does Rabbel feel about that?" Crilen was skeptical.

Panla loosed a heavy sigh. She looked out of the transport window as if she were deciding whether to dignify the question with an answer.

"Rabbel understands," she finally scowled at him with haughty disdain.

"Hmm." Crilen rubbed his chin with a forefinger. "A godless man leading a godless rebellion respecting the piety of his allegedly godless girlfriend. You must be the best double agent I've ever seen, or the Break must be in serious trouble because Rabbel would have to be an idiot!"

"Mr. Len!" Panla became furious.

"But I don't think he's an idiot." Crilen continued. "Because I've seen how he looks at you. I know the feeling he has in his eyes. There's a look a man has when he's craving something he's never had. And there's a look a man has when he's longing to hold on to something he's had, and is deathly afraid of losing."

"So you're a mindreader?" Panla scoffed.

"No." Crilen shook his head. "But I've been there."

"Well you haven't been here!" Panla pointed at her chest. "You haven't been where I'm sitting. Oh, you seem to think you're so very smart, but you have no idea what's going on with me. No idea, at all! Maybe you're just confusing me with something that happened between you and your wife again. I see how you look at me…confused and yearning. Maybe you need to snap out of your twisted little delusions about her and me and face reality for a change."

Her voice reverberated through his marrow. Under any other circumstance, he'd have launched into a searing invective of his own. But as he opened his mouth, he suddenly chose to say nothing. He slumped back into his seat and drifted into reflection.

Panla could see immediately that she had, in her fury, opened a mortal wound, never healed. She regretfully abandoned the confrontation, closed her eyes momentarily and took a deep breath.

"I'm sorry." She looked up and reached across for his hand. "That was totally wrong of me."

"No, no." Crilen's thumb rubbed her fingers. "I started it. What you and Rabbel do or don't do is none of my business."

"And what happened between you and your wife is none of mine," Panla added.

Crilen gazed deeply into her passionate brown eyes. It was like the end of any number of arguments he'd had with his wife. No matter how brutal or bitter the confrontation, she was always the one prepared to sow the peace.

"The sad thing is," Crilen said, holding her hand, "nothing happened between my wife and I. Nothing bad. It was all so damned perfect."

Panla reached up with her other hand and touched his shoulder.

"It must have been a wonderful thing to have had someone know you so completely and love you for it." Her soothing voice sounded a bit sad. "Someone who cared about your soul. Someone who needed you just as God made you. I can't imagine that."

Crilen could see what she was thinking.

"Mrs. Tem," he started, "why did you marry a man who was so wrong for you?"

"Oh, I didn't think he was so wrong at the time." She smiled her regret. "But I could see the flaws as soon as we met. And, if I'd tried to, I could have foreseen where we were heading before he ever proposed to me.

"But I guess, deep down, the problem was that I never thought I could ever find a man as perfect as my father, so I didn't even try. When I think about it, maybe I tried to find someone completely unlike him so I wouldn't consider it a competition. Crazy, isn't it?"

"And they say males don't make any sense." Crilen smiled.

"Touché." Panla squeezed his hand.

Silence fell between them, each, waiting for the other to say or do something.

"I wish we could love like adolescents do," Panla said finally. "Full of wonder and innocence. We all become so jaded by experience, scarred and gun-shy by having seen too much of the world. After a while we just think and reason our way out of loving anything because it never seems to make perfect sense. I really don't think God meant for love to be a wise thing. Moral perhaps, but not calculated and dissected. It's just suppose to happen…like kids colliding on the playground or something. You look up and, smash, there it is."

"But in a lot of ways," Crilen added, "I think the scars help us appreciate love all the more. When I was younger, I didn't have any idea. It was all just inexplicable floods of feeling, but I can articulate my love now. I can revel in its beauty and splendor because I understand it and cherish it more than I actually could during my marriage. Experience and perhaps loss, teaches you to appreciate the depth, richness and rarity of true love. I think that's the virtue of maturity."

"Hmm." Panla nodded. "Maybe God never intended us to capture a perfect love in this life. When we're young and full of blind passion, we lack the depth to appreciate what we have, or, sometimes, even the wisdom to choose wisely. Yet, when we get older, our wisdom becomes a barrier that blocks us from our deepest passions. Our rapturous desires wind up constricted by practicality. It doesn't seem fair, does it?"

"Did you and your husband ever think about children?" Crilen wondered.

"Yes." Her expression jumped as she looked at their fingers together. "But my schedule became increasingly rigorous. That and I found out that I can't have them anyway."

An emotional surge of deja vu twisted Crilen's stomach.

The door between the center and rear cabins swished open and Linnfeld's short round body popped in. Panla and Crilen hastily broke their clasp, and her lead attendant acted as if he had witnessed nothing between them.

"How are you feeling, Mrs. Tem?" he asked with dutiful concern.

"Better." She laid back across her seat again.

"One would think that if you hold a luncheon to honor someone, you might go to some length to ensure that you don't poison them in the process," Linnfeld said as he flipped through his note pad.

"Next time, we'll pack our own," Panla responded and winked at Crilen.

Crilen noted the sudden shift in her mood. He couldn't tell if it were real or some automatic defense mechanism she'd conjured up to keep herself from falling into a depression.

"As you wish," Linnfeld answered without lifting his head. "Now, regarding the interview…"

"The interview will be fine." Panla waved her hand.

"Yes, I'm certain it will be," Linnfeld concurred, "but bear in mind that Ms. Libbi Trullup is a shamelessly liberal, agnostic, media hitwoman. She, along with much of the popular news, have been slanting away from the Cathedral for nearly a twinmoon. She'll be looking to make you appear both narrow and obtuse."

"Well, there's nothing wrong with narrow." Panla smiled and shrugged. "Narrowness allows one to stay focused on the proper path, don't you agree, Mr. Len?"

"True," Crilen answered, undividing his attention. "Personally, I've come to realize that while the cosmos offers infinite possibilities, that doesn't necessarily mean that we should partake of them all. I mean, it seems that alternate paths only increase the likelihood that one can become lost."

"Well said," Panla commended him. "You can stay on the narrow path or take your chances on routes that may lead to nowhere. Nowhere you'd want your soul to wind up, certainly."

"Very good," Linnfeld continued to scribble notes. "Keep that sword sharp. I have a feeling you'll be needing it. By the way, I'm also having a little trouble plotting our course to Mr. Mennis's tavern later this evening. Are you sure we should keep that appointment?"

Panla glanced at Crilen. The questions which had spawned their argument flashed over her expression.

"We must keep the appointment." she became serious. "We can't let them feel neglected or we'll lose them. Besides, my husband has other things to track with his spare time. We'll keep the hotel reservation in the central north and route any com calls from there to our auxiliary transport. It'll be a long night, but we don't have much choice."

"Very well." Linnfeld folded his lips, turned and crouched through the doorway leading back to the center cabin. The door swished shut behind him.

"Don't I get consulted?" Crilen watched her recline to her original position.

"Consulted about what?" She sounded bored.

"Consulted about whether I consider it safe for you to meet with Rabbel," he answered.

"It's not a matter of consultation, Mr. Len." She closed her eyes. "We're going and that's that. And I consider it a foregone conclusion that you'll do everything to make my visit as safe and secure as possible. That is why you're here, isn't it?"

"But how do you know one of these anti-religious zealots won't try to bump off the Deliveress?" he asked.

"Well, for one thing," Panla sounded like a teacher filling in a tardy pupil, "none of the zealots know that PJ is the Deliveress. Only Rabbel's closest associates know that. As far as everyone else is concerned, I'm just Rabbel's influential girlfriend from the north who provides them with a little moral support."

"And how do you know you can trust Rabbel's associates?" Crilen wondered.

Panla opened her eyes and sat up again.

"Because you're right about one thing." She pushed to sound confident. "Rabbel is in love with me. And, while I'm not totally comfortable with his little crew, as long as he feels the way he does, I don't think I have anything to worry about."

"Not very fair to Rabbel, is it?" Crilen sounded oddly sympathetic.

There grew a tinge of sadness on Panla's face as she looked away for a moment. Her conscience appeared to be wrestling mightily with her resolve, but finally, she turned and met his eyes again.

"No. It's not fair to Rabbel," she conceded. "Just like it's not fair for millions of people to lose their souls' salvation because their cathedral has betrayed their faith. It's not fair for people to conclude that God has no law simply because the man-made laws of the cathedral are ridiculous. It's not fair that God should be shunt by those he loves in favor of popular entertainers and media propaganda. None of it's fair, Mr. Len. But you were right when you talked about the soldier calling down friendly fire on his own position to destroy the enemy around him. It's not my intent to be killed. And its not my intent to kill anyone else. But this is a war. And if there come casualties as I lay my life down for my Lord in Heaven, then so be it!"

Panla turned away, took a deep breath and closed her eyes again.

"It's not that I don't care for Rabbel," she continued. "I'm very fond of him. He's like a big cuddly forest creature. The kind you'd read about in children's books. Warm and courageous and dedicated...and even heroic. And you can't help but admire how devoted he is to his cause and to the people who follow him. If I weren't who I am, knowing what I know, I might even love him for the kind of man he is. But the truth of the matter is, I can't. I just can't. He's a fine man, but he's a lost soul. I don't know whether it was his time in the military or some other personal tragedy he suffered, but he's declared himself an enemy of God. A hater of God. And while I know that I'm supposed to love my enemies, I must also acknowledge that he is my enemy...and never mistake him for anything else."

She paused a moment and awaited Crilen's response. She was growing accustomed to his challenges. But the cabin fell silent this time. And, when she concluded that no rebuttal was forthcoming, she adjusted herself against the cushions and the tension in her expression peacefully smoothed away.

Crilen found himself adoring her all the more as he privately reflected upon her words. A sense of impending dread wrapped itself around his fixation as the haunting stench of Aami's death played wickedly upon his senses.

XIV.

"And now, the show." Yolo smiled to himself, clicking on his ten by ten meter visual monitor as he neatly tucked a large glazed muffin into his copious cheek.

The dark, beautifully sculpted, angular face of a pert young newswoman filled the screen. Her shimmering blonde hair swirled and curled about her head like a prize-winning flower arrangement. Her bright make-up was as finely drawn as the hand-painted colors of an expensive porcelain dinner plate. Her pointed chin and her padded shoulders were, of course, professionally squared to the camera. Still, her make-believe journalistic expression belied her depth and rather mirrored that of a spoiled girl denied sweet candy just before her supper:

Newswoman: Good afternoon, everyone. I'm Egs Bloyt. We have more on that accident in the northeast quadrosphere. It has now been confirmed that a vehicle containing actor Finx Melder and sand surfer Preppi Deyz has been destroyed in a fiery one-vehicle collision with a fuel tank. Both Finx Melder and Preppi Deyz have been confirmed dead at the scene. Melder was 36. Deyz was 20.

We now have a live feed from the site of the accident. It's dark, but you can still see the smoking husk of Finx Melder's vehicle protruding from that blazing fuel tank which exploded on impact. It almost looks like something out of one of his films. Unfortunately, this is very real and two people have died.

YBS correspondent, Tol Bulchette is with us from the scene. Tol, what can you tell us about what's happened?

TB: Thank you, Egs. I don't have to tell you that this is a staggering tragedy. Finx Melder is, or should I say was, THE most influential artist of our generation and was at the peak of a magnificent career. He'd won an unprecedented six Golden Icons over the past decade for his acting, writing and directing in such powerful, but controversial films as *Knock it 'til you Try It, The Embalming Room, Bius II* and *Sister's Lingerie*. He was also reportedly working on an upcoming project wherein he was to star in the biographical film *Trixon*, a historical docu-drama about the Accommodant who tried to unilaterally take over the world's government through propaganda, treachery and coercion. The buzz was that this, too, would have gotten a lot of consideration from the Golden Icon committee.

And, likewise, Preppi Deyz captured our hearts and imaginations during last twinmoon's World Games where she dominated the sand-surfing competition and won a record four Gold Pins. Her sweet cheerful smile on the victory podium will be forever etched in our memories.

Melder and Deyz were rumored to have just begun dating, but sources close to the couple say it was true love. Many felt that they were perfectly suited for one another and it was only a matter of time before they would have gotten married. But now, we'll probably never know if their storybook romance could have had a happy ending.

EB: Any word as to the cause of this accident?

TB: Well, we've heard that Finx may have engaged the entertainment media in a dangerous high-speed chase. It's been well-documented that he's always had kind of a love-hate relationship with the media and this might be an outcropping of that. But we also know that Finx fancied himself as a bit of a daredevil who reveled in various forms of brinkmanship. Who knows? Maybe he was showing off for Preppi or playing some kind of game. It's hard to say at this point.

EB: Any possibility that drugs may have played a role in this?

TB: Well, it's too early to tell, but we all know that Finx had a long history of drug problems going back some fifteen twinmoons. He was rumored to have cleaned himself up over the last several months, but as we all know, relapses can occur at any time. Certainly, if drugs were the cause of the accident, this would compound an already horrible tragedy.

EB: I understand that Finx is survived by his children.

TB: Yes, Finx is survived by seven children from five previous marriages.

EB: How horrible for them. Our wishes and prayers go out to his children.

TB: Yes, we must think of the children at a time like this.

EB: And what about Preppi? We all remember those images of her parents and siblings embracing at the Games last twinmoon. Have they been found and contacted?

TB: Preppi's brother Bucki was told of the accident by reporters, but declined to comment. We understand Preppi's parents are vacationing on the family's private island off the northwest coast, and authorities haven't been able to reach them as yet.

EB: Well, hopefully, they'll see this broadcast and contact the authorities themselves.

TB: We can only pray that they will. In the meantime, the world has lost two of its brightest, shining lights. Who knows if or when we will ever recover. And now, with a look back on the life of Finx Melder, is our YBS Eastern Bureau chief, Proptz Rotz. Proptz?

PR: Thanks, Tol. Finx Melder was born in a tough, southwest, working-class town where his father was known as Melder the Welder. The early twinmoons of his childhood were not easy ones. Both parents drank heavily and his father was shot to death by his mother's boyfriend during a domestic dispute. But shortly thereafter, Mrs. Melder stopped drinking and moved her and her son out to the northeast coast. There, Finx's mother worked as a waitress and cleaning woman on the underbelly of society's upper crust.

It's been said that a young Finx showed great imagination and talent during these formative twinmoons. Though little of it was exhibited in school, where he was often found to be absent for weeks at a time. After struggling to make ends meet, Mrs. Melder and her teenage son moved in with model-actress Bedda Phlatbakker. Mrs. Melder and Phlatbakker were said to have become good friends. But no one foresaw that Bedda and Finx would soon become much, much more. By the time Finx was sixteen, he and Bedda Phlatbakker, twenty twinmoons his senior, were having a torrid love affair, and, finally, decided to get married. Disapproving and heartbroken, Finx's mother moved out and was not heard from again until her death eleven twinmoons later. Phlatbakker helped Melder get into the theatre. But their relationship soured when Phlatbakker found that her daughter Skiza, thirteen, had become pregnant and that Melder, by then eighteen, was the father. Melder eventually married Skiza Phlatbakker and they had two more children. But trying to support a family made Melder, who had broken off his work in the theatre, depressed. So, after three and a half twinmoons, he moved out and asked Skiza for a divorce.

Melder drifted into the cult of Uno-Octagonalism, the religious organization which believes that the self is connected to the universe at eight specific points of awareness. It was at a spiritual rally that Melder met folk singer, Durt Dinga. The two quickly fell in love and wed after only a few short months. Melder had two more children by Dinga. And it was during this time that Melder began heavy experimentation with drugs and alcohol. He and Durt were known to throw parties that lasted for weeks, neither one of them seeming to get more than an hour of sleep. Still, the two seemed quite happy, and Melder was making a name for himself in satellite situation comedies. But then he was dealt a crippling blow: Durt slipped into a fatal seizure on stage at the Accommodant's Ball. Some say that Melder, then twenty-four, became a dark, brooding, and almost ghostly figure. A drugged-out vagabond, according to his former manager. But for better or worse, this period also spawned some of his best early work. Melder took a small role in the film *Spit and Duck* and turned it into its most noteworthy performance:

Clip: "Hey, over here! Missed me! Hah!"

This won him a Golden Icon Best Supporting Actor nomination and the notice of writer-producer, Giggi Gondoleda who would eventually make him a star. It was Gondoleda who cast him in *Knock it 'til you Try It*. The story of a young male who spurns homosexuality until he, himself, falls in love with another male

Clip: "I...I never thought it could be like this!"

Under a maelstrom of criticism from the religious right, Melder won his first of six Golden Icons for this performance and quickly became the most bankable mega-star in the industry. His princely handsomeness coupled with his charisma and wit made him both an artistic and popular force people couldn't seem to get enough of. He and Giggi married a week after *Knock it*'s release. Their award-winning collaborations over the next decade included the *Embalming Room* where Melder played a handsome drifter in love with a lonely young woman trapped in her family's funeral parlor business:

Clip: "These people may be dead on the outside, but baby, inside, you're as cold and dead as they come!"

Then came the historical epic and box office smash, *Bius II*:

Clip: "If God will not show himself willingly, then by hell's fire, I'll claw myself to the heavens...and drag him back to the earth with my bare hands if I have to!"

And the unforgettable satire, *Sister's Lingerie*, about a man who loses a bet with his sister and has to wear her underwear for a day, but winds up liking it:

Clip: "Is it really unmasculine to wear satin and lace...if it feels good?"

Unfortunately, the string of hits and awards and wealth did not bring stability to Melder's personal life. Though they continued to collaborate and soar professionally, Melder and Giggi divorced after *Bius II*. Insiders say that Giggi was humiliated by Melder's sexually and chemically addicted exploits. The two insist, however, that the parting was amicable. Leaving yet another wife and two children behind, Melder soon married Yanga Blas, his co-star from *The Embalming Room*. But a twinmoon later, Melder landed in jail for badly beating his fifth and, what turned out to be, his final wife. After six months in prison, however, Melder went into rehab, claimed to have found God and appeared to finally be coming to terms with his own mega-celebrity. I spoke with him only a month ago:

Interview clip: "Twinmoons ago, I like, fell into this huge thing. And I didn't know what it was, but everybody was telling me I was this great guy! And I had trouble with that. I didn't buy it, y'know? I didn't buy it! But...but now I'm okay with it. Now I'm fine, y'know?"

Melder met Preppi Deyz while on vacation at an oasis resort. It's said that in the weeks they knew each other, it had blossomed into a true love. He, with his worldly charm and experiences, she, with her homespun innocence and warmth. Now, the only positive epitaph we can place upon this tragedy, is that they died together...and perhaps died happy.

Proptz Rotz, for YBS News. Egs?

EB: Thank you, Proptz. Once again, you're looking at a live shot of the back end of Finx Melder's vehicle, lodged into the side of that blazing fuel tank. You can see that firefighters are trying to put out the flames, but as you can imagine, it's got to be very hot in and around that fuel tank.

Meanwhile, responses have begun to trickle in from around the world:

Giggi Gondoleda: Finx was my best friend. And he was the greatest talent this world has ever seen. Irreplaceable. Simply irreplaceable. I will miss him as a friend. And the world will miss him as a great performer who always spoke for the common man.

Yanga Blas: I loved him madly. I still wear our wedding necklace. He was so kind and gentle and caring. He was just getting his life back together…and now this. I wish I could tell him how much I love him.

Accommodant Tem: We all learned so much about life through the work of Finx Melder. We learned how to be fathers, sons…friends and lovers. We learned how to laugh. We learned how to cry. We learned how to stand tall in the face of adversity. And, most importantly, we learned how to live life to its fullest. His legacy will live on forever. I'm sure Finx is looking down on us from Heaven today, smiling that signature smile, knowing that he left the world a better place than he found it. God Bless.

Skuddy Dult (frequent co-star): Finx, I know you're up in Heaven lightin' a big one for the Dultster, man! I just hope people never forget all the joy and hope you gave us, buddy! Never forget, man! Never forget!

Fuchsia Moon Phlatbakker-Melder: My dad was, like, the greatest dad. I mean, like he wasn't always around, but he was around when I needed him, you know? And he showed me that life is about living. And that you can determine your own destiny by just doing your own thing and not worrying about what other people think of you. And because of the way he died, I will miss him, but I'm, like, not really sad, you know?

Feggie Limpwist (film critic): Melder recreated the industry in his own image and changed the world. He didn't just win six Golden Icons. He was the Golden Icon, a standard by which all other people will be measured. I'm going to ask that the industry strongly consider renaming the Golden Icon Award the Golden Finx Award. It's the least the industry can do to preserve the memory of the greatest performer the world has ever known.

EB: Once again, this is a shot of the vehicle of actor Finx Melder, who died in a one-vehicle collision with a fuel tank late last night. Sand surfer Preppi Deyz also perished in the accident. Presently, we have no details as to the funeral arrangements for either, but reporters are pursuing details and we'll have them for you as soon as they are made available to us. In the mean time, stay with us. We'll have more complete coverage of this tragic event in just a few moments.

Serene, reflective music chimed as the screen faded into a slow-motion collage of Finx Melder waving to crowds and giving his most memorable performances. Next, the images became frozen as his name and dates appeared at the bottom of the frame.

Fade to grey.

Suddenly, the noise of squealing children chasing an animated candybar sales creature, blared into view.

Yolo pressed the mute button and poured himself a liter of some black tarrish, foaming alcoholic beverage.

XV.

"So, Rabbel," Reza popped onto the seat next to Rabbel Mennis, "how've you been?"

Rabbel's face was a black stone carving of brooding vexation. His dark, cavernous eyes appeared hypnotized by the dry red, boulder-laden landscape which scrolled past the transport's tinted window. His heavy jaws were clamped and sealed with taut disdain. The impassive lines of his wrinkled forehead were like thick crevices rippled across cooling molten rock.

No one in their right mind would think to bother him now.

"Rabbel?" Reza tilted her head to and fro attempting to prompt a response, a blink, or something.

"PJ." Rabbel thought to himself. "Peej, marry me, you goddamned bitch! Marry me right now and everything will be fine. You wouldn't have to hide anymore. You wouldn't have to run anymore. I'd take care of you and protect you from anyone and anything. We could both be happy for once in our lives. Happy together. Happy forever. But you insist on sticking to your goddamned precarious balancing act. Insist on risking it all. What are you waiting for? We both know you can't keep up the charade much longer. But you'd rather risk everything we could have together. Why?"

Rabbel could feel Panla's shoulders under the palms of his hands. He could taste her neck, her lips, her breasts, her navel, her thighs. He could smell her hair. He could see her eyes casting hope into his soul. He could sense her salving voice melting through the pain and loneliness in his cast-iron heart. Then he watched her leave, angry over a rewritten flyer. And the emptiness in his gut, left his conscience fractured.

Rabbel felt cold moisture against the left side of his face. Sprinkles of moisture drizzling from another world. The images of Panla recessed and he reached up to touch his cheek. More water sprayed against the back of his hand.

"Hel-loooo." Reza giggled as she reached into a cup and flicked water into Rabbel's face. "Catatonic leaders give me the cramps!"

Rabbel snapped his head around like an angry alligator. Reza lurched backward, spilling the cup of water across her lap.

"Fuck!" she cursed under her breath. "Is this runny shit-cruise ever going to end? Hey, I've got my pipe. Want a hit? I mean, I'd rather be humping a bed of needles than spend another hour on this rolling dildo."

"What did you think you were doing?" Rabbel found himself momentarily amused by Reza's accident.

"Rabbel Mennis: always making me wet." Reza wiped between her legs. "I can't believe you did that!"

She lifted her skirt, checked her underwear and looked up at Rabbel.

"Hey!" she frowned. "Don't look, pervert!"

"Right." Rabbel rolled his eyes and carelessly turned back to the window.

"Well, fuck you, Mister PJ pumping thick prick!" Reza tossed her skirt back over her legs.

"Excuse me?" Rabbel lazily turned his head back toward her.

"You heard me!" Reza poked her finger into his shoulder. "You sit around moping about Miss Pearly Pussy, when there are plenty of girls who'd grease your skillet...hey, got a light?...grease your skillet and sizzle-fry that frown right off your lace baster!"

"Reza..."

"I mean, what's so special about Panla Phlegm? I bet she can't even do half the things I've been doing since I was ten. Probably doesn't even want to. That's a bloody coming shame, if you ask me. Got a light? And, if she cares about you, she should be willing to...I am fucking soaked...satisfy you anyway you want! I would!"

"Reza." Rabbel shook his head. "If you're looking to get thumped, there are plenty of people on board here who'd be more than willing to oblige."

"What makes you think I want to be thumped?" She paused and smiled as if the suggestion were absurd. "Or did you say, humped? Humped would be nice. Actually, thumped, I can handle too."

"Whatever." Rabbel closed his eyes and disconnected her.

"You don't like me, do you?" Reza sounded unhappy.

"Reza," Rabbel mumbled, "just shut up and go away."

"Wow." Reza shook her head. "I knew it. You lure me into this left wing cuckoo pit, spend up my spunking trust fund and you don't even like me. What the fuck? Am I the dumbest jizz-faced lather twat or what?"

"Well," Rabbel reluctantly responded, "you're not the dumbest. In fact, that's what's disturbing about you. You're not dumb at all."

"True." Reza smiled. "But I'm a total...you have a light? I'm a total hormonal autistic. I mean, why am I here, right? I could be gang-skanking some fraternity party at my dado's alma mater and studying to be some flirt-skirt lawbooker. Or I could be some rich boy's birthing orifice and just eat, sleep, fuck and spew children without ever having to close my legs. But no. Here I am, shit-cruising the rock jungle, posting propaganda, planning assassinations, screwing people I hate, doing drugs that suck, getting my ass kicked by the psycho-lesbian beastwoman, and watching the only man I want to fuck me, who won't fuck me, act like he hasn't shit in ten twinmoons over some stuck up sugar-shitter! I mean, for me this gig is really starting to smell like grandma's dying piss, you know?"

"Well, you're free to go visit your grandma anytime you like," Rabbel grumped.

"Grandma's dead! Aren't you listening?" Reza pounded her fists on her knees.

"Sorry."

"Rabbel!" Reza grabbed him by the collar. "Don't you understand? I need you to tell me why I'm here. Doesn't that mean...shit, I am so wet...anything to you?"

Rabbel's face slacked with weary annoyance.

"Reza, I know why you're here." he forcefully clutched her hand and removed it. "And you know why you're here."

"No, tell me!" Reza's voice quivered with anxiety. "You tell me!"

"You just said yourself." Rabbel responded with disinterest. "You like screwing men you hate. You like doing drugs that suck. You like getting your ass kicked and you like being rejected by men who won't fuck you because you're so fucked up. You like the rebellion, but you don't really care what the rebellion's about. You only care that it's not about the people who might really care about you. You like the danger and the violence and the fact that we could all be killed. And you like that it's a plain fact that everyone's only using you until there won't be any you left. You're a sick, spoiled, masochistic little girl with a trust fund. And you actually hate the fact that you were born pretty and protected from all the ills of the world. That's a pretty fucked-up universe you live in, hmm?"

Reza's jaw dropped open as she fashioned a knowing chuckle.

"You're wrong!" She tossed her head back and tried to assert herself. "You're so wrong. I love the Break, I love it so much! I love it because fucking God was nowhere to be found when my acne-cocked brothers raped me. God was nowhere to be found when my neuron deficient mother left me for the sewer plumber. Or even when my pet died. Are you going to smoke with me? I love the Break because here I can be myself, my real self. And no one tells me that I can't or that I shouldn't! There's no hypocrisy here, only purpose. And the purpose is to give the world back its…shit, I need a towel.. freedom. Freedom from the goddamned Texts and the goddamned Cathedral and goddamned lying, brother-fucking God!"

"Whatever." Rabbel murmured as his eyes closed. "What…ever."

Reza jumped up from her chair and snarled like an angry child, but Rabbel took a deep breath and remained still, as if there had never been a conversation. Finally, Reza decided to go wake up Durn for another round of miserable sex. She pouted and stomped off.

Meanwhile, Leesla had sequestered herself in a rear booth with the com speaker.

"Hesh!" she whispered excitedly. "Hesh, baby, I've been trying to reach you for days."

"I know," a quiet female voice answered her.

"Well, where have you been?" Leesla asked.

"Um, not home." The voice answered

"No shit, Hesh!" Leesla laughed quietly. "You've been partying like a madwoman, haven't you?"

"No." the voice answered, "no, not really."

"No?" Leesla became concerned. "Then what, then?"

"I dunno."

"You don't know? Hesh, it's me. You can tell me. What's wrong?"

"Nothing's wrong."

"Bullshit! I've been calling the flat for three days and there's no answer. I've been worried sick. You say you haven't been partying and you tell me nothing's wrong. Now I know you. What's going on?"

"Um, I don't know if I can talk about it."

"Hesh, goddamnit! If you can't talk to me about it, then who can you talk to?"

"I dunno."

"You dunno? Shit, Hesh! It's me. Leesla. You know, the woman you live with? The woman you love? What the fuck is this?"

"It's fucked up."

"Are you sick?"

"No, no, not really."

"Because if you're sick, whatever it is, I can get help. I've always told you that. Rabbel has connections. That north bitch of his? She can get you anything. Won't cost a coin! Just tell me what it is and we'll fix it."

"I'm not sick!"

"Then what the fuck is wrong with you?"

"Nothing's wrong with me. I just…wasn't around. And when I was around, I just didn't feel like answering."

"I'm out on assignment, and you didn't feel like answering? What the fuck is that?"

"Like it really matters if I answer or not. Either it's you, calling to tell me when you're going to be home, or it's someone else telling me that you got arrested or you're dead or…"

"Arrested or dead? When's the last time that happened?"

Silence.

"Hesh? When's the last time? And haven't we been through all that? Baby, I'm not going to get killed and I'm not going to get arrested again. We are taken care of. Rabbel knows his way around and he's connected in high places, sister."

"I know."

"Well, if you know, then you're not being straight with me. What is going on here?"

"I don't want to talk about it on the com."

"What, you think someone's listening?"

"No. It's just that this is really personal."

"This what?"

"This…Fuck, Leesla! Why are you being so goddamned difficult?"

"Me!? I just called to talk to the lover of my life. But instead, I get weird, secretive shit."

"I'm not being secretive."

"Then how come I don't know what the fuck's going on and you're telling me you don't want to discuss it on the com?"

"I care about you."

"I love, you too! So let's cut the bullshit"

"I'm pregnant."

Silence.

"Leesla, did you hear me? I'm pregnant."

"I heard you. Um…so…when…"

"Around a month ago…I guess."

"A month ago."

"Yeah. Um…you were real busy and we weren't really seeing a lot of each other right around then."

"So you thought you'd break the vegetarian diet and try some meat?"

"I guess. Look, Leesla, I'm really sorry…"

"You don't have to be sorry, sweetheart. I understand. I got latched a couple of times before I made up my mind to go veggie for good. Any girl can make a mistake. The main thing is to get it taken care of."

"Leesla…"

"Rabbel will hook you up. We'll get it taken care of tomorrow. It's no big deal."

"Leesla…"

"Hesh, don't be scared. I'm not mad. And it'll be okay. Serves me right for neglecting you."

"But I want it."

"Want it!? Want what?"

"The baby."

"You…you…want the baby?"

"Yes."

"Oh, Hesh, honey, we can't have a baby now. I'm in the middle of a lot of shit! You're going to need me around if we're going to do something like this."

"Leesla, it's okay. The father wants the baby, too."

"The fath…! What the fuck does he have to say about OUR baby?"

"Leesla…Oh god, Leesla, when are you coming home? We need to talk."

"We're talking right now!"

"I know. But this is fucked up."

"Yeah, well it won't be fucked up for long. When I get back there, I'll tell Mr. Meat and Tomatoes where he can take his shit!"

"No!"

"No? Hesh what the fuck are we talking about?"

"Oh Leesla…shit!"

"What?"

"Um…this guy, I like him."

"Ohhhh c'mon, Hesh! We've been through too much for you to get crazy on me now."

"I'm not crazy."

"Then what the fuck do you call it? Fucking around with a little meat is one thing, but you say you love this guy?"

"I didn't say I love him. I just like him. He's nice and we get along."

"And we don't?

"Of course we do, but this is something different. Way different. I can't explain…"

"Can't explain? Can't explain that you want to throw away our life together because you think you're in love with some…!"

"He's a good guy, Leesla. A really good guy."

"Told you how fucked up you are, living with another female?"

"No, not at all. I told him I have a roommate, but I didn't tell him about you and I."

"Roommate? You fucking bitch!"

"Leesla, it was totally innocent! We met at the book shop. He asked me to coffee and we just talked."

"You don't get pregnant talking."

"I know, and it was just curiosity at first. I hadn't been with a guy for four or five twinmoons. But he was so different. So different than I remember it being with the guys from school. It was the deepest…"

"I bet it was real deep!"

"Fuck you, Leesla!"

"Oh, now it's 'Fuck you Leesla!' Yeah, fuck you, Leesla for fighting for our life together! Fuck you, Leesla, for not sitting at home on your skinny little ass reading poetry, getting stoned all day and sucking some bookstore stalker's cock behind your lover's back! Yeah, fuck me!"

"Leesla, I don't want it to be like this."

"Like what? Like WHAT?"

"You're my best friend."

"Friend? That's all I am to you after all these twinmoons? A fucking friend?"

"You're more than a friend. More than a sister. I care so much about us. I always want you to be part of my life."

"Hesh, I always wanted you to be my life."

"I know."

"So what am I supposed to do now?"

"I…I don't know. Come home, I guess."

"Come home to what? My friend?"

"I don't know. I need time to think."

"Oh, Hesh. Goddamnit, you can't do this! You can't love that fucking guy and you can't have this baby! If you want me to take the blame for not being around…for neglecting our relationship, I will. It's all my fault! But I love you. God, I love you so much! I can't lose you, now."

"I better go."

"Hesh!"

"We'll talk when you get back."

Silence.

"Okay, Leesla?"

"Yeah. Yeah, baby. We'll talk. We'll get this shit right."

"I'll see you."

"Hesh, I love you."

"I'll see you, Leesla."

The soft click from over the com was like the deafening echo of a loud gunshot. Leesla sat crumpled in the corner, holding her stomach with one hand, tightly clutching the com-speaker in the other.

XVI.

"Baloni's Walk reduced to a single song!" the Lord Regent seethed.

"Have I missed something?" the Holy Inquisitor frowned.

"Missed something?" the Lord Regent cried out. "Missed something? Why no, I supposed not. If you, of all people, did not notice that the Scrolls of Baloni were not even addressed, let alone read in their entirety in the ancient language, then I guess you didn't miss a thing."

"Is that what has your robe in a wrinkle?" the Holy Inquisitor scoffed. "I didn't miss the reading of the scrolls because, like everyone else, I realize that Baloni's Scrolls are little more than a tedious reconstruction by Deliverer Bius II of every pebble, insect and blade of grass he might have seen during his journey to the Lord's Summit. The reading of those blessed scrolls, which takes at least an hour and half, dilutes the very significance of Baloni's accomplishment. The important fact is that he overcame monstrous obstacles to obey the will of God. The genus of foliage through which he hacked or the color of bugs which he squished are of no spiritual relevance whatsoever."

"Deliveress Jen conspires against us." the Lord Regent warned.

"Conspires?" the Holy Inquisitor questioned. "Where is your proof of a conspiracy?"

"What more proof do I need?" The Lord Regent's restrained voice echoed against the stone walls of the sanctuary. "I knew her father. I knew his mind. He railed against every Cathedral tradition till his dying breath. I know what he instilled in her."

"She has served us faithfully." The Inquisitor frowned. "She has served the Deliverancy as few have ever served before."

"She has served herself!" the Lord Regent charged.

"She's more popular with the masses than any Deliverer has been in three centuries," the Inquisitor countered.

"Yes, SHE is more popular!" the Lord Regent shook his hands. "But worldwide, Cathedral attendance is the lowest it's been in over a hundred twinmoons. And the migration away from the Cathedral grows exponentially!"

"You blame her?"

"Who else??" the Lord Regent nearly shouted. "She leads Baloni's Walk, yet disdains it with her gingerly motions and gestures. A Deliverer should march and splash proudly through the manure as Baloni did. A holy, undaunted spiritual leader, face covered and caked in the muck of the ages!"

The Inquisitor swallowed and grimaced, but said nothing.

"She quotes the CDR, but with no emphasis upon its meaning!" The Lord Regent railed on. "She forsakes the ancient language in favor of her own blasphemous, contemporized translations! And she carries herself, not as a divine descendent of Bius, but as a contumacious usurping guttersnipe!

"Lord Regent!" the Inquisitor became incensed. "Perhaps it is you who has become vulgar."

"Because I speak the truth?"

"No," the Inquisitor snorted, "because your unseemly hatred and jealousy has laid bare the wickedness in your heart and revealed your soul as little more than a blackened pit of envy."

"Envy?"

"Panla Jen, half your age, voted unanimously to the Deliverancy!" the Inquisitor folded his arms and leered down his nose. "She leapt over you and into the throne with nary the effort you exert to tie your robes. Leapt over the right hand of the late Deliverer, Reg En. And no one even cared or noticed that your life's ambitions were swept away by the hem of her holy garments."

"Ambitions?!" the Lord Regent's mouth fell open as his eyes bulged. "My only ambition is to serve the Deliverancy. And I have been so privileged and blessed to have done so from the right hand of the throne. And, know you, that if I had truly coveted the position which she so brazenly defiles with her unholy manners and her corrupted ideals, I would have seized the opportunity...No...allowed the accolade to be bestowed thus."

"Then why didn't you?" the Inquisitor asked doubtfully.

"Because I am an iron girder, not some fanciful, decorative pillar. I am the foundation, not the facade. Let some other be lavished by praise, imprisoned by public duties and indoctrinated protocols. I serve the Deliverancy at its roots! At the core of the Text and its Addendums! I have been the humble backbone of the Cathedral for thirty-seven twinmoons. More twinmoons than our dear Deliveress has been alive! And, unlike her, I know that the Glory belongs to the Cathedral, not the individual. I know that the strength of the Cathedral lies not in the alleged charisma and popularity of its Deliverer, but must remain focused upon the production and growth of its patronage. We can't do God's work if our tills are left bare. We can't fill the coffers on empty pews. It would be well if the Cathedral could survive on faith alone, but the reality is that our survival, in the real world, is driven by the power of hard currency. But to our dismay, Deliveress Jen's reign is fraught by the sewing of dissonance."

"Because she questions?" the Inquisitor cut in.

"Because she questions everything...publicly!" the Lord Regent grimaced. "From the legitimacy of Bius I to the sanctity of the CDR to the relevancy of our most sacred rituals, she places doubts in the minds of everyone who follows her!"

"Many say that her willingness to question blind tradition is what makes her so popular," the Inquisitor noted.

"Questions without answers?" the Lord Regent cried. "Does the father question himself before the child? Does the Admiral question himself before the oarsmen? If Deliveress Jen has so many doubts regarding her faith she should abdicate! It's only proper! But instead, she lays low her own faith and all of the faithful with her. Which, needless to say, provides propitious opportunities for the Break.

"The first thing people tell themselves is that if they are ambivalent in their faith, they should not invest. And if they can't invest, then they shan't attend. And, when they cease to attend, they become severed from their promises to Cathedral doctrines and their obedience to the Text. They soon justify their faithless quagmire by concluding that all religion is little more than a mish-mash of fanciful, conflicting rubbish. One cannot be expected to commit to any principle with certainty because there's always another side of the coin. Soon, you have an amoral agnostic populace preaching hollow amoral agnosticism. And what does amoral agnosticism beget you but enabled hedonism, sin and a world which knows no God at all. No God but the one each individual chooses to make up in his or her own mind. There's a word for that kind of society: ANARCHY!"

"Lord Regent, you're overreacting....slightly," the Inquisitor offered.

"Watch her!" the Lord Regent pleaded. "Listen! Listen to her carefully worded statements! Listen to her cleverly guised embellishments! If you hear nothing that distresses you within the month, your office may have my job instead of hers."

"I'll have neither." The Inquisitor recoiled at the notion.

"Neither?" the Lord regent scowled. "Neither, my dear Inquisitor? Do tell me, what is your job?"

"My job is to ensure the congruity of the Cathedral according to doctrine," the Inquisitor recited.

"And you see no incongruity 'twixt the Deliveress and myself?" the Lord Regent asked as if the obvious were being overlooked.

"I see no incongruities but that of which you speak," The Inquisitor answered firmly. "I shall not act solely upon frail accusation and loose innuendo."

"Frail?" the Lord Regent whispered disdainfully. "Loose? I see. Then you would wish things to continue as they are: God's Cathedral, nothing more than a bleeding, dying casualty, prone upon the battlefield of souls. You see the wounded before your very eyes but will do nothing to stop their gushing blood which splatters about your feet. A cry for help, ignored. A cry for life, left to die. My dear Inquisitor, a mortal wound cannot heal itself. It must be tended to. The shrapnel must be removed. The infection, eradicated."

"Yes, but one does not cure that which is not ill, lest it become ill from malpractice!" The Inquisitor became annoyed.

"But I have shown you the ill!" The Lord Regent's voice shook. "Look upon the lesions. Look upon the discoloration of flesh. The shriveling of limbs. Look!"

"I see with my own eyes, Lord Regent, not those which you would wish me to have." The Inquisitor frowned. "Deliveress Panla Jen loves the Cathedral more than any of us. She selflessly and tirelessly abandons her own personal interests for the sake of this institution. That would include her marriage to the Accommodant, which teeters precariously upon uneven footing. You should know that if she had compromised the Deliverancy, in the very least, to steady her positioning in the Mansion of the Accommodant, I certainly would have acted swiftly to bring about the abdication you seek."

The Lord Regent tossed up his hands in exasperation.

"My dear Inquisitor." He closed his eyes tightly. "You quest for the giant beast in the hive of insects! You search for a chip of ice in a blast furnace! If you look very hard for something where it is least likely to be found, I dare say you are most likely to never find it.

"She despises her husband! There's nothing to be found there! What she loves is her self-absorption with the Texts, HER interpretations of scriptures. That is where her treachery lies!"

"Proof!" the Holy Inquisitor bellowed. "Give me proof or hold your tongue!"

"Proof." the Lord Regent simmered. "Proof. I'll give you proof. I'll give you more than you want. And when I'm done, not only will you be forced to end her reign, but I am quite certain that the public...the praying, paying faithful public...will demand her head."

"So you say," the Inquisitor sneered.

"So it will be," answered the Lord Regent.

XVII.

"What's the problem?" Panla addressed Linnfeld as he glumly re-entered the sparsely decorated YBS Studios waiting room.

"We've been pushed back a half an hour." he answered curtly.

"Pushed back?" Crilen sounded stunned.

"That's right." Linnfeld plunked himself down into a thickly cushioned chair. "Pushed back. Back-burnered. Or, in the kinder vernacular, momentarily delayed."

"Momentarily as in 'go home, we'll call you'? Feebie, a sturdily built young female attendant, wondered aloud.

"Not quite so dismissive." Linnfeld offered a wry smile. "More like 'Make the Deliveress comfortable and have her ready to go at a moment's notice.'"

"That's ridiculous." Crilen dropped his arms. "How important do you have to be to have your interview aired on time?"

"Based upon what I've been told," Linnfeld pinched the tension from his sinuses, "you have to either be a famous dead actor or a famous dead athlete...or both."

"What do you mean?" Crilen shook his head.

"Take a seat, Mr. Len." Panla casually gestured. "He's talking about Finx Melder and Preppi...Tees, is it? Anyway, they were killed in a media chase last night."

"Media chase?" Crilen looked clueless.

"Yes, a media chase." Panla sat neatly and crossed her legs. "A time-honored sport amongst so-called newspeople who believe it is completely necessary to hound, harass and pry into literally every aspect of someone's private life merely because they're famous. Like pornography, it's the devil's conceptual perversion of free speech.

"You can hide in your home with the doors locked and the blinds drawn and be perfectly entitled to your right to privacy. But go out to the store or to get a bite to eat or to visit relatives and you enter the domain of imminent intrusion. That is, the media's right to record and photograph anyone they choose as often and excessively as they like. And for no small profit, mind you. Occasionally things may get a little testy if a reluctant subject does something unseemly, like resist. In this particular case, Mr. Melder tried to outrun them and the media chased he and his date…to death. Literally."

"For a picture?" Crilen stammered. "They had their lives taken…for a picture?"

"Don't sound so surprised, Mr. Len." Panla fiddled with her bangs. "It is quite horrible but it does happen now and again."

"For a picture?" Crilen couldn't place the relevance amid the expanse of all his galactic experiences.

"I believe that's what Mrs. Tem said." Linnfeld said, trying to break the cycle.

"For a picture." Crilen finally concluded. "What kind of society places so much emphasis on the pursuit of simple celebrities, that lives are taken?"

"A very sick one, I'll grant you." Panla yawned. "But there seems to be quite a bit of money in mortal idolatry. And, like drugs, alcohol and prostitution, if there's the slightest hint of public demand, the streams of supply become boundless regardless of any moral ramifications."

"Give the public what they want." Linnfeld smiled. "The first rule of free commerce."

"Well, at least I hope they apprehended the assailants." Crilen shook his head.

Panla, Linnfeld and the other attendants broke into light laughter.

"Assailants?" Linnfeld smiled. "In order for there to be assailants, one must prove that there has been a crime."

"But they were chased to their deaths, correct?" Crilen frowned.

"No question." Panla inspected her nails.

"And this media chase was the cause," Crilen reasoned.

"Absolutely," Linnfeld concurred.

"Well, where I come from," Crilen was vague, "if you chase someone to their death, you're responsible for that death."

"You must be from the real world." Feebie chimed in. "'In the world of fame, fortune and commercial flesh-peddling, the rules are totally different. The law doesn't apply when the media wants a story."

"No touch, no crime," Linnfeld added. "That's the way it works."

"So a gang of so-called journalists can stalk an innocent person to the brink of insanity or even to their death and there's no recourse?" Crilen sounded astonished.

"None." Linnfeld clasped his hands together.

"So why haven't there been hordes of these media gangs chasing us?" Crilen asked. "I'd think that the Deliveress and wife of the Accommodant would warrant a thorough hounding."

"They used to." Panla sighed and closed her eyes. "Then we got elected and they had to back off."

"Executive privilege," Linnfeld added. "It doesn't stop them from putting out skewed or slanted material, but if you stalk the Accommodant, or any member of his family, you get shot. A matter of government security, you see."

"So the people who make decisions affecting millions of lives around the world are allowed to retain their privacy, but silly irrelevant celebrities aren't." Crilen sounded annoyed. "I don't think I want to know anymore."

"You don't." Linnfeld sighed and brushed at the seams of his trousers.

"It'd almost be nice to be irrelevant." Panla sat up and tried to remain alert.

"Respectfully, Mrs. Tem," Linnfeld shook his head. "you wouldn't know how."

"Respectfully, Mr. Linnfeld," Panla mocked his sturdy, dutiful, inflections, "you're probably right."

Crilen smiled and tried to make eye contact with her, but she didn't care to pay him notice at this particular juncture.

"Feebie," Panla spoke across the room, "I think I'm getting a little hungry after all. Could you see if you could scare up some fresh fruit or something?"

"Yes, Queen Mother." The young woman's white freckled face snapped to attention as she rose to her feet and waited to be officially dismissed.

"Anyone else?" Panla pointed to Linnfeld, then to Crilen, then to the other female attendant leaning next to a lamp along the wall.

"You know me." Linnfeld thumbed, impatiently, through an outdated periodical. "Whatever's edible."

"Fruit's fine." Crilen nodded.

"Nothing." Genna, the other attendant looked bored.

"Very well." Panla gestured. "Dismissed."

Feebie pivoted sharply, pulled open the door with an almost masculine assertion, and confidently stalked out into the corridors in search of fruit, beverages or whatever else might be suitable.

Crilen wanted, very much, to use this unscheduled gap to sit nearer to Panla and engage her in another private conversation. But with Linnfeld and the other attendant present, he could sense she wouldn't receive him in quite the same personable manner as she had aboard the transport. In fact, she couldn't. So he settled onto a comfortable chair directly across from Linnfeld and opted to open a more general discussion to pass the time.

"She called you Queen Mother." Crilen said, sounding almost like a media interviewer. "But Linnfeld calls you Mrs. Tem. Why is that?"

"Feebie and Genna both came up through the Cathedral orphanage." Panla spoke with fond reflection as she glanced up at Genna's dark, reserved features. "When they graduated theology school, they became Text Instructors and junior officers at the Cathedral. When my husband got elected to the Accommodancy, I asked them if they'd like to get out and see a little more of the world, observe how our life with God balances against the cruel realities of secular politics. With some prodding, they agreed and I brought them on board as my personal attendants."

"And Linnfeld?" Crilen asked.

"Right here," Linnfeld chimed in, not wanting to be discussed in the third person. "I came with the wallpaper and the carpet stains."

Panla and Genna both smiled.

"I'd been an attendant to the wives of the Accommodants for twenty twin-moons." Linnfeld said proudly. "I'm an expert. So when the Tems came into the Accommodancy, naturally, I was retained. And, not that I'm an irreligious sort or anything like that, but I've always referred to the Accommodants' wives as Mrs.. That's just the way it's always worked. Of course, now that I have the added duty of First Attendant to the Deliveress as well, not to mention her other goings on, this has easily been the most challenging, rewarding, hair-raising assignment I've ever enjoyed. Most of the Accommodants' wives have been more concerned with shopping, decorating or entertaining. But this one? I've got three identities, three schedules, the media and the world's law enforcement to worry about. If it weren't for the fact that she's so bloody right all the time, I'd much sooner take her over my knee for all the trouble."

Linnfeld wagged a finger at Panla, then buried his weary grey-white features into his wrinkled hands.

"So what was the story behind my predecessor?" Crilen threw out another topic which he felt had been left incomplete.

Linnfeld glanced up at Panla. Panla glanced back. Genna shifted her weight against the wall and looked down.

"Moll," Panla finally said with heavy regret.

"Moll?" Crilen probed. "Was that her name?"

"Yes," Linnfeld answered. "Moll Shen."

"Moll was my best friend." Panla's eyes stared into nothing. "My best friend since the second day of grade school. We'd been together for almost thirty twin-moons. Moll was…sacrificed."

"Sacrificed?"

"When I was in the preliminary stages of making contact with Rabbel and The Break, Moll ran interference. Quite understandably, Rabbel was suspicious of me, and with good reason. How could the Deliveress of the Cathedral possibly want to support his insurgent band of left-wing atheists? Moll was the one who worked it all out. She took a lot of risks in those early days, but she believed in me and was willing to do whatever it took to get Rabbel and I together. Well, after several months of Moll running back and forth between Rabbel's tavern, the Cathedral and the Accommodant's mansion, Rabbel and I were finally able to get together and come to an understanding about what we wanted for the world. Unfortunately, it was also during this time that my husband's security had begun to track Moll's movements. I think it was some sort of security rivalry. They felt threatened by Moll because she was very, very good. Better than they were. So they recorded everything she did for a period of several weeks…Com calls to Rabbel, meetings with Rabbel, everything. When they thought they had enough, my husband had her arrested for both treason and, ironically, endangering my life."

"But you weren't implicated." Crilen concluded.

"No." Panla slumped in her chair. "Moll had insisted upon taking all the risks early on. She even went so far as to tell me that she thought PJ was a very dumb and very dangerous idea. Well, when she got caught, she was careful to gauge what the government knew. And when she figured out that all they knew about was her, she gave herself up and convincingly absorbed all of the blame. She even went so far as to publicly renounce her faith and her friendship with me. That hurt the most. Moll loved God, and I loved Moll. She avoided a trial, and any investigation that might have exposed me, by pleading guilty to treason. I was able to get her life spared, but she'll likely spend the rest of her days laboring in the Ponder Gulag."

"Then I can see why you were suspicious of me." Crilen sympathized.

"Were, Mr. Len?" Panla's eyes narrowed. "You've convinced me of who you're not working for, but I'm still very suspicious of your intentions."

"The Accommodant made certain he drove the process of finding Moll's replacement," Linnfeld added. "If he has any suspicions at all, your position would be the perfect spot to place an informant."

"True." Crilen's eyes darted between the two of them. "But if that were the case, I already have enough information to have all of you busting rocks with Moll by the weekend."

"That's not funny." Panla seemed wounded by his insensitivity.

"Sorry," Crilen apologized.

"The issue with you is," Panla continued, "you already know enough to destroy us. So there's no point in our concealing anything from you. Destroying us doesn't seem to be your aim, yet, you certainly are collecting information for some well-hidden agenda. Care to illuminate? We have the time."

"I can't." Crilen met her eyes. "And if I did, you wouldn't believe me anyway. It just wouldn't make sense to you. All I can say, again, is that I've been assigned to you and I'm here to help."

Linnfeld loosed a heavy sigh. Panla shook her head and dismissed his inscrutable explanation with a backward wave of her fingers.

An impassive silence filled the room, then a mounting commotion outside the door lured everyone's attention. Voices were approaching. And one very deliberate and resonant voice asserted itself over all the others.

"I'll only be a moment." the dominant voice bellowed as the waiting room door creaked open.

Slowly, like the revolution of a giant celestial body, the ponderous figure of Yolo Pigue eclipsed the doorway. He looked older, larger and heavier than anyone had recollected him to be, but his unfettered arrogant smirk, along with the bolts of well-tailored fabric which comprised his neatly pressed accouterments only intensified the powerful aura of his imposing presence.

"My dear Yolo! You're looking fit!" Panla cut through the moment with all of PJ's mischievous charm.

"Why, thank you, Queen Mother." The rolling layers of sagging flesh which were his jaws spread slowly to form an mendaciously affable smile. "How is our good, faithful Accommodant these days?"

"He is well and sends his best wishes to our most honest media baron." Panla never lost the glint in her eye.

"And who better than so honest a fellow to judge one so honest as I," Yolo chuckled. "As with all of your choices, my dear, you selected, for a husband, a man with extraordinary and insatiable prowess."

"My dear Yolo," Panla parried, "I blush to think that my husband should brook such high praise from so insatiable a man as yourself."

"An insatiable man, perhaps, good lady," Yolo's grin was now plastered across his face, "but my insatiability pales by comparison to the plaudits our good Accommodant has won from the fairer sex...at large."

Panla blinked twice as the tips of her frozen smile suddenly threatened to melt away.

Linnfeld loudly cleared his throat to gain her a moment to collect herself.

"The fairer sex?" Panla could only waltz to Yolo's lead.

"Why yes!" the large man gloated, veiling a light twist of malice. "Surely your neglect of your husband's well-chronicled affairs haven't left you ignorant of his very public courtship of the planet's female persuasion. A virtual orgy of good-will toward the feminine populace. Indeed, the Accommodant has revealed himself a man of varied and dynamic passions where females are concerned. But then, of course, as they say, 'The wife is always the last to know.'"

Yolo's massive form shook confidently as he chuckled down at her, though he never lost contact with the anger simmering behind Panla's brown eyes.

Linnfeld wanted to intervene, but could only stand aside and witness the bludgeoning exchange of bitter pleasantries.

Likewise, Crilen wanted badly to singe Yolo's vicious arrogance, but clearly, this was neither the time or the place for a pyrogenic display of chivalry, lest he also expose his cover.

"Queen Mother, you act as if I've surprised you with the obvious." Yolo suddenly feigned sympathy. "Surely a man of Accommodant Tem's charisma and charm is bound to leverage his powers of seduction where they serve him best. Were I, or any man, in his position, I venture to say that any of us would take the same liberties."

"Mr. Pigue," Panla's indulgence wore thin, "what my husband does..."

"Is his own business." Yolo finished the sentence. "Just as your affairs are your own. But we are talking about the right of public domain aren't we? And if it, in any way affects the public well-being, people have a right to know of such goings on, don't you agree?"

Panla's jaws tightened. Her mounting ire illuminated her contempt.

"I mean it would be one thing, entirely, if the Accommodant were a private citizen, embarking upon such openly inviting flirtations." Yolo's eyes narrowed as he played upon every fold of Panla's unraveling composure. "But after all, this is politics we're talking about. Isn't that so, Queen Mother?"

"Politics?" Panla seethed under a controlled whisper. "Politics? How so?"

"How so?" Yolo smirked innocently. "How could it be anything else? The endorsement your husband has garnered from the Female Activists Coalition will all but assure him of a second term in office. Gaining their support a full twin-moon before the official start of his re-election campaign was a stroke of brilliance! In fact, I credit the man with embarking wholly upon his re-election campaign midway through his inaugural victory celebration. A politician's politician! A credit to the political species, you have to agree."

The word politics echoed at the cross section of Panla's racing thoughts. Yolo had been talking about politics, not her husband's stream of promiscuous liaisons. Not openly, anyway. Yolo had coldly woven a cruel, gouging paradox into the fabric of meager political chit-chat. And, in so doing, had managed to rook her frailest emotions with humiliatingly effortless aplomb.

Crilen watched the light dim from Panla's eyes. All of her energy appeared to drain downward, dispersing directly into the carpeted floor.

"Did I miss something?" Yolo smiled innocently as he lapped up the dour expressions which surrounded him.

"No." Panla said quietly, "I guess I did."

"You? Miss something?" Yolo placed his heavy hand on her padded shoulder.

Panla froze like a woman about to be raped. His merest touch stung like a malevolent and vulgar intrusion. And she could smell the pungent stink of a recent meal billowing from his labored breaths.

"You're a busy woman, I'll grant you," Yolo offered unsettling consolation. "but I can't imagine anything getting past you, unless you plotted it thusly. Your husband is a shrewd man, but I would never underestimate the emissary of God, Queen Mother."

"Mr. Pigue," Crilen's voice interceded, "have we met?"

Yolo dropped his hand from Panla's shoulder and turned to look at him. Crilen could see Panla exhale as she took a step backward and collected herself.

Yolo peered deeply into Crilen's face, hurriedly eyeing every line and contour with careless self-importance. "I don't believe so." Yolo snorted and looked away.

"Not at the diner?" Crilen tried to shake his memory.

Yolo looked back at him and squinted, pretending as if he were actually making an effort. Crilen thought he detected a glimmer of recognition, but if there was, it remained well hidden.

"No, I'm afraid not, dear fellow," Yolo answered matter-of-factly. "Though a good number of people pass through the diner from time to time. Unless we spoke at length, I'm afraid I've failed to commit you to memory, Mr...."

"Len," Crilen answered. "I'm Mrs. Tem's new security head."

"Len...Len..." Yolo's heavy jowls twitched. "I'd remember a strange name like that. Not from around here, are you?"

"No sir," Crilen answered.

"Well, Mr. Len, guard our Queen Mother with your life." Yolo nodded. "Actors, musicians and athletes aside, she is the most compelling and newsworthy figure in the world. The last thing anyone needs is for some grimy rebel or delusional lunatic to lay low so compelling a centerpiece."

"Yes sir," Crilen responded blankly.

"Don't you agree, Queen Mother?" Yolo called to her back.

"You'll get no argument from me." Panla wished him gone.

"No argument from you?" Yolo chuckled. "Imagine that."

Yolo revolved slowly, then tottered steadily toward the door.

"My apologies for the delay." Yolo seemed almost genuine. "It wasn't at all my idea that these two iconic placebos get themselves killed last night. Nonetheless, we live in a world where the public demands to dine on its dessert before we can serve the main course. Therefore, I respectfully beg your indulgence."

"I understand," Panla responded knowingly.

"And do go easy on our poor Libbi Trullup when she poses her questions." Yolo waved adieu. "She's not well-equipped for the kind of sparring that requires intellect."

Yolo narrowly slipped past the door as it quietly closed behind him. Once again, they could hear the sound of his muffled voice as he resumed a stream of commands to his staff members who trailed after him.

"Pleasant." Linnfeld sighed as if he had been holding his breath the entire time.

"The Devil," Crilen sneered before he could catch himself.

"Not the devil." Panla wearily returned to her chair. "Just a well-heeled member of the board."

XVIII.

Newswoman: Hi everyone! Egs Bloyt, back with you. Once again you're looking at a live shot of actor Finx Melder's sports vehicle protruding from the side of a blazing fuel tank. Melder, along with his companion, sand surfer Preppi Deyz, was killed in a single-vehicle accident when he apparently lost control of his vehicle, speeding through the city streets. No details as to the cause of the accident have been determined at this time. Some have said that Melder was trying to avoid a handful of persistent reporters, but that has not been substantiated. Witnesses, however, say that Melder was attempting some sort of stunt, lost control and crashed.

We now have our YBS Eastern Bureau Chief, Proptz Rotz, with more on the impact the tragic death of Finx Melder will have on the world. Proptz?

Proptz Rotz: Like a changeling borne to our richest fantasies, Finx Melder was an evolutionary revolutionary. From moment to moment he seemingly altered his form, his shape, his identity, and all of us hastened quickly to bask in the glow of each incarnation. To say merely that Finx was a trend-setter would be understating the influences of a man who destroyed and reshaped the core of our culture, time and time again. What world leaders and businessmen attempted to achieve through elaborate schemes designed to capture the public imagination or sway mass appeal, Finx could accomplish with a smile and a wave while sipping soup in a sidewalk cafe.

The Finx Phenomenon began with the release of *Knock It Til You Try It*. His character's transformation from a stodgy conservative lawbooker to a philosophical, free-spirited, bisexual lover captured the imagination of the world. Millions of men and women dyed their hair pink and grew flowing manes of curled locks. They tore away the buttons from their shirts and their pants and strutted the club scenes turning society on its ear. The fact that Melder himself flaunted this image in real life for nearly a twinmoon only fueled the explosion of imitators. Soon, fashion designers were marketing buttonless clothing and seatless trousers that stores couldn't keep on the shelves. Melder's most popular line in the film: "I won't shun what I haven't done" also became a trendy catch phrase which is now well integrated into our everyday language.

Still, some felt that Melder, like so many before him, was a mere flicker of light upon the pop culture continuum. But during the filming of *The Embalming Room*, Finx shed his flowing locks in favor of a black flat-cut and a pointed goatee. And like the law of natural selection, the many millions of pinkened manes around the world soon relented to closely-cropped hairstyles, ragged white tunics and black leather boots. Indeed, the new Melder legions stormed into predominance like a newborn race of angry, underclass foot soldiers. By the time *The Embalming Room* actually hit theaters, the new Finx and his new tough look were already in full stride. And his performance as a bitter, lovelorn drifter from the wrong side of the tracks was, of course, electrifying. Tragically, re-enactments of the violent scene in which Finx raped his co-star, actress Yanga Blas, also became a domestic trend across the globe. Incidents of rape and rape-murder increased sharply. The most notable case, wherein the family of a slain girl tried to sue Melder and Producer Giggi Gondoleda because the killer claimed he was living out a sexually graphic scene from the film, dominated headlines for months. Eventually, the suit was dismissed and Melder won another Golden Icon. But the actor was said to be distraught over being blamed for the rash of sexually violent incidents, so he resolved to alter his image once again.

Melder disappeared from the public eye for nearly a twinmoon. When he re-emerged, it was with a thick beard, a shaven head and long pastel robes. Many speculated that he had undergone a religious conversion to cast off the demons of his personal miseries. But as it turned out, he had merely embarked upon an intense study of his latest upcoming role: The legendary second Deliverer, Bius II. Melder wanted to silence his critics who claimed he had built his popularity upon the portrayals of "freaks and punks" so he took on the monumental lead in a classic historical drama. Though wholly criticized by the Cathedral as wildly inaccurate, Melder's *Bius II* set box-office records. His huge following, as expected, turned out in droves. But surprisingly, this film also became widely appealing to religious moderates creating an entirely new wellspring of Melder fanatics. In fact, the Cathedral itself became a reluctant benefactor of the very film it denounced. Cathedral attendance rocketed nearly twenty-five percent during the first several months of *Bius II*'s release. And some suggest that Cathedral profits rivaled that of the film's production studio. In either case, Melder had indeed attained the status of an Icon. Though, when questioned about the impact of religion in his own life, he quoted infamously, "Gods don't need religion, we create our own." Perhaps it was a mere publicity ploy, as a predictable firestorm of controversy ensued. But Finx Melder never offered a retraction. And the greatest irony was that, while he had paved the way for a religious revival around the globe, Melder himself fell deeper into sex and drug addiction. His month-long binges became legendary in the tabloids. His frequent run-ins with law enforcement only heightened his reputation as a rebel. And his defiance of death from frequent overdoses fortified his aura of total invincibility.

During this turbulent period, Melder still found time to write, direct and star in another hit film, *Sister's Lingerie*. Looking gaunt and often disoriented, Melder staggered through the satirical comedy, who's haphazard production was dubbed "the all-drug festival", and into three more Golden Icons for his story of a male who becomes obsessed with wearing female undergarments. As expected, another fashion trend took hold as millions of males donned white lace and peach-colored silk as evening outerwear. The cross-dressing sensation seemed madly outrageous, but as one Melder fanatic put it, "Who cares as long as the ladies dig it? Women want to do Finx, and any guy who gets gussied up like Finx never spends his nights alone, y'know?"

In addition to his on-screen persona and his after-hours nightlife, Finx was also influential in the political arena. He spoke out against the sale of hand weapons in the south. He spoke out for the protection of animals in habitat preserves. And, of course he was a strong proponent of sexual liberation and reforms from the Cathedral. Some say he was the real emblem of the Break. In fact, many felt that Melder may eventually have moved away from the performing arts and into politics, where the sway of his influence may have been incalculable. Tragically, we'll never know. All we're left with today is the immortal memory of a great man who touched us all and died well before his time.

For YBS news, this is Proptz Rotz.

Newswoman: Once again, you're looking at a live shot of the vehicle of Finx Melder protruding from the rear of a blazing fuel tank. Hours ago, Melder and girlfriend Preppi Deyz crashed headlong into the fuel tank at a reported high rate of speed, resulting in a huge explosion taking the lives of both occupants. We'll be back with continuing coverage in just a moment.

XIX.

The Market.

What difference did it really matter whether the populace continued to embrace the church, or if the Break burned every cathedral to the ground, heralding the brave new age of a secular society devoid of monotheistic worship? Who's to say whether one man's invisible deity is any better than another man's flip of the coin? Life, after all, is more a matter of chance than fate. And, of course, only hard work, a good education and a steady stream of current and reliable information skew the odds toward the most fruitful yield of one's assets.

The Market.

Who gives a goddamn about Finx Melder? Yes, he was talented. Yes he was popular. And, most importantly, he generated mountains of capital for the parasitic executive pimps of the entertainment industry. He was an optimal entertainment commodity, to say the least. But he's dead now. Can't we change the damned subject? And shouldn't the people in the entertainment industry be more concerned with who will fill the gaping chasm left in the box office revenue stream? Shouldn't everyone be more concerned about which studio gains or retains economic leverage as a result of this fortuitous financial sinkhole? Tributes and tears and film fans crying in the streets. Where are people's priorities?

The Market.

It's the Market that matters. Without the Market there is no mass entertainment. There is no food. There is no running water. There is no clothing on people's backs. There are no jobs. There are no modern conveniences. No currency. No global economy. No energy sources. No mass communication. No institutions of higher learning. No land development. No housing. No pretty little wife. No grinning little children. No scratching, salivating pet to greet you at your door. And no doors, for that matter. What would the blithering idiots do then? Sharpen their blunt spears for the morning hunt? Rake the meat from the bones of dead vermin while they huddle over their dwindling fires in their damp dark caves? Hump the nearest four-legged animal that doesn't have the will to protest the intrusion?

Wyel sneered at the monitor as the promise/threat of further coverage of the Finx Melder story scrolled beneath a loud, flashing advertisement for yet another world-shattering sporting event. No news on the Market. But then, all of the recent news on the Market had been bad, anyway. A veritable horror show, wrought with gloom and guesswork.

Of course, the economy in the south had always been poor. In fact, the Market's vitality appeared to thrive on the steadily high mortality rates, the steadily rampant birth rates, the steadily declining property values and the steadily laughable fifty-percent rate of unemployment. But the Market hadn't begun to stagger until the Break emerged as a viable force in the world's conscience. People, north and south, began to question every dormant facet of their long, complacent lives. They began to question their Regents. Question their Governors. Question the Accommodant. Question their allegiance to societal mores as well as to God and the Cathedral. And, most assuredly, they had begun to question every precept of the Deliverancy.

Civil unrest. Ethical vacillations. Ideological instability running a low fever. Turbid paradigms, hurtling the Market into cancerous uncertainty.

Uncertainty: the Market's most terminal state of ill health.

Draxford Wyel, CEO of the Travails Group, had received a specious communiqué from Piddel, CEO of Citadel Corp., informing him that their much anticipated insurance/bank merger would be postponed until the Market "comes back." A cryptic epitaph chiseled onto the tombstone of a proposed, hundred-billion-coin business venture, which had had success and profitability chomping to burst from the contractual gates of dividend heaven. Every signature assured itself accolades of genius from the business community, and an electronic pot of gold beamed coin into their bank accounts in large, tidy increments.

All the wining and dining with contemptibly self-important little men and their vacantly arrogant little wives. All the condescending to proposals from ambitious young incompetent professionals, over-eager to outshine their counterparts with overblown, melodramatic boardroom productions worthier of a surreal theme-park ride than a professional business meeting. All the speeches and glad-handing and compromises and published propaganda and government bribes. All the months of weaving and sowing and rooking and manipulating every conceivable variable but the stars into alignment.

The Market.

Frozen like a confused, dumbfounded behemoth lost in a blizzard of conflicting ideological banter. Stalled like a massive, magnificent, mechanical marvel of engineered brilliance…out of oil, gears smoking, grinding, gnashing, squealing to an abrupt and unseemly halt, with an indeterminate amount of repair pending.

Interest rates rising. Stock prices falling. The indebted in default. Divestiture, the order of the day. Economic chaos exponentially mounting on a global scale. If this weren't the harbinger of the world's end, nothing could be.

And all due to the uncertainty of the Market. If the masses could make up their minds, then the Market could react accordingly. The doors of opportunity would either open or close, rather than continue to flap in the breeze like a warped screen door. Old opportunities would fade, but new deals would be brokered in their place. The capital shell game could begin anew. And the fraternal maestros of the sport, amongst whom Wyel considered himself anointed royalty, could grow their glorious profits, unimpeded by the broken shards of society's crisis of identity. Unimpeded by the mad, crippling uncertainty of the Market.

Wyel involuntarily clenched his teeth as he poured himself another drink. He stared deeply into the trembling brown liquid as it settled smoothly into his glass. He wondered what all the fools in the streets would say about their God, or their godlessness, if they could fully comprehend the gravity of their impact on the omnipotent and all powerful Market and the inverse effect the health of the Market would have on them all.

XX.

Libbi Trullup rocked anxiously in her chair as her hairdresser counted the brush strokes under his nervous breath. Her shimmering black coif which cupped symmetrically around her bright white cheeks was as pointed and flawless as the fine lines of an ink drawing. Her pointed nose was powdered. Her luscious lips were ruby red. Yet the tension darting behind her otherwise affable blue eyes belied a woman struggling fitfully, to conjure up her professional façade, lest the facade take irrevocable flight for parts unknown.

She rehearsed her confidence in the mirror time and again, to assure herself that it would be there for the cameras. She practiced her pseudo-intellectual austerity, balancing it with a supercilious, jocular air which would allow her to gracefully transcend anything she could not understand. But despite her strongest efforts, her starkest apprehension still managed to chip and nick at her fraying resolve: the fear of having her renowned and convincing veneer flayed before the scrutiny of millions of broadcast viewers.

And, of course, there was the nagging question: Why had Yolo chosen her to interview the Deliveress, to begin with? Did he honestly believe she was the best person for the job? She wanted to believe this was true, but at the core of her reason, she could not delude herself into embracing so clearly false an accolade. In the journalistic pecking order of hard news, Libbi was, at best, a distant tenth behind the true luminaries of the profession. She harbored an abundance of confidence in her natural charm, her assassin's wit and her madeover imperfections, but the fit for this particular assignment felt far too untidy for her to feel anything other than bowel-twisting anxiety. Kowtowing with celebrities was one thing. And sniping mercilessly at special interest leaders or corporate chairpersons was always a satiating delight for her vast, but fragile ego. But while a journalistic inquisition of the spiritual descendent of the world's Cathedral carried considerable appeal to her vanity, she foresaw that the dross of such a confrontation would bear the fetid stench of a nauseating disaster.

It was easy for Libbi to envision humiliating circles run round her by the most powerful and charismatic figure in the world. Optimistically, she might manage to salvage a stalemate for herself. Or, with sorcerer's luck, she could even wring out a miraculous victory on style over substance. But realistically, Libbi knew this was a battle which she would never win in earnest. For even though religious doctrine now wobbled under an unprecedented sociological siege, Panla Jen Tem remained as popular a symbolic icon as ever in the eyes of the ambivalent masses. Even those who openly resented her beliefs still adored her for her intrinsic beauty and her natural grace. Libbi envisioned herself shrinking to little more than a decorated, empty eggshell beside a monolith. Worse still, she was convinced that very few would forgive an impertinent journalist for any soiling of the hallowed robes of the admired and beloved Deliveress of the world.

Libbi tensed as she saw her burgeoning career as a broadcast personality imperiled by the sheer weight of the task which lay before her. It was an ascent to the gallows which would make a decapitated, bloodless corpse of her carefully crafted public persona.

Then, like the heavy dragging lid of a concrete coffin, a chilling and horrible thought finally revealed itself to her: Yolo under the auspices of having selected her for a spectacular opportunity, had insidiously offered her up as little more than a bundled sacrifice before a smoldering volcano.

"Damn him!" she cursed. She had been so smart, so shrewd and manipulative. She had covered every possible angle to protect herself. She had won ratings if not respect. She had established her niche, her value, or so she thought. It was inconceivable to her that it could still come down to one cold crude fact after all the twinmoons of hard work and maneuvering: She should have slept with the fat bastard when he had offered her the chance.

"Goddamnit!" Libbi's blaring voice exploded throughout the dressing room. She jettisoned a flurry of white cards up into the air. Simultaneously, the hairbrush flew from the hairdresser's hand and went clattering across the dressing room floor.

"Where the fuck are my fucking questions?" Libbi shrieked. "I need my goddamned questions and I need them right now!!"

A startled, obsequious little man in a mechanized headset which covered his eyes and his ears popped up from nowhere at the arm of Libbi's chair.

"What have you done now?" The man's voice warbled with irritation.

"What have I done?" Libbi yelled, searching for the man's eyes behind two wired, protruding reflective lenses. "Your fucking moron copy editors gave me the wrong god damned questions!"

"Those are the questions you asked us to prepare, Libbi." the man said trying to calm her.

"No, Mr. Dar," Libbi pounded her fists onto the arms of her chair, "those are the questions I asked your people to prepare yesterday! But since I didn't get any sleep last night, I stayed up and wrote out an entirely new set of questions that I handed the stupid copy fuck this morning! These are wrong, wrong, wrong, wrong, wrong!"

"All right, Libbi." Dar fiddled with the mouthpiece stem which sat a centimeter from his lips. "I'm sorry, we'll find the questions. I'll be right back!"

Dar scurried off, frantically blurting commands for a studio-wide search for Libbi's "new" questions.

Meanwhile, the hairdresser returned, picking puffs of dust from the bristles of his brush.

"Shit!" Libbi covered her face with her hand.

"No sleep last night?" the hairdresser timidly inquired. "Not a good idea, girl."

"Well it wasn't my idea exactly." Libbi tried to blink back the tears that would ruin her makeup. "There's this guy…"

"Uh, oh. Here we go." the hairdresser patted her on the shoulder.

"I met this really cute guy at a midtown club last weekend." Libbi rolled her eyes. "I buy him a drink. I dance with him. He makes a few moves, so I pay for dinner. Then I sleep with the guy. I pay for the hotel. I pay for breakfast, and, now, he won't return my com calls. Can you believe it?"

"Sounds like he got the all-expense-paid pass into Libbiland, if you know what I mean." The hairdresser winced as he inspected his work.

"Expense-paid?" Libbi rolled her eyes. "Shit! Was I wrong? To pay, I mean? Three weeks ago, I read this article in *Vaginopolis Monthly* that said if a female wants to show a guy that she really likes him, she should pay. Show him that you're not afraid to take control. Be the aggressor. And I make more money than most guys I meet so, I figure, why not? Pay, I mean. So I do that, and now this fucking gigolo who never even told me his real name won't even call me back. Like I'm a goddamned spunk receptacle he found in the bottom of a prophylactic dispenser! I mean, did I intimidate him? I thought we had great sex! And I was conversational, but not too pushy! I initiated the oral sex, but I didn't demand to stay on top. And its not like I asked him for any kind of commitment. But I didn't exactly think I was buying a one-night mystery fuck either! I mean, I didn't think I was buying anything, really. I just wanted to pay! Pay and have a good time. Now I feel like some goddamned whore…again. Only, a whore who pays, for god's sake! Fucking prick! Fucking males! Life sucks with 'em…and you can't suck without 'em!"

"I heard that!" the hairdresser's dark features lit up momentarily.

"So, last night, I couldn't sleep because I'm thinking about that guy," Libbi continued, "and this musician I interviewed last month who said he's going to be in town next weekend and wants to get together again. During his last show, we had a sweaty little quickie backstage before the encore, but nothing serious. But now he's going to be in town for two whole days, so I think I want to go for it. See what happens! Why not? Life's short, right? Only, he's a superstar! And people are always trying to get things off of him, especially females. And I don't want him to think I'm like that. Some kind of fame-humping parasite, y'know? So…what happens if I pay?"

"Then don't pay." The hairdresser tilted Libbi's head.

"Right." Libbi frowned. "I don't pay and I'm just another road-slut looking for a free ride. I mean, I'm not looking for a relationship. But it would be nice if we could have a really good time and get to be really good friends."

"Then just tell him that, up front." The hairdresser teased Libbi's bangs with his fingers.

"Up front?" Libbi's mouth dropped in horror. "If I'm up front, that'll ruin everything! If I tell him anything up front he'll think I have expectations. Guys like that hate expectations."

"And if you say nothing…"

"Then my expectations might be fulfilled because he'll act as if I don't have any expectations, get it?"

"Uh huh." the hairdresser met her eyes in the mirror.

"Hey, you're not just kissing my ass, are you?" Libbi sulked.

"No ma'am." He smiled.

"Well, are you just pretending to agree with me or what?"

"No, ma'am."

"Then why are you just standing there, grunting like some brain-dead valet?"

"Maybe I really agree with you."

"Oh, fuck you! You don't agree with me. You just want to finish my hair and get the fuck out of here."

"No, not really."

"Then say what's on your mind before I tell Dar to fire your skinny ass."

The hairdresser grimaced and sighed, and began packing up his brushes and combs.

"Oh, look, I'm sorry, okay?"

"You don't need to be sorry, Ms. Trullup," he said. "I'm finished. You look great."

"But I asked for your opinion!"

"Yeah. Yeah, I know." The hairdresser met her eyes in the mirror. "Well, if you must know, I don't understand why a beautiful, famous, all-together woman like you is so worried about a couple of silly bed buddies…or this interview."

"I'm not worried about the interview." Libbi frowned, raising her voice. "Once they find the goddamned questions I wrote…"

"Okay, okay." The hairdresser held up his hands. "I just think you need to remember one thing: You're Libbi, goddamn it! Nobody can fuck with you! I've seen you make CEOs look like grammar school drop-outs. I've seen you reduce corporate lawbookers to sniveling primates. They don't pay you the big bucks for nothing! The only person worried about whether you got your shit together or not, is you. You're the best! You're the queen! You're Libbi, goddamn it!"

Libbi met her own lost gaze in the mirror.

"I'm Libbi, goddamn it!" she spoke forcefully.

The hairdresser patted her on the shoulder and quietly left the dressing room. Libbi tried desperately, to peer into the crux of what being Libbi really meant.

Meanwhile, in the guests' dressing room down the hall, Panla eased out of her chair, grimaced wearily and lifted her brows at Crilen and Linnfeld.

"I feel terrible." She shook her head.

"You look wonderful," Linnfeld complimented her.

Crilen nodded passively, but observed that she did look spectacularly luminescent for a woman who had been running full throttle since the early morning hours. The day's itinerary was only half completed, but had borne the burden of two days full. Thus far, she had been assailed by a horde of patrons and reporters outside St. Baloni's Medical, sung to and consoled a ward of terminally ill patients, delivered a short, but rousing speech to a women's political organization and been, for all of her trouble, summarily food poisoned by the most renowned caterer in the region. All of this, and still the most daunting maneuvers of the day's trek lay ahead of her.

"Well, I did learn something from Mother." Panla sighed at the irony. "She said that there's nothing wrong with crying or vomiting all day so long as you never do it in front of an audience. Muster an hour or two of perfection for the public, and the rest of the day's misery can be all your own. Thus!"

She curtsied, bowed and fashioned the pert, but intellectually engaging countenance she would carry before the worldwide audience.

"Are you nervous?" Crilen asked.

Crilen could sense Linnfeld and the other attendants stop still even before the echo of his query died away.

"Now what?" Crilen thought.

Panla smiled knowingly, pushing an air of confidence hard upon the segue of discomfort which threatened to sour the positive aura that had filled the room. With a casual flip of her hand, she calmly dismissed his notion of nervousness altogether.

"Really, Mr. Len." Panla caressed the minor transgression with her eyes. "Just when I'd thought you'd figured me out entirely, you go and say something so terribly silly."

Crilen's face went blank as reality became disoriented by another profound wave of vivid reminiscence. The cadence of her words were, to him, an incantation conjuring the remnant of a familiar scene, played to conclusion years ago. At the intersection of past and present, he could feel Aami preparing herself for a comparable public engagement. Then, as now, he had been overpowered by his protective instincts, wishing to cradle her delicate sensibilities from the cruel malevolence of her weighty opposition. Yet it was she who rebuffed his gravest desires to shield her as she brandished her own armor of indomitable independence. In the end, he found himself humbled to the point of embarrassment, much like the father who had come to discover that his grown daughter, frail in his fantasies, was far more than competent to defend herself.

"Are you alright, Mr. Len?" Panla's voice echoed through his lapse. "You look rather ashen all of a sudden. You weren't fouled by the luncheon fowl, were you?"

"No." Crilen's eyes snapped clear. "No, I'm fine. And I didn't mean to imply that you weren't ready."

Panla read his expression and recognized where his mind had wandered off to. But for the sake of her time and his privacy, she opted not to delve further into his personal digression, for now.

"I've been down this road many times, Mr. Len." She patted him on the shoulder. "This is the easy part. Blessed assurance is a wonderful thing to have in this world of ours. When you hold God's irrevocable truth in your heart, there can be no debate. There can be no doubt. All that remains is to teach and illuminate all the other souls you come into contact with, so that they too, may share in the same comfort and knowledge, and not fall prey to the caprice of the devil."

"The caprice of the devil." Crilen thought. Through his years, he had seen the devil's caprice roar through the sentient universe like a sprawling, raging web of noxious poison, withering souls, by the billion, upon the honeyed scents of abject damnation. Enticements, contemptuous of all circumspection. Libidinous, gratuitous seductions for the recklessly avaricious worshippers of lurid, hedonistic narcissism. Vitiated souls, serenaded by the orchestras of Hell, preening thoughtlessly to the pronouncement of their final sentence: Eternal death by secular indulgence. Truly the devil's caprice was well-mated to the singular, mortal, wanton obsession with the lure of ephemeral rewards. On some worlds, it had been succinctly defined as temptation.

"Very well." Crilen's arms felt numb at his sides. He wanted to hug her.

"I'm glad you approve, Mr. Len," Panla mocked him warmly.

The dressing room door popped open and an odd-looking man with a strange electrical apparatus attached to his head peered in.

"We're ready for her!" Dar frantically gestured.

Panla squared her shoulders and waited for her attendants to take their places.

"You'd better make your rounds" Linnfeld suggested to Crilen. "Just in case. You never know."

Crilen had already inspected blueprints of the building and gone through the personnel files of everyone working at YBS studios, but Linnfeld was right. Stranger things could happen. Through the years, through the cosmos, Crilen had seen many stranger things with his own blazing eyes.

Linnfeld stepped in front of Panla; Feebie and Genna took their places behind her, completing their formation. Without a word, Linnfeld took the first step toward the door and Panla, Genna and Feebie walked behind him, stepping in a synchronized rhythm which fell just short of mimicking a march.

When everyone had departed, Crilen stood alone. He decided to reconnoiter the building one last time even though he sensed no immediate dangers. No immediate dangers. But the ghosts of impending dread still nagged his conscience, and caused the pyrogenic flames beneath his flesh to simmer with anxiety.

XXI.

Mivins ran as fast as he could; the larger adolescent boys were not far behind. He was frightened for his life, but he knew if he could reach the cathedral, Churchlord Farpal would protect him.

Out of the corner of his eye, he saw Joxo and Beb round the corner as they yelled more threats. They were gaining on him fast.

"Drop the books!" Mivins thought as he felt his legs tire. "Drop the damned books!" But he wouldn't drop the books. They were his love. They were his passion. They were his lifeline to all the other worlds of fantasy and knowledge he coveted. Without the books, he was nothing. Without the books, he was no better than his pursuers.

Mivins ran past the food market, looking in the front window hoping the owner would notice the lopsided chase and come to his aid. Unfortunately, he saw the storeowner preoccupied in conversation with another adult at the front counter. He thought of stopping, but if he tried to enter the store, it would give the older boys just time enough to intercept him. And the pummeling he would receive with those wooden clubs before he reached the door would not be worth the storeowner's belated intervention. Mivins begged his weakening legs for just a little more strength to continue on.

His throat and lungs were raw as he rambled down a narrow alley between the store and a vacant renovation site. It was a shortcut to the cathedral. There had to be somewhere to hide in the trash bin, the overgrown brush or the construction equipment he'd seen there previously.

"You've got a date with the devil, you little shit!" Joxo yelled as he and Beb stopped and watched the tiny Mivins struggle down the alley.

"This is pathetic." Beb tapped his club on the ground, smiling at their quarry. "Why doesn't he drop those books?"

"Because he's too good to drop his books." Joxo sneered. "Too smart."

"Yeah." Beb smacked his club against the alley's stone wall. "Too smart for his own good."

Mivins could see his pursuers shrinking in the distance as he staggered to the end of the alley and ducked from view. Were they going to give up the chase and let him live another day? Doubtful. The thickening phlegm wheezed through his chest and up the back of his throat and he could taste the blood in his mouth from sheer exhaustion. Maybe that was their real plan…to chase him to death. That way, they could always claim they never touched him.

The smaller boy could see the cathedral across the yellow, overgrown field. He could even make out Churchlord Farpal's robed figure jogging up the stairs to the front entrance. One hundred meters or so, and he would survive.

He heard the heavy footfalls of Joxo and Beb come thundering down the alley. To him, the bigger boys sounded like large, swift predators. As Mivins heart pounded through his sternum, he sadly realized they'd been playing with him all along. He looked up at the cathedral once more, and, suddenly, the distance seemed to measure a full kilometer. Panicked, he glanced at the large trash bin, a thicket of tall grass and a large four-wheeled piece of machinery sitting unattended in the mud.

Mivins decided to go for the trash bin, but before he could move, he felt a violent jolt shove him from behind the shoulders, causing him to fly forward into the air and land, chin first, onto the rough concrete. As he crashed hard and rolled over onto his neck, his tangled legs hit the ground backwards. Blood dripped from the gash on his chin and damply stained his yellow tunic with dark crimson. Strangely, his first thoughts were of the books he had been carrying. They were now scattered across the back lot, pages riffling in the breeze. Then he looked up and saw Joxo and Beb standing over him, predatory smiles carved across their faces.

"You've really fucked up, Mivins." Joxo poked the small boy with his club. "All that shit you've been talking around the neighborhood."

"What s…stuff?" Mivins quaked, failing badly to collect his composure.

"SHIT!" Beb yelled. "The man said shit, not stuff, you little homo!"

"I'm not a homo." Mivins looked down.

"You talkin' back to us?" Joxo smacked the boy against the ankle bone with his club.

"No!" Mivins winced as a sharp pain shot through the marrow of his leg.

"Then you're a homo, aren't you?" Beb laughed.

Mivins remained silent and tried to take inventory of his scattered possessions.

"Hey!" Beb violently jabbed the smaller boy in the face with the blunt end of his club. "I asked you a question."

Mivins heard his nose crack. He could feel the swelling begin almost immediately and the blood flowed over his lip, staining his teeth.

"Oh shit!" Beb chuckled. "Oh, man, Mivins, I didn't mean to do that. Of course it does match your chin. Kind of like a mustache and beard."

Joxo and Beb both laughed as they shook each others' hands and tapped the barrels of their clubs together.

Mivins unsteadily attempted to rise to his feet, but Joxo snapped around and viciously smashed his club into the side of Mivins' left knee, causing a loud popping sound which was accompanied by the boy's loud squeal. Mivins rolled over onto his side, clutching his leg as tears flowed from his eyes.

"I haven't done anything!" the smaller boy cried.

Joxo twirled his club up onto his shoulder and smiled. "Well, that's just a plain old lie now, isn't it?"

"You just don't think the way the rest of us do, Mivins." Beb smirked. "That's a big problem. My folks even think that your folks need to move out of the neighborhood. We don't need your uppity bullshit telling us how we're supposed to live!"

Mivins moaned, clutching his numb, twisted leg.

"Only good thing about your family is the way your little sister fucks!" Joxo nudged Beb.

"Yeah," Beb giggled, "She's screwin' half the guys at school."

"Not bad, considering she's only nine!" Joxo cackled.

"No!" Mivins cried. "Why are you doing this to me?"

"Did he just say no?" Beb smiled at Joxo.

"Yeah. He's callin' us fuckin' liars!"

"His old man's a fuckin' liar," Beb sneered. "Thinks his whole family is better than everyone else."

"Must be something about all those books." Joxo reached down and picked up one of the books Mivins had dropped. "What is all this shit, Mivins? What good is it?"

"It's bullshit." Beb glared down at Mivins. "Isn't it?"

Mivins tried again, to struggle to his feet, but his dead, swollen knee wouldn't cooperate. He wiped under his chin with his sleeve and a large smear of thick, drying blood appeared on his forearm. He licked over the top of his mouth and could taste more blood as his nasal passages became completely blocked. Sitting on the ground, he looked back at the cathedral, over the tall yellow grass, into the alleyway and around the renovation site for a policer or anyone who might come to his aid.

"He wants the Churchlord to help him." Joxo grinned. "Isn't that funny?"

"Well, we know he doesn't need any fucking Churchlord." Beb teased. "Maybe there's something in that book that can help him."

"Well, let's see." Joxo tore out a fist full of pages and wadded them up in his hands.

Beb dropped his club and knelt down behind Mivins. He reached around the smaller boy and locked his forearm under Mivins' chin, forming a choke-hold. Mivins struggled to catch his breath when Joxo knelt in front of him and jammed the wad of paper into Mivins's mouth with his fingers.

"I don't think it's helping," Beb observed sarcastically.

"Yeah. Well maybe this will."

Joxo grabbed his club by the barrel while Beb pinned Mivins arms to the ground. Joxo carelessly jabbed the handle end of the club directly into Mivins's eye. It was difficult to tell how badly the eye had been damaged as blood squirted out and formed a small blackish-red pool in the socket.

"Whoops," Joxo chuckled. "Missed."

Mivins struggled to spit out the paper so he could yell when Joxo's second attempt to stuff the wad of paper almost broke Mivins's cheekbone. Beb positioned himself to hold the boy's face steady. With one final stab, Joxo jammed the paper wad deep into Mivins's throat as if he were punching home a stake.

Mivins writhed on the ground, kicking and choking as he reached into his own mouth to pull out the obstruction before he suffocated. His pallid complexion, stained in his own blood took on a nauseating shade of blue.

"Damn, Mivins." Beb picked up his club. "Look at you."

Joxo and Beb met each other's eyes, gazing as if each were waiting for the other to blink. Beb cocked his club behind him, and, with every ounce of his strength, smashed Mivins squarely across the forehead. The odd, disturbing sound of Mivins crushing skull momentarily chilled the two adolescents. They stared in awe as the involuntary spasms of death quivered through Mivins' trembling limbs.

"Ouch." Joxo tried to laugh.

"I think I'm gonna' be sick." Beb stared at the body.

"What for?" Joxo frowned. "His family didn't belong to the Cathedral. My dad said his old man is a Break sympathizer and his mom's got IVC from sex with too many strangers. This is God's work."

"Yeah," Beb answered with no inflection.

Joxo grabbed Beb's club and walked over to the trash bin. He tossed both of the bloodied clubs in, then jostled the garbage until they sank somewhere toward the middle.

"What about him?" Beb sounded scared.

Joxo scanned the area for moment. An idea flashed over his face.

"I saw this in a film." Joxo grinned. "As Finx Melder would say, 'This has to look like an accident.'"

Joxo reached down and lifted up Mivins's feet. He beckoned Beb to grab hold of the boy's arms. Together they hauled the corpse over to the renovation site and dropped the body onto the conveyor feeding the metal rollers of the four-wheeled machinery.

"My dad runs one of these." Joxo hopped behind the controls. "Get out of the way."

Beb stepped back from the machine as Joxo scanned the controls. A loud ignition filled the air and the heavy machinery belched itself to life. While Joxo fiddled with the controls, Beb watched as Mivins's dangling arm vibrated in unison with the machine's churning engine.

"I got it!" yelled a smiling Joxo. He punched a button and the conveyor whisked Mivins's body up into the heavy metal rollers. For a brief and sickening moment, Mivins head skittered and skipped against the rollers as clumps of hair, flesh and bone flew up into the air. All at once, the boy's corpse was snatched up into the large rollers and jammed the machinery, causing the gears to screech and whine.

Beb no longer *thought* he was going to be sick; Beb *was* sick. He turned away to vomit in the tall yellow grass as he heard Joxo triumphantly howl with mad pleasure. The sound of the grinding engine shut down. Once Beb finally straightened up to compose himself, Joxo was at his side, patting him on the back.

"What's wrong, kiddo?" Joxo smiled.

"That was really nasty." Beb shook his head.

"You know something," Joxo rubbed Beb's neck, "It was. But somebody's got to keep the devil from taking over. Mivins's whole family is full of fucked-up people who don't believe in the Cathedral, the Chieftains or any of those things that keep our way of life together. They're bad people. They don't give a fuck about God, and God doesn't give a fuck about them. So why should we care?"

"We shouldn't."

"Damn right." Joxo swatted Beb on the shoulder. "Now let's get the hell out of here before somebody wanders back here and asks us what happened. I'll see you on Solemnday at Cathedral."

Beb and Joxo quietly jogged back down the long alley. When they reached the end, they shook hands and Joxo went into the store for candy and sportcards.

Meanwhile, the pages of Mivins's books continued to flap in the lazy early evening breeze.

XXII.

YBS Studios.

"Hello. It's the bottom of the hour and I'm Egs Bloyt with the latest news. World renowned actor and six-time Golden Icon winner Finx Melder is dead tonight…the victim of a one-vehicle accident. He was thirty-six. You're looking at a live shot of Finx Melder's sports vehicle as it protrudes from a blazing fuel tank. As you can see, firefighters and rescue workers are on the scene, but both Finx Melder and his companion, world champion sand surfer Preppi Deyz have been confirmed dead. Witnesses say that Melder, known for his fast-paced life-style, was traveling at a high rate of speed when he lost control of his vehicle, crashed through a barricade and flew over an embankment into the giant fuel tank, resulting in a huge explosion.

"It has not been determined whether Melder, known almost as much for his addiction to drugs as his brilliance as a performer, was under the influence of any foreign substances. Though we now have reports from leaks close to Melder that he had failed to attend any of his scheduled drug-counseling sessions over the past few weeks, and many described him as seeming sluggish and disoriented at a recent charity function several days ago.

"Meanwhile, the world is in shock and mourning this evening. We'll have more news on this catastrophic tragedy as information becomes available on this YBS station. Now, stay tuned for *Nailing the Newsmaker* with Libbi Trullup and her very special guest, our Deliveress and First Lady, Mrs. Panla Jen Tem."

The lights dimmed over the sitting news anchor until all that was visible was a shadowy silhouette of her swirling mane, her padded shoulders and a pair of feminine hands busying themselves over a darkened desk prop.

The cameras panned left to an adjacent, illuminated studio set where the figures of two well-dressed women, sitting across from each other in cushioned, swivel arm-chairs, scrolled into view.

A powerful militaristic drum solo broke the momentary silence. Then it flowed, all too smartly, into a contemporary, up-tempo woodwind jazz melody.

Simultaneously, the standard YBS network letters tumbled from all directions to the center of the screen. With choreographed computerized precision, the letters metamorphasized into lavishly self-important fonts, spelling the word

"Newsmaker" with the faces of famous figures superimposed within each letter. Then, with the staccato explosions of an automatic rifle, large grey nails shot into the "Newsmaker" word, impaling its letters to a stony reddish background. Finally, a metallic mass of nails crawled into view, arranging themselves to complete the animated logo for *Nailing the Newsmaker*.

As the music reached a crescendo and the visual was firmly etched into the viewers' minds, a booming, authoritative, grandfatherly baritone stated: "This is Nailing the Newsmaker. And here is our host, news commentator Libbi Trullup."

On cue, Libbi's brash, irreverent smile faded into view as she assertively engaged the camera.

"Hey, World. Good evening." she began. "I'm Libbi Trullup, and welcome to another edition of *Nailing the Newsmaker*. Our guest today is perhaps the single most influential person on the planet. She is married to our sitting Accommodant, Klin Tem. And she is also the spiritual leader of the world's Cathedral. All this, and she's obnoxiously beautiful and not even thirty-five twinmoons old. I'd like to welcome Deliveress Panla Jen to our program.

"Welcome, Mrs. Tem." Libbi extended her hand.

"Thank you." Panla smiled warmly, taking Libbi's fingers. "I'm pleased to be here."

"Well, we'll see." Libbi wisecracked and threw a knowing glance to the camera. "But first I'd like to offer my condolences to the families of Finx Melder and Preppi Deyz who died in a horrible accident earlier today in the northeast quadrosphere. They were both such beautiful and talented people. I don't think the world will ever recover from their loss.

"Did you know either of them, Mrs. Tem?"

"I really didn't know Miss Deyz at all." Panla fielded the question with minimal, obligatory interest. "But I understand she was a marvelous athlete. And, of course, we're all familiar with the work of Finx Melder. I have to agree. They'll both be missed tremendously."

"You never met Finx Melder, though?"

"I believe my husband met him a couple of times, but I never had the pleasure." Panla answered flatly. "I do recall that the Accommodant was most impressed with Mr. Melder's creativity."

"I met Finx once." Libbi smiled and rolled her eyes. "But I won't get into what we got into. A very, very creative man, indeed."

Panla nodded respectfully.

"Oh, I'm sorry." Libbi popped herself on the side of the head with the heel of her hand. "Here I go again. The most powerful woman in the world and you're probably wondering what kind of bimbo are you stuck with for the next hour."

"No. They told me." Panla finally met her eyes with a glint of PJ's mischief.

"Ohhh. Touché, Mrs. Tem." Libbi offered the camera a devilish smirk. "Touché. Well now that we know that we're both bitches, I guess we should get on with it."

"By all means." Panla's face subtly intensified.

"By the way, for all the wonderful religious people out there, yes, I know I just called the Deliveress a bitch, but it was only in jest, so spare us all the sanctimonious tears and jeers. It was only a joke. Get it?"

"I've been called worse," Panla added.

"And on this program!" Libbi chuckled, patting Panla on the leg.

Panla kept her hands folded in her lap and smiled pleasantly.

"So what's this whole Break thing about?" Libbi jumped into her first question.

"Well it's pretty well-documented that there's a radical faction who disagrees with the precepts of the Cathedral," Panla answered. "They feel that God and religion are just a contrived means by which the repression of individual freedoms has been institutionalized."

"Well, isn't it? I mean, I'm not saying it's all bad, but isn't most of it just stuff that was made up centuries ago and then we got locked into this pattern of trying to uphold a bunch of outdated morals and ideals? I mean, why should we believe in the Chieftains? Weren't they just a bunch of guys who claimed to have had some sort of religious experience? And didn't they really use their tale of some meeting with God to put the world under their heel?"

"Well, first, the Chieftains were more than a 'bunch of guys.'" Panla's demeanor became very serious. "At that time, they were the nine great warlords who ruled the hubs of ancient civilization—each bent on destroying the others so that his kingdom could grow by conquest. But on the same morning, spread hundreds of kilometers apart, God spoke to each of them in their own native dialects, and instructed them to meet at the Temple of Chry by four nightfalls. There was no mass communication in those days. There was no physical way that any godlike impostor or fleet of impostors could have spanned the globe in a single day and unerringly convinced each Chieftain where and when the Lord's Summit would take place. And each was forewarned that if any one Chieftain failed to attend, God would destroy the entire world. Not even the shrewdest charlatan would have gambled on those stakes. Thus, the only plausible explanation for what really happened is that they were each individually summoned by God Himself. And so they came."

"Right. They came and they schemed out this really ingenious way to rule the world by consortium." Libbi chided with a rambling lack of respect.

"God instructed them," Panla continued, "to carry His law back to their people or face the destruction of the world. These nine most powerful warlords returned to their lands, not as conquerors, but as teachers. Instructors in the word of God. They put down their swords, gave away all their wealth and chose to rule only through the wisdom God had imparted to them. Three of their kingdoms collapsed into anarchy when the subjects saw that they would no longer be ruled through brutality and coercion. All but a couple of the Chieftains ultimately died deposed and penniless. Why would these powerful men who held the world in their hands do this to themselves if the instruction of God had not been written on their hearts? Were they mad? I think not. The only logical explanation is that they really did receive God's word at the Chry Temple."

"That, or those Chieftains suckered themselves into a really bad plan." Libbi tossed her witty skepticism to the viewing audience.

"You could try to look at it that way." Panla gestured. "But you have to understand the history of the Chieftains' relationships with one another during that time. Muntor, the strongest Chieftain with the most fertile lands and the most powerful army was one of those Chieftains who died destitute. Months before the Lord's Summit, his soldiers killed Baloni's son during what was considered a routine border skirmish. In retaliation, Baloni had Muntor's wife and four daughters kidnapped, slaughtered and gutted. He sent the butchered remains back to Muntor in a beast-drawn wagon that took four days to deliver the rotting mutilated corpses, ravaged by scavengers along the way, back to Muntor's territory.

"Overcome by grief, hatred and a lust for revenge, Muntor swore that he would have Baloni's head by twinmoon's end. And he literally had all the means to crush Baloni and his small army whenever he chose to. Muntor had no incentive to make peace with anyone. His personal seers told him that the death of his family was actually a sign that he should wage war on the entire world, starting with the annihilation of Baloni and all of his subjects. The only thing that interceded to save Baloni and his people from a savage genocide was the Lord's Summit. If you were Muntor, only God could have made you sit down, forgive and make peace with the murderer of your wife and daughters, when a bloody vengeance and world domination would have been so much simpler and so much more rewarding."

"Oh, but come on, Mrs. Tem." Libbi shrugged and shook her head, "We really don't know what happened at that temple. All we have is the word of these Nine Chieftains, their writings and their so-called laws."

"And we have their actions," Panla added. "The nine most powerful men in the world have a meeting, and, as a result, choose to throw away every object and belief they've ever lived for in favor of a philosophy of love, peace and obedience to our Lord in Heaven. A philosophy that rails against hedonism, violence and materialism, the very principles upon which their kingdoms had been built. I submit to you, that none of the Chieftains, collectively or individually, were equipped with either the rationale or the inclination to adopt such a totally foreign philosophy without divine illumination. Before the Lord's Summit, this planet had never seen an ideology that approached the notion of a free and peaceful monotheistic world. That God spoke to these warring, conquering, barbaric warlords, as they claimed is the only way that any of what followed makes any sense at all."

"True. But then, we could use the notion of God to explain just about anything we can't explain." Libbi smiled condescendingly. "I mean, why don't men like to talk after having sex? Is that God telling them to roll over and snore like a hump-backed swine? Maybe."

Panla was stunned by how Libbi so frivolously unraveled the pertinence of their discussion. Moreover, she wondered how a mass audience could just as easily digest this bawdy banter over a truly meaningful dialogue. But then she considered her husband's campaign for the Accommodancy: A six-month parade of specious buzz words and hollow catch phrases that somehow enthralled the voting masses. That, and she thought of the world's most popular contemporary entertainment form, the sex-com: bawdy, enabling half-hour satellite vignettes, which beckoned the slacking amoral public to mindlessly chuckle itself into witless slumber every evening.

"And speaking of sex," Libbi played on the moment, "what's wrong with premarital sex? Isn't the position of the Cathedral just a tad archaic? I mean, sex is the most important thing a married couple has. And, presumably, the person you marry is the only person you're going to sleep with for the rest of your life, right?" Libbi winked aside to the camera. "So don't people owe it to themselves to choose the right sex partner? And isn't premarital sex the only way you can really be sure?"

"Well, I have to disagree with you. First of all, sex isn't the most important element in a marriage."

"It's not?" Libbi's mouth dropped open. "Well it's certainly the most important part of being single, I'll tell you that!"

"Really, Libbi, I can recommend a good cathedral for you." Panla patted her on the arm.

"That's okay." Libbi tossed back her hair. "Church guys are too tense for me. The single ones, anyway. Of course, after a few twinmoons of being cooped up with their little missionary maids, the married ones can be pretty wild. But then, afterwards, they lay their whole religious guilt trip on you. Run, girls! Thanks, but been there."

Panla smiled and nodded, more in acknowledgment of the humor than in commiseration with Libbi's depraved sentiment. After a slight pause, she plowed on with her thought.

"Love is actually the most important element," Panla said calmly. "Anyone could have superlative sex with a prostitute, but love would never enter into the equation. The client satiates his or her lust, the whores satiate their bank accounts and that would be the whole of it. Sex, plain and simple. But love is found in the heart, mind and soul, not in the burning lust of our loins."

Libbi wiggled in her seat and smiled.

"The problem with premarital sex," Panla continued, "is that you have all these people believing that sex is the key, when, in fact, sex is the trap. When you're constantly trying to trade up for that perfect sex partner, how do you ever know when to stop?"

"Don't ask me," Libbi deadpanned. "Trade up. Trade down. Right now, I just wish I had something to trade."

"But how often do you see sex partners force themselves through an otherwise incompatible relationship because they've fallen dependent upon good sex? Or how often do you see people fool themselves into believing that love *is* sex, only to find that when the sex runs its course, it's time to fall in love with someone else?"

Libbi's confident smile remained frozen across her face, though the light in her eyes dimmed slightly.

"God's law is designed to protect all of us from ourselves," Panla stated. "To lust is mortal nature. None of us are immune. But God says that unless you honestly love a person and are willing to commit to this person for the rest of your life *first*, then having sex with that person is nothing other than a selfish abuse of one of God's greatest gifts. Love is more than a passing fondness, fancy or obsession. What makes love the most enduring, beautiful force in our universe is that it is a commitment. And what is a commitment but a promise? And what is the

ultimate promise but one that is made to God? And if you should make this ultimate pledge for a permanent union with another person, should this not be called
a marriage? Certainly, anything beneath so high a covenant is nothing other than
soul rendering, self-indulgent abuse."

"So, you're telling me," Libbi tilted her head, "that the only man you've ever
had sex with is your husband."

"That's correct." Panla nodded.

"No playing medical in the bushes after study hall at grammar school?" Libbi
rubbed her chin. "No wild partying in the boys' locker room shower after a big
win? No series of alcoholic binge sleepovers in the campus frat houses? No regret-
table road trip with your ex-boyfriend and six of his horny buddies that your girlfriends warned you not to go on?"

"I'm afraid not." Panla smiled, shaking her head.

"Whew! Me neither." Libbi grinned and winked at the camera once more. "At
least, not twice. Live and learn, I say."

"Twice would certainly be excessive," Panla answered light-heartedly.

"Yeah, well, a girl's gotta uphold her reputation." Libbi nodded. "Especially
when you get around like I do."

"I'll pray for you."

"Don't do that, Queen Mother." Libbi held up her hands and pleaded. "Every
time a member of the clergy prays for a woman, she winds up pregnant."

There were a few audible chuckles from behind the cameras.

"But seriously," Libbi turned to Panla, "I respect the fact that you say you've
only been with one man. I don't get it, but I respect it. Why does it bother you
when I tell you that I've been with, uhh, more than one man?"

"It doesn't bother me."

"But you said you'd pray for me. Obviously, you disapprove."

"It's not for me to approve or disapprove," Panla clarified. "God is the only
one who can make those determinations. I said I would pray for you because I
know that God does not approve of such behavior, and I would hope that anyone
stranded outside the arc of His Word would find salvation before it's too late."

"God doesn't approve?" Libbi frowned. "Who are you to say what God does
or does not approve of?

"I'm the Deliveress." Panla stated with royal confidence. "But beyond that,
before that, I was a student of the Text. I diligently studied God's word and
applied it to my everyday life. And when I followed His path, I seemed to always
find myself feeling much better about this life and the world we live in. Whatever
the outcome, I could sleep soundly knowing and trusting that I'd acted within

the Lord's commandments. But whenever I stepped outside of His word, I always found myself sad or angry or confused or hemmed in by trying to serve the things of this world rather than He. That's a lonely abandoned feeling I wouldn't wish on anyone. Not even you, Ms. Trullup. That's why I pray for you…and everyone."

"Well, you certainly are the Deliveress." Libbi appeared unmoved. "But the fact remains that there is a huge world out here that's becoming increasingly disenchanted with the reins the Cathedral has tried to place on individual freedoms. In particular, the freedoms of women. If a man steps out of bounds, people might say it's wrong, but they forgive him because he's a man. But when a woman steps out of bounds, whatever out of bounds really is, she's branded, labeled and sometimes ostracized by society. Why can't females have it the same way males do?"

"First of all, you're talking about secular standards." Panla explained. "I certainly do agree with you that society places a double standard on masculine and feminine virtues or the lack thereof. But the Text doesn't make any such distinction between the genders. God doesn't differentiate between the fornication of males versus the fornication of females. Sin is sin, regardless.

"Of course, when you speak on the rights of women to be equally as sinful as men, and judged accordingly, I find it tragic that in this world we live in today, females believe that there's only one thing worse than being a whore and that's being a virgin. Chastity has been convoluted into a synonym for cowardice and it's really quite sad. I wish more young women could realize how society is goading them into self-exploitation like calves to the slaughter. They should understand that secular society's spiritual misery certainly wants all the company it can find and that their corruption only enables the jealous corrupters."

Libbi shrugged as if Panla had spoken to her in a foreign language.

"And, while I'm on the subject," Panla continued, "I also take great exception to the liberated notions of the modern female who believes that she has to work like a man, earn income like a man and wrestle for the top position in the bunk in order to assert her value."

"Mrs. Tem, this is a family show," Libbi playfully reprimanded.

"The modern female proclaims her equality only when she grapples successfully with males on traditionally male turf. Yet it's most often these same modern females who are more lost and confused as to their blurred identities within our society than any other faction. The traditional female understands her role very plainly and begs only that her vast, unquantifiable contributions not be devalued for mere lack of a salary. And you certainly don't see males losing any sleep over a desire to annex traditional female roles. Only the modern liberated female can't figure out what portions of her self-worth lie within her family or within her business portfolio. Hence, she becomes the proverbial mistress of all trades and a master of none. Neurosis and insecurity follow hard upon the condition."

"Well, listen to you. You should write a book." Libbi flipped back her hair again.

"Too many have been written on the topic already," Panla answered. "It's an abhorrently prolific industry considering the fact that their rabidly devoted female patronage never do manage to properly right themselves. They just hop and skip from journal to journal, scratching for secular answers to the aching in their souls...all the while, lining the pockets of publishers who flourish on the tautology of conflicting resolutions. If any of these self-help scribblings ever actually amounted to a resolution, it'd cost the publishing houses a hundred billion coin. That's why they don't want to print Texts anymore. Because they know that the Text is the only self-help any of us really need. Unfortunately, an increasing number of people's Texts are being used more as decorative antiques than for practical application."

"Well, there goes the whole self-help industry down in flames." Libbi snickered. "Tens of thousands of our most learned, educated counseling professionals can't possibly be right."

"We do live in a time where the wisest people in the world are the greatest fools." Panla met her eyes.

Libbi paused for a moment and tried to ingest the comment, then she merely reclaimed her assertive facade and smiled broadly as if she had won the exchange. "'Fools.'" Libbi sounded disappointed. "Don't you think addressing people in those terms is just a bit beneath you? And don't you think you're being just a tad judgmental?"

"I don't think it's beneath me to point out that scholars who believe that mortality holds dominion over itself is a foolish notion," Panla said. "As creatures of free will, we choose our path, but only God can choose our destiny. Anyone who claims otherwise is either a fool or in collusion with the devil."

"Sort of a narrow view, don't you think?" Libbi questioned.

"When I think of things that are narrow, I think of things that are well-focused," Panla responded. "There shouldn't be any shame in being focused upon a faith that makes sense."

"Hmm. Well, when I think of narrow, I think of someone who's very limited."

"Are there no limits?" Panla queried.

"Only the ones we place on ourselves," Libbi smiled proudly.

"Very well." Panla leaned back in her chair.

"Oh, c'mon. You don't agree with that."

"No."

"So you're judging again, aren't you?" Libbi accused. "Religious people just can't stop judging. It's like you're not secure unless you're tearing someone else down. This may be a stupid question, but don't you see anything wrong with being so judgmental?"

"Yes."

Libbi lurched backward in amazement.

"That is, if I were being judgmental," Panla continued. "It's wrong for any person to condemn. Only God can do that. But it would also be irrational for me to fail to acknowledge fundamental differences between right and wrong."

"Yeah, but see, how can you say what's right and what's wrong?"

"I don't say what's right and what's wrong. That would make me like all the other amoral anarchists out there making up their own rules. No, I let God tell me what's right or wrong and respond accordingly."

"So when your God tells you to hate homosexuals, then its okay," Libbi challenged.

"God doesn't tell me to hate homosexuals."

"Then I suppose you love them?"

"Very much, as a matter of fact."

"Oh Mrs. Tem…please!" Libbi scoffed. "I've heard your comments. I've read your quotes in the media. The Cathedral's position against the homosexual lifestyle is well documented."

"The Cathedral is opposed to the lifestyle, but it has nothing to do with hate." Panla clarified. "Again, the Text tells us that males with males and females with females is unseemly in the eyes of God. And I concur because it is impossible to build enduring families through such relationships. Historically, they have always been a breeding ground for rampant infidelity which leads to virulent strains of incurable diseases. Frankly, it doesn't take a theologian to see the inherent biological and sociological pitfalls involved."

"But why is it any of your business what they do? Can't you just do your monogamous missionary thing and leave other people, who want to experience life a different way, alone?"

"As if we don't occupy the same planet?" Panla shook her head. "As if we don't occupy the same neighborhoods? The same medicals? The same workplaces? The same society? Would that that were true. But as much as some wish to deny it, all of our lives are inherently intermingled on more levels than we can calculate. The impact of our individual behaviors is not limited to the few or the individual, but to everyone. The harm they do to themselves, and it is harm, affects all of us…medically, financially, culturally, spiritually, etcetera. There's no getting around it."

"So if you're so worried about diseases affecting the whole planet, why do you oppose funding for IVC research?"

Perturbation flickered through Panla's expression.

"The Cathedral does not oppose funding for Internal Viral Consumption," Panla said sternly. "We oppose the proportion of funding that goes to this sexually transmitted, fatal disease, when there are myriad other deadly, unpreventable illnesses which are getting shoved aside because they don't have the strong media outlets that IVC does. Cellular Inertance continues to be the number-one malignancy on our planet and has been for the last two centuries. And while scientists have developed many drugs to treat CI and slow its progression, we're still fighting to figure out what genetic codes trigger the illness and what treatments will lead to a complete cure. On the other hand, IVC is a totally preventable illness that effects roughly ten percent of the proportion of people who will someday suffer from CI. Yet IVC receives an equal amount of government funding for drugs, research and hospices. It's a horribly unfair practice and the Cathedral simply can't in good conscience, support this disparity."

"Does this have anything to do with the fact that your own father died of CI?" Libbi feigned a sympathetic tone.

"No." Panla showed little emotion. "I loved my father dearly. But I'm the Deliveress. It would be unconscionable for me to elevate my personal interests above the Cathedral's."

"Then you aren't concerned with the fact that IVC is a readily transmittable disease that's rapidly becoming the world's newest plague?"

"My dear, let's not prevaricate," Panla corrected her. "IVC is not readily transmittable. It's sexually transmittable. The only way you get it is through intercourse or some other form of prolonged intimate contact with someone's genitalia. And the only reason it's spreading so quickly is because of the sociological shifts we're seeing in sexual mores toward more open and promiscuous sexual relationships."

"So because it's a sexually-transmitted disease, the people who die from it are somehow, less important," Libbi grimly concluded.

"That's not true." Panla became mildly annoyed. "No one is less important. But we are talking about people who willfully engage in reprobate behaviors knowing full well what the consequences could be. IVC has no cure, but monogamy, if not abstinence, goes a long way toward the prevention of this disease. Intelligent, moral, preemptive behavior is the cure. Certainly, if you offered such an option to the millions of CI victims around the world, most would gladly choose whatever measure of avoidance necessary to keep from cutting their lives short.

"But the even greater irony here, is that Cathedral missionaries were the first to petition the government for grants toward the research of IVC. That was about twenty twinmoons ago when the disease was running rampant through the impoverished southern townships. Nobody cared then. It was considered an illness of the poor and the ignorant. I even remember being appalled by discussions of natural selection by so-called scholars and members of the media. But then the virus found its way into the decadent lives of our entertainment community, and, quickly, everything changed. Once popular entertainers started contracting and dying from IVC, finding a cure suddenly became an urgent worldwide obsession. Celebrity benefits and foundations dedicated to the eradication of IVC have become a multi-billion coin industry. Every fundraising effort is a public spectacle. And the government has nearly been extorted into accountability to do its share, so naturally, against the balance of reason, it has accommodated.

"Meanwhile, the Cathedral thought it saw an opportunity to reinforce the Lord's wisdom regarding sexual conduct and the logic of personal responsibility. It made perfect sense that if people conducted their private affairs as God has asked us to, we might isolate and possibly eradicate the disease. Unfortunately, the Cathedral's view was impugned by our irreligious rivals as another impractical attempt to impose its will on the freedoms of the masses. God's way meant calling one's self into accountability for one's own behavior. A cure, on the other hand, would allow society to continue embracing the popular media culture's ideal of wantonness and vacant secular agnosticism."

"Hmm" was all Libbi could muster. The meat of Panla's answer sailed past her, but she managed to take hold of the tail of it, and construct another question.

"Now what do you mean when you talk about the media culture?"

Panla glared momentarily, then reached forward and picked up the glass of water set aside for her. She took a short sip and regathered herself. She knew the producers deplored prolonged pauses, but this was her way of protesting Libbi's tactic of covering her lack of comprehension by contriving new questions from Panla's answers.

Deliberately, Panla placed the glass back onto the table and straightened the hem of her dress at the knee. "I apologize." Panla smiled. "This is a talk show. I thought you'd do more of the talking."

Libbi blinked twice; she was still trying to organize Panla's previous answer in her mind. By the time she realized she'd been insulted, Panla had picked up where she'd left off.

"This may surprise some people, but I have nothing against technology or uncensored mass communication," Panla finally answered. "Obviously, they're wonderful tools that are making everyone's lives much safer, and information more accessible. But I deplore the use of these tools by the media and entertainment communities to warp and propagandize our world's values for sheer profit. It's not enough that they peddle sexual and material fantasies. The danger lies in seducing an audience into believing that no level of selfish excess is wrong. That greed and capriciousness are virtuous aspirations for anyone truly seeking to maximize their potential. The media culture takes our basest desires and invites us into a guiltless partnership with moral anarchy. Moral anarchy that does little else but fill the very coffers of the media/entertainment industries."

"As opposed to the coffers of the Cathedral." Libbi shook her head, smiling into the camera "Sca-ry. Pick your poison. So where do words like patience, forgiveness and tolerance fit into the picture? I'm hearing a lot of dogma, but I don't seem to hear much of these other ideals one might attribute to the Cathedral."

"Well at the risk of sounding cliché, patience certainly is a virtue," Panla answered. "To say that none of us should ever be patient with one another presumes that none of us should ever require the patience of someone else. It's easy to become frustrated with someone's ignorance..."

"Like mine?" Libbi baited.

"I don't find you frustrating," Panla smiled warmly. "A bit challenging, but I would never lose patience with you. Just as a child learns to make judgments as it matures, so, too, do we all continue to learn and grow, intellectually and spiritually, at our own pace. Along the way, we all falter and stagger and stumble while others seem to breeze past without a care. But in the long run, we take our turns at leaping ahead or falling behind. That's why universal patience is an absolute necessity.

"Likewise, as imperfect creatures, if we are to be forgiven by God, and we all must be for our daily transgressions, conscious or otherwise, we should also exhibit a willingness to forgive anyone who transgresses against us. Even our enemies. Especially our enemies."

"Do you forgive members of the Break even though they hate your guts and want to tear down everything you stand for?"

"I forgive them because, like all of us in our willful transgressions, they simply know not what they do," Panla said solemnly.

"Even Rabbel Mennis?" Libbi frowned. "I get the impression that if he were sitting with us right now, he'd jump across this set and wring your neck. He's as much as said so."

"Anyone can forgive a friend." Panla pushed back her bangs. "But God asks that we forgive and love our enemies as well. This requires a great deal of strength. But if you've ever looked into the eyes of someone who has knowingly, intentionally wronged you and said, 'I love you and I forgive you,' their reaction is usually all the proof you need that the Lord's word is true. Certainly, it's much more disarming than saying 'I hate you too.' Think about it."

"Unless, of course, that person," Libbi grinned, "is a violent ex-boyfriend who's been stalking you for the past six months, in which case, 'I hate you' would have to be the appropriate response, along with a heavy dose of acid spray and a swift kick you-know-where!"

The production crew, again, burst into laughter.

"Seriously ladies," Libbi continued, "if you ever f...screw up and use the L-word during sex, make sure you have that acid spray handy for your getaway. Believe me! It beats having to hide in a witness protection program later on. My god, I had to wear a mustache and coveralls to work for nearly a month, remember that? Met some cute policers, though. It was almost worth it, but not quite. Anyway, where were we?"

Libbi paused a moment and riffled through her cards. "Okay. Patience, forgiveness, tolerance. You've skated around the first two. What about tolerance? Do you consider yourself tolerant?"

"Not particularly." Panla met her eyes.

"You answer that as if you think that's a good thing." Libbi sounded accusatory.

"Not all things necessary appear good to our mortal sensibilities," Panla stated. "Being tolerant sounds nice, but in its truest context, it means that a person who is tolerant must accept things that are contrary without challenge. To endure any and all things with no measure to the Lord's word is an utter contradiction to the laws of evangelism. There is no virtue in tolerance for the sheer sake of being tolerant. Tolerance for those who rail against the traditional family unit? Tolerance for those who believe that freedom is an end instead of a means? Tolerance for the liars who misrepresent God to the masses? Tolerance to a media that tilts or embellishes every other truth? Tolerance for the pridefully ignorant? Tolerance for the intellectually vain? Tolerance for those who monger the recreational abuses of alcohol and drugs? Tolerance for a government too impotent to stand up for things it knows are right?"

"Impotent?" Libbi smiled and rolled her eyes. "An interesting choice of words to describe our government by our own First Lady. Is there something you care to elaborate on, Mrs. Tem?"

There were a few stifled chuckles in the studio followed by what seemed like an eternity of silence.

On the inside, Panla was mortified. To this point she'd given a virtuoso performance, deftly, if not eloquently, fielding every challenge and distraction Libbi Trullup had conjured against her. Now she had handed her adversarial host a better weapon from her own mouth than anything Libbi had been able to manufacture on her own.

"I'm sorry, but since you brought up the subject, you have to admit that by reputation, impotence is not one of the Accommodant's shortcomings." Libbi drilled the topic for all it was worth.

"Dear, I was making a figurative reference to our tolerance for the government's political posture on pertinent subject matters." Panla didn't appear to struggle. "And I think its important to note that the word tolerance never, once, appears in the Text."

"That's great," Libbi fanned her hand, "but what do you make of all the stories surrounding your husband's sex life, which of course includes your sex life, I'd imagine."

Panla didn't feel the humiliation Libbi was hoping for. She'd privately resigned herself to the failings of her marriage twinmoons ago. And the media had already publicly made substantiated ridicule of their relationship, citing evidence of the Accommodant's numerous ongoing affairs. But the fact that many of her Cathedral loyalists had chosen to show public embarrassment on her behalf made it a horrifically unwieldy subject. She had expected something like this, but no prepared answer or statement could easily tidy her image as a wife, misused.

"My husband and I continue to work on our marital issues," Panla finally stated.

"Together?" Libbi's eyes brightened facetiously.

"Yes," Panla answered firmly, "together. It's very hard to do in public life, but despite what the media thinks it sees and hears, we're very committed to each other."

"Do you ever see any strange women around your husband at weird hours in the mansion and wonder who they are?" Libbi probed deeper.

"I know everyone who enters the premises." Panla contained her displeasure with the line of questioning. "There's nothing strange about anyone, that I've observed."

"Everybody's strange, Queen Mother." Libbi touched Panla on the wrist. "You've only been with one guy, but trust me, they are. "And speaking of trust, how do you keep tabs on him; know what he's up to when you're so busy yourself?"

"I don't keep tabs on my husband." Panla's voice became terse. "I trust him. A marriage without trust is no marriage at all."

"So he's promised you that he's not going to fool around anymore and that's good enough, or you just don't want to know?" Libbi put on her face of false journalistic concern.

"He hasn't promised anything. I trust him. That's it." Panla tried to bury the subject.

"Well, some people think you should just leave his sorry ass and run for the Accommodancy yourself."

"I understand their sentiment." Panla fought to hold her composure. "But I believe in my marriage. And, aside from that, I already have a title. I don't think the Deliverancy and the Accommodancy could ever be occupied by a single person. Dutiful service to one would invariably lead to neglect of the other."

"Interesting." Libbi shuffled her notecards. "So how do you and your husband co-exist philosophically with agendas that are so radically different?"

"Well I wouldn't say they're radically different," Panla offered. "The Accommodancy is assigned to preserve the planet and accommodate the will of the people. The Deliverancy is assigned to preserve God's will on the planet and save as many souls as possible. In the end, we both serve the betterment of our world."

"True," Libbi's brows danced, "but what about times like now, when the will of the people comes into conflict with what you say is God's will? People are looking to experiment and grow in areas that the Cathedral disagrees with. Who prevails in that situation?"

"The law of the land says that the people may choose any direction they wish for themselves," Panla acknowledged. "It's the Accommodant's job to see that this happens. Still, the laws of God remain constant. My job is to prevail upon the world the importance of upholding those laws."

"So you and Mr. Tem don't fight over the passage of laws like the substance legalization bill?" Libbi wondered.

"We have our spirited discussions, but in the end, it makes no difference what we say to each other. It's a matter of what society chooses for itself that must be accommodated."

"But didn't you once say that the people don't know what's good for them?"

"I believe I said that the masses don't always know what's good for them," Panla clarified. "This is especially true when God is excluded from the decision process."

"So you, in effect, don't believe the people are capable of making decisions for themselves without the Text," Libbi concluded. "Aren't you then, advocating some sort of theocracy?"

"Absolutely not. Theocracies don't work," Panla stated flatly. "There have been a few instances in our history where Deliverers seized governmental control by 'divine right' and tried to force the doctrines of the Cathedral down the world's throat by military force. Predictably, what they got was a hideous and bloody series of revolutions followed by centuries of irreligious secularism. I firmly believe that society belongs to the people, but I assert that the people belong to God. Hence, the only way God's blessing shall have dominion over society, is if society chooses to accept it. Through enlightenment, not coercion, the world must choose its Lord. Otherwise, only Hell can truly reign."

"Divine rights." Libbi flipped over another card. "I always hear that phrase used in describing the Deliverancy. What is that, exactly?"

"The Ascension of Divinity, or divine rights, as they're commonly referred to, was instituted by Bius II. It links the succession of the Deliverancy directly to the Nine Chieftains who met with God and chose the first Deliverer. It affirms that God's will on the planet will be done through the Deliverancy. Whatever a Deliverer shall bind in this world, shall be bound in Heaven. It also asserts the divinity of the Regents and Churchlords as the layman's conduit to our Lord in Heaven. Obedience and prayer to them are necessary to gain God's grace."

"So you think, as Deliveress, that you are, in effect, a direct descendent of God?" Libbi leaned back and rubbed her chin with the tip of her finger.

"No. I think of myself more as a curator of God's office," Panla replied modestly. "Overseeing that God's will is properly conveyed."

"According to Addendum? Text? Voices? What?" Libbi gestured.

"Sorry, dear. I haven't heard any voices." Panla fashioned a warm, but admonishing expression. "But the Text and the Addendums are the keys."

"And what if, as we often hear, the two conflict?"

"It doesn't happen at all with the proper interpretations," Panla responded

"And, if all else fails, you can just make up your own Addendum, isn't that right?" Libbi smirked. "Bind your own opinions in Heaven according to doctrine?"

"I haven't done that."

"But you could."

"I choose not to."

"Why? Most of the other Deliverers have. Why not leave your stamp on God's word like everyone else?"

"Because the point is not to leave my stamp on God's word. It's to see that God's word is interpreted and disseminated in the context for which it was intended."

"But isn't every scripture open to interpretation?"

"Poor interpretation, certainly."

"But who decides what's poor? And please don't say 'God does.'" Libbi tilted her head and swiveled in her chair.

"Unfortunately, interpretation is left to mortal minds." Panla picked up her glass of water. "But for hearts that are true and minds that are learned, poor interpretation is never an issue."

"Hmm. You don't sound like any other Deliverer I've ever heard or read about." Libbi smiled. "Believe me, that's a good thing. But then some charge that you aren't exactly the traditionalist you should be."

"Well, every Deliverer has had his or her critics, Ms. Trullup." Panla placed her glass back onto the table. "I think that some are resentful that I head the Cathedral but reside in the Accommodant's Mansion with my husband. It's an unusual circumstance. All I can say is that I wasn't about to get a divorce just because Klin won the election. And I certainly wasn't going to abdicate my holy responsibilities to the Cathedral either. Frankly, I think the arrangement has been beneficial to both institutions. There's certainly a great deal more empathy between the two now than there ever has been."

"True." Libbi smiled. "And at least now, when the Deliveress says she's getting screwed by the Accommodant, we can take it literally. At least, I hope so."

Without forethought, Panla released an audible sigh and fell back in her chair, recrossing her legs.

"Losing patience with me yet, Mrs. Tem?" Libbi rolled her eyes at the camera and smiled again.

"No." Panla shot her a piercing stare.

"No, but the last person who looked at me like that, I had to take out a restraining order against." Libbi popped her eyebrows up and down. "I thank you for your patience."

"Don't mention it," Panla answered dryly, but tried to soften her expression.

"Okay. So now that I've totally pissed you off, I'm going to switch to an easy question that we're hearing echoed throughout the world. How can the church assert that their way is the only way? Aren't there many paths to God?"

"That's two questions, dear." Panla found PJ's affable mischief.

"See!" Libbi sat up in her chair and gestured playfully. "I was trying to be nice!" Libbi gave a wicked stare toward someone off camera. "Oh, it's a little late, my director just said to me. Fine. Take her side. Are you trying to hit on the Deliveress? You better not be. God'll strike you dead. And if he doesn't, I will. "Now where were we?" Libbi straightened her blouse.

"You asked me how the church could assert that there's only one way to God," Panla paraphrased.

"Oh, that's right," Libbi sneered off-camera, then smiled pleasantly to Panla.

"Well that sounds nice," Panla started her answer. "God is so large and all encompassing and the world is filled with so many possibilities. Certainly there must be many ways to touch Him, to know Him, to reach the many facets of His glory. But scripture tells us that there is only one way...His way. And all other paths lead to destruction. It's like a great labyrinth wherein only one path leads to the center. All other pathways, long and short, may take you somewhere, but eventually they lead to a dead end.

"Some people feel that life should be lived for material prosperity. Monitor our bank balances and investments and we'll always be well. But have you ever tried to buy happiness? The pleasure of purchase has a very short lifespan. Consider the parable of the man who is given everything in the world he asks for. God gives it to him. But the man is never satisfied with what he has because he's constantly yearning for things he doesn't have. Eventually, the man becomes so sickly obsessed with his fear of losing all the possessions he's amassed that he finally begs the Lord to take it all away and end his miserable, insatiable life. Wealth and possessions can't fulfill us.

"Some of us try to use career to fulfill us. But what are mortal accomplishments in the infinite spectrum of the universe? Less than nothing! And does God favor the fortunate over the unfortunate? Does God rank us on our secular promotions or successes? Does a failure in our career place us farther from the love and glory of God? I think not."

Libbi frowned and nervously bit a nail.

"Some of us try to fill ourselves up through sexual gratification," Panla continued, "but what does this physical act mean to God? Are we esteemed by the creator through the mindless ecstasy of our flesh? Sex is a gift from God, yes! One to be shared by loving married people. But why would the creator of all things measure us by such pleasure? And are people who measure their own happiness through sex really fulfilled as living souls? By what reason would God see them as such? None, most likely.

"And, of course, we have people who try to define their happiness and existence through affirmation from the majority. Yet what should we do when we find ourselves scorned by the majority, alone and separated from the majority by some personal dilemma or insight? There comes a time when all people must walk alone with only the Lord to guide them. People are wonderful, but they are not so lofty a sentience that we should invest all of our trust in them. That must be reserved for our Lord in Heaven. Only the path He offers us leads to salvation. And truly, how often does humanity step outside the path of His righteousness, and find itself entangled in miseries conceived of our flesh by the devil? The theory of many paths is a trick. But the Lord lighteth the one true course."

Libbi sat with her head tilted against her fingers. She smiled and shook her head in amazement.

"Wow." She slapped her cards onto her lap. "You have the most beautiful way with words. I don't agree with much of what you have to say, but you sure do say it well. Must be all that Text reading."

"You should try it," Panla spoke pleasantly.

"Maybe, when my ratings slip." Libbi chuckled. "Actually, I could get your ratings up, if I could get you to loosen up a little. I'd have people flocking back to the cathedrals. You and I could collaborate on some Cathedral Addendums. Spiked heels and mini-dresses in the pulpit. Or maybe create a Sin Day. You know, where everyone is all pious and boring five days a week, but on the sixth day, God looks the other way and everybody just cuts loose and blows all the sin out of their system."

"Do you think twenty-six hours would be long enough?" Panla played along.

"For me or for most people?" Libbi laughed. "For most people, twenty-six hours should be more than enough. For me, since we're friends, maybe you could get me a special dispensation or something."

"So we're friends now?" Panla raised her eyebrows

"If you tell me where you shop, we're friends for life," Libbi fawned. "You're the best dressed damned religious woman I've ever seen. It makes me sick. I bet you were a serious tease in school."

"Not really."

"Are you kidding? You're a serious tease now."

"No." Panla smiled. "At school, I left all the teasing to girls like yourself."

"Hah!" Libbi chuckled. "What I did in school would never be mistaken for teasing. When I broke hearts, it was the real deal, honey."

Libbi's eyes then drifted past the camera. "Yeah, I know your brother went to school with me. How do you think you got this job?" Libbi smiled. "It sure as hell wasn't anything you did."

The production crew again, broke into laughter.

Panla quietly swiveled in her chair and wiggled her foot impatiently.

"Do the Regents give you these kinds of hassles?" Libbi finally took her attention away from the crew.

"Not the same kind, but they have their ways of getting under your skin when they decide to." Panla answered. "We keep each other on the straight and narrow."

"Yeah, well it's all wide and crooked here, minds, out of the gutter, please!" Libbi shook her head as she flipped to another card. "So tell me, what exactly do you mean when you talk about disdaining secular treasures?"

"Well, think about what I've said already." Panla settled back, confidently. "Do you really think God is going to care how much money you made when he passes judgment upon your soul? Do you really think he's going to care whether you lived in a shining mansion or a filthy tenement? Do you think he's going to judge you on your salary receipts? Judge you on the kind of restaurants you dined in or the vehicles you bought? Do you think he's going to care whether your spouse was handsome or beautiful? Do you think the creator of our universe is going to be preoccupied with whether your clothing had designer labels in them? Or where you earned your diploma…or if you earned a diploma? The only thing God cares about is your naked, nurtured, penitent soul. The soul that you bring before him. The soul that will be colored by your faith, obedience and love."

"My god, I think I'd actually pay to hear you speak," Libbi marveled.

"I speak for free every Solemnday," Panla offered. "Come to the Bius Basilica."

"No, I'd rather pay. I'd hate to gyp God for a good show," Libbi cracked. "But tell me, if secular treasures aren't important, why does the church claim that a large gift from someone who's wealthy buys that person a higher reward in Heaven?"

"You're referring to a doctrine instituted by the Deliverer, Odyus VI." Panla lifted her chin. "It's based on the belief that one who gives a large gift to the church better enables the church, by that gift, to do God's good work, and, there-fore, assures themselves of a greater place in Heaven."

"Then, according to this, maybe a rich person can buy their way into Heaven," Libbi challenged. "My god, I've still got a chance!"

"It…It's not that simple." Panla seemed hesitant for the first time. "Certainly that person would also have to be a believer in our Lord."

"But that's not what the Addendum says."

"No, but that's what the Text says."

"Then there seems to be a little conflicting information, doesn't there?"

"Not if you refer back to the Text's original intent," Panla emphasized.

"So we should just throw out Odyus VI's Addendum?"

Panla froze for a moment. She knew exactly what she wanted to say. Yes! Throw out Odyus VI's Addendum. Throw out all the damned Deliverers' Addendums and get back to the word of the Lord. But she held her convictions in check.

"It requires a lot of study," Panla said with a tinge of resignation.

"More study than most people are willing to bother with," Libbi dismissed. "Now let me ask you this: Aside from the fact that you don't live at Bius Basilica, do you feel that you're forsaking any other traditions or rituals?"

"Again, that's a matter of interpretation," Panla treaded lightly. "I don't think you can find a Deliverer who's been truer to the Text than I have. However, I do admit that when it comes to some institutional rituals which I find cumbersome, I'll slight toward being more of a minimalist."

"By minimalist, do you mean trim off some of the fat on the baloney?" Libbi chuckled. "I mean, no wonder they call it Baloni's Walk. Hungover and stoned out of my mind, I wouldn't walk through a swamp of manure in a million twin-moons. Of course, there was that guy I dated who owned the swine farm…and we did drink a lot that one night. Hmm. Never mind."

"I wouldn't use the term trim." Panla's jaw became tense. "The symbolic meaning of Cathedral rituals is inviolate. I just don't believe in making a show of things that take emphasis away from the Word of God."

"Well call it what you will," Libbi flipped her hand, "in show business, we call that trimming. And, according to some critics, you're leaving a lot of the old Deliverers on the cutting-room floor. Which leads me to my next question: Are you at all sympathetic to the Break?"

Panla's hands felt cold and numb. Her heart pounded violently against her sternum. It was an innocent question which begged a grave and hideous truth. She had come to defend the Cathedral, and, to that end, she expected to be labeled a rigid, morally passé clergyman. But this question struck far too close to home. Sympathy for the Break. Any Deliverer with a clear and singular conscience would have no trouble answering the question, but Panla Jen Tem did have sympathy for the Break. Almost as much sympathy for their disillusioned souls as she had love for her Lord in Heaven.

Panla's face hardened into a mask of royal disdain. It was a cold unwavering countenance that would make her assertions irrefutable.

"I feel sorry them," Panla stated firmly "We should all feel sorry for them. Rabbel Mennis and his followers are lost, Godless creatures. Terrorist propagandists leering alongside the devil's throne of evil, lapping their jowls for the souls they seek to corrupt and destroy. We should be wary of them. But more importantly, we should offer them our love and our prayers."

"That and a major chill pill." Libbi nodded with a big smile. "If you don't like Cathedral, don't go. But leave your homemade bombs and your cheesy little leaflets at home!

"Hey world, we'll be back in just a moment."

XXIII.

"Now there's a woman who needs a good hard sadistic fuck!" Juds blew smoke from the side of his mouth as he watched *Nailing the Newsmaker* fade to a commercial break. "That bitch needs to know the joy of feeling her kneecaps cracking against her collar bones for a few hours."

"Which one?" Mongeer looked quizzical as he refilled Juds's glass.

"'Which one?'" Juds glared mockingly at his bartender. "Y'know, Mong, if you didn't own this bar, you'd be out on the street selling used prophylactics. You're dumb as a fuckin' brick, you know that?"

"I'm dumb as a fuckin' brick?" Mongeer leaned over the bar and pointed his finger. "Who got drunk and tried to take home the man/she?"

"Oh, two twinmoons ago!" Juds threw up his hands. "Two twinmoons ago and you still gotta throw that in my face. Like you haven't taken home your share of farm animals to that mudpit you live in. You probably stopped me from picking up the man/she so you could take him home for yourself, you sick sodomistic fuck!"

"I don't live in no mudpit."

"Did I say mudpit? I'm sorry. I was being kind. It only looks like a mudpit. 'Shit hole' is the word I was groping for!"

"Well, it don't stop you from comin' over all the time." Mongeer slammed a half empty liquor bottle back onto a shelf.

"That's because your shit hole's the only place you don't serve watered-down booze like this colored sugar water you just handed me." Juds slurped his drink and turned up his nose. "If the company wasn't so bad, and the women weren't so ugly, I might actually stop coming here!"

"Yeah but nobody else around here has the big screen monitor." Mongeer gestured proudly.

"I wouldn't say that too loud." Juds smirked. "I saw the repo-guy's vehicle parked next door."

Mongeer turned and frowned. "You're a real funny guy tonight, Juds".

"If I could stick my dick in that Deliveress, I'd be a fuckin' riot!" Juds took another drag from his cigarette. "Look at her. She has no idea what it means to really get fucked. No idea! And has the nerve to act like she doesn't give a shit, like that makes her better than us."

"I like that Libbi." Mongeer smiled. "That's the one I want."

"Yeah, there's a lot of miles on that hot little body." Juds reached into a small dish and tossed a nut into his mouth. "I bet you can't even get any friction, her shit's so loose. Now that's what I call a female professional. And I ain't talkin' about her interviewing skills. I bet her oven's always on."

"On high." Mongeer added.

"Yeah." Juds snickered. "But does it self-clean? I bet not. She likes bein' a filthy little celebrity skank. You can tell."

"You can smell." Mongeer laughed as he hand-dried a wet mug.

"Yeah!" Juds chuckled and drained his glass.

"So what brings you here this time of evening?" Mongeer asked. "It's a little early for you, isn't it? Business slow?"

"No." Juds pushed his glass aside and popped a short drag from his herbal cigarette. "Actually, just the opposite. Business is pickin' up. Pickin' up fast. In fact, if things go as well I think they will, I might be lookin' at early retirement. Go buy me a little place on the northwest coast. Drink myself silly. Chase horny little skinny rich girls all day and night. If that's not Heaven, God's out of his fuckin' mind!"

The front door jingled open and three ominously stealthy men in dark suits and brimmed hats entered the room. Juds's ghost-white expression shifted from a buzzing cockiness to a chilled rush of pallid anxiety.

The three black-faced strangers stood and inspected the front room from ceiling to floor with a militaristic precision which bordered on paranoia. The front man extracted an electronic device from his lapel pocket, pressed a button and a strange, alien whistle sounded for several seconds. He studiously read something on the face of the device, appeared unmoved by the data and, with the slight-of-hand of a magician, secreted the instrument back into some part of his black clothing.

When the three approached, the two flanking members leaned over the bar, looking for anything that might seem out of place to them. Meanwhile, the man in the center, the one apparently in charge, stood next to Juds and looked him sternly in the eye as if to x-ray his disposition by reading every line, dimple and crevice in his face.

"Can I help you?" Mongeer finally spoke.

"Uh…Mong," Juds smiled nervously, "I think this is for me. Um, we're going to go over to that booth over there and have a little talk. Why don't you grab us a few house ales and bring 'em over, huh?"

"Yeah, sure." Mongeer answered as he watched Juds pop off his barstool and greet the three men with the handshakes of a used-car salesman.

Juds herded his three associates over to the farthest corner booth. There, he anxiously leaned into his pitch as the three robotic strangers listened intently.

XXIV.

It was a struggle for Crilen not to immerse himself in the interview as he observed the broadcast from the YBS Studios control center only a few meters behind the *Nailing the Newsmaker* set. From what he'd allowed himself to hear, however, Panla was holding her own, which was hardly a surprise.

But his job wasn't to fret over Panla's precarious political position or to fawn over her bedazzling resemblance to Aami. His job was, only in part, even to protect her from all harms' way. What he couldn't afford to lose sight of was that he had been assigned to save the entire world. A world which, according to his taunting, antlered host on the asteroid, had already destroyed itself several centuries ago.

What pivotal moment would decide the fate of this world? And how would he know when to act? Was saving Panla's life the key? Or was killing someone else, like Yolo, Rabbel or the Accommodant, the event which would save this planet from irrevocable obliteration? Or, Crilen shuddered to think, would his intervention cause Panla's death, releasing this world from its preordained demise?

Certainly, the mad, antlered alien had offered, at best, veiled clues. And, to this juncture, no extraordinary, world-shattering opportunities had presented themselves, other than to avail himself to Panla and her intricate revolutionary plan to heal the sentient souls of the world. So for now, a resigned Crilen continued to focus on the micro-aspects of his security assignment and hoped that something would leap to the fore very soon.

Intergalactic travel had made Crilen an expert in the behaviors of assassins, bombers, abductors and thieves under guise. Regardless of the race or species, there was a duplicity of movement the perpetrator of a criminal act could rarely conceal once observed. There was always that dull and common task they would have to appear to be doing in the open. Yet there would also be some other action or movement which they couldn't allow anyone to witness. A deceitful act, betraying the character in costume. An act, within plain view, which had to be ignored by everyone on the premises.

Menial camouflage was a universal terrorist favorite. No one of any import wished to burden their gaze with a person mopping the floor, cleaning the lavatories, dusting the furniture or repairing a fixture no one had noticed needed repair. Such lowly tasks were usually invisible to the average intellect, ascribed a dull, filtered, sublime place in the consciousness alongside inanimate objects and background noises. Hence, a good criminal in character usually relied upon carrying out his or her performance shrouded by the apathetic antithesis of all scrutiny.

In the hallways of the broadcast floor of the YBS Studios building, Crilen had observed many such menials, going about their duties with an unflinching innocence. The people in coveralls carried on like people in coveralls. They weren't at all concerned with who watched or observed them do anything. Rather those who did not move about in an entranced robotic fugue, seemed most preoccupied with prolonging their tasks until it was time for them to go home. Or they would poke fun at one another to make the banality of the day move faster along.

By contrast, activity in the studio control room moved at such a brisk and synchronous pace, there was no room for the insertion of an impostor or zealot with anything on his mind other than the production of a seamless broadcast. Anyone dallying about would immediately be exposed by their blatant uselessness much like a miscolored piece from the wrong puzzle.

This left the fringe areas of the studio where guests, executives and entourages lingered about with no special purpose other than to take in the interview and get a live glimpse of the most important woman in the world.

The guests had been identified and cross-checked. Most of them were family members of YBS production staffers who wanted to see the Queen Mother and First Lady in person. The only entourage on hand was the one of which Crilen was a part, namely Mr. Linnfeld, Genna, Feebie and himself. And there were the executives in the dark green suits, overdressed for any occasion with no other purpose in mind other than to look excruciatingly self-important. Too self-important even to interact cordially amongst each other. All except for one.

At first, the pale lad with the pasted, oily hair looked like just another young corporate cretin, condescending his way up the ladder to nowhere by ingratiating himself to anyone who seemed important enough to matter. He was dressed for the part and mingled effectively. He shook hands, smiled affably and appeared to know almost everyone. But there was a chord of disharmony in the rhythm of his performance.

Whenever the pale young executive turned to interact with someone new, the individual with whom he had just conversed would turn and appear to ask someone nearby something about him. After the third time it happened, it became clear that while he was talking to everyone, no one really knew who he was.

Then there came one final bit of incrimination.

Three, maybe four times, the pale affable young executive would look toward the studio set where Panla and Libbi continued their discussion. In those instances, his eyes would suddenly harden with a flash of cold, rueful contempt before he would slip back into his gregarious cover.

Crilen knew the look all too well. It was a look that had cost billions of lives.

Crilen scanned the room for prospective accomplices. He looked up in the skywalks and in every nook of the studio for someone who might be choreographed with the pale young executive's movements, but there didn't appear to be anyone else. Whoever this was, tonight he was working alone.

Crilen stepped up behind Linnfeld and spoke into his ear.

"We have someone," he whispered.

Linnfeld nodded discreetly and moved sideways to pass the message along to Genna and Feebie. Their job would be to get to the Deliveress immediately and take her out of a predetermined exit, in the event any commotion broke out.

Crilen walked the perimeter of the studio until he placed himself directly behind the cluster of dark green suits. The pale young executive was talking and gesticulating to another executive who seemed more annoyed than engaged.

"Excuse me, sir," Crilen spoke into the young executive's ear, "may I speak with you a moment?"

The young executive turned, looked Crilen up and down, then disdainfully turned away, trying to continue his vacuous monologue.

"Excuse me." Crilen placed his hand on the young man's shoulder.

"Hey, buddy, what's you're problem?" he whispered as he attempted to jerk away.

"I'm security for Mrs. Tem." Crilen held him with a firm grasp. "I'd like to have a moment of your time."

"Look, pal, do you know who I am?" The young man became indignant.

"No." Crilen glared into his face. "Does anybody?"

The young man's complexion became even more pallid as he realized his cover had been blown.

"Outside," Crilen whispered, "now."

With nary a sound, the young man complied as Crilen held him by the suit jacket. They exited the studio, into the hallway. There, things became heated in more ways than one, as Crilen slammed him against the wall and held him there.

"What are you doing here?" Crilen's eyes blazed crimson.

"What in god's name…?" the young man became fearful. "Your eyes!"

"I wouldn't worry about me," Crilen snarled. "What are you doing here?"

"I can't breathe." the young man gasped as he squirmed.

"Not breathing will be the least of your problems if you don't start talking." Crilen pressed him into the wall until the plaster popped.

The young man's face went from fear to an odd rage of his own.

"There's a bomb." He choked and gurgled for breath. "That bitch is dead!"

"Bomb? Where?" Crilen's hands grew hot as the smell of the young man's smoldering suit became noticeable.

"What….(cough)…what are you?" the young man rasped.

"Where's the bomb?" Crilen raised his voice.

"She's got to die!" The young man clenched his teeth.

"Not tonight!" Crilen jerked and slammed him into the wall again.

The young man let out a loud scream and reached up to touch his shoulder blade. Crilen dropped him to the floor and watched him curl up into a contorted ball of pain.

"Tell me where the bomb is," Crilen demanded, "or you won't live to hear the explosion."

"All…all right." The young man struggled to catch his breath. "All right."

The head of the YBS Studios building security approached the scene.

"You got this under control, Mr. Len?" the ponderous, stocky man asked.

"This gentleman hid a bomb somewhere." Crilen answered.

"What? We need to evacuate the building!" the security head gestured frantically.

"Maybe not," Crilen spoke intensely. "He was right behind the set conversing with executives when I grabbed him. Unless he was planning to commit suicide,

I'm pretty sure we still have some time especially since he's going to tell us where it is. Isn't that right?"

The young man was still panting heavily, trying to catch his breath as he righted himself against the wall.

"How did his suit jacket get burned?" the security head wondered aloud.

"He was smoking." Crilen stared down at the young terrorist. "Now where's the bomb?"

"Over...over there." The young man pointed toward a handle on the wall.

"What is that?" Crilen asked.

"Just a garbage chute," the security head answered.

"Check it," Crilen ordered.

The security head toddled over to the garbage chute and carefully pulled open the handle.

"Wouldn't that be something." Sweat formed on the head of security's black face. "Boom!"

He looked down the dark chute and didn't see anything. He stuck his arm inside and didn't feel anything either.

"Where?" Crilen demanded, yanking the young man to his feet.

Crilen pulled him toward the chute and shoved him toward the opening.

The young man offered a weary smile as he slowly reached inside.

"You were reaching in the wrong spot." His alto voice was still rasped. "You were reaching down instead of up. Only I could swear I didn't have to reach this far."

The young man leaned a little further.

Crilen sensed they had just made a mistake.

The young man dove head first into the chute and was gone.

"Damn!" Crilen shouted.

"Evacuate?" the security head strongly suggested.

"Not yet." Crilen frowned. "This leads to the ground level, doesn't it?"

"Yeah."

"Notify Mr. Linnfeld and your staff, but give me three minutes." Crilen ran toward a hall window.

"Okay, but..."

Before the security head could finish his sentence, Crilen was out the window. The security head ran to the open window and looked down. All he could see was the busy street, six stories below.

Downstairs, the young man fell out of the chute and crashed into a half-full metal garbage dumpster. The fall was disorienting, but he quickly sat up and hastened about his task. He removed a small electronic box from his back pocket and punched it on. He removed two thin wires from around his calf under his leg. He plugged the ends of the wires into the box. He ripped open his shirt, took the sharp prongs on the other two ends of the wires and stabbed them into his stomach.

The pain was actually less excruciating than he had expected it to be as blood ran down the front of his pants and into the garbage. Feverishly, he punched the final sequence codes into the box when he sensed a bright light and a wall of heat rise up over the dumpster. He snapped his head around and saw a man engulfed in flames hovering directly above him.

"Oh, Lord in Heaven," the young man gasped.

"So you're the bomb," Crilen's voice echoed above him.

"Y...yeah," he confessed. "I...I've been chemically treated. Bio-molecular fusion. All I need...."

"...is an ignition source." Crilen was familiar with the theory.

"Yeah," the young man answered, looking into Crilen's burning crimson eyes amid the pyrogenic flames.

"You're a member of the Break?" Crilen surmised.

"The Break?" the young man's voice was exacerbated. "Not in a million twin-moons!"

"Then why are you trying to kill the Deliveress?" Crilen demanded.

"The Deliveress?" the young man smiled nervously. "The Deliveress? I'm not here to kill the Deliveress. I love the Deliveress! I worship her! I'm here to kill that heathen bitch, Libbi Trullup! I'm so damned tired of listening to her spread her sick, corrupt morals all over the planet with that God-hating show of hers. She's a vicious evil woman doing the devil's work. She deserves to die and I'm sending her straight to Hell where she belongs!"

"But if you do it this way, you'll kill yourself and the Deliveress, too." Crilen was taken aback by the young man's true purpose.

"I want to die with her." Tears began streaming down the young man's face. "She's so beautiful. And the Lord loves her so much. She'd go straight to Heaven. And I love her so much, the Lord would take me straight to Heaven with her."

"What makes you think that?" Crilen frowned. "Aren't suicide and murder sins? The Deliveress might go to Heaven, but don't be so sure you won't find yourself lying in a hot sweltering lava bath with Libbi Trullup when all the souls are tallied. You may think of yourself as some noble crusader, but the truth is, if you detonate yourself and destroy this building, you'll be nothing less than a mass murderer."

"No!"

"Yes." Crilen's body flashed and flickered with flames. "Doesn't the Text tell you to leave God's enemies to Him? Doesn't the Text tell you that suicide and murder are wrong? What do you think the Deliveress would say about what you're doing?"

"Shut up!" the young man screamed as his lips started to quiver. "You're working for the devil! You're trying to confuse me with trickery and deceit!"

"I'm trying to save your life."

"You're trying to save that whore, so she can go on spreading her lies, weaving her web of iniquity!"

"Don't be a fool," Crilen growled down at him. "If you've got a problem, let someone help you. I can let you talk to the Deliveress herself, if you'd like."

"Liar!" the young man shouted. "I've talked to the Deliveress. She knows who I am. She doesn't talk back, but she knows me. She knows me and she loves me! And she understands what I have to do!"

The young man's thumb pressed a button on the electronic box he held and there was a soft beep that chimed over the echo of his voice. The desperately confused expression on his face disintegrated into a ferociously violent explosion that swelled up from the metal dumpster.

Instinctively, Crilen blasted a pyrogenic wall of pressurized heat over the swelling explosion. The sudden concussive impact nearly blew him out of the air, but he felt the redemptive urge to save every life in the building above, including the life of Panla Jen Tem, who may as well have been Aami.

The roaring fires blasting downward from every pore of his body drove the force of the explosion back down into the dumpster. The dumpster itself glowed bright red, then yellow, then gradually collapsed, melting into a large steaming pool of hissing molten metal.

Crilen extinguished his flame and alighted at the edge of the destruction. A rather large murmuring crowd gathered behind him, but he didn't notice. Most of them had been waiting for an opportunity to witness the Deliveress and First Lady depart the YBS building and enter into her private transport. They had been treated to a bonus in the form of a loud, condensed explosion which quaked the very ground beneath them, and the resultant remnant of the event in the form of a large hot pool of liquid metal.

Crilen ignored the crowd. He was preoccupied with whether he had accomplished his mission by squelching this attempt on what turned out to be Libbi Trullup's life rather than Panla's. Panla, of course, would have died as well. So, in effect, he had saved her life. He looked around, expecting the asteroid to reappear along with his antlered benefactor. But nothing happened. The streets, the people and the murder plot he had just squelched were still all too real and present. He wanted to shout out to It and ask if the bloody game was finally over. Just then, he felt a hand on his shoulder.

"What the hell happened here?" the YBS security head asked.

"He blew himself up," Crilen lamented. "I tried to talk to him, but…he seemed determined to die tonight."

"Hmm." The security head observed the smoldering liquid metal pool. "Not much of a bomb. Looks like all he did was melt a trash container…and himself along with it. These idiots always get it wrong. They scare a bunch of people, but they never pull it off."

"Right." Crilen preferred not to detail how he had contained the massive explosion with pyrogenic energy.

"Well, at least we didn't have to evacuate the whole darn building." The security head smiled. "That's a royal pain."

"I'm sure it is." Crilen looked at him. "But you were right before. We should have. He was willing to kill himself and anyone else unfortunate enough to be in the neighborhood. Next time you have a gut feeling about evacuation, you'd better do it. If I was wrong, it would have cost us thousands of lives."

"Probably not." The security head yawned. "These wackos never get it right. They're like school kid vandals. All they do is get hurt or killed and leave a big mess for the adults to clean up. I'll call the city urban unit. They can ice this down before it turns into a fire."

"Right." Crilen was dismayed by the security head's ignorant attitude toward the near catastrophe.

"Well, the interview's over." the security head informed. "Too bad I missed most of it. The greatest things in the world happen right under my nose and I wind up missing half of them because I'm working right here. Hopefully, my wife recorded it and I can watch it tonight."

"Excuse me?" Crilen broke his deep thought.

"You'd better get up there." The round-bodied man smiled and scratched his head. "It's time for her to go. I'll send you folks the bill for the damage. Mr. Pigue ain't payin' for this."

Crilen just shook his head. He almost ignited his body again, when he realized, like the religious zealot, he, too, had a cover that needed to be maintained. He straightened his jacket and weaved his way through the crowd toward the front entrance.

He hoped he would find himself back on the asteroid at any moment. But the longer it took for nothing to happen, the more he was certain his work had only begun.

XXV.

On the flat wall monitor, Libbi Trullup's broad smile was replaced by a collage of moving pictures advertising a YBS special which would pay homage to the legacy of Finx Melder. The motions of video remained, but the audio was abruptly muted. The lights were dingy and dim. And the air in the room was thick and musty with the heavy thoughts of rogues.

"Creatures?" Leesla's clipped inflections broke the silence in Rabbel's office. "Terrorist propagandists? Is this what you wanted to see? Is that what you wanted to hear?"

Rabbel resembled a brooding stone sculpture set behind the wooden desk; his thick heavy brows converged like dark storm clouds hanging over his piercing, inset stare. The muscles in his jaws were taut. His black dried lips were as flat and sealed as those etched onto the face of a statue chiseled out of coal. His large forearms remained draped over the arms of his chair. He was perfectly, unnervingly still, staring at the muted wall monitor as if every word and syllable of the interview were replaying in his head.

"She's not with us, Rabbel!" Leesla raised her voice, to shatter his trance. "Did you hear her? She's…not…with us. She's telling the whole world to feel sorry for us like we're a gaggle of parasite lunatics who belong in a padded cage! She's…"

With frightening suddenness, Rabbel ferociously slammed his huge fist into the center of his desk.

The tall, angular Leesla was jolted into silence.

"What did you expect?" Rabbel's voice growled through his clenched teeth. "Did you think she was going to renounce the Cathedral on worldwide satellite and trumpet the cause of a gang of political outlaws?"

Leesla folded her arms and swallowed her own mounting anger.

"Of course not." She attempted to sound contrite.

"Panla has a lot of pressure on her," Rabbel justified.

"And we don't?" Leesla's long arms unfurled like a pair of giant wings.

Rabbel held up one finger and met her eyes with a dark scowl. Leesla folded her lips and her arms again, then released a sigh of frustration.

"We're all under a lot of pressure." Rabbel jabbed his finger into the desk. "But Panla had a role to play and she had to play it to perfection. Anything less might have caused suspicion."

"Yeah, she's playing a role, all right." Leesla sneered as she leaned back and banged the her head against the wall in exasperation. "Only she wasn't playing any role in that interview. That was the real her. The one that's going to fuck us. But when she prances her ass down here in that tight little leotard you like, that's when she's playing a role. A role that's leading us calves right into the slaughter-house."

"Damnit Leesla!" Rabbel jumped to his feet. "What has she done to you?"

"I should be asking you that question." Leesla met his eyes.

"No." Rabbel pounded his fist onto the desk again. "What in the hell has that woman ever done to you? What in the hell has she ever done to any of us?"

"Shit, Rabbel." Leesla shook her head. "You really don't get it, do you? It's a fucking set up. You're not supposed to know. Not until it's way too late."

Leesla spoke in the earnest voice of a friend cajoling Rabbel to consider Panla's betrayals behind her overtures of love and devotion.

"Did you listen to her tonight?" she continued. "Did you really listen to her? That girl was preaching. Point by point...preaching...as natural as a baby cries for its mama's teat. At every turn, she defended the goddamned Cathedral as if she were defending her own life. What does she do when she comes here? Tells a few dirty jokes. Slums and slurps with the 'terrorists' for a few moments. Then climbs into your pants and plays you like a one-note wind instrument!"

Rabbel stepped around his desk and moved angrily toward her.

"What?" Leesla glared at him defiantly. "You're going to kick my ass...for her? My ass, that I lay on the line for you everyday, right here in this place? Can you say she does the same? Or is she always somewhere else, doing her double talk, doing us in?"

"I think I see the problem." Rabbel squinted. "This is about Hesh, isn't it?"

"Hesh?" Leesla frowned.

"Reza says she dropped you this afternoon." Rabbel read her face as he spoke.

"Ugh! That eavesdropping little c...!"

"Well?"

Leesla took two deep breaths and ran her fingers through her wild dark mane. Any thought of Hesh felt like a sharp kick to the stomach. But she wasn't going to wrestle with those feelings now.

"This isn't about Hesh." Leesla's nostrils flared. "This isn't about personal relationships. This is about the Break. This is about our survival. If the Break dies, Hesh and me are dead anyway. If the Break dies, you'll never taste your precious PJ again...in Heaven or Hell."

"Well if this isn't about Hesh, then why do you hate Panla so much?" Rabbel demanded.

"I hate her because she hates us. You see her as you want to see her. And because they believe in you so much, everyone out there sees her as you want to see her. But I see her as she really is: a user."

"What about all the money she's brought in?" Rabbel gestured. "Money skimmed right out of the Cathedral treasury! If the Lord Regent or anyone else found out, she'd be imprisoned for the rest of her life!"

"That's why the money doesn't come from the Cathedral treasury," Leesla conjectured. "It's probably coming straight from the Accommodant's surplus."

"You have a hyperactive imagination, Leesla."

"It takes one to catch one," Leesla sneered. "PJ's the one with the imagination. I watch her eyes. I don't melt in them. She will destroy us."

Rabbel wanted to punch Leesla's head through the wall. Panla was everything to him. More to his dark conscience than even the Break. But if he were the backbone of the movement, Leesla was its throbbing heart. To her, the Break was more than a cause. It was a glorious crusade to her ultimate liberation; the liberation denied her by both the wavering government and the hypocritically monolithic Cathedral. Rabbel's ideals rode on the Break's success. But for Leesla, her every breath depended upon it.

He reached out and placed his heavy palm on her lean muscular shoulder. Leesla flinched for a moment, knowing Rabbel's temper could make him do many violent things. But surprisingly, his touch was gentler than she ever imagined he could be…except with *her.*

"Leesla," Rabbel's voice was an intense whisper, "I swear to you I will not let you down. I will not let any of these people down. I'll die first! And if you're right…and it comes down to a choice between Panla or the Break…I will not let her or anyone else come between us and our right to be free. Free of any religion. Free of any false god."

"I know." Leesla wrapped her long arm around his thick neck and placed her chin on his shoulder. "I know. I just needed to hear you say it. I just needed to be sure."

XXVI.

Her dressing room was dim and deserted. From across the room, the lighted mirror still illuminated the bright lavender chair and dresser which had, earlier in the evening, served as the command center of her war chamber. It was here that Libbi Trullup had prepared for the greatest professional challenge of her life. Her hair and make-up had been perfectly detailed. Her brash and shameless queries had been the most direct and deconstructive of her career. Her divertive ducks and her masterful parries left her outwardly unscathed...apparently. She had masterfully melded her renowned irreverent humor to an unflinching display of cocksure self-confidence. Yet now, inexplicably, Libbi found herself huddled into a tiny corner, knees clutched to her chest, herbal cigarette twisted in her lips, shivering like a frightened and betrayed political prisoner awaiting the hour of her execution.

She cursed as she knocked over her stemmed crystal glass, spilling her fourth drink into the shaggy pink carpeting. Sadly, in pursuit of blinding inebriation, her crippling fears of an hour ago were still no less vivid.

As the interview had concluded, she was buoyed that her once pristine guest seemed less so, worn down and frustrated by Libbi's warping wall of filters wrapped crudely around every clear and logical response her opponent could muster. Had she been allowed to press on indefinitely, Libbi was certain she could have eventually cracked and crumbled the polite and stately Deliveress into a fit of ranting, cursing rage. She'd certainly accomplished it before with guests who'd had much less to defend than Deliveress Panla Jen Tem, First Lady of the Accommodancy.

But after she and the Deliveress had exchanged their final pleasantries, with Panla, maddeningly courteous, dignified and certain to the final handshake, something in Libbi came quietly unhinged. It wasn't enough that she had "won" all of the arguments and obstructed her adversary's religious discourse. She wanted the world to see this guest broken, teary-eyed and defeated. Or at least, she wanted them to hear her adversary concede a single point which she'd lost in their hour-long interview-turned-debate. Though, in her darkest fantasies, Libbi really wanted to watch this queenly, sanctimonious snob stumble and break an ankle or be bloodied by a jab to the face from some zealous Break sympathizer. She wanted anything other than to merely stand by and observe the Deliveress march out of the studio with her attendants and security in tow, bearing a demeanor which inferred that the interview had already been jettisoned into her least relevant and distant memories.

"How dare she still sashay out of my studio with her nose in the air," Libbi simmered. "I kicked her pointy virgin ass, didn't I? She should have to blow every guy in the building, then crawl out on her bleeding hands and knees."

Upon the Deliveress's departure, the studio staff offered Libbi an obsequious round of applause for a job well done. Individuals approached and praised her on her caustic wit and her journalistic genius. One staffer even confided that he could see the crumbling spires of the Cathedral reflected in the Deliveress's "broken" gaze as the hard-lined questions and racy repartee eroded the Queen Mother's "delusional" resolve.

But then there was Yolo. The bloated, wrinkly, wart-faced media monarch idled quietly in a shadowy corner, leering at his charge with a devilishly carnivorous expression that shook her spirit to the point of making her dizzy. An evil contentment filled his gaze toward her as the red smoke from his herbal cigar billowed thickly from his wide upturned nostrils.

All at once, Libbi's surging confidence whisked out of her like a tissue snatched up in a windstorm. She suddenly remembered Yolo had hand-picked her for an assignment he could not have believed she was qualified to do properly. He had set her up for failure. Staked her for the sacrifice. Now he was gloating quietly to himself, like a master puppeteer watching his broken marionette take one final bow.

He was pleased. But she brooked no comfort in his ugly, insidious pleasure. To Yolo, the world was a game board and every piece had its value. To win a larger piece from the enemy, smaller pieces were always expendable. Yolo had held back his larger pieces and used her in their stead. Used. "Used up." Her anxiety gnawed at her. Nothing had ever been said or implied along such lines but her career meant everything to her. And now she was certain it was over. Over unless she could glean from him the measure of the sacrifice she had made at his behest.

Libbi finally broke free of the condescending little crowd that had encircled her behind the cameras, and slowly, bravely approached Yolo Pigue.

His cold, placid expression did not change as their eyes locked through his enveloping crimson haze of cigar smoke. She felt her skin begin to pimple as both the cigar smell and a more personal, stifling stench repulsed and suffocated her senses. He was a grotesque and beastly giant of a man whom she could never have envisioned as handsome, even as a youth. Though a lifetime of physical unseemliness had apparently allowed him to fortify a powerful intellectual confidence, moored by a galaxy of logical inward assertions. In middle age, he mastered the role of an imposing omnipotent monstrosity, with his layered sagging jowls, his bolts of fine-tailored clothing and a piercing, egomaniacal gaze.

Libbi felt a nauseous trembling in her stomach. The same as she had felt twenty twinmoons ago when she'd given over her adolescent innocence to a male twice her age. She had never again felt so used or violated. But this evening, the cruel, debilitating sensation returned full bore.

"Good evening, Yolo." She masked her fear behind a smile borrowed from her public persona.

"Hmm," he grunted, looking over her head.

"Well, everyone here seems to think it went pretty well." She cast her line for a compliment.

"Everyone here works for you, dear girl." The contentment on Yolo's thick lips diminished slightly. "Don't be foolish. You could defecate in your guest's lap and screech primate mating noises for an hour and they'd laud it to your face so long as the ratings remained favorable."

Libbi wanted to be angry, and, normally, she would have been. But tonight her stark terror had chased away every morsel of pride and strength she had ever owned.

"Well," Libbi's chest heaved with a sigh of feigned confidence, "I believe it went pretty well myself."

"And everyone who believes as you do will think so." Yolo snorted disdainfully. "That's the best we could have hoped for."

"What?" Libbi was lost by his answer.

"I'll want to see you in my office in the morning." Yolo exhaled another thick smoky cloud. "Good evening."

Libbi smiled nervously, nodded and expected him to depart, but it quickly became apparent that he had excused her from the studio rather than himself. She smiled again, nodded again, and promptly exited, a complete emotional wreck.

Now she sat alone on the floor of her dressing room, drunk and quaking madly, with an imaginary pendulum swinging over her veiny little neck. Morning, she thought. He would see her in the morning and concoct a reason to flush away her career. A career about which she had built her entire life. She could find another job, but anything other than YBS would be a humiliating and unbearable plummet from the pinnacle of success. Suicide crossed her mind, but there had to be another alternative that would rescue her from the precipice of oblivion. There had to be some act or gesture that would redeem her sudden disposability. There simply had to be…something.

Several floors above, Yolo squatted and sunk slowly into his wheezing leather chair as the fumes of raw flatulence roared violently into the still air of his large, lamplit office. Everything had gone perfectly; everyone had played out their part predictably. For a moment, he dared fancy himself a sort of god. A god of settings and scenes and perceptions. But then he belched up a gastrocolic chuckle and scoffed at the sheer lunacy of such grandiose delusions.

"Demi-god, perhaps." He lapped his lips with his tongue. "For were I imbued with total omnipotence, I would have certainly, by now, affected repairs on this horrible heap I abuse for a body.

"But alas, though not a god to be sure, I needn't be, to observe that the globe remains peopled by a mass of malleable sentients who bear all the collective depth of a dry wading pool, peppered with twigs, leaves, pebbles and all manner of unweighty debris. What shiftless intellect. What bestial predilections. They see the Deliveress in plain view, brandishing morality for a higher cause. No, the highest cause: The will of God, Himself. She offers the world a clear path to peace, love, joy and eternal bliss in exchange for the warmth of an…annoying fellowship and the minimal sacrifice of mammonistic addictions, the pursuit of which lead only to exhaustion and misery more often than not. Were she not so obscenely genuine about it all, one might mistake her goodness as little more than a tawdry affront. But she feigns nothing and the world couldn't care less. Not that they don't concede that she's on to something positively marvelous, if not altogether miraculously reasonable. But the toll is so steep. In order to partake of the Queen Mother's glory, one must forsake the King Father of earthen pleasures. How rudely unappealing! To cast off our selfish gluttony in the realm of the present in exchange for the abstract uncertainty of eternal bliss elsewhere, unseen. A fool's fantasy. Of course, she did recant that the wise are the fools and the fools shall be wise in her Heaven. I wouldn't doubt it. Though I can hardly envision myself a fool on either plane, lest fiction surrenders to us, this earnest, beneficent God, after all.

"But what does it matter when the masses choose to dally upon much shallower reflections: 'What am I going eat'? Where am I going to drink? Who am I going to bed that would impress the neighbors?'. These are the golden virtues which elevate us above incarceration at the local zoo, for no animal has the civility to care what another animal thinks. Vanity is the acid test of our higher evolution. 'What do I own? Where have I been? And who's going to affirm the merit of my vast or modest accomplishments?' With so much weighing upon the mortal mind every waking hour, how should anyone be expected to make time to dwell upon the translucent expectations of a creator? And if such a creator even existed wouldn't it behoove he, she or it to simply smack us on the hind quarter and overrule our narcissistic obsessions rather than to test us?

"I'm sure the Deliveress could answer all such confounding queries. But to her chagrin, very few have any desire to comprehend them. Oh, sweet and noble queen, how courageously you pinch the dagger's point against the pulsing vein of your own melodic throat. You wager your flesh for the souls of millions. What conviction! What yearning to convey a truth so few care to grasp! Your religious pedantry rings silently in the ears of the deaf. Your revolution hasn't enough soldiers to hoist up your flag. You're so bright, yet you fail to realize that morality is no longer etched upon the transcendent tablets of eternal constancy. Rather, morality is now as ephemeral as the latest cut of evening gown. For every convolution of decency, a season…so that all the convolutions may have a turn. How democratic. Praise be to the Accommodant. It's all such a bloody mess.

"But then, bloody messes are the boon of the media business. Ask Finx Melder and that silly dead girl. Everyone is so preoccupied, supplicating upon the death of this junkie/thespian and his muscle-legged concubine, that they haven't taken notice of the greater forces aligning themselves for control of the world. They know the players, but they refuse to acknowledge the stakes. They refuse to believe that Rabbel Mennis, the Deliveress, the Accommodant and, clandestinely, myself hold the keys to the world's survival. The masses prefer to embrace the hollow notion that life will continue to stagger along its merry path, regardless of which ideology holds sway. Shiftless intellects, indeed."

Yolo swiveled around to the wooden bar behind his desk. From the bottom cabinet, he withdrew a liter-sized pewter goblet. He looked up and quickly scanned the marble counter containing his favorite liquors. With all the care of a skilled laboratory technician, he plucked the first bottle and filled the bottom of the goblet, calibrating the amount carefully with his eyes. He added a second and a third until the dark liquid concoction filled the goblet, three-quarters to the lip.

"Fortunately for myself, all that matters are the coins. Ethics and morality are immaterial. Rights or wrongs are the stuff of children's storybooks. The media has no marketable interest there. That the tale is disseminated at optimum entertainment pitch is all that matters. Pace and perception are everything. Large numbers must be mesmerized by the drama so that large profits can be harvested from the sponsorship. This is the bane of reporting the truth. As they say in the marketplaces, let the consumer beware."

Yolo hoisted the large goblet to his lips, delicately holding the stem in his fat fingers with a grace that belied his girth. With a tip, he splashed and swished the liquid into his large throat with the deep plunging sound of a washtub drain. Within seconds, he set the empty goblet down with a visceral finality.

"Ahhhhhhhwuuuuuup." Yolo gasped, suppressing another resounding belch.

Abruptly, the intercom chime jingled.

"Yes," Yolo frowned and bellowed at the interruption.

"Your evening meal has arrived," responded a female voice he didn't recognize.

"Rather early, aren't we?" Yolo was intrigued, yet suspicious. "And, besides, I don't recall placing the order, yet."

"It's something out of the ordinary, sir." the voice answered. "Something you're certain to enjoy, compliments of the house."

"Hmm. Games, is it?" Yolo sounded annoyed. He punched up the security scanner to be certain the solicitor wasn't carrying any weapons. The word "clear" flashed green on his monitor.

"Very well, you may enter," Yolo huffed. "But if this is just some lewd solicitation for air time, I'll have you thrown off the roof, understand?"

"Oh, it's lewd, alright." The voice began to sound oddly familiar. "I guarantee a decadently delicious evening."

Curiosity deepened the fleshy ripples of Yolo's countenance as he released the remote lock and the door chimed open.

A slender robed female with dark bell-shaped hair sauntered slowly into the room. Yolo could not immediately identify the silhouetted figure but her gait was obscenely seductive, though just a bit unsteadied by the taint of inebriation. Under her arm was a large silver tray. The enrapturing aroma of a spicy meal intermingled with sweet perfume accosted his senses.

The woman leaned forward into the desk lamp light and loudly slammed the tray onto the center of Yolo's desk.

"Dinner is served," she said as her head doddered to and fro. Her black hair swung in perfect symmetry around her white cheeks, but her colorful make-up was a mess: two oblong circles of navy painted unevenly around her eyes and a red zig-zag of lipstick smeared carelessly across her mouth.

"Libbi." Yolo sounded as stunned as a demi-god would allow himself to reveal.

"I know you wanted to see me in the morning," Libbi smiled with her eyes slit, licking her fingers, "but I thought I would rather see you tonight."

"I see." Yolo was astonished by his own loss for words.

"No, you don't." Libbi giggled and almost fell over. "Not yet."

In spite of her drunken state, Libbi executed a nimble maneuver, rolling herself over onto the silver platter she had placed on Yolo's desk. She sat up, loosened the robe and tossed the garment back over her shoulders revealing an even more startling surprise. Libbi had dressed herself in thinly embroidered panties and a bra, stuffed with a tantalizing variety of fruits, vegetables and meats.

"Dinner?" A slip of saliva rolled from Yolo's lips.

Libbi laughed and threw back her head. She snapped her neck forward, flinging her dark hair over her eyes.

"Dinner," she groaned in a deep seductive voice as he reached forward and fingered a breast with his thick paw.

"Ah, ahh." She flicked his hand away with her fingers. "You have to wait for me to read the specials! Up top, on this side, we have an assortment of imported fresh fruits, sliced with whipped cream and honey. On the other side we have fresh stir-fried vegetables in a sweet wine sauce prepared with peppery southern seasonings. Around my neck is a knotted sweet crescent loaf, fresh baked and oiled."

Yolo cleared his throat, licked his lips and let slip an ounce of drool. But the show had only begun.

Libbi swung her legs forward.

"For our main course, we offer a choice of flame-broiled drumsticks." She gestured toward the pieces of meat suspended from her calves by her black stockings.

"Or," she spread her legs far apart revealing the dripping meats bulging through her panties. "we have an assortment of flesh tenderloins, roasted medium rare…just the way you like to eat it."

Libbi dabbed her finger into the bloody juices running between her thighs. She leaned forward and moistly tapped Yolo on the tip of his large snout.

"And for dessert, my precious?" Yolo inquired as he hastily reached into his drawer, pulled out a large napkin and stuffed it into his wide collar.

"Custard mousse with hot melted fudge…anywhere you like." Libbi smiled and laughed, running her shaking fingers through her hair.

"Hmm." Yolo reached out with his giant hands and jerked the silver platter and Libbi forward. "This will be quite a feast, indeed, my dear. Quite a feast, indeed."

"Bon appetit." Libbi leaned forward, clutched his sagging jowls and licked him passionately across his fat salivating lips. "Bon appetit."

XXVII.

The atmosphere in the transport's rear cabin was decidedly tense. Even more so, than it had been before the interview. Crilen sat across from Panla feeling uncomfortably useless as he watched her pour over the show's transcript with a glowing laser marker in her hand and a flat electronic pad resting on her lap.

"Damn," she cursed privately, inscribing notes and drawing circles.

"I wouldn't worry," Crilen said, trying to calm her. "You did very, very well."

Panla continued to scroll through her electronic pad as if she hadn't heard him. She cursed and marked her copy again.

"Mrs. Tem," Crilen addressed her.

Panla simply lifted her eyes into space and quietly muttered parts of the transcript back to herself as if she were the only person in the cabin.

"Mrs. Tem." Crilen raised his voice.

She let loose an exaggerated sigh fraught with wearied annoyance, but still continued working as if she hoped he would go away.

"Panla," Crilen spoke once more.

Panla slammed down her laser pen.

"What?" she tersely acknowledged him without looking up.

"I said I think the interview went very well," Crilen reiterated. "I don't see the need for you to…"

"Mr. Len," she curtly interrupted him. "Have you been paying attention to anything that I've said to you today?"

"Yes." Crilen was taken aback by her tone.

"Well, then, you should realize that because of this interview, I'm going to have a lot of questions to answer from both Rabbel Mennis and the Lord Regent, if not the Holy Inquisitor himself. Surely, you can understand that, can't you?"

"Yes, Mrs. Tem, but…"

"But nothing!" she raised her voice. "This may be a game to you, but this is all very serious business for me."

"Panla, I just thought you'd find it comforting to know that you didn't lose any ground to Libbi this evening."

"Of course, I didn't." Panla's voice shook with tension. "Libbi Trullup is a rootless immoral media assassin. Nothing more. The day a mixed-up harlot like her gets the best of me is the day I hang myself from the Cathedral belfry."

Panla paused for a moment, then looked up at Crilen with frustration and fatigue in her eyes.

"Although it is getting harder," her voice cracked just a little, "to tell the difference between a woman like Libbi and a woman like PJ. I mean, I'm beginning to lose track, myself."

Crilen frowned at the analogy.

"Oh, please, don't look at me like that." She slammed the electronic pad onto the seat next to her. "It's beginning to wear very thin."

"I'm sorry." Crilen wanted to find some way to settle her. "It's just that if PJ were all that you were, I might agree. But PJ's just a role."

"Is she?" Panla glared at him. "How do you know? Have you been reading my mind again?"

"Panla…"

"It's Mrs. Tem, please," she interrupted again. "You're starting to forget your place. You're my security, not my psychologist. You'd do well not to try to comprehend things you can't begin to understand."

"Yes, Mrs. Tem." Crilen folded his arms and leaned back.

Panla observed him angrily, then closed her eyes as if she, again, wished him to vanish.

"I just don't understand who you're supposed to be." She was exasperated. "You barge into my life acting like the kind of man my Churchlord told me I was going to marry when I was fourteen. Unfortunately, as I got older, I came to the very adult realization that those men only exist in romance novels and fairy tales, and so I married my husband instead. Now you come along, and, in one day, you're making me very sick if you really must know the truth. I wish to hell you'd just leave."

"Mrs. Tem…"

"You're a little tardy, Mr. Len. I said leave!" She took up the transcript again.

"But…"

"GET OUT!" she shouted and angrily flung the electronic pad at his head.

Crilen easily ducked out of the way. Then, without thinking, he picked up the transcript and twirled it right back to her, striking her in the chest. Without looking up, he stood and stormed out of the rear cabin.

By contrast, moments before, the mood in the center cabin had grown rather daft.

"What I don't understand," Linnfeld sat slumped in the corner with his jacket undone, "is that if you like him so much, why don't you say something?"

Genna smiled as if the answer were patently obvious.

"Why does she have to say something?" Feebie leapt to Genna's defense. "Why can't he simply be a male and ask her out?"

"Well, maybe he doesn't want to," Linnfeld huffed and rolled his eyes.

Feebie and Genna looked at each other and started to laugh.

"What?" Linnfeld gestured. "What did I say?"

"Last week, he almost slammed the transport door shut on the Queen Mother's leg, he was so busy flirting with me." Genna grinned.

"Oh, that's hilarious," Linnfeld deadpanned. "The world comes to a grinding halt because of a derelict chauffeur's raging hormones."

"Oh, they're raging, all right." Feebie chuckled. "He was actually dumb enough to ask me if I'd find out her favorite flower. Then he begged me not to tell her that he said anything. Like I'm really not going to tell her! Duh!"

"So now he just acts really embarrassed every time he sees me." Genna laughed. "What a dope!"

"So even if he asked you out, you'd just humiliate the poor boy by making fun of him," Linnfeld offered.

"I might." Genna smiled. "No, I would."

"Then what's the point?" Linnfeld threw up his hands.

"The point is," Feebie shook her finger, "if he wants to go out with her, he should ask. He shouldn't sit around waiting for her to ask him."

"Especially since she's not interested." Linnfeld sighed.

"Who said that?" Genna looked at Linnfeld as if he'd just concluded that the world was flat.

"He's a stud." Feebie smiled.

"But he's got to do the manly thing and cough it up!" Genna wagged her finger.

"So you actually would go out with him if he asked?" Linnfeld sounded confused.

"After I picked myself up off of the floor." Genna fell back and smiled.

"Then I'll go tell him." Linnfeld moved to stand up.

"Don't you dare!" Feebie jumped up and pushed him back in his seat.

"I just want to save everyone, including myself, any more aggravation!" Linnfeld pleaded.

"The only thing you're going to save is your life, by sitting back down and not breathing a word of this conversation, do you understand?" Feebie looked almost threatening.

"Whatever you say, Miss." Linnfeld playfully acquiesced. "Just please don't hurt me."

A stoic and disquieted Crilen entered the cabin like a cold stiff wind. Quickly, everyone fell silent. Crilen tried to unobtrusively place himself into the setting, taking a seat next to Feebie without a word. But everyone could immediately see on his face that there had been real trouble with the Deliveress.

"Maybe you ladies should run along and torture our driver a bit more." Linnfeld eyed Feebie and Genna.

Feebie wrinkled her nose and all but stuck out her tongue at the lead attendant, then she and Genna snickered to each other and exited through the front cabin toward the driver's compartment.

"Did I interrupt something?" Crilen sat awkwardly cramped in his seat.

"What you interrupted doesn't qualify as anything." Linnfeld sat forward and shook his head. "Believe me."

"Hmm." Crilen took his word for it.

"So she let you have it, eh?" Linnfeld offered a wry grin.

"How could you tell?" Crilen couldn't deny it.

"The high-heel marks all over your face and chest for one thing." Linnfeld smiled. "That kicked-in-the-groin expression you had when you sat down, for another."

"I see."

"Don't read much into it," Linnfeld consoled. "She likes you. But the way you'd been hawking her today, I'm surprised it took her this long to blow. Plus, she's always a bit tense just before we go see Rabbel. Being the First Lady suits her. And being the Deliveress comes as second nature, but the PJ thing, its hard. Oh, she'll pull it off, all right. And she'll make it seem effortless. But therein lies the strain. Even though it doesn't seem like much of a stretch, PJ has to be everything Panla isn't…morally. PJ can be just as charismatic and royal as Panla, but she has to pretend that she hates the one thing she loves more than anything: God."

"So what about her and Rabbel, anyway?" Crilen digressed slightly.

"Rabbel's quite smitten," Linnfeld confided.

"And her?"

"She's doing what she has to do."

"Which means?" Crilen's eyes narrowed.

"I know what you're asking." Linnfeld drew himself up. "And the answer is: I don't know. Frankly, I don't want to know."

It wasn't the answer Crilen wanted to hear, but he continued his line of questioning before his expression could betray any feelings on the matter.

"And what about you?" Crilen probed.

"Me?" Linnfeld chuckled with amusement. "I'm just a lifetime civil servant…whose gotten a little tired of the status quo. In another life, I was a non-believer who attended Cathedral religiously. The more I went, the more I hated it. But I went because that's what my wife insisted we do."

"So what happened?"

"To me or to my wife?" Linnfeld spoke with a glint in his eye.

"Both."

"Ah. Well my wife died from CI ten twinmoons ago. And with that, I pretty much concluded that the Cathedral hadn't done her or me very much good, so I divorced myself from all things spiritual and concentrated on being the best attendant I knew how to be. Not altogether fulfilling, I must admit. In one breath, I didn't want to believe in God at all, and, in the next breath, I was always cursing Him in the middle of the night for the emptiness echoing through my soul. But then the Tems came to the Accommodant's Mansion and I met Mrs. Tem for the first time. On the road, we had a series of long talks that helped me finally accept my wife's death and made me see things with a broader perspective. Over time, I eventually became her confidant and…co-conspirator, if you will."

"She's very persuasive, isn't she?" Crilen concluded.

"Mr. Len," Linnfeld spoke with a quiet, but resplendent joy, "I'd lay down my life for that woman. For twinmoons I was so angry because my wife's death seemed so premature and senseless. Then someone sits down with you and makes beautiful heavenly sense of it all. Now I know my wife didn't die for nothing. Can you imagine the peace and comfort that knowledge brought to my soul?"

Crilen leaned back and stared out of the window…into the black evening darkness. The haunting echo of a dying woman's final scream rang through the well of his ears and dried the center of his tongue.

"No, Mr. Linnfeld," Crilen answered, "I can't imagine."

XXVIII.

Newswoman: Hello everyone. I'm Egs Bloyt. You're looking at a live shot of the sports vehicle owned by world famous actor, the late Finx Melder, engulfed in flames and protruding from a blazing fuel tank. Melder and his companion, sand surfer Preppi Deyz, died in an accident late last night there in the northeast, when Melder apparently lost control of his vehicle, smashed through an iron gate, flew over an embankment and crashed into the side of that fuel tank, which caused an horrific explosion that could be felt kilometers away.

As firefighters continue to battle the roaring blaze, it's about an hour away from dawn on that side of the world. And we understand that the bodies of Finx Melder and Preppi Deyz have been taken to the Metro Morgue where a large crowd has gathered. Our YBS Eastern Bureau Chief Proptz Rotz is on the scene. Proptz, what's going on there?

PR: Well, it's an absolutely amazing scene here at the Metro Morgue. Literally thousands of fans have shown up here to pay their last respects to the greatest actor/genius of our time, Finx Melder. Some people are re-enacting scenes from his most notable films. Some people are even dressed up like Bius II or his characters from *Sister's Lingerie* or *The Embalming Room*. It's turned into a veritable Finx Festival here at the morgue.

EB: Proptz, has there been any problems with security so far?

PR: Well, a couple of overzealous fans did initially attack the rescue workers as they attempted to transfer Melder's remains from the ambulance to the morgue.

One man snatched away part of Melder's burned hand that was dangling by a piece of flesh and a huge fight broke out over possession of it. Meanwhile, the rescue workers were literally trapped with the bodies in their vehicles by the pressing mob of fans. But since then, things have quieted down a bit. Policers were called in. Melder's body was safely transferred into the coroner's cold chamber. And we can assume that an autopsy is being performed, as we speak.

EB: What's the need for an autopsy at this point?

PR: Well, its just one of those things you have to do when someone is dead, Egs.

EB: But we pretty much know what killed him. He was roasted by a giant fuel tank explosion!

PR: That's true, but there is some speculation as to whether Finx might have been high on some drug. He hadn't been going to rehab. He'd been ducking out on his counselor. It's possible that this tragedy may be attributable to his long fight with substance abuse. A fight he was apparently losing. Only the coroner's toxicology report will tell us for sure.

EB: So in the meantime…

PR: In the meantime, fans are celebrating the life and death of Finx Melder with much the same verve and energy that he exhibited throughout his acting career. I don't think the Metro Morgue has ever been a more popular place. It's quite a spectacle.

EB: I see you've got some folks closing in on you.

PR: Yes, (chuckles) I do. Sir, you're all decked out in lingerie like Finx's character from *Sister's Lingerie*. What brought you here this morning?

Man 1: I…I…I dunno. Finx, man, he…he changed a lot of lives. He did so much for people and…..taught us valuable lessons about life, y'know. To just be yourself and….y'know?

PR: Okay. And what about you, ma'am?

Woman 1: Finx was so hot. I've seen all his movies, like forty times. Even *Spit and Duck*! And we met him once at a hotel and he was so nice and down to earth. And he signed all of me and my girlfriend's stuff. And we're like, really gonna miss him so much!

PR: Thank you. Now wait. I think I know this young lady over here. For our fans at home, we hope you recognize folk singer Lesandra Diik. What brings you out on this cool morning?

LD: Well, I got to know Finx quite well when he was married to Durt. Y'know, Durt Dinga. And when we were doing the Godless Goddess Festival tour, I remember hanging out with Finx on the road and we had these really deep philosophical conversations real late at night and he and I got to be really tight. So I thought I'd come out, sing a few tunes for the fans, you know. Sing some of Finx and Durt's old favorites.

PR: That's great. But you also have a new recording coming out, or is it out already?

LD: The song's out. The anthol will be out next month.

PR: And it's called?

LD: *Lick It, Don't Prick It.*

PR: Well, you're looking a little pricked right now. What's the scoop?

LD: Yeah, I guess so. Well, actually, I'm separated from my third husband, I'm dating a female roadie and I'm carrying the child of our opening band's drummer. Love's a little hectic right now, but life's copacetic. Know what I mean?

PR: Well, hopefully, we'll get to hear you sing a little later on.

LD: Stick around. This is for Finx!

PR: Okay. Egs, as you can see this is a very special morning at the Metro Morgue.

EB: It certainly is. We look forward to hearing Lesandra sing later on. Hang in there.

PR: You bet.

EB: As we again view the sight of Finx Melder's burning vehicle, lodged into the side of that blazing fuel tank, we turn our attention to the other person who lost her life in that fatal crash last night. A young lady who's athletic brilliance lit up so many lives at last twinmoon's World Games: Preppi Deyz. Here to remember Preppi for us is sports commentator Blank Duhforge. Blank?

(poignant music)

BD: Thank you, Egs. I remember meeting Preppi Deyz at the Sand Surfing Junior Championships ten twinmoons ago, along with her parents. She didn't win first prize that day. But even then, you could tell that there was something so very special about this little girl with her bright cheery smile and the shy giggle she brought before the wall of cameras and microphones. When I asked her parents why she wasn't sad with fourth place, they said Preppi loved sand surfing so much that she would never let something like losing get between her and having fun. Well, over the next several twinmoons, Preppi had lots of fun. And she had fun winning. Time and again she would shatter world records, crossing the finish line with a wave and a smile that would become familiar to all of us by the time she was sixteen.

But just as it seemed that nothing could go wrong for Preppi, tragedy struck. Preppi's great-uncle died in a nursing home at age eighty-seven. A week later, she sprained her knee during a practice run. Her world was suddenly collapsing all around her. The injury forced her to miss the World Games that twinmoon, yet she bravely stood on the sidelines and cheered the loudest for her teammates as they brought home two silver pins. But four twinmoons later, Preppi's time had finally arrived. Blossomed into the beautiful young woman we always knew she would become, she had also honed her skills as the ultimate competitor. This time, no adversity could rob her of her date with destiny. Our hearts soared as she won four gold pins in each of her four events, gliding across those sun-splashed, mountainous dunes with her golden hair fanning behind her like a the silken veil of a princess on her wedding day. Our bellies warmed as she stood atop the dais, receiving her four gold pins with that bright cheerful smile that said to the world, winning isn't coming in first in a sporting event. Winning is simply the joy of life. We will miss Preppi Deyz, not because she was some brilliant superstar or ideological icon. Tonight, that accolade belongs to another. Rather, we will miss Preppi because she was one of us. A daughter, a sister, a friend who taught us how to love, and, more importantly, how to smile.

(poignant music fade)

EB:(sigh) I'll always remember that smile. Thank you, Blank. After a short break, sociological expert Dr. D'lood will rank the films of Finx Melder in order of their cultural relevance. And then, our staff of film critics will rank them in order of their artistic merit. It should be interesting. Stay with us.

XXIX.

Crilen saw Aami crossing the street with a large book bag slung over her shoulder. Her shimmering dark hair was shoulder length, longer than he had seen it in years. She wore a familiar, oversized yellow pullover sweater with puffed long sleeves and her cursive initials embroidered on the front below the center of its ruffled collar. Her short plaid skirt swung well above the knee, while her flat brown loafers glistened in the hazy sunlight, as though they had never been scuffed or soiled. With a perky hop, she bounced up on to the curb and strode across the campus green with all of the confidence and aloofness of a stately young heiress from a faraway realm.

Crilen hastened to intercept her, but felt the threads of his own clothing loosen at every seam. He stopped, looked down at his knees and saw holes where he was certain he'd sewn patches. He saw his bare toes poking through the front of his tattered shoes, not recalling when they had worn to such raggedness. He looked at his hands and they were oddly filthy; black grime lined the nails and crevices of his fingers. He even detected a strong odor about himself that he prayed would be, at least, diluted by the next gentle breeze.

Courageously, he still continued onward and overtook her at the base of a statue shaded by a giant tree. He mustered the fortitude to call out to her in a strong and audible voice, but she never broke her stride. He chased after her and called her name again, but she continued on, unfettered. Stunned by her blatant indifference, Crilen could neither believe she could not hear him nor would he accept she had chosen to ignore him. He reached out to touch her, but his grasp was rudely eclipsed by the broad back of another man.

"Hey, hot stuff." The young man spoke in a grating, enthusiastic alto.

"Spart!" Aami turned and smiled eagerly as the larger man eyed her with a wanton lust that made Crilen bristle. Spart was, if nothing else, her perfect masculine counterpart as a purely physical specimen. His short wavy hair was pasted perfectly to his scalp. His bulging shoulders were broad and square. His clothes were pressed and well-fitted. And his single-minded affability, though loathsomely shallow, was polished to the degree of refinement befitting a suitor of Aami's social strata.

Aami tossed her book bag to the ground and threw herself around Spart's thick, muscular neck. Spart wasted no time working his hands up the back of her bare thighs, beneath her skirt, kneading and mushing her firm derrière with his fingers and palms. Crilen was appalled and distraught at the sight of this violation, but Aami only squealed and laughed gleefully. Crilen grimaced as he watched Spart tumble the both of them into the shaded grass as they began tongue kissing and groping one another madly.

Humiliation enveloped Crilen. He perceived the rustle of every leaf on every tree as the laughter of nature deriding his mounting sorrow. He turned to walk away, wishing rather to gaze upon his own funeral than to witness another moment of Spart and Aami mauling and pawing in romantic splendor.

But then, a familiar, haunting cackle warped and fractured reality.

Crilen turned back and met Aami's eyes for the first time. She was laid on her back with her arms and legs clutched rapturously around Spart. She looked toward Crilen with a taunting, supercilious expression he had never seen on her face before. He glanced at Spart who was also glaring at him with a toothy, lascivious grin as he rode her with slow, deliberate, swiveling pelvic thrusts.

The vulgar coitus on the open campus green left Crilen feeling numbed with horror and shame for his future wife. But as he observed them, there was something about Spart which grew even more disturbingly surreal. Spart's heavily muscled arms shriveled down to thin bones covered by a stretched layer of torn opaque skin. The teeth of his smile became jagged, sharp and carnivorous. Large, pointed antlers slowly sprouted from bleeding scabbed holes at the temples of his skull. His eyes suddenly appeared as deep blackened alien pools of dark deviltry and mischief.

Crilen looked at Aami again; only something there had changed as well. The color of her flesh had now drawn to a creamy smooth, unblemished white. In fact, it wasn't quite Aami any longer. It was PJ. Or perhaps it was Panla. Or, perhaps, she had now become all and the same.

With Spart's next thrust, Aami's blissful expression was violently jolted into a pained contortion of misery and anguish. She yelped as a large vein popped across her forehead. Instinctively, she tried to scream, but began choking and coughing instead as something long, bloody and living lurched from her open mouth and thrashed randomly against the sides of her face. Like the feasting predator he had become, Spart savagely bit down on her throat to squelch her piercing lamentation.

Enraged beyond endurance, Crilen felt a sudden burning fire rip up his spinal column, across his shoulders and over the crown of his skull. The hot pyrogenic sensation was familiar, but displaced in time. Before he was even conscious of it, his entire body was aflame.

"Get off!" he yelled at Spart/It.

"Make me," Spart answered with It's mocking inflections.

Crilen's hands burst into blazing fiery torches. His anger consumed him with the vision of blasting Spart/It into a scattered trail of scorched ash and black cinders.

"Last chance." Crilen's eyes glowed molten red.

"For me?" Spart/It growled a chuckle and jerked Aami's head around to face Crilen. "Or for her?"

Crilen froze as a horrible, familiar fear washed over Aami's terrified features.

"I can't," he lamented to himself. "God of the cosmos, I can't. Not again. But I have to do something. Something! Something!"

"Something like what?"

Crilen's eyes popped open as he lurched forward from his seat and fell onto the transport cabin floor. Disoriented, he looked up and saw a head of strawberry-orange hair surrounding a concerned face hovering over him.

"Are you all right, Mr. Len?" It took a moment for Feebie's voice to register in his mind.

Crilen squinted up into the cabin lights, then over to Feebie's freckled white face. He could feel the auxiliary transport's engine droning through his back, and he could see the impression of his body molded into the vacated leather seat just above him.

"No wonder you passed out." Feebie stepped away. "It's hot as hell back here. Mind if I buzz open a window?"

"No," Crilen groaned as he sat up on the floor.

"You're not getting sick, are you?" Feebie reached over and touched his forehead. "You're burning up."

"Not likely." Crilen took her hand away. "I'm fine."

"Tough first day?" Feebie offered him an excuse.

"Long first day." Crilen crawled back onto his seat.

"You conked out the moment we switched vehicles. You're going to have to learn how to pace yourself." She lifted the lid of a large, boxed container and pulled out a small clear bottle of blue liquid. "Here, have one. It'll cool you off."

Crilen frowned at the contents.

"What's wrong?" Feebie looked at him strangely.

"I've always had trouble thinking of anything blue being good for you," Crilen commented.

"It's just enriched juice." Feebie shook her head and handed him the bottle. "What color's the fruit on your side of the world?"

Which world? Crilen thought.

"Never mind." He took the bottle and flipped open the top.

"It's hard to keep up with someone leading a triple life." Feebie spoke of Panla's trebled existence. "I have enough problems keeping up with my one. Today, I slept on the way to YBS. I usually try to nap in the middle of the afternoon because I can never sleep once we head for Rabbel's."

"Why's that?" Crilen wasn't really concentrating on the conversation as he drank.

"Because Rabbel's tavern scares me," she said grimly. "Everything's all wrong there. The people. The music. The food. The drinks. The violence. The crap pasted on the walls. Rabbel. Even PJ. It's all wrong there. It's like everything there is from another planet or dimension. I mean, they hate God, for crying out loud. How can anyone who cares about anything feel right there?"

"How does Mrs…I mean, how does PJ do it?" Crilen asked.

"I don't know." Feebie sighed. "I honestly don't know. I think I understand what she's doing, but then we get down there and she changes. She's a different person. She's like them."

"Isn't that the point?" Crilen offered.

"Yeah." Feebie folded her lips. "Yeah, I guess so. But when I think of her sermons at Bius Basilica and then I see her sitting on that tavern stage with that long hair, playing to that hateful mob, it really makes me sick inside. I guess I can't explain it. Maybe you'll see for yourself tonight. Then, maybe you can explain it to me."

Crilen drifted into the last images of his dream. Spart/It taunting him with Aami/Panla impaled by his tormenting, perverted grasp.

"Mr. Len?"

"Excuse me." Crilen blinked himself back into real time. "I had a rather wild dream."

"I heard you." Feebie's brows rose. "You had to do something, you said."

"Yes."

"Do you have flashbacks?" Feebie questioned. "I hear a lot of ex-policers have flashbacks from all the ugly things they've had to see."

Crilen pondered the irony. She had no idea of the magnitude of ugliness he'd witnessed throughout the universe. He wondered, for a moment, if It was really omniscient enough to be orchestrating this entire elaborate plot.

"Let's just say it's a good thing flashbacks weren't part of my interview for this job." Crilen smiled. "But then again, maybe it's a requisite."

Feebie looked at him strangely.

"So where is Mrs. Tem?" Crilen finished his bottle and handed it back to her.

"She and Mr. Linnfeld are meeting in the rear cabin," Feebie answered hesitantly. "Actually, I think they expect you to be there."

"Wonderful." Crilen rose slowly, shaking his head.

"Sorry." Feebie smiled sheepishly.

The door to the rear cabin slid open and Crilen ducked through.

As he entered, Linnfeld was sitting with his back to him. He looked up at Panla and was taken aback by her cosmetically subtle, yet sublime transformation.

She was dressed in full PJ regalia. The black refracting leotard clung to every curve of her lean figure as its deep incandescent properties caused his eyes to strain before he could adjust. Her hair was tied back and blended into a long pony-tail extension. Her eyebrows were neatly arched and thickened by black marker. Her lips were colored a very blatant shade of scarlet red. And an oversized, jeweled bracelet hung from her left wrist sparkling brightly, twinkling with every movement.

"Well, it's about time," she huffed without looking away from Linnfeld.

"Sorry," Crilen apologized and took his place next to the lead attendant.

"Sorry." she mocked disdainfully without looking at him. "I guess sorry is all I should expect from anyone my husband would hire. But even he would find it unconscionable for my security head to doze off during the most critical point of the evening. I think I'll mention your lapse to him when we get back."

"By all means," Crilen frowned, "and you can tell him where we were going when I lapsed."

Panla's head snapped around as she angrily stared through him with a chilling contempt which seemed completely out of character. If her eyes had been lasers, he would have felt a pair of holes burning straight through the back of his head.

"Fuck off, Mr. Len." she cursed him.

The harsh remark stunned Crilen and Linnfeld. A momentary silence tightened the bands of tension gripping everyone.

"As you wish…Queen Mother," Crilen finally responded.

Panla jumped up from her seat and lunged as if she were going to strike him. Linnfeld stepped between them and gently held her by the waist until she reluctantly dropped back to her seat.

"Let go of me!" She fitfully shrugged Linnfeld's hands away.

Linnfeld held up his hands and eased away.

"You're finished, do you understand?" she pointed at Crilen. "I don't give a damn who you work for or what you're doing here. After tonight, you're finished!"

Crilen sat in quiet astonishment as their eyes locked once more. PJ snapped off the connection with a sharp breath, a dismissive roll of her eyes and an irritated shake of her head.

"Does he need to be here?" she said to Linnfeld.

"I'm an Attendant, not a bodyguard," Linnfeld answered concisely.

"Well, neither is he!" Panla hissed. "He's a sneaking, delusional, misbegotten…"

"That's enough!" Crilen's angry voice thundered. "I'm not the one playing dress-up roulette. You are! I'm just the poor dupe who was hired to protect you. That is, to protect you from yourself apparently. But whatever childish role you choose to play, I'm still going to make sure you get home safely. Whether you want to or not."

"Whether I want…?" Panla spoke through clenched teeth. "You ignorant cretin! Do you have any idea…?"

"PJ," Linnfeld interrupted. "I think you and I have gone over everything. Perhaps I can brief Mr. Len while you get prepared for our arrival."

Panla scowled bitterly at Crilen, as her chest heaved. She fell back against the cushions and stared out the dark transport window.

Crilen was surprised at how deeply this exchange unhinged him. He had never fought with his wife so bitterly. She had never cursed him with so dismissive a contempt.

"Fine," she relented grudgingly. "But Mr. Len…"

"Yes." Crilen stood to excuse himself.

"If you try to eavesdrop on anything I'm doing," her hands dug into her seat cushions, "I'll tell everyone in that building that you're a government spy and set them on to you. If I do that, you'll feel your dead body thudding against the floor before you hear them draw their weapons. Do you understand me?"

"Understood." Crilen met her eyes one last time. "Only I wouldn't have my back to Rabbel when you 'set them on' to me. Otherwise, that loud thudding body you hear…might be your own."

He turned and pushed past Linnfeld, exiting the rear cabin.

For an instant, Linnfeld thought he smelled smoke.

XXX.

The willfully corrupt never identify the vile corruption within themselves. Rather, with impunity, they embrace the delusion of their entitlement and justification, fueled by their lust for glory and their poorly concealed, amoral instinct for self-preservation.

The Accommodant stepped down from the parliamentary podium amidst a sea of ingenuous applause which thinly veiled the contempt of his legislative adversaries. For every camera, a bevy of smiles were pasted beneath the dead eyes of politically mendacious souls. The illusion of harmony and accord was purveyed to a mass audience like the staled staging of a monotonous lie which apathy no longer cared to question. And, indeed, what choice was there but to fall neatly into the queue behind the Accommodant's convincing recitation of an impassioned plea for the confirmation of his new World Judiciary candidate? What would the planet think if so fine a man, as the Accommodant had so enthusiastically endorsed him, should not be placed upon the world's highest legal bench? They would pointedly question how any legislator with a heart in his bosom could not be moved by the specious, yet tearful story of the candidate's bout with CI, the loss of his wife in a vehicle accident and the nurture of his handicapped adult offspring?

What legislator's reason could outweigh so moving a performance, in spite of the candidate's personal views favoring the eradication of Cathedral symbols from public property, the elimination of Cathedral teachings in public schools, the limitation of Cathedral advertising, deregulation of personal weaponry, legalization of non-addictive hallucinogenics, termination of unwanted unborns and government funding for non-profit existential educational programs?

"Un-Godly," whispered one clapping parliamentarian. "The devil's will, bundled warm and fuzzy."

"We sanction the glory of Hell for our luxuries," another commented quietly as he smiled and waved to the passing Accommodant.

"But it is an election twinmoon," a third legislator sighed under his plastered smile. "If we don't give the people what they want, we'll all have to go out and actually work for a living. I like my free limo. I like my paid vacations. I like the fresh tender, long-legged university girls on my staff. And nothing beats living in a fully-furnished lakeside villa, mortgage-free. I'm not paid to vote my conscience, gentle friends. I'm paid to give my district what it wants. If the whole goddamned world wants to become a cesspool, I doubt I'll live long enough to see it anyway. I've got my own cesspool to worry about. And I'm not about to piss it away for a vote of conscience that nobody really wants."

"Indeed," The first legislator nodded, "it's the people's fault, not ours. If the people wanted morality we'd certainly give it to them. If they wanted traditional families or socially temperate sexual values, that's exactly what we'd give them. If they wanted the Deliveress's stamp on every law of the land, we'd welcome her, with open hands, to the Parliamentary floor."

"With exactly the same enthusiasm with which we greet her husband," added the second legislator.

"Which is exactly the point," the third legislator concluded. "People don't want rules today. Certainly no rules that get in the way of a good romp. The laws of the land should equate to no laws of the land, manslaughter not withstanding. A fair amount of anarchy and social decay are sure to follow, but that's better than appearing to be closed minded in this day and age. Why the other night, I heard one of those new satellite preachers refer to God as a bisexual hermaphrodite. He said 'who are we mortals to say what's what? Anything is possible. All things are possible'."

"And, even if its nonsense, that's what the people really want," the second legislator affirmed. "Let's never lose sight of that."

"Amen." The first legislator watched as the Accommodant greeted Allabel casually before exiting the floor. "Our good Accommodant understands these things. That's why he's so popular with the masses. Amen."

"Amen." The other legislators dropped their synchronized smiles with the dimming of the camera lights.

CONCERTO DUPLICITÉ

I.

The atmosphere in the tavern was heavy and putrefied by the wafting haze of herbal smoke and the bitter stench of stale alcohol. The lights along the room's perimeter were dimmed over the booths, the bar and the stage. It was, otherwise, pitch black where the dense contingent of patrons milled about, laughing, growling, cursing, fondling, and bumping one another as PJ held court.

On stage, she was perched upon her customary stool amid the leaning wooden instruments momentarily abandoned by their musicians. Tonight, the buzzing crowd was more transfixed than usual by their commiserating compatriot/benefactor from the north. They had grown fondly accustomed to both her polished irreverence and her flagrant contempt for the Cathedral. But this particular evening, for whatever reason, PJ was in a rare form that electrified the rebellious contingent even more.

"So where's my fucking drink?" she yelled into the darkness as the crowd laughed, loudly echoing her request with a barrage of obscenities.

Linnfeld, Feebie and Crilen tried to remain passive as they sat at the bar even though the grumbling patronage slowly turned their mounting discord upon the three. Hurriedly, Genna derailed the smoldering standoff, whisking across their bough, carrying a large glass of bright red liquor above her head.

"I've got it." Genna sounded genuinely apologetic to everyone in the room.

The mass of bodies parted for the young woman as if she were rushing to deliver an ancient artifact to a sacred altar. PJ, the high priestess, popped off of her stool and stepped to the edge of the stage, waiting with her hands on her hips, glowering an admonishing scowl. Genna obsequiously held up the glass with two hands. Only after an uncomfortable, overlong and demeaning pause did PJ finally crouch down to accept it.

"Well, don't spill it!" PJ shouted for the crowd as she reached for the glass. "You get any of this on me and you'll be washing your hair with the rest of it. Do you understand?"

Genna steadied her hands and bowed her head as PJ pulled the large drink from her grasp.

"Thank you, dear!" PJ tilted her head and mocked the young woman with a broad smile and an exaggerated flutter of her eyelashes.

Genna respectfully turned away and tried to maneuver back to the bar area as the crowd shoved and jostled her, cursing and yelling at her for disrupting PJ's monologue.

"That was so mean," Feebie whispered, tightening the hood of her cape over her head. "I hate this."

Genna finally burst through the raucous crowd and nearly fell into Feebie's arms. Crilen leaned over to Linnfeld. "Is this normal?" he whispered into the lead attendant's ear.

"The crowd or her?" Linnfeld kept his eyes on the stage.

"Both," Crilen answered.

"Well, tonight is rather tame for this bunch." Linnfeld grimaced. "Last night, they had Reza's father in here. I guess he meant to drag his daughter out into the street and whisk her home to safety. For his trouble, the poor man got beaten within an inch of his life. I can't say I see any suicidal sacrifices roaming around here tonight...except us, that is."

Crilen remembered the thrashing Durn had given Reza's father.

"What about Pan..." Crilen stammered, "I mean PJ? Is this normal?"

Linnfeld leaned back and met Crilen's eyes with deep concern.

"She's on her fourth drink and we haven't been here an hour, Mr. Len. That certainly isn't normal for her. I'm afraid things aren't quite right."

"Any suggestions?" Crilen whispered.

"We can always drag her off stage, blow everyone's cover, fight our way out of here and risk getting ourselves killed." Linnfeld said with resignation.

Crilen ran the scenario through his head; the probable results were not attractive.

"Right," Crilen sighed.

"For now, I think the only thing we can do is…our jobs," Linnfeld continued. "We'll do the attending and you'll do the securing. And we'll all just pray that nothing actually goes wrong."

Meanwhile, on-stage:

"Did you see the Deliveress on the monitor tonight?" PJ's amplified voice echoed as she climbed back on to her stool.

The crowd booed and hissed.

"She said she's only had sex with one man." PJ shook her head and frowned. "Of course they didn't ask her about the thirty or forty churchmaids she's been slapping around with that three-dm dildo."

Loud shouts and cackles flew freely.

"And Libbi forgot to ask her about those low-hung bulls they keep out in the Cathedral farmyard."

"Suck it!" a hoarse male voice yelled from the back.

"I do have to admit I'd have loved to have been the interviewer, tonight," PJ gulped from her glass and adjusted her posture. "'My dear Deliveress, are those rug burns on that homophobic tongue of yours? And Mrs. Tem, if a churchmaid takes a ramming with a dildo is she still considered a virgin? What about the Lord Regent? Oh, yes, darling, I know he's a he, but that doesn't really answer the question, now does it?'"

The crowd's maniacal laughter mounted.

"'And Mrs. Tem, can a lady tongue the testicles of a two-ton bull and still be considered a virgin?'" PJ tilted her head with an expression of girlish mischief. "'Oh, I'm not asking for myself, of course, I'm asking for a friend. Oh, you say only IF she's a lady. Yes, ladies don't swallow, they just swish and drool. I see.'"

The dark room broke into a bawdy uproar of wild hysterics that segued into thunderous cheers and fervid applause. PJ, however, remained quietly upright on her stool as she poured down another gulp from her glass. She paused, looking out over the room with a winsome reflection no one could really interpret.

"So where the hell is Rabbel tonight?" her neck wobbled slightly.

There was a subdued response from someone just off stage.

"Excuse me?" PJ leaned forward cupping her ear. "He's what?"

The voice quietly repeated itself and PJ's head popped up with mirthful embarrassment.

"'He's off, wanking!' the gentleman says." PJ giggled to the person off stage. "And the worst part is, he told you and not me. Should I be jealous?"

The crowd chuckled, uncertain whether it was good to laugh at anything which poked fun at Rabbel.

"Oh, did I hit a nerve out there?" Panla looked up with a serious gaze. "You sound as if someone just told you that there's no God or something. I guess that'd be a comfort to some of you. Well, maybe there is and maybe there isn't. But one thing's for certain: you can't deify flesh and blood. Rabbel…and me and you…we're all just mortals. Flawed, imperfect and maybe just a little bit insane. If you're looking for perfection, you certainly won't find it in this life…unless you do something absurd…like pick up a Text or some such nonsense."

"Fuck that!" a screeching female voice decried.

"Right." PJ's playful glint returned to her eyes. "Well, on that philosophical punctuation, I have to leave you with one last story involving the hierarchy of the Cathedral. I swear to you, this is true."

The crowd roared and applauded.

"After a full day of prayer and confessions, the Lord Regent throws on a hat and overcoat and wanders down to the local brothel."

"Yeah!" someone belched from the audience.

"He walks in the front door of the brothel," PJ continued "and the madame says 'Oh, how good to see you again.' The Lord Regent quietly holds a finger up to his lips and whispers to the madame, 'The usual.' The madame claps her hands and out walks a pretty little boy, about nine or ten. The Regent smiles, licking his chops and off they go up the stairs to a private room. Well, the Lord Regent is all eager and horny when he walks past a room with the door slightly ajar and to his shock he sees the Deliveress! He stops dead in his tracks and enters the room where he sees a bedroom full of men and women laying around half-dressed.

"'What are you doing' the Lord Regent asks the Deliveress.

"'Don't worry. I'm saving minds,' she says to him.

"The Lord Regent is stunned, but he's got that little boy waiting for him out in the hallway so he hurries out before she asks him the same. Later in the evening, the Lord Regent, feeling quite refreshed after a good bloody ramming, goes down to the sauna. This time he sees the Deliveress lying naked between two females. The Lord Regent is shocked.

"The Deliveress says, 'Don't worry. I'm saving bodies.'

"The Lord Regent nods respectfully and backs out, not wanting to think about what he'd just seen. Later still, the Lord Regent sees a closed door with a sign that says Oral Sex. He gets excited and barges into the room only to find the Deliveress on her knees in front of a male, holding his organ up to her face.

"Stunned for a moment, the Deliveress recovers and smiles saying 'Don't worry, I'm saving souls.'

"Despondent, the Lord Regent decides to go back to the boy's room until he can settle down. But he's just too upset, so he gets dressed, runs down the stairs and pays the madame. He runs out the front where he sees a taxi waiting outside. Unfortunately, when he gets close enough, he looks into the back seat and sees the driver humping the Deliveress, her legs flopping in the air. 'Queen Mother!' the Lord Regent shouts. 'Are you saving another mind?'

"The Deliveress rolls her eyes and says, 'No.'

"'Are you saving another body?' the Lord Regent asks her.

"'No', the Deliveress answers as her feet bang and slap against the inside of the taxi's roof.

"'Are you saving another soul?' the Lord Regent's voice became strained.

"'No.' the Deliveress' smiled. 'But don't worry, I am saving cab fare,' she said as she pushed down the taxi driver's trousers, exposing his bare ass. 'Hop in. He says you love splitting rides!'"

The crowd offered a low groan as they reveled in their disgust.

At the bar, Feebie hung her head, slumped her shoulders and rocked unsteadily as if she were going to vomit. Genna grabbed hold of her; Linnfeld thought he saw Feebie wipe away tears.

"Are you all right?" Linnfeld asked her.

"I'm out of here," Feebie sniffed, cleaning away Genna's helping hands.

"Where are you going?" Linnfeld spoke authoritatively.

"Out." Feebie looked inconsolable. "Out of here. Away from this shit."

"You can't wander off." Linnfeld pointed his finger. "It's not safe."

"I'm not wandering off." Feebie became agitated. "I'm just stepping outside. I'll be by the transport. It may be a little dangerous, but I'll just count on the Lord, thank you. If He wants me to get raped or killed tonight, so be it. One thing's for sure: I know He doesn't want me hanging around in here anymore."

Before Linnfeld could command her to stay, her hooded figure had pushed into the crowd and melted from view. He considered going after her, but his priorities changed instantly when the sea of bodies parted once more, and yielded the dark, stout, figure of Rabbel Mennis.

"Mr. Linnfeld, good evening," Rabbel offered an affable nod and extended his large black hand.

As Linnfeld felt his hand engulfed by Rabbel's, he couldn't escape the discomfort he had always felt in the presence of the powerful leader of the Break. Not that there was any hint of dishonesty in Rabbel. On the contrary, this was certainly a genuine man of great honor. But within those stolid virtues, laid a black storm of harsh, inexorable will purposed by ideals wholly juxtaposed to anything that would soothe a Godly conscience. The sensation of their brief encounters always left Linnfeld feeling the cool chills one might only expect to suffer in the company of the devil. Fortunately, Linnfeld's twinmoons of experience in diplomatic circles, rehearsed him well in the art of facades.

"As always, a pleasure to see you again." Linnfeld was almost jocular in his greeting, shaking Rabbel's hand enthusiastically. "Of course you remember Genna."

"Of course." Rabbel nodded his acknowledgment.

"And here we have PJ's new security lead, Mr. Len." Linnfeld tried to gloss over the introduction.

Unfortunately, Rabbel paused, immediately scrutinizing Crilen's face for lines of recognition.

"Hmm." Rabbel stepped in front of Crilen and clasped his hand with a piercing stare. "Have I seen you before, Mr. Len?"

"We haven't met, sir." Crilen returned the gaze respectfully.

"I didn't ask you if we'd met." Rabbel held his hand with a mildly perceptible force. "I asked if I had seen you before."

Linnfeld swallowed hard. Genna held her breath.

Crilen paused a moment, then smiled a tight, confident grin of his own.

"I was a policer in the south for eleven twinmoons." he inspected Rabbel's own scrutinizing gaze. "If we met, I'm sure it was under…forgettable circumstances."

"Indeed." Rabbel nodded. "I would agree. So, how did you manage to become…privy to so much, so quickly?"

Crilen didn't flinch.

"I was a friend of Moll's," he answered with feigned regret in his voice. "She recommended me. PJ approved."

"I see." Rabbel left no indication whether the answer was satisfactory or not. He released Crilen's hand and severed their tense connection, glancing toward the stage.

"Is she still upset with me?" Rabbel asked Linnfeld with the sudden paradoxical tone of a smitten young suitor.

"She recognizes the necessity of your alliance," Linnfeld answered. "As for her mood, I'd say merry…with a pinch of venom."

"Very well." Rabbel sighed, and headed for the stage.

Crilen observed him guardedly.

"Mr. Len, you're an accomplished liar," Linnfeld smirked.

"Mr. Linnfeld, you're an accomplished diplomat." Crilen watched the crowd part for Rabbel Mennis.

"Liar. Diplomat. Synonymous, more often than not, I'm afraid." Linnfeld turned to order himself a drink. "You certainly can't be very good at one without a fair measure of skill in the other."

On stage:

"Oh!" PJ visored her eyes with her hand. "It looks like my ride is here. Better drink up."

The patrons applauded and whistled.

"But first let me leave you with one serious thought and I really mean it this time. Our movement has become a peaceful one. Because of that, our rivals haven't a clue and the government hasn't a case. Stay strong. And stay faithful. We aren't a threat to anyone except the enemies of liberty. All we want is a society that doesn't check its conscience in front of an idol or a statue. The truth resides in our heads and in our hearts. As long we don't let them take that from us, we will always be free."

The tavern burst into rousing applause as PJ held up her large glass in tribute. She put the glass to her lips and drank deeply, draining the remaining half with a series of large gulps. Rabbel stopped at the edge of the stage and looked up at her. PJ finally set down her glass and regarded him with a reprimanding scowl. Without warning, she danced to the lip of the stage and jumped several meters, landing cradled in Rabbel's arms. Rabbel tried to hide both his joy and his embarrassment, but all was lost when she threw her arms around his thickly muscled neck and kissed him tenderly on the cheek for everyone to see.

Serenaded by laughter and cheers, Rabbel carried PJ back through the crowd, past the bar, and into his rear office.

Linnfeld refused to look. Crilen, meanwhile, could not tear his eyes away.

"Why don't you stop staring?" Linnfeld set down his glass.

"I'm supposed to be her security," Crilen answered, boring a hole through Rabbel's office door.

"That's right," Linnfeld snorted, "you're her security. But you're baring the face of a jealous boyfriend."

"Excuse me?" Crilen finally snapped off his fixation on the door.

"I love her, too." Linnfeld put his hand on Crilen's shoulder. "Not romantically, of course, but the same way Feebie and Genna do. She means everything to all of us…as a spiritual leader and as a friend. But you're falling into something I wouldn't wish on my worst enemy.

"She's a wonderful woman. A beautiful woman. But she's rather married, don't you think? And doesn't her spare time seem to be just a bit congested with two or three full-time careers aimed at balancing the spiritual fate of the entire planet? And don't take this the wrong way, but in any case, what makes you think a woman like her would fall for a man like you? Let alone after one day. She may have confided in you. She may have held your hand. But I'd wager she's doing a lot more than that with Rabbel Mennis right now, and she doesn't give a damn about him.

"You're another listener for an unhappy wife. Another shield for the queen of the world. But the more you think of her as a woman, the less likely you are to succeed at whatever it is you're here to accomplish. Man to man, I advise you to get on with your job. Don't undo yourself for Mrs. Tem. I won't say she's not worth it, but the question is: Are you?"

Linnfeld's pointed words were dull in Crilen's ears, as his smoldering eyes lured themselves across the dark, tavern tableau…back toward the sealed door of Rabbel's office.

II.

YBS Studios.

EB: Hello, everyone. I'm Egs Bloyt. You're looking at a live shot of the blazing fuel tank, which, hours ago, was ruptured and ignited by the careening vehicle of actor Finx Melder as he lost control speeding through the city streets. Dead tonight are Finx Melder and the magnificent legacy he had only begun to build, and his companion, world sand surfing champion Preppi Deyz. We understand that firefighters are debating at this hour whether to continue trying to put out the blaze immediately, or, for safety reasons, merely contain the fire and allow it to burn itself out. Apparently, there is such a dense concentration of fuel at the epicenter that the intensity of the flames and heat are making the battle extremely difficult and dangerous. We promise to keep you apprised of any developments regarding this incredibly tragic story, so please remain with us for further updates.

Now, via global-link, I have the head of Avarice Studios, Mr. Nob Bobr. Nob, thank you for joining us.

NB: My pleasure.

EB: Now, aside from the fact that Finx is an irreplaceable icon who was literally the core of our contemporary culture, what does this immeasurable loss mean to Avarice?

NB: Well, in pure coin alone, there's no telling what the financial impact on Avarice Studios will be. There's the domino effect. We invested over a hundred million coin in Finx's contract. And our vendors, in turn, invested billions into our studio because of the irrepressible drawing power of Finx Melder. With Finx gone, our investment in Finx obviously falls by the wayside, along with some portions of the contractual commitments to us from those who invested in Avarice because of Finx.

EB: Is it a certainty that all of the vendors for Avarice will simply demand their money back and walk away?

NB: Well they can't just walk away. Our lawbookers are in discussions now as to how we can minimize any losses and retain the largest proportions of those contractual commitments.

EB: Weren't those commitments tied directly to Avarice Productions that featured Finx Melder?

NB: Not necessarily. Our lawbookers are in the process of making that determination.

EB: Well, if not, will Avarice be in financial jeopardy?

NB: Absolutely not. We were heavily bonded and insured against the prospect of Finx's untimely demise. We all loved Finx, but as business people, we had to underwrite his lifestyle. Either way, we'll be fine. It's a great loss. He was a great asset. And personally, he was a great friend. But as a corporate entity, we'll be fine.

EB: There are rumblings and rumors that allege Finx was being chased and hounded by the media and that this might have somehow, if true, contributed to this accident. Do you blame the media for his death and are you going to pursue any legal action?

NB: First of all, I think I'd be remiss if I didn't first extend my deepest condolences to the families of Finx Melder. Finx left behind some beautiful children whom I know he was planning to devote more time to during the upcoming twinmoon. Wonderful, wonderful children. My prayers go out to those children and their mothers. It's such a shame.

EB: Yes, we'll all certainly pray for them. But Mr. Bobr, what do you make of the charges that the media may have somehow been involved?

NB: Egs, in my business we simply can't afford to dignify rumor, hearsay or innuendo. I don't know what business can. I've known Yolo Pigue for forty twinmoons, and, while we've had our differences, I've never known any of his journalists to act irresponsibly. We don't always like what they have to say, but that's the flipside of having a free press in a free society.

EB: Are you saying you don't think the media caused the accident?

NB: I'm saying that it doesn't sound like we have nearly enough evidence to indicate what really took place one way or another. Until we get all the facts, we should reserve judgment.

EB: Amen. That's so refreshing to hear in an age where journalists are blamed for everything. Now tell me: Has the studio made any memorial plans for Mr. Melder?

NB: Yes. We've already set up a trust for Finx's children we're calling Finx Linx. Anyone at home who wants to contribute 25 coin or more will get a collage poster of Finx's films and receive a monthly newsletter on how Finx's children are progressing as they try to grow up without their father. Also, we're in discussions with YBS Media to produce a live broadcast of Finx's funeral from the Bius Basilica to every monitor around the world. And this is not just going to be a funeral. This is going to be a star-studded event that no one will ever forget. A tribute to the most popular icon who ever lived. I certainly think Finx would have wanted to go out that way.

EB: But Finx was a renowned atheist. Will there be any problem with the Deliveress or the Cathedral hierarchy allowing Finx's funeral to take place there?

NB: Egs, what I've learned is that when money talks, the Cathedral walks. Finx may have been an atheist, but Avarice is going to buy his way into Heaven with the funeral to end all funerals. Even God will have to stand up and applaud the show we're going to put on. It's going to be spectacular!

EB: Do you think there will be a protest over use of the Bius Basilica for the funeral of a man whose life was opposed to everything the Church stands for?

NB: I would hope not. When Finx was portraying Bius II in a sprawling epic film that sharply increased religious interest and attendance around the world, where were those critics?

EB: I recall there was some criticism.

NB: A small amount. But Finx did more to line the coffers of the Cathedral than all the Churchlords, Regents and Deliverers over the last half century combined! I'm not a particularly religious guy, but I have to believe that God is smiling on Finx for that great work despite their philosophical differences. I'd be willing to bet that God is overjoyed to be receiving one of his most triumphant children up into that great kingdom in the sky, as we speak. Even God can't deny Finx's greatness! And if God can't deny the greatness of Finx and the people can't deny the greatness of Finx, I don't see how a few stodgy religious protesters, out of step with contemporary thought, can deny Finx the star-studded burial he deserves in the world's most impressive edifice.

EB: What does the Deliveress make of this plan? Has anyone spoken to her?

NB: My people are talking to her people and we really don't anticipate a problem. From what I understand, she's a huge Finx fan and she can certainly appreciate a good show. That's what Avarice is all about. Positive entertainment with a happy message that makes everyone feel good about themselves. What more can the world ask for?

III.

"Oh wow! Hi! Kiss me!"

Before Crilen had any time to react, Reza had swept her bony young arms around his neck. Her glistening green lips smashed, pumped and rotated themselves against his mouth with an astonishing industrial-strength suction, which registered well off any biological p.s.i. scale he could think of. The only point of comparison he could conjure was the bite of the seven-meter eels from the planet Shakir, whose giant mouths latched onto their victims' torsos and drained them of every last molecule of H2O. At least, by contrast, Reza provided a surfeit of moisture. When she finally did uncouple herself from Crilen's face with a thin stream of slime trailing between them, he wondered whether his lungs would ever dislodge themselves from the vacuum knot which had formed in the base of his throat.

"You remember me, right?" she smiled brightly, kneading her fingers into the sides of his scalp.

"Uh…" Crilen stammered with his back pressed uncomfortably against the bar.

Linnfeld rolled his eyes and picked up his drink. "I'll be around," he said, patting Crilen on the shoulder sympathetically.

"Wow." Reza watched Linnfeld hastily wedge himself into the crowd. "Who spunked on his hemorrhoids?"

The contorted metaphor humored a smile across Crilen's lips before he could catch himself.

"See! You do remember me!" Reza hugged him, pressing her narrow pelvis forcefully into his. "Mmm. And I think you like me!"

Crilen reached up and gently unraveled her arms from around his neck. Reza's expression immediately dropped into a wounded, girlish pout as if a steady teenage boyfriend had abruptly broken off their schoolyard romance.

It was easy to read the injury in her white oval face framed by her pressed green curls. Her large brown eyes welled up into a theatrical mixture of anger and despair. Her mouth quivered and drooped with a childish, adolescent dejection. Crilen easily assessed her as an aesthetically cute, yet erratically manipulative, young woman. Though, while in tune with her unevenly orchestrated performance, to her credit, he still found himself groping for an apology undeserved.

Just as he opened his mouth to make amends, Reza surprisingly spun about and side-kicked him in the stomach as hard as she could. The action was violent and precise. However, the disparity in size and weight sent her twirling backward, bouncing onto the floor, leaving Crilen towering above her, stunned but unmoved.

Several tavern patrons passively observed the humiliating scene, but no one bothered to interrupt their drinks or conversations to intercede. Two men casually stepped over her prone figure, diverting only a pitiless sidelong glance as she remained sprawled on the bar room floor, clutching her right knee for effect. Reza even gestured for general assistance, demonstratively stretching up her arms to the open air, but everyone carried on about their business with nary a wink of concern. It became harshly apparent that neither help or sympathy were forthcoming.

"Shit me!" Reza exclaimed, finally picking herself up and dusting off her bright pink mini-dress. "You are fucking hard. Why don't you just split my head open on the bar?"

"You might like that." Crilen eyed her with bemusement.

"I might like a lot of things." Reza licked her fingers and leaned onto the bar, arching her back. "But then again, that's me. I like lots of things and lots of places and lots of people. There's nothing wrong with that. I mean I hate limited people, don't you? I mean people who limit themselves. I mean, there really aren't any limits until we put limits on ourselves, you know what I mean? Limits are pathetic. I hate limited people. I'm not limited. Never have been. Never will be. Want a drink?"

"I…"

"Do you like these boots?" Reza nodded down to her spike-heeled, pink and blue ankle boots. "They don't kick for dick, but they're cute, I think. Two, please!"

Reza pulled out a tiny green and pink spotted patent leather pocketbook. She popped open the flap and pulled all matter of trinkets and wadded junk out onto the bar.

"Bleeding jizz!" she cursed. "Where the fuck…? Oh, never mind."

Reza jumped up and snagged a clear vial of pills just before they rolled off behind the bar. She thumbed open the cap and poured in an indiscriminate number of orange capsules into the palm of her hand. Then, with a quick motion, she dumped them into her mouth, popped the vial closed and raked her scattered possessions off the bar and back into her pocket book.

While she hastily tucked the pocketbook onto the drooping belt around her waist, she sensed Crilen's eyes on her.

"Medicine, okay?" She looked up and tilted her head with a sassy smile. "Medicine for my little problem, that's all."

Crilen nodded with a dubious acknowledgment, then looked for the bartender.

"Oh, eat my grandma, you stinking shit-smear!" Reza hissed. "You think everybody who takes pills in a bar is getting off for recreational?"

"You can do what you want," Crilen responded with indifference.

"Ever heard of IVC?" Reza's large eyes became angry. "Well, I've got it! And since I can't digest anything solid without pain and puking, the drug helps me maintain my weight and coagulate the internal bleeding. The virus is still eating through all my pelvic organs. And it scorches like a brother fucker when I have to spray, but at least I can still have fun."

"I'm sorry," Crilen said as this knowledge added depth to her waif-like thinness.

"Don't be sorry." Reza smiled as their drinks arrived. "Life is still a roast! And, besides, you didn't burn me. Maybe Durn did…he's got it. Or maybe I burned myself. Whatever. What's done is done. At least I'm free."

"How so?" Crilen was genuinely intrigued.

"I love this drink!" Reza leaned over and sipped. "If it came out of a cock, it'd be a perfect world."

Crilen could only stare at her as she was fully prepared to digress into another galaxy of thoughts unless he reeled her back into focus. It was difficult to determine whether she was so thoroughly elusive by design or flaw.

"How are you free?" Crilen asked with sharpened clarity, cutting down her room to ramble.

"Oh, shit, are sure you want hear this?" Reza slumped. "You're fun. I want to have fun."

"Too late." Crilen met her eyes. "I'm intrigued."

"By me?" Reza laughed. "I thought you were deeper than that."

"Maybe not."

"Well, hold your breath." Reza arched up on her stool, crossed her legs and slurped a short swig from her glass. "This is Reza's Theory of Life. It probably sucks, but it's all I've got.

"The way I see it, everyone is so totally monked with what food or drink or habit will kill them and what food or drink or habit will make them live forever, like that's really fucking possible. But the truth is, that most of the people you see who live forever are miserable fucking cowards who never had a good gushing orgasm in their lives! Shriveled up little wieners and gashes with virgin livers and lungs, chained up in that rusty iron chastity underwear they have welded into their heads. But when it's all said and done, a good vehicle wreck can kill you just as fast as anything else. Good boy, Bad girl…what spunking difference does it make? Look at Finx Melder. Everyone wanted him to straighten up…dry out…stop doing drugs…stop banging off with his gaggle of sexers. What for? All of a sudden he's dead for none of the reasons people thought he would die. An accident. Boom. Dead. So fuck it! I've got IVC. Whether I die sooner or later, what's the difference? The key is to live every moment like it's your last. That's how I get the most out of life!"

Reza leaned forward and spoke lowly as if she were disclosing the solution to a treasure map.

"The one universal truth," she looked as serious as Crilen had ever seen her, "is that nobody promises you a future two minutes from right now. So you've got to live fast and come as hard and as often as you can. Otherwise, there's just no point."

With that conclusion, Reza tilted her head, held up her glass, rolled her eyes contritely and drank.

"And what would God make of that?" Crilen offered.

"Lube that wad and lick me, will ya?" Reza frowned and slammed down her glass. "I should have pegged you for a statue blower. Too many questions, not enough love. You jizz-spitting religious wankers think you know everything."

"On the contrary." Crilen stirred his drink. "We're just wise enough to realize how little we know. How little we'll ever know."

"I know what you don't know!" Reza smirked and eyed his crotch. "But you can know a lot more if you promise not to be gentle."

"Really," Crilen smirked.

"No, not really." Reza tossed back her head. "You have it in you, but you won't let it out. I don't go down the shaft unless the mine's open. Otherwise it's all hassle and no hurt."

"Hurt?" Crilen's eyes narrowed. "What does hurt have to do with anything?"

"Oh my god, you are from another fucking planet!" Reza cackled and shook her head fitfully. "Burn that Text and get a life! Hurt is the point! Okay. Here's Reza's Theory of Life, Part II: If it don't make you hurt, it ain't worth the squirt!

"Before I was even twelve," she recalled with a disquieting fondness, "I learned that sex is the only thing that hurts the right way. Hurt with no thinking involved. With sex, you just go with it. Everything else is so shitty fucking complicated! But sexual hurt is simple, direct and spontaneous, and it isn't a bad thing. I mean, it can be, but everyone knows there's bad hurt and there's good hurt. Bad hurt is like getting whacked in the head. Not that I haven't been bludgeoned a few times, but who can enjoy sex with throbbing head trauma, you know? It dulls your ability to feel.

"But good hurt is ass-licking wicked! I love that wild nasty strained hurt that rips through every muscle in your body like a spasm of lightning. I love that helpless, vulnerable, defenseless hurt, where I feel like some dirty sweaty psycho could take my life while he's inside me and I can't begin to do anything to stop it. Totally dominated at the mercy of some menacing sadist who uses his cock for a ten-ton mining drill, tearing through me like he doesn't care if I live or die. He wants to hurt me and make me miserable. Feeling like he's going to snap my arms or break my neck! Pushing pain and fear through the pit of my stomach, down the crack in my ass, burning the muscles in my thighs and tearing all that thick torturous agony up into my slit 'til I scream for him not to stop. Sometimes that hurt feels so prick-sucking good, I shit on myself! And, frankly, I know that brings me closer to God's stiff wiggler than anything in the universe! A fuck of a lot closer than any book can get me."

Crilen was speechless.

"Whup!" Reza burst into a perky mischievous smile. "I can tell by the silence, I'm a sudden disappointment to you. Sorry. That's the way it is."

"I see." Crilen looked up thoughtfully. "To each, his or her own."

"Amen, brother!" She swatted him on the thigh.

"But what I don't get," Crilen continued, "was the whole scene with your father the other night."

"You mean, last night." Seriousness encroached upon Reza's devil-may-care expression once more.

"Last night," Crilen corrected himself. "Your father came in here looking for you. And he absorbed, what I would hope was, the beating of his life because he wanted to take you away from all of this."

"Oh suck the puss out of my grandma's tits, you loser!" Reza sighed angrily. "I told you last night, that Da-do likes to put on a big fucking self-righteous broadcast to make himself look like some sort of stake-humping martyr. He was jizzing in his pants while Durn was busting his face. That, and I'm sure he was trying to exorcise some kind of egotistical guilt trip over being such a shit-licking lousy da'. Fuck him."

"Maybe." Crilen sipped from his glass. "Probably. After all, you know him better than I do. But what you didn't explain is why you were crying."

Reza's thin body heaved with a deep sigh as she giggled, looked up at the ceiling and shook her head.

"Crying?" she frowned. "Crying for Durn to kick his testicles across the room."

"Is that what that was?" Crilen looked at her. "I recall hearing you yell things like 'stop' and 'no'. And I could swear I saw you crumple to your knees when you looked into your father's bloodied face."

"I was pretty drunk last night." Reza looked down into her glass. "I'm sure I was acting totally stupid. After all, I talked to you, didn't I?"

"Yes, you talked to me," Crilen answered. "And you were rambling on about a few things, but I didn't get the impression you were drunk."

"Well, so what?" Reza's lips tightened as she nodded stressfully. "Whatever!"

"Well, I just thought you were more than a little upset to see your father take that pounding," Crilen concluded. "It bothered me and I didn't even know him."

"Well, it was disgusting." Reza chuckled nervously. "Da-do can't fight at all. My brother kicked his cock three twinmoons ago in front of that prepubescent whore-sore of his. And my brother's a limpy. I don't know what he was thinking to come here, knowing he'd get beat to puss like that. What an idiot."

"But you were crying," Crilen noted again.

"Well, that was Da-do, okay?" Reza glared at him. "I can hate the runny fuck and still not want to see him get cracked like that, can't I? Don't you have a Da?"

"I did." Crilen reflected. "And he and I used to argue about a lot of things. But a strange thing happened as I got a little older. The more I lived and experienced life, the more I learned that he wasn't really as wrong about most things as I'd thought."

"Didn't that just twig your wig?"

"At first." Crilen smiled. "But after a while, it just made me proud. I was actually proud that my father had been right about most things. And that he'd cared enough to fight my young ignorance every step of the way."

"Well my fucking Da…"

"It hurt to watch your father lose, didn't it?" Crilen continued. "He came all the way down here because of you. Because he loved you and he didn't want his daughter staying in the middle of this mess. And you knew he was right, and you wanted him to win so badly, but you also knew he didn't have a chance in a bare-knuckle bar-room brawl. And you couldn't stand it. I mean if he was wrong, and you hated him as much as you say…"

"You are so lost!" Reza hissed.

"But you knew he was right. And you wanted him to, somehow, triumphantly scoop you out of here and haul you back to that imperfect little home of yours because now you know that home wasn't quite so bad. But Durn crushed him. Resoundingly crushed him. And your Da had to be dragged out of here in a bleeding heap of bruises and welts and missing teeth. So you both lost. Him, out there. And you, in here with these people, living this miserable masochistic life you really hate."

"I don't think I like you anymore." Reza's expression grew cold as her voice became barely audible.

"You play the role of a confused little girl trapped by a world of degradation." Crilen leaned into her personal space. "But you're not dumb. You're actually rather ingenious. An ingenious little masochist who works very hard to ensure that things never turn out quite right. God made you special, but you'd rather spit in God's face in favor of a life and death of self-inflicted hurt and suffering. Bad things don't happen to you. You just make it seem like they do. You maneuver the circumstances surrounding you so that some form of misery will always be the result. And, for anyone stupid enough to get close to you, they get a heavy dose of misery too. Their penalty for loving you more than you love yourself, like your father. And even poor stupid Durn."

"Durn does not love me!" Reza laughed and threw back her head again. "He's my protection, sort of. He likes to watch me tongue the spunk, so I let him. That's as deep it gets. Or as deep as he gets. Take your pick."

"Reza…" Crilen took her hand.

"I don't want to talk about it anymore." Reza jerked away. "Oh, Durn! Honey."

She turned her back to Crilen as Durn appeared out of nowhere. With no words between them, Durn's dingy paw crawled between her legs as she extended her tongue to his and kissed him with a drooling lust that dribbled between their chins.

Durn opened his eyes momentarily and winked at Crilen.

Crilen slid from his stool and decided it was time to walk the bar's perimeter…as far from Reza and Durn as he could get.

IV.

"Enough is enough." Mr. Pont failed to invigorate another listless cliché while recording dictation from his cramped kitchen nook. "I've tried to stay as far away from this ideological conflict as I can, but it appears as though neither side will rest until all of us are drawn headlong into their sickening melee of blind hatred."

Mr. Pont sat alone under the dingy amber ceiling lamp. He thoughtfully fidgeted with the last remnant of a dried corner of bread which teetered on the edge of a chipped plate. The plate was stained by a smeary swamp of browned condiment, gnawed gristle and dried yellow peas. The cuffs of his wrinkled shirt were unbuttoned and unevenly twisted above his knobby wrists. His cracking tenor voice strained to fill the air like the delusional wail of a self-anointed monarch reigning majestically over his own private utopia.

Indeed, within the walls of his narrow, grey apartment, his empirically unimaginative convictions were irrefutable. No authorities, experts or zealots could contradict him here. No angered or offended patrons would make rebuttal. Even the soft, sagging folds of flesh about his sunken waist felt firm and taut with none present to deride its ill-condition for what it was. In his mind, he was a lean and scholarly sculpture of mortal insight and intuition, particularly when compared to the mountainous rumbling girth of his loathed employer, Yolo Pigue. In this vacuum, he was both the ingenious orator and the awestruck audience riveted on his personally profound philosophy. In this vacuum he was the crowned ruler of the world. Though by tomorrow, few who bothered to read his daily editorial would share in his ethically diluted delusion. As was more often the case, they would subconsciously borrow a morsel of thought or a smidgen of rankle, and witlessly synthesize their own beliefs for their morning debates in the cafes and their fractured inarticulate evening commentaries in the restaurants and pubs.

Still, this modest, if not imperceptible, effect on the world view suited Mr. Pont well enough when multiplied by millions.

Mr. Pont, though eminently qualified in his own mind, was not the ruler of the world. His dubious career had been built upon extrapolation and prevarication betwixt shadow and light with the addled ideological elusiveness of a quasi-religious parliamentary candidate, grifting for the highest votes. He ruled nothing other than perception. Yet, for his starving journalistic libido, this nearly sufficed. As fat, contemptible Yolo had schooled him twinmoons ago: "There are powers which rule the world, and there are forces charged to discolor it. A journalist can never be a power in the truest sense, but he can always ply the forces of shade, hue, pattern and contrast to reshape any perception of reality. Today's right is tomorrow's wrong. Yesterday's evil can be the golden virtue of our future." Yolo always demanded that the force of journalism be utilized for optimum effect.

Yolo. It was through the grand media mogul that Mr. Pont learned it was possible to wholly hate and admire an individual concurrently. Yolo had taken him under his wing and taught him the arcane nuances of the media trade. Yet, in so doing, Yolo revealed himself a misanthropic monster of fathomless proportions, devoid of either conscience or spirit. To Yolo, the media was a soul-less amoral living mass, feasting indiscriminately upon the storied lives of its subjects with no ulterior desire other than to perpetuate itself into infinity.

Recently, however, an empty and weary Mr. Pont considered why the force of the media couldn't be used in the service of mortality rather than the other way around? Why couldn't this force be used to teach mortal beings to stand tall, strong and independent? Why couldn't it be used to simply do what's right, as right was perceived by Mr. Pont, of course?

As his atrophied moral notions resurrected themselves, Mr. Pont more frequently ran far afoul of his enormous mentor. Yolo routinely scoffed and ridiculed him for his moralizing "pseudo-journalistic" recalcitrance. Scoffed and ridiculed, but strangely enough, never fired. Free in fact, every day, to say or write whatever he chose. A disquieting freedom. Outside of his omnipotent vacuum, Mr. Pont often sensed that because Yolo allowed it, the media force was actually weaving his part into a broader tapestry, too intricate and subtle for him to perceive. But how many moves could a mortal mind contemplate on this grand game board of infinite possibilities and maintain one's sanity? He knew he was less than a player, yet more than a piece. An influence, perhaps. An influence he doubtfully hoped Yolo had underestimated.

"On one side, we have the Deliveress and her religious order," Mr. Pont resumed his soliloquy, "demanding that all people's ties to the church must remain inviolate."

He leaned back in his kitchen throne and pensively tilted his chin toward his audience. "That is to say, they were absolutely positively right two thousand twinmoons ago. And in our ever-changing world with its ever-changing dynamics regarding the mores of our species, they are still twice as right today! Let's forget about all of the progress that females have made over the centuries in becoming the true equal partners of we once, arrogant and ignorant males. Let's forget about the fact that millions of people find true loving companionship outside the bonds, or chains, if you will, of matrimony…before, during and after their sanctimonious marriages. Let's ignore the Churchlord sex scandals that have crumbled this planet's religious foundation, ruined the lives of hundreds of thousands of our children and revealed the irreparable perversion of past generations of children who are our ancestors.

"Instead, let's just keep stomping through the animal manure, or fasting until we pass out on Holy days. And let's ride ourselves into manic depression the rest of the time with repressive moral guilt bludgeoning away at our sanity and our happiness. Don't any Cathedral worshippers wonder why the Deliverancy won't do for itself what it always asks of others? Examine itself, expose its faults, admit to its transgressions, lay down its iniquities, and avow the choice of a brighter path? In the face of its own antiquated notions of moral behavior, why can't this institutional monolith be big enough to admit to its mistakes and correct them, rather than remain insistent upon its divinity and infallibility? Instead, the Church continues to mutate into an aloof and distant oppressor. A dictatorial viceregency of God who no longer knows or cares for its subjects. Subjects who, alas, are finally mustering the courage to revolt.

"On the other hand, we have the revolt or Break: admirable in its zeal, if not for its substance. The elusive Rabbel Mennis and his soldiers of social insurrection are openly defiant and insistent that the government confine and restrict the Church. Chop off its tentacles of influence and seal it away behind the great doors of the Bius Basilica as one would entomb a living monster in an archaic mausoleum. But then do what? Has anyone heard their solution? Has anyone seen their road map to paradise? Down with God and up with…people? More legal drugs? More alcohol taverns? A shorter work week? A shorter mini-dress? Appealing prospects, all. But has anyone in the Break actually told us what comes next, after we burn the Deliveress at the stake, shred the Texts into confetti, and convert every standing church into a super pub or sports arena? An insurrection leading into the unknown is nearly as frightening as another century under the benevolent heel of the Deliverancy.

"Of course, it would be so easy to dismiss the Break's absence of tangible ideals were it not for an alleged underground network of support and funding from the affluent north. Where, in the past, anti-religious movements had never carried much weight against the establishment, large influxes of capital, have given Rabbel and his minions the sharpened teeth to gnaw through the public's apathy this time around.

"Which brings us to the largest and most significant variable in the equation: the public apathy, formerly known as the public conscience. The average person, as I have observed, just isn't into all of this philosophy. They're not into God and prayer. Nor are they into a declaration of revolt. The average adults just want to eat when they want to eat, belch when they want to belch, laugh when they think they're supposed to laugh, and have guilt-free sex whenever the opportunity presents itself. And they absolutely do not want anyone passing judgments on the how, when or where they should choose to do any of the above. Which is not to say that the average person, liberal as they wish to appear, doesn't want rules and boundaries to protect their liberties. Otherwise, the liberty of one person or persons would invariably crush the liberties of someone else. Rules and the enforcement of such are necessary fail-safes which allow society to avert certain anarchy.

"So everyone wants law and order. Liberal law and order, we hope, but law and order nonetheless. Which is where our fine government comes into play.

"The Accommodant's job is to accommodate. That is, accommodate all beliefs and all values, so long as they do not attempt to over-run each other. If you wish to go to cathedral on Solemnday, you're free to do so. In fact, I still recommend it, just to be safe. But if you'd rather roll out of bed and walk your pet or stagger around, naked in your own living room half the morning, that's perfectly legal as well. Again, the average person falls between these two categories. Most of them want to do what's socially acceptable, with just a smidgen of individuality to justify their own existence alongside someone else's. Not wholly irreligious, mind you, but certainly not so fanatical about the Almighty that they appear obtuse or uncurrent. They neither want God meddling in their daily lives, nor do they wish to dispatch with him altogether. Basically, the average person is looking for remedies on an as-needed basis…a drunken binge or sexual rampage when things are too tense and prayer and humility when things get…impossible. Frankly, I see nothing wrong with this.

"The Deliveress speaks often of moderation. She claims that the church is not repressive at all, but merely a proponent of moderation. Moderation until you ask for a moderate religion. Then she changes her tune. Likewise, the Break speaks in absolute tones. 'No more God. No more Religion.' And they should add to their battle cry 'No more Answers'.

"To resolve this impasse, I propose the adoption of a new word conciliatory to all parties. That word is Tolerance. Like the Accommodant, who works diligently to accommodate the dreams and desires of all people, so, too, must each individual. Hatred of irreligious people is no more acceptable or fruitful than hatred of those who purport to love God. Ideological zeal will do nothing but tear the world apart. Better we should all while away our days snoozing lazily on a park bench, than slit each other's throats over philosophies. The religious philosophers swear that they're right, and they may be. But don't impose your dubious righteousness on the freedoms of those who think you're wrong! Likewise, if you don't care for religion, simply be fair enough to let it and its proponents alone! What do you care if they slog around in manure once a twinmoon and walk around bearing their guilty burden? What do you care if they think the Deliveress is God? What do you care if they're praying to a god who's just not there? Isn't that their problem?

"Tolerance may be the one holy word that saves us from ourselves! It represents the ultimate compromise that allows everyone to thrive and coexist peacefully. Tolerance means that we do as we choose and accept the choices of our neighbors. We may disagree with our neighbors, but we tolerate their opinions and beliefs as we would expect them to tolerate ours. After all, only God knows who's right and who's wrong in the end. And for those who don't believe in God, what is there to worry about in any case?

"Tolerance is certainly a far better state than that of hatred or persecution. The Deliveress will tell you she loves her enemies. But you can be certain she doesn't love homosexuals or drug users or art advocates whose lifestyles threaten to derail her agenda for a cold, antiseptic, robotic, utterly unattainable perfect mortal race. She needs to realize that the Cathedral's view cuts off and alienates the majority of the modern world. Societies change. People change. Religion must change with the times and tolerate the evolution of values and relationships. Otherwise, the Cathedral will be lost. And perhaps any hope of any positive relationship with God will be lost as well.

"In a tolerant world, there's a place for everyone. In this sage wisdom we acknowledge the presence of an opposing viewpoint and move on to more important ideals like the food in our stomachs and the well-being of our loved ones. Ideals that neither God nor godlessness can resolve. Ideals that only a tolerant people, working for the common good of all, can bring to fruition for an enduring and prosperous civilization.

"Thank you for tolerating me."

Mr. Pont clicked off his recorder and considered whether there was any more to say. Then his sunken belly groaned and he grimaced, having to acknowledge that the final chord of his extrapolating diatribe had indeed rang hollow. He stood, grabbed a periodical from the shelf beneath the drainboard and shuffled to the bathroom.

V.

Libbi awoke to a nauseating darkness that smelled horrible.

For an hour and a half, his raw flatulence had hissed, spit and gargled into a stingingly putrefied atmosphere that now stank like a biological sewage dump.

A full hour and a half.

Libbi wasn't certain whether she had merely fallen asleep, passed out from alcohol consumption or lost consciousness under the weight of asphyxiated duress. As she rolled her head from the damp malty pillow, she considered herself fortunate she hadn't choked on her own vomit…or his.

Libbi had gauged Yolo's culinary addictions accurately enough. But she had grossly, with emphasis upon gross, underestimated the large man's stamina for the consumption of flesh not devoured. Thus their altogether humiliating sexual encounter left her feeling like little more than a small primate creature, recently wedged through the briny clogged intestine of a large sea mammal, having all the nutrients of her self-worth extracted during the process.

In hindsight, trussing herself up, a la carte, had only added insult to her injury. Aside from her flesh being soaked and permeated by the reeking stench of his personal odor which oozed and dripped from every fold of his sagging skin…every pore of his sweating blubbery pulsing girth, aside from the intrusions of his thick lapping salivary tongue which harbored the unbelched effluvium of his wheezing gaseous gullet, her hair was caked with the sticky remnants of honey, fruit and whipped cream. Her arms, legs and feet were flaked with the dried juices of bloody rare meats. And she now found the sweet wine sauce prepared with peppery southern seasonings personally discomforting in the wake of Yolo Pigue's rapaciously consumed feast.

All of her muscles were tired and sore from supporting so disproportionate a rider. She peeled herself from the sheets and tried to ignore the wide array of discolored squalor their unseemly frolic had left behind. As her mind cleared the alcoholic fugue which had brought her to this "daring" foray into corporate politics, she tried desperately to reconstruct her fragmented reasoning for so suddenly pursuing the utterly repulsive media baron to his bed.

"Oh my fucking god!" she sat up, fighting her dizziness. "That goddamn interview."

All of the debilitating insecurity she had hoped to exorcise returned full bore.

With increased alertness, she looked around the room for Yolo, whose notable absence made the claustrophobic room feel suddenly spacious. She scanned the wreckage of tangled clothing and twisted bedding, but could only make out shreds of what she had worn to Yolo's office hours earlier. Through the bedroom door, she heard the pattern of his voice in his office. He was already back to work at a wee morning hour she couldn't be certain of.

"And, now, for my exit," she quipped with a nervous, ragged sigh as she stood and looked for something to put on. The post-intercourse exit had rarely felt so daunting a task: Find something to put on and emerge from your employer's bedroom stinking of dried regurgitation and caked with food. Enter his office where he had already resumed working and either fill your departure with idle chit-chat pertaining to work, curtsey and bow thanking him for a lovely evening, or slip away with no words other than a meek, yet femininely resilient "Good night, sir."

The choices were nearly as unpalatable to her as their "love-making" had been.

On the other side of the door, a world away, a satiated and invigorated Yolo Pigue conjoined himself with his media machinery. Even before breakfast, information was always the first meal of the day. Through his window, the night's twinmoons still loomed, but in the eastern hemisphere, sunrise was already several hours past, and the story of the dawn had to be prepped as daylight scrolled westward.

"Proptz," Yolo drew a deep breath, "you have the look of a domestic predator who's just devoured the household pest. I sense that I should either be mightily encouraged or prepared to restoke the lawbooker budget for another legal suit."

"Um, both actually." Proptz Rotz's long pale face winced sheepishly from Yolo's monitor. "You're really going to love hating this. Watch."

Yolo's screen went blank momentarily. Then the cue serial numbers of raw stock news footage jumped across a darkened background. The next image was that of a peaceful sun-splashed front porch on a modest provincial dwelling. The wholesome setting was beautiful and utterly tranquil...until the black leather-clad stick figure of Proptz Rotz appeared, microphone in hand, clogging purposefully up the front steps.

"My sweet, contemptible demoness," Yolo whispered as an anticipatory smirk bowed his jowls. "What now?"

Proptz paused at the front door and snapped her head around to offer the camera one final gleefully gaunt, open-mouthed leer before she slipped into character. She transformed herself to an erect, professional paragon of journalistic integrity as she urgently rapped her scrawny bare knuckles against the dwelling's front door.

"Mr. and Mrs. Deyz?" she called out, knocking frantically. "Mr. and Mrs. Deyz? This is Proptz Rotz with YBS News. We wanted to get your reaction to the leaking story that your granddaughter, Preppi, survived the crash!"

Yolo drew a sudden heavy breath, and choked a phlegm-gargled cough as his bulging eyes riveted on the monitor.

Proptz continued to call out to the grandparents of Preppi Deyz with all of the intonation of an angel of hope heralding great tidings from the kingdom of Heaven. She even turned and spun before the camera with the perfectly calibrated exasperation of a person, yearning, desperately, to do good. She called out again, maniacally thumbing the door chime as if an entire world depended upon what the people inside did next.

The door cracked open, ever so slightly, and the meek silhouetted figures of an elderly couple could be faintly detected as Proptz cajoled them into the daylight.

"Alive?" the elderly Mr. Deyz quivered.

"Yes, yes. It's okay," Proptz whispered in a tender nurturing voice.

"How is that possible?" Mrs. Deyz spoke, on the verge of tears.

"Listen," Proptz leaned into the crack, "my name is Proptz Rotz and I'm the Eastern Bureau Chief for YBS News. I have a camera outside and we'd like to talk to you about your granddaughter."

"Well, this is shocking news." Mr. Deyz fought his skepticism under labored breaths. "They told us she was dead."

"I know, I know." Proptz nodded and backed away, luring the couple out into the open line of fire.

The guileless, elderly couple toddled out of the door following Proptz like trained circus animals being led by dangling morsels of food. The cameraman slowly, stealthily crept closer to the drama as Proptz maneuvered the grandparents into position.

"So tell us," Mrs. Deyz gesticulated with impatience, "tell us about our granddaughter. Tell us about Preppi!"

"Well, Mr. and Mrs. Deyz," Proptz signaled the cameraman, "I was actually hoping you would tell us more about your granddaughter."

"What do you mean?" Mr. Deyz became unsettled.

"I mean, there are rumors now circulating that Preppi Deyz was a hermaphrodite." Proptz bluntly floored the couple without a flicker of hesitation or remorse.

"Hermaphro...what?" Mrs. Deyz's voice became shrill. "What in the world...?"

"They're saying that five twinmoons ago at the World Games, your granddaughter was found to have dual sets of genitalia." Proptz spoke succinctly. "A hermaphrodite. That is the real reason she missed the games that year isn't it?"

"For the love of mercy!" Mr. Deyz's wrinkled face became a contorted mask of ancient rage.

"She had a surgery when she was a child," Mrs. Deyz reflected, "but that was twinmoons before..."

"Then you're saying Preppi Deyz was not a hermaphrodite?" Proptz held the microphone tightly between the mouths of the elderly couple.

"Well…" Mrs. Deyz wasn't sure how to respond. "I guess at one time…"

"Young lady!" Mr. Deyz interceded angrily. "You came to us…"

"To talk about your late granddaughter." Proptz cut him off.

"Late?" Mrs. Deyz's hands shook as she covered her mouth. "But you said she was alive, that she'd survived…"

"What I said was that there was a story about your granddaughter surviving the crash." Proptz shook her head as if the elderly couple had forgotten the common rules of a child's game. "It's a rumor! A story someone is trying to circulate. Preppi Deyz was blasted to sizzling chunks of stew meat. I was there!"

"Stew meat?" Tears welled in Mrs. Deyz eyes.

"Was Finx Melder her first male lover?" Proptz continued with her questioning.

"What…what kind of question…?" Mr. Deyz's fury broke into short breaths.

"Preppi was renowned for her little lesbian flings, Mr. Deyz." Proptz chuckled. "She was a jock's jock. Actually, as a hermaphrodite, I guess she had more jock than most ladies on the circuit."

"You…you…" Mr. Deyz gasped.

"What do you mean by jock?" Mrs. Deyz cried in outrage.

All at once, Mr. Deyz was on his knees, clutching his own throat with one hand while clawing at Proptz Rotz with the other. Proptz leapt backward and the elder man spasmed forward, toppling down the front stairs. Mrs. Deyz let out a horrified shriek as blood spewed from Mr. Deyz's gashed forehead and poured over the concrete steps.

Proptz appeared shaken momentarily, but quickly gestured to her cameraman, as she hopped over Mr. Deyz's sprawled figure.

"That's a wrap." Proptz smiled as her gaunt face closed in on the camera lens and winked. "Call the medics and get some good post-trauma footage. I'm outta here."

Yolo's monitor went blank, followed by a quick procession of serial numbers flickering across his screen. In another instant, the thin pale live portrait of Proptz Rotz reappeared with a mischievously ambivalent smile.

"Well, there you go." She chuckled. "The grieving grandparents."

"To say the least." Yolo snorted a thick red cloud from his cigar. "Compelling theatre, my dear. Excellent work. What's our damage?"

"Minimal." Proptz's dark circled eyes turned serious for a moment. "The old man's had a history of breathing problems. They can't nail us for that. The only bad thing is he nearly brained himself on those concrete steps. He's in a coma. That could get expensive."

"Damned masons," Yolo commented casually. "We didn't build the stairs. Sue the damned masons. Anyone who builds residential stairs out of concrete should be sued into a pauper's grave!"

"Of course the only real witness was the grandmother, and she's such a yipping senile twit, I don't think she'll ever be able to tell the same story twice. We may be free and clear," Proptz smirked wryly.

"You are a princess, aren't you?" Yolo chuckled. "If you ever tire of field work, I'm sure I can get you a studio slot. We have an opening."

"Yolo, are you finally proposing?" Proptz fluttered her eyelashes.

"Not for all the steak and pastry in the world, princess." Yolo grinned. "Besides, pill junkies make poor wives. And I don't fancy you a particularly good cook in either case."

"Then I guess I'll keep playing the field, 'Herr General.'" Proptz winked.

"Carve and dice that footage into something palatable, my dear." Yolo leaned back in his chair. "Tasty morsels of scandal and woe. I want to see that old man's choking, bleeding face on every monitor in the world by mid-morning, western time."

"Aye, sir!" Proptz smiled and the desk monitor faded to a view of the Eastern news feed, jabbing relentlessly, from one Finx Melder image to another.

Yolo's mind delved into the exponential calculations of how the Finx Melder death could be fissioned and conjugated into gripping tentacles of serial programming. The movie angle. The popular cultural angle. The drug-abuse angle. The religious angle. The anti-religious angle. The romantic angle. The family angle. The icon-worship angle. The corporate-entertainment angle.

"A cacophony for clueless consumption." Yolo grinned and exhaled a giant red cloud into the air. "How delectable."

With his large forefinger, he punched his controller and the blank desk and wall monitors bloomed into glowing colorful portraits of Panla Jen Tem as she had appeared during her interview on *Nailing the Newsmaker*. He turned down the sound a bit and simply watched her speak, watched her move. With an eye, practiced in the interpretive art of reading moods behind the masks of his subjects, Yolo measured Panla's physical responses to each and every question posed to her.

What topics prompted her to lean forward? What subjects caused her to settle back? At which points would her eyes start to smolder with conviction? Whose names caused the muscles in her jaws to tighten? Dismissive at some turns, emphatic upon others. Often, her words aligned in complete juxtaposition to her gestures. Yes, this woman could say all of the right things, but she was certainly hiding some gargantuan inner-conflict under her religiously impenetrable "armor of God." But what? Something evil? Hardly. Something mad? Improbable, despite her gender. Something…

"So do you really think I convinced everyone about her?" Libbi's intrusive voice blared even as she tried to speak softly.

Yolo tensed with dismay over the abrupt interruption, but he quickly recovered his evenness and swiveled around to face her. He made no initial acknowledgment of her filthy, haggard appearance as she stood next to his desk wearing a badly stained bedsheet tied around her tired slouching body. His rigid indifference, in and of itself, was enough to make her uneasy.

"Of course not." Yolo finally snorted, lifting his cigar to his lips. "Anyone who liked her will certainly like her all the more. And anyone who was predisposed to disliking her won't be swayed by her sanctimonious sermonizing, one way or the other. I'm afraid the net effect, as is always the case with interviews of this nature, was nil."

The wafting red cigar smoke marked an unsettling silence between them.

"Ohh." Libbi quaked as she felt her heart pounding heavily in her chest. "Oh, I'm…so sorry. I thought that I'd…shown everyone how…empty all of her religious pomp really is. Y'know…made her…squirm in front the audience. Flinch a few times…"

"Yes, yes." Yolo chuckled through his red cloud. "I'd say you made her uncomfortable, brought her out into the light a bit. That was certainly my intent. But really, my dear, if I'd wanted her discredited or besmirched, don't you think I'd have hired a professional for the job?"

Libbi felt as if she had been punched in the stomach.

"I…What?" her hands shook as she clutched at the sheet around her body.

"You are the diva of digressive decadence." Yolo's expression fell serious. "A vamping voice-box of gutter wit, adorned in high-heeled pumps, skimpy skirts and silken blouses to accentuate the points of your protruding…professionalism. Females of your ilk have been espousing such traits as 'professional' for centuries, although I'm certain that journalism wasn't the trade. So, alas, I can understand your confusion. We now live in a modern society where a woman, so accoutered, can pass herself off as anything she wishes with a modicum of competence and a reasonable proclivity for prompting an erection."

"Y…Yolo, I don't deserve that." Libbi tried to firm her resolve.

"You aren't deserving, I agree," he said with a heavy sigh. "A horrible waste of words on my part. Why bother? After all, look at you. Has anyone on this planet sunk to lower depths in the past twenty-six hours? You've degraded yourself with a man who physically repulses you just to save a job that was never in jeopardy...until now, that is."

"Now?" Libbi was dumbfounded.

"I knew your limitations." Yolo spoke with dry contempt. "You performed just as I expected you to. But this? This, I must say, was a disappointment. Your tramping woman-of-the-world arrogance was one of the few things I ever respected about you, but now I see you barren, frightened and fractured beyond shame. I'm afraid this changes everything. I don't think I can use you anymore. I think *Nailing the Newsmaker* needs to go away, and you along with it."

"B...but my ratings are still good, Yolo! They're still good!" Libbi leaned forward and thumped his desk as her sheet came undone.

"Yes, they are, but a program that no longer exists can't generate any ratings, can it? Soon you'll be an afterthought in the analogs of medialogs. A few months later, we'll rename, recast and retool your old program with something the critics are bound to say is 'fresh intelligent and breathtaking.' A hot new skirt will pander her journalistic plunging neckline, snow-capped smile and death-defying salon coiffure to the panting patronage. She'll be the perky sorority sister antithesis to your egomaniacal glitter-whore. Grand timing, wouldn't you say? And I have you to thank, after all.

"Tonight, your dithering insecurity proved to me that the day of the mega-tramp has run its course for the time being. The art of programming is for myself to see the end before the audience does. And you are definitely finished. Of course, if I'm wrong...well, I can always walk into any night club, step into the first men's room stall and yank a newer, younger mega-tramp off her knees and into the limelight. The scenario does ring familiar, doesn't it?"

"Oh my god." Tears began flowing freely down Libbi's pale cheeks. "I don't believe this!"

"You wouldn't." Yolo leaned back in his leather chair. "But remember not to call when the stiff cold winds of reality do find you. Good night, Ms. Trullup."

"Yolo, I..."

"Ms. Trullup!" He glared through her with volcanic finality.

It was over. Just like that.

Libbi looked up to the ceiling, swaying and swooning for the strength to merely exit without collapsing. She took up the stained sheet, held it close to her body and slowly shuffled her way toward the door.

"Ms. Trullup, I believe you're leaving with something that belongs to me." Yolo addressed her in an even tone which nearly belied all that had just transpired.

She froze for a moment and hung her head.

"I don't wish to sound callous," he continued, "but the maid does hate it when she finds the bedding sets mismatched."

Without turning her head, Libbi untied the bedsheet and dropped it to the floor. She folded her arms over her bosom and trudged out into the corridor stark naked. The large wooden door closed and locked itself behind her.

Yolo lifted his eyes and looked down at the bedsheet in the floor.

"A pity." he smiled to himself.

Then he punched the console on his desk and resumed working.

"Mr. Nil."

"Yes sir," a dutiful voice answered him.

"Please, note press release: 'Libbi Trullup has left the *Nailing the Newsmaker* program for unspecified reasons'. Note to production: 'During her absence we will be broadcasting reruns'. BAD reruns, Mr. Nil. The only thing worse than an outdated interview is an outdated interview that's hideously boring. See to it."

"Yes, sir."

"Oh, and a note to Mr. Pont on his prospective commentary on Tolerance: 'Mr. Pont, your article is dim, vacant, shallow and utterly ridiculous. It's bound to be a smash. Print it.' And Mr. Nil…"

"Yes, sir?"

"Gather the fellows for breakfast at the diner this morning. I have some theories on the queen hag Deliveress I'd like to toss about."

"Yes, sir."

Yolo finally opened his mouth with a voluminous yawn that rolled into a thunderous belch. He clicked up images of Panla Jen, and started to dissect them more closely.

VI.

Juds entered Rabbel's tavern with his new, mysterious, darkly clad associates.

Thirty weapons of varied sizes, shapes and configurations instantly appeared out of the crowd and trained themselves on Juds's spindly frame, from forehead to pelvis. The music screeched to an eerie silence.

"So," Juds swallowed hard, then smirked into the maw of weapons, "who do we have to fuck to see Rabbel Mennis?"

For a moment, the glaring mob appeared ready to blast Juds and his cohorts straight back through the door, but then, the crowd parted and the tall, black, angular figure of Leesla strode forward with her own weapon pointed directly at his throat.

"Who are they?" Leesla's eyes narrowed as she looked down at the smaller man.

"Honey, I don't ask you where your hairdresser buys the weed killer he uses on your head, so why the fuck should I tell you anything?" Juds's cockiness remained steady. "We're here to see Rabbel."

"And I'll ask you again," Leesla's clipped syllables snarled through her long clenched teeth, "who are they? And one more wise-ass comment from you, and no one in this room will ever know or care."

Juds smirked again as if ten insults had just flashed through his mind, but this time, he held his lips tightly until he could force himself to be cooperative.

"Interested parties." Juds said. "Interested parties who can make things a helluva lot easier than they've been. Interested parties who can help you guys change the world. Go tell him that. We can wait."

Leesla stroked the side of his chin with the glistening blue barrel of her slender weapon. She hadn't killed anyone in so long; her murderous lust craved to see Juds die. But her intellectual reason deferred to her role in this revolutionary drama, and she knew that no one could be killed in Rabbel's tavern without sanction from Rabbel himself.

"You and your pallbearers can wait, little man…and you will." Leesla backed away with a threatening stare, then pushed toward Rabbel's office.

"Must be fuckin' his girlfriend," Juds said to the semi-circle of weapons as beads of sweat formed on his forehead. "And if he's not and she's here, I'll fuck her!"

The crowd parted again and little Reza stepped through and approached him.

"That's all good and gunky." Reza tip-toed her fingers up his chest. "But would you fuck me?"

"With all that prep-school dementia swirling around under that green hair?" Juds sneered. "I wouldn't fuck your scrawny ass with the wrong end of a broken broom handle!"

The crowd of weapons broke into laughter as Juds momentarily ingratiated himself to the hostile gathering.

Out of nowhere, Juds found Reza's high-heeled boot buried in his groin. He crumpled to the ground immediately and the laughter escalated. The dark-faced men Juds had brought with him remained still, their hands at their sides. Their faces registered no emotion other than a tinge of mild impatience.

"Where's that smart mouth now?" Juds could hear Durn's voice in the distance.

"I don't know," Juds gasped. "But you could use something smart."

Juds could hear Durn's angry footfalls make their way toward him. Before they arrived the unexpected sharp kick of Reza's pointed boot knifed into his rib cage. Then, before he could process that pain, Durn was upon him, yanking his contracted body back to its feet.

"I think you could use a little taste of that paste, lil' man." Durn smiled a yellow, toothy grin through his unkempt growth of beard. "Shut you up real good."

"Give it to him!" Reza instigated. "I want to see him shit his liver, the impotent inbred."

"Inbred?" Juds wearily looked at Durn. "She MUST be talking about you."

Durn punched Juds squarely in the mouth and Juds fell back into the three dark men who had accompanied him.

"See." Juds spoke as they held him up. "I told you they know me. They don't like me, but they know me."

"Don't be so hard on yourself." a deep authoritative voice cut through the escalating commotion. "We're always hospitable to our friends until they bring friends we don't know."

Rabbel Mennis parted the crowd without a gesture. He glared at Durn, then flinched his muscular left arm. Durn scrambled back across the bar as if he'd been struck. Rabbel looked down his nose at Reza, and the incurably brash young woman in the green hair looked away as if she'd been viciously scolded.

The pack of rebellious tavern patrons quietly sheathed and holstered their weapons. When the room resettled itself, Rabbel stepped forward to inspect Juds and the three men he had brought with him.

"I've had my fill of strangers tonight." Rabbel read each of their faces. "Every strange face increases the odds that one of them is either a spy or an assassin. New faces showing up at critical moments is a bad omen, Juds. I hope you have an excellent reason for bringing them here, other than to be killed."

"Uh...yeah." Juds tried to stand erect as he rubbed his ribcage. "I generally don't set people up for dates with death unless there's a little money in it."

Rabbel did not smile.

"But...uh..." Juds continued, "anyway, these guys are very, very serious about what you...we...are doing here and they can offer some major support. Major."

Rabbel looked into the dark expressionless faces of the three men again.

"Your weapons," Rabbel said. "Leave them here and follow me."

"Weapons?" Juds laughed nervously. "You think I'd bring three strangers to you carrying weapons? These guys…"

Each of the three men standing behind Juds withdrew a large three-barreled hand weapon from his coat and handed them to Leesla, who was impressed.

"Aw, shit, guys." Beads of sweat formed on Juds forehead.

"Gentlemen, step into my office." Rabbel turned and led Juds, Leesla and the threesome back toward the rear of the tavern.

"Scary." Durn watched from the bar.

"Cute." Reza snaked her tongue across the front of her perfectly aligned teeth, and ordered another drink.

VII.

"She is NOT okay." Crilen growled under his breath.

"I can assure you she's fine, Mr. Len." Linnfeld motioned for Crilen to return to his cabin seat aboard the transport.

"She's a complete mess," Crilen spoke emphatically. "It's all starting to get to her! The Cathedral. The Accommodant. The media. The Break. Rabbel, in particular. It's all wearing her down."

Linnfeld looked at Crilen with an indicting expression.

"Rabbel, in particular, Mr. Len?" Linnfeld recited. "Well, therein may lie the problem. As I've alluded to you before, I think it's quite obvious you're letting your feelings for Mrs. Tem get in the way of your responsibilities. You're not here to supervise her health and well-being. That's my job. Your job is to keep her alive—plain and simple. If you can't keep that straight in your mind, then perhaps this isn't the job for you after all."

Crilen leaned back in his seat and tried to separate his emotions for Panla from his objective observation that she was suffering mightily under the strain of bearing a trebled identity. Yes, it singed his sensibilities every time he watched Rabbel's thick, battle-worn hands come to rest on her narrow waist. Certainly, it burned his molten blood to watch her smile at Rabbel and kiss him with a warmth that bore her deepest affection. And it seared his heart to watch this elegant lady spew slurred vulgarities for the amusement of a raunchy immoral crowd of irreligious cut-throats, knowing that every word from her lips ran contrary to the core elements which comprised her spirit. But he was positive his overlapping fixation upon Panla had little to do with his mounting concerns over her mental state.

An hour ago, she had emerged from Rabbel's office looking flushed and invigorated. But once outside the tavern, she nearly collapsed into an exhausted state of recriminatory depression. Then she flew into a wild, defensive rage, ordering the driver to return them all to the Accommodant's Mansion, hours away, rather than to their reserved hotel nearby. At last, she stormed back to her private rear cabin and demanded, unequivocally, to be left alone for the duration of the trip.

She was so much like Aami. But he had never seen his wife wall away the world as Panla did. It was hurtful to watch such a brilliant woman be driven away from those who cared for her, rather than into their loving arms. Perhaps this is where the two women diverged. Or perhaps, still, this was merely a side of Aami which had never been tortured by the rigors of public life...and rebellion.

"All right, Mr. Linnfeld," Crilen gathered himself, "you know how I feel about her, and that's all well and good. But if I can set that aside, I'm telling you that she isn't acting rationally. And this life she's trying to lead is tearing her to shreds."

"I see." Linnfeld clasped his fingers together and squinted at him. "Mr. Len, how long have you been in charge of Mrs. Tem's security?"

"It doesn't take years...er...twinmoons to see..."

"How long?"

"One day," Crilen admitted.

"Barely one day," Linnfeld clarified with emphasis. "I count twenty-two hours out of a twenty-six hour day. Me, on the other hand? I've been at this particular cloak-and-dagger duty for almost a full twinmoon. A few more, before this whole Break business started. For your information, there've been evenings when I've carried that young lady, whom I love dearly, out of that bloody tavern, draped over my shoulder, with her vomit running down my back! From there, I would deliver her, powder fresh and prim, to the bed of that abominable husband of hers, for reasons truly known only to them. Then, by daybreak, I would find her dressed in the royal garb of the Deliveress, standing before a throng of worshippers at the altar of the Bius Basilica, delivering a mass so powerful, it could wring tears of joy from Heaven itself!

"By the afternoon, she would be back in the guise of the First Lady, delivering another speech or cutting another ribbon or visiting the southern regions where there are millions of sick and impoverished. By nightfall, she might finally catch an early nap. Then she'd pick up a book or click on a monitor and start sorting through how she might save the whole bloody world all by herself again.

"I wouldn't recommend the life she lives to anyone, but this is who she is. This is what God's chosen for her. And I'd bet my soul to Heaven that the world will be a better place for her sacrifice…even if it is tearing her apart."

"That's funny." Crilen sounded suspicious.

"Funny? How?" Linnfeld drew himself up in his seat.

"Because when she was downing her fourth drink on stage tonight, you were the one who said things weren't quite right." Crilen frowned. "I don't believe she's gotten drunk like that before. Not in a place where a million things could go wrong at any moment and she'd need her wits about her. Not when she could slip up and say the wrong thing to the wrong person, stone sober, and lose her life. You were just as concerned as I was tonight. Only now, you're lying as if everything was normal. Why? Why do you want me to think things are perfectly fine when clearly they're not?"

"Because you're distracted," Linnfeld answered flatly. "As I said before, her behavior isn't your concern. Only her safety."

"Then what are you going to do for her?" Crilen asked.

"Nothing," Linnfeld replied, settling back.

"Nothing?" Crilen responded. "And you say you love her?"

"More than anyone," Linnfeld answered. "More than anyone, except God. But as much as I care for her, if I put my feelings for that dear girl ahead of my allegiance to Him, what would that make me?"

A disquieting silence hung between the two men as they dwelt upon the fate of the world in Panla's delicate hands. Her irrevocable path was an encapsulated tunnel from which there were no outlets, save the very end. If this were true, Crilen was further perplexed as to why It had placed him on this assignment. The outcome was far from certain, but there appeared be no alternatives to affect in the interim. Surely, his role as a fiery shield could have been filled by virtually anyone else up to this point.

"So you're saying we shouldn't help her at all?" Crilen finally responded.

"I'm saying that if God wishes to intervene, He will," Linnfeld spoke seriously. "But our intervention had better be for the good of every soul on this planet, and not just one person's flesh and blood."

A sacrifice for the souls of millions, Crilen thought. A sacrifice for the souls of billions. Had not his own wife made the self-same sacrifice when he blasted from their bed in a roaring pyrogenic ball of fire, screaming into the cosmos to save worlds. What had been sacrificed for all of the souls upon all of the worlds he had rescued from dictators and despots and self-anointed demi-gods? What had been sacrificed but the flesh and blood of the woman he loved more than all the billions upon billions put together?

VIII.

Rabbel sat in silence as he stared across his desk at Juds and the three dark men whose faces remained as stone. Leesla leaned against the wall at her usual perch, waiting for the Break leader's powerful voice to render judgment.

Juds's hands were leaving a damp stain on the thighs of his trousers as he waited for the final word. Rivulets of sweat formed on his sloping forehead. His beady eyes were dilated with anxiety. Either Rabbel would take this very sweet deal to form an ironclad alliance or he would order them out into the back alley and have them killed and disposed of for compromising his relatively clandestine, rebellious enterprise.

Of course there was no reason for Rabbel not to take the deal, Juds thought. Unlimited funding. Unlimited information. Unlimited weapons. Shields from legal harassment or prosecution. No more envelope-stuffing and leaflets posted on the bulletin boards of coffee shops and colleges. No more covert cajoling and pleading for contributions to the cause from wealthy, ethically fad-conscious, half-hearted Breakphiles. No more mosquito-bite terrorist tactics which, most often, resembled the actions of wayward teen thuggery. Now they could finally declare war on the Church and wage it unimpeded. The ideological underground could finally come out of the closet and mark itself as a credible socio-political force. A sweet deal, indeed, Juds fretted. But what if...

"I accept." Rabbel's sneering lips barely moved.

"Yahhhh!" Juds leapt from the sofa and accidentally banged his head against the low ceiling.

The three dark men stood and approached Rabbel. Rabbel stood and extended his hand.

"To freedom." Rabbel clutched each of their palms, one by one. He reached into his desk drawer and plucked out three golden pins bearing the Break symbol of the dagger through the Cathedral dome.

"Wear these when you walk among us." Rabbel welcomed them into the fold.

They each nodded.

"Juds," Rabbel spoke to the pale sweat-soaked man who looked as if he'd won a marathon, "take our new allies out to meet their comrades. They can reclaim their weapons...and the drinks are on the house."

"Rabbel," Juds grinned from ear to ear, "you will not be sorry! In three or four twinmoons, you'll be the fucking Accommodant!"

"In three or four twinmoons," Rabbel offered a faint smile, "I may not have to be."

"Yeah." Juds patted him on the shoulder. "Great. Um, come out and celebrate with us?"

"In a few minutes." Rabbel returned to his seat. "Leesla and I have a few housekeeping items we need to tend to."

"Sure." Juds smirked at Leesla. "Y'know, I may get so drunk tonight, I might be willing to make a real woman outta you."

Leesla uncoiled her limbs and hissed at the smaller man. Wisely, Juds hastened his dark clothed companions out of the office before violence ensued.

"Leesla," Rabbel called to her.

She paused at the closing door, clenching her fists. She forced herself to disengage from Juds's taunt and regathered her equilibrium.

"So, what do you think?" Rabbel consulted. "What do you really think? If I've overlooked something, it's not too late to have them…taken care of."

Leesla dropped her long arms to her sides and sauntered over to a chair next to his desk. She turned the chair around backwards and sat down, coiling herself around the back in a manner that resembled a jungle predator perched upon a tree limb.

"I think," her long white teeth formed a carnivorously sinister grin, "that this is more than we could have ever dreamed of."

"Even though they represent the government," Rabbel stated.

"Especially because they represent the government," Leesla affirmed. "Rabbel, if they were going to betray us, they could have bulldozed the entire block in one motion. Knocked down the walls and firebombed everyone of us to ashes. And it would have been glorified in the media as the destruction of the world's most rebellious terrorist cell which threatened the foundation of civilization. But they didn't. They didn't because they believe in us. They believe in us and they need us!

"Rabbel, you know as well as I do that you are as much a symbol of sentient free will as the Deliveress is a symbol of all the chains which bind free will. When people hear your name, yes there is fear. And there should be. You are the declared enemy of all the old ways of thinking. But you are also a champion of a new way of thinking, a new way of living. Self-determination rather than some totally unreliable, contrived, phantom god, fabricated to take credit for all of the good in the world while reflecting all of the bad back onto our own natures. The world is tired of being mind-fucked by the Deliveress and the Cathedral and her Text and her clergymen and her Baloni shit-sloggers. These are modern times full of modern ideals that must be allowed to express themselves, without impediment!

"The Accommodant knows this. Why do you think he sent them?"

"Perhaps because of her." Rabbel stared blankly into his steepled fingers.

"Her?" Leesla gestured angrily.

"Yes, her," Rabbel affirmed tensely. "This could be some elaborate way for him to get her away from me."

"Oh, Rabbel." Leesla slapped her forehead. "Rabbel Mennis, this deal has nothing to do with her!"

"A jealous husband?" Rabbel murmured. "One who knows where his wife spends her evenings? Don't be so certain."

"Rabbel," Leesla lowered her voice, "the Accommodant doesn't know anything about PJ. She's told you that. And from what all of us know, he barely has time to keep tabs on himself, let alone a wife he doesn't even love. You're projecting your feelings onto his."

"Maybe." Rabbel sighed. "But the government has spies."

"There are no spies in your tavern." Leesla shook her head. "We've made the consequences of spying rather unseemly, don't you think?

"Yes. But what about that new security man of hers?" Rabbel countered. "He was hand-picked by the Accommodant. She said so."

"And she also told you he's an old acquaintance of Moll. Moll's the one who got him the interview. The Accommodant and his staff have no idea."

"So it seems." Rabbel closed his eyes.

"So it is," Leesla responded. "But the greater question now beckons: Now that we're aligned with the Accommodant, why do we need PJ at all?"

Rabbel's eyes opened again.

"What do you mean?" His thick black brow wrinkled.

"I mean that we have our benefactor," Leesla pleaded. "We have the ultimate benefactor. What do we need with a dubious woman and her dirty jokes and her constricted resources? We don't need her to bring down the church from within anymore. Now we can knock it down with sledge hammers and the best wrecking equipment government coin can buy!"

"She's with us," Rabbel answered. "She's risked everything to be with us. I'll let her know and she can join us. I'll make it part of the deal. I'll tell the Accommodant…"

"What?" Leesla interrupted. "Have you lost your mind? You can't tell her anything. If she doesn't already know, that's because the Accommodant doesn't want her to know. Which leads me to another conclusion you must consider: Here is a husband and wife who share the same bed, making overtures to you for supposedly the same cause. Yet they know nothing of each others' sentiments? Rabbel, they don't have to love each other to share the same agenda. Empowered couples have used each other for centuries to reach a common goal. If not romantically, then politically. If they were on the same side, she'd have brought him in a long time ago or he'd have recruited her. If both of their ambitions were truly to bring down the Cathedral, what need would either side have for us?"

"Then what are you saying?" Rabbel grew annoyed.

"I'm saying what I've been saying for nearly a twinmoon." Leesla's enunciations became clipped. "She is NOT with us. She never has been. And she never will be. I don't know what the game is, but her goal and our goals are not the same."

"You have no proof of that," Rabbel snarled.

"This last interview, for one thing," Leesla reminded him. "She defended her god as if her life depended on it."

"Did you expect her to announce that she'd joined the Break on worldwide satellite?"

"I don't ever expect her to announce any such thing, except to that roomful of people out there," Leesla answered coolly. "I expect her to string all of us along until her little plan is ready to be sprung. Then, all of us will be expendable."

"You have a devious mind."

"I am a lesbian, Rabbel, but I'm still a female." She smiled.

"PJ's a female," he countered, "only I can't believe that she could ever be deceitful."

"Oh really?" Leesla shook her head. "What do you think she's doing when she alters her appearance to come down here? She's deceiving her followers, your followers and the entire world."

"That's different," Rabbel responded. "She's doing this out of nobility."

"Probably." Leesla grimaced. "But who's idea of nobility are we talking about? Yours? Or something else having to do with that god of hers?"

"She feels the same way we do about God". Rabbel became agitated. "She hates the Church. You've heard her carry on about all the rules and restrictions and hierarchy."

"Has she ever said, 'I hate God'?" Leesla questioned.

"No," Rabbel pondered, "not in so many words. But its obvious. She wouldn't come down here and break every covenant she's sworn to uphold, if she didn't hate that god and the Cathedral and everything it stands for."

"But then she always has to leave," Leesla reminded him. "Have you ever asked yourself why PJ won't join us now? Right now? If she did, do you know how many people would follow her? Millions! Millions who are waiting for any excuse to break away from the manacles of the Church would follow her straight to us. Millions who don't really give a goddamn about their 'God', but would follow her to the ends of the world simply because she's pleasant and pretty and wears nice clothes. But she won't do it. She won't. Don't you find that just a little discouraging? Just a little suspicious?"

"She can't," Rabbel's voice trailed off. "She can't. Not yet."

"Are those your words or hers?" Leesla stood and walked toward him. "My god, Rabbel. You're waiting for PJ, the Deliveress, to deliver you people when she doesn't have any people to deliver. Not to us. Not ever. The Accommodant is ready to deliver them now! That's what makes sense for your people out in the tavern…and the rest of the world, for that matter."

"I think your jealousy is getting the best of you," Rabbel grumbled.

"Jealousy?" Leesla scoffed. "I wouldn't trade places with that woman for all the herb in the north. I know where I stand. And I like how that feels. I'm not confused and groping for answers in the heavens. My answers are right here, on solid ground in the palms of my hands. And everyday I break just a little more sweat, which inches me closer to having everything I want."

"Have you heard from Hesh lately?" Rabbel eyed her vindictively.

Leesla stopped to catch her breath as she glanced at the ceiling. She looked back into his dark brooding face with an angry scowl of her own.

"I love Hesh," Leesla spoke crisply. "And I believe that the Break represents our freedom to be together as a loving couple. But if Hesh ever came between me and this cause I fight for, I wouldn't let her. I couldn't let her. You see, I know that the Break is bigger than me and Hesh. It's bigger than Durn and Reza. It's bigger than Rabbel Mennis or PJ or Juds or three government operatives lurking around in dark suits. The Break is about the future freedoms of generations to come. You used to understand that."

"I still do!" He pounded his fist and snarled.

"Do you?" Leesla eased back. "Then prove it. Prove that PJ isn't more important to you than everything we're fighting for. Prove that you won't sacrifice all of our work for one person who doesn't honestly share your vision for the freedom of the world.

"Rabbel. I know you love her. It disturbs me to see you bewitched by this woman, but who is anyone to question the feelings in another person's heart? That, in and of itself is what the Break is all about. I'm free to love Hesh. You're free to love PJ. But the difference is whether you love PJ more than your ideals and principles. Without our ideals and principles, there isn't really much left to a sentient creature is there? Without our reason, we become more animal than civilized. And what we are fighting for is a new civilization. A free civilization. Isn't that more important than your feelings for one solitary person? Individually, it's a horrible sacrifice to make, but you are the one who declared war on the Church. And in war, we're all bound to lose some of the people we love. PJ must be one of those people, Rabbel. She's become a luxury our movement can no longer afford. I dare say she may even be a liability.

"I mean, imagine if one day, in a tender moment of marital reconciliation, she convinced her husband to kill you. Can you imagine? I can! The two of them, nestled warmly under their satin sheets, in their opulent mansion, reminiscing about their star-studded wedding reception. They'd pause and ponder the fate of the savage rebel leader who wants to uproot the status quo and turn the world upside down. 'Things were so much more pleasant before that Mennis came along.' they'd say. You, of all people should know how convincing she can be. All she'd have to do quake in his arms and speak tenderly into his ear and your life…our lives…would be over. As if we'd never existed. Then he could go on accommodating and she could continue preaching her gospel of the ghost god to apathetic skeptics who care more about what their neighbors think of them than some invisible entity up in the sky."

The muscles in Rabbel's iron jaws tensed and writhed. His eyes became fixed upon no object but Leesla's strong words.

"I don't like P.J.," Leesla continued, "I don't trust her. But more important than that, I can honestly say that I love the Break more than I hate the Deliveress. Is your love for the Break that strong?"

"Of course it is!" Rabbel growled, suppressing a shout. "Of course it is."

"Then kill her, Rabbel," she spoke in a low consipiratory whisper. "Kill her. The only thing standing between the defeat of the Church and the freedom of the world is Panla Jen Tem. No one else."

"And what would the Accommodant make of the murder of his own wife?" Rabbel glared into space.

"Today?" Leesla speculated. "Not much. Tomorrow, who knows what sentiments may turn on the passions of bedfellows. Whatever you decide, I wouldn't waste much time, though. If she learns of our new alliance, there are things she can do for our dear Accommodant that I trust you would never consider."

As her words trailed off, Leesla uncoiled herself from around the chair. She uncharacteristically leaned forward and kissed Rabbel Mennis on the forehead.

She turned and exited his office making nary a sound. Rabbel, remained in deep thought, his catatonic stare piercing the emptiness.

IX.

"Proptz Rotz! She is great!" The Accommodant cackled from his bed as he watched the first broadcast of Preppi Deyz's grandparents being tormented on the front steps of their home.

"She's a monster!" Allabel laughed, swatting him across the arm as her bare legs caressed his beneath the covers.

"That's what I call real journalism," he snickered. "It was beautiful. She nearly kills the old man, sends the old lady into hysterics and never lays a hand on either one! And she even got blood. Unbelievable!"

"I think you're a monster, too." Allabel leaned over and bit his ear. "What she did was cruel and unnecessary."

"Well, there you go again." The Accommodant rolled on top of her and pinned her wrists to the pillows. "There you go making moral judgments about what's right and what's wrong. Just because you think something's wrong doesn't make it wrong for everybody."

"You honestly believe people watching that think what she did to that poor old couple was right?" Allabel struggled meekly under his weight.

"After they get through laughing their heads off, I'm not sure anyone'll care." He smiled seductively, captivating the younger woman's eyes. "Some people might call in and complain. Most people will just be glad they have something new to joke about around the office water spout. But either way, you can't be judgmental and say Proptz Rotz is a bad person or did a bad thing. She was just doing her job and some people got hurt. It wasn't bad. It wasn't good. It was just something that happened, you know?"

"So if everybody's good with it, I shouldn't worry about it?" Allabel smiled whimsically.

"Pretty much." He gave her a short kiss.

"Life is so simple, isn't it?" She chuckled under her breath.

"It can be." He smelled and licked her neck. "Unless you choose to heap two thousand twinmoons of moral philosophy on top of every other topic like some-body I know."

"So is that how you stay so popular with the...masses?" Allabel writhed beneath him.

"A trick of the trade." He finally let her hands loose. "In the old days, a politi-cian took his values to the people, and then the polls determined whether that politician was going to get elected. Well, I just reverse the formula. I read the polls first, then tailor myself around what the polls say the people want. No candidate with a head full of convictions could ever defeat someone using my strategy. That's because nobody with real opinions could ever hope to agree with as much of the majority as a candidate who builds his opinions around the majority itself. It's straight math. I call it 'playing to win'."

"So do you know any other tricks of the trade you'd like to teach me?" Allabel smiled brightly and stroked his grey-haired belly.

"Oh, I think I know a few." A cunning grin crept across his lips. "In fact, I think you might love…"

The Accommodant stopped, mid-sentence. His head snapped up like a startled deer out of the brush.

"Hey. What…?" Allabel was confused.

"Shhh!" he gestured, listening intently. In his eyes, Allabel could see he was hearing something, but no matter how hard she tried to sort through the voices on the satellite monitor, what his trained ears detected was totally inaudible to her.

"Shit!" the Accommodant cursed.

"Klin, what are you…?"

"Shit! Shit!" he cursed again, groping through the covers for the control to mute the monitor completely.

The relaxed, sensual mood in the room crashed. The warmth of their playful moments whisked from their bedsheets as the cold, biting winds of tension and fear snatched up all the comforts of their intimacy.

Finally, Allabel heard something, also. Distant footfalls in the upper corridor. A light, purposeful, echoed march, ticking closer and closer against the marbled tiles. One person. High heels. A woman. A woman walking in the precise, inexorable staccato cadence of a symphony conductor's metronome. Louder and louder now. Very near. Approaching this room.

The Accommodant noted the hexagon chronometer on the wall and cursed again under his breath.

The cruelly distressing footfalls clapped to a stop. The mounting anxiety in the bedroom became torturously taut. A busy shadow flickered under the large wooden doors. The glistening brass handle snapped downward with a gut-twisting jolt. The bedroom doors burst open.

"GOOD MORNING." Panla shouted to the stunned, naked couple frozen to still life.

The only sound in the large luxurious bedroom was the oiled hush of the wooden doors gliding closed behind the First Lady until they loudly latched shut again.

Panla, as always, looked as fresh as the brightest spring morning, adorned in her two-piece peach-toned bouclé ensemble with a ruffled white pill-box hat and matching gloves.

"Oh my god," Allabel gasped and scrambled off the far side of the bed, onto the floor, searching frantically for her clothes.

Panla's expression remained eerily calm and impassive. It was as if she had merely walked in on two children, frolicking under the covers past their bed time.

"W...Why did you come all the way home tonight?" The Accommodant's voice was rasp with indignity.

Panla's expression brightened with an amused smile. She slowly walked toward her dresser, pulling her gloves off, one finger at a time. She stopped in front of the mirror and checked her make-up. When she was satisfied she was completely in order, she turned slowly to address her husband.

"Tonight?" her soft voice echoed in the high ceiling. "Why. it's one hour from sunrise. It's morning."

"You know what I mean," his voice cracked. "You weren't due back until just before noon."

Panla tilted her head as if there had been an honest misunderstanding.

"Oh," she remarked casually, "how rude of me. I'm sorry, darling. It was just a matter of semantics. I wasn't looking forward to a long morning trek, so I thought I'd rather get a fresh start from home. You do understand, don't you?"

The lines in the Accommodant's face hardened into greyed crevices of raw vexation. It was a very private, personal expression of contempt which the politician always kept hidden from a public audience.

"Well," Panla's dark innocent eyes widened with contrition, "I can see I've made you unhappy."

"Damn you, Panla!" the Accommodant seethed. "You know damn well..."

"Oh Queen Mother!" Allabel popped up from behind the bed, hopping toward Panla on one shoe as she attempted to slip on the other. "I am so sorry! I am so very, very, very, very sorry!"

Her skirt was twisted sideways and her blouse was hooked eschew leaving an uneven tail hanging out of the front. Her hair was scattered and matted. And her lip coloring was still badly smeared. Yet what stood out the most to Panla was Allabel's facial expression, awash with an unharnessed, wide-eyed regret...and fear.

"Queen Mother!" Allabel dropped to her knees and clutched Panla's hand. "Please, please, please forgive me for this...this absolutely hideous, self-indulgent...disrespectful, stupid transgression. I am not really this kind of person. Really, I'm not! I...I just love politics and I really love my job on the staff and your husband....the Accommodant is such a beaut...um...wonderful man...not that you don't already know that...but I really, really, used some really bad judgment in letting things go a little too far. It's not his fault. Well, not totally. And I'm an adult and I know that it's so wrong to sleep with another woman's husband! That is, a married man. Or I think, any man I'm not married to, actually. And I just fell into this. It was so stupid and so evil and so wrong, I can't believe this is me!

"And I'm so sorry for not going to Cathedral. I've blown it off for twinmoons and I can't really say why...except this job is so great and such a high for me that maybe I didn't think I needed you...it...cathedral, I mean. But I am so ashamed! So embarrassed! This is such a mess! And I think I'm going to Hell for this...but I'm just not that bad a person. And I really try to do good things. And I just don't want this to be what you think of me! And I don't want you to hate me! And....I'm just so sorry!"

Allabel began sobbing as she threw herself around Panla's waist. A startled Panla found herself compassionately running her fingers through the young woman's rumpled hair.

The Accommodant, meanwhile, crawled wearily out of bed and stood naked, staring at the two women in disgust. He snatched a long, leaf-embroidered silken robe from the bedpost and tossed it around his body.

"Whenever the shit comes down, you all stick together, don't you?" He looked on the scene disdainfully. "Unbelievable."

"This isn't me." Allabel lifted her head up to Panla. "You have to believe that this isn't me. I don't do this kind of thing. I am so, so, sorry!"

"I know," Panla said in a hushed voice. "When Manucus slaughtered a woman and her young son for the coin in the woman's purse, and spent the coin on a sack of wine, and drank the wine in one short afternoon, three days later he witnessed the funeral procession for the woman and child he had slain. And no one but God knew what he had done and no one might have, but that he fell to his knees out of grief and remorse and confessed his crime to the family as they passed by. A crowd gathered and quickly decided that he should be vivisectioned for his crime. But the husband, who had lost his wife and young son, stepped forward and asked the angry mob, who amongst them had not sinned. And they all fell silent. The husband then helped Manucus to his feet and entreated him: "Sin no more for the Love of God, and Heaven shall be yours.' Manucus was overwhelmed by this incredible display of mercy. And he never murdered again, he never drank again, and he became the founder of the second of the original Nine Tribes.

"Allabel, is it?" Panla helped the young woman to her feet.

"Yes, Queen Mother," She continued to hang her head.

"Sin no more for the Love of God and Heaven shall be yours."

Allabel lifted her head and met Panla's eyes. It might have been better if Panla had struck her, Allabel felt. For this instruction from the Deliveress bore an even greater burden for the ultimate salvation of her soul.

"Yes, Queen Mother," the young woman sniffled. "Thank you."

Allabel paused for a moment and thought to say something to the Accommodant, but oddly she sensed no reason to speak or look back. Instead, she exited quietly, leaving her corruption withering in the Accommodant's disheveled bed.

The door closed quietly; the world's First Couple were now alone.

"So you still know how to fuck up a good time," The Accommodant said as he poured himself an early morning capper. "Even on your feet."

"Well, darling, I must say I'm surprised." Panla walked slowly toward him. "I believe that girl was actually sentient. Not your usual fare."

"You call that sentient?" he snorted. "One minute she's screwing me, the next minute she's praying to you. If that's what passes for sentient on this planet, then the whole world needs a frontal goddamn lobotomy."

"Hmh!" Panla laughed to herself, then moved toward the bed. She sat down, crossed her legs and glanced at the silent monitor.

"Poor world." She sighed, tilting her head. "Finx Melder is dead. So young and handsome and talented. How will we ever survive without him?"

"You didn't answer my question." The Accommodant threw back his drink, then set down the triangular glass.

"What question is that?" Panla closed her eyes and wound her neck wearily.

The muscles in the Accommodant's jaw became pronounced as he fought down his temper. His wife knew all the casual gestures and responses that would set him off if he wasn't careful. She had already laid the mines and now he had to step carefully to elude the detonations. He tried to focus on the political chessboard always playing in his head to guide him clear of a losing skirmish.

"The question was," he said through clenched teeth, "why are you home so early?"

"Oh, Klin, darling I answered you." She sounded politely impatient with him. "I told you…"

"I know what you said!" He interrupted as his chess pieces quickly toppled from their tenuous positions. "Now let's cut through all the bullshit!"

"Really, must you swear?" she scolded.

"Yes!" the Accommodant scowled. "Yes! With you, I need to curse and swear and shout some feeling through that thick frozen hide of yours!"

"Frozen?" She regarded him with PJ's sassy aloofness. "Are you certain?"

The Accommodant was stunned by this subtly, uncharacteristic taunt. There was a brash, almost sensuous looseness about her which he had never seen before. He might have found it arousing were her behavior not arousing his suspicions more.

"Maybe 'frozen' doesn't apply anymore," he probed more than apologized. "Maybe we're talking about a thaw?"

"No." She gazed at him playfully. "No thaw for you, I'm afraid. Where you're concerned, the ice has only begun to crest."

"I see." The Accommodant became even more suspicious. "So, are you finally fucking someone Queen Mother? Fucking someone behind my back? Maybe one of your quasi-religious she-buddies in that kinky little entourage of yours?"

He had hoped to box her back into her rigid sensibilities. He knew that no matter what she truly felt, she would never compromise, even in private, her adamant devotion to faith and decorum. Foisting depraved vulgarities upon her clear shield of enduring righteousness had become nuptial sport for him. Unfortunately, this particular confrontation continued to evolve in hues of disquieting unfamiliarity.

"Men," she sighed with a weary huff. She looked at him with an earnest contempt he had never seen from her.

"Am I fucking someone?" Another wry smile under angry eyes colored her expression. "My dearest husband, the only person I'm fucking is myself by staying in this marriage."

The Accommodant had to blink. He didn't know whether to strike her, call a psychiatrist or pour himself one more stiff drink before breakfast. It was as if he had been blindsided by a completely new adversary disguised in a familiar enemy's uniform. Who was this woman?

Trying hastily to absorb her scathing candor on the state of their wedded bliss, he opted for the stiff drink, stepping to the dresser where the platinum tray and crystal decanter sat next to the giant monitor in front of the bed. He refilled his glass, then turned to his wife whose cool, playful expression had now fused into a white porcelain mask of fiery contempt.

"Join me?" He tried to make a peace offering.

"Lord in Heaven." She closed her eyes. "This sopping drunken lying immoral lecher! What was I thinking?"

"I could ask myself the same question." He started to sip, but suddenly regarded the glass as an affirmation of her indictment. He set it down and pulled his robe tightly over his chest. "A spoiled, frightened, passionless virgin…do you remember that night? I felt like I'd pried open the legs of a five-twinmoon-old girl and raped her you cried and whined so much. And, frankly, it never got much better. How did I ever manage to find a female who hates sex as much as you do?"

"Ask your whores, they could tell you." The anger in Panla's eyes deepened as her voice remained even. "If you ever once considered love rather than sex, you'd have your answer…to a lot of things."

"Love!?" The Accommodant threw up his hands. "You want to talk to me about love? What the hell does love mean to you, other than some dream of screwing the man upstairs when you're dead? Honey, I'm made out of flesh and blood. Maybe you're not! But I have needs like everybody else on this goddamn planet. And if my wife's not going to meet those needs, I have to go where real people have real feelings. People who aren't caught up in some deluded fantasy about God that turns every earthly pleasure into guilt-ridden arbitrary sins!"

Panla bounced up from the bed and stepped toward him. Her sudden, uncharacteristic movement was genuinely frightening. She shook and quaked as if she were prepared to commit murder.

"Sins…are not…ARBITRARY!" she yelled loudly into her husband's face. "They are NOT! And if you think you can con the whole world into believing that they are, or that the Text is open to specious, criminal interpretations, I will stop you cold! I will stop anyone who tries to slander or blaspheme the irrefutably good and just words of our Heavenly Father! Do you understand me?"

The Accommodant backed away, stunned by the intensity of her tirade. There was clearly something amiss here. And he was ill-prepared to handle it.

Finally, he managed to stammer: "Honey, I…I think we should…"

"I never asked anything of you as a husband but to be yourself!" The sting of her sharp feminine voice pierced like a rapier. "But you could never even figure out who you were. It was always about what other people thought! First, you were this successful lawbooker. But then, you let people talk you into politics. And from there, you let power-mongers and interest groups shape you into anything they wanted! You became nothing more than whatever the latest ad campaign said you were. And, behind closed doors, you realized that you didn't have to stand for anything at all except your id! Your libido!"

"That's out of hand!" The Accommodant raised his voice.

"Is it?" she shouted with rage. "You mean it's not all about this?"

Panla placed both her hands on the side of the large video monitor and with all of her hidden might, pushed it off of its stand, crashing and exploding in the middle of the bedroom floor. A spark and a puff of smoke billowed up from the dead appliance lying between them. Even she was momentarily taken aback by the sudden violence, but not enough to retreat from purging her frustrations.

"Some very well-meaning people stand up for manmade principles or ideals." She was nearly out of breath. "Others only stand up for themselves. A foolish few honestly think they're doing good when they blindly stand up for someone else. While the righteous, we stand up for God. But you? You proudly stand up and waft in whatever direction the wind sways you, like a weed or a ball of lint. How could anyone ever love you for that?"

The giant bedroom doors burst open. Standing in the doorway were Crilen and two heavily-armed mansion security officers, poised for action. They immediately took in the scenery of domestic wreckage as the Accommodant and the Deliveress stood, rankled, but in perfectly good health. Crilen gestured for the two officers to remain at the door. He approached the couple respectfully, noting the buckled, smoldering monitor on the floor.

"An accident." The Accommodant chuckled nervously. "Everything is perfectly fine."

"Oh, yes." Panla didn't attempt to hide her disgust. "Everything is absolutely wonderful."

She glared at her husband one last time, then flickered a glance at Crilen. She tugged on the bottom of her jacket, swallowed hard, and proceeded to march out of the bedroom with the same royal air with which she had entered.

Crilen watched her depart with increasing concern. He looked back to the Accommodant who was smiling.

"Wives." He shook his head at Crilen.

"We'll get someone up here to clean this up," Crilen said with stone-faced professionalism. He pivoted and followed after Panla before her footfalls disappeared from earshot.

"Mr. Len." The Accommodant halted him with authority.

Crilen stopped in his tracks, silently cursing the momentary delay. It was just long enough for him to be certain Panla would be long gone. Dutifully, he turned and faced the highest elected official on the planet.

"Yes sir?" Crilen came to attention with his hands clasped behind his back.

"You seem to be in a hurry." The Accommodant's tone was serious. "Is there something going on with Mrs. Tem that I need to be made aware of?"

"No, sir," Crilen answered flatly.

"I see." The Accommodant paced toward the dresser and scooped up his glass. He sipped very slowly as if to savor the moment's peace. The sun had not yet risen and it had already been a very long day.

"So how was your first day on the job?" the Accommodant asked him.

Crilen quickly filtered out any thoughts of PJ, which would taint his response. "Brisk," he answered.

This time the Accommodant swigged from his glass and worked the liquid with his mouth before he swallowed hard. He smiled that affable politician's grin Crilen had seen during his job interview. At that time he wasn't sure if the Accommodant could be trusted. Now he was quite sure of him.

"Brisk?" the Accommodant spoke with a chuckle. "Brisk? All her days are brisk, Mr. Len. She's got a dual life: First Lady to the Accommodant and Deliveress of the Cathedral. That's enough to make anyone's days brisk. What I'm asking you is if anything unusual happened that might have upset her yesterday."

"Well, there was the food poisoning," Crilen answered evenly.

"Food poisoning? What food poisoning?" The Accommodant frowned.

"The luncheon menu did not exactly agree with her," Crilen recollected. "The fowl was apparently foul."

"Her and that weak stomach." The Accommodant shook his head. "I don't know why she ever eats out. Anything not prepared by that goddamn Cathedral chef is too something for her digestive system. And she wonders why I won't take her to dinner. What, so I can watch her pick through her plate looking nauseous all evening? I can think of better things to do and better people to do it with. Anyway, was that it?"

"Well, the interview was very stressful," Crilen added. "Especially having to field so many difficult questions, after feeling sick the way she did."

"The world thinks she's so damned tough." The Accommodant sipped again. "Whine your ears off, did she?"

"No, sir." Crilen remained rigid. "She seemed to feel things went pretty well under the circumstances. Although the evening got a bit dicey after the bomb exploded."

"Bomb?" The Accommodant's eyes widened. "What bomb? An attempt on her life?"

"Not exactly, sir," Crilen answered. "Actually, it was an attempt on the life of the talk show host. The young man was actually a mad religious zealot, in love with the Deliveress."

"Why wasn't there any news of this?" The Accommodant was shocked.

"Probably because once the media found out it was an attempt on one of them, they figured a grass-roots attack on the media would not make them look as....popular as they'd like to appear."

"Grass roots?" the Accommodant asked suspiciously. "How do you know?"

"I spoke with the young man briefly, before he...blew himself up."

"Hmm." The Accommodant rubbed his chin. "You're lucky you weren't killed, let alone my wife, who was poisoned, interrogated and nearly blown to cold cuts. No wonder she's acting strangely."

Crilen did not reply.

"So when did she make the decision to leave the southern continent and come home?"

Crilen's mind jumped for a moment.

"Southern continent, sir?" Crilen tilted his head slightly. "We weren't on the southern continent. YBS studios is...."

"Okay, okay." The Accommodant fanned his hand and finished his drink. "I was just playing a little geography game with you. But still...I can't understand why she ordered you all back here so early in the morning."

"I think," Crilen said phrasing carefully, "that Mrs. Tem may be suffering from a mild touch of exhaustion. At least that's what I could ascertain from my first day with her. She seems very stressed and very exhausted."

"Well, if she'd spent the night in her hotel instead of sneaking home, 600 kilometers in the dead of night to spy on me, maybe she'd have gotten some rest," the Accommodant snorted. "Don't get me wrong, Mr. Len. I love my wife. But every marriage has ground rules. And I can't be held responsible if she wants to drive herself crazy trying to stretch those rules. I had some business to attend to with a member of my staff tonight and that segued into a little...playtime. Nothing unusual. It happens. You understand. Cute young girl with stars in her eyes wants a taste of life at the top. So I give her a taste. What am I supposed to do? Tell her to go back to her little condo and blow the coffee house clerk? Hell no. I did what any man in my position would do: I gave a young protégé a midnight ride in the seat of power. A chance for a talented and aspiring young lady to sup on the fruits of her political prospects. Two consenting adults having an instructive evening of recreation after a hard day's work. That's all. And Panla knew damn well what she might run into when she showed up unexpected like this.

She knew damn well! So if she's stressed or tired or exhausted about something, what the hell am I supposed to do about it?"

"Nothing, under the circumstances." Crilen absorbed the Accommodant's reasoning without emotion. "Perhaps, if there were a way to prune Mrs. Tem's schedule..."

"Well, like you said," the Accommodant cut in, "there's nothing I can do about it. I don't make her schedule. Talk to Mr. Linnfeld about it. Maybe he can do something."

"Yes, sir." Crilen nodded dutifully.

"And, Mr. Len." The Accommodant stepped closer and lowered his voice. "I understand that my wife has a very...appealing personage. The people who work for her wind up becoming extremely dedicated to her and her causes. I know you're a religious man. There's nothing wrong with that. But if my wife should ever engage in any activity that you might consider...a threat to this world's...peace or balance, I would expect you to notify me, as the Accommodant of this planet, immediately. Do you understand?"

"Yes, sir." Crilen didn't flinch.

"Her job is to represent the best interests of the Cathedral." the Accommodant said softly, "but my job is to accommodate everyone. The majority rules. Do I make myself clear?"

"Very clear, sir."

The Accommodant smiled and took note of Crilen's rigid posture. "Religious mumbo-jumbo aside, Mr. Len, man-to-man, I think you might be a little on the stressed side yourself. If I were you, I might go find myself a little piece of ass to take the edge off. Do you some good. Trust me. If you ever want my help, I know some very, very discreet sources of pleasure and relaxation. God'll never know."

The Accommodant winked and patted Crilen on the shoulder, snickering as if they were old buddies.

"I'll remember that." Crilen lifted an eyebrow and nodded.

X.

"Once again, you're looking at a live shot of the back end of Finx Melder's vehicle, lodged in the side of that blazing fuel tank," the monitor blared throughout the diner.

"Oh, to hell with Finx Melder!" the short waitress exclaimed as she worked her way around the table, setting down glasses of juice for everyone.

"Very likely, I'm afraid." Yolo Pigue's broad morning smile made curved indentations in his large sagging jowls. "Assuming you believe in that sort of thing. There certainly wasn't much our late hero de jour didn't do to qualify. For Hell, that is."

"Murder." Mr. Pont picked up his glass and gave Yolo an irked, sidelong glance.

"I beg your pardon, Mr. Pont." The media giant raised his heavy brows.

Mr. Nil sighed and looked up at the ceiling. The waitress shook her head and glanced toward the grill. Mr. Pont had ordered his daily spanking early this morning, and it usually wasn't a pretty thing to observe. Fortunately, Yolo did seem to be in a more forgiving humor...thus far.

"Murder." The thin pasty-complexioned columnist held his ground. "He didn't commit murder. Maybe he just ran out of time, eh?"

"And then again, perhaps not." Yolo raised a finger as the waitress tucked an extra large napkin into his wide collar. "Toxicology may yet complete Mr. Melder's sordid personal portfolio. If they find he was under the influence of another unprescribed pharmaceutical, and it's likely, they will, he may yet be charged with the homicide of that insufferably sweet girlfriend of his, post mortem."

Mr. Pont's expression wrinkled in disbelief.

"A shame he didn't survive her," the large man continued. "An idiotic show-trial would have made for spectacular theatre! Something we haven't enjoyed in a good while. A celebrity murder trial, that is. All the famous witnesses putting on their finest jewelry for their most challenging and pitiable performances: attempting to act like themselves. Every morning is like a movie premiere, limousines lined up around the block with famous faces posing for pictures under the canopy, feigning genuine concern as to the outcome. 'I'm here to support...' they always say. Support. Exploit. Blood-suck. The difference is negligible in the entertainment community. And of course, the clamoring cretins at home are never savvy enough to see through the insipid charade. Ratings soar to the moons, and all the masses comprehend is some spontaneous drama unfolding without a script. At least no script anyone ever actually sees!"

"The last one was the murder of that bit-part com-com actress ten twinmoons ago," Mr. Nil snickered.

"Oh, yes!" Yolo chuckled aloud. "A deliciously rancid affair! The defense built their entire case around the fact that she had infected so many males with IVC, that any one of hundreds had strong enough motive to bury that sickle into her throat. And that without accounting for the secondhand wives, girlfriends and homosexual lovers who had peripheral interests in her demise. The lawbooker reasoned that killing her was akin to wiping out a virulent plague and that his client, some poor brutish athlete who's name escapes me, had done the entire world the same service as any scientist who had cultured a life-saving cure in his laboratory."

"She was hot." Mr. Nil cupped his hands in front of his chest.

"Until the night in question." Yolo slurped from his pitcher-size glass.

"And he was acquitted!" Mr. Nil shook his head.

"Of course," Yolo snorted. "By law, the jury had to be comprised of twenty-one people who had no prior knowledge that any of the most famous celebrities in the world existed before the trial began. Thus, the entire planet watched, in stunned amazement, as the verdict of a multi-million coin litigation was held hostage by a room full of semi-retarded, agoraphobic imbeciles whose impaired intellects were scarcely capable of processing more than ten words a minute. Once again, the dim tax-paying populace got what it paid for."

"They kept asking for the crime scene photos," Mr. Nil snickered. "One of the jurors even accused policers of omitting pictures of the actual murder. 'Where are those other pictures?' he kept asking. Like the cops were there during the murder and then said 'Okay, killer, you can go now. We're just going to take a few more shots of the bloody corpse, thank you.' Scary."

Mr. Pont stared glumly at his boss and co-worker. The snouted king and his obsequious henchman were at it again. Yolo Pigue was as weighty an opponent in debate as his physique, so Mr. Pont always resented Mr. Nil piling on.

"God took a lot of fine performers from us as a result of her behavior," Mr. Pont started, "but she didn't deserve to die the way she did. And we shouldn't make light of what wound up being an awful tragedy in the eyes of God."

"Oh, don't drag God into the conversation." Yolo's heavy glass clunked onto the table. "Especially when you're woefully ill-equipped to defend he or it!"

"Or she." Mr. Nil chimed him.

"She?" the large man frowned. "Only if you believe that all creation must ooze from some writhing cosmic vaginal cavity. That's a rather stupidly narrow-sighted mammalian notion of the universe."

Mr. Nil's mouth dropped open, but nothing came out.

"Now firstly, why should God consider murder a tragedy?" Yolo turned up his nose. "As the creator of all things, I should think he'd have an ample supply of matter to replace each and every one of us a thousand times over. Let alone some diseased, mindless, coin-a-dozen strumpet who wasted every second of her life twisted into one sexual contortion after another. Secondly, why should 'God the almighty' care about another bungled trial? Aside from the fact that our flimsy mortal laws are not his laws, the Text painstakingly reminds us that 'God' sees all, knows all and will get us all in the end for our 'evil' deeds. So I wouldn't really worry about some 'God's' feelings. 'He' allegedly has matters under control, I'm sure."

Mr. Pont could only frown as his biscuit crumbled between his fingers.

"In any case, we're talking about actors." Yolo continued, "Thespians. Those people don't believe in any hard and fast god or religion. They simply can't. If they did, they'd have to abandon their convoluted, vacuous lifestyles. Then what fun would be art? Crimped and shorn by moral shears, no self-respecting artist could ever hope to make a living. Today's entertainment must be violent, vulgar, and, if all else fails, naked. That is the bane of artistry. Notions of God are shunned like a terminal contagion. Take a look at any modern art exhibit. Any satellite program with high ratings. Any film or modern stage production. The thespians have convinced the world that God has become passé. A pity. Not for the sake of religion, mind you. But once upon a time, art was actually an elegant thing. Not the artists themselves, but art once had a graceful, dignified substance. All of that has changed now."

Yolo sat back and stared distantly, as if he were gazing into a fond part of his own past.

"Up to about a hundred twinmoons ago, most performers were little more than traveling rogues," Yolo reminisced beyond his years. "Their rag-tag troupes delighted our ancestors for an evening or two, usually in some cramped, dingy little theatre, and then their wayward caravans would ramble on to the next town for a night or so, with relatively modest fanfare. Creative people, yes. But the life of the performer has always been shrouded in decadence, transience, insatiable excesses and tragedy. The only difference between now and then is that they used to die in the gutters, penniless and forgotten. Now they die in posh hotels, mansions and luxury condominiums. And their shallow rotting carcasses are outlived and outweighed by their recordings, which posthumously canonize the rehearsed and scripted segments of their, otherwise, ludicrous existences."

"You never had a favorite actress, Yolo?" the waitress set down utensils as she passed.

"More than my fair share, good lady." The large man's girth rocked with a tinge of glee. "But if you're asking me if I ever staggered off to the theatre to worship one of them, I'd sooner worship the wind."

"How can you say all of that with a straight face?" Mr. Pont threw up his hands. "Without entertainers...actors, actresses, commentators...Yolo Pigue

Communications and Yolo Broadcasting Systems wouldn't have an audience. And you wouldn't have an empire!"

"Indeed." Yolo splashed a half-pint of juice into his mouth and gargled it down. "But the grinder needn't respect the meat. The colon needn't respect the bowel."

"Forgettin' your surgery, Yolo?" the waitress stopped and frowned. "I seem to recall quite a bit of respect right around that time."

"Ah yes, my dear woman," the large man smiled wickedly. "How kind of you to...remind me. But even then, it wasn't a matter of respect. Rather it was an...unpleasant negotiation of disposable waste. Much the same as the negotiation of a celebrity contract. A sumptuous consummation inevitably dumped and flushed."

The waitress shook her head, rolled her eyes and toddled off to the kitchen.

"Like Libbi," Mr. Nil smirked and slumped in his chair.

"Libbi?" Mr. Pont was puzzled. "What happened to Libbi?"

"On hiatus." Mr. Nil grinned.

"Hiatus?" Mr. Pont was stunned. "Her interview with the Deliveress was her highest rated show ever."

"A career choice." Yolo shrugged. "She needed to get away for awhile. I concurred."

"You slept with her," Mr. Pont concluded with disgust.

"Really, Mr. Pont," Yolo quaked with satisfaction, "have you no shame? I am a modest man who prefers to keep such matters private. But if you must know, it was she who approached me without overture. A pitiable display, all told. And not at all satisfying. I found our girl Libbi was even roomier than had been rumored. It was something like fitting on an worn old glove with all of the stitching come loose. It was rather like that, I'm afraid. Hiatus was the only remedy."

"Wushhhhh!" Mr. Nil mimicked a flushing sound.

The waitress returned, skillfully balancing plates upon platters with an ease that belied her diminutive stature. She placed two small plates in front of Mr. Pont. She placed one normal-sized plate in front of Mr. Nil. Then, disproportionately, the rest of the morning feast belonged to Yolo Pigue. Two dozen links of large thick sausages, a mountain of fried fruit, a towering stack of honey-covered toast, and a whipped sculpture of swirled eggs at the center of it all.

Yolo licked his chops, but hesitated and gave the waitress an admonishing glare.

"The rest is coming." She mopped her brow and placed her hands on her hips. "How many times do I have to tell you, we only have one grill, Mr. Pigue. One grill!"

Yolo smiled knowingly and took up his utensils. The surgery and smelting commenced as he tossed out a question to his subordinates.

"So," the large man spoke as he chewed, sausage grease flying from his mouth, "what did you fine gentlemen make of that interview with the Deliveress, anyway?"

Mr. Nil sat and pondered what answer would please his employer.

Mr. Pont dove in instinctively. "It was encouraging." the thin man nibbled from his biscuit. "I sensed a compromise in the Deliveress. She knows that the Cathedral can't endure if it remains rigid and inflexible, so she's willing to compromise for the sake of her own survival. I think that's a reasonable position to take considering the declining appeal of organized religion."

"An awful observation, Mr. Pont," Yolo blustered as a clump of meat fell from his mouth. "That's merely what you wanted to see. Mr. Nil?"

"I saw just the opposite," the pudgy, round-faced assistant carefully weighed in. "It was a claw-fight. Deliveress Jen wasn't giving any ground. Neither was Libbi. Two arrogant females with polar-opposite points of view who couldn't agree on anything. The only thing missing was a giant mudpit. Otherwise, I didn't get anything out of it. But it was fun watching both of them squirm a little. I guess you could say Libbi did a good job making the Deliveress uncomfortable. That was different."

Yolo plowed through the giant egg structure at the center of his plate with an over-sized spoon and dumped the large green/yellow mass into his mouth. He pushed the wad into a large cheek and held it there.

"Well, the Queen Mother certainly wasn't comfortable, that's true." his voice became garbled with food. "But it wasn't any of Libbi's doing, I assure you. There was something else at work. As if our sweet young pious little hag had difficulty defending her title."

"I thought she defended herself very well." Mr. Pont sipped from his glass.

"Quite right for a change, Mr. Pont," Yolo snorted, "but as always, your listening comprehension has failed you. I didn't say she had difficulty defending herself. I said she had difficulty defending her title. She said all of the things a Deliverer is supposed to say, but there were moments where her conviction faltered."

"Yeah, I saw that," Mr. Nil chimed in.

"Sure you did." Mr. Pont scowled at his associate.

"Gentleman, please." Yolo smiled and shook his head at the petty bickering. "Let's not lose our focus. What I mean to say is that I believe there are conflicting forces at work, warring in the bosom of our Deliveress and First Lady. I can't tell you the crux of it just yet, but I'm certain there's something amiss."

"There's nothing wrong with the Deliveress." The waitress dropped off another bowl of sausages. "I'll tell you what's at work here. You just hate women, Yolo. Listen to yourself. A cranky old bachelor who probably had his big old heart broken one time too many. Now you're old and mean and full of whiny old bitterness."

Yolo's eyes widened as he watched the waitress whisk by and make her way over to another table.

"Have you ever considered a position in journalism, my dear?" Yolo called to her.

"What, and be indentured to you?" She smiled. "You don't have the coin!"

"Well I'll have you know I make little fuss over never having been married." Yolo splashed another pint of juice into his large mouth to clear his throat. "And I haven't a misogynistic bone in my body. Though, if I had my druthers as to whom I should appeal least in this world, I would choose females over males, children or beasts. After all, the camaraderie of males is irreplaceable in the male equation. It's only from such peers that a male can receive affirmation that he belongs to the fraternity of males. Present company excluded, of course."

Mr. Nil shifted uncomfortably in his seat as the food fell from his utensil. Mr. Pont merely flipped his brows and bit into his biscuit.

"The affection of children," Yolo continued, "is the most innocent form of sentient, guiless warmth a person may ever experience. Children know little of selfishness or deceit and nothing of egocentricity. The corruptions of maturity are alien to them. They simply like what's good and hate what's bad. It's not much more complex than that."

"Spoken like a man with no children." The waitress rolled her eyes and busied herself clearing the table next to them.

"And as for animals," Yolo ignored the comment, "could you imagine if every creature you came across brayed, howled and hissed it's contempt at you in its own secret animal language? You'd done nothing to them but happen by, and yet there'd be this id-driven bestial screeching of disapproval of you, for all to bear witness to. I can't imagine a more unbearable condemnation from nature.

"But females? I beg you, what boon do we gain from the love of a woman when all the sweating and grunting is done? A woman is fickle, jealous, insecure, and, in the end, the embodiment of deceit, betrayal and inconsistency. What gains a man by the love of such a creature?"

"I wager you'll never know." The waitress patted him on the shoulder.

"Nor would I care to," Yolo chuckled, "nor would I care to. For how is a man to know when a female loves him? Her scope of trickeries and deceptions knows no bounds. The best a fellow can do is not concern himself with love at all."

"Hah! Males are the big liars, Yolo," she admonished him with a glare.

"Feminist propaganda, dear lady." He chuckled and quaked as the joints of his chair squeaked their protestations. "Feminist propaganda. Females are by far, the greatest liars. In fact, they are such artful liars that they even lie about the notion that men are better liars to deflect this obvious attribute from their own lying natures. When a man lies, you can be certain it's about one thing: Sex. He either lies to get sex or he lies to conceal sex. But when a woman lies, no one can begin to fathom the whys or wherefores which motivate her tangled tale-spinning. It could be for a myriad of frightening reasons or rationales, sex being the least of it!"

"That's right," the waitress scoffed as she refilled his giant glass. "It's all propaganda. A big conspiracy."

"Well, I wouldn't say that it rises to the level of conspiracy." Yolo stabbed the pile of toast with a skewer. "Everyone knows the truth, but women simply won't own up to it. They'd rather obscure their reason in circular tautologies of self-help and insipidly inane male persecutions. The entire female periodical industry is wholly built upon telling women that all of their shortcomings are strengths. And while males should love them no matter how fat or ugly they are, it's never going to happen. So it's better to be humped than respected, because getting humped is who and what they are. And having been humped and dumped, of course, they proclaim every selfish right in the world to drive everyone around them insane with their subsequently incongruous, wanton behavior."

"Oh now wait…!" the waitress' dark features became enraged.

"And lest you dispute me on this count," the media giant rolled on, "my publications division makes four billion coin every twinmoon printing just the sort of feminine tripe I abhor. Females, by far, comprise my most profitable patronage."

Yolo grinned as he chewed. Then, tragedy struck.

"Fine. No sauce for you." The waitress snatched a bottle of dark yellow sauce from the table, turned on her heel and stalked away.

Yolo dropped his utensils on the table and watched with a sudden forlorn expression as the short stocky woman disappeared through the swinging kitchen doors. For an instant, he was a child who had just had his favorite toy snatched away. He was nearly at a loss for words. Nearly. But then his brows wrinkled and he took up his instruments again, pretending as if the crippling loss of his hot sauce meant little to him.

"You see, there." Yolo tried to mask his inconsolable pout. "Wanton behavior. Inexcusable."

"So you think the Deliveress is up to something?" Mr. Pont tried to lasso his attention.

"Mr. Nil, go fetch my sauce, would you?" Yolo fought to keep his face from darkening into a stormy grey mask of perturbation.

Mr. Nil grimaced and swallowed hard. "But nobody's allowed back…"

"FETCH MY SAUCE!!" Yolo slammed his open hand on the table. Every dish and utensil jumped and scattered.

Mr. Nil popped up and briskly headed for the kitchen. He didn't know what he was going to do once he entered the diner's forbidden sanctuary, but he knew if he didn't emerge with the media giant's sauce he might as well keep walking straight out the rear exit. Where his journalistic talents crossed with such assignments as this remained uncertain, but he knew sitting at the right hand of the most powerful media force in the world was still excellent work, even if the salary lagged, along with his pride.

"So you were saying?" Yolo picked and flicked at his toast.

Mr. Pont cleared his throat and offered his query again.

"You think Deliveress Jen is hiding something?" he paraphrased himself.

"To say the least." The large man skewered three sausages, then extracted them with his tongue and teeth. He continued to talk as he gnashed his food to molecules. "Some personal torment screaming to burst forth. But it's a mystery. If she were a he, I might be on to something. But she is very she and I haven't a clue for the moment. All we can do is poise our troops to strike when the moment is at hand."

"I can't believe the Deliveress has anything to hide." Mr. Pont folded his arms and tilted his head with skepticism.

"That's because you're like most of the so-called faithful". Yolo reached for his giant glass. "You're like the blind, deaf beast with its head sunk between its shoulders, loping along in the herd, with only the stink of the rectum in front of you to serve as your life's compass. A true independent thought frightens you more than the devil. You fear it may separate you from the loping stinking herd and you'll be left all alone to question your solitary judgment absent the sway of the majority. Better to think of the Deliveress as an infallible statue born of paint and plaster than to think of her as a living creature, vulnerable to the same frailties we all suffer. That lets you sleep at night. And we all know a good night's sleep is the most important thing, even if it is couched in blissful ignorance."

"Well," Mr. Pont lowered his eyes and tried not to shake, "it's better than believing in nothing. I can't believe in nothing. I'd rather believe in her."

"Hmh." Yolo shook his jowls and snorted coldly. "I'm sure the majority would agree with you."

The kitchen doors burst open.

Mr. Nil emerged and scurried back to the table, the jar of sauce held gingerly in his hands. He set the jar down in front Yolo and Yolo immediately observed the jar was smeared with blood.

"What in the world…?" Yolo inspected the jar of sauce with amazement.

"She…she had this…fork!" Mr. Nil held up his bloodied hands. "A huge fork!"

The waitress emerged from the kitchen clutching a long pointed utensil with sharp prongs, twelve centimeters in length. Her surly expression was that of a lioness who had justly defended her den.

Yolo looked at her, then at the jar, and then at Mr. Nil's bloodied hands. His girth quaked with laughter that loudly reverberated throughout the diner, out onto the sidewalk and probably down the street some distance.

Mr. Nil smiled also, chuckling painfully as he dabbed his bleeding wounds with a napkin.

Mr. Pont could only fashion an impotent stare as he pondered the mortality of his faith.

XI.

The Bius Basilica:

Panla stared at her gold sequined robe spread beautifully along the wooden pegs on the wall of her large private Cathedral sitting room. She eyed its shimmering layered plumes wearily. The thought of donning its crass, gaudy betrayal of her true love for God made her feel that bearing a chained wooden stock around her neck would be less burdensome. Rather than continue to bear the crown of her false secular divinity, she would find more comfort being cast into the street as Dinthois the Accused had been…ragged clothes, cut and swollen feet, bruised and blistered face, chained to the stocks as people hurled rocks and animal excrement at him for their scorn…and their justification.

In the Text, Dinthois was a merchant, wrongfully accused and convicted of theft by a local government who favored his rival. His possessions were sold and his store was burned to the ground. He was sentenced to wander the town streets for thirty days with his head and wrists clamped in stocks, forbidden to speak of his innocence. For the first four days he stumbled aimlessly as the townspeople spat upon him and pelted him with anything they could find.

But on the fifth day, Dinthois staggered to the town center where he collapsed to his knees and prayed continuously for the remainder of his sentence. For the next twenty-six days, the townspeople who had ridiculed and derided him began offering him food and water as he prayed, but Dinthois would not acknowledge anything but his penitence to Heaven. On the final hour of the thirtieth day, Dinthois, emaciated and frail, was released from the stocks and finally accepted aid from those who had first scorned him. At that same hour the employee of his rival confessed to committing the crime at the command of his employer. The government imprisoned Dinthois's rival and restored to Dinthois everything he had lost. When asked if he had prayed for the truth to be known, Dinthois replied that God reveals all truths in His own time. He had prayed only that he could learn to love and forgive his enemies and accusers. As God bestowed his heart with love and forgiveness, no other sustenance was needed or required. His soul's hunger had been filled by Heaven.

"God grant me the love and peace of Dinthois." Panla muttered to herself. "For today, I have neither."

Her fingers felt numb and rigid as they reached up to undo the first silver button on her suit jacket. She looked into the tall framed mirror mounted on the wall and saw an expression on her face she had never seen before. Her eyes resembled those she'd witnessed on starving orphans in the Southern slums…lonesome, longing and desperate. Drained of conviction and light, she too, felt lost.

Nothing was the way she wanted it to be. Her marriage was a humiliating, farcical ruin. Her position as the Cathedral Deliverer was a hypocritically burdensome sham. Her role as the Break benefactor/co-conspirator was a torturous ethical ruse. And her relationship with Rabbel Mennis had become a spiritually rapturous defilement of everything her entire life stood for. In the eye of a tornado of conflicting ideals, the fight to remain focused on her ultimate objective was the only strap preventing her sanity from snapping loose.

"God first," she comforted herself. "A loving personal relationship with God for every sentient soul on the planet. Before the Cathedral. Before the Deliverers or Regents or Churchlords. Before institutions or secular interests. Before writers or singers or actors or philosophers. Even before family or friends. God and His word above all other things."

She took a deep breath and felt better. Her drawn, weary expression found a flicker of the old light. Still, it troubled her that it now required effort to bring herself back into a frame of mind which had always been second nature. Perhaps this was a by-product of feigning servitude to multiple masters.

And then there was the dilemma of Mr. Len: thoughtful, truthful, patient, strong and wise in his faith, and protective in a manner inconsistent with a mere sense of duty. Too loyal to be a spy, yet too evasive to be just security. In many ways, he was adorably intrusive, as one might hope a husband would be. In this, she envied his late wife. Yet there remained an aura of mystery about him which she, regretfully, had no time to sort through. She was compelled to trust him, but could not fathom to what end.

As her head finally started to clear, her private desk com chimed with the sound of an antique hand-bell. Who would call her now? Who would call her here? Her husband was beyond apologies. Linnfeld always came by in person. The Lord Regent was on the premises and had no reason to call, and the Holy Inquisitor only rang under the direst of organizational circumstances. Part of her became unsettled again; most of her was simply curious. She pressed the privacy button and picked up the handset.

"Yes?" she answered authoritatively.

"Peej," a deep voice responded through the receiver.

It was Rabbel.

"Wh…Why are you calling me here?" Panla whispered in shock. "Do you have any idea how dangerous it is to…"

"Fuck dangerous," he growled. "It's all dangerous now."

He sounded as if he'd been drinking.

"I can't talk to you." Panla's voice shook. "I'll see you in a few days."

"Come stay with me." Rabbel's tone was almost desperate. "It's all shit without you. I love you. I can take care of you. You don't need to fake any of this bullshit any longer. We can be together right now."

"I can't!" Panla exclaimed in a hushed voice.

"Why not?" Rabbel shouted through the receiver.

"Because the timing is all wrong, dear. We've talked about this." She fell into exasperation.

"You've talked about it." Rabbel sounded betrayed. "I think you're full of shit. I think, maybe, we're shit!"

"Don't say that, darling. You know how I feel." Panla hung her head.

"I thought I did," he spoke with increasing aggravation, "but maybe I'm just getting the picture today."

"Today?" Panla fought to keep her voice down. "What's so different about today? Everything was fine last night, wasn't it? What's changed other than you sounding as if you haven't gotten a wink of sleep?"

"Everything's changed," Rabbel said cryptically. "You've got to come tonight. If you don't…"

There was a prolonged pause. Panla wanted to slam down the receiver, but was frozen by the silence.

"If you don't," he started again, "I don't know if it'll be safe for you anymore."

"What? Is that a threat?" Panla felt her heart pounding.

"It's the way things are going," Rabbel answered. "I love you, Peej. And we need you. Do what you think you have to do."

There was a short click and he was gone. Panla stood clutching the receiver as a rigid tension made her entire body feel petrified.

"Was that Rabbel Mennis?" a voice came from nowhere.

Panla jumped and spun around to see the old Lord Regent standing hunched in front of her, his long wine robe settled around his sandaled feet.

"Lord Regent, what are you doing in my room?" she said, lifting her chin with royal indignation.

"Queen Mother," the old man smiled hauntingly, "I asked you a question first."

"I don't care what you asked." Panla glared at him. "You have no business here."

"Is not my place at your side, Queen Mother?" He continued to leer with a foreboding grin. "Does not this room belong to the entire Cathedral?"

"Technically, yes. But you know…"

"What I know," the Lord Regent interrupted, "would astound you."

His voice cracked like a creaking hinge. His ominous demeanor chilled her to the marrow.

"Really, Lord Regent, this is neither the time nor the place," Panla scowled bravely. "If you have yet another critique of how I do things for the greater good of the souls of this planet, feel free to take your complaints to the Holy Inquisitor. I'm sure he'll be quite amused as always."

The Lord Regent's pale wrinkled features brightened like the visage of an evil ancient ghost musing in his own dark deviltry.

"Amused by private conversations with Rabbel Mennis?" He raised a brow and bulged an eye. "You slander our Holy Inquisitor's sense of humor."

Panla was subconsciously alarmed by the context in which the Lord Regent referred to Rabbel. What did he know? How could he know?

"What makes you think it was Rabbel Mennis?" Panla fussed with her jacket in the mirror.

"You spoke his name."

Panla paused for a moment. The call had taken her by surprise. She had been careful to keep her voice low, but had she spoken his name?

"He threatened me," Panla hastily conceded, couching her position in a bluff.

"Before or after you met with him last night?" The Lord Regent spoke in a gratified, accusatory tone.

"My dear Lord Regent, I think you're imagining things." Panla folded her arms and unconsciously began tapping her foot.

"It doesn't take much imagination to figure out who PJ is: Panla Jen." He nodded with a knowing, crooked smile. "In fact, even our myopic Inquisitor will be able to piece those letters together, don't you think?"

The blood had started to rush to her head. Panla thought she was going to faint.

"This game is wearing thin, Lord Regent." Her expression became grim. "What is it that you want from me?"

"From you?" He grinned ruefully. "Nothing. From the Holy Inquisitor? Your head. And I will have it."

"My head on rambling hearsay?" Panla frowned. "Perhaps milord would do his faith a greater service by retiring. Retiring quietly before the Board votes to have you committed."

"The Board." the old man quaked with laughter. "The Board will have many more concerns than committing an old fool once they've heard everything I have to say. Our Deliveress, consorting with Rabbel Mennis and his God-hating minions under cover of night! Our Deliveress, spewing drunken blasphemous obscenities to a hedonistic mob of terrorist thugs! Our Deliveress, a married woman, sworn to the service of our faith, slinking off into private chambers with that filthy, sinful soldier of the Devil! I think the Board will certainly have a very dim view of whomever should be brazen enough to level such charges, but I think the Board's view of the accused will be a grave one. Very grave. Unless, of course, you or PJ, or whomever, chooses to deny all of these facts which we both know to be true. Then, there will be a formal hearing. Your staff will be asked to testify. Travel and communication logs will be audited for validity. My dearest Queen Mother, can all of your tracks be covered? Will all of the stories corroborate? And, if not, will the Board be inclined to look the other way based upon your Jivenché clothing labels and your mass appeal? Or will the lies and deceptions begin to stumble over themselves until God's truth sets all of us free?"

"We are negotiating with them." Panla failed to lie convincingly. "I…we…"

"Negotiating?" he chuckled. "What could you possibly be negotiating that would require the complete exclusion of the entire Cathedral hierarchy?"

Panla could feel the blood surging up through her neck, pushing painfully into the sides of her skull. Suddenly, it was all over. She was wrong. He was right. She was trapped.

"Lord Regent." Her hushed voice quaked as she unwittingly gripped the back of an ivory chair. "If you do this, you'll destroy the Church."

"I will destroy the Church?" he exclaimed loudly. "I? And what have you and Rabbel Mennis been plotting? An initiative to build a new Cathedral on every street corner in the south?"

"It's very complicated." Panla closed her eyes. "Very, very complicated. If you'd look around this place, you'd see. Here, we honor the works of mortals. Statues honoring Deliverers. Services honoring traditions. Addendums and decrees pushing us farther and farther away from the Text! Farther away from God! Farther away from the souls He wants to save! I would never do anything to betray the word of our heavenly Father. You have to believe that!"

"I don't have to believe anything you say, Queen Mother." The Lord Regent's face hardened. "It's not up to me, but you'd better be prepared to explain your position to the world. I'm sure the planet is going to have a lot of questions when all of this…ugliness…comes to light."

"Lord Regent…." Panla couldn't piece together what she wanted to say.

"Queen Mother." He held up a finger to his lips. "You have a service to conduct in a short while. It will probably be your last. Do whatever you think would make your Father proud today. I meet with the Board this afternoon."

The old man turned slowly and ambled out of the room with his hunched head raised and his gait jaggedly triumphant.

When he was gone, Panla collapsed to her knees and tried to pray, but she broke into sobs and wept profusely.

Meanwhile, in the southeast quadrosphere:

"Rabbel?" Leesla poked her head into the Break leader's pitch black office and spoke to the back of his chair. "I think this has to happen now."

"Do it." His heavy voice cracked. "Tell them to make it clean and quick for her sake."

Leesla smiled a toothy carnivorous grin and closed the door.

XII.

The Bius Basilica was the grandest, most ornate sacred edifice on the face of the planet. In all his journeys through the cosmos, Crilen could recall few structures which rivaled its majesty. It's gold, crystal and ivory surfaces glistened and sparkled like a mammoth jewel reflecting back into the glowing sunlight, radiating the spirit of its earthen splendor into the grand foyer of Heaven. It's monetary value, though calculable, was insignificant by comparison to its symbolic representation of this mortal realm's reverence for its faith. Through centuries of wars, both political and holy, no act of violence toward a member of the church's hierarchy had ever been recorded within its sacred walls. So revered, even by non-believers, was this hallowed sanctuary. For the religious, this was the Lord's home. For the irreligious, it represented a seminal secular architectural achievement, stirring a love and tranquility for any and all who entered through its gates. Even the rhetoric of the Break made only figurative allusions to bringing down its great walls. Were they successful in their bid to unravel two thousand twinmoons of institutionalized religion, no one actually considered that the building itself would be violated. Rather, it might become a museum or a library or a concert hall, but never destructed or disassembled; such would universally be perceived as a mad, unconscionable desecration.

Crilen stood in the Basilica's western courtyard, just inside the tall iron gates. A gentle breeze rustled the towering trees shading the garden pathways. He momentarily mused in the sweet scent of floral nature which romanced his dormant senses from their cold inter-stellar slumber. No iron asteroid rocks for pillows here. No metallic sand ground beneath his nails. No blinding burning starlights or hostile inter-galactic spacecraft searching for a live random target. This was a rich and ebullient world spewing the conjugations of organic life from every crevice. It was so difficult to imagine this planet fallen into the broken ruins of the asteroid belt where It had found him over a day ago.

But now was not the time to mourn futures past. He needed to remain focused upon futures alternative. Futures where Panla would live. And, perhaps, a future where he and his wife, Aami, could live and love again.

He decided to forego the mid-day service. As fixated as he had become on Panla's resemblance to his wife, he needed time away from her to ingest everything else he had witnessed over his first day as her protector. Everything else, arranged in a sequence which would allow him to save her when the time came…along with everyone else living on this ideologically conflicted world.

The Cathedral security appeared thin by contrast to the importance of their subject. Armed guards in ancient period garb patrolled the common areas looking diligent, but callow and untested. Crilen could easily envision their defenses crushed by the first wave of any zealous armed insurgence. Then again, the magnificent structure they guarded seemed to provide an intangibly surreal protection of its own, as if Heaven were the true defender and God's timeless wrath would rend all of its enemies. Unlike the other venues where the Deliveress had traveled, Crilen's keenest instincts felt no element of danger for her here. The sensation was almost mystical.

He checked in with Linnfeld who concurred that Panla Jen Tem was safe for the time being. Then he quietly strolled through the iron gates and out onto the cobblestone streets of the old city to take in a more pedestrian view of this imperiled planet.

The buildings outside the Bius Basilica were very old structures of blue-grey stone and cracked brownish brick. They were clean, sturdy buildings which had weathered centuries of tenants and tumult; their rustic character easily transcended time and technology. It might well have been five centuries past were it not for the satellite nets on the roofs and the occasional squeals of two-wheeled solar/electronic vehicles whizzing along the distant roadways.

He wandered to the end of the first block where he came upon a broad public square with a large antiquated marble fountain in the shape of a gigantic horned feline beast. Young children in formal Solemnday clothing frolicked around slow-moving elderly clusters of adults who gingerly moved through the bustle of activity. Families sat around the rim of the fountain, absorbed in the peace of their leisure. Young couples sat, holding hands or embracing, absorbed in the peace and romance of one another.

There were ragged musicians playing wind and string instruments as they stood with straw baskets at their feet to receive spare donations. Thickly bundled wayfarers with no particular talents, other than the retelling of their particular tale of woe, drifted from pedestrian to pedestrian begging for whatever charity anyone would offer.

There were a variety of domestic animals which Crilen hadn't had the time to take notice of before. Some were a mixture of hairless reptilian canines. Others were feline creatures with bird-like heads darting, ducking and pecking playfully at passersby. Most were pets, leashed and collared in some fashion. Others roamed in small pairs and threesomes, abandoned to their wandering fates.

Crilen loosed a sigh as he allowed himself to absorb the mortal tranquility of this planet for the first time. Amongst the common inhabitants, it was difficult to perceive that this world was torn by factions of godless rebels, an indomitable religious hierarchy, a dubious government agenda and a media playing upon real life as if it were some tasteless drama tailored by the greed of advertisement sponsors.

Crilen considered that most beings in the universe yearned for some role in a simple living portrait like this one. But in order to attain a lasting peace, complex ideological wars had to be fought. Fought and won. Without such conflicts, intervals of peace become only a deceitful mirage that veil the steep and arduous climb towards the undeniable truth of life, spirit and the godly principalities which govern all things. Crilen wished this humble old square could be life's destiny, but he knew it was only a quiet rest stop along destiny's journey. A stop where only the lost could live forever.

In the short distance, Crilen saw a kiosk. He walked toward it and gradually smelled the sweet aroma of baked fresh breads. Food across the universe varied greatly from planet to planet, but there was something truly universal about the baking of bread. There were only so many ways to prepare loaves, biscuits and muffins. Only so many ways to converge dryness and moistness into culinary harmony. Only so many ways to transform a lump of dough or paste into a warm, sweet, delectable masterpiece.

"What do you like?" the wrinkled, leathery black-faced man in a floppy toque asked.

"All." Crilen smiled at the selection. "I wish I could have one of each."

"So do I." The kiosk owner tilted his head with a condescending smile under his bushy grey mustache. "But what do you like?"

Crilen's senses were overwhelmed by the smells and designs of bread decorating the quaint wooden cart. Part of him wanted to sample something exotic, but another part of him wanted to select something that would remind him of his childhood. Indecisively, he looked up at the kiosk owner who nodded and smiled.

"Take your time." The owner understood.

"Sorry." Crilen was embarrassed by his own bemusement.

"S'okay," the old man replied.

Crilen finally spotted the one pastry that touched his memories the deepest. A flaky light brown triangular scone that resembled those steamy warm biscuits his grandmother would draw from her stone oven. He found himself reminiscing about those days as a youth, when the taste of fresh, warm bread could make or break an entire evening. His grandmother was like the guardian priestess of a great stone temple, and those biscuits were edible treasures born from the great fires of creation.

He reached for the last scone. But a small hand sifted under his arm, around his ribcage and plucked it away before he could close his fingers on it. Crilen spun about. Before he could confront the little scavenger who had rooked him, the smiling boy winked smartly, flipped the vendor a coin, ripped away a corner of the scone with his bright white teeth and scurried back toward the large fountain to rejoin his young playmates.

"Sh...!" Crilen marveled at the boy's speed..

"So how was service today?" the old man dusted away some crumbs from the edge of the kiosk.

"Excuse me?" Crilen watched the boy melt into the leisurely Solemnday portrait.

"The Deliveress." The man raised his voice with emphasis. "Was she beautiful today?"

Crilen hesitated for a moment. It was an odd question pertaining to any mass or service.

"Oh," Crilen adjusted his focus, "I didn't go, actually."

"What?" the old man's eyes lit up and rolled as if it were unthinkable. "How could you not go? Me, I have to work. But you? Why would you be so close and not go see her?"

"Well, actually I work for her."

"You know Deliveress Jen?" the old man exclaimed with sudden reverence. "You know her? Like a real person, you know her?"

"Well...yes." Crilen was surprised by the man's reaction. "Not very well. But I..."

"She knows you by name?" The old man shook his head. "You sit down with her and have conversations?"

"I have..."

"Sweet Lord in Heaven!" the old man clasped his hands together. "You are blessed! She is so beautiful! She is a wonderful, sweet lady! An angel from Heaven!"

"She's a fine woman." Crilen offered.

"Fine woman?!" the vendor's mouth dropped open as if Crilen had uttered a profane insult. "She is the reason I live. The only reason I look to Heaven. Without her, I am dead! Without her, I go back to the way I was!"

"Without God, you mean." Crilen tried to mask his disapproval.

"God?" The old man wearily rolled his eyes heavenward. "What is God? I cannot see God. I cannot smell God. I cannot feel God. If God is so good, why do children die of diseases? Why do criminals become millionaires? Why are politicians allowed to lie to us, and cover their lies with more lies? And why can't we do anything about it but vote for new liars to replace the old liars? If God is so good, why is there so much poverty and starvation and crime in the south? Is God only for the northerners? Northerners with money? If God is so good, why he let my daughter marry that bum who drinks and beat her? Why she have to get divorced and my grandkids have no father to look up to? If God is so good, why did my father get his hand chopped off by robbers so he couldn't work no more?"

"The world was never meant to be a paradise," Crilen answered earnestly.

"No, I tell you why." The old man rapped his knuckles against the kiosk. "God is not good. God is not bad. God simply don't give a damn. We're like his little pets in a glass jar. Every now and then, he shakes it up to watch us roll on our backs and squirm a little bit, then he goes away and comes back when he feels like it. But he don't care."

Crilen's eyes narrowed slightly.

"But Deliveress Jen," the old man's face brightened, "she loves the whole world. She's so beautiful and intelligent, but she loves the whole world anyway. She don't need us. She grew up rich! She could have married a physician or a businessman, and laid around having babies the rest of her life. What would it matter? But no. She preaches and teaches and smiles on us with that wonderful smile. She loves each and every one of us. Even that no good husband she got. If God was good, he would not have let her marry that man. But it don't matter to her. She does good things all of the time! And she is so lovely and polished. She speaks like a poet. Never a hair out of place. And always something good to say. Always telling us to hope. To live for another day. I would die for that beautiful woman. She is a living miracle."

The old man's fondness for the Deliveress was not lost on Crilen. He, too, had become ensnared by the charisma of Panla Jen, but there was a reverence in the vendor's tone that stepped beyond reason. Or perhaps far beneath it.

"What about the Text?" Crilen offered.

"What about it?" The old man waved his hand. "It's all a bunch of mumbo-jumbo. Outdated. Conflicted. The dreams of shepherds. The lies of kings. I remember the Deliverers before Deliveress Jen. Tired, greedy, old mumblers. I could barely keep my eyes open. And they always looked so sick and miserable. If I wanted to look at sick and miserable, I could look in the mirror! I did not need their misery on top of my own. During those days, the only words I listened to were the ones in my own head. If I was hungry, I ate. If I needed to use someone, I was nice. If I was forced to take something, I took it. I was young, mean and tough. But I was not happy. Then Deliveress Jen appears with her angel eyes. Her gentle voice. She is the embodiment of goodness. I said to myself that if this woman commands me to be a good person, then I will do everything I can to be good."

"But she is only a person," Crilen reasoned. "An extraordinary person, but flesh and blood, all the same."

"Hmh." the vender became slightly irritated. "You ask me about God. Well, I believe that God sent her to us as a living example of perfection. An example of what we can all be if we try. I tell my daughter to try to be like Deliveress Jen. I tell my grandchildren to try to be like Deliveress Jen. I tell them to be kind and learned and charitable…like Deliveress Jen. Deliveress Jen is more than a person. She is the way we all should be. All of us. If we were all like her, this world would be a perfect place."

A romantic crosswind caressed Crilen's reason. "You may be right." Crilen answered softly, "but the Deliveress loves God. I think that's the perfection we should be striving for."

"So beautiful." The old man chuckled to himself and sighed. "Such a beautiful lady."

If there had been any semblance of a debate, it was over. The vendor was content with his perspective. Crilen went back to searching the kiosk for a bread that would connect him with his childhood. He finally settled on a small loaf which resembled a series of chained links, knotted and baked together. It was an unusual design, but the texture reminded him of home. He picked up the loaf, wary that another child might intercept his reach at any moment. He searched his pocket for his Accommodancy credit identification.

"No, no." The old man held up his hands. "It's free for you. You know Deliveress Jen. It's like a visit from Heaven today. Instead, you tell her that the old man in the square loves her, and that he always will. You do that for me."

Crilen. nodded. "Thank you, sir. I'll tell her."

"God Bless you." The old man smiled, stretching the deep lines in his face.

"God keep you," Crilen acknowledged.

XIII.

EB: Hi, this is Egs Bloyt. You are looking at a live shot of the blazing fuel tank where actor Finx Melder crashed his sports vehicle at a high rate of speed last night. Apparently, Melder and his new girlfriend, sand surfer Preppi Deyz, were joyriding through town when Melder lost control, crashed through an iron gate, flew over a steep embankment and impacted, like a missile, into the side of the giant fuel tank you see in your picture. Both Finx Melder and Preppi Deyz died in this horrible accident. Finx Melder leaves an irreplaceable void in all of our lives as a performer as well as a true icon of our contemporary culture and consciousness. Today, the world is paralyzed. Schools and some businesses are closed. People are milling around the streets, searching for answers and direction.

But now we learn that things may be even worse than we thought. Something we all hoped would not be true has now become the center of the investigation as to the cause of this devastating accident. On hand is our tireless Eastern Bureau Chief, Proptz Rotz, whose been covering this story for YBS, almost from the moment it broke to the world. Proptz, before we get to this latest news on this horrible story, I wanted to compliment you on the touching piece you did with Preppi Deyz's grandparents. I was nearly in tears. Such a wonderful piece. I hope they're both going to be all right. It's a good thing you and your crew were there to help when they broke down.

PR: Well, Egs, this is a tough job, especially on a day like today. We just happened to be in the right place at the right time. I'm just praying that Mr. and Mrs. Deyz are going to be all right. They're such a sweet old couple.

EB: I'll be praying as well. But Proptz, what's the story now, from the Metro Morgue? We understand some preliminary tests have come back regarding the toxicology examination of Finx Melder's remains.

PR: Yes, we have a very preliminary report regarding the cellular blood content of Finx Melder at the time of his death. And, as we feared, it appears that Mr. Melder was heavily intoxicated by a mixture of chemicals yet to be completely identified. What we do know is that Finx Melder's chemical content read .28 in the preliminary cellular blood scans, which would make him virtually unconscious at the time of the accident. One chemical which has been identified is Equinide, a paralytic chemical used by veterinarians when they euthanize race animals. Equinide has recently been listed by authorities as a base for any number new chemical cocktails being cooked up by the upscale nightclub crowd here in the northeast. It's been responsible for several dozen deaths in the last twinmoon.

EB: This is absolutely horrible!

PR: Yes, it is. Finx was such a brilliant man, and yet it appears as though he had a death wish which finally fulfilled itself. If the accident hadn't killed him, it's almost a certainty that the drugs would have.

EB: What about Preppi Deyz? Are we to assume that she was riding in the passenger seat with a man who was semi-conscious, careening through the streets on a mission to die? I mean, she hasn't been linked to any drugs, has she?

PR: From everything I've heard and everyone I've talked to, Preppi was absolutely not into drugs. She was very particular about her health and her conditioning.

EB: Then she just sat there and did nothing?

PR: Well, apparently so. That is, from everyone I've talked to, Preppi was in absolute awe of Finx Melder. He was older. She'd grown up watching his films. He had a charisma that was very mesmerizing, especially to a girl like Preppi, who hadn't been exposed to that sort of man and his world. Friends of Finx Melder tell me that Finx could appear very lucid and reassuring moments before he'd pass out from alcohol or drugs. I just don't think Preppi had any idea what she was into until, of course, it was far too late.

EB: What about reports that there was some sort of chase going on that might have pushed Finx Melder into recklessness?

PR: I've heard that rumor, but I can't find anyone to substantiate it. One witness did say that they saw a male kind of slumped over as the vehicle hit the iron gate. Then they heard a female scream, and that was it.

EB: Really horrible.

PR: I'm afraid so.

EB: Well, Proptz, we thank you again for staying on top of this very emotional and difficult story for all of us. I'm sure you could use some sleep.

PR: I'm going to try as soon I'm able to get a little more information here that can shed more light on this terrible tragedy.

EB: Well, good luck, Proptz.

PR: Same to you, Egs. Hang in there.

EB: We will. People at home, we'll be back in just a few moments.

(Poignant flourish, followed by the smiling faces of Finx Melder and Preppi Deyz, with the dates of their births and deaths, fading in before the break.)

XIV.

The Lord Regent exited the Bius Basilica's eastern gate feeling an exuberance he hadn't felt since he'd been a young Churchlord given his first parish. It was the joy of ascension. The joy of singular recognition and acknowledgment. The joy of a life's worth of servitude to the Cathedral and its Addendums. A joy marred only by the insufferable succession of younger and younger Deliverers who made him appear more and more a religious relic rather than a chosen spiritual leader sanctified by the grace of Heaven.

Throughout his entire life, there had always been some lacking measure of charisma which stalled his popularity. Handsomeness, in his youth; grace, in his middle years; warmth, in the twilight of his service. There had always been some intangible reason for him to be passed over for the Deliverancy. Until, finally, *she* arrived and dealt him the most humiliating blow of all. Panla Jen Tem was ten twinmoons the junior of his youngest niece, yet her knowledge of history and the Text was exceeded only by the banks of computer memories stored in the bowels of the Bius Basilica. And she was beautiful. Beautiful in all senses of the word. Beauteous in her piety. Beauteous in her charity. Beauteous in the rhythm of her recitations of verse and song. Beauteous in her ability to spin any casual garment into high fashion simply because it adorned her lithe frame. To the world, she was a living angel, a saint anointed in the rains of Heaven, while he remained like an inanimate, hump-backed, time-worn antiquity. A clerical ghost, white-washed in anonymity by the Cathedral's sprawling bureaucracy. A vulgar fate for one who thought himself the living embodiment of the CDR: Complicity. Duty. Reverence.

Complicity to the laws of the Cathedral. Duty to the offices of the Church. Reverence for the succession of the Deliverancy and all of the Addendums bound to the world.

He had served longer than anyone alive. Longer than the Holy Inquisitor. Longer than any of the so-called elders of the Board. To himself, the Lord Regent was more the living symbol of everything the Cathedral stood for than any other breathing soul. And, finally, he would prove it to the world. He would prove Deliveress Jen a traitor to her faith. And his reward would be to revel in the glory of the remainder of his days perched upon the golden bejeweled throne of the Deliverancy. Amen.

As he struggled to balance himself on his cane, the bustle outside the gate unnerved him. So many people crossing…racing in so many directions. He remembered a time when the world seemed so less hectic, so less confusing. It wasn't the age of his bones that discouraged him; it was the contemporary fashion of the world which was his nemesis. So little time for the old pleasantries. So little respect for the old ways. Everyone, scurrying off to wade in the cesspools of modern follies. Scurrying off to fornicate with the foolish fads of the day. No one taking time to reflect on the laws of the Church. Chaos. Unruly, spiteful chaos. It was as distasteful as it was disorienting, which is why he rarely ventured out into the world at all.

"I shan't be long, my sweet palace," he muttered as he looked back at the glistening Basilica spires. "Wait for your humble servant. Wait for your humble king."

As he stepped to the curb, his aged senses were jolted by the sharp skidding metallic sound of a pair of spinning transport wheels blistering against the cobblestone road. As dust kicked up and the people along the walkways drew back, he looked up and saw a small, open, two-seated, pea-green mini-vehicle racing in his direction. He hastened his aching joints backward a step to be sure he wouldn't fall in its path. However, as the vehicle drew nearer, it screeched to a wild, tail-spinning stop as the occupants smiled menacingly at him, evil mischief twinkling in their eyes.

The driver was an odd-looking, scantily clad young girl with a round white face and green locks of hair twirled symmetrically around her forehead and cheeks. Her protruding breasts heaved under her skimpy pink and navy halter as she clutched the controls in her tiny gloved hands. The passenger, by contrast, was a scruffy, thin, pale, older male with yellow receding hair scattered wildly about his scalp. He wore dusty dark leather from his neck down as far as one could see and appeared unbathed, for some duration, from the inside out.

To the Lord Regent, the girl appeared to be a sweet but unholy young woman from an educated well-to-do home, but the male was clearly a convict of some sort. A miscreant on leave from a lengthy incarceration, the Lord Regent considered. Together, the couple was a disquieting dichotomy of modern secular decay. He wanted no part of them but he couldn't hurry away fast enough.

"Holy Father!" the girl called to him with a sweet intonation which mocked him. "Father, we came to see you."

The Lord Regent could not sever his lock on the young girl's eyes. There was a lure of honey in her corrupted innocence. A sensual decadent lure polluting his ingrained sexual piety. She smiled and arched her bare leg up to her chest so he could see it.

"Come here, silly!" she beckoned to him, giggling like a devilish teen nymph.

The Lord Regent hesitated. A hushed voice from his conscience told him to flee. "But where?" he thought. The old man shuffled one hesitant foot forward.

The scruffy man rose up from behind the girl. He was holding something metallic in his hand, but the Lord Regent refused to believe it was a weapon.

"Father," the man grinned, "I hear the angels in heaven have tits the size of field melons and pussies that taste like raw filet. Well, I got good news, ya virgin old fuck. You won't have to come in your diapers anymore, 'cause I'm about to make you the stud of your wimpy wet dreams!"

The scruffy man lifted the object in his hand.

The Lord Regent was suddenly very certain it was a weapon, but his feet wouldn't move. He quickly covered his head with the sleeve of his wine robe, and he tried to think of a prayer. There was a loud explosion and he felt an alien pain burn through his ribcage as he lost his equilibrium. In another instant, he felt his skull smack hard against the concrete. He heard screams of terror from all around mixed with the sound of trailing laughter as the vehicle's wheels squealed loudly under the roar of a racing engine.

"They shot him!" a voice called out.

The Lord Regent lay sprawled against the pavement waiting for the numbing cold of death to overtake him, but other than the pain in his side and the ache in his head, he felt better than he thought he should.

Two faces appeared over him: a church maid and a Cathedral security officer. He recognized both of their faces as casual daily acquaintances, but he wasn't sure if he had ever learned their names.

"Lie still," the security officer said. "Help is coming."

The church maid knelt down and took his hand. "Our Lord is with you, Father. Pray with me."

Her touch was gentle; her words caressed his soul. The blinding fear that he would not reach the Board with his news of Deliveress Jen's secret betrayal subsided. The alarmed anguish over the prospect of not fulfilling his lifelong dream to ascend to the Deliverancy dissipated.

Then, his nerves started to sting. The small wound from the pellet which had pierced his flesh, felt as if all the tissue around it were on fire. The searing acidic pain raged up under his armpit and down over his pelvis into his groin.

The Lord Regent screamed, but the wail choked in his throat and a thick fountain of red blood gushed up from his mouth into the face of the church maid who tossed aside his hardened, contracting hand in horror.

The small crowd which had gathered around the scene recoiled as the protruding veins and blood vessels in the Lord Regent's face burst crimson spurts through his crackling, bubbling flesh. His body unleashed a nauseating low groan. His bulging eyes sunk back into their sockets and liquefied into melting orbs of swirling blood and mucous. At last, the flesh on his jaws drew tighter and tighter until it snapped and ripped away from the bone, shriveling into the gaping orifices of his wet bloody skull.

His robes steamed and smelled the putrid stench of burning flesh cauterized into woven fabric. His chest cavity wilted. What remained of his head liquefied and smoldered into a hot black chemical scorch etched into the pavement.

Panla, tightly surrounded by armed security, arrived only in time to see the bubbling smear of pulp hissing into the cement amidst the remnant of the Lord Regent's wine robe. The putrid odor was stifling. But even worse, was the full knowledge of who was behind this murderous act, and of her complicitous role in a horrifying death.

She grew dizzyingly nauseous as two security guards caught her just before she collapsed.

XV.

The pea-green vehicle whizzed through the narrow urban streets, a blur leaving a dusty litter-swirling tailwind in its wake. Its oversized engine hummed like a racing baritone siren as its screeching pair of wheels wove and skidded through traffic, blindly searching for a straight path to freedom. Unfortunately for its occupants, the ensuing chase resulting from their very public crime was not going well at all. For every alarm-blaring policer vehicle they managed to elude, two more appeared at the next intersection and filled in the thick wall of pursuit closing behind them.

"You stupid cunt!" Durn yelled. "You missed the fucking turn!"

"No, I didn't!" Reza cried.

"Yes, you did!"

"No, I didn't!"

"Yes, you did!"

"No, you alco-fucking-holic noodle-prick, I didn't!" Reza shrieked at the top of her lungs as she slammed her fingers into the control panel, averting a fatal crash into the side of a solid stone building. "Fuck!"

"The first turn out of the square woulda led us straight out of the city!" Durn looked back at the dark emerald policer vehicles closing in. "We'd have been gone before anybody knew what happened."

"I did not miss that turn!" Reza's lips quivered. "Leesla fucked up. There was no turn."

"I saw it back there!" Durn yelled. "You missed it! You were too goddamned busy laughing and waving!"

"No!" Reza's recrimination warmed her inner thighs.

"Yes, you whiny little snatch!" Durn cocked his fist. "You fucked up. And now we're fucking dead."

Tears filled Reza's eyes as her arms burned with excited tension. Her heart pounded violently against her sternum with exhilaration and fear. Emotionally overcome with delirium, she still managed to maneuver the small vehicle through the city streets with masterful aplomb in the face of diminishing odds.

Just ahead, she saw a dense cluster of flashing policer vehicles blocking the next intersection. Another six or seven pressed hotly from behind. She pulled back on the brake lever and twisted the steering controls, sending the two-person craft spinning wildly toward a crowded pedestrian walkway.

"We're dead!" she heard Durn yell.

There were bumps, thuds and screams as bodies flew and fled in all directions. A large window violently exploded as their vehicle entered the building. Giant shards of glass rained onto them as dislodged metal poles swatted at their heads from every angle.

Reza could feel slivers of glass in her shoulders and cheeks as she tried to open her eyes to regain control of the wildly careening vehicle. She squinted to see that the windshield was smeared with blood and partially obstructed by the writhing body of a middle-aged male. His arm was freshly severed and he shrieked mindless obscenities as he flopped, across the swerving vehicle's hood until he finally slid away. She glanced over at Durn who was now shivering with a tensed expression of terror, his eyes bulging with naked fear. He hunched in his seat, fresh scars marking his forehead and chin. He clenched his yellowed teeth tightly, anticipating a final fatal impact.

But for Reza, the whirlwind of chaos became surgingly orgasmic. As her pounding heart took away her breath, a burning spasm tortured the pit of her stomach. She was the epicenter of a swirling tornado of random disaster. The queen of a sado-masochistic catastrophe mounting to crescendo. The bombardment of pain and fear and danger came faster than her enraptured senses could beg for. She gasped lustfully, licking the blood which gushed from her broken nose. She prayed silently that this cascading ecstasy of horrors would never end.

Thump, thump! The wheels bumped over two more bodies.

Smash! Through another glass door.

Slam...crunch! A wooden desk exploded across the hood.

A scream and a thud! Reza smiled, marveling at a limp woman's body flying through the air.

"What a ripping bloody thrash!" she writhed in her seat.

She looked down at Durn who looked fearfully up to her as if she had transformed into a monster.

"Rip me." Reza purred through her bloodied green lips. "Rip me raw."

With a decisive push, she shoved the lever to maximum and relinquished the controls. The engine roared to a loud piercing whistle as she dove onto Durn, thrusting madly into his shaking petrified body.

On the other side of the city block, a squad of policers stood with their weapons poised for the pea-green vehicle and its assailants to emerge from the building. Commanders stood intently as the crashing noises from inside the structure drew closer. Snipers crouched at the ready, waiting for the first flinching signal to open fire.

To their surprise, when the outer glass wall of the building blew apart, it became instantly clear that the pursuit was over. The flipping, hopping vehicle came skipping out, bounding end over end, fragments of metal and glass spewing everywhere from its disintegrating chassis.

At this unexpected culmination, the commanders did not utter a sound. The snipers withdrew their weapons and stood slowly as they watched the husk of pea-green wreckage ram thunderously into a stone wall and bounce backward, creaking to rest in a hissing, mangled heap.

Crilen arrived only to see the end. A moment ago, he had allowed himself to enjoy a pastry within the serenity of the city square. Now he followed a trail of carnage which had led him from the Lord Regent's smoldering robe to the destructive wake of the vehicle which had ripped indiscriminately through a building of offices, shops and innocent people.

And here lay Reza....or what was left of her.

Only ragged slivers of skin from her neck kept her dangling head attached to her torso. Her arms were twisted and broken into bone-wrenching contortions, torn unnaturally from the elbow joints. Her lean thighs were split open by her snapped and protruding femurs. Her bloody ribs poked through her leather vest. A ragged crimson cavity yawned where her stomach had once been; her organs lay spilled and spattered on the street. The right side of her skull was crushed, and the remaining flesh on her deformed face hung from the bone like a melted rubber mask. The only thing which remained familiar was the green hair, frayed and shorn from her bloody scalp and the scraped and bloodied ankle boots fitted to her twisted, lifeless feet.

Crilen knelt down and touched the heel of her boot. The same heel she had playfully ground into his abdomen the day they had met. She was like a child...a confused, lost, angry, corrupted, but delightfully playfully adolescent. He remembered the tears in her eyes as her father endured Durn's merciless pounding. He remembered the grimaces she would force into smiles every time Durn touched her body. And he remembered her recalcitrant objection to any role God could ever play in her miserably tortured young life.

Crilen had seen millions of deaths across the cosmos. Sometimes the deaths would come in mountains of rotting slaughtered corpses whose stench would putrefy fifty-square kilometers of smoldering battlefield. Other times it would be on a more personal level; an ally or enemy whose life-force would quietly evaporate before his very eyes in the midst of a soulful dialogue. Sometimes the agony of millions would reduce him to tears. Other times, the end of a single wasted soul left him bitter more than sad. Today, he wanted to feel nothing. Nothing for the smiling young woman of the rambling profanity. Nothing for the girl who had chosen eternal death over life long before this afternoon. He wanted to feel nothing. But for reasons that bewildered his compassion, he felt sorrow.

"What a mess," a policer commander stood next him.

"Yes," Crilen's jaw stiffened, "she owed herself better than this."

"She owed the Lord Regent." The commander sounded annoyed. "She owed the dead and injured people in that building she just rolled through."

Crilen continued to stare at her mutilated remains.

"Did you know her?" the commander asked.

"In a manner of speaking."

"Who the hell was she?" The commander's brows wrinkled.

Crilen rose from his knee and breathed a heavy sigh. He recalled his debate with It; a debate he was certain he had won at the time.

"Filler." Crilen shook his head. "Water between the rocks."

The commander was a poor audience for the melodrama. He received Crilen's metaphor as little more than faint mumbling without context.

"So, who are you?" the commander asked as he watched policers and medics gradually filter into the scene of carnage.

Crilen paused for a moment; he had nearly forgotten his guise.

"My name is Len. I'm the lead security for Mrs. Panla Jen Tem," he finally answered. "The Deliveress."

"Moll's replacement?" the commander said with recognition and fondness for Crilen's predecessor.

"Right." Crilen finally lifted his eyes from Reza.

"Well," the commander observed the exposed mortar and broken windows of the building, then the crushed pea-green vehicle, "looks like you're doing great so far. Is Mrs. Tem dead yet?"

Crilen bristled, but before he could manage an equally toxic response, "He's alive! Unbelievable!" Two armed policers in black uniforms popped up from behind the partially demolished concrete wall approximately twenty meters from the wrecked vehicle. Each held an arm of a battered, bloodied and more disheveled than usual Durn.

"Bring him!" the commander shouted.

Crilen watched as the policers half-dragged a staggering, stumbling Durn toward them. His face was flecked and pitted with cuts from debris. His scraggly yellow hair was stained with a long, thick gash of oozing dried blood. He also looked as if he were missing some teeth under the scruffy, unkempt beard, but Crilen wasn't sure if this were new or something he simply hadn't noticed from their previous interactions.

The commander regarded Durn with dutiful, military disgust. He looked down at Durn's trousers and became even more indignant.

"Button him," the commander ordered in a low taut growl.

Durn looked down at himself, and his pasty blood-stained face broke into an ugly yellow grin.

"Jealous?" Durn smiled as a clot of blood rolled out of his nose.

The commander stared directly through him, unmoved by the inane vulgarity.

"What's your name, boy?" the commander asked firmly.

Durn wobbled and blinked his eyes as he appeared to play upon his own disorientation.

"Well," Durn answered with a mild slur, "I'm actually feeling a little woozy. I don't know if I can answer any..."

"Durn," Crilen interjected. "His name is Durn."

Suddenly, Durn's eyes focused again and he gazed directly at Crilen.

"Hmm. Don't I know you, too?" Durn's face shifted into a gaunt mask of mischief.

"No," Crilen answered, suddenly realizing Panla's cover could be blown in the next couple of sentences.

"Something about the Deliveress....or....First Lady..." Durn grinned as the swelled flesh above his left eye split open.

"I work for her." Crilen wanted the conversation to end quickly.

"Oh, I know that." Durn folded his lips sarcastically, eyeing the breast-shield of the commander.. "I know alllll about that."

"You know each other?" the commander asked.

"Durn was in Moll's files." Crilen met Durn's eyes. "A Break recidivist."

"Yeah." Durn smirked at Crilen as he pushed weakly against the policers holding him. "And I know you, too. More than you want me to know you, mister."

"How?" The commander's suspicious nature immediately kicked in.

"We're old drinking buddies," Durn deadpanned. "Slammed my head into the bar a couple of times."

"What bar?" The commander shifted into interrogation mode.

Durn glanced at the commander, then looked at Crilen again. Durn became fully aware of what his next answer might mean to the Break, if not the entire planet. The window of relevance was sobering. But exposing Crilen meant exposing Panla. And exposing Panla would not please Rabbel at all. A scheduled judicial death sentence would be much gentler than an agonizing contract killing in prison.

"Bar?" Durn's face appeared confused. "I didn't mean to say bar. I think I meant car. Down south I used to steal rec-vehicles. Policers like him didn't take kindly to my...vocation. I got a knot on my noggin every time I got busted. I got a hard head."

"Policers like Mr. Len?" the commander sounded like someone who always considered everyone a link in the web of conspiracy. "How do you know Mr. Len was a policer?"

Durn smiled darkly at Crilen as if he were going to regurgitate every secret his cracked skull could no longer hold. But then he looked over at the commander and shook is head.

"He's a policer, all right." Durn licked the blood from his lips. "He's got that same arrogant, ass-grinding bug pinching his nuts."

Durn turned his doddering head toward the commander. "Just like you...sir."

The commander immediately became incensed.

"Are you going to tell me how you know each other?" His inflections grew tighter.

"Satellite." Crilen answered dryly. "Virtually everything Mrs. Tem did yesterday was on satellite. He must have seen me with her."

"Yeah." Durn blinked to retain his consciousness. "Yeah, that's it. I saw him on a leash following that religious bitch of his."

"Well, you'll learn all about what it means to be a bitch where you're going," the commander sneered. "Murdering the Lord Regent is going to cost you your manhood and your life...in exactly that order. Get him out of here!"

The two policers holding Durn lifted his limp body and turned to drag him away to a nearby transport.

"I have one question for Mr. Durn," Crilen spoke up.

The policers stopped and turned their prisoner back toward him.

"The Deliveress...Mrs. Tem," Crilen sounded grimly serious, "was she on your...list?"

Durn lifted his wobbling head and smiled his hideous yellow smile one last time.

"She wasn't on my list." Durn chuckled madly. "Nah! She's on Rabbel's. Y'hear? She's on Rabbel's list! Ha!"

The commander scowled and gestured for his men to take Durn away.

"Hey, don't I get a medic?" Durn called out loudly. "My organs feel like they're about to fall out of my ass! I'm bleedin'! I got rights! I need some attention!"

One of the policers sidekicked Durn in the knee. The loud popping sound of tendon snapping from bone was followed by a girlish yelp. With one motion, both policers dumped Durn into the rear of the dark navy transport, and the bulky five-wheeled vehicle pulled away.

She's on Rabbel's list. The words echoed in Crilen's head. Was this a lie? Was this a random taunt? Or was this a numbing portent of the end of this world?

XVI.

The Accommodant leered at the chaotic hand-held images shaking across his office monitor. A mob of angry religious protesters gathered at the site of the Lord Regent's assassination. What remained of the chemically scorched body was removed, but a wine-robed effigy now laid in its place, draped over the etched shadow of what had once been a living being.

Many of the gatherers inside the Bius Basilica gates sang mourning hymns in the ancient language, honoring the slain Lord Regent. However, their peaceful harmonic songs were undermined by the taint of an angry rising chant by protesters: "Break the Break! Break the Break!"

Pushing, shoving and a slow surge of rancor built upon itself as the crowd multiplied with every passing minute. Soon, the armored policers and Cathedral security officers were struggling to push back the swelling sea of outraged religious patrons who hurled rocks and profanity at anything signifying secular authority. The direction of the uprising was uncertain, but its intensity was disturbing.

"Our role is to uphold the will of the people," the Accommodant observed grimly. "To preserve the rights of expression in whatever form they may take. But those religious folks are a little out of hand."

"I agree, sir." Obseq handed the Accommodant a triangular glass of his favorite liquor. "They should trust the government to handle this."

"Thank you, son." The Accommodant accepted the drink and took a short sip his eyes remaining fixed on the pictures being broadcast from outside the Bius Basilica.

"Sir. About Allabel…" Obseq interjected.

"Allabel quit this morning." the Accommodant spoke firmly.

"Quit?" The youthful staffer fought to contain his glee. He lamented the missed opportunity to sleep with his equally young colleague, but the opportunity for advancement pleased him more.

"Don't sound so surprised." The Accommodant looked up from his giant wooden desk. "You saw how contentious she was in our meetings. She was a smart girl, but she just didn't get it. Girls like that need to stay home with their daddies. Stay home, get married, have babies and keep the hell out of politics."

"I know what you mean," Obseq responded with a short snicker.

"Do you?" the Accommodant eyed him wearily.

Obseq swallowed hard. "Well, in college a lot of those girls…"

"This isn't college, son." The Accommodant turned back toward the large monitor. "And I'm not the Dean of poli-sci. The shit you see on that monitor isn't a case study. This is real. It's happening right now. And there isn't any course guide with all the answers in the back to gift-wrap us a passing grade. Even Allabel knew that much."

"Yes, sir." Obseq felt like he'd just gotten himself fired in the first five seconds of his new staff position.

"And unless you plan to grow yourself a firm pair of tits and a soft round little ass, you'd better be ready to do her job twice as well, you understand?" The Accommodant frowned at his half-empty glass and wrinkled his lips.

"Yes, sir," Obseq said trying to retain some enthusiasm in his voice.

"What we have before us is a crisis." The Accommodant leaned pensively in his chair. "The religious radicals have crawled out of the box, the anti-religious fanatics are trying to blow them to kingdom come, and now the people are caught in the middle. There's nothing worse than when the people get caught between two extremes. They get polarized. They get forced to make difficult choices. And nobody wants that. People just want peace. People want their steady incomes, their backyard barbecues, their drinks and their sex partners. They don't want their lives cluttered up with a lot of complex ideology that's going to wake them up with a headache in the middle of the night. They don't want to know who God is or isn't. They just want breakfast, lunch, dinner, new stuff to replace old stuff, a good chuckle and a great fuck every now and then. That's the will of the people.

"Not this." He gestured toward the monitor in disgust. "Murder and rioting. Violence and hatred. That's what you get with religion. People are intrinsically good, especially during a good economy. It's only when you make them step beyond their scope that they get tangled up in messes like this…trying to figure out creation, trying to figure out what the big plan is. It's all so damned fruitless. The only thing that matters is feeding your family and being with your loved ones. What happens along the way is a coin flip. There is no rhyme or reason to it. It's just life, that's all. That's what makes this planet great. That's what's going to keep this planet great."

"I couldn't agree with you more, sir." Obseq said dutifully.

"I'm sure you could if you really tried, son." The Accommodant stood and patted him on the shoulder. "I have to meet with my security staff to figure out the best way to defuse this mess. In the meantime, you'd better go fetch me a better bottle of gold stuff. Otherwise, the next time I see you, you'd better be wearing high-heels and some sexy lingerie."

The Accommodant exited the room.

"Yes, sir." Obseq didn't know whether to smile, grimace or clean out his tiny office on the first floor. Upon reflection, he decided to scamper down to the galley stock room and search for a better bottle of liquor.

XVII.

"Pre-empted? But someone just stole Finx Melder's body!"

"Yes, yes, Proptz. Sumptuous celebrity gore. I commend you." Yolo creaked his chair and billowed forth another toxic cloud of heavy red smoke. "I promise, your…journalistic efforts shall not go to waste. I suggest you keep your crew on top of this debacle you've created and arrange the facts in whatever manner suits you. Our good Lord Regent's death has bought you some time to revise the history of your actor's demise. You should be relieved. This way, you can dispense with the random splashes of absurdity. Now, you'll be able to quietly compose and rehearse your concerto duplicité for an audience clamoring for a news story which resembles a digestible fiction rather than raw niblets of incomprehensible fact. You can crimp the truths that will detract from your composition and extend the perceptions that will enhance it. Knowing your imagination as I do, I'm certain it will be award-winning material that shall leave the gullible global gallery agape in witless wonder."

"Are you telling me that my crew and I chased the most famous entertainer in the world to a fiery, spectacular death for absolutely nothing?" The woman's voice cracked with amazement.

"I wouldn't say so." Yolo lifted his heavy brows with a smile. "After all, the likelihood of you being tried for murder is virtually nil at this juncture. That's something, isn't it?"

"It wasn't murder," Proptz scowled defiantly. "It was journalism."

"Perhaps, the murder of journalism." Yolo chuckled. "Either way, I wouldn't be eager to make your plea to a judicator if I were you."

"Goddamnit, Yolo." The deep circles around Proptz's eyes appeared to sink deeper into her bony white cheeks. "The fucking Lord Regent does not have hundreds of millions of fans! A religious old coot whose name nobody can remember gets blasted by some radical joyriders and that's more important than exploiting the death of a superstar? When Finx Melder died, the world market went into convulsions. Schools shut down. People stayed home from work to watch the media. Now, you're telling me that this mercy killing of God's grandpa is more important?"

"Yes." Yolo's jowls bowed slightly. "Yes, it is. You see, you underestimate the relevance of God's grandpa and the like. He's only the first berry tumbling forth from a cracking cornucopia. I can…taste it."

Yolo's eyes became momentarily fixated upon a procession of events only he could vaguely envision. He rolled his giant tongue around the insides of his large opened mouth, making the fleshy wet smacking sound of a suctioning organic orifice.

"Ooo, baby." Proptz turned up her nose and lips.

"I beg your pardon?" Yolo's expression snapped back to the present.

"This cracking cornucopia that's shoving my amazing story into the toilet," Proptz tersely responded through her long clenched teeth. "What are we talking about? A string of assassinations?"

Yolo's girth quaked with a soft chuckle and a malevolent twinkle in his eye.

"Assassinations," he grumbled mockingly. "No doubt a plot line culled from our late Mr. Melder's résumé, hmm? Well…your notion isn't entirely without merit. There may be another carcass or two painted onto the landscape before it's done. But there's much more afoot than the weighty matters of life or death. In fact, the dead and departed will have the best of it. If all unfolds as I sense it will, the living shall pay the greatest toll and the realm of ideals will suffer rudely.

"Choices. Soon, the public will have more choices than it will know what to do with. And of course, when I have my way, they'll never know."

The flesh from Proptz's skeletal cheeks sunk even further into her jaws. The big man was on to something, but he had an annoying talent for bragging about things without revealing the object of his boast. Meanwhile, her media murder turned media spectacular was now being relegated to a media special with an air-date "to be determined".

With a perturbed scowl, she picked open the front pocket on her black leather jacket and pinched out a pair of large purple pills.

"Well, great for you, Yolo." Proptz peevishly flipped the capsules into her mouth. "Me? I'm getting some sleep. My crew can milk the Melder loonies. In the mean time, I can produce a docu-fucking-special in a coma and I'm about to prove it. Good night...sir."

Yolo's monitor flipped blank, but he didn't even notice his Eastern Bureau Chief was gone. His mind was preoccupied by the tactical positioning of all the world's game pieces...with Panla Jen Tem at the center of the board.

XVIII.

As the golden twinmoon rose against the scarlet western dusk, the dull noises of waning civil unrest echoed through the carved ivory walls of the Bius Basilica. The policers had rooted out the most virulent troublemakers. What remained were a handful of vociferous, albeit toothless lions amongst a crowd more comprised of the curious than the indignantly outraged. The soothing intonations of reverent song continued, harkening the souls gathered within the Cathedral gates to pay homage to the late Lord Regent's decades of service to the institution. The polyphonic harmony resonated like an abandoned angel's voice in a world falling fast from God's Heaven.

Panla sat on the edge of the velvet-cushioned chair in her dressing room surrounded by Crilen, Linnfeld and Genna. Her hair was tied back into PJ's long ponytail extension. She was again clad in PJ's black refracting leotard and slippers as she slouched forward with her elbows resting on her knees and her long fingers kneading the flesh on her temples. Her cream-white face was reconfigured into PJ's arching eyebrows and bright scarlet lips, but the mischief and energy of the Break collaborator was strained out of her slender figure. The transformation was incomplete.

"He knew everything," she said, just above a whisper.

"How could he know everything?" Linnfeld huffed incredulously. "He bluffed you. He tricked you."

"I deserve a little credit for intelligence." Panla glared angrily at her lead attendant. "I wasn't bluffed or tricked by that tired old man. He was hateful, mean and blatantly subversive, but guile wasn't one of his traits. He knew. He knew. And, what's worse, *they* knew he knew."

"But you said you'd just finished talking to Rabbel," Crilen offered.

It was obvious how badly shaken she was. Crilen achingly wanted to hold her. As with his late wife, he knew exactly where his touch would soothe the tension from her delicate muscles. But on this planet, he regretfully understood that this female would not stand for it. Panla was not his wife. Crilen was not her husband. So he forced his arms to remain firmly folded across his chest and endured her suffering.

"That's right." She shook her head as her large eyes peered into nothing for an answer. "Rabbel and I talked, but there wasn't any indication of anything like this."

"He didn't threaten you?" Crilen asked pointedly.

Linnfeld and Genna both looked at Crilen with surprise.

"No," Panla answered quickly. "No, he didn't threaten me. Everything was fine."

"Why would you think Rabbel threatened her?" Genna sounded confused.

"Because when I spoke to Durn this afternoon," he watched for Panla's reaction, "he gave me the impression that the Lord Regent's murder was only the beginning."

Panla did not react.

"Beginning of what?" Genna shrugged.

"Curious." Linnfeld rubbed his chin. "Do you think the Lord Regent could have gotten his information from Rabbel himself? You know, plant a dangerous seed, giving you up to the Lord Regent, to frighten you. Then promptly erase the information by erasing the Lord Regent. You said Rabbel called you."

"Yes," Panla responded wearily.

"And then the Lord Regent suddenly appeared in this room as soon as the conversation ended," Linnfeld reconstructed.

"Yes," she answered again.

"Who's to say that Rabbel Mennis didn't tell the Lord Regent to hide in your dressing room? Then he called you at a prearranged time so that the Lord Regent could hear everything," Linnfeld proposed.

"But the Lord Regent would never conspire with Rabbel Mennis," Genna reasoned. "Not even to bring down the Deliveress."

"True." Linnfeld paced the room. "The Lord Regent would never knowingly conspire with Rabbel Mennis. But what if he didn't know? What if he thought it was merely an anonymous tip from a concerned citizen? That bait, he'd take in a moment. And I'm willing to wager that our guileless Regent couldn't contain himself once he saw a clear opportunity to bring down his only obstacle to the Deliverancy."

"Possibly." Crilen frowned, unconvinced. "We may never know for sure. The only thing we can do is proceed on the facts we have. We know that Durn and Reza were sent by Rabbel to kill the Lord Regent."

"How do we know that?" Linnfeld questioned. "Maybe they were taking orders from Leesla."

"I doubt it," Crilen rebutted. "You know this cast of characters better than I do, but I'd wager that if Leesla started making a drastic move like this without Rabbel's blessing, she'd have been dead before the Regent's robe stopped bubbling. No. Rabbel sent them, all right. We just don't know why. All we know is that Durn was pretty pleased with himself, and wasn't bashful about blurting that Mrs. Tem would be next."

"But everything was fine when we left there last night, wasn't it?" Genna sounded frightened and increasingly confused. "I mean, we were all getting along, right?"

"Mrs. Tem, would you say that was a fair assessment?" Crilen asked, observing Panla carefully.

Panla continued to stare into space. Her expression was completely blank as if she were lost in a trance.

"Mrs. Tem?" Linnfeld knelt down in front of her.

Panla's body lurched backward with a sudden jolt. She looked up and around, confused as though she didn't recognize a single person in the room. Then, gradually, her eyes cleared. She ran her fingers through her bangs and glanced around apologetically.

"That's it." Linnfeld climbed to his feet and put his arms around her slumped shoulders. "We're not going anywhere. Not tonight."

"No!" Panla pushed his arms away and jumped up. "Absolutely not! We have to go, don't you see? A man was murdered this afternoon. Murdered because of me! And the killing won't stop unless I do something. I have to see Rabbel. I have to find out why he had the Lord Regent killed. I have to fix things before they get any worse, before any more people die!"

Crilen observed a desperate strain in Panla's face he had never witnessed in her or his wife. Again, he was certain the weight of treble duty was crushing her emotionally. Especially now that her meticulous calculations for the reformation of the Cathedral were collapsing into a random heap. Linnfeld was right; she needed rest. But how could you rest the heart and lungs of the world without causing harm to the entire planet?

"I'll go," Crilen resolved. "I'll go alone."

There was a pause in the air; no one knew quite what to make of the suggestion.

"And do what?" Panla hissed with haughty royal indignation. "Sell us out? Come back and tell us 'the coast is clear' so we can follow you into an execution? For all we know, you're the one who set the Lord Regent up! Strange how not one bloody thing has gone right from the moment you mysteriously appeared in Rabbel's tavern that night! Hired by my husband to protect me? Do you really think I believe that? All this mystery and double talk from our great protector! You 're nothing but a lying, murdering…!"

"Mrs. Tem!" Linnfeld interrupted.

Panla was nearly out of breath. She spun around violently and returned to her chair. She plunked down and bowed her head, tensely clasping her fingers behind her neck.

Linnfeld's round face grew increasingly despondent over Panla's behavior, but all he could do was make suggestions.

"Mr. Len," the lead attendant put on his most diplomatic demeanor. "I'm sure your offer was well meant, But Mrs. Tem has a point. Of all the people involved in this operation, you are the newest and the one we know the least about. It's not a matter of whether we trust you, but perhaps more a matter of whether Rabbel would trust you. This is a very delicate situation and the only one qualified to handle it properly is Mrs. Tem. Besides, you wouldn't be doing anyone any good if you went down there and got yourself killed. We'd have to dig through all the old résumés again to replace you. That could take weeks and I don't think the world can wait that long. Please realize that you may be here to protect the First Lady, but in Rabbel's tavern, she's there to protect the whole world."

"Mr. Len," Panla's voice shook as her eyes welled with tears, "I'm very sorry. Very sorry indeed. You're a bit of a mystery, but I know you're here to do good. I'm certain of that. This is just a very critical time and I can't ask others to do my dirty work for me. I have to be the one to handle this."

"Thank you, Queen Mother." Crilen nodded respectfully. "As I've said before, I'm here for your security. That's my job. And I could never consider your work dirty."

Panla blinked, looked away and tried to distance herself from the compliment.

"Mr. Linnfeld," she wiped under eyes, "you've known me a long time. I know I haven't been myself lately, but you understand why I have to go down there tonight, don't you? The Lord Regent was murdered. A precious life was taken. And, directly or indirectly, I'm responsible. I've got to do whatever I can to ensure that there won't be any more killing, whatever it takes. And if God really wants my life this evening, there isn't anything anyone can do to stop it. He could strike me dead this instant and all the security or precautions in the world couldn't stop it. I won't be prevented from doing the right thing because I'm afraid. Cowardice would be the antithesis of my faith in Him."

An anxious silence chilled the room. There wasn't anyone among them that felt proper about what needed to be done. Crilen knew the feeling all too well. The eerie cold draft of impending death wafted into the air like the suffocating odor of poisonous fumes; a sickening sensation that some or all of the people in this room would not be alive come morning. He looked long and hard at the delicate curvature of Panla's figure. She appeared as a living, irreplaceable art object, soon to be shattered and ground to dust under the boots of an iniquitous barbarian horde. She appeared as his wife, again offering her innocence and trust to a hideously violent, unseemly demise.

Perhaps now was the time to reveal himself for who and what he was. He could reveal to them the roaring cosmic fire he commanded in his veins. He could save Panla and force Rabbel Mennis into abject capitulation. He could overthrow the hellishly immoral Accommodating government and install a just and righteous governing body. He could reduce Yolo Pigue's prevaricating and manipulative media empire to a mound of flickering ashes. He could even anoint Panla Jen Tem the Queen of the world and threaten horrible retribution upon anyone who would oppose her.

After all, he had done such things many times before in his earlier days, when his rage was hot, his wisdom was young and his heart was broken by the death of Aami. He had left the charred, crackling skeletal remains of brutal pagan despots standing cauterized, mid-speech, on their smoldering palace balconies for all the oppressed millions to bear witness. He had buried Godless armies under raging torrents of molten rock blasted from the sides of mountains. He had leveled the temples and churches of countless charlatans on hundreds of worlds and driven trillions of depraved souls into their deserts to re-search God's truth, or die in the trying.

He had been a cosmic judge and destroyer of destroyers to save sentient souls throughout the universe. But in so doing, he learned that the free-will of living sentient creatures cannot be usurped even for a greater good. They must be taught, not tortured. They must be learned, not slain. They must be shown the narrow precipice upon which the fate of their souls rest. And they must be counseled compassionately in the compositions of love, wisdom and faith that will either sanctify or condemn their lives eternal. They must become willing servants of God rather than the cowering slaves of a force they fear.

Crilen commanded the fires of a living star. He could reshape the entire civilization of this planet in a single day. But at what cost would such stellar butchery set this world aright? What grand harvest of souls would find their way to Hell by such planetary carnage? Alas, he found himself a soldier in a world which required a surgeon. It was clear that only the supple grace of Panla Jen could save this planet, if he could simply find the means to keep her alive.

"All right," Crilen spoke decisively, "we go. But we go carefully. We have to square our ledger with Rabbel tonight, one way or the other. It's the only way to know where everybody stands."

Linnfeld grimaced as if he had hoped Crilen would have found a way out of following Panla's lead. Genna shifted her weight from one leg to the other and tried to mask her mounting fear.

"Thank you, Mr. Len." Panla stood and placed her hand on his shoulder. "I wouldn't want to do this without you. In fact, I'm not sure that I could."

A tingle goose-pimpled Crilen's sensibilities; her touch was so much like Aami's. So familiar. How could this woman whom he had known little more than a day be capable of moving him so intimately. "Because that's how you choose to perceive her," It had told him.

He reached up and touched her hand. He wanted to hold it forever, so he removed it gently, and pushed the delusion aside.

"I'll have the driver meet us in the tunnel." Linnfeld excused himself wearily. "See all of you down below in five minutes. I have to go check my will."

As the lead attendant exited, Panla noticed Genna was shivering.

"Genna," Panla said in a tender voice, "it's going to be all right."

Genna looked up sadly and met her eyes.

"Queen Mother," the young woman spoke in a shaking whisper, "I don't want anything to happen to you. If something happens to you, I'll die. I will just die."

"Ye of little faith?" Panla smiled warmly and wrapped her slender arms around her attendant and student. "If something happens to me, I would expect you to live. God would expect you live. This is all so much bigger than any single person. And I am just a person. You know that, don't you?"

"Yes." Genna nodded.

"Then you pledge your faith to Him, and let God worry about what happens to me." Panla caressed Genna's arms affectionately.

"Yes, Queen Mother." The young woman tried to recover herself.

"Very good." Panla smiled and held her eyes with assurance. "Now where in the world is Feebie?"

Genna's eyes widened. Then she looked down again.

"Genna?" Panla looked at her quizzically. "What's happened to Feebie? Where is she?"

"She…" Genna's voice trailed off into deep regret, "she…she's not coming."

"Not coming?" Panla could not hide the hurt in her expression. "What do you mean she's not coming?"

"She's out." Genna lowered her head. "She quit. She's done."

Panla clenched her fists at her sides subconsciously. Her jaw tightened at the stunning news that Feebie, daughter and sister to her, had abandoned the cause.

"She loves you." Genna looked up with tears in her eyes.

"Not enough, I'm afraid." Panla rubbed her temple again. "Very well, then."

Panla turned, walked to her closet and yanked out a large black shawl. She hastily tossed it over her head and swept out her hair from the opening. She glanced at Genna and then at Crilen. With resolve, she stiffened her expression into a stoic mask of assertion.

"I'll be along in a moment." She gestured for the pair to exit. "Make sure no one sees you."

"Is there anything I can help you with?" Crilen asked.

"I'll be along." Panla smiled off-tempo. "I need a moment alone. You do understand?"

Again, there was something amiss. But there were too many layers of complexity to the woman and not enough time to decipher them all.

"Always," Crilen answered, caressing her angelic profile with his eyes.

He took Genna by the arm and gently guided her out of the room.

XVIII.

The Swanky Skank Nightclub in the upper northwest continent:

Tropical island music pounded into the warm post-Solemnday night as the young and affluent mingled carelessly amidst the clinking of glasses and the murmur of superficial chatter.

"Goddamnit!" Libbi cursed as she slumped against the patio railing overlooking the neon reflections of nightlife in the cold river below. "What am I supposed to do with my life?"

"Jump in, I guess." Juds lifted her up by the arm, lit her herbal cigarette and handed her another drink. "Go 'head! Just jump in and say I quit! Say life sucks, and I can't deal, so I'm gonna' check out."

"Sounds good to me." Libbi whistled a stream of pink smoke from the side of her mouth, then gulped half her drink without tasting it. "I mean, where the fuck does Yolo, Fat Pig, get off firing me? He tells me to do an interview. I do the interview. He tells me it was exactly what he wanted. Everybody should be happy, right? I even sleep with the big fat, disgusting, sweating, farting old hog…just to be safe…and he fucking fires me! My ratings were good. My ratings were great! I'm the best he's ever had…in the studio, that is. I mean not had in the studio, but…"

"I get it." Juds smirked and petted her on the rear end.

Juds had just arrived in the northwest, his brokered deal between the Break and the Accommodant government having netted him the heftiest payday of his hustling amoral life. He'd decided to finally take his seedy, smalltime action to the big city for a dose of rest and relaxation amongst the well-to-do. He figured a pocket full of cash and a few well-placed lies would net him some uptown female playmates to crystallize his depraved curbside fantasies. What he hadn't counted on was meeting *the* lady herself: the one and only Libbi Trullup, news talkshow diva, wafting away in the breeze of another late pre-dawn evening of "glamorous" bar-hopping.

She looked great…for a depressed, inebriated female in her late thirties, dressed the part of a spoiled debutante tart half her age. Her figure was lean. Her thick dark hair was flowing and shimmering in the twinmoon light. Her skimpy skirt was under-designed and overpriced. Her multi-colored reptilian pumps looked store-bought new. Yet, her drooping pouchy face had certainly seen better days. As she haughtily blew another stream of smoke into the air, she was the perfect portrait of an assertive, modern career gal on one of those particularly bad and lonely nights, searching desperately for a bloody train wreck she could call her very own.

Juds was delighted to meet her in such a state. A sinister smile curled his lips. All he was missing were good intentions and the bib overalls of a railway engineer.

"I was so great, doing that interview." Libbi pounded her fist against the wooden railing. "She was like, 'God this and God that and I only fuck my husband once a fucking twinmoon and I'm totally happy because God loves prudish snobbish stuck-up little repressed bitches like me, because its God's will!' And I was like, 'Honey, if God is making you this uptight, you need to quit the faith and find yourself a man who's gonna turn the heat back on, 'cause your oven sounds like an icebox that hasn't had a damn thing in it in a very long time!'"

Juds turned away, snorting, coughing and laughing.

"Well, that's what I should've said anyway." Libbi smiled, stroking him across the back. "I tried to be respectful, for all the good it did me."

"Sorry," Juds cleared his throat, "you are a fucking riot."

"I know." Libbi chuckled playfully and slurped from her glass again. "I'm the vaginal discharge of wit! That's what one reviewer wrote about me. What the fuck is that? If I was a male, would I be the spurting semen of satire? The slapping schlong of shtick? I mean, goddamn! What are these people thinking?"

"Who the fuck knows?" Juds rolled his eyes.

"Who the fuck knows?" Libbi repeated unevenly. "And who cares? I am still sexy. I am still hot. And I will work again!"

"No doubt." Juds leaned over, pushed his pelvis into hers and kissed her on the neck.

"Whoa, wait a minute." Libbi wobbled against the railing. "What did you say your name was?"

"Finx." Juds smiled and kissed her again.

"Oh, bullshit!" Libbi laughed out loud. "Your name is not Finx. Finx is Finx's name. Not yours."

"That's my name!" Juds held up his hand. "Swear to god."

"That is such bullshit." Libbi cackled loudly. "Finx is a goddamn stage name made up by Finx Melder. Nobody's real name is Finx."

"Look, my name is Finx." Juds pretended to be perturbed. "My mother gave me that name. She happened to think it was a great name for her baby boy. Melder's mom probably stole it from my mom. We both grew up in the same town, y'know."

"Oh yeah. For sure!" Libbi spilled part of her drink on Juds. "Oh fuck…sorry."

"S'all right." Juds brushed the beaded liquor from his shiny new silver two-piece suit.

"No…no…" Libbi seemed suddenly frustrated, "I am such a fucking klutz. You look so great and you're being so nice and I'm just fucking up all over the place."

"Hey, babe." Juds smiled and lifted her chin with a curled forefinger. "I'm the one who's fucking up. I blow into town, hoping to meet a beautiful young lady. My dream comes true, and then I can't tell her how I feel. Story of my life."

Libbi paused for a moment. It was definitely amateur night and his lines were horrendous. He was clearly a hungry hustler from the wrong side of the planet, with no guile or polish to compensate for his pock-marked pick-up attempt. His name wasn't Finx and she knew every word from his mouth was a lie. He wasn't too ugly. Just too slick, raw and untrustworthy. He might have been a rapist. He might even have been a serial killer. But most likely, he was just a dumb horny guy on the make, too stupid to realize he was playing out of his depth. The sad thing was she really didn't care tonight. Anything...anyone was better than being sober and alone with tormenting realities howling through her skull.

"So, what did you say you did for a living?" She touched his shoulder with the back of her fingers.

"I'm a wholesaler." Juds smiled confidently. "Been working my butt off for the last six months down south. We're making so much fucking money. This is the first break I've had to get away on a mini-vacation. Not much time for a social life, y'know?"

"So what do you wholesale?" Libbi smirked seductively. "Drugs?"

"Hey, do I look like a drug dealer to you?" Juds raked his fingers through his slicked back hair.

Libbi eyed his suit, then rolled her eyes sarcastically. She took another drag from her cigarette and smartly spouted another stream of pink smoke into the air.

Suddenly, the playfulness bolted from Juds's eyes.

"Y'know, you are one stuck-up, snobbish, rotten little cunt, you know that?" Juds sneered. "I may be just a guy from down the way, but I don't take that kind of shit in my own backyard and I sure as hell ain't gonna take it from a used-up bimbo like you. Fuck this!"

With a snap of the wrist, Juds flicked the remainder of his drink over the railing and slammed down his glass.

"See ya." He turned and stalked away, disappearing into the crowd.

Libbi had to blink to try to remember what part of the conversation she had missed. The abrupt abandonment stunned her dulled senses like an open-handed slap in the face. It was the last thing she needed. She had already lost her job. She had stumbled woefully in seducing Yolo Pigue, and now she was even failing at getting picked up by a loathsome stranger. Her insecurity grew into a canyon. The emptiness made her nauseous. Her esteem couldn't bear another loss, no matter how shoddy the prize.

She flicked her herbal cigarette away and went after him.

She overheard someone actually chuckle, "Go get 'im, Libbi!" as she hurried through the crowd looking for the thin, pasty man with the receding hairline in the shiny silver suit. Juds had just begun to sidle up to a pair of younger fresher faces when she finally caught up to him.

"Hey!" she touched him on the shoulder. "Excuse us, girls."

She hooked him by the arm and led him away.

"I'm really sorry." Libbi pleaded with an apologetic smile. "I speak before I think. It's my job. You know, that old vaginally discharged wit of mine?"

"Don't worry about…"

"Listen." She pressed against him and lowered her voice. "I'd really like to be alone with you. Really. I've never met anybody like you before, and I didn't know exactly what to say. I…I feel like I owe you an apology…and maybe a little more because of how I acted out there."

"Yeah." Juds smiled and kneaded her ass with his fingers. "Yeah, you do actually."

He swept his arm around her shoulders, claiming his trophy. She secured her arm snugly around his waist and kissed his pitted, weather-beaten cheek. Together, they sauntered briskly out of the Swanky Skank and into the symbiotic abuse of their hastily forged union.

XIX.

The bright morning's promise for this Solemnday had fully degraded into a grey evening wake for the afternoon of destruction and death. The shadowy first floor wreckage of the downtown office building Reza and Durn had smashed through, was now a sprawling spotlit urban crime scene.

"Heathens." Policer Fembletun stepped carefully over a fallen metal beam. "This is the work of heathens, here."

His partner shook his head as he knelt down and tried to examine another pool of blood sprinkled with tiny fragments of glass and concrete dust. The thin light from his finger beacon did not provide sufficient illumination for him to reconstruct what had happened; his brow wrinkled with a tinge of aggravation.

"I need a light over here!" Bales called out into the cavernous remains of the pulverized structure.

"Just a minute!" an echoing voice answered from a short distance away.

"Yeah, just a minute." Bales grumbled to himself. "Take your time. I can't think of anything else I'd rather be doing."

"Yep." Fembletun's smooth black face was filled with awed consternation. "Only heathens could do something like this."

"Heathens?" Bales stood up and confronted his partner. "Heathens? Why does everything, every crime have to have a religious connotation with you?"

"Because every crime has a religious connotation." Fembletun cracked off a large splinter of wood from a shattered desk and tossed it carelessly to the ground. "Where God is present, no crime is possible."

"Uh oh, here we go again." Bales shined his light on a bloody trail of wheel tracks striped into the ripped and frayed hallway carpeting. "The perpetrators were obviously non-Cathedral-going folks because they committed murder and mayhem, right?"

"And because they killed the Lord Regent," Fembletun reminded him.

"Oh, yeah." Bales's opaque complexion greyed in the dim dusty lighting. "Of course they might have been pissed-off Cathedral-going folk who just didn't like the Lord Regent."

"Not possible." Fembletun kicked aside a mangled metal chair.

"Not possible?" Bales flipped his finger light up toward the ragged ceiling. "How come?"

"Because Cathedral-going people wouldn't kill the Lord Regent." Fembletun followed Bales' light with his eyes, then glanced at his partner quizzically. "And what the heck are you looking at? The perpetrators drove in off the street. They didn't come flying through the ceiling."

"I know." Bales continued his scrutiny. "I'm just a fan of modern, glitzy, low-budget building materials, that's all. The first lawbooker who glances at the insurance reports is going to make himself a very wealthy body-bagger. There's no way this beam should have come crashing down like this. And that desk came down from the floor above. This poor bastard fielded the worst split-second dilemma in the history of desk jockeys: Get run over by a vehicle plowing through your office or eat a shiny wooden 600 kilo desk crashing through the ceiling from the second floor. Whatever happened to 'coffee or tea before I snooze away the afternoon'?"

"A heathen death at the hands of heathens." Fembletun shook his head.

"Oh, so what did this guy do to deserve to get killed by psychos?" Bales became annoyed.

"Today was Solemnday." Fembletun frowned. "If this guy had been at Cathedral instead of working for a heathen company on the Lord's day, he'd still be alive."

"So this is his fault?" Bales tilted his head in disbelief.

"I'm just stating the facts." Fembletun returned a look of irony. "Cathedral: live. Work: die."

"And what about the Lord Regent?" Bales gestured animatedly "He was at Cathedral today. He's at Cathedral every day. It didn't do him a whole helluva lot of good, did it?"

"The Lord Regent was a son-of-a-bitch. Everybody knew that," Fembletun replied.

"So he deserved to die, too?" Bales grew exasperated. "How can you say that about that pious old man?"

"Because it's true," Fembletun answered evenly. "And I didn't say he deserved to die. I'm saying that him being a rat-bastard son-of-a-bitch made him a prime target for murdering heathens."

A dumpy uniformed policer approached the partners carrying a thin, ten-meter metal stem with a blaring bright light on the end that lit up fifty square meters. He planted it directly behind Fembletun and Bales, then tottered back into the darkness without a word. Both men had to shade their eyes until they could adjust to the intense blast of illumination.

"Thanks for the scorched retinas." Bales squinted painfully.

"I also remove toe nails using dull rusty hand tools," the dumpy policer's fading voice echoed.

"I'll call you," Bales deadpanned.

"You would." Fembletun stepped into the brightened wreckage with his hand visored over his brow. He followed the trail of bloody wheel prints out into the cracked marble atrium.

"So you're saying that since there was a crime here, God was nowhere to be found?" Bales shouted to his partner.

"What?" Fembletun cupped his ear.

"You're saying that since there was murder and mayhem all over town today, that God took the day off!" Bales raised his voice and paraphrased his question.

"That's ridiculous. I didn't say that." Fembletun scowled. "God is everywhere all the time."

"But you said that crime is impossible where God is present, right?" Bales restated. "God must've blown town some time around noon, don't you think?"

Fembletun slowly crunched his way back through the rubble, frustrated by noting nothing other than the obvious vehicle/building collision debris.

"God is everywhere all the time…except in the heart of the heathen," Fembletun clarified. "When a heathen is loosed in God's world, God can only mitigate the damages. Save the souls that want to be saved. Other than that, the devil has lease."

"That doesn't sound very omnipotent, to me." Bales snorted.

"That's plenty omnipotent, if you want to get to Heaven." Fembletun's eyes became stern and fixed on his partner. "In the end, Heaven's all that matters. Not all this…stuff."

"So that's it? Heathens and saints? Heaven and Hell? All bagged up in neat little packages?" Bales shrugged his shoulders.

"That's pretty much it," Fembletun affirmed without a doubt.

"So that girl and her boyfriend who killed all these people, they're both going to Hell," Bales concluded.

"There's not a doubt in my mind." Fembletun shook his head. "Of course the guy has time to repent. But from everything I've heard, he's not the type. The Devil's holding a reservation for that loser and I'm sure he'll be more than eager to hop the first ferry to perdition's patio party. He'll say: 'Looks fun! Smells great!' He'll be too stupid to see he's the main course in the barbecue pit until it's way too late."

"Hmm." Bales gazed out over the carnage reflectively. "I guess I just can't see the world in black and white. I look everywhere and I see shades of grey. A little bit of good and bad in everyone."

"That's because you never go to Cathedral," Fembletun lectured. "If you went to Cathedral, you'd know what I'm talking about. My Churchlord, he's a saint. Where my Churchlord is present, nothing but good follows him everywhere. People smile. People give. Even the heathens are disarmed because they sense that something good's in the air. Same thing with the Deliveress. She's the living embodiment of holy goodness on this planet. Where Deliveress Jen is present, no wrong is possible. God set it that way so that we would have living examples of perfection to follow. She's perfect because God is in her all the time.

"Now you take those heathen murderers. God wasn't in them. They did a ghastly murderous thing because they never knew God. They think they're serving themselves by rejecting the Lord, but in so doing, they just become slaves of evil, heir to do devilish things."

"Okay, fine." Bales conceded, for the moment. "But how do you explain what happened to the Lord Regent?"

"The Lord Regent was a son-of-a-bitch," Fembletun stated flatly.

"I know, but you said he wasn't a heathen," Bales countered. "Why did he have to die such a horrible death?"

"Because some people who are saved are still sons of bitches," Fembletun shot back confidently. "They serve the church, but they just aren't likable. They put off a bad vibe and pretty soon some heathen is looking to settle a score. Sometimes they get a pie in the face at the Cathedral picnic. Sometimes they get shot full of flesh-eating chemicals. Only God knows why."

"Hmh." Bales shook his head. "Well I feel sorry for you religious types. I think most religious people are just plain jealous of us free-thinkers. You guys spend way too much time worrying about what people who don't agree with you do and think."

"I'm not worried about what you think." Fembletun chuckled. "The question you should be asking yourself is why you're so worried about what I think? Why are you bothered by my faith in God, my faith in Heaven. If you're so secure about being a free-thinker, you should be able to look me in the eye and tell me I'm a fool. Tell me that you're a hundred-percent certain that I'm dead wrong. But you can't. You just believe in doing what you feel like doing, and justifying it any way you can to keep yourself feeling good. But deep down, you know He's up there, watching, taking note on all you free-thinkers. And, just like the people we bust everyday, you hope that ignorance of His law will buy you special dispensation. A remedial cloud in Heaven for people who just didn't feel like being obedient. If you really feel that's what God meant for all of us, don't be sorry for me. Be sorry for yourself. The Devil's got a cell waiting for you."

"I don't think this is a good discussion." Bales rolled his eyes with a long sigh.

"That's all right." Fembletun looked his partner in the face. "You're not alone. A lot of people try to believe in things they can't defend."

Fembletun started to walk away.

Bales lifted his head up and smiled at being baited into continuing the conversation.

"All right. So, if you live this so-called perfect life according to the Text, nothing too bad is ever going to happen to you?" Bales concluded.

"I believe that." Fembletun said thoughtfully. "Look at Deliveress Jen. She's beautiful. She's intelligent. She loves God. She never says or does anything wrong. With the exception of being married to the Accommodant, her life is a perfect model for all of us to follow. And even her tolerance of him is a Godly example of marital faith and fidelity. She can't fall. God won't let her. Where she is present, no crime is possible. God is in her heart and always will be...unlike the heathens who did all this here."

"Well, I'm glad it's all so simple." Bales looked down and searched for more reconstructive evidence.

"It really is," Fembletun spoke confidently. "If everyone were like Deliveress Jen, the world would be a perfect place. We wouldn't have to be shuffling around in the middle of the night, diagramming a crime scene. We could just go home, play with our kids, snuggle up with our wives and sleep with both eyes closed."

"Like Deliveress Jen?" Bales smirked.

"Yeah." Fembletun smiled. "Some day. Just like Deliveress Jen."

"Some day? You mean, with all this wisdom, you don't sleep with both eyes closed yet?" Bales chuckled.

"Not with all the heathens running around loose," Fembletun lamented. "With two teen daughters in midschool? Not anytime soon."

XX.

PJ's entourage arose from the four sliding doors of the long black, missile-shaped luxury transport. Crilen observed the orange and yellow reflections of the twinmoons glowing along the vehicle's smooth rounded hull like a broad starscape mural, mirroring all stellar pathways to every corner of the infinite universe. It was a miraculous portrait of home, this dark enveloping ocean of distant stars and moons and planets glittering overhead. His awe of the creator of the vast cosmos, in all of its wondrous molecular detail, grew with every moment he gazed upon its splendor. Billions of years of history. Billions of years of exponential futures.

And yet, within all of that, the relevance of everything which would happen in the next hour to a handful of sentient beings on a single planetary speck in a tiny little building was beyond measure in scope and significance. So few would ever know or care what happened here. Less than one one-hundredth of one percent of every sentient creature in the universe would ever know that this particular world had even existed. But God would always know. God would always care. The destiny of every single living soul mattered to this omniscient and omnipotent creator. What incomprehensible genius, the maker of us all. What unfathomable love we owe.

The warped, chipped, weathered doors of Rabbel's tavern, inset in mortared stone and shadowed under the vestibule lamp, resembled the entranceway to an enormous gothic mausoleum. Only the driving acoustic music, the clinking of glasses and the swells of bawdy laughter from within betrayed the cool, still, ghostly whisper of death chilling the night air.

Panla took two steps away from the transport, then looked back as its smoked glass door whirred shut behind her. She turned away and swallowed as if she would never look upon her stealthy secret conveyance again. She stood still for a moment and lifted her chin as she stared resolutely into the tavern doors. Her eyes were narrowed with piercing resolve as they looked down her slender, flaring nostrils. Her shoulders were squared bravely, her arms hidden beneath the black shawl which dangled beneath her waist. The aura around her was less luminescent than usual. Almost eerily earthen…and gravely foreboding.

This was the first time Crilen had seen her for several hours. She had remained sequestered in her private compartment, away from him and the others for the entire journey. He had worried about the physical and psychological strain she had exhibited. He had worried about what emotional stability she would bring to her meeting with Rabbel. He had worried about whether he would be able to protect her in a hostile nest of volatility and violence. Gazing upon her now, a portion of his fear dissipated on the sudden sturdiness of her lithe figure which seemed to draw intangible fortitude from a powerful source unseen. He almost understood it. In his mind, he could picture her bursting into a beautiful cosmic flame, preparing to blast the minions of deviltry back to the molten pools of Hell. She was clearly prepared to do battle this evening. And she was not about to let a gathering of rabid secularists scare her from the fight. PJ had not made the trip this evening. Nor had Deliveress Jen. Panla had taken their place. The only question which was problematic was whether this woman had come to win or to die.

"Mrs. Tem....er....PJ...." Linnfeld appeared carrying a thick jacket. "I strongly advise that you take a moment to place this protective garment under your clothing. It's the same material your husband wears when he travels south. And other Deliverers have..."

"Mr. Linnfeld." Panla looked upon him warmly. "And a helmet for my head? Armor for my arms and legs? Where is your faith, old friend?"

"In this shell-proof garment, for the moment." Linnfeld was sweating profusely.

She smiled at her lead attendant with an expression of lifelong appreciation and fondness. She hugged him for an extended moment, kissed him on the cheek and ordered him to put the jacket away. Desperate tears welled up in Linnfeld's eyes as his shoulders slumped. He walked back to the vehicle and tossed the protective jacket in an open door behind the driver.

Genna approached her. Panla put her arm around the young woman and kissed her on the forehead.

"She's saying good-bye." Linnfeld's voice whispered behind Crilen. "Can you feel it?"

Crilen's own suppressed fears blossomed full again.

"Couldn't you find any way to keep her from doing this?" The elder man's white face was a swollen picture of despair.

"Couldn't you?" Crilen frowned.

Linnfeld's eyes became sad and disconsolate. They had all tried their best to keep her from being exactly where she stood, but her logic and convictions had won out then, just as they had a moment ago.

"She says you're here to do something," Linnfeld sighed with resignation. "I hope to God, whatever it is, you do it in there tonight."

Crilen felt the stinging licks of his wife's death beat against the chords of his soul. There had been no warnings then. No opportunity to choose an alternate path. It had all happened so quickly. One moment they were making love, the next moment she was dead. And he was hurtling a 100,000 kilometers into space, anguished and bewildered.

By contrast, here he'd had two full days to gather information and build an impenetrable fortress around Panla Jen. Yet the pathways of this past present seemed cosmically unalterable, as if the piece had already been written. And any discordant alteration in its tapestry would unravel the fabric of every living soul on the planet, plummeting their world into something even worse than the annihilation which had resulted in the asteroid belt. Thus, she remained exposed to fate. And time was now very, very short.

"I'll do whatever I have to do to save her life." Crilen placed his hand on Linnfeld's shoulder. "I'll do whatever I have to do to save this world."

"I'm sure you will." Linnfeld's expression was dubious. "But we might need an army this evening, and I needn't remind you that we have no reinforcements in this neck of the woods."

"Gentlemen?" Panla called in a commanding tone. "Are we ready?"

Linnfeld straightened himself and tried to put on a confident air that would get him through the door and to the bar for the stiff drink that would settle his nerves. He walked toward Panla, nodded his head and led the group toward the tavern entrance.

Linnfeld pushed open the dingy squeaking doors. Crilen was the first to enter. Genna followed. Panla was behind her. Linnfeld brought up the rear.

The lights were dim as always. The tavern was packed and buzzing. The air was thick with herbal smoke. The smell of worn leather and stale alcohol fouled the aroma. Panla's jaw set tightly; her eyes simmered with contempt. As PJ, she had pretended well to enjoy this putrid atmosphere. Tonight, she concealed none of her loathing for it.

Suddenly there was a loud festive growl from the far end of the bar.

Crilen's hands grew hot as he quickly surveyed the surroundings for danger.

The entire room exploded into fervent cheers and spirited applause.

"The fucking Regent's dead!" shouted a female dressed in nothing but vertical leather straps. "Death to the goddamned Cathedral!"

Linnfeld's expression was jolted into stunned bewilderment. Genna recoiled subconsciously and cringed. Crilen continued to scan every set of hands for weapons, every pair of eyes for malevolence, but the mood of the gathering was

347 DONALD I. TEMPLEMAN

gruffly congenial. All, that is, except one leering, angular dark face perched against the far wall near Rabbel's office. It was Leesla.

The tall sinewy woman locked a hateful gaze on Panla that could have melted steel to steam. It was a raw and dangerous look. The look of a murderer.

"Yeeow!" a female voice shrieked behind him.

Crilen spun and saw Panla calmly looking over her shoulder. Following her gaze, Crilen witnessed that poor Genna had been drenched with someone's spilled drink.

"I've got it." Linnfeld touched Crilen's arm. The lead attendant reached through the crowd toward the bar for a dry towel. Then, like the old father he had been, he wiped the young woman's face and rubbed Genna's head like he was drying his daughter's hair by the poolside.

It was a common barroom mishap, but to Crilen, it felt like a diversion or a rehearsal for something sinister. He reached across to take Panla by the arm; he wanted to keep her closer. But as he touched her, she shrugged his hand away.

"I'm all right!" she said with curt annoyance.

With total disregard for protocols or safety, Panla plunged through a wall of drinkers and stalked toward the stage. Crilen hurried behind her. The crowd started a deafening chant: "PJ! PJ! PJ! PJ! PJ! PJ!"

As always, the motley gathering parted for her, forming a makeshift aisle leading to the spotlit stage. The musicians abandoned their instruments. Her customary stool was set in its regular place.

Just as she came within a meter of the stage, a large burly giant stepped in front of her and cut her off. Panla was startled as she stopped on her toes and stumbled sideways before regaining her balance. This type of confrontation had never happened before, and, for the first time all evening, a flicker of fright crossed her countenance.

The tavern hushed silent.

Crilen interceded immediately and put himself between Panla and the towering white-faced male. Crilen's brows furrowed deep ridges into his forehead. His eyes flashed a molten red before he was able to suppress it. The giant simply looked down and smiled, revealing rotting and dangling teeth. He extended his giant paw which held a strange looking rag doll.

"For luck," the giant droned in a slurry baritone. "Rub my buddy for luck. I always get good luck when I come to see you. Things always go good. I got a new job last month. Got me a girl last week. Could you give me some more luck before my luck runs out, PJ? Please?"

Crilen felt Panla brush past him as she stepped forward to confront this wall of a male and the tattered object of his superstitions. She looked up into his large features, tightened her lips and narrowed her eyes.

"No!" she sneered. "No, I will not!"

With that, she ducked under the giant's elbow and concluded her march to the stage. The giant male appeared confused. His slow mind didn't know whether to be angry or sad. The crowd decided for him, whistling and jeering as Panla hopped up on stage, tossed aside her stool and pirouetted to face them. She tensely wiped her palm across the front of her shawl.

The hoots and curses intensified as the crowd shifted into an uneasy hostility. Panla stood frozen before them, her nose and chin lifted proudly as she glared down at their taunts with royal contempt.

"What the hell happened?" Linnfeld suddenly appeared next to Crilen with Genna in tow.

Crilen swallowed hard as he watched Panla absorb the crowd's profane derisions with the blatant defiance of a proud indomitable martyr. He was certain someone would throw something eventually. But they never did. Then he remembered, this was still PJ: Rabbel's woman. She knew they wouldn't dare.

Or did she?

"Mr. Len?" Linnfeld whispered urgently. "What is going on?"

"It's over," Crilen answered him.

Linnfeld looked up at the stage and tried to assess whom he saw. Certainly it was not PJ. And there were only trace elements of the Deliveress, devoid of her spiritual serenity. What he saw was another woman with whom he had become increasingly familiar in recent days: a very angry, emotionally tried Panla Jen Tem.

"Oh, how fickle we are this evening." Panla's clear voice cut the tavern's noise to silence. "Cheers for the murder of the Lord Regent. Cheers for the death of a lost young girl."

"It's all right," a voice yelled. "Reza couldn't fuck for shit!"

The crowd laughed and chuckled as they heaped defecation upon the disturbed girl's memory.

"But I cast aside a stupid doll, and suddenly you're all in a rumple." Panla continued intensely. "Why so, I ask you? Don't all of you cast aside God with less consideration than I rejected a bundle of fabric and stuffing? I come down here week after week and listen to everyone rail about how ridiculous religion is. How evil the Cathedral is. What a sanctimonious bitch the Deliveress is. How nothing that has anything to do with faith in our Lord in Heaven has anything to do with you. You say there's no God because you can't see him. You say there's no God because he doesn't speak to you. You say there's no God because there's poverty and suffering and death. You say there's no God because you think everything he says gets in the way of you having a good time!

"You say: 'I can't drink enough because of an unseen God. I can't party drugs because of an unseen God. I can't have sex with anyone I want because of an unseen God. I can't lie and cheat and murder and steal because an unseen God tells me it's wrong. I can't be selfish because the unseen God tells me to be charitable. I can't hate because the unseen God tells me to love.'

"And, yet, you believe in unseen luck. You believe in unseen karma. You believe that God is shit because you claim that you can't see him. But when you're all done burning religion down to the last ember, the unseen is exactly what you do believe in. Only yours is an unseen force of convenience that requires you to do absolutely nothing. And, in return, you expect it to always perform some random magic in your favor. You say that believing in a God you cannot see is illogical. I ask you, how illogical is it to believe in anything else you cannot see? Does it make sense that God would give us His word to study, live and die by in a Text? Or does it make more sense that God would conceal himself in a deck of cards or a lottery stub or the mind of a psychic or the law of averages or the stitching of a lucky doll?"

"Fuck off!" a loud voice echoed in the background.

"Hey, PJ, I think you need a drink!" another voice yelled.

The crowd chuckled uneasily.

"And where do you go when this life is over?" Panla continued with no acknowledgment of the growing restlessness turning against her. "The Text says that there's a Heaven and a Hell and spells out what you need to make of yourself to wind up in one place or the other. But of course, this is all Cathedral propaganda, am I right? Yet most, if not all of you believe that there is something after this life. And whatever it is, you hope that it's pleasant and that you won't have had to do anything particularly special to get there. After all, we are talking about eternity, aren't we?

"Only, what about the bad people? And what is a bad person anyway? We reject God's plan, and yet we somehow think that something is going to keep the bad people out of our private little make-believe afterlife. What might that something be other than God? And, if it is God, wouldn't God have guidelines and requirements for access into His eternal kingdom? If not, any semblance of an afterlife would resemble pretty much what we experience in our daily lives. Saints and sinners coexisting in the same realm, only forever and ever. You'd have good days and bad days. You'd have your friends and your enemies commingled for all time. It doesn't sound like much to look forward to, does it? In fact it sounds rather like the miserable life you've already led. Is that our immortal destiny? Does that make sense to you, really?

"I came to you people because, like you, I know that the Cathedral stinks."

"Yeah!" a voice cheered from the darkness.

"It's full of corrupt, lying, unscrupulous bureaucrats who's only concern is to fatten the company trough." Panla's voice shook. "They don't believe what they say and they rarely say what they believe. And, in either case, their godliness is so far removed from the true living God, that the Nine Chieftains would barely recognize their own two thousand twinmoon-old faith. Thus, the Cathedral's failings have resulted in people like yourselves: Lost. Secular. Empty. Dead."

"You want dead, bitch?" a clipped cadence yelled from the side of the stage. It was Leesla, her long sinewy limbs climbing onto the platform. The tall dark woman drew a large glistening blade.

Startled, Panla stared directly into the face of her attacker, but froze.

A bright burst of fire shot from the audience. It struck Leesla's hand, forcing her arm to swing upward. The blade flew up from her hand, lodging itself into the wooden ceiling.

Panla took a step backward as a confused, hunched-over Leesla turned away, clutching her burned hand. Rabbel appeared out of nowhere.

Leesla squinted at him with a pained expression scrawled across her face.

"Do you hear what she's saying?" she whispered in agony.

Rabbel grabbed Leesla by her wild scraggly hair, straightened her up and punched her in the face. The tall woman's body went sprawling into the standing crowd.

"I heard," his deep voice rumbled.

Crilen had foiled Leesla's attack with an imperceptible stream of fire, but he now had to hurriedly assess Rabbel Mennis's intentions. If he went after the stocky muscular leader of the Break in a tavern full of heavily-armed constituents, it might mean death for everyone. But if he were too passive...

Rabbel wore a deep black angry scowl as he stared at Panla. He extended his large open hand to her, not tenderly, but as a command he insisted she follow. Panla, shaken, backed away and looked out into the crowd again. They jeered and howled obscenities. Some yelled for Rabbel to kill her. But as the volatility of everything around her continued to escalate, somehow, Panla regained her composure. She returned Rabbel's scowl with an angry penetrating glare of her own. She turned back on the crowd.

"You're all fools!" she spat.

Rabbel strode across the stage and snatched her by the wrist, lifting her off her feet. He stepped down into the crowd, pulling her carelessly behind him.

"This is over right now!" he growled and led her toward his office.

Crilen stepped in front of them.

"Mr. Mennis." Crilen spoke with threatening authority. "You need to let her go."

Rabbel halted in his tracks as a wild anger pinched his deep dark expression. It wasn't the look of a venerable leader now. It was a look from another time in his life. A time when he'd been a wild young rogue in the southern streets, building his reputation on the stacked carcasses of vanquished rivals.

Rabbel gently released Panla's wrist. An evil and dangerous smile etched itself into the deep lines of his pitch black face. Rabbel looked Crilen up and down as if he were just another ignorant street punk who was unaware he was about to have his life taken.

Meanwhile, in his own mind, Crilen could already see Rabbel's scorched, smoking skeletal remains curled up into a fetal collection of cauterized bone. It would be the easiest kill he'd ever done…in defense of Panla, in memory of Aami…all the better. Rabbel had no idea what cosmic forces he was about to unleash on himself.

But then, Panla stepped between the two men and put her arm around Rabbel's waist.

"Oh Rabbel darling, did I make a mess of things?" she offered herself apologetically. "I'm so sorry, sweetheart. It's been such a mad day."

Crilen was stunned.

Rabbel peeled her arm from around his waist and regained a full grasp on her wrist. His dark brooding face softened into the more rational and charismatic leader of the Break. His self-control gradually returned, although there was no hint of mercy or forgiveness in his deep disapproving eyes.

"Get in my office," Rabbel growled at Panla.

Crilen reached forward and pulled her back by the other arm.

"She's not going back there." Crilen's expression was grave. "We're leaving. We're leaving right now."

Panla frowned and jerked her arm away from Crilen.

"Mr. Len," her face grew angry. "you are not in charge of our delegation. Step out of line again and you're fired. See to the others. That's an order."

Rabbel's eyes tossed Crilen another warning as his hand tightened its hold on Panla's wrist.

Crilen was at a loss. It was as if every force of reason in the universe were conspiring against him. As if Panla welcomed her march to the gallows. Perhaps she viewed her own death as the only way to escape the failure of her plans for Cathedral reform. Certainly if she disappeared behind that office door, he knew he would never see her again. Not alive.

But if he interceded now, how would it effect the future/past of this planet? Was this the moment in time for which It had chosen him to intervene? Would saving Panla from certain death at the hands of Rabbel Mennis be the key to the salvation of this world? Or would her martyrdom?

Crilen could not be sure, but he certainly knew what his heart was telling him: he could not bear to lose his wife again.

"You're not going in there." the words nearly choked in Crilen's throat.

"Mr. Len," her eyes narrowed, "I'm not her. You don't belong here. Go back wherever the hell you came from and leave…me…alone!"

Crilen felt as if he had been kicked in the stomach. His knees felt like gelatin as he watched Rabbel tow Panla through the parting crowd and toward his office. She glanced back to him one last time, before she was pulled in and the door sealed behind them. It was a deep and sorrowful glance, but he couldn't interpret its meaning. Maybe it didn't matter after all. Maybe this was how it was intended to be. The lamb had run off with the devil…to be slaughtered. Amen.

"My God," Linnfeld's voice quivered with sadness, "she's gone. That's it. She's gone."

"Not necessarily." Genna sniffed back tears. "She's smart. She knows him. She's talked her way around him before. She'll do it again."

"We'd better find a way out of here." Linnfeld grimaced with resignation. "If he kills her, we won't be worth a red coin in this place."

"He won't." Genna hung her head. "He can't. He loves her, doesn't he?"

Crilen stood stone still. This could not be all that It had asked him to do. He'd lived out a million scenarios throughout the universe, and he knew that there was no poetic rhythm in any of them. But this felt odd. Awkward. Maddeningly askew. Backwards.

"Take them and bind them," a short clipped voice spoke in a broken lisp. "We'll let Rabbel decide what to do, once he's done with her."

Leesla held a bar rag to her swelling lips as she spoke through her long blood-stained teeth.

Two large men seized Genna. Two more grabbed Linnfeld and pressed him against the wall.

"Go get the driver." Leesla signaled randomly to the throng with her long fingers.

"Aren't you forgetting about me?" Crilen's eyes simmered.

Leesla tried to smile through her split, swollen lips, but the expression was malformed. So she licked over the top of her mouth with her tongue and spat a large clot of blood at Crilen's feet.

"We have them," she spoke confidently. "We have her." The tall woman nodded toward Rabbel's office door. "You aren't going anywhere."

She was right, and Crilen hated it.

"You like her a lot, don't you?" Leesla approached him cautiously. "In fact, I think you love her. I know the look. The longing. It's so pathetic when a man can't take 'no' for an answer. She wants him, not you. He's going to kill her, and she knows it…and she still wants him. She'd rather die begging at his crotch, than live staring into your fawning watery-eyed face. How does that feel?"

Crilen's jaw set solid. He was still mulling over his options. A voice was telling him to burn a fiery path into Rabbel's office and whisk her away, but something else kept him still.

"Why don't you tell us how it feels!" Genna shouted to Leesla as she struggled against her captors. "What happened to that little cutey you used to huddle in the corner with? She hasn't been around lately. She must've gotten tired of your fawning watery eyed face…and that scarecrow scatter-hair stuck all over your head!"

Leesla's expression twisted into a primal rage. "You are going to die first, you little…"

"!!KROKOOW!!"

The deafening, concussive explosion of a weapon reverberated from Rabbel's office.

Crilen bolted past Leesla in a haze of smoke and crashed through Rabbel's door. He clung to the door frame praying that he didn't see exactly what he saw.

Panla was sprawled in a corner against the wall, her white face spattered in crimson blood. Her large brown eyes sat open in frozen amazement as a swirl of smoke billowed from a huge hole in the chest of her garments. A tear fell from her eye, but there was no other sound or movement from her body as she lay still.

Rabbel stood, facing his fallen love. His dark face was a deep rich impassive carving of black coal. His inset eyes showed no emotion, no hint of regret.

Leesla pushed past Crilen and into the office to comfort her liege.

"Rabbel." She stepped in front of him. "Rabbel, don't despair. It had to be done. It had to be…"

Rabbel's hulking frame tottered for a moment then the great leader of the Break tilted and fell, slamming his thick black skull against the sharp corner of his desk. He rolled over onto the cold wooden floor of his office and came to rest...stone dead.

Leesla dropped to her knees in disbelief as the organs from Rabbel's gut-shot torso spilled out onto the floor with a dying groan.

From across the room, came a sharp, shivering gasp.

Panla's mouth hung open as she fought to learn how to breathe again. Overcome with shock, she shook involuntarily as her fixed eyes never blinked. A large copper-metallic hand-weapon toppled out from under her shawl. The ascending smoke from its barrel twisted into the air and quietly dispersed.

Crilen dove down by her side and touched her. He could barely believe she was alive.

"Panla," he whispered.

Her arms and legs remained rigid; her eyes were still locked on the air.

"Panla." He shook her.

Her arms relaxed slightly, but the network of veins in her long neck protruded as though they would explode at any moment. She slowly turned her frightened bewildered gaze toward him.

"Lenny?" she whispered softly.

A savage animal roar cut through the odd silence. Crilen looked up and saw the wild hate-filled eyes of Leesla boring through them.

"Kill them!" she shouted madly. "Kill them all! Kill them now! Kill them!"

Before the command even finished, four heavily armed figures leapt through the office door. There were several more behind them. They aimed their weapons at Crilen and Panla indiscriminately.

Crilen didn't wait for the weapons to discharge. His body burst into golden flames; his hands ignited into swirling amber torches. A hot wall of fire spiraled from his body, covering the attackers. Leesla and the gunmen spun and staggered out of the office, tossing aside their weapons and patting away the flames that immersed their clothing.

The entire office became engulfed in flames except for the corner where Panla remained huddled and petrified. Crilen extended his right hand, and, with a burst of fire, blew through the mortar of the outer wall. He extinguished his left arm, lifted Panla to her feet and rocketed them up and out of the tavern; over the buildings and into the night sky.

Where they could possibly go from here, he had no idea.

NAKED &
IRREVOCABLE

I.

THIS IS A YBS NEWS LEAK FROM YBS STUDIOS:

Newswoman: Good Morning. I'm Egs Bloyt. The world is a cauldron of turmoil and confusion as dawn breaks over the northwest. What most of you know, is that yesterday afternoon, the Lord Regent of the Cathedral was murdered outside the Bius Basilica gates by two assailants alleged to have ties to the Break. One of the assailants died while fleeing from Policers. The other was captured and remains in custody.

What most of you don't know, as we have just learned from our leaking sources, is that Rabbel Mennis, the elusive, dangerous driving force behind the anti-religious Break movement has been assassinated by a member of his own following at his southwest stronghold. Details are sketchy at this moment, but sometime after midnight, Rabbel Mennis met privately with one of his aides behind closed doors. The aide, a trusted confidante, apparently shot the Break leader with a hand weapon and killed him. The assassin then detonated some sort of explosive and escaped through a collapsed outer wall. He is still at large at this hour.

Adding to all the mystery of these two recent murders is the sudden disappearance of Deliveress and First Lady, Panla Jen Tem. Mrs. Tem has not been seen or heard from since she conducted the Solemnday Services at Bius Basilica yesterday afternoon. Neither the Holy Inquisitor acting Lord Regent, or spokespersons at the Accommodant Mansion can verify her whereabouts or assert whether she is safe or even alive. When asked whether Mrs. Tem had gone into seclusion for her own protection, aides said they were not aware of any such action being taken nor did they believe that it would have been necessary. They added that were she considered to be in any danger, both the Accommodant Mansion and the Bius Basilica were fully capable of providing the security needed for her to continue her public duties.

While her whereabouts are unknown, one inside leak at the Bius Basilica stated that the Deliveress and her attendants made an unscheduled departure from the Cathedral sometime early yesterday evening. There was no travel itinerary scheduled and there has been no communication from any member of her traveling party. As a result of her sudden, inexplicable disappearance, her scheduled breakfast at the Accommodant Mansion with a parental advocacy group this morning has been postponed. Meanwhile, religious worshippers around the world find themselves anxiously fearful that the Deliveress may also have met with foul play.

If you include Finx Melder, four of the leading public figures in the world are either dead or missing. It is an alarming revelation which begs the question: What is the mood of our Accommodant this morning? And what, if anything, can we do to protect him from these seemingly spurious, fortuitous events affecting the lives of our leading citizens?

We now bring in our Accommodant correspondent, Ruff Flough. Ruff, has there been a statement from the Accommodant yet?

RF: Nothing official yet, Egs. The Accommodant is said to have had late night meetings with labor parties and is only now en route back to the Accommodant Mansion under heavy security. According to people who have spoken with him, he is very upset and distraught over the sudden disappearance of his wife, Mrs. Tem. He can't understand why she would have disappeared without telling anyone. Like any husband who is deeply in love with his spouse he just wants to see her returned safely in light of all of the death and mayhem that has struck the planet over the last couple of days. We understand he will be making an official statement upon his return.

EB: Ruff, has the government made any connection between the death of Finx Melder, the Lord Regent and Rabbel Mennis as of yet?

RF: Well, while the timing seems a bit odd, I think they, like us, seem to feel that the death of Finx Melder was an isolated, untimely celebrity tragedy. Finx had no real socio-political affiliations. He lived by his own rules. He did as he pleased without any obvious social agenda other than to make films and win Golden Icons. It's said that his sympathies were certainly in line with the Break, but he never really publicly or privately supported anything they did. We're talking about an incredibly troubled and self-absorbed genius who tried to rise above the commonness of normal life. He certainly fought against the censorship and ratings of his work, but it doesn't appear that his death had anything to do with religious politics.

On the other hand, it's very obvious that the murder of the Lord Regent was politically motivated. You've got two alleged trigger-people with strong Break ties identified by scores of witnesses. Then, less than twelve hours later, you have the apparent murder of Rabbel Mennis. And that's followed by the disappearance of Deliveress Jen. It all begins to add up to the manifestation of an exploding war of ideologies which has been brewing for some time.

EB: Is the Accommodant in any danger?

RF: It's impossible to tell at this point. Twenty-six hours ago, if you had told me someone would assassinate the venerable Lord Regent, my response would have been: 'What for?' But when you line up his death with that of Rabbel Mennis, things begin to fall into place very quickly. The one thing the Accommodant does have in his favor is that he has never really committed to a firm opinion in one direction or the other. His vague convictions have made him moderately popular with both sides of the electorate. Remaining on the fence may very well save his life.

EB: Deliveress Jen has been missing since early yesterday evening, several hours after the Lord Regent's death. Do you think there was, perhaps, a retaliation on the part of the Cathedral against the Break?

RF: I hate to speculate, Egs. But it seems highly improbable that Rabbel Mennis was murdered in retaliation. At least not by anyone involved directly with the Cathedral. As I'm sure even you know, murder was one of the first offenses abolished in the Text when it was written by the original Nine Chieftains. The Cathedral clearly stands against death sentences for murderers, against the murder of the living unborn, and even any form of physical aggression against their enemies. The notion that the Cathedral could somehow be mixed up in some sordid underground war is unimaginable.

The more likely scenario is what we've already heard bits and pieces of: Someone close to Rabbel Mennis either betrayed him or simply snapped in a heated argument and killed him. The Break is supposedly comprised of some pretty volatile and eclectic characters. In their arena, it's likely that anything could have happened.

EB: Hmm. How frightening.

RF: Yes indeed.

EB: Ruff, we'll come back to you as the Accommodant prepares to speak to the world.

RF: I'll be here, Egs.

EB: Thanks. We're going to take a short break here, and, when we come back, we're going to discuss the makings of this ideological war. Who's to blame? Does religion engender hatred and violence even though it espouses love and peace? Or is it the only thing holding most of us together in a world clamoring for moral anarchy?

We'll be back in just a moment.

II.

Crilen looked up from his craggy perch and watched the orange twinmoon fade into the dawnlit eastern horizon. There was something in the orbit of these dual lunar satellites which troubled him, but he had no time for a scientific celestial analysis now.

To the west, the rising sun illuminated the rocky ledges and jagged spires, making their natural reddish hue luminesce like an artists' surreal embellishment. He did feel very much at home in the solitude of the planet's rough-hewn badlands, but then he reminded himself that this was a past world and there could be no logic in attempting to take up residence in its history. No logic at all, but that which was captivated by a solitary female.

Ten meters below, Panla was curled under a rocky shelf, asleep in the red sand. The spatter of Rabbel's dried blood still stained her white cheeks and chin. Her dark hair was eschew from their short fiery flight from the tavern. Her black leotard and slippers were coated and discolored by the windblown dust from the arid breezes which howled eerily over the sprawling landscape. It was a truly incongruous portrait: An elegant, deposed queen, displaced and severed from all the civilized comforts of her royal trappings. Abandoned to the random cruelties of raw nature like a rare indoor flower, uprooted from her fine pottery and flung carelessly onto a coarse plain of infertile dried clay.

Her mouth was opened slightly, revealing a glimpse of her front teeth; her brow was gnarled with tension, causing a vein to protrude from her forehead. Crilen had saved her life. But what would he do with his now marred sculpture of the spiritual feminine ideal?

His mind was awhirl. The more the scenario progressed, the less he understood any of it. He thought he had been sent to save Panla Jen's life. And he had. But he was still locked in this planet's past. His antlered alien guide had not drawn him back to their asteroid meeting place.

Meanwhile, the pristine life he had been sent to preserve had now taken a life. A female whose faith appeared to render her incapable, if not indifferent, to self-preservation, had premeditatedly executed a dubiously defensive, violent crime. A murder which ran contrary to everything her entire existence had stood for. Up to that moment she had appeared a perfect, albeit troubled, servant of God. Troubled and tried much like himself. Yet wiser, stronger, and nobler, so he had thought.

For Crilen, death on a galactic scale had always been a viable alternative in the preservation of the just. The violent eradication of evil was often a necessity for the survival and salvation of a world, even if it meant killing millions. But in some corners of the universe, he had found enlightened pockets of faith which commanded peace, love and even martyrdom in the name of the Lord. In these places, the murder of the soul was more reviled than the rendering of flesh and blood. They who lost their lives for the Lord's sake would find everlasting life in God's Kingdom. Killing, unsanctioned by Heaven, would save the flesh, but condemn the unrepentant soul for all eternity. Crilen was certain Panla's faith abided by the latter. But if that were true, then what had she done?

Panla exhaled a long peaceful breath as her closed-eyed countenance softened. She unfolded her limbs from their fetal lodgings and stretched outward with a light groan. She opened her eyes, blinking quickly to protect them from the blowing dust. Shielding her eyes, she cautiously rolled upright, then carefully opened them again. She glanced in every direction for anything that looked familiar, but became confused.

"Good morning," Crilen greeted her from his perch just above.

His vaguely familiar voice startled her as she quickly spun about and looked up toward him.

"Who….?" She wasn't sure she recognized him. "Mr. Len?"

"Yes." He smiled, stood and jumped down to her level.

Crilen extended his hand to her, but she stepped backward and gasped. She looked frightened by him.

"Panla, its me," he tried to reassure her, "it's just me."

"You were on fire." Panla's eyes widened with fear. "What's happened? What is this place? Am I…dead?"

"Relax." Crilen held up his hands. "You're all right. We're fine."

"That's not an answer." She continued to back away. "What's happened to your face? Your eyes? Your clothes?"

Crilen held up a hand and examined it. It was no longer black. His flesh had reverted back to the indigenous grey pigment of his home world. He examined his clothes and found his form-fitting burgundy tunic, black pants and boots had also returned. He ran the palm of his hand over his scalp and it was, again, bald and smooth. He touched the tips of his ears and they were pointed. Alas, he did not require a mirror to tell him his eyes were glowing the color of hot, molten rock.

"Panla, I need to explain to you…" he started.

Panla spun away from him, dropped to her knees, closed her eyes and prayed aloud in breathless recitation: "Oh, Heavenly Father, forgive me for the evil wickedness in my soul. I love thee and ne'er meant to defy thee or violate thy will. I have sinned to so base a measure that I know my soul may be lost, but I pray for those whom you charged me to nurture. Let not my wicked failure lead them to eternal death. Let not my…"

"Panla!" Crilen pulled her up by the arms and shook her. "Look at me. Feel me! You are not dead."

Panla slumped in his grasp and sobbed. "Lord demon, do not tempt me with your deceit. I will endure your ravages! I will defy your tortures! I will…!"

Crilen lifted her by the elbows and spun her around.

"Look at the sky!" he commanded. "To the east, do you see it? That's the setting twinmoon. Your twinmoon. The twinmoon of your planet!"

Crilen then kicked up the dirt in front of them.

"This is dirt!" he spoke firmly. "Dust! Dirt! Soil! The soil of your world! Do you feel it under your feet?"

He reached behind her head and pulled apart the extension of hair clipped to the back of her scalp.

"Here." He took her hand and slapped the bundle of hair into her palm. "This is PJ's hair. The hair you've clipped to your head a hundred times. Why would you still have a useless bundle of hair if you were on your eternal walk?"

Crilen turned her to face him again. He took his forefinger and raked it across the side of her face.

"And this" he held up the dark smear, "this is the blood of Rabbel Mennis. Rabbel Mennis, the man you killed last night!"

Panla stared at the dried bloody finger as her lips started to quiver. She stared, recoiling from it in horror. She turned away, collapsed to the ground again and loosed a sorrowful wail of anguish as she laid her face against the red soil and cried. It was not the response he had intended.

It reminded him of that tragic night at the hospital with Aami. She had just miscarried their baby. They could still have others, but at that moment, the death of their unborn child was the center of their crest-fallen, grief-stricken universe. It would have been the first grandchild. Their families were devastated. And, at the very bottom of misery's well, was his wife, seemingly crushed and broken beyond all consolation or repair. He had never seen her so disconsolate. So mournful. So lost.

In the days that followed, however, Aami gradually reclaimed her world through a remarkable strength and faith. Enough so that Crilen came to rely upon her strength to get him through their painful loss. But he never forgot her outpouring of sorrow that first evening. It ranked almost as painful a memory to him as the day she had died.

Here, however, there was a difference.

Aami lamented the loss of an unborn child under circumstances over which she had no control. Panla lamented the commission of a murder spun from her own ill-woven web of socio-political-religious machinations, by which she had become rooked and ensnared. Aami was an innocent victim of circumstance. Panla Jen, on the other hand, was a victim of her own maneuverings, manipulations and miscalculations. It seemed cruel to conclude she was the source of her own undoing, but regardless of her benevolent intentions, that was exactly the case. He was sorry for her; his heart ached at witnessing her suffer. But he did not grieve with her. This was not his wife.

He knelt beside Panla in the red dust and gently caressed her neck and shoulders. He struggled to find the words which would console her.

"Sometimes," Crilen spoke in a soothing voice, "sometimes a very good person has to do a horrible thing to protect something that's good. Sometimes wrong people, evil people, force us to choose actions we'd take back in an instant if we had the chance. Sometimes, when we combat evil, we can't help but get the stench of evil all over us. At frozen moments in time, you can't tell who's good or who's bad by their actions. It all begins to run together and we're left trying to understand if by using evil means to eradicate evil, do we serve the devil's bidding?"

The question seemed to touch an intellectual chord in her. Panla's tears quietly subsided as she slowly lifted her wet, weary face from the ground. She rose up on her hands and knees and hung her head. She stared into the earth as if she were attempting to draw some semblance of composure from the very ground.

He saw flashes of PJ and then the Deliveress struggle for control of her countenance. Then the First Lady tried to fight her way to the surface. But in the end, a very tired and exhausted woman with no facades closed her eyes and swallowed deeply.

"What happened to your face?" she asked very deliberately in a voice just above a whisper.

"This is what I look like," Crilen fumbled to explain. "This is who I really am."

"And what is that?" she droned wearily.

"A…being….not from your world." he answered.

"Of course," she responded sarcastically, "it was obvious. Staring me in the face the whole time. A being from another world. How silly of me. The bursting into flames should have been my first clue. And the flying was a dead giveaway. So, you're from the planet of the…fire people?"

"No," Crilen replied. "I was a scientist. A scientist who used himself as an experiment. It turned out to be a mistake. There's no one else like me."

"So there won't be an invasion?" She lifted her head with her eyes closed. "Not that this planet couldn't use a good invasion right about now."

"No," Crilen sensed his wife's satirical wit. "not today anyway."

"That's good." She wound her neck around slowly. "Then we'll hit you with the garden hose and that'll be the end of it. We can't have two rotten days in a row, can we? I mean, a murder is bad enough. But to have the whole planet invaded by aliens the very next day? That's positively uncivilized. Catastrophes need spacing, otherwise life gets just a little too depressing, don't you agree?"

"How can I not?" Crilen answered. "I've seen it happen."

Panla opened her eyes and looked up at him.

"What kind of experiment were you conducting anyway?" she frowned.

"Pyrogenics," he replied. "The controlled genetic fusion of charged atoms and plasma with biological life forms."

The corners of Panla's mouth twisted sideways. "Why?" she asked innocently.

"At the time," he gestured feebly. "it seemed like a pretty important thing to do. "

"Being on fire?"

"More like being fire, actually," he clarified. "Those days…those ambitions…..it's suddenly a lifetime ago. Research grants. Research patents. Notoriety in the journals. Breaking new ground no matter where the broken ground led me. It's kind of hard to explain now, but it was very important once upon a time."

"So what are you doing here?" She wiped the wet tears with the back of her hand. "What do you want with me?"

"I'm not sure I can tell you," Crilen answered.

"Still?" She glared up at him in disbelief. "After all that's happened? You're still not sure you can tell me?"

"I'm not sure I can tell you," Crilen rephrased, "because I'm not totally sure myself. I thought I was sent here to save your life. I've done that. But it hasn't been made clear to me what's supposed to happen next. The fact that I haven't been drawn away from here tells me that whatever I'm supposed to do isn't finished."

"Drawn?" Panla sighed with reservation. "Drawn where? Can't you just leave?"

"Not really," he replied. "You see, this isn't just another place for me. It's another time. I could fly from here to the other end of the galaxy and still be centuries from home. I have to wait until I'm drawn back to my own time, my own reality."

"So you're telling me you're from the future?" Panla sounded as though she were piecing together a dubious fiction. "Then you already know what happens here."

"No." he frowned. "I'm not from this planet's future. I have no idea what your history is...was...like. I've been sent to affect it, but I really don't know what I'm supposed to do other than to stay with you."

"Oh." Panla's shoulders slumped "Well, maybe you can be my jailer. Or maybe my executioner. There won't be much of me left to stay with once the truth is out. You should have let Leesla's men kill me. Then it would already be over."

"You don't believe that." Crilen knelt down and touched her shoulder. "I don't believe that."

"I killed Rabbel!" She raised her voice, "I murdered him in cold blood! You just said so yourself!"

"Not in cold blood," he responded. "You put an incredible amount of pressure on yourself. Literally, the pressure of an entire world. You allowed yourself to get backed into a corner by a dangerous man you hated, who threatened your life. And with every soul on the planet hanging in the balance, you did what you had to do. I understand. I've been there. I've killed more enemies of God and truth than I can count, and it never feels right. But when I look at the lives, the souls that were saved as a result, I've always known I've done the right thing."

Panla never met his eyes as he spoke. She remained slouched and forlorn, staring into the red soil in timeless reflection. A sad, smile lifted the sides of her mouth. Another tear fell from her eye.

"You really are a rather naive thing for someone who's been sent through time to save me." Her voice quaked. "I wish I were worthy of the nobility you try to cast in my name, but you've got it wrong. Rabbel…"

"He was a strong and powerful man," Crilen interrupted. "And he adored you. There was only one way for you to control him as long as you did. The time you spent alone with him had to be horrifying—emotionally, spiritually…"

"No! No! No!" She pounded her fist into the ground. "You're trying to make me out to be this inhuman paragon of virtue, Mr. Len. That's not who I am. Maybe your wife was, but I'm not!"

With both of her hands, she reached out and grabbed one of his.

"Don't you understand?" she pleaded. "I liked having it off with Rabbel! It wasn't ugly or repulsive or disgusting! I liked being with him! It was wrong, but I liked it!"

There was a moment of silence as Crilen's expression went blank. He had suspected what had taken place between Panla and Rabbel behind that office door, but he had held out hope that he had been wrong. Now, there it was from her own lips. Abruptly, he pushed her hands away, rose to his feet and turned his back to her.

"You lied," he murmured in a dry baritone. "You were in love with him."

"No!" Panla stood.

"No?" Crilen turned on her. "No? This enemy of God? This hater of God? This man you declared as your enemy? This man I watched you dance with and coddle and disappear behind closed doors with for hours on end? And all the while I stood by, believing your hypocritical rhetoric about fidelity and sacrifice and calling down friendly fire on yourself to destroy your enemies. You seethed at me for even suggesting that you were sleeping with him. You told a planetwide satellite audience that the only man you'd ever been with was your husband! How many lies…?"

"What was I supposed to say?" Panla cried out with her fists clenched. "To you? To the world? 'Yes, I'm the Deliveress of the Cathedral, and, yes, I love the Lord God, but I'm also having sex with the leader of the Break, who hates God, by the way. But never mind me. Don't do as I do. Do as I say. I'm only mortal flesh and blood, after all.' How would that sound? What would that make me then?"

"A woman who tells the truth," Crilen stated flatly.

"Oh, grow…up!" Panla shouted. "Virgin? Whore? Liar? Saint? Are those the only choices I have? Are those the only possibilities there are? Black? White? Good? Evil…?"

"Right. Wrong." Crilen cut her off. "The possibilities are endless. But in the end, there's right, and there's wrong. You've said it yourself. Or was that a lie, too?"

"It wasn't a lie," Panla conceded.

"Then why are you trying to justify having sex with Rabbel?" Crilen accused angrily.

"I'm not trying to justify it." Panla sighed, closing her eyes wearily. "I'm just trying to explain it."

Crilen folded his arms as a light blue flame illuminated his scalp and his eyes flashed a seething red. He wouldn't admit it, but she sounded more like his wife now, than she ever had.

Panla noticed his external alien mood change, but nothing alien seemed to matter.

"I was not in love with him," she continued. "I wasn't imprisoned by him either. I wasn't raped or forcibly taken by him. And, in my heart, I tried with every measure of my soul to resist him. I prayed so hard before the first night we wound up together. But I wanted it. I needed it. My entire life had been so bound up in rules and responsibilities and logic and wisdom...and godliness. You're right. I knew the difference between right and wrong. I've always known, as far back as I can remember. The order of everything always made sense and I was thankful for it. But there was a part of me that was dying inside. I'd lived a virtually perfect life in plain view of the entire world, but I was dying.

"I was, and still am, married to a man I loathed more and more every day we were together. I was his trophy in public and his stress receptacle in private. One of his many stress receptacles, I might add. Sex was grueling and cold. I hated it. He only cared about himself, you see. But I thought that since I loved God more than anything else, it didn't matter. What greater love could there possibly be?"

"None."

"True," she concurred, "there is none greater. But we are living creatures. Imperfect, living, sinning creatures. When I met Rabbel for the first time he was so full of power and rebellion. Every word he spoke ran contrary to everything I believed. But when he looked at me, spoke to me, there was this masculine gentleness I'd never experienced before. He could command a room full of vicious mercenaries, and then look at me with warmth and tenderness, and touch me the same way. I never knew how alone I had been my entire life until I was alone with him. We shared nothing important, but everything else in the world. We could laugh about simple things...dumb things...secular things. We made each other happy in the ways that matter least to God, but most to creatures of flesh and blood. It was all so wrong, Mr. Len. But it was something I needed more than anything at the time.

"But the problem was that he fell in love with someone I wasn't. He fell in love with PJ. He fell in love with the girl who wanted to knock down the Cathedral, but he wouldn't acknowledge the woman who loved God most of all. As long as we remained in our vacuous fantasy we were fine, but whenever we stepped into the real world, the problems were insurmountable. I could see it. He couldn't. In the end, he was willing to give up everything he believed in for me, but there wasn't any way for me to do the same. My world was built upon a rock. His was built upon the…"

"Sand." Crilen finished.

"Sand." Panla nodded sadly. "And so he became less and less patient with me. And my plan became more and more disjointed as a result. I needed the Break to bring down the Cathedral. But if he couldn't have me, then neither one of us was going to get what we wanted. I wanted a peaceful rebellion, but Rabbel believed in terrorism. Then the Lord Regent found out everything somehow. Rabbel threatened to kill me. Then he had the Lord Regent murdered, and I could tell that was only the beginning. Murder. Terrorism. Anarchy. That was never part of the plan. It was supposed to be an ideological war, not a bloody one. I didn't see any other way to stop things from getting worse. So I offered my soul to the devil to save the world. I was ready to die, but I was going take Rabbel Mennis with me. I thought….I thought that maybe both of our deaths would invalidate the Cathedral and the Break. Maybe some Godly compromise would be the result. A rough and ragged resolution that would lead to the reform I had hoped for."

"Murder, suicide…" Crilen's voice trailed off.

"I know." She sighed despondently. "It's quite a revelation. You spend your entire life thinking you stand for everything that's good and just in the world, and you wake up one day and find that you've done nothing but the devil's bidding."

"I've been there, too." Crilen swallowed.

"Then I'm glad you understand." She reached over and touched him on the shoulder. "It's not to late, you know."

"What do you mean?" Crilen grasped her fingers.

"Well, I think I've been a big enough disappointment to you by now," Panla whispered. "I'm a big phony disappointment to the whole bloody world. I don't even think God would take me at this point. Don't you think it's time for me to die?"

"What?" Crilen's face contorted with disbelief.

"Kill me, Mr. Len." She lowered her eyes. "It's the only answer. Then this will be over, and you can go home."

Crilen snatched her and shook her causing her head to snap backward. His eyes crackled with fire.

"I did not come here to kill you!" he snarled into her face. "And the Lord you profess to worship does not want you to quit on Him now!"

Crilen shook her again and shoved her to the ground.

Panla bounced on her backside. Her eyes widened. She sat up, too shocked to gather a response.

"Now where are we?" he growled angrily.

"I...don't know." She lowered her head, gingerly rubbing her rear end. "You're the one who brought us here."

"It's your planet!" He pointed in a circular motion. "Tell me where we are!"

Panla lifted her head as if it was the most difficult task in the world. She didn't need to follow his gestures. Now that she had gathered her faculties, she knew exactly where they were.

"The Thanaton Desert," she huffed wearily. "You flew us to the Thanaton Desert, fifty kilometers southwest of Rabbel's. I've never been here, but I recognize it."

"You need food and a bath and somewhere we can hide out for awhile," Crilen stated.

"I'm the Deliveress, not some master fugitive on the run!" Panla became indignant. "I have no idea where to..."

"Don't lie to me," he scowled. "PJ would have a pretty damn good idea where to hide out."

"PJ's dead." She hung her head.

"Then hold a séance!" Crilen raised his voice.

Her body tensed up as if she wanted to simply make herself disappear. Another swirl of dust blew across them and she shielded her eyes again. He wasn't going to kill her and they couldn't stay in the desert forever.

"What about Genna and Mr. Linnfeld?" Panla folded her lips. "Are they dead?"

"They're either very dead or very alive," Crilen answered bluntly. "Leesla will either kill them or use them. Either way, I'm not taking you back there and I'm not leaving you alone. Keeping you safe is why I'm here."

The unknown fate of her friends' lives seemed to weigh her down even farther. Everything was suddenly out of her control.

"I think I know a place," she finally conceded.

"Good." He nodded. "I can fly us there. Point the way."

She lowered her head again, but before she knew it, he was pulling her to her feet by the arms.

"God put us here for a reason." Crilen brushed the dust from her bangs. "Let Him use us."

A fiery flash kicked the red dust up into a spiral swirl and they departed in a bright golden streak which shot into the sky and arced toward the horizon.

III.

"Nothing hinders the media like true morality." Yolo smiled broadly. "False morality is a wonderful implement. It enables every simpering twit to declare him or herself just, no matter how base or absurd the ideal. Empty circular debates erupt with a mad frenzy. And media sales explode as the amoral populous spins round and round about, chasing its own wagging tail like a flea-bitten cur.

"But true morality…God's morality…it's so straight and clean and narrow. It elicits a dull, soothing calm which simply doesn't translate into sales or ratings. Fear, fascination and vice feed the media maw. With the Cathedral out of the way, the insentient masses will have only themselves to rely upon. And we will show them how to do it. Ratings will soar and so too shall the profits. After all, the easiest way to purchase a man's soul is to give him everything he prays for, even if, in the end, it destroys him. Of course, self-destruction is none of our concern. Self-destruction is a matter of free choice. And choice transcends any notions of right or wrong."

Mr. Pont could feel the pressure twisting in his neck. The big man was feeling his oats this morning, and he could sense that the worst was yet to come. It was days like this that no one had ever warned him about when he chose to major in journalism some twenty-odd twinmoons ago. Days when he would be sitting at the left hand of power, repulsed by everything it stood for.

"You're talking as if someone dropped a warhead on the Bius Basilica and blasted it to smithereens," Mr. Pont spoke, fighting to curb his disgust. "The last time I checked, the Lord Regent was dead, but the building and everything it stands for was still intact."

Yolo closed his eyes and exhaled. His girth expanded and contracted. He took a deep drag from his giant cigar and released a stinking thick cloud of foul red smoke.

"Is it?" The large man smiled knowingly.

"Yes, it, is." Mr. Pont asserted.

"And where is our dear Deliveress today?" Yolo's body rocked with a slight chuckle.

"Safe, I'm sure." Mr. Pont licked his lips nervously. "She's not dead. I know she's not dead."

"I never suggested that she was." Yolo's heavy brows lifted. "But I'm willing to wager that death might be preferable to her at this juncture. In fact, suicide may well yet be an option. And, as for the Cathedral, it is a pile of rubble. You just can't see it."

"Well I can't wait until the Deliveress shows up safe and sound." Mr. Pont became testy. "Then you'll see what's lying in rubble."

"Hmh!" Yolo chuckled. "Well, I certainly agree with you there. I can't wait for our dear queen hag to surface, either. Then we will see exactly who and what lies in rubble for certain."

Mr. Pont could not contain himself from growing visibly annoyed.

"Oh, come now, Mr. Pont," Yolo teased, "let's not resort to childish pouting. It's unbecoming to a man of your twinmoons. And it's not as if you've lost at some contest. There is no competition between you and I. You're a servant in my employ. A media menial who's unqualified opinions are published to serve a higher purpose: Mine. Jostling yourself about as if we were combatants is a waste of good common sense on your part. Settle back and collect your wages. I'm not going to fire you. You're far too valuable a source of amusement for me to waste the effort. Besides, life is rather short, isn't it? You mustn't dwell fiendishly on issues you haven't the power to affect."

The intercom chime on Yolo's desk jingled.

Mr. Pont shifted his weight but could not muster the courage to stand up and storm out.

"Mr. Nil?" Yolo spoke to the intercom.

"She's here, sir." Mr. Nil's obsequious enthusiasm beamed through his voice.

"Excellent." Yolo's waggling jowls bowed with a broad smile. "Has she been waiting long?"

"An hour and a half longer than you promised," Mr. Nil answered with a whisper.

"Splendid." Yolo's ponderous frame rocked with a chuckle. "Splendid. Show her in."

Mr. Pont was completely lost as to what "her" could make Yolo so giddy.

The giant wooden doors slowly drew open. A sturdy, tall young woman with a bright white face, freckles and shoulder-length, strawberry-orange hair entered the room. Her white blouse was neatly pressed. Her woolen skirt hung well below her knees. Her brown tie-up shoes made her look every bit the Cathedral school teacher she had once been.

"Ms. Feebie Bleik," Mr. Nil handled the introduction, "I'd like you to meet Mr. Pont and the great Mr. Yolo Pigue."

"Pleased to meet you." Feebie lowered her eyes and spoke just above a whisper as she extended her hand.

Yolo took her fingers and held them with gentlemanly aplomb.

"Please sit." Yolo gestured her toward a large ivory chair with burgundy velvet cushions.

Mr. Pont watched the nervous young woman sit daintily upon the seat as if it might jump up and bite her.

"Something to drink?" Yolo smiled an ingenuously hideous smile.

"No, thank you." Feebie tugged at the hem of her skirt.

"Very well." Yolo ponderously maneuvered back to his desk and wedged himself into his large leather chair.

"So, have we met before?" Yolo queried, mendaciously.

"Not exactly." Feebie tried to raise the volume in her quaking voice. "I was here a couple of days ago with Mrs. Tem. You came by the waiting room before the interview, but we didn't exactly meet."

"I see." Yolo doused his smoldering cigar in his marble ashtray. "So what brings you back here today?"

"Well," Feebie tried to compose herself, but felt tears welling in her eyes, "I just felt…"

"It's alright, dear." Yolo gestured for Mr. Pont to hand her a handkerchief.

Feebie took the cloth and wiped under her eyes, then rubbed across her nose. She stared into space for a moment, still wondering whether she was doing the right thing.

"You were saying?" Yolo prompted her.

Feebie looked up and around at the stern faces of Mr. Nil, Mr. Pont and Yolo Pigue. They glared like salivating beasts eyeing their cornered prey. There was nothing in this room she could trust, but there hadn't been much she'd been comfortable with for some time, anyway. She prayed that God would now be her guide.

"I just want to tell the truth." Feebie finally threw her hands out with exasperation. "I just want everyone to know the truth…about everything. The lies have been such a burden. I was brought up to believe that the 'truth shall set you free'. Well that's what I've come to do: Set myself, and everyone else, free. It's time for God's truth. That's all that matters now. God's truth."

Yolo met her eyes and nodded in the affirmative.

"Amen, young lady." Yolo licked his lips rapaciously, "Amen."

IV.

"Are you sure we have the right address?" Crilen warily inspected the squalid urban blight surrounding them.

Compared to the four-way intersection at which they stood, Rabbel's tavern had been located in the most glitzy sector of a teeming metropolis. Crumbling stone storefronts with dirty, smeared windows lined the boulevards. Weeds sprung from every uneven cracked concrete crevice, and the curbs and walkways were littered with crushed tin and filthy paper garbage.

Loud, pounding music throbbed from open upstairs apartments and rickety cruising transports packed with lean wild youths. A bedraggled middle-aged shopkeeper stood under the ragged canopy of his liquor market, the deep lines in his wrinkled white face castigating the missing regulars who hadn't shown up for their daily refill. Meanwhile, two slovenly buxom females in scant, thin dresses cackled loudly, waving, jiggling and cursing at familiar passersby.

Another disheveled man clung to a lamppost as he stared angrily into space, a thin herbal cigarette wagging between his tight chapped lips. He pinched the cigarette from his mouth momentarily, and ejected a bright green clot of saliva from his left nostril, stinging the hind of a rodent scampering in the gutter beneath his feet.

"Yep." Panla sighed without reservation. "This is the place."

Out of nowhere, three shirtless teens pushed between Crilen and Panla on a dead run. The one in the lead tried to hop over a corner bench, but flipped over the back of it and landed face first onto the concrete curb with a sickening smack. His dark face spewed a pool of blood into the street. In another instant, the two pursuers were on top of him. One snapped the silver chain from around his neck as he bled. The other rummaged through their fallen quarry's pants pockets, then pulled off his shoes and tucked them under his arm. Together, the triumphant pair of mugging scavengers loped away from the splattered barefoot victim, cackling and screeching at one another in resplendent victory.

Crilen's fist ignited with the concussive sound of an industrial torch.

"Mr. Len," Panla said quietly, "we were looking for somewhere to hide. Remember?"

Crilen opened his flaming hand at his side, and the fire disintegrated into twirling plumes of smoke.

"We should help the boy." Crilen simmered.

"We should." Panla touched his shoulder. "But if we try to help every boy, girl, man and woman who gets pummeled here tonight, we might as well set up shop until the policers hand us over to the government."

Crilen frowned at the sight of the shoeless, semi-conscious boy gurgling and writhing in a pool of his own blood. The shopkeeper and the two females came across the street to tend to him. The shopkeeper gently kicked the youth over onto his back with his foot. The two women dabbed his gashed, swelling face with a white towel.

"He'll be all right." Panla pushed against Crilen's tensed back. "Come."

Panla moved quickly along the uneven walkway with the same purposeful march he remembered from when she had powered into her busy itinerary as First Lady two days ago. Her strides were assertive and urgent. She appeared to know precisely where she was going, but it was also clear she did not want to remain on these open, mean streets any longer than she needed to.

They approached a small gathering of males standing outside a storefront, laughing, drinking and cursing. One large man eyed her hungrily until he met Crilen's threatening alien scowl following closely behind her.

"Damn, man," the large white male spoke, holding up his bottle disarmingly, "relax, brotha', or whatever you is."

Crilen snapped off the eye contact as Panla turned sharply and skipped cautiously through a thickly weeded alley littered with twisted metal junk.

"I thought you knew where you were going." Crilen became concerned as he hopped, less gracefully than she, over the discarded wreckage.

Panla did not answer.

They reached the end of the alley and found themselves standing in a clearing of tall wild grass. A hundred meters in the distance stood a sagging three-story sandstone structure which looked as if it had been weathered by a thousand twin-moons of natural elements.

The building's stones were bleached sandy brown by the sun and worn down to rounded edges by all manner of precipitation. Still, this urban edifice of indeterminate age appeared solid and sturdy enough to withstand another millennium if it had to.

"Finally." Panla breathed a heavy sigh of relief.

She hopped and danced through the tangled grassy field. Crilen wanted to fly them both to the front stairs, but realized it would only draw attention.

She seemed to know where every uneven hill and hole laid beneath the grass as she gracefully bounded from side to side with perfect balance. Crilen tripped and stumbled several times, turning a foot, then an ankle. The pain was less of an issue than his clumsy embarrassment.

"Hmh." Panla turned and looked at him as she reached the base of the stony staircase. "I had you pegged for the rugged, outdoor type. Oh well."

Crilen frowned.

"I'm very outdoor." He pointed skyward with a broad circular motion. "I'm from outer space, remember? But I don't think hiking through abandoned, lumpy, urban underbrush counts."

Panla smiled in earnest for the first time in days. Not a smile of sad irony or a forced smile for some public audience. This was an easy unguarded smile. Even with Rabbel's blood still staining her cheeks, she bore a deeper resemblance to the warm, affable Aami he had loved than the PJ he had met in Rabbel's tavern.

However, it was as if she could read his thoughts as their eyes locked. She abruptly chased the smile back inside of herself, turned away and hurried up the cracked and broken cement stairs.

Crilen became frustrated with himself for remaining so adolescently smitten. His rational mind repeatedly warned him against affection for Panla, as had Panla herself. But "this is how you interpret her," his alien facilitator had told him. He wished that he could interpret her differently so that he could concentrate more clearly on his assignment. An assignment that promised to reunite him with his real wife through some time-space-continuum magic conjured by the alien from the asteroid. Yet there was something about Panla Jen that made her seamlessly inseparable from his memories and visions of Aami. Unfortunately, unraveling the complexity of this reincarnation required more introspection than he had time for.

He joined Panla at the top of the stairs and immediately heard the echo of a different type of spirited music emanating from within. The rhythm was relentless and forceful. There was a steady beat of clapping and stomping. The voices were raw and untrained, but soaring through unified chords with a power and precision that was stirring.

As if drawn in by some gravitational force, Panla slowly entered the vestibule and walked reverently into the illuminated sanctuary. Crilen scanned the open field and then the sky to make sure no one had pursued them, then he followed Panla into the building.

The sanctuary was a circular three-story cavern. It was starkly decorated with only a miniature wooden spire of the Chry Temple suspended above the choir-stand behind the pulpit. The ceiling and walls were colored white with blackened wooden trusses girding them in a succession of tall arches. The shuttered rectangular windows, five meters tall, swung on rusted hinges. The navy floor carpeting was worn through to the wooden boards. The sparsely populated pews were also wooden and outlined through their dark finish by smoothly worn rounded edges.

In the pulpit was a thin metal podium that would have looked more appropriate at the elbow of a string musician. Three males sat in tall high-back chairs, in varied degrees of absorption, nodding in cadence to the music churning and swirling all around them.

Behind the three males, in the choir-stand, was a collection of the very old and the very young, with only a smattering of representatives from a middle generation. The faces were black and white, male and female, all swaying and singing in a wave of glorious synergy.

Panla closed her eyes, spread her arms wide and laid her head back. Crilen braced himself to catch her, certain she would fall backwards at any moment. But she never did. She simply stood, arms stretched to Heaven as if the waves of music were permeating and cleansing every molecule of her body.

Crilen also found the music stirring. The energy surging through this house of worship was closer to his experiences from his homeworld than anything he had witnessed on this planet thus far. It reminded him of the days in his childhood when his father would drag him to worship, and he couldn't wait until all the noise had ended. So much preaching had been little more than a tiresome intrusion on his young imagination. An obstacle to the endless, alluring possibilities of the cosmos. But when he thought of this particular aspect of his impetuous youth now, he was embarrassed by his obstinate ignorance. There had been so much his father wanted to teach him about the nurture of his soul. So much about God and Heaven his father held dearest. But the arithmetic of secular logic and science always separated them. And the two stubborn males never reconciled, even at the very end.

The choir's song finally dove and swooped through the pews, soaring to an immaculate conclusion. As the echo of the last note faded, Panla lowered her arms, smiled broadly and led the smattering of applause from the audience.

A tall, black, lanky man with a head of neatly cropped white hair stood up from the pulpit and looked toward the back of the sanctuary. A big smile jumped across his face as he recognized Panla standing in the aisle. She rose up on her toes and waved back to him like a spunky adolescent girl.

The tall man moved slowly toward the podium and shuffled his notes.

"We thank all of you who could make it to our Epi-Solemnday service this morning." He spoke in a deep rich baritone. "I know that some of us believe that

Solemnday is the only day we're supposed to think about God, and that all the rest of time is time for us. But I know, and hope you know, that there is no time for us. That is, all of our time is God's time. And even though you may not be with Him all week, He is certainly there with you. You may not want to acknowledge Him. You may not want to obey Him. But when you disobey Him, you just better realize that He's still right there with you all the time. And when you come to Cathedral on Solemnday with your chest puffed out, holding the hands of your family and smiling at all your friends, they may not know where you've been and what you've been up to all week….and I won't know…but you better believe that God knows. So the pretense is meaningless. Take that fake smile off your face. Take the puff out of your chest. Bow your head as low as it will go, and pray, because you need to. We all need to. He knows what you've done and He knows where you've been every minute of every day from the moment you were born. So you just better pray."

Panla quietly slid into the last row of benches, never moving her eyes from the speaker. Crilen moved in next to her, scrutinizing the sparse crowd for potential danger.

"I want to take a little time this morning and talk to you about worship. I know some of you are saying that I don't talk about anything else. But I'm going to talk to you a little differently this time. Instead of talking to you about worshipping God as he asks us to worship Him, I'm going to talk to you about worshipping God as we choose to worship Him.

"You see, in the Text, God is very clear about how He wants us to receive Him. He is very clear about how He wants us to obey Him. He is unyielding in the precise way in which He asks us to love Him because, after all, He has always loved us from the very beginning.

"But there is another type of worship out there by those of you who claim to be of the faith. And it has nothing to do with the Text. It has nothing to do with what God wants. Instead, it has everything to do with what *you think you want*. I call this, mortal worship.

"Mortal worship is the attempt by mortals to worship God in a way that is convenient for them. Forget about what God wants. Forget about what God says. Forget that you are only a tiny speck of dust in God's grand universe. To the mortal worshipper, your life isn't about God. Instead, it's about you and what you think you want from Him.

"Some of you believe that because you enjoy certain things, then God must also be pleased by your secular indulgences. You're having sex with someone who makes you feel good, and I'm not talking about your spouse. Or you enjoy getting drunk or getting high or cursing other people or taking advantage of other people or the pursuit of social status or doing whatever it is in life that makes you feel good…irrespective of what your conscience fears is displeasing to our Lord in Heaven. You say: If God says I can't have this thing or I can't do that thing, then God isn't God and He's not with me because He won't let me be happy the way I interpret happiness, even if your happiness is built on a tower of sin! Well I have to tell you that He is with you, but it's you who is not with Him. What you've done is relegate what little faith you have to that hellbound cliché that 'If this is wrong, I don't want to be right.' You may not admit it, even to yourself, but that's where you are. You'd rather be wrong and pretend that what you do is condoned by God through your fictional interpretation of scriptures you probably haven't even read. You'd rather let sin run rampant through your life and pretend that you're right with God than to offer yourself up to the truth of our loving Lord in Heaven.

"There are those of you who come to God only because you believe that if you mouth enough prayers and songs, go through the motions of charity and fellowship with no love in your heart, then the Lord will eventually reward you with what you think you need. Note: I said, 'Reward you with what you think you need.' He's going to give you that new job or that new home or that new vehicle or that new relationship you've been staying up at night dreaming about.

"First, let me make the observation that some of you actually have the audacity to believe that you know what you need. In fact, since you obviously don't believe that the creator of all things has an ounce of sense with respect to your life, you believe you have to tell Him what you need. Some of you even demand that He give you what you…think you need. And if you don't get what you…think you need…then you decide that God's against you or that you haven't worked hard enough or that you just don't have good luck.

"Well, my friends, you've got to realize that you can't fool God by going through the motions to earn what it is you think you need. God isn't your mother or father asking you to take out the garbage or clean up your room or do your homework for an allowance. You can do the will of your parents with ulterior motives or hard feelings and they may not even know or care so long as you do as you're told. But God cares much more about what's written on your heart. If you go through the motions for God, you're wasting your time. All those hours of charity work mean nothing to God if it wasn't done out of love for your Heavenly Father. He knows when you're just going through the motions, so don't bother. Stay home. Take an afternoon nap. Going through the motions will not get you any closer to God or Heaven or…what you think you need.

"And, before you turn your back on God because he won't give you what you think you need, let's talk about what you think you need for a moment. I can look back on my life and think of more than a dozen times in my life where I knew I wanted or needed something that was going to make my world a happier place. If only I could have it or her. And when I didn't get that thing or that woman, I felt shorted or jilted or forsaken. But time always orchestrates a clearer perspective. And looking back, I think of all the blessings I would have missed if God had given me what I thought I needed instead of what He knew I needed. If God had answered my prayers when I was twenty, I'd have been married to that beautiful actress on satellite with the bad drug habit. I saw her on some talk show the other day and she's not even beautiful anymore and she's still addled with drugs, sleeping with passing acquaintances and tragically unsaved. What did I know about what I wanted? I praise God that He gives me what He knows I need instead of what I think I need, because if He didn't, my life would be a mess. He's always been a little wiser than any of us. Amen. The Text says 'He knows what you have need of before you ask Him'. So I don't ask Him for anything anymore except what He wants for me.

"If your relationship with God is built on what you think you want, I beg you to reconsider. He was here before we were born and will be here long after we're gone. He knows us better than we know ourselves. He loves us better than we love ourselves. We need to trust Him...only trust Him...every day of our lives.

"Now, some of you believe that if you develop a good relationship with God, that means you should never have to suffer. That's more of that scriptural fiction people make up in their heads. The Text, in fact, tells us that we are likely to suffer in this life. But thankfully, the Text also tells us how to survive and grow from our suffering through faith. Again, none of us think that we need to suffer. But if God allows us to suffer, we should never betray our faith in His wisdom. The salvation of our souls depends on it. If the devil should offer you peace, prosperity and comfort all the days of your life and God would only offer you pain, suffering and affliction in this world, to whom should you commit your immortal soul?"

"Amen," Panla whispered solemnly.

"Finally, within the Cathedral structure, there are those of you who worship your mortal leadership instead of your Father in Heaven. You worship the Deliverer. You worship the Regent. You worship the Churchlord. You worship the leader of your Text study group. You worship the soloist in the choir. You may even worship your friend, relative or spouse who brought you into Cathedral in the first place. This is understandable since the Cathedral itself has obscured our relationship with God through rituals and doctrine and patronage to the egocentric secular Cathedral hierarchy. Unfortunately, if any of these flawed mortal persons should fail or fall before your eyes, then, too, does your faith. The element of faith which is most difficult for many of us is to effectively worship that which is unseen instead of our brothers and sisters we can touch and feel. Deep down, some of us wonder if God really is out there, or if we're just casting our breath up into the dead winds of the universe. As a result, we latch on to someone whom we make the hub of our faith. Unfortunately, we mortals are all bound to sin because it is in our self-serving natures to do so. So what happens if your "hub" or Text study leader gets arrested for public drunkenness? What happens if your Churchlord, and this is just hypothetical, friends, gets caught having an affair with an underage girl? What happens if the Deliverancy is cast into the midst of some hideous scandal? Do we lose our faith in God because of the natural failings and imperfections of others? Or do we pick up a Text, actually read it sometime, and build our faith in direct line with our Lord and savior so that no single person's failure can knock us off our course to God's Heavenly throne?"

Crilen continued to search the faces of the parishioners on hand. Recollection of the bombing incident at the YBS studios two days ago made him wary. He did not want a repeat performance of a zealot or martyr getting close to Panla.

As his gaze ran up one wall, across the pulpit, up into the balconies and down again, he noticed Panla nodding in affirmation with large tears rolling from her tightly closed eyes. Her fingers clutched the back of the bench in front of her. He could see the recrimination for her plan gone awry flooding through her again with a grand measure of pain and anguish.

Crilen gently touched the nape of her neck and ran the palm of his hand down her back to comfort her.

Another five minutes passed and the sermon came to a close. Panla lifted her head, wiped away her tears and smiled to Crilen, politely touching his hand graciously for his consolation.

"These people show a lot of energy," Crilen observed. "But they don't appear to be very sophisticated in their faith."

"But they love God, Mr. Len," Panla spoke in a choked whisper. "To the Lord in Heaven, those who are wise in the ways of the world are made fools. And those who are fools in the world, but rich in their faith, are as the wisest in the universe. There's a misnomer that those who are the most well-schooled in the Text and its academic interpretations have the best relationship with God simply because they know so much. What rubbish. Look at these people…naked, innocent, showered in Heaven's light. Look at me…covered in the blood of my murder victim. In the end, my knowledge didn't do me an ounce of good. Where was my faith, Mr. Len?"

The tall dark man in the pulpit stepped down and slowly made his way up the aisle, smiling and shaking hands as he went along. He stopped at the last row of benches and greeted Panla with a broad, ageless smile.

"Panla Jen!" He took her by the shoulders, then hugged her like a father. "Lord almighty, look at you!"

"Hello, Father Rouan." She smiled humbly and lowered her eyes. "I've brought a friend along. This is Mr. Len, my security lead up north."

"God Bless you, Mr. Len." Father Rouan smiled broadly, with a firm handshake. "Wonderful to meet you."

The man made nothing of Crilen's alien appearance.

"Mr. Len, Panla's father was my best friend in grade school." He looked at her proudly. "We knew she'd go far. We just didn't know all the blessings the Lord had in store for her."

Panla lowered her eyes.

"So what brings you back here today?" the tall elderly man asked. "Did they finally give you some vacation?"

"No," Panla said softly. "As you can see, I'm not exactly dressed for vacation. There's been some trouble. Big trouble. We need a place to stay until we can sort things out."

"Panla, you're my daughter, you know that." Father Rouan was warm and firm. "This is your home. And if there's trouble you and I can't figure out, we'll just give it to the Lord and let Him sort it out while we get you cleaned up and find something to eat."

"Thank you." Panla collapsed into his chest with a big hug. "Thank you so much. But I think you need to hear what's happened before you decide to take us in."

"I don't need to know." Father Rouan smiled earnestly. "But if you need to tell me, I'll listen."

A tear fell along the side of her nose as she looked up into his assuring gaze.

"I did all I could, and it wasn't enough." Her voice choked. "I used everything I knew and it still went wrong. I tried so hard…"

Father Rouan rubbed her shoulders as if calming a despondent child who had scraped her knee on a playground.

"Well, then, I guess it's time to let God do all He can do," he said tenderly. "That's usually the best way to solve things, isn't it?"

Panla looked at Crilen, signifying she needed time alone with Father Rouan. She and the tall elderly man held their embrace and walked together toward the front of the sanctuary for some privacy.

Nothing had changed outside of these walls since their arrival, but somehow, Crilen felt just a little better as he watched Panla abandon her pride and inner strength in exchange for a greater power which had been standing alongside of her before the day she had been born.

V.

"Leethla, it's a bad idea." The skinny, androgynous male quaked and lisped.

Leesla uncoiled her long angular frame from her stool. She had converted one of the tavern's bathrooms into a makeshift office. Rabbel's office, burned and exposed to the street by Crilen's fiery blast, had to be sealed with curtains of plastic. A barstool now served as her seat of power. A covered sink served as her desk. The wall urinals were covered with piles of papers and notes salvaged from Rabbel's melted cabinets.

Leesla's swollen mouth, where Rabbel had punched her, contorted with rage. The bald, burned side of her scalp, where Crilen had singed away her wild hair, glistened in the torchlight. Her dark clothing was still smeared with blood from the burial of her lord and liege, who had been shot dead in the dark hours of the morning. Her dreams shot dead by that vile arrogant queen from the north whom she had always hated so intensely.

Needless to say, she'd had a very bad night. As Leesla attempted to salvage what remained of the Break, the last thing she was in the mood for was contradiction. Her eyes widened with fury, beaming like golden lanterns from her black, sweaty face.

"You contemptible quivering cock-queen!" she hissed through her bloody teeth as her clipped voice echoed against the porcelain tile ceiling. "You are going to stand there and contradict me? I...I...fucking bled for you last night! Rabbel Mennis died for you last night! Died for you, so that you can stand there in lipstick and high-heeled shoes dreaming about sucking another male's ugly misshapened penis, and contradict me?"

Leesla reached into the front of her pants, drew a weapon and shot him in the leg.

He toppled to the floor with a loud yelp.

Leesla walked over to him and glared as he tried to hold in the blood gushing from his wound with his jeweled fingers.

"Rabbel Mennis is dead, but semen-sucking leeches like you live on!" she cursed and shot him again.

"You leech...faggot....fuck!" Leesla shot him once, twice, three more times before the lavatory/office door burst open and three armed men entered with their weapons drawn.

The men stood in stunned silence, staring at the bloody, dying, wheezing carcass on the floor.

"That's right!" Leesla slapped the face of one of the men. "This isn't an office! It's a fucking execution toilet! Get this slutty male whore out of my sight! And anyone else who wants to argue can argue with this!"

She fired another round into the ceiling. A clump of plaster fell and knocked out the torch on the wall. It was suddenly dark.

"And get me some fucking light!" She fired her weapon again. The three burly men scampered out of the dark lavatory/office, carrying the bloody corpse of her upstart advisor.

"What a shame. He was so pretty," Linnfeld spoke sarcastically to the armed men as they hustled past. "Perhaps the lady requires a nap?"

"Shhh!" Genna pulled on the roped bonds which joined their chairs together. "She shot our driver. Now she's killing her lieutenants. That doesn't give your smart mouth very long odds!"

"Like I care," Linnfeld scowled at the tavern walls.

"Maybe you don't, but I do," Genna whispered. "I want to live."

"Live or die, I could use a good night's sleep," Linnfeld sighed carelessly.

Leesla stormed out of her "office", her head and shoulders dusted with white fragments of plaster. She was still holding the weapon whose barrel was smoking from rapid discharges. She angrily approached Linnfeld and stopped directly in front of him. Her dark, angular, features leered perniciously into his round white face.

"You." She scowled intensely. "You were that goddamned PJ's valet?"

"Valet?" Linnfeld's tired features found new life. "I don't know the first thing about pressing and folding female outer garments. And I couldn't match a pair of female shoes if they came in one size and two colors. I may have opened a door or two for the lady, but I never picked lint. I was her lead attendant, not her hand maid."

"You have a big mouth," Leesla seethed. "Maybe you'd like another one on the back of your head."

"No, thank you." Linnfeld frowned. "I'm watching my weight. I can barely control my consumptive urges with the one."

A psychotic rage flickered across the tall woman's features as she lifted her weapon.

"Is there something we can help you with?" Genna intervened, sensing her back was in the line of fire.

Leesla's attention suddenly altered.

"What did you say?" She slowly stalked around the pair of chairs and leaned her face next to Genna's.

"I....I just thought that you might want something from us?" Genna's voice quaked nervously.

"Hmm." Leesla's expression tightened like a black latex mask. "Suddenly you are so accommodating. Nothing like the loud, brash whelp who thought she knew so much about me last night."

"Oh. I'm....I'm sorry about that." Genna's heart pounded heavily in her chest.

"Don't be sorry." Leesla grinned a horrible grin through her swollen, scabbed lips. "I actually thought it was very sexy."

Leesla clutched Genna by the head with her long fingers and pressed their mouths together with a prolonged, suffocating, drooling kiss. She pressed the warm barrel of her weapon between Genna's legs. She snatched Genna by the hair and snarled into her face.

"You wanted to know where my girlfriend, is?" Leesla's eyes bulged wildly. "Why...she's right here! She's you! When this is all over, you are going to be my new little heifer. I'm going to be your big bad daddy! And you're going to like it. When I'm done with you, you'll have to make yourself like it. You'll be begging your god to make you like it. Because I'm never...going...to go away. Understand?"

"I believe you were going to ask me something," Linnfeld interceded.

"How sweet." Leesla smirked as she moved away from Genna. "The fat little valet, making a rescue. Too bad you won't always be there for her, hmm?"

Leesla stood straight and slowly stalked back around to the front of Linnfeld's chair.

"But for now, I do need your help. I need to contact the media directly. Rabbel was good at planting stories and leaflets, but I want to go directly to the source with our story. I want the world to know what's been done to their Break movement. And I want them to know whose hands are covered in the great Rabbel Mennis's fallen blood!"

Linnfeld could not conceal his contempt for the tall angular woman and her seething secular convictions. He really didn't care what happened to himself; life had been good and he knew the Lord was waiting. Unfortunately, he couldn't say or do everything he wanted to because he knew his actions would endanger Genna's life. He took consolation in the knowledge that if he gave Leesla everything she asked for, the downfall of the Break would not be far behind.

Rabbel had played the media shrewdly, releasing calculated statements and performing acts of vandalism or terrorism couched in arguable justifications. He never told anyone what to think or what to believe. He simply offered enough questions for people in doubt of their faith and discontented with the Cathedral to waiver toward something more tangible and immediately gratifying.

Leesla, on the other hand, was a volcano of amoral venom on the verge of indiscriminate eruption. No logic. No reason. No direction, other than to defecate her personal pain and convictions onto as wide an audience as her imagination could conjure. In the hands of Rabbel and PJ, the Break was a delicately dangerous piece of machinery, poised to topple the world's most powerful institution. In the hands of Leesla, the Break was rapidly becoming little more than a haphazard implosion destined to destroy nothing other than itself.

Linnfeld couldn't wait to see it.

"Well," the flash in Linnfeld's eyes betrayed an otherwise, calm demeanor, "I used to make all of the media arrangements for Mrs. Tem, the Deliveress. Under the extraordinary circumstances in which we find ourselves, I'm certain my contact at the YBS studios should be able to facilitate the audience you're looking for rather quickly."

Leesla tried to read the treachery in his immediate cooperation, but it was concealed by her own headstrong incompetence, the last place she would ever think to look.

"All right," she responded uneasily. "You make your call. But we will be watching and listening to every word you speak. At the first sign of signals or betrayal, my new lover will be the first one to die. And then I will slit your throat."

Linnfeld smiled with absurd affability. "Of course."

Leesla wanted to kill him immediately for his inscrutable mocking expression, but she would wait until after her message was dispatched to the waiting world.

VI.

Father Rouan's cathedral was secure, but as the afternoon wore on, Crilen wondered if he could say the same for Panla herself. It hadn't been seven hours since she'd asked him to execute her for her treason, infidelity and the murder of Rabbel Mennis. And though she appeared to have found some comfort in the asylum of Father Rouan's house of worship, she was still emotionally distressed. Suicide seemed improbable, but he'd learned that anything remained possible with Panla Jen, her love of the Lord notwithstanding.

Crilen trudged up the creaking wooden stairs of the cathedral's boarding wing. The antiquated building was fairly well maintained in that it was very clean, but natural wear was evident on every wood and plaster surface. The smell of old curtains and carpeting was pungent, and the loosened balustrade felt as if it would collapse under the palm of his hand. He reminded himself not to ignite his flames in this old structure; the insides might roar to ashes before the sound of the first alarm.

A skinny, pallid old man greeted Crilen at the top of the stairs. He was as thin and wispy as a translucent ghost. He wreaked of alcohol, but nodded cordially.

"God Bless you, son." the old man said, clutching his tattered and wrinkled version of the Text.

"God Bless you," Crilen returned.

The old man smiled and nodded as he gingerly took the first stair of his descent. His tired body moved as if it had been battered by centuries of harsh and difficult living, but something in the way he held up his head and smiled indicated that all wounds would be healed.

Crilen turned and started down the narrow hallway.

"Fourth door from the window," he remembered. For whatever reason, he was nervous. He hoped he would find her on more emotionally stable footing. They had been through so much already. Yet he sensed that the most difficult challenges were still ahead of them and she would have to be steady to survive the socio-political mines.

The door was cracked open. He didn't know whether to knock, enter or speak.

"May I come in?" he called through the warped wooden door.

"Yes!" a crisp female voice answered.

Crilen entered the tiny bedroom and was taken aback by yet another seemingly miraculous Panla Jen transformation. She stood before him barefoot, wearing a long plain white gown fitted loosely about her shoulders. Her bright smiling face was washed clean of Rabbel's blood. Her short dark hair was still wet and swept back away from her face except for a curled tuft feathered over her forehead. She appeared immaculately refreshed with all the dark trappings of PJ figuratively tossed kilometers behind her. The only things that belied her sudden rebirth were the puffed circles under her large brown eyes, which were still deeply troubled by all that had transpired the night before.

"Is there something the matter?" Panla asked, conjuring a playful smile. "You can't see through this, can you?"

"No." Crilen tried not to stare through the garment. "It's just that my wife..."

"Owned a hideous, ill-fitting frock just like this one and it was your favorite, right?" she finished the thought for him.

"Not exactly," Crilen corrected her. "Aami had a habit of getting into my things when a certain mood struck her. The last night we were together, she was wearing one of my lab shirts. Sorry to bring her up again."

Panla tossed her arms at her sides with an apologetic sigh.

"You don't have to apologize for loving your wife." She stepped forward and touched his arm. "I'm the one who should apologize for being so callous. I'm suddenly in a rut. I can't seem to shake this villainous coil that..."

"You don't have to apologize either," Crilen interrupted her. "Not when you're making such a lovely recovery."

Panla hesitated and blinked for a moment. His response was out of chord with the weighty matters still traversing her thoughts. She followed his eyes which were still fixated on the gown. She looked down at herself, feeling naked and exposed. She was well-covered, but his penetrating eyes made her feel completely bare. A flushed awkward embarrassment suddenly warmed her neck and shoulders.

"Lovely?" She looked down and checked herself again. "Mr. Len, are you...flirting with me?"

Crilen smiled in a way that was familiar to her. On his alien countenance was an unmistakably male expression.

"Must be the pheromones." His brows lifted as he stepped toward her.

"Pheromones?" She burst into a girlish laugh, backing away. "Whose?"

"I'm not sure. You tell me." His voice was low and almost serious.

The warmth in Panla's neck crept up the back of her skull.

"Well," she smiled, pushing her fingers through her hair, "I think I left my pheromones back in Cathedral school. So, by the process of elimination, that leaves..."

"The two of us," Crilen continued, moving forward.

"Oh, Mr. Len," Panla sighed nervously. "I'm not your wife. I'm not anything you could possibly want. Do you have any idea what kind of woman you really need?"

"Yes." He gently touched her bare shoulder. "The kind of woman who loves God more than she can lust for any man."

Panla's mouth fell open.

"Was your wife that kind of woman?" She closed her eyes and absorbed his caress.

"I'm not sure." He breathed heavily. "Maybe. I was so different then. If she was, I wasn't capable of appreciating her for it."

"It's a shame."

"That you couldn't appreciate her?" Panla fought to recover herself.

"No." Crilen touched her cheek. "No, actually I was thinking it's a shame that you've never experienced the kind of love I'm talking about. A man walks through life so full of himself, so full of all those masculine things he thinks are so important: Science. Sport. Law. Commerce. Politics. He doesn't even realize he's only half of who he should be...until *she* comes along. *She*, this delicate, whimsical, unpredictable creature who doesn't make a world of sense to him except that he loves her. He needs her. When she isn't there it's like God strikes cold the warmest aspect of his soul. She's the reason he feels. The reason he cares. The reason gentleness and subtlety have meaning. The reason he finally pauses to admire that beautiful parallel feminine dimension of life he's only now able to see for the very first time. The world turns another hue, vibrant and luscious with a sobering joy he always feared to comprehend."

Panla trembled.

"You are so beautiful," he spoke in a whisper. "You don't have to let this world make you its martyr. You deserve someone you can love who loves you more than anything under Heaven."

He leaned forward to kiss her, but she leaned backward and turned her head away. Crilen pulled her closer, but she continued to lean away. He shook her.

"Look at me." He spoke between clenched teeth.

She bowed her head.

"I said, look at me!" He raised his voice and firmed his grasp, but she refused to look up at him.

He pushed her backward and toppled them both onto the bed. She yelped with surprise and shock as he pinned her beneath him and leaned his face as close to hers as he could without touching.

Unable to escape, Panla slowly turned her head toward him and met his longing gaze. She wasn't frightened by the blazing red flicker in his alien eyes. Crilen could see in her expression that a large part of her very much wanted this to happen. Part of her even believed it should happen.

But then she spoke in an earnest whisper: "Another round of adultery for the fallen Deliveress, Mr. Len?"

"I don't see it that way." Crilen ran his nose up the side of her long slender neck.

"But that's the way it would be." She closed her eyes. "I'm married."

Crilen was frozen by those words. He looked up directly into her eyes again.

"Your marriage is an unholy union," he said in a deep passionate baritone. "A union on paper, yes. But one the true living God never sanctioned, and you know it! Without love there can be no commitment. Without commitment there is no marriage.

"And your affair with Rabbel was a mistake. Nothing more. A political ploy turned to lust. You've said as much. The Lord in Heaven knows that, too! Where I come from…out there…you're not bound by secular judgments. You're bound by the naked truth under the gaze of God Almighty."

Panla tensed and dug the heels of her hands into his chest.

"But I'm not from out there, Mr. Len!" She raised her voice with exasperation. "I'm from here. This planet. I can't declare my independence from my mortality and fly off into space because you say so. I have to obey what God has revealed to me, not you. Besides, I'm not her, Mr. Len."

"I know that!"

"Then don't dishonor her memory." The tone of the Deliveress returned to her voice. "Don't dishonor yourself. And don't dishonor your love of our Lord in Heaven."

Crilen paused, then hung his head. She was right. He didn't want her to be, but she was exactly as righteous as the woman he could love most could ever be. Slowly, he rolled from on top of her.

She sat up and didn't go very far.

"One should never commit adultery." She rubbed the sides of her head. "Not for love. Not for loves lost. Not even for love of Him. Every sin, no matter how well-intentioned, diminishes our bond with Heaven. I'm learning, first-hand, just how intolerable that can be."

Crilen sat still, staring into nothingness.

"Lenny," she suddenly sounded exactly like Aami, "I wanted to do this."

"I know." A frustrated Crilen winced.

"Sinning with Rabbel was one thing." Panla touched his arm. "Performing my marital duties was another. But you're the only thing I have left between Heaven and the world right now. The only decent thing. I can't destroy that, I just can't."

"I understand." Crilen pushed his fingers into his forehead. "I just wish…"

"That you could make life perfect?" Her voice was soothing. "That you could make things so that you or I would never feel any pain? That we would never suffer any setbacks?"

"Why not?" Crilen turned his head and regretfully stared into her eyes.

"Because that's not real life, Lenny." She slipped her hand onto his cheek. "Because setbacks are part of life, and no one can get through life avoiding them. So, instead, we have to find the strength and the wisdom to deal with them when they come. That's how we make it. That's how we survive."

"I never want to lose you…" The words choked in Crilen's throat as another breeze of deja vu swept over him.

"Never say never, Mr. Len." Panla touched his fingers. "Only God is forever."

There was a knock at the door.

Panla and Crilen jumped to their feet and found opposite ends of the room.

"Come in!" Panla tried to sound matter-of-fact.

The door creaked open and Panla recognized the young smooth dark face of one of the choir members. The boy looked at Panla, then looked at Crilen, then looked at Panla again.

"I…I can come back." He started to pull the door closed.

"That won't be necessary." Panla lifted her head and assumed an authoritative tone. "Mr. Len and I were reviewing some issues. Business issues. He was just on his way out."

On cue, Crilen straightened his tunic and strode toward the door.

"Well," the boy continued, "Father Rouan actually wanted both of you to come downstairs. He says there's something on satellite you'll want to see. They're talking to a lady who knows you. I think her name is Feed…Feek…Fee…"

"Feebie?" Panla's eyes widened. "Feebie's on satellite?"

"I think that's her name," the boy answered indifferently. "Orange hair. Kind of…"

Still barefoot, Panla bolted past Crilen and the boy, and glided down the stairs. Crilen charged after her, sensing that all secrets were about to be made known.

VII.

The red smoke from Yolo's cigar built up a hellish crimson haze amidst the shadows behind the cameras. He stared intently at his prize catch as she revealed all the splendidly sordid details of Deliveress Panla Jen Tem's secret life to a worldwide audience.

The petite, stylishly attired young female interviewer sat perched upon her cushioned stool with all the regal sanctimony of a media dauphine, newly seated to the throne room of the king of the communication world. Armed with the prepared cues of Yolo's staff, she launched each carefully configured question like a streamlined missile designed to pierce and detonate for optimum destruction.

Feebie, by contrast, felt naked and uncertain before the glare of the studio lamps, the swiveling sea of reflecting camera lenses and the swooping microphones buzzing about her head like large pernicious insects. Something in the balcony of her conscience screamed "Traitor!" as she fought truthfully to answer every question posed by her beautiful young interrogator. She couldn't fathom why her Godly intentions tasted like poisonous venom dripping from her honest tongue, but the bitter flavor of betrayal was unmistakable.

"So Deliveress Jen and Rabbel Mennis were having a sexual relationship?" The interviewer's ensemble of expensive betrothal jewelry sparkled and glared in Feebie's eyes.

"Y...Yes." Feebie's voice quivered.

"You saw them have intercourse?"

"No."

"She told you they had intercourse?"

"No."

"How do you know they were having intercourse?"

Feebie closed her eyes and prayed silently to herself. Was intercourse even the point? Was intercourse the reason she had come forward?

"Ms. Bleik?" the younger woman pressed with haughty journalistic impatience.

"They spent a lot of time alone in Rabbel's office," Feebie clarified.

"So?" the interviewer snorted. "Anyone can spend time with someone behind a closed door. It doesn't mean that they're having intercourse. How do you know that Deliveress Jen and Rabbel Mennis were having intercourse?"

"Um, well, I was also responsible for Mrs. Tem's wardrobe," Feebie stammered reluctantly. "Her PJ wardrobe often showed clear signs that intercourse had taken place."

"By signs you mean stains, secretions, that sort of thing?" the young woman queried unflinchingly.

Feebie swallowed hard. The swarm of microphones edged closer.

"Y...Yes," she answered sheepishly.

"I see." The interviewer notched her victory with a well-rehearsed grimace. "Did the Deliveress ever show any sign of remorse or regret after having intercourse with Rabbel Mennis?"

"Um, I'm not sure I can answer that." Feebie grew vexed by the line of questioning.

"Was she gleeful? Giddy?" the young woman pursued with a straight face.

Yolo quaked with a silent chuckle.

"I wasn't monitoring Mrs. Tem's moods." Feebie's expression tensed. "I considered it a private matter between her and Mr. Mennis. My purpose was to support Mrs. Tem in her cause."

"And what exactly was her cause?" The interviewer rapidly keyed in a new line of prepared questions on her electronic hand prompter.

Feebie paused again. The cause had been so clear at the start: Reform the Cathedral. Return to the Text. But then there came Panla's scurrilously profane and vulgar monologues against the Cathedral. Drinking and carousing into the late night hours with God-hating criminals and sexual deviants. Panla's licentiously, adulterous affair with Rabbel Mennis. Propaganda. Vandalism. Terrorism. And, finally, the hideous murder of the Lord Regent. Was there anything left of their once holy cause to justify the evil they had done?

"Was she trying to destroy the Cathedral?" The young woman filled the silence.

Feebie lifted her head and came to attention. "Destroy is too strong a word."

"Forging an alliance with the Break?" the interviewer questioned. "An organization whose stated purpose is to destroy the church? If Deliveress Jen was meeting with the leader of the Break and having sexual intercourse with the leader of the Break, wouldn't it be logical to conclude that Deliveress Jen's cause was the same as that of the Break's?"

"Not necessarily." Feebie tried to assert herself.

"Was she trying to convert the Break?" the young woman scoffed with a toss of her shimmering salon-sculpted mane. "Was she trying to cleanse Rabbel Mennis through ritual coitus?"

"No." Feebie closed her fists. "No, that wasn't it at all."

"Then what was this cause?" The interviewer leaned forward. "It was clearly outside the boundaries of anything sanctioned by the Cathedral. Obviously, the Deliveress wanted it kept secret. She even created this false PJ identity. Was this some attempt by the Deliveress to start her own religion? Did it involve a government coup? Was she attempting to make herself into some sort of demagogue of a new ruling order?"

"No." Feebie gestured. "There was no political agenda. She wasn't trying to create a new religion. And she wasn't trying to convert the Break...at least not directly. She was using the Break..."

"Using?" The young woman's mouth hung open with the revelation of a new word to manipulate. "You mean Deliveress Jen was using Rabbel Mennis? Using the entire Break movement?"

It sounded horrible. Panla Jen as a sinister and manipulative viper, using and deceiving witless, decadent villains for her own, even baser purposes of villainy. Yes, Panla had used Rabbel and the Break. But here, the inference grew utterly unseemly.

"Maybe, a little." Feebie tried to couch the implication. "But her purpose wasn't to destroy the Cathedral. Mrs. Tem loves God. Mrs. Tem loves the Text. Her cause was to bring about reform in the Cathedral, to get away from the rituals of the Deliverancy and get back to the meaning of the original Text."

"And she was going to accomplish this by having sexual intercourse with Rabbel Mennis?" The interviewer's smooth young features frowned skeptically. "By murdering the Lord Regent? I haven't read my Text in a while, but I don't think any of the Chieftains wrote about the virtues of adultery and murder."

"No." Feebie sighed and hung her head. "No, they didn't. It all went wrong somehow. It started out for all the right reasons, but somehow it all went wrong."

"The Deliveress went wrong," the young woman concluded for her audience. "It's not the first time power has corrupted, nor will it be the last."

"She wasn't corrupted," Feebie murmured.

"Excuse me?" The interviewer's brows lifted. "We didn't get that."

"She wasn't corrupted." Feebie raised her voice. "It all went wrong. But it wasn't because she was corrupted. It was something else."

"Oh. Well, maybe it was love?" The young interviewer broached the topic sounding coldly inexperienced.

"Love?" Feebie was taken off guard.

"You know: Love." The young woman sounded slightly annoyed. "Maybe the Deliveress fell in love with Rabbel Mennis."

"I...suppose it's possible." Feebie found herself wandering into uncertain waters. "But it didn't seem that way."

"Then it was just sex." The interviewer lifted her head and peered down her nose.

Feebie paused. There was no correct answer. In fact, the questions weren't even correct. What she witnessed between Panla and Rabbel was neither lust or love entirely. It was about the cause, the mission. It was PJ playing her role.

Using Rabbel. Using the Break. Using them for the reform. But these answers sounded no better than the sordid answers the perky young media dauphine was already funneling to her audience.

"I don't know." Feebie finally retreated. "I don't know what to tell you."

"I understand." The young woman reached across and touched Feebie's hand. "It's all so very sad."

Feebie's flesh pimpled and crawled under her beautiful young interviewer's ingenuous caress.

"So when were you first aware that Deliveress Jen and Rabbel Mennis plotted to kill the Lord Regent?" the interrogation continued.

"I had no knowledge of any plot," Feebie answered in earnest. "I was in the Cathedral library studying when a commotion broke out. I ran downstairs, hurried outside to the Cathedral gate and could see the Lord Regent's robe smoldering in the pavement with a large crowd around it. I didn't know exactly what'd happened until the media described the assailants. Then I knew Rabbel was responsible."

"You knew the assailants," the interviewer concluded.

"I'd met them, yes," Feebie conceded. "They were part of Rabbel's inner circle."

"Rabbel and Deliveress Jen's, you mean."

"No," Feebie stated flatly. "Rabbel's inner circle. Mrs. Tem was very leery of Rabbel's associates. She only trusted Rabbel. Myself, Genna, Mr. Linnfeld, the chauffeur, Moll, and recently, a Mr. Len were Mrs. Tem's inner-circle."

"So you're saying you don't know when they planned the murder?" the young woman hedged.

"I'm not even saying that they planned the murder." Feebie frowned. "Mrs. Tem doesn't believe in murder. She was constantly wrestling with Rabbel to tone down the vandalism and some of his rhetoric. The idea of Mrs. Tem being mixed up in the murder of anyone is inconceivable. She cherishes life. She taught all of us that. Even the lives of our enemies, she taught us to cherish."

Behind the cameras, Yolo quaked with satisfaction. "Excellent," he chuckled to himself.

"Then you don't know what's happened?" A facade of pitiable sentiment appeared on the interviewer's innocent face.

"Happened?" Feebie became confused. "I don't know what you're talking about. What's happened?"

"Well," the young woman paused for effect, "we received a confirmed report from the south that Deliveress Jen is the person who murdered Rabbel Mennis in cold blood last night."

Feebie felt as if she'd been struck in the head with an axe. The frame of her entire reality felt like it was crumbling from within. The sea of lenses and microphones twisted and lurched forward to capture her stunned reaction. She tried to remain calm, but her hands started to shake. Her lips tightened as her mind struggled to process this incongruous tragedy and simultaneously fashion a cohesive response.

"Wh…where's that coming from?" Feebie appeared disoriented, looking past the cameras. "Who…who said that?"

"A female who calls herself Leesla," the interviewer answered calmly. "Do you know her?"

"Y…yes," Feebie answered weakly. "She was…Rabbel's lieutenant."

"The body was positively identified minutes before we went on the air." The young woman slipped into reporter mode. "Rabbel Mennis, the renowned, elusive leader of the Break is confirmed dead, and it's been alleged that Deliveress Jen murdered him during some sort of quarrel."

"Wait!" Feebie placed her fingers against her temples. "This isn't making any sense. Mrs. Tem killed Rabbel Mennis? That's not possible! She wouldn't….she couldn't…Where is she? What does she say?"

"According to this Leesla and other eyewitnesses, she and the Mr. Len you mentioned escaped and are still at large."

"This is crazy!" Feebie stood up. "You're all making this up. I know Mrs. Tem! I know her! That's impossible!"

"Ms. Bleik, we thought you knew…"

"Bullshit! How could I know? You had me in that room for the last three hours!"

Yolo signaled to the technicians to cut to commercial. Within seconds, the broadcast signal lights dimmed and the warbling comedic music of a restaurant commercial echoed in the background.

As technicians moved onto the set to calm and restrain Feebie, the pretty, petite young interviewer popped from her stool and made her way toward the massive media monarch.

"What did you think, uncle?" She beamed before the giant man who was engulfed in red cigar smoke.

"Yara, you were spectacular." Yolo's pouchy jowls bowed with pride. "Sweetly, innocently, connivingly lethal. You have all the makings of a seminal satellite journalist."

"Do you think Mom was watching?" Yara smiled brightly at her uncle.

"My sister rails mindlessly about the 'immoral' bent of what we do here." Yolo grinned. "But I can't imagine her ignoring her only daughter shining at the epicenter of the world's biggest story. I can assure you, she was watching. Spewing her mad disapproval at the monitor screen, but watching nonetheless."

Yara Pique, the stage name of Yara Pigue, bounced on her toes and patted her uncle on the belly. She scurried off to the company of her stage entourage who brushed the lint from her suit, refreshed her heavy make-up and teased her swirling hair.

Yolo tottered his way to the studio set where Feebie bickered and wrestled with the dutifully indifferent technicians. As his wide presence became apparent, the technicians froze respectfully, then retreated. When the media giant and the strawberry-orange-haired woman were alone, he spoke.

"I'm sorry we had to surprise you with that bit of information on the air, but it couldn't be helped." he spoke with mendacious sentiment. "It's the way this business works sometimes. You do understand, don't you?"

"I want to know what's happened to Mrs. Tem," Feebie fumed. "I want to know how they can accuse her of murder!"

Yolo held up his large hands and gestured for Feebie to calm herself.

"I understand your concerns," Yolo spoke empathetically. "We're only piecing together the details ourselves. This Leesla woman is a dreadfully crude source of information, but everything we know thus far points to the fact that she's telling the truth. Policers confirm that Rabbel Mennis was killed by a weapon blast to the chest. Witnesses confirm that Mrs. Tem and Rabbel Mennis were alone at the time it happened."

"What about that Mr. Len?" Feebie pleaded for a more plausible suspect. "We didn't know anything about him. He showed up two days ago. Couldn't he have…"

"The reports say he wasn't in the room when the shot was fired." Yolo confirmed. "Our leaks also say that you have him to thank for your precious Queen Mother still being alive, wherever she is. He's apparently very good at what he does. Mr. Len supposedly throttled several of Rabbel's men and whisked our dear Deliveress to safety before they could retaliate."

"What about Genna and Mr. Linnfeld?" Feebie asked.

"Hostages." Yolo lifted his cigar to his lips. "Only this Leesla doesn't seem to know what the ransom is quite yet. She's a hideously amateurish creature in these matters, I'm afraid."

"Oh, God in Heaven." Feebie slowly slumped back onto her stool.

"Don't fret, Ms. Bleik." Yolo released a cloud of smoke over a repressed belch. "You've done the right thing here today. You're telling the truth. That's what you wanted. I'll see to it that the authorities are lenient with you in consideration of your well-meaning cooperation."

Yolo turned with the slow deliberate movement of a revolving celestial body and tottered carefully away from the studio set. Yara Pique magically appeared from behind the eclipse of his large oval frame. She was already perched, ramrod straight, on her stool studying the next series of questions on her hand-prompter.

Feebie stared blankly as her thoughts careened through the chaos of maddening events just revealed to her. Rabbel Mennis, dead? Panla Jen, a murderer? Genna and Mr. Linnfeld, hostages? It was an insanely morose jumble of tragedy. Then she heard a studio technician count down to air: Five...four...three...two...one...

VIII.

"Ooowaaww!"

"Ooowaaww?"

"Ooowaaww!" Libbi Trullup repeated as she shifted her weight on her barstool and blew pink smoke straight up into the air.

"That was it?" Her former studio hairdresser sounded astonished.

"That was it," Libbi confirmed. "The last thing he ever said to me was 'Ooowaaww.' He rolled over. I got up and went to the bathroom. When I came out, he was gone. No note. No 'Have a nice life, skanky bitch.' Not even money. Nothing. If it weren't for the dry jizz all over my back, I'd think I imagined the whole thing."

"That's cold." The hairdresser fanned his hand and sipped from his glass.

The mid-afternoon drink and pickup crowd was gathered at trendy Defecatto's By the Barge, a glass and neon restaurant along the river overlooking the shuttling trash barges servicing the city's sewage dumps. The rank odor of garbage and waste actually blended well with the aroma of pan-fried fish, liquor, perfume and cigarettes. At least, that's what the owners sold to their fad-conscious patrons at the grand opening three months before.

Normally the music would be pounding so hard no one could think past the last luscious torso that happened to walk by. But on this particular afternoon, nearly everyone holstered their libidinous indulgences to take in the stunning news of Rabbel's death and the breaking story of the secret life of Deliveress Jen playing on multiple screens throughout the restaurant.

Nearly everyone.

"Ooowaaww!" Libbi shook her head in disbelief. "I mean, I've never been great at relationships, but the last thing he says to me is an ejaculatory groan? Shit! I give my disposable inserts more consideration than that."

"I know what you mean." the hairdresser sighed as he followed the male bartender's buttocks with his eyes.

"At least Yolo had the decency to totally humiliate me, fire me, and send me out into the corridors ass-naked." Libbi frowned. "At least that had some kick. But this guy, I don't even think I got his real name, treats me like a used prophylactic. Like I wasn't even a person. What ever happened to the bogus chivalry of the one-night screw? A peck on the cheek? An 'I'll call you' when they don't even have your code? Or that glorious epitaph: 'You're the best piece of ass I ever had'? What ever happened to the token effort to make it seem like something? Even a prostitute gets a handshake and a little pocket change. Even animals give each other a good-bye lick. What do I get? 'Ooowaaww.' I swear to fucking god, it's the end of civilization."

"You're probably right." The hairdresser winked and smiled at the baffled bartender.

"And that little bitch niece of Yolo's is cashing in on my work." Libbi pounded her fist on the bar.

"My bitch ex-boyfriend is doing her hair." He lamented, rolling his eyes. "But that's all right. He's got IVC. He ain't long for this world."

"I knew the Deliveress was lying to me!" Libbi gestured, nearly knocking over her drink. "I knew it! As soon as someone tells you that they're not doing it, they're *really* doing it. And definitely with someone they don't want you to know about."

"You got that right."

"Everybody's gotta' do it with somebody," Libbi declared. "Everybody. Celibacy is the biggest load of crap since….that!"

Libbi's finger followed a long rusty barge, overflowing with sewage, as it slowly trawled down the river.

"When a male says he's not doing it, he's either doing himself or doing another male." Libbi took a drag from her cigarette and blew another spout of pink smoke into the air. "Not that there's anything wrong with that."

"Sho' ain't." The hairdresser winked at the increasingly uncomfortable bartender.

"And when a female says she's not doing it," Libbi continued, "she's not only doing it, but doing it with someone that embarrasses the living shit out of her so bad, she'd rather people think she's a lesbian or a tool freak or blowing the neighbor's pets. It's usually that bad."

"Case and point." The hairdresser nodded toward the monitor where Feebie was concluding her interview.

"Exactly." Libbi gulped her drink. "The Deliveress, screwing the leader of the Break! Then she kills the poor bastard! What? Was she feeling guilty because his dick was too big? And she had the nerve to talk to me like I was fucked up. Take a look in the mirror, honey! That 'god' bullshit was just a smoke screen. You're drippin' juice in all the wrong places just like the rest of us."

"Speaking of which," the hairdresser pointed to a surly muscular male sitting alone at a table by the window, "isn't that the athlete who stalked you a few twin-moons ago?".

"Oh, my god, it is." Libbi perked up in her chair and doused her cigarette. "And he is looking good."

"True," the hairdresser observed, "but he was looking good the last time 'til he broke your jaw and lit your condo on fire."

"Oh, he was on those hormone supplements back then." Libbi fanned her hand. "I hear he's a coach now. Coaches don't do hormones. In fact, coaches can actually get it up."

Libbi hastily rummaged through her purse until she found her laser makeup kit. She quickly touched up her face with thin beams of light, then checked herself in the bar mirror.

"You are sexy sauté!" The hairdresser winked at her. "Only make sure you get more than 'Ooowaaww' this time."

Libbi popped off her barstool and pulled the hem of her short tight dress over her taut thighs. She smiled slyly. "You know, maybe if I get two or three 'Ooowaawws' he won't need to say anything else."

She eagerly strutted across the room to greet her once-and-future abuser. His solemn scowl broke into an affable smile. He was genuinely glad to see her. He tightly flexed his large fists under the table as she sat down and started to chat.

Meanwhile, hundreds of kilometers to the southwest:

"Ooowaaww!" Juds chuckled. "She got up and went to the shitter and I got the fuck outta there!"

"Puh-thetic." Mongeer grinned as he flipped a couple of empty bottles into the trash bin behind the bar.

"Pathetic would have been an upgrade." Juds gulped his drink and shook his head. "She's famous, she makes all this money, she ain't bad looking, but underneath it all, she's a drunk half-a-coin lay on the skids. Go figure! I mean, I'd a' been more turned on if she blew me off. But there I was, a sack o' shit among royalty and she dragged me back to her condo like I was a bag o' gold. Yikes! Females are fuckin' scary. When they get that masochistic complex shit going, you don't know what the fuck's gonna happen. They could yell 'rape' or start planning the wedding. Who the fuck knows? Huh! Hah!"

"So ya just get outta there." Mongeer smiled as he refilled Juds's glass.

"Ya got that right." Juds scratched the pasty pits on his jaws. "Let the next idiot deal with her. I may be horny, but I ain't stupid."

A dark heavy-set female sitting next to Juds picked up her drink and walked away in disgust.

"The truth hurts, don't it, honey?" Juds yelled at her back.

"Go fuck yourself," she shouted with an obscene gesture.

"Don't got to, babe!" Juds sneered. "I can't unhook my belt in the toilet without the sound drawin' whiny sows like you from under the sandwich trough. No, babe, you go home and fuck yourself and pretend its me through those lonely tears that'll be runnin' down those fat cheeks o' yours."

"Shhh!" Mongeer grabbed Juds by the arm. "Be nice. She's a regular."

"Yeah, she's a regular all right." Juds and the female exchanged one last angry glare. "A regular sweat-beast off the wild plains."

"Okay, I hear ya." Mongeer assumed his role as the peacemaking bar owner. "But I thought you were supposed to be in a good mood."

"I am." Juds kicked the side of the bar and rubbed his forehead.

He had successfully brokered his big deal between the Break and the government. He had just returned from a triumphant sexual escapade with one of the most famous females in the world. His bank account was full, for the time being. All his debts, monetary or otherwise, had been settled. And he was free and clear of any imminent legal proceedings against him. His uneven life was presently in the best condition he could recall within recent memory. But somehow, he felt empty.

"I don't know." Juds finally forced a smile onto his tense face. He looked up at the large monitor screen behind the bar and saw "Cathedral Crisis" pulsating in large red letters.

"So what about that?" Mongeer tilted his head.

"Un-fucking-believable." Juds smirked. "I knew something was up with Rab-bel, but I had no idea he was screwing the Deliveress. He acted funny when you mentioned her name, but I had no idea. I heard he had some rich girlfriend from up north who was helping him out, but who could've figured it was the Deliver-ess herself? I mean, it doesn't even make any sense. She's doing services at the Basilica in the afternoon and doing Rabbel at night? Fucking crazy. Fucking broads!

"And meanwhile, the Accommodant is jamming himself into every pair of lace panties he can get his fingers into. If this is leadership, no wonder the whole world's fucked up." Juds rapped his knuckles nervously against the bar. "You'd think the people who are always telling us what we should be doing could at least live up to their end of the bargain, right? But no, the whole goddamn world is one big hypocritical shit hole. Pisses me off."

Mongeer looked at his seedy, longtime patron quizzically. In the worst of times, he had never seen Juds so serious. "Well," Mongeer offered with a feeble smile, "at least you got laid, right?"

Juds tried to immerse himself in that whimsical thought. His eyes flickered, trying to recapture their cocksure contentment.

"Yeah." Juds shook his head and lit an herbal cigarette. "Yeah. I guess that's the point, right?"

IX.

Detective Fembletun sat at his desk, examining the reports and pictures on his hand-held field recorder. He followed the path from where Reza and Durn's vehicle had crashed through the building and smashed through offices and corri-dors, all the way through to the solid concrete wall that had abruptly ended the violent mayhem. The physical evidence spoke for itself. Buckled metal. Splin-tered wood. Shattered glass. Shredded carpeting. The pictures of the contorted, bloodied, dismembered remains of the victims also spoke for themselves. One minute, it had been just another boring day on the ground floor of an office mall. The next minute, chaos, horror and death. There wasn't any mystery here. The sequence and consequence of events were cruelly obvious. Even the motive, such as it was, required little analysis. The perpetrators were being pursued by policers. The girl at the vehicle controls panicked and they crashed, plowing through a crowded building. None of this required Fembletun's intellectual attention or detailed analysis, but he prayed that it would somehow distract him from a greater matter that chiseled at the moorings of his soul.

"Face it, partner," the voice of Bales abruptly jarred his concentration, "Deliveress Jen is a whore."

The words stung like boiling acid poured down the middle of his back. Fembletun spun around in his chair and jumped to his feet. His dark, bald scalp glistened under the office lamps as the veins across the crown of his head appeared to tighten. A thunderous anger crackled in his eyes as he leaned nose to nose with his partner.

Their eyes locked. Fembletun, on the brink of violent, explosive aggression. Bales, smugly taunting like a mischievous brother who knew exactly the worst wounds to exacerbate.

"Deliveress Jen…is not…a whore," Fembletun growled through his clenched teeth.

"Of course she is," Bales replied with a grin. "It's all over the media."

"The media is wrong!" Fembletun yelled.

"How do you know?" Bales stepped back calmly and folded his arms.

Fembletun held up a finger as the black scowl on his face intensified. "I just know."

"You 'just know'?" Bales chuckled. "She's been sleeping with the leader of the Break for nearly a twinmoon. Her own attendant just said so. Did you 'just know' that?"

"I don't care what her attendant said." Fembletun gesticulated angrily with gnarled fingers. "Powerful people have powerful enemies. The media's been after her for twinmoons. Now they pay one of her disgruntled trustees to stab her in the back. That's all this is!"

"And she's a murdering whore," Bales piled on. "What a paragon of piety. She not only took a lover outside of her marriage, but she murdered the bastard."

"And I suppose you have evidence to that effect?" Fembletun threw up his hands.

"I don't, but the media does." Bales shook his head. "Do you honestly think Yolo Enterprises would risk their credibility by tossing out these types of allegations against the most prominent religious leader in the world? Yolo Pigue's a cold-blooded eel, but he didn't get where he is by being a fool. They've got their facts and I'd bet my last coin that every bit of it is true."

"Tried and convicted in the media?" Fembletun pointed toward a silent monitor mounted into the wall. "Is that how we do our job now? Whatever fat Yolo Pigue tells us is the gospel, no questions asked?"

"You know that's not what I mean."

"Oh, I know what you mean." Fembletun paced back and forth. "As long as the media is telling you something you want to hear, you don't care if it's fact, fiction or a blatant lie. To hell with the rights of the accused!"

"Rights of the accused?" Bales white face lit up. "Is that what we're talking about? Is this a conversation about rights? Or is this more about your Queen Mother getting caught with her bloomers down around her ankles?"

"You watch it." Fembletun pointed his finger in Bales's face. "The Queen Mother is an anointed descendant of Bius the first! She is descended from God to lead all of us to Heaven. She'd even save a bastard heathen ignoramus like yourself if you ever repented! So I suggest you show a little respect."

"Respect?" Bales scoffed. "To who? For what? Some hypocritical, sanctimonious female who got tangled up in a political murder-sex scandal? I don't respect that. I bring that to justice and hope it rots in prison for a very long time. That's what I'm paid to do. That's what you're paid to do. We've seen this kind of thing a million times on every level of society. Just because she occupies some religious office you happen to worship doesn't make her any less mortal or any less guilty."

"You don't hear what I'm saying!" Fembletun's voice rose. "She...she is the Deliveress! She is incapable of adultery...murder...."

"She's a person." Bales shook his head. "You can call her whatever you like. You can dress her up in whatever titles make you feel good. But underneath the fancy headdress and the golden plumes, is just another person. A person susceptible to the same ills, the same rights and wrongs, the same sins...as anybody else."

Fembletun turned away from Bales, clutched the rim of his desk and lowered his head.

"She anointed my daughters." Fembletun's hushed voice quaked.

"She also murdered Rabbel Mennis." Bales placed a hand on his partner's shoulder. "At least, it certainly looks that way."

"And we know looks can deceive," Fembletun answered.

"For her sake, let's hope so." Bales patted Fembletun on the back and walked toward the exit. "In a way, she probably did the world a favor killing Rabbel. But she broke the law, not to mention her own antiquated doctrines. Maybe she had a good reason. A good secular reason."

Bales hesitated for a moment, waiting for another response, but all he received was silence and the back of his partner's black bald head. With a sigh, he finally closed the door behind him.

The muscles in Fembletun's tense jaw tightened. Then he opened the drawer of his desk, pulled out his unused Text, and searched for a prayer that would soothe his conscience and bring all truth to light.

X.

Yolo Pigue, Mr. Nil and Mr. Pont adjourned to the broadcast control room. The interview with Feebie was doing exceedingly well; the reputation of Deliveress Jen was rapidly disintegrating into a scandalous heap of tawdry hypocrisy. Ratings were soaring, and it was only the beginning of a raging media firestorm which would burn through every aspect of life on the planet. Now, it was only a matter of deciding what next to toss onto the bonfire.

Leesla's angry, bruised, burned face appeared on an auxiliary screen.

"GYAK!" Mr. Nil recoiled from the visual image.

"Hooh!" Mr. Pont sounded as if someone had punched him in the gut.

Even Yolo gasped audibly with dismay. The thought of beaming so wrenchingly unappetizing a visual to a worldwide audience made him queasy.

"The person who said that we should never judge a lady by her appearance ne'er laid eyes upon this." Yolo grimaced. "Although the term 'lady' appears inapplicable."

"No wonder she hates God," Mr. Nil snickered. "I could finger-paint a face on my ass and it'd look better than that."

"I'll curb my imagination." Yolo sighed. "Let's make this one an 'audio only'. Nothing ravages the ratings like the miscarried mien of a frightening female. You do recall that female sports league that lost us a billion coin a few twinmoons ago, don't you? They were splendid athletes. As splendid as the gender allows, that is. But once they worked up a lather, they appeared collectively, a hideous flock of flailing, knock-kneed fowl. Hips, elbows and unkempt hair flapping chaotically about. The viewers fled in droves. It was a politically affirmative feminist fad that died violently, devoid of male patronage. It took months for that mindlessly filthy teenage beach drama to repair the damage to the time slot. Ratings always judge the ladies by their looks, I'm afraid. There's nothing that can be done about it. Audio only, Mr. Nil. Audio only, I beg of you."

"Yes sir," Mr. Nil snorted with a quiet chuckle.

Meanwhile, on the studio set, Feebie was prepared to bolt. She needed to see Panla but she had no idea where Panla was. She needed to find out what was being done to rescue Genna and Linnfeld. Her spiritual family was in mortal crisis. And here she was, on a plush satellite broadcast set, stoking a tasteless albeit world-shattering scandal that was betraying everyone she truly loved.

"Well," Yara Pique shook her golden mane like a famished debutante having just hostessed afternoon tea in her sun room, "the world thanks you for your courage in coming forward today. God be with you."

Feebie's flesh crawled upon the hearing of so ingenuine and vacant a religious sentiment from this amoral media assassin.

"God be with you," Feebie responded as the cameras panned away from her perturbed scowl.

As soon as she was certain she was off camera, Feebie stood up and stalked off the set. She was immediately greeted by a pair of government officers in black suits who spoke with her briefly and quietly escorted her out of the studio.

"A very brave woman who will have much to answer for," Yara sanctimoniously concluded the segment as she checked her hand-prompter. "But now I understand we have a member of the Break on audio. To whom am I speaking?"

"I am Leesla." The cold clipped tones reverberated through the studio speakers.

The sharp haunting voice cut through Yara's confidence like a machete. Four syllables from the intense Break lieutenant and the young interviewer suddenly appeared frightened by something alien and monstrous. She reached down and nervously scratched her calf, then fidgeted with her prompter.

"And, um, Leesla, exactly who are you?" Yara tried to sustain her confidence.

"Who am I?" The crisp deliberate female voice was a mad blend of insult and amusement. "Who am I? I...am the leader of the Break!"

Yara swallowed hard. It was as if she were speaking to the bogey woman. And she hadn't even seen Leesla's face.

"You...are the leader of the Break?" The young interviewer's voice shook. She cleared her throat. "Um...I assume you are the new leader of the Break as of Rabbel Mennis's demise?"

"That's right!" The voice intensified. "The great Rabbel Mennis has been murdered by your evil Deliveress Jen. Now, the Break will have its revenge. Rabbel will not be the last casualty in our battle for freedom from the religious oppressors! What happened to the Lord Regent will look like mercy when we're finished with the Cathedral and its followers. They'll be begging to fry in acid!"

Yara Pique's large eyes glanced beyond the cameras with childlike fear welling in them. She suddenly looked like a lost little girl who needed her mother to take her home, but all she could see was the large outline of her uncle shrouded by a drifting haze of reddish smoke. She desperately needed some sort of reprieve to regain her composure, but knew full well that rescues were not her uncle's style. She took a deep breath and forced herself through another question.

"So you admit that the Break was responsible for the murder of the Lord Regent?" Her voice continued to quake.

"Proudly." Leesla's voice rolled like thunder. "He and his ilk have been murdering souls for centuries. We considered it a direct act of self-defense from religious poison!"

A stunned shudder murmured through the studio.

"Those are very strong words." The young interviewer swallowed hard. "I don't know if killing is ever right..."

"That's because you've never had to!" Leesla cut her off. "Your pampered hetero-centric life isn't under siege. Switch places with me and you would feel as I do!"

Yara's hands started to shake as she quickly searched for another question on her prompter.

"Um...well...we know that the Break has a history of opposition to the Cathedral," she continued unevenly, "but what can you add to the story of Deliveress Jen and Rabbel Mennis that Ms. Bleik didn't already touch upon?"

"That traitorous orange-haired spy only told part of the truth!" Leesla snarled. "Rabbel Mennis was a good and honest leader, but he fell prey to Panla Jen's evil, seductive, religious, heterosexual wiles! Anything wrong done by the Break was done at her behest. Rabbel never intended to bomb statues or buildings. He never believed that violence would solve anything. It was all her doing. He was a peaceful man who only wanted to see the Cathedral exposed for what it was so that people could dispense with religious nonsense and begin to live free lives. Freedom to embrace the arts and the sciences without the imposition of religious influences! Freedom without insane deference to some made-up god created by oppressive warlords millennia ago! Females with females! Males with males! The right to adopt and mold children! Equal rights for concubines regardless of age or gender! Alcohol and drugs without laws or regulations! Freedom for the individual to choose! The right to choose, goddamnit!"

Yara froze. Gossip and scandal were one thing. She had learned at an early age that the world fed insatiably upon the dross of adultery and infidelity. But this rain of hardened ideals...philosophy, beliefs...these were concepts which had no definition in her world. She viewed them as too substantive to be taken seriously in her comfortable young life. She wanted no part of them. She wanted her fiancé, a massage and a bubble bath.

Her hand-prompter fell from her lap with a sharp clattering noise. A technician crawled alongside her chair and retrieved it just beneath the camera's view. He poked it between her fingers and she took it up hastily. With a grimace she couldn't suppress, she glanced up and down until her next question finally appeared.

"Um…again….strong words," Yara repeated herself. "But exactly where does the Break stand now?"

"Stronger than ever," Leesla's voice thundered confidently. "As great as Rabbel was, he allowed himself to be ensnared…sidetracked by that religious vixen. His death has served as a lightning post for the dawning of a great new age. Women with women. The right to choose! The end of God as an oppressor of our freedoms! This is what we fight for! And within the next twenty-six hours, we shall have it."

"So soon?" Yara cringed. "How can it all happen so quickly?"

"We have hostages!" Leesla's spoke triumphantly. "Hostages from the Deliveress's murdering criminal entourage. Cathedral loyalist swine. They deserve to die for their hypocrisy. Die as Rabbel died for all our freedoms. But I believe that you can always make something good out of something bad. My grandmother raised me to be a positive person. So I…we…offer the Cathedral a deal: Renounce your God and your Texts and your rules and laws and all of the shit that's destroyed the freedoms of this planet, or we will slit the hostages' throats and declare a bloody war on all Cathedral persons and property everywhere in the world. No male, female or child will be safe from what we do next! We will strike immediately and often! But you will never know when or where until it is too late! I believe in choice, so this is the choice I offer to our oppressors!"

"Oh my." Yolo's expression luminesced with a pensive glow.

"She's crazy." Mr. Nil recoiled in amazement.

"She's mad." Mr. Pont affirmed with dismay.

"She's magnificent." Yolo lapped his sagging jowls. "Frightfully, shockingly, hideously magnificent. If she hadn't just tattooed a government bullseye on her forehead, I'd offer her an audio contract. A pity. We'll have to live in the moment. Signal to my niece to keep this going as long as she can. Scandal begetting terrorism begetting worldwide fear! Tell the marketing department to triple the advertising rates! We're in the midst unfolding the greatest story ever told. See to it, Mr. Nil!"

"Yes sir." Mr. Nil jumped up and sprinted out of the room.

Mr. Pont sat, rubbing his temple, trying to compose his next commentary for the late edition and his morning program.

XI.

"Well, who the hell put her in charge?" the Accommodant shouted into the round metallic blue combox sitting on his large wooden desk. "And who told her she could talk to Yolo? Rabbel's carcass isn't even cold yet and she's turned this whole thing into a goddamn satellite circus. It's a mess! A goddamn, idiotic, run-away thunder bus! We offered them the best deal imaginable! Weapons, immunity, all the coin funding they could ever spend on their war against the Cathedral, and now, this psychotic lunatic is destroying weeks of planning. Destroying her own goddamn movement!"

"I'm afraid all of this was unforeseen," a deep monosyllabic voice answered. "Your wife's involvement was a variable no one anticipated. And the assassination of Rabbel Mennis was a fortuitous event."

"How come no one knew that my own wife was fucking that scheming boor?" The Accommodant's tone became pronounced. "My own wife. The most famous and influential female on the planet, fucking the most renowned insurgent scum on the planet and none of my intelligence sources pick it up!"

"We were never asked to monitor the movements of the Deliveress." the deep voice responded unemotionally.

"Now there's an excuse!" The Accommodant pounded his fist onto his desk. "I don't ask, so you don't do! I didn't ask you to wipe your own ass this morning…did you do that? Did I really need to ask the worldwide intelligence net to keep an eye on the Deliveress and First Lady? Isn't that something I should expect from 'intelligence'?"

"Mr. Accommodant," the deep voice remained even and respectful, "it was your initiative that insisted upon private security for Mrs. Tem. Our posture surrounding the Deliveress and First Lady was a defensive one at your insistence. She was, in your own words, predictable and above the necessity for surveillance. The security which you insisted upon screening and hiring yourself, was deemed by you to be all that was necessary."

The muscles in the Accommodant's tightened jaw rolled angrily.

"So do we have any idea where my wife is at this moment?" he asked with a perturbed sigh.

"No, sir."

"And do we have any idea what this Leesla might do next?"

"No, sir."

The Accommodant leaned back in his chair and ran through the political calculations flickering in his head. Whatever he did next had to be popular with the masses. It had to be something simple. Something the majority of the world would understand and embrace…blindly.

The clandestine support of the Break had made ingeniously wonderful sense. The world had grown weary of the Cathedral's oppressive proselytizing. Rules on top of rules. Rules burdening virtually every personal behavior. Rules demanding the suppression of individual freedoms in favor of a ghost of a God whose so-called promises had been fabricated over two millennia ago. The world had been chomping at the bit for its independence from the tiresome weights imposed upon it by an ancient, antiquated religious order. Properly funded and controlled, the Break could have easily brought about the shift in social mores the Accommodant would have packaged into a political renaissance all his own. A loud party on every street corner. Sex, anywhere, anytime, with anyone, without guilt or condemnation. Infinite choices of legal recreational drugs and alcohol to rocket the economy into frenzied prosperity. Accommodations unprecedented by any Accommodant in the history of the planet. They would build statues in his honor. He would be immortalized.

Even Yolo Pigue and the powerful media would have him to thank for stripping away the bonds of piety vicariously imposed upon it by the Cathedral. No programming would be deemed too lewd or vulgar. Entertainment and art would be constricted only by the boundaries and joys of secular perversions. The entire world would swell to a paradisiacal state of insatiable orgasmic addiction to hedonistic pleasure. And the credit for this liberation would be his for all eternity.

But it had to be done the right way. Otherwise, those with a moral conscience might actually see it for what it was and cast shadow upon this amoral light. Guilt and fear would supersede the libidinous mischief imprisoned in every soul. The masses would go scurrying back to their dark repressed little corners, prop up their cathedrals and Churchlords, and insist that the moral fabric of society be fortified in the name of the holy Deliverers.

The Accommodant froze upon the thought. Holy Deliverers. His holy wife. His holy wife, suddenly at the heart of murder and scandal. Without the Break, the masses would return to the bosom of their Queen Mother. Only now they would find that bosom cankered and rotted with the open lesions of falsehood and hypocrisy. If everything rumored about his wife were found to be true, then perhaps the Break had outlived its usefulness. Perhaps, the public ruin of his pious, Text-clinching, God-loving wife would serve him better. Who best to exemplify the futility of the Cathedral than the Deliveress who turned her back on everything it stood for? Adultery. Treason. Murder. She would have to die for those transgressions. And with her legal and justifiable execution, the masses would justifiably fly far from the failed religious institution and into the new age of secular freedom.

The Accommodant smiled.

"Alert the Armory," he said in a tight whisper.

"Sir?" the deep voice replied.

"Alert the Armory," the Accommodant repeated in an audible voice. "The Break are holding innocent hostages. Those terrorists are holding innocent hostages. We've got to rescue our people and bring them home. Let the media know that we've just learned the whereabouts of Rabbel Mennis' hideout."

"But sir, we've always known where Rabbel's…"

"I said 'let the media know that we've *just* learned the whereabouts of Rabbel Mennis's hideout. And let them know that I also flatly reject all rumors concerning my wife's involvement with the Break or Rabbel Mennis. Tell them that Panla Jen Tem is the most beautiful and honorable female on the face of this planet. That she is the moral beacon and guiding light for every soul on this planet. And, as her husband, I love her more than life itself and pray to God Almighty for her safe return to our home."

"Sir," the voice responded, "may I respectfully note that the evidence against Mrs. Tem is mounting. She…"

"Just tell them!" the Accommodant shouted and severed the connection.

X.

Father Rouan's office was a small and modest room in the center of the pitted, sandstone cathedral structure. But the office ceiling was a glass dome that always revealed the light of the sun or the rolling clouds or the brownish overcast or the twinmoons and the stars. It wasn't constructed with sentiment derived from the Text, but the view always made him feel closer to the heavens during his moments of study, meditation or prayer.

Today, however, there was nothing in the sky that could console the venerable cathedral leader or his guests. The cruelties and consequences heir to flesh and blood had closed in all around them.

Panla sat next to Father Rouan on the worn pastel sofa in his office, clutching his large paternal hands as they both sadly stared at the monitor. Crilen leaned against the doorway, mindful not to allow his smoldering temper to ignite a pyrogenic fire that might incinerate the combustible interior of the entire complex.

On the screen was another stern-faced journalist interviewing Durn from behind the diagonal metal bars of a prison cell.

"So tell us again what you believe the reason was for Deliveress Jen's murder of Rabbel Mennis." The interviewer leaned toward Durn with an overly serious, inquisitive scowl carved into his twisting brows.

Durn rubbed the coarse hairs of his scraggly unkempt beard and smiled a horrible yellow-toothed smile as his mischievous eyes met the camera.

"She killed Rabbel because he was jealous of me and her," Durn snickered. "She was sex-crazy. She just couldn't get enough of me, but she also had this nympho-freak power trip going. Doing the Accommodant. Doing Rabbel. It got her high or something. Then she'd break down and cry to me and start clawin' like a scared animal 'til I gave her what she wanted. It was wild!"

"Oh, Lord in Heaven." Panla hopelessly collapsed onto Father Rouan's broad shoulder.

"This is ridiculous." Crilen frowned. "The media's throwing out any ludicrous information they can find, like raw meat to starving carnivores. By the time they're done, nobody sitting at home will be able to separate the fact from the fiction. Durn's a psychotic murdering terrorist. How can anyone believe a word he says, let alone air his lies all over the world?"

Panla slowly lifted her head. Her eyes were darkened and distraught from all she had absorbed over the past two days. She wasn't certain whether it was Durn's lies or the actual truth which stung her more, but she was definitely at the end of her endurance.

"I'm a murderer, Mr. Len," Panla said with resignation in her voice. "And a whore. And a traitor. Should anyone listen to me?"

Crilen felt the heat rise up the back of his neck. He couldn't stand the sound of her voice…Aami's voice…degrading herself so roundly. They all knew the circumstances were far more complicated than that, and he was growing tired of reminding her.

"You're not a murderer." Crilen tried to lift her with the conviction in his voice, "We'll prove it. You were defending yourself in a nest full of armed radicals and mercenaries. Rabbel had threatened your life. Leesla had just tried to kill you."

"And Rabbel came to my defense." Panla closed her eyes and shook her head with exasperation. "He wasn't armed, Mr. Len, and I didn't care. I came to kill him that night. That was the only reason I wanted us to go there…so I could kill him and put an end to the whole bloody charade. So that no one else would have to die like the Lord Regent, or Reza, or those innocent people in that building. The only thing that went wrong was that I survived. I didn't have an escape planned. I didn't want one. If Rabbel's people killed me, I didn't care. I just wanted it to be over. Thanks to you, it's not."

"You're welcome." Crilen frowned.

The mood in the room grew deeply pessimistic.

"Well we've had just about enough of this thing." Father Rouan stood up, leaned forward and flipped off the switch to his dusty, outmoded satellite monitor. "Whenever I want to lose sleep over what's right or wrong in the world, I watch the media. Whenever I want to sleep like a baby, I read an hour of Text with a glass of juice and a slice of pie. Then God tucks me in and I don't have to worry about who's lying and who's not; who's guilty and who's not; who deserves to live and who deserves to die. That's not my concern. All I worry about is my service to the Lord and guiding as many souls into Heaven as I can muster. Everything else is not my business. That's God's business so I just leave it to Him."

Panla fell back on the sofa and stared into space. Crilen shifted his weight and continued to frown.

"Hmh," Father Rouan observed, "I remember when I took myself so seriously. Young and self-important. I thought the whole world revolved around every little choice I made. Turn right: Joy and salvation for the world. Turn left: Death and damnation for everyone. Every day was like that until I nearly lost my mind, not to mention my family and my parish. That's when I learned that I needed to hand my burden over to God and not worry about the things I couldn't control or change. God didn't make us to bear all the burdens of the world. If your faith is truly in Him, your burden will always be light."

Panla continued to stare. Crilen continued to frown.

"Yep," Father Rouan sighed and shook his head, "I sure remember those days. Pie and juice are downstairs when you get the universe all figured out."

The tall elderly man leaned over and kissed Panla on the cheek; he nodded to Crilen. With the swaggering shuffled gait of an elder statesman at peace with the universe, Father Rouan exited his office.

There followed a prolonged silence. Crilen didn't know where to begin.

"Genna and Mr. Linnfeld are still alive," Panla said. "That's some good news anyway. You were right. Leesla's using them."

"As hostages." Crilen looked up. "They're still alive, but there's no telling for how long."

"True." Panla sounded at a loss. "But we can't do anything. They're surrounded."

"'We' can't do anything," Crilen responded, "but I can. Leesla's out of her mind and out of her depth. There's no telling when she'll decide that the hostages are more trouble than they're worth."

Panla lifted her gaze as she read what was running through Crilen's mind.

"You're going to go back?" She sounded distressed.

"I should have gone back immediately, but you were my first priority," Crilen said evenly. "That's why I'm here, remember? But now that you're safe, I fully intend to get them out."

Panla sighed and hung her head again.

"Mr. Len, you're uncommonly heroic, cleaning up after me," she said softly. "I'm the one who led them to their deaths."

"You really insist on tearing yourself down, don't you?" Crilen grew annoyed. "Is this what your faith means to you? Defeat? Death? Total abdication of every gift the Lord ever gave you?"

"Apparently so." A tear rolled down her cheek. "I'm among the living dead now. You have no idea what that's like."

"True," Crilen's jaw set, "except when my wife was incinerated in our bed because of my own selfishly reckless experiments. It never crossed my mind that when I experimented on myself, I was experimenting on both of us. 'One flesh', remember? I blasted myself right out into the cosmos...a mutated freak never to see anyone I knew or loved ever again. That seemed like a damn good time to quit, but I didn't. Thank God for that. Because if He had quit on me, I wouldn't be here with you now."

"Lucky you," Panla responded.

"I don't believe in luck," Crilen responded, "and neither do you."

"So what then?" Panla finally met his eyes.

"I'm not sure." Crilen knelt down and placed his palm on the top of her leg. "But you and I were brought together for a reason. Across time, space, dimensions...whatever. We were brought together for some purpose and only God knows what it is."

"And your alien benefactor," Panla added.

"Maybe." Crilen nodded. "But one thing I do know is that I can fix this world. I can shut down Yolo Pigue's media machine. I can toss your husband out of office, into the streets and expose him for the lecherous political cur that he is. I can bury the Break so deep into the ground that no one will ever remember it existed. And I can set the course of the church in the direction you envisioned. No more secular rituals or Addendums. No more institutional hierarchy claiming divine rights. Just souls and the Text and God in Heaven, the way it was meant to be."

"And what do I do?" Panla touched his hand.

"When it's over, you come with me." Crilen pleaded with his eyes. "You come with me and be my conscience and help me with my work. Our work! There's an entire universe out there that needs us, that needs you!"

"Outer space again?" Panla closed her eyes and frowned.

"'Outer space' to someone who's never been there." Crilen smiled warmly. "But when you see it, you'll know that it's the grand canvas of creation stretching out into infinity. Countless worlds, countless civilizations, countless souls in need of illumination."

"And how would I get from place to place?" Panla shook her head. "Flap my arms? Cling to your fiery neck and hold my breath as you fly us around the universe?"

"Ships are easy." Crilen rubbed her hand. "I'll build you a palace that will move through the stars at the speed of light. Faster if you like."

"So then, what would I be?" She gazed at him with fond pessimism. "Your partner? Your lover? Your…?"

"My wife." Crilen squeezed her hand.

Panla froze and fell back on the sofa. It was far too much for her to absorb.

"The wife that I need. The husband you deserve." He slid up next to her.

Panla closed her eyes and shook her head: "Isn't this the wrong time, the wrong dimension? None of this is your home."

"My home is with you." He tried to capture her gaze.

"I'm married," she reminded him.

"I'll make him grant you a divorce. When I'm done with him, he'll be begging for one."

"The Cathedral forbids divorce." She shook her head.

"Does the Text?" he countered.

Panla buried her face in her hands while Crilen gently massaged the nape of her neck. He had all the correct answers, except the one that properly aligned her heart with Heaven.

"This is too much, Mr. Len." Panla sniffed back another tear. "I need to think about it. You're asking me to change my entire existence and I need to think about it. Go save Genna and Linnfeld. We'll talk about it again."

Crilen leaned toward her and tried to read any sign of a decision behind her eyes. He could see something running through her mind but he couldn't decipher it. It resembled the grave and decisive look she had worn at the Basilica the night before they'd gone to Rabbel's tavern for the final time. He wanted his answer, but he knew better than to press a female into revealing anything before she was ready to do so. All he could do now was rescue Genna and Linnfeld and hope for a favorable decision upon his return.

He stood and took her up by the hand. Together they walked out of Father Rouan's office. She rested her head on his shoulder as they strolled through the empty cavernous sanctuary toward the doors leading to the open field just outside.

As they stepped through the outer doors and into the twinmoon light, the warm evening air caressed them. Panla looked up to the stars and stared as if seeing the sprawl of the universe for the very first time.

She was so beautiful as the gentle night breeze rolled through her white gown and flicked through her short dark hair. He lightly touched her bare shoulder and kissed her on the cheek. Their fingers separated. He walked down the stone stairs and made his way to the center of the field. His body glowed a luminescent red, then burst into white/yellow flames. In another instant, the ground beneath him appeared to explode. She watched his body shoot up into the sky, circle once overhead and dart over the black, starlit horizon in a bright streak of golden light.

God. Space. Alien souls. And the world she would leave behind. There was much for her to think about indeed.

XI.

The commotion outside the Bius Basilica was a protest rally wrapped around a religious revival, impaled by blind justification, fueled by raw mortal rage. All avenues leading to the Basilica were overrun with people loitering, meandering shouting and marching. The pandemonium built upon itself like a murky combustible storm set to consume or obliterate anything or anyone that wandered into its inexorable, destructive path. Lines of policers and security pushed back the shouting factions in an attempt to keep them separated. Only it was impossible to discern which faction was a danger to whom. Or who belonged to which faction. Or how many factions there really were.

A young female swung a fist at her Churchlord. A father clutching a Text spit at his son. A mother wept as her three children shouted profanities at her from all sides. A husband clutched his lover and pushed away his wife. Break supporters paraded signs depicting the martyrdom of Rabbel Mennis. Three looters tried to pry a section of ancient carvings from the Basilica wall. Patches of shouters celebrated the liberated decadence of Panla Jen. Others loudly declared her innocence and hurled rocks and bottles at anyone who spoke against her piety.

Small platoons of media snaked in and out of the roiling throng, extracting any morsel of sensational copy that would elevate a career or boost the YBS ratings.

"Who needs God or religion?" a lanky, balding, pallid young male spoke into a journalist's microphone. "It does more harm than good. If we just love and respect each other, we wouldn't need to pretend there's a higher power."

The sprawling swarm was a daunting and volatile one. There was a feeling in the air that an explosion of mass violence was imminent. Any policer who had not been called upon to control, herd or disperse the swelling population outside the Basilica gates had to be thankful for any other assignment that would take him far from the disturbing scene.

Any policer except a restless Fembletun, who pushed angrily through the crowd, making his way toward the Basilica's northern gate. Like an unthrottled machine, he plowed impatiently over anyone who blocked his path. More than once, a displaced demonstrator would turn back toward him, ready to make a physical challenge, but under the long beige policer's coat and the wide brimmed hat, was a dark foreboding grimace etched into his black features. It was the countenance of a person with death in his heart. It was not a look to be trifled with unless one were prepared to be killed or commit murder.

Fembletun shoved past the final wall of protesting patrons and found himself facing the embattled Basilica security, shoulder to shoulder with his fellow policers wearing their dark uniforms and riot protection.

"I need to get in," Fembletun said forcefully into the face of a cathedral security officer.

The security officer's attentions were divided by two crying females who claimed they had been robbed and assaulted by a band of roving young males. Both females tried to simultaneously give their accounts of what had happened as the besieged officer simply shook his head and tried to divide his attention with everything else that was going on.

Fembletun impatiently pushed past the security officer who mumbled for him to stop, but Fembletun was already beyond the gate and making his way up the tall staircase toward the entrance of the Basilica.

He jogged the steps with a rigid, militant determination. Entering the outer vestibule, he pulled open the tall wooden doors and witnessed a sparse gathering of cathedral patrons scattered throughout the bowl of the main pews surrounding the empty triangular spotlit pulpit in the center. By contrast to the loud noises clashing outside, the mammoth, sacred sanctuary within these holy walls was dead quiet. It was as if he had stepped out of the world and into the vestibule of Heaven.

It was a prayerful cradle of soothing tranquility. Unfortunately, tonight, he really didn't care.

"Okay, everyone!" Fembletun's voice ruptured the reverent quiet. "I need to see the Holy Inquisitor right now! Has anybody seen him?"

The individuals, violently snatched from their prayers and meditations, looked up with dismay and disgust.

"Shhh!" one person hissed at Fembletun.

"Look, I know this is inconvenient for all of you," Fembletun's voice reverberated through the ornately carved triforiums overhead, "but the Holy Inquisitor is the acting Deliverer and I need to speak with him. Has anybody seen him? Anybody?"

No one responded as they all stood still in stunned indignation.

Fembletun reached inside his long coat. He withdrew a large glistening pewter colored firearm and held it high. There was a smattering of squelched shrieks as everyone ducked down between the benches.

"This is a very serious matter." His voice was loud and steady as he purposefully strolled down the aisle. "None of you are going to get hurt, but I have to see the Holy Inquisitor!"

The mood in the enormous main basilica sanctuary shifted to one of terrorized disbelief. This was the last place anyone ever expected to witness an act of violence, let alone the brandishing of a lethal hand weapon. Everyone noted Fembletun was a policer, but there was something eerily unsettling in his irreverent demeanor that convinced them this had nothing to do with law enforcement tonight.

Frustrated, Fembletun's jaw set like an iron vice. He stalked up the pulpit stairs and stepped under the spotlights illuminating the lavender carpeted stage. He tossed aside his wide-brimmed hat and pulled off his long coat. The lights glistened on his smooth black scalp as the veins lining his temples writhed with tension. He scornfully scowled at the smattering of hunched-over patrons, who now knelt in fear rather than penitence behind the benches.

"I don't know why you all are hiding," he spoke in a mild tone. "I said that none of you are going to get hurt. And when I say that no one is going to get hurt, I mean that no one is going to get hurt! I wouldn't lie to any of you. Lying isn't in my nature. I believe in telling the truth. Because once a person starts lying, he has to tell more lies to prop up the first lie. Pretty soon he starts lying and lying and lying until his entire reality is just one big fat lie. You ask him his name or where he's from and even he's not sure if he's telling you the truth anymore because he's grown so accustomed to lying every time he opens his mouth.

"I have a lot of experience with liars. In my line of work that's all you see. Witnesses lie. Perpetrators lie. The media lies. Lawbookers lie. Judiciaries lie. Politicians lie. I've even had my fellow policers lie straight to my face! My brothers in arms. But underneath all the layers and layers of lying…is the truth. The truth.

My job is still to get to the truth. I face a wall of lies ten meters thick and I still have to get to the truth! Why? Because some father or mother or husband or wife or child is RELYING on me! They're relying on me to tell them who killed their loved one. They even want me to tell them why! And I don't get paid extra for 'why'. But they need to know who. They need to know why. They need to know the truth so that they can get on with their lives and not be stranded in a black hole of grief with a bunch of unanswered questions! They need to know the truth! The truth! The only thing in life that separates reality from fiction. The only thing that separates our lives from our nightmares! The only thing that separates mortality…from God. Truth.

"And you all come here looking for the same thing. You all come here looking for the truth. I know, because I do. I did. I came here because I knew that the Deliveress would always tell me the truth. This glorious, beauteous, pious lady who disseminated scripture like rivers of poetry flowing from the heavens. She wouldn't lie to me. She couldn't lie to me. Not the Deliveress. Not the anointed chosen servant of the Lord in Heaven. Not her. She was above lies. She was beyond it. She had heard the Heavenly Father's voice! She had touched the hem of His garment. She could never lie to me…and my friends…and my neighbors…and my wife…and my daughters. She could never…."

"You were looking for me." A deep authoritative voice echoed from the pews. Slowly a tall robed figure appeared under the light at the edge of the stage. His deep-set eyes were shadowed by the bright lights shooting down from the high ceiling. His thick grey beard neatly decorated his worn dark flesh. A bejeweled burgundy toque sat on his head. His fingers were peacefully clasped together.

"Holy Inquisitor?" Fembletun squinted, realizing he had never actually seen him in person.

"Yes." The elder male nodded solemnly.

Fembletun straightened his arm and pointed his weapon directly at the Holy Inquisitor's head. There were more yelps and shrieks of fear from behind the benches.

"Get your ass up here!" Fembletun snarled.

"Let these people go," the Holy Inquisitor said firmly.

"Let them go?" Fembletun cracked a smile. "Let them go? These people aren't my hostages. They're your hostages. As far as I'm concerned they can leave anytime they want."

Fembletun stepped back and called out into the torchlit sanctuary surrounding him: "You hear that? You're all free to go! I didn't lie to any of you. Now, get the hell out of here! Right now!"

There was a bustle of movement followed by a hasty shuffle and scuffle of feet as everyone in the pews stood and quickly ushered themselves toward the exits.

However, one older woman stopped and shouted back, "What are you going to do to him?"

"I'm not sure yet, ma'am." Fembletun rubbed his bald head and re-aimed his weapon at the Holy Inquisitor. "I usually let the Lord be my guide, but I'm freelancing tonight. So get your ass outta here."

The old woman frowned and moved slowly toward the exit.

"I thank you." The Holy Inquisitor nodded respectfully.

"Don't thank me," Fembletun spat angrily. "Your gratitude is something I don't want or need."

He stalked to the edge of the stage and went down two steps. He grabbed the Holy Inquisitor by the neck of his robe and dragged him back up to the pulpit. With a violent thrust, he shoved the older man to the floor, then dropped to his knees and pointed his weapon directly into the Inquisitor's face.

"What am I supposed to tell my wife and daughters tonight?" Beads of sweat formed on the crown of Fembletun's head.

"I beg your pardon?" The Holy Inquisitor struggled to catch his breath.

"My daughter is fifteen," Fembletun snarled. "Some boy at school has been sniffin' around our house lately. Young hungry little cub, looking for his manhood in my backyard. I understand. I been there. And my daughter's pretty. Real pretty. Prettier than her mother. She's smart, too. And headstrong. It may be hard for you to imagine, but I think she gets that part from me. So when I tell her that this boy doesn't have an ounce of sense beyond that hard little knot in his drawers, she thinks I'm being…'obtuse'. Obtuse! My little girl actually used that word on me. 'Obtuse,' she said. The whole thing was almost funny.

"But you see, she's serious about this boy. At least she thinks she is. And that's a very serious matter. If I tell her she's not in love, she'll ask me how do I know. If I tell her she's too young, that'll bounce right off all that biology eating away her resolve every time she sees that horny skinny little punk. If I tell her to worry about getting pregnant, she can't even comprehend that it could ever happen to her. She's a teenager, so she's got all the answers, you know? But when I tell her that the Deliveress says that 'Thou shalt not fornicate,' it means something. It means that it's not just her obtuse daddy worrying too much or trying to keep her from having a little fun. It means that there's a plan out there that's been set into motion long before any of us were ever born that we have to adhere to. A heavenly plan. A Godly plan. A plan that supersedes the wants and desires of any single individual, including me or her.

"It works. She's a good girl. My wife and I think we've done a good job. But today, it's all gone. Wiped away. How do I explain to my daughter that everything we've been telling her is a lie? How do I explain to my daughter that the Deliverer I've been quoting to her is a murderer, an adulterer and a traitor to all the values we built our lives on?

"For that matter, how do I explain to my wife why I've been dumping twenty percent of my salary into this place when our vehicle craps out every five-thousand kilometers? When four people have to fight for one shower every morning in our cramped little hut? When our marriage is strained and I can't even take her on a second honeymoon up north because it's not in the budget? And what's going to stop her from taking that guy at her job up on his offer to put a little excitement in her life while I spend my nights sniffing dead corpses and crime scenes to put food on the table?

"My wife likes to point out the Churchlord scandals…celibate leaders of the cathedral molesting and mutilating the lives of young children. I used to tell her, the Deliveress doesn't approve of that and she'll do anything in her power to stop it. The Deliveress is the perfection of our faith, so don't worry. She'll make it all right. I don't know what to tell her now.

"And how do I tell my youngest that it's wrong to steal or pick on people smaller than her? That it's wrong to lie to the teacher or anyone else on this planet, for that matter? That this life isn't about what we take for ourselves, but what we give back, and that we shouldn't expect anything in return for goodness or charity? How do I explain that there is still such a thing as goodness and evil? And that it really does matter whether you're a heathen or a saint?

"How do I explain that everything I've ever heard in this building still holds water? How do I explain that the Deliveress is a liar, but we should still do everything she's been telling us? How do I do that? What am I suppose to tell my family when I go home, tonight, Holy Inquisitor? I need to know. Because if you don't give me a good reason, a damn good reason, I don't think I need to go home at all. Not when I don't have any more to offer my family than a pack of lies. Does this make sense to you?"

The Holy Inquisitor looked down the barrel of Fembletun's weapon and into his angry eyes. He didn't see the eyes of a murderer or a madman. He saw the eyes of a father and a husband locked in a desperate struggle to save his family any way he could.

"The Text," the Inquisitor spoke clearly. "Do you read it?"

The fire in Fembletun's eyes receded just a little.

"You own one, don't you?" the Inquisitor continued.

"Y…Yes."

"And you read it?" the Inquisitor repeated.

Fembletun's eyes darted from side to side. He knew that he had read…some of it, but he wasn't sure where or when.

"No?" the Inquisitor proceeded.

"Yes," Fembletun answered. "Yes. All the time. Whenever we come here. The Deliveress reads. Then we read some…"

"That's not what I meant, officer." the Inquisitor was firm, but respectful. "Do you read it; study it…at home…at work…at lunch…in transit…anywhere else but here?"

"Why would…?" Fembletun started.

"Because that's where the truth lies." The Inquisitor gently guided the barrel of the weapon away from his face with the back of his hand. "It's not about this building of crystal and ivory and gold. It's not about the righteousness of the Deliverancy. It's not about the history carved into these hallowed walls. It's not about rows upon rows of statues of mortal saints lined up out in the Basilica corridors. It's about the Text. It's about the Word of God. It's about what was preached to the denizens of this world centuries before our traceable ancestors were ever born. It's about the miracles chronicled therein. It's about the laws to be obeyed and the promises that will be kept and our faith in the Lord in Heaven. The actions of a single person, even one bearing the Deliverer's robes, can never supersede what God has written in our hearts and our minds and our souls.

"The Text is where you'll find your truth. Here…within this grandiose edifice…with our titles and our teaching…we merely attempt to be the curators of it. We are not a law or truth unto ourselves, and we certainly do not exist to be worshipped. There is no divinity in buildings or symbols or statues or flesh. The only divinity is in God Himself. A Churchlord or Deliverer is heir to flaws, fallibility, temptation and sin, just like anyone else. Only the true written words of the Lord, The Text, is perfect and eternal"

A trickle of sweat ran down the side of Fembletun's confounded expression.

"No." Fembletun gestured with his weapon and stood up. "No, no, no, no, no! That is not what I have been hearing for the last twenty twinmoons! That is not what the Deliverer who baptized me taught! That is not what the Deliverer who married my wife and I taught us. That is not what Deliveress Jen has been saying for the last four twinmoons. That is not what Cathedral law has said for the last two millennia! You are wrong, man! You are dead wrong! You are…"

"It doesn't make sense to you?" The Holy Inquisitor sat up and gathered his robe. "If what I've just told you doesn't make sense, then what does? What does in these times?"

Fembletun pointed his weapon at the Holy Inquisitor again as his dark face contorted in anger. His finger slid along the trigger as the sweat continued to roll down the sides of his face.

"Hey!" a familiar voice echoed from the rear shadows of the sanctuary.

Fembletun quickly spun around and saw the silhouette of his partner Bales standing with five other policers who had their weapons drawn.

"What's going on tonight, partner?" Bales held up his empty hands and moved slowly down an aisle toward the pulpit.

Fembletun's tensed rage slowly drained out of his limbs. His face sank into a resigned pitch of irony. He lowered his head and chuckled with a wry smile.

"Bad night, I guess." Fembletun stroked the sweat from his scalp. "Bad fucking night."

"Yeah, I guess so." Bales stopped at the base of the stage. "You uh, want to put that thing down before you blast someone you used to like to Heaven or Hell?"

Fembletun looked down at the weapon in his hand. He weighed it for a moment. Then he flipped the barrel into his fingers, reached down and handed the butt end to Bales.

"Thanks, buddy." Bales took the weapon and met his partners eyes warmly.

Fembletun turned back and glared despondently at the Holy Inquisitor.

"You people...you can't mess with people's lives...people's souls...like this." He pointed with his finger. "Those people out there in the street need to hear what you just told me."

"It's not that simple, my son." The Inquisitor shook his head. "We have centuries of addendums we have to adhere to. Centuries of traditions. We can't change everything over night."

"It's changing already!" Fembletun's voice cracked. "With or without you, with or without God, it's changing. If this place won't tell us the truth, who will?"

The Holy Inquisitor met his penetrating gaze, but said nothing.

"Let's get out of here." Bales reached up and touched his partner's arm. "You know how I hate these places."

"I'm beginning to understand why." Fembletun frowned, shaking his head. He picked up his hat and coat and wearily trudged down the stairs.

"Hmm." Bales patted him on the shoulder. "I thought you, of all people, had more faith than that."

Fembletun glared up at the Holy Inquisitor one last time.

"I do." He replaced his hat on his head and pulled on his coat tightly. "Sometimes you just have bad nights. Tomorrow? God only knows."

"You're hopeless." Bales shook his head.

"No." Fembletun released an exasperated sigh. "That's the beauty of it. Nobody's totally hopeless. Not even you."

Bales took his partner gently by the arm and looked up at the Holy Inquisitor. "Are you all right, sir?" Bales said to him.

The Holy Inquisitor climbed to his feet with a gaunt, breathless expression and gingerly adjusted his toque. "I'm well." the elder man nodded. "Some counseling sessions with the faithful tend to be more…volatile than others."

Bales looked back at the intense expression etched into Fembletun's face. He nodded to the Holy Inquisitor; the Holy Inquisitor bowed his head slightly.

"Good night, sir." Bales gestured with a flick of his fingers.

Fembletun and Bales strode up the aisle together. The policers parted. The two men exited the sanctuary and returned to the world.

XII.

Leesla was feeling confident. She was feeling powerful. It felt so good to finally air her unbridled opinions to the world without restraint. Rabbel had always held her back. She admired his leadership and charisma, but he had always held her back. Kept her from speaking her mind even within the tavern walls. She detested how inhibited and ponderous his calculated decisions seemed. Yet he had the gall to confide in Panla, the woman who betrayed and killed him.

Foolish male.

As far as Leesla was concerned, Panla's relationship with Rabbel had polluted the Break and diluted their strength. Panla had been a virus with an agenda all her own, which crippled the movement from within and consumed its leader. But those days were over now. The Break was finally hers. The hearts and minds of the world would soon follow.

The tall angular woman stalked down the steps to the dark storage cellar where her captives were bound and seated back to back. She glared at Mr. Linnfeld with an evil smile and shook her head menacingly as if to convey that his life would soon be over. She saucily swiveled her pointed hips around to Genna's chair and straddled the young woman where she sat.

Leesla had changed into a form-fitting pink leather vest and matching skin-tight trousers. The buttonless vest hung open as her dark breasts swung loosely over her bare stomach. She eyed Genna with a predatory leer as she licked her long teeth smiling hideously through her bruised and scabbed lips. She stood, peeled down the front of her trousers and pushed her pelvis into Genna's face.

"Like the smell?" Leesla purred through her clenched teeth. "Like the taste? I hope so. For your sake, I certainly hope so. You see, your fat old friend here has no chance. He was made with all the wrong parts. But you, my precious little sweet, were made to order. I wanted you the first day I laid eyes on those sweet little teats of yours...and that pouty little mouth. I knew from the first moment..."

"You didn't ask me if I liked the smell," Linnfeld interrupted. "And I can bloody well tell you that it smells like the dead sea-rhinos we used to gut when I was in the Ocean Corps. Of course, the stink was understandable. They died from bowel blockage, so when we cut them open..."

"You shut up!" Leesla shouted as she snapped her pants back up onto her hips.

"I've heard better seductions grunting out of zoo cages, lady," Linnfeld continued. "The sad thing is you just don't get it. You don't have to believe in God to realize that you've got your britches on backwards. Females go with males. Round peg, round hole! And they usually bathe at least a few days before intercourse. Most animals at least roll through a damp mud hole before..."

Leesla picked up the first wooden stool she could grab and smashed Linnfeld across the head with a mad, shriek. One of the legs broke off in her hand. She glared wildly at Linnfeld and was about to strike him again when she saw him slump down in his bindings unconscious, a large bleeding gash swelling on the side of his head.

"Mr. Linnfeld?" Genna called as she struggled to look over her shoulder. "Mr. Linnfeld?"

A breathless Leesla stepped back around and stood in front of Genna. With a wild swing, she savagely slapped the younger woman across the face.

"Your friend is dead!" Leesla snarled. "And you will be too, unless you change your heart!"

Genna dropped her head and sobbed.

A twisted rage contorted Leesla's shining dark face.

"Leesla." A muscular, bearded man appeared in the cellar doorway.

"What?" Leesla shouted.

"There's a very large government vehicle hovering outside." He looked concerned.

She rolled her eyes from side to side for a moment, processing what he had just said.

"Ah." Leesla's frown stretched into a leathery confident smile. "Our friends are here to reward us for my performance today."

The tall dark woman leaned over and pinched Genna by the chin.

"You see, my love." She smiled. "You'd better get on the winning side. The game is rigged."

Leesla flipped Genna's chin with her finger. Genna recoiled in revulsion, the tears still streaming down her dark cheeks. Leesla turned away, pretending she didn't notice how deeply repulsed Genna was.

"Keep this door locked," Leesla commanded a tall muscular female. "Don't kill the fat one yet. When he regains consciousness, I'm going to make him sorry he was ever born with a penis."

"Yes, ma'am." The large woman frowned uncomfortably as she noted Linnfeld's bleeding head wound.

"So," Leesla turned to her male compatriot, "have they said anything?"

"No." he sounded worried as they started up the staircase. "No one has approached the tavern, and this vehicle is quite large. The sound of the engine alone is making the front door rattle."

"Hmm," Leesla thought aloud as they entered the main floor and strode to the front of the tavern where hundreds of Break mercenaries and followers stood with grave expressions etched on their faces, "Perhaps with all of the changes around here, they felt a need to send a larger delegation. You know the government. They love to throw their weight around, show everyone who's boss. Because I'm a female, maybe those males want me to come out and suck them off before they continue their support of our cause. They should know better. But if they're going to play hard to get, I can be very diplomatic when I decide to be."

Leesla stretched over the bar and pulled out a large black rifle with two steel canisters lodged under the barrel.

"They want to play games?" Leesla smiled at her charges. "Then we can play very dangerous games. Cover me."

Everyone looked at each other, unsure of what Leesla had planned. But the small army drew their weapons as Leesla pulled open the front door and marched purposefully out into the dimly lit street.

She had never seen or felt anything quite like it. This government vehicle was larger than any conventional transport she had ever heard of. And the drone of the idling engine vibrated steadily through her sternum, up the tendons in her neck and down into the wells of her eardrums. It's wing span was at least fifty-meters wide. It's black metallic hull glistened in the twinmoon light. There were no windows visible. Only the government flag etched into its coned nose and two incandescent blue lights flickering from the tips of both wings were notable. It hovered hauntingly above the street, facing the tavern. It's intentions were ominous at best.

Leesla confidently held her rifle at her side in a non-threatening manner as she approached the craft. She smiled and waved at it as if she were greeting out-of-town relatives who had come to visit for the weekend.

Behind her, a metal garbage canister crashed as a homeless man in rags scurried out of the dark alley adjacent to the tavern and took off running as if Hell were at his heels. Leesla spun around and aimed her weapon, but when she realized what the noise was, she laughed anxiously and returned her gaze to the hovering craft.

"Well," she spoke above the engine's hum, "if anyone is in there, you're making people a little bit nervous. We're all friends. Everything is the same as when Rabbel was here. Maybe even better. Why don't you set down and come in and drink with us? We have so many plans for this wonderfully changing world of ours.

"And," she held open her vest and cupped a hanging breast in her hand, "when we're done, we can party the night away. We know how to par-tay! Hah!"

The large hovering craft ascended about ten meters, then angled its coned nose and wings roughly forty-five degrees toward the ground. Its engine vibration hummed louder…deeper. Leesla opened her mouth and worked her jaw to keep her eardrums from popping. Mechanized horizontal shutters on the wings whirred open as the flickering blue lights intensified into long blinding slits of incandescence.

She squinted and covered her eyes with her forearm.

"What the fuck are you doing in there?" she cursed and raised her weapon. "We're on the same side! I have given you more than you asked! We are going to change the world!"

With a deafening crack of lightning, four concussive explosions burst from the wings of the government craft. Leesla fell backwards and rolled, covering her head with her weapon as she hastily scrambled to try and orient herself.

With her chin pressed against the concrete she saw four metallic, clawed cylinders, approximately five meters in diameter, geometrically embed themselves into the four corners of the stony front of the Break's tavern. There was a loud hissing noise. After several suspenseful seconds, she heard commotion and scuffling from inside the building followed by shouts and screams of terror, anguish and desperation.

The front door to the tavern burst open and what appeared to be a large male came staggering out into the street, howling like a wounded animal, his six-meter barreled weapon dangling loosely in his hands. Leesla tried to make out who it was, but as she focused on his features, she was horrified.

His eyelids were melted shut as his flesh appeared to peel and sizzle, revealing bloody mucousy cheekbones and lipless teeth. His hair ran down the sides of his head like blades of clipped grass washing away in a water stream. His clothing smoked and sizzled, commingling with his burning, puckering flesh. He randomly fired two rounds from his weapon before his knees collapsed, separating from his standing shin bones, and he smacked the ground in a moist motionless smoldering heap.

The acidic mist wafted from the open tavern entrance and stung Leesla's nostrils. She struggled to her feet and watched for the next several minutes as a moaning herd of hundreds of bloody, skinless, featureless Break mercenaries flushed out into the streets and collapsed, one on top of another. It was a monstrously swift, hideous and stunning genocide. A ghastly extermination of all her hopes and dreams.

"Nooo!" Leesla screamed tearfully as she stumbled to her feet. "No! You can't! We are your future!"

She saw something shoot from the right wing's opening and heard it whistle past her, striking the ground. She looked down behind her and saw a one-meter saw blade embedded in concrete. She growled and tried to aim her weapon back at the craft. She tried to lift the sight up to her cheek. She tried again. She looked down and saw her bloody weapon and her severed arm twitching harmlessly at her feet.

Leesla wanted to laugh at this final sickening symbol of their total betrayal and uncompromised defeat, but the acidic cloud had already started to eat away her own flesh. She tried to speak one last time, but felt only a large clot of bloody regurgitation push up into her throat. She doubled over and vomited, watching organs she'd never seen before splatter on the ground in front of her. Her sight blurred. Her equilibrium disintegrated as she thought she had started to float. The last thing she felt was her numbed skull smack against the concrete pavement.

The dark government craft descended again, nearly to ground level. A small launch silo mechanically emerged from the crown of its hull. There was a loud blast and a missile streaked over the piles of smoldering bodies and crashed through the tavern's front door. A large explosion inside caused the outer walls of the structure to creak and collapse.

Munitions within the tavern popped, streamed out in random directions and exploded loudly.

In the cellar Genna tried to pray through the noise of thundering carnage above her and Mr. Linnfeld. A section of ceiling collapsed next to their chairs. She could see a sky of flames through the hole overhead. The smell of acid suddenly burned the inside of her nose.

"I love you, Lord," Genna whispered and closed her eyes.

There was another explosion. She opened her eyes and the side of the basement wall had collapsed in a ball of fire. She saw an odd movement within the gold and white heat, something living. She thought it was a member of the Break covered in flames, but the body moved closer and extinguished itself. It was Crilen.

"It's time to go." Crilen snapped their bonds with a combination of pyrogenic heat and raw strength. He pointed Genna toward the smoking hole in the wall.

"What…what are you?" Genna stammered.

Another section of ceiling exploded above their heads

"Go!" Crilen commanded

She jumped up and started to run toward the smoking exit. Crilen gathered up Linnfeld and hurried after her. In another instant he snatched Genna by the arm. His legs burst into flames and he rocketed the pair up through the subterranean tunnel he had burned, then skyward as Rabbel's tavern churned into a burning pile of rubble and ruin.

Fifteen hundred kilometers away:

"The hostages could not be saved, sir," a monotone voice said over the Accommodant's combox.

"Did anyone try?" The Accommodant drummed his fingers on his desk.

There was no answer.

"Forget it." The Accommodant sighed. "We'll take care of it. We can frame this any way we want to. We can say the hostages weren't really hostages, but defectors. Or we can say our personnel found them among the dead with their throats slit like Leesla said she was going to do. Whatever. We know how to pitch these things to the media. Just make sure those jackals get enough superficial access to our handiwork. We'll all be heroes by morning."

"Yes, sir," the voice replied.

"And good job handling my wife." A vile grin curled the Accommodant's lips. "It's all coming together very nicely."

XIII.

The orange and yellow moons sat beautifully against the bright starlit evening sky. If this particular planet could find no peace this evening, at least there was the appearance of a cosmic solace everywhere else in the universe.

A streak of golden light arced up from the distant horizon of lowrise buildings and hurtled closer and closer to Father Rouan's cathedral until it landed in the open field at the base of the stairs. The bright light extinguished into a cloud of smoke and revealed three living figures.

"Where is this?" Genna dropped to her knees in the tall grass to catch her breath.

"Panla's here." Crilen held on to Mr. Linnfeld and started toward the front steps. "She'll be glad to see you. Come."

Crilen hauled Mr. Linnfeld's bulk up the stairs with little effort. He was finally feeling his first twinge of optimism since he had come to the asteroid belt where this planet once orbited. While the timing of the Break's destruction troubled him, their destruction had been inevitable. And he had managed to save Panla's closest friends and associates. She would certainly be overjoyed to see them safe and relatively sound.

Genna wearily followed behind him, anticipating the reunion with her Deliveress and teacher. A harried relief was just beginning to sink in on her. However, when the trio reached the top of the stairs, Crilen froze.

He looked at the front of the building. It was centuries old and pitted, but he now saw fresh scars. He smelled fresh burns. He looked back down the stairs and noted multiple boot prints and blood stains that had not been there two hours ago. His optimism turned to dread.

Crilen hurried into the front entrance and found the once, illuminated sanctuary pitch black. He gently set Mr. Linnfeld down in the center aisle and gestured for Genna to tend to her injured colleague and stay put.

He wasn't concerned with being ambushed by the enemy. Whatever had taken place here was long over. He was much more concerned with where Panla was and if she were injured or killed. He'd left her side for less than an hour, but perhaps those mere minutes had yielded the deadly interval he feared.

This impoverished southern town was certainly prone to a high measure of crime and violence, yet Crilen sensed nothing domestic or random in the air. Whatever happened had been quick, precise, organized and trained. And there was only one organized, trained, armed force that would have any reason to assault a defenseless cathedral: The Accommodant military.

He reached the pulpit area and nothing was disturbed. It was oddly illuminated by the amber twinmoon light beaming through the tall, opened windows lining the three-story walls. The wooden Chry Temple spire suspended above the ministerial chairs hung in quiet serene perpetuity as if no secular action which transpired beneath it could ever alter the foundation of Heaven.

"Ohh!" A loud groan suddenly echoed throughout the cavernous sanctuary.

Crilen snapped around, following the reverberation back up the aisle from which he had come. He could see the outline of Genna kneeling with Mr. Linnfeld's head in her lap as he stirred. The portly attendant's groan of pain was actually a good sign. Consciousness was always preferable to...

"Mr. Len," a voice whispered close to him. Crilen spun around again and Father Rouan's white hair shown brightly in the dim moonlight.

"Father?" Crilen spoke.

"Yes, yes," the tall old man spoke softly, "come this way."

Crilen followed the broad slumped shoulders of Father Rouan over creaking floor boards until they reached a door with a sliver of light showing beneath it. Father Rouan pushed the door open; six or seven people huddled around a fresh bloodied corpse lying on a tattered cot. Crilen could only see the pallid blood-stained bare feet until he moved closer and the teary-eyed mourners parted for him to see.

It was a boy, perhaps in his early teens, with a large hole ripped through his side revealing broken, cauterized ribs and blackened severed organs setting in a pool of drying blood.

"He threw a rock," a woman who might have been his mother cried into her clasped fingers, "he threw a rock and they killed him."

"They tried to kill us all," a man said. "They fired their weapons at us as we dragged his body inside."

"Who fired their weapons?" Crilen looked up at Father Rouan. "Who killed him? And where's Panla? Is she all right?"

Father Rouan's black complexion was ashen and grave. The assurance he had worn so comfortably a few hours ago was shaken.

"She's gone," he answered, his eyes still fixed on the boy's body.

"Gone?" Crilen frowned. "Gone? Gone where? With who? Did she escape?"

"She called them," Father Rouan looked up and met his eyes, "right after you left. She called them and they came and took her."

Crilen dropped into a chair as the support of his legs was cut out from under him. His heart kicked in his chest. His mouth hung open as his head dropped back and struck the wall behind him.

"When you both arrived here, she told me that this is what she would have to do," Father Rouan continued. "She knew you wouldn't let her go, so she waited for you to leave."

The vision of Panla and Crilen together crumbled into a horrifying image of her martyrdom.

"You didn't try to stop her?" Crilen's quaking voice fought down his anguish. "You didn't talk her out of it?"

"The truth will set her free, Mr. Len." The elder man's voice was firm. "There's no other answer."

Crilen's eyes flashed coal red. His fists burst into blazing yellow torches. Everyone in the small room jumped up and pushed backward into a corner except for Father Rouan.

"They're going to kill her!" Crilen shouted angrily, blasting a smoking hole through the plastered wall. "Don't you understand? They're going to drag her body through the streets, crucify her as a traitor to the world and put her to death! Do you understand that?"

With all of his cosmic rage, Crilen tried to stare the elder man down, but Father Rouan stood still and strong in silence.

With a curse under his breath, Crilen extinguished his flame, turned and stalked out of the room leaving a cloud of grey smoke in the dark doorway. He re-entered the cathedral's sanctuary and stormed up the aisle toward the outer door. Sitting in the last pew was Genna holding a bloodied, semi-conscious Mr. Linnfeld.

"What did she say?" Genna asked innocently. "Can we see her?"

Crilen paused for a moment, staring through the open door into the starlit sky framing the silhouettes of buildings in the distance.

"She's not here," Crilen spoke through a clenched jaw. "She's not here any-more. She…"

He had to fight back the flood of sorrow that so vividly rekindled the emotions surrounding the death of his wife.

"Apparently," Crilen forcibly steadied his voice, "she turned herself in."

"No!" Genna clutched Mr. Linnfeld's body tightly. "Why?"

"I'm sorry." Crilen shook his head. "Tell Mr. Linnfeld I'm sorry. It looks like I've let you down."

Tears formed in Genna's eyes as she whispered a prayer and rocked Mr. Linn-feld like a large child in her arms.

Crilen slowly trudged out into the open air. His body burst into a hot, bright explosion of light on the cathedral stairs. In another instant, he was streaking back over the horizon.

XIV.

Newswoman: Good morning, everyone! I'm Egs Bloyt. An extraordinary series of events last night has led to the apparent destruction of the anti-religious terrorist organization known as the Break and the capture of deposed Deliveress and First Lady, Panla Jen Tem. We have two reports for you. We begin with Fab Hipe in the southwest quadrosphere.

FH: Thank you, Egs. The Accommodant government has been searching for the secret hideout of Rabbel Mennis for over a twinmoon. Last night, they found it. And in the wake of the violent assassination of the Lord Regent and the subsequent deaths of several office workers killed by the fleeing perpetrators, action was swift and decisive.

Shortly after the YBS interview with the Break's new leader, Leesla Luuz, the government was able to trace the signal of her transmission back to a renowned urban nightspot in the most dangerous corner of the southwest's largest city. The area was said to be so violently hostile that even policers had sealed off the area, writing it off as too violent to be controlled. The government had suspected this as a possible stronghold for Rabbel Mennis but could never gather enough intelligence to verify his precise whereabouts. Last night's direct communication with YBS studios gave the government the opening it had been waiting for.

After the interview conducted by our own Yara Pique, the government armory dispatched a Z-3000 stealth combat unit to the location where the transmission had been traced. Government operatives tried for an hour to negotiate the release of the Break's hostages and terms for a peaceful surrender, but Leesla flatly refused any form of compromise. After communication was broken off, several heavily-armed Break mercenaries flooded out into the streets and began firing upon the Z-3000. With that, the government had no choice other than to return fire and settle the matter decisively. From what we can see here, the tavern, which served as the Break's nerve center, has been completely destroyed. We've been told there were no survivors. The Break mercenaries chose to fight to the death rather than be captured.

EB: Uh…what about the hostages?

FH: In light of what we've learned about Mrs. Tem's involvement in all this, the government tells us that they have serious doubts as to whether Lindell Linnfeld and Genna Klos were hostages at all. The com link established between YBS studios and the Break used a high priority security coding that could have only been provided by Mr. Linnfeld. Whether that coding was provided under duress or not was problematic, but the Accommodant viewed the stakes as being too high to be lured into a game of prioritizing the rescue of potentially false captives.

EB: Has the Accommodant said anything regarding this apparently successful operation?

FH: Yes, he has. He released this brief statement that reads: "A threat to our liberties and freedoms was eradicated last night. While the principles of our world are built upon the accommodation of differing viewpoints, we can never sanction the violent and murderous acts of any group or individuals who use death and destruction as a means of attaining their goals. The Break claimed to offer the world a new alternative, but their actions were as old and vile as the original sin. Rabbel Mennis, Leesla and their criminal mercenaries have been wiped from the face of the planet. Our children awaken this morning to a safer world full of all the free choices they will always be entitled to."

EB: Amen. Thank you Fab. But the destruction of the Break wasn't the only leaking news last night. Deliveress Panla Jen Tem was captured in another daring siege that happened several kilometers away from the fall of the Break. Miks Faks has the details. Miks?

MF: Good morning, Egs. I'm outside the Ponder Gulag just a few kilometers north of the Bius Basilica. Here is where some of the world's most infamous and heinous criminals are incarcerated. Mrs. Tem was brought in a few hours ago, surrounded by heavy security which still had trouble holding back a very large, mostly hostile crowd. Mrs. Tem, wearing little more than a white gown and metal shackles around her wrists and ankles, could be seen through security shields as bottles, rocks, food and animal excrement were hurled in her direction. She appeared very worn but oddly defiant in her posture. Despite the flying debris, she continued to hold her head very high and regal as we've grown accustomed to seeing her. She kept her eyes fixed forward and tried to appear every bit the religious martyr rather than someone who's about to face trial for treason and murder.

EB: How was she captured?

MF: According to my leaks, the government was tipped off by someone residing at the old southwest cathedral where she was hiding. When government officials arrived at the cathedral, they were greeted by small-arms fire which they were able to overcome with relative ease. Officials stormed the cathedral, secured their position and conducted a room-by-room search until they found Mrs. Tem hiding in the corner of a men's' lavatory stall. She was arrested with little resistance and transported here early this morning.

EB: Any word on her accomplice, this Mr. Len?

MF: No one seems to know where the mysterious security head has disappeared to. Supposedly, he'd gone out for groceries just before government officials showed up. He probably saw what was going on and fled into the night. My leak says it's only a matter of time before he's caught, but his crimes are relatively trivial compared to the charges Mrs. Tem faces over the next several weeks.

EB: Any word from the Accommodant on the arrest of Mrs. Tem?

MF: Unofficially, a leak close to the Accommodant says that he is shocked and saddened by the turn of events and prays that none of it is true. Either way, he loves his wife very deeply and vows to stand by her no matter what happens.

EB: What a great man.

MF: Indeed.

EB: Thanks, Miks. In other news, an unrelated tragedy struck when fourteen girls died in a fire at a prestigious Cathedral boarding school in the northwest. A dormitory caught fire in the wee hours of the morning. Five of the girls escaped unharmed, but the other fourteen were ordered locked in the burning dorm by their schoolmaster when they attempted to leave the building without their virginity pins. According to a Cathedral Addendum, all females are expected to wear their virginity pins in public until they are married. While the 400-twinmoon custom is practiced only sporadically around the world, Cathedral schools strictly enforce this rule as law. The schoolmaster stated that locking those girls in the burning dorm was the most difficult test of faith he has ever faced, although not nearly as difficult as the multiple murder charges he could face pending further investigation.

When we come back: Who stole Finx Melder's body? Some say it's all a publicity stunt and the actor is still alive. Others say it's just another sick example of cult-hero worship. His fans say they don't care. They just can't get enough of that Finx Melder memorabilia and are willing to pay whatever it costs to be a part of history. We'll have more in just a moment.

MORTAL TRUTH

I.

The orange moon hung in the east. The yellow moon shone brightly to the west. The twinmoons sat in perfect juxtaposition to one another, mounted over the evening landscape like incandescent stage lights balanced for optimum effect to illuminate the large cast of commingling characters playing out their parts in the world below.

An acoustic jive samba comprised of flutes, horns and percussion echoed over the crisply manicured acreage of Yolo Pigue's sprawling estate. The festive jazz danced over the high walls of iron rods and prickly brush with vain bravado, teasing and taunting the uninvited who strolled curiously along the outer boulevards. Exclusivity brashly mocked all plebeians within earshot. And that was how Yolo liked it.

Behind the secured walls, a vibrant din of lively conversations, clinking crystal and swells of haughty laughter billowed from the open patio doors which led out into the garden of marble fountain sculptures surrounding a large octagonal swimming pool. Female guests in form-fitting strapless gowns and sparkling jewelry were interspersed among important-looking males in dark suits, decorating the gold stone walkways.

A brigade of orange-jacketed chefs manned the stable of grills, broiling up every meat and vegetable culinary concoction imaginable and those were just the appetizers. All the guests' dinners would be individually tailored to their palate like a fine imported garment measured and contoured to a perfect fit. A la carte was the order of the evening and the menu was every dish in the world.

Just inside the two-story glass patio doors, Yolo sat at the center of the enormous ballroom, elevated a step above his guests on what appeared to be a giant velvet throne surrounded by a rotating carousel of hors d'oeuvres and drink, hastily replenished by an efficient staff of mindful servants.

A blissfully contented smile bowed Yolo's copious jowls as he admired the ostentatious festivities. He removed the large herbal cigar from his lips and lifted a liter-sized crystal goblet to his mouth. With a large gulp, he splashed the wine into his wide throat, spilling nary a drop. He released a long subtle belch as he set the goblet down and lustily scanned his personal buffet for the newest arrivals.

Yolo zeroed in on a freshly furnished tray of large dough pastries bulging with oily sausages and red-hot vegetables. He reached out with the greedy zeal of a spoiled child let loose in a candy factory.

"Splendid party!" a tall thin older man interrupted Yolo's predatory descent.

Yolo's thick paw halted mid-reach. His expression was chilled with annoyance at this unforgivable intrusion. He glanced up and saw the face of Wyel, the CEO of his highest-paying sponsor, the newly merged Citadel Group. The media giant mendaciously reframed a mien of contentment and greeted the loathsome corporate cannibal like an old and dear acquaintance.

"Wyel, Wyel." Yolo stood and extended his hand over the rotating hors d'ouvres. "My dear friend, Wyel. Good of you to come!"

Wyel's pallid features bore the gaunt sunken cheeks of a time-worn mortician, yet his eyes bore the crisp gaze of a tireless and ruthless assassin. Indeed, he was both. He reveled in presiding over the financial death of his corporate victims. Acquiring vibrant billion-coin companies, stripping them bare of their assets and souls, and selling the corpse to the highest bidding scavenger for a tidy exponential profit was all he lived for.

"I wouldn't have missed this for the world, Yolo." Wyel grinned ingenuously. "It's not every day that the world's leading religion gets flushed into oblivion by a shrewd twist of journalistic acumen. You've done a masterpiece. I'm jealous."

"Oh, you give me too much credit." Yolo chuckled, watching despondently as the meat pastries disappeared behind his chair. "I only presented the facts. I only aired the truth. What comes of it is beyond anything you or I could ever decide."

"Come, come." Wyel plucked a vegetable stick from the rotating console. "The modesty of a cub reporter doesn't suit the maestro of media machinations. The public may gobble up your innocent reporter-of-the-facts facade, but this is me you're talking to. I've seen your scripts on how history will unfold months before it actually does. You don't report history, you create it…like an author or a playwright. If there were a God, I'd be afraid to guess that he's probably you."

"If there were." Yolo smiled. "Alas, I lament to reveal to the world that all there is and ever has been are ambitious characters set upon the planet by accidents of nature. Deliverers, Accommodants…"

"…CEOs and media barons," Wyel concluded the thought.

"A pity." Yolo chuckled. "The world wants to believe there is a moral force governing the destiny of their lives and souls. A compelling fiction we can't seem to shake. Everyone wants there to be something incredibly good waiting for us at the other side of the rainbow, but if you've ever chased a rainbow, you know that it always evaporates into little more than a cloud of mist and a muddy bog full of insects and animal dung. Reality. That's what they'll have henceforth: the cold muddy bog of reality.

"My scripts, as you say, project that once the queen hag Deliveress is executed for her crimes, the masses will have all the justification required to release themselves from the clutches of the obscenely abstract Cathedral ideology. They'll stop searching for answers in the heavens and start searching for answers within themselves. Of course, the average pedestrian is usually lacking greatly in the area of substance, so eventually they'll need a new god to follow. A god that enables their vices. A god that reconfigures the composition of right or wrong to the standard of whatever makes them feel good today."

"Sounds profitable." Wyel's thin mouth spread into a cold, dreadful smile.

"Programming without any boundaries of moral constraint?" Yolo tipped his large goblet. "The possibilities will be as endless as the revenue stream."

"The market was down when that Finx Melder moron got himself killed a few weeks ago," Wyel concurred, "but when the Break was taken down and the Deliveress was captured, the uncertainty dissipated, people began to invest, and the market has been rolling along ever since. Very profitable, indeed."

"Only the beginning, I assure you." Yolo smiled confidently. "Only the beginning."

"So what about an interview with the Deliveress?" Wyel asked curiously. "There has to be profit in that. You've already tripled my rates. Why not a special bonus broadcast featuring the fallen Panla Jen Tem? She is your prize carcass of the hunt, after all. You should have her mounted and stuffed for your mantle when all this is done."

Yolo's bushy brows bounced playfully at the thought. Then he sighed, suppressing a belch, and nodded.

"Unfortunately, the former Deliveress has what's known in our business as charisma," Yolo lamented. "Too much of it, I'm afraid. And because she's foolish enough to have true convictions, she's very likely to say things contrary to our cause. And because she's beautiful and brave, the masses won't care what she says. They'll follow her. Straight into martyrdom, they'll follow her. It would make a spectacular splash in the short run, but in the long run, there would be this moralistic pall coloring her demise with something dreadfully optimistic. People would be racked with religious guilt and start questioning the whats and wherefores of life, god and all such rubbish. They might even begin to think for themselves.

"The masses: thinking for themselves. Imagine that. Instead of riding the crests and eddies of amoral values, they would start to ask those difficult questions which can only be answered by the Cathedral Text. They'd start to believe in the beneficence of a higher power. They'd start to believe that they are accountable for their actions, in plain view, and in private. They'd start the piety/morality cycle all over again. How obscene. How unprofitable. No, my dear friend, no interview with the queen hag Deliveress. It's bad enough they're going to allow her to speak at her trial. Airing anything she has to say works contrary to what you and I are seeking to achieve. The only thing I want now from that harpy is the recorded image of her disgraced death-wail for all the world to see, over and over again. A bloody, garish portrait of the futility of it all. Then they'll be keen to bolt in whatever direction I lead them, so long as it's far flung from everything she ever stood for."

Wyel grinned with sinister delight as he plucked a long-stemmed glass from a passing server's tray.

"And I thought I was cold and calculating." Wyel sipped from his glass.

"Don't worry." Yolo chuckled as he observed the wrapped sausages rotating back toward him. "We share the title. We merely play separate sports by the same rules, you and I. Commerce? Communication? We are the champions of a global symbiosis."

"And the Accommodant?" Wyel lifted his chin.

"Merely a pawn in the game." Yolo grinned. "A very replaceable pawn. And he knows it. He'll follow our lead as he always does and adapt accordingly. His slithery politician's survival instincts are nearly as acute as his libido. That's in my script as well."

The two men laughed, then gazed out over the bustling crowd of invited guests.

"So I hear you're not all cold and calculating," Wyel said. "I heard you picked up Libbi's hospital bills after that horrible beating she received from that raging neanderthal a few weeks back."

Yolo rolled his eyes and shook his jowls.

"Yes, well, it was the least I could do." The large man grimaced. "It being such a sordid public spectacle. Tossing a stark-naked woman off a hotel balcony and into crowded rush hour traffic in broad daylight? Not that such brutality doesn't cross every man's mind, but how tasteless. Whatever happened to slipping a girl a tranquilizer in her drink and booking her on a twilight train to parts unknown before sunrise?"

"Ah, the good old days." Wyel grinned. "We were gentlemen."

"Yes, indeed," Yolo reflected fondly. "Anyway, the charity for this fallen strumpet was worth a kilometer of good will. She was a former employee, after all. It showed the public that we really do care even if we don't. Perception, you see. Perception is the key."

"Excellent party, Mr. Pigue," a female voice intruded.

Yolo and Wyel turned their heads and observed a beautiful, statuesque young lady in a strapless red gown, accompanied by a shorter young male with a ghostly opaque complexion and spiked yellow hair.

"Egs Bloyt." Yolo smiled, shifting his weight to relieve the flatulent pressure building in his seat. "They finally pried you away from that desk. How good of you to come."

"How good of you to give me the night off." Egs smiled back, running her fingers through her thickly swirled golden mane. "This is my boyfriend, Sving Schlonger."

Yolo and Wyel greeted the young man with courteous disregard.

"So, who's here tonight?" Egs leered over the large gathering trying to soak up familiar faces.

"Friends, colleagues and a few rivals looking for employment." Yolo snatched up a pair of the sausage pastries.

"I enjoyed your work a few weeks ago." Wyel eyed the young woman's cleavage with dry, lecherous, grandfatherly lust. "Balancing the Finx Melder story with the Break and the Panla Jen mess was remarkable journalism."

"Thank you." Egs smiled, sizing up the powerful old billionaire. "It was everything you dream of when you're studying to be a journalist...the interviews, the sudden news leaks, the shocking revelations. I was amazed at how I was able to hold it all together."

"And I wasn't." Yolo grinned as sausage grease spilled from the side of his mouth. "I know talent. I pick the best. You were more than equal to the task."

"Thank you, Mr. Pigue." Egs nodded, clutching her boyfriend's hand tighter.

"Well, there's plenty of food." Yolo gestured the couple kindly away.

"And some for his guests as well," Wyel cracked as he unabashedly stripped the young woman naked with his rapacious glare.

Yolo winced momentarily, then conjured a chuckle.

Egs glanced uncomfortably at Wyel. She lifted her boyfriend's hand and tugged him purposefully into the crowd.

"Yolo!" A shrill female voice cut through the din of music and conversations. "Yolo Pigue, you're gonna dance with me!"

A short, round butterball of vivacious middle-aged female energy parted the crowd near Yolo's makeshift throne.

The large woman, an even match to Yolo's proportionate girth, shimmied and quaked, snapping her fingers as her thick high heels pounded thunderously into the marble floor with the force of iron-shod hooves under the weight of some overfed farm beast. Her white hair was styled in a mountain of curls which came to a meter-high peak, held in place by a silver tiara. The bright collection of glistening jewelry around her neck and wrists caught every spectrum of light and blasted blinding sparkle-lasers in all directions. Her copious cheeks squinted her eyes and jiggled into her neck with frightful enthusiasm. Her body was poorly restrained under a sheer, peach, silk evening gown, through which every unbound fold, nipple, wart, crevice and surgical scar could be viewed by anyone too stunned to look away. As she sashayed toward Yolo, her sagging breasts, thighs, stomach and miscellaneous rolls all slung and flopped in random directions with the chaos of a holiday circus float full of jiggling clowns performing random stunts.

Wyel hastily threw back his drink.

"Time to mingle, old boy." The pale, gaunt billionaire fashioned a quick smile before he bolted. "Ciao!"

Yolo could barely move his lips before his only line of defense ducked away into the crowd of party revelers.

"Long time no see!" the woman bellowed.

"Good evening, Massilee." Yolo's expression went blank.

"Great party!" The large woman leaned against the hors d'oeuvres carousel causing its motor to grind and whir to a halt. "Oops! Sorry."

Yolo rolled his eyes and sighed.

"Oh, these look good" The woman grabbed a pair of sausage pastries; biting into both simultaneously as she swayed and danced in place. "Oh, my god, these are fantastic! Almost as fantastic as you, lover man!"

"Really, Massilee." Yolo sighed again. "Must you?"

"Must I what?" The large elder woman jiggled to the rhythm of the music, snapped her fingers and winked at a male young enough to be her grandson.

"Must you get voraciously inebriated and make a spectacle of yourself?" Yolo spoke in a hushed voice.

"Spectacle?" Massilee cackled. "Spectacle? How else am I going to get you to take advantage of me?"

"I wouldn't know." Yolo grimaced.

"Oh, c'mon," she pouted playfully, "it didn't stop you thirty-five twinmoons ago."

"Thirty-five twinmoons and hundreds of kilograms ago." Yolo struggled to keep his voice lowered.

"Like father, like son." Massilee picked up a glass and noisily slurped her drink. "You like 'em young and skinny, tight and pretty. Well, let me tell you something: It doesn't last forever! And it's not supposed to. So you better get real, sonny boy. Otherwise you'll always be a big old, rich lonely bachelor!"

Yolo discreetly and repeatedly fingered the silent alarm on his chair signaling for security to take her way. Massilee bent over and mooned the crowd.

Out on the patio Mr. Nil and Mr. Pont were cornered by Ded Stanc, veteran political correspondent.

"You boys missed the good old days!" The frail, hunched-over, dark skinned Stanc shook his finger, spilling his drink on their shoes. "I was a Churchlord thirty twinmoons ago, but I wasn't making any fucking money. So I went into real estate. And I still couldn't make any fucking money. So I got into news, see. Local news. That's when I met Yolo. He was leaner and meaner in those days, but he taught me everything.

"Yolo taught me how the media can fix elections. It's so simple! You take a poll. You tell people that the poll, any friggin' lame-ass poll, says this person's going to win by this percentage. Then you show the person smiling, shaking hands, working the crowd and acting confident, like they've already won. You show the other guy acting concerned, looking glum like he's already lost. In people's minds that guy, even if they were going to vote for him, becomes a loser. And nobody wants to waste their bet on a loser, even if they don't really like the winner. They say, 'Well, this guy's going to win, so I guess I might as well vote with the majority.' That way, with a clear conscience, when they're chit-chatting around the water spout in the office, they can always say they voted for the winner. I can't tell you how many elections we turned using that strategy. Half the parliament owes us their chairs!"

"Wonderful," Mr. Pont grimaced.

"Oh, shit, here she comes." Mr. Nil looked across the patio.

"What?" Mr. Pont turned, severing his connection with the obnoxious old man.

"The wicked skeleton witch of the northeast." Mr. Nil shook his head ruefully.

Both men witnessed the pale, black-leather stick figure of Proptz Rotz stalking toward them with a long toothy grin stretching the flesh over her pointed cheekbones.

"Living proof of what happens when your diet consists solely of pills, smokes and diarrheotics." Mr. Nil whispered to Mr. Pont as he extended his hand to her. "Hey, sexy lady."

"Why, if isn't Yolo's two favorite little scrotum-lickers." Proptz smiled as she took a puff from her herbal cigarette and hissed smoke through her teeth.

"You must be thinking of that whore who runs the eastern bureau." Mr. Nil smiled. "What's her name? Killed that famous actor last month…"

"I have no idea what you're talking about." Proptz clenched her teeth and lifted her chin. "Finx Melder died in a horrible accident. My people just happened to be in the neighborhood. It was timely journalistic fortune, that's all."

"Like the interview with Preppi Deyz's grandparents?" Mr. Pont added on. "Is he out of a coma yet?"

"Well," Proptz folded her arms over her sunken chest, "I do believe I'm sensing more than a modicum of professional jealousy. I've been nominated for six awards for my coverage of that world-shaking event. If it weren't for this bloody Panla Jen scandal, I'd probably win."

"'Bloody Panla Jen.'" Mr. Nil smirked. "How dare that arrogant Deliveress bitch and the fall of our world's leading religion get in the way of the glory of your dead actor. Life stinks, doesn't it?"

"Almost as much as this dull, stodgy, middle-aged soirée." Proptz rolled her eyes and rocked on her spiked heels. "Where are the goddamn drugs?"

Mr. Pont shook his head, jammed his hands in his pockets and looked away.

"Yara's bringing 'em." Mr. Nil lowered his voice.

"Oh, great." Proptz sighed in disgust "Who put the powder-puff princess in charge of scoring some good shit? If I'd known that, I could've brought…"

"Don't worry about it." Mr. Nil held up his hand. "I was in a fraternity with her fiancé. He'll handle it."

"The old man doesn't like dope in the house." Mr. Pont frowned.

"Are you kiddin'? He invited you, didn't he?" Mr. Nil chuckled.

Proptz burst into laughter, leaning forward and placing her arm around Mr. Nil's neck. Their foreheads came together and they laughed fiendishly into one another's face.

"If he catches us, we're fired." Mr. Pont became serious.

"If he catches us, he has to fire his niece," Mr. Nil smirked. "That's the point."

"What is wrong with him?" Proptz gestured as if Mr. Pont were some oddly disjointed art object.

"He's just pissed because his sweet little Deliveress didn't turn out to be all that he thought she was," Mr. Nil answered.

"Oh." Proptz looked Mr. Pont up and down. "One of those. I didn't think we had any of those kind working for us anymore."

"We don't." Mr. Nil grinned. "He's converting."

"Thank god." Proptz blew a stream of smoke into the air. "If you want to worship something, worship the fat man in the chair. It's better for your career, trust me."

"Meaning?" Mr. Pont became annoyed.

"Meaning I'm a bureau chief and I haven't even slept with the old bugger." Proptz tilted her head with a hint of arrogance.

"See. I told you, you don't have to do the old man." Mr. Nil put his arm around Mr. Pont's shoulder.

Mr. Pont shrugged him off.

"Fortunately for you, he likes females." Proptz smiled. "Fortunately for me, the northeast elevation gives him bad bowels."

"And he hates pill junkies," Mr. Nil jabbed.

"He loves my work," Proptz sneered, "and *my* work doesn't include fetching his danish and his toilet tissue."

"Drugs are here." Mr. Nil craned his neck, ignoring the insult.

Yara Pique and her fiancé could be seen inside the patio doors greeting her uncle at his throne. Mr. Nil, Proptz Rotz and a reluctant Mr. Pont started to snake their way through the crowd to greet the boss's niece and spirit her away as soon as they could.

II.

Her cell was a dark, squalid, stone dungeon.

From the barred window ten meters above, a sliver of orange twinmoon light shone faintly against the coarse sooty cement walls. A small flickering encaged torch on the far wall provided the balance of dim light along with what scarcely passed for a heat source. The air was, otherwise, cool and damp, wreaking of rotting sewage from the leaky plumbing dripping through the stained, cracked ceiling overhead. It was a harsh and spartan setting insidiously designed centuries ago to grind the will of its inhabitant into dust.

Her bones ached from the discomfort of her unpadded iron bunk. Her bare feet were numbed cold by the gritty, stone floor whenever she stood and paced to keep warm. Tonight it was chilly enough to see her own breath. She coughed raggedly and felt the pain of thick congestion raking up through her lungs.

Panla sat in the corner of her prison cell with a single tattered blanket draped around her bare shoulders. She wore only the thin white cotton gown she had put on the day she had arrived at Father Rouan's Cathedral. The once fresh garment, which had seemed to outwardly reinvigorate her sullied aura, was now reduced to a wrinkled, dingy frock. It was the only clothing she had been allowed to wear for over a month.

She rested her forehead on her knees and tried to hold her hands across the back of her head to meditate and pray. But the heavy chains around her wrists, designed for a male ten times her musculature, caused her arms to drop to the ground in utter fatigue.

With her mind, she attempted to block out every unpleasant assault on her corporeal senses, transcending the fears and pains in her body, reaching her spirit out into eternity where she could feel God's blessed and loving caress. She strained mightily to conjure vivid recollections of every personal sin she had ever committed and offered them penitently to Heaven for forgiveness and grace. She would do this every waking moment her concentration would allow, until she literally lost consciousness from the effort.

Concentration, however, was a luxury in the Ponder Gulag. Rodent vermin scurried in and out of the cracks in the walls and bore no fear of making physical contact with sleeping or motionless figures much larger than themselves. Crawling under garments and bedding was an endless game of forage and harassment.

When an icy evening wind wasn't rattling her heavy wooden cell door, the lumbering warders would bark loudly to one another, slamming and banging gates and furniture with untimely, jarring abruptness. Some of her fellow prisoners would shout back in rebellion and a prolonged profane argument would ensue. It often concluded with the growls and whimpers of a sadistically, overlong and merciless beating. The warders made certain the protest was never worth the pain.

There was one burly, bristle-faced warder who took particular enjoyment from blurting vulgar threats into her cell through the tiny peephole in her door. He would chuckle coarse obscenities at her while she used the open concrete commode next to her iron cot. And when he entered the cell to bring her food, he would set the tray down on the floor and lasciviously fondle his crotch, making kissing noises as she hunched in the corner waiting for him to leave. Fortunately, he would always be accompanied by another sentry who would finally persuade his departure, but his filthy words and grotesque gestures stayed with her long after he had gone. Not even the mercenaries and miscreants at Rabbel's tavern seemed as hellishly depraved and threatening as her jailer.

Prayer, more than ever, became her refuge. Her titles were gone. Her followers were gone. Her plans laid in ruin. Prayer was all she had left. But tonight, for reasons she could not fully grasp, her fiery protector Mr. Len hovered at the forefront of her thoughts. She did not fantasize about an elaborate rescue. She had reconciled that death was the only way to publicly atone for her crimes. But she couldn't escape the guilty conviction that she had betrayed her alien benefactor. Betrayed his trust, his confidence, and perhaps more. Nearly the entire time they had been together, it was she who fretted over whether he would betray her and her cause. Yet, in the end, he had proven more loyal to her than perhaps she had been loyal to herself, or her faith.

What had she done in turn? Betrayed the core of her own professed beliefs through adultery and treble-faced deceptions. Deceived him in murdering Rabbel. Endangered his life, and her attendants, in a desperate attempt to amend her crumbling plan for Cathedral reformation. Deceived his devotion, yet again, in calling the authorities to arrest her while he rescued Linnfeld and Genna. The raw recrimination made her heartsick. She knew that only God could absolve her of her innumerable transgressions, but her mortal conscience felt a sorrowful longing to square matters with this alien male who had come through time and space to protect her and, like an innocent boy at a school dance, fallen in love with a feminine ideal she couldn't uphold.

A heavy door in the distant corridor opened, then shut. A steady echo of footfalls slowly marched toward her room. It was not the normal rumbling heavy-booted gait of one or two sentries. It was an orderly procession, and the sound of the shoes against the stones were more light and civilian.

Panla rose from her squat-legged position and slowly barefooted across the freezing floor. The heavy chains dragged behind her making the effort nearly unmanageable. The procession stopped at her door. She heard the congenial murmur of a familiar voice. She smelled the faint aroma of a familiar cologne. The door burst open. Her heart sank.

It was her husband.

The Accommodant stood in the open doorway looking fresh, pressed and powerful. Behind him stood Obseq, a young attendant she vaguely recognized, and a member of the Accommodant security detail. She saw the momentary shock in his eyes at her appearance, filthy, drawn and disheveled. But he held to his official posture until he could conjure the false facade of a caring and loving husband.

"I need to be alone with my wife." He feigned an authoritatively concerned and restless tone.

The sentry who had made all of the vulgar gestures toward Panla stared blankly at attention. With a military competence he had never exhibited before, he gestured the Accommodant into the cell, closed the door and ushered everyone else away.

As the heavy door locked tightly behind him, the Accommodant's mask of sympathy quickly melted away. His earnest gaze became one balanced between victory and contempt.

"I'm ashamed of you," he finally spoke in the tone of a father whose high repute had been brought low by association with the wrongful deeds of his wayward child.

Panla felt as though she were on the verge of collapse until hearing these words. A sudden rage welled up in her that was so deep and personal, it took all of her spiritual strength not to lunge madly for his throat with her bare hands.

Instead, she exhibited an outward calm, drawing herself up and meeting his eyes with the strength and conviction she knew he abhorred. She cleared her scratchy throat and addressed him forthright.

"Good," she answered him coldly. "Now you know how it feels."

The Accommodant's jaw fell before he could catch it. When he finally did, he recovered himself with his signature politician's smirk of irony. An expression that usually signified absolutely nothing, but always looked confident and condescending toward the opposition in front of the media. This was the vacuous political front he always knew to put on to rile her contempt. It was a better response to his wife than anything he could have said.

"Look at you," he said nodding his head with a smile. "What would your dead parents say? You're a mess. Chained to the floor like some godforsaken criminal. Your career is ruined. Hell, your life is ruined. And you don't smell so great either. They're going to try and convict you of murder, sedition, high treason against the Cathedral and lord knows what else they can dredge up. You are finished, honey. In fact, you may not realize it…but you're dead."

"Well," Panla scowled into his smirking face, "you should be quite pleased. You'll be rid of me and have more sympathy and females at your beckon call than you'll know what to do with."

"Oh, I always know what to do with 'em." The Accommodant grinned. "And, frankly, I have that already. But what I really need, strange as it may sound, is for you to live."

"What?" Panla was taken aback. "Why?"

"Because you're still popular, for the most part." The Accommodant sighed. "I mean, you're finished as a religious leader, there's no doubt about that. But your fall has been a huge gain for everybody who always thought organized religion was a bunch of bullshit. You're a hero to those people. Living proof that all the Cathedral's sanctimonious moralizing is nonsense and always has been. Now every female who used to harbor religious guilt about sleeping around knows you're just as low-down and raunchy as they are. Those gals are free to do whatever they want now. And every guy can look at you and say 'She's not so holier than thou. She's the kind of broad who likes to do it.' Of course, I won't tell if you won't.

"But the point is, I can't save the Deliveress. But if you let me save my wife, the First Lady, together we can usher in a new liberated age, the likes of which the world has never seen. Freedom. Tolerance. Choice. Everything people really want. You'll be idolized by billions. The world loves a fallen angel. That, they can relate to. And of course, because I'm your adoring, loving husband who came to your rescue and never lost faith…well, let's say it beats the hell out of playing the role of dumbfounded, betrayed widower.

"You can walk out of this jail right now and climb right back into that designer wardrobe of yours. I've got new witnesses lined up around the corner, ready to tell the world that you didn't kill Rabbel Mennis. Since I had all the real witnesses vaporized, who are they gonna believe? I can rewrite the last twelve months of your entire history if you let me. I can have my people document a plot where Rabbel, Leesla and your old buddy Moll conspired to make it look like you were involved with the Break, when in fact…"

"Stop!" Panla interrupted. "Just stop it."

The Accommodant froze, looking surprised that he wasn't allowed to finish out the pitch for his scheme.

"Where have you been?" Panla's shoulders tensed with exasperation. "Ten twinmoons of marriage and it's like you weren't even there. You have no idea who I am. You married me, but you've never had any idea who I really am. The whole world could see it, but you managed to miss it somehow. I'm not a title.

You may be, but I'm not. It's not about being the Deliveress. It's not about being the First Lady. It's about Him!"

"Who?" The Accommodant frowned.

"God!" Panla pleaded. "God in Heaven, don't you understand?"

The Accommodant's expression grew dark.

"Yes, I have fallen." Panla shook her chained hands. "But through my innumerable sins, I have yet stumbled upon the salvation of the world. If God made me the Deliveress, and I am imperfect, I submit to you that the Deliverancy is imperfect! That is what the world needs to know. That there is no perfect answer in flesh and blood. The perfection and salvation lies in Heaven!

"I won't lie. Not again. Not for you. And not for myself. I know right from wrong, my husband. Do you?"

The Accommodant winced. He started pacing to and fro.

"Right from wrong is going to cost you your life." he spoke across the ideological chasm.

"Wrong from right is going to cost you your soul," she glared unwaveringly.

The Accommodant's jaw locked in wearied anger. She had an answer for everything. A sweet-sounding, oh so holy, answer for everything. Through the course of their entire relationship, he had never been able to offer her any morsel of himself she deemed more valuable than her wretched faith. Not even the conjugations of sexual pleasure he had mastered over a lifetime of multiple partners and experiences. Something was always in the way. Her ideals. Her piety. Her goddamned god! She would not even accept her own life from him.

He turned away, then violently swung back and struck her with the back of his fist.

Panla flew backward from the impact and landed, head and shoulders against the stone wall, in a dazed heap.

"I've wanted to do that for a long time!" The Accommodant pointed at her as she fought to sustain consciousness. "You think you're above me? Too good to enjoy my success? Too good to enjoy our bed? Too good to accept my offer to save your life?"

The flesh around Panla's eye had already started to swell, but she drew herself up on her elbow and met his scornful rage.

"If I save my life now, I will lose it," she said clearly. "If I lose my life for His sake, I will save it."

The Accommodant knelt down and pinched up her chin.

"You're going to die you spoiled, delusional, sniveling cunt," he growled under his breath. "And your religion is going to die with you. Have a nice life, or what's left of it. Maybe you can psych yourself into thinking those spikes are God's loving hands when they shred your body into bloody paste."

Panla met his eyes once more.

"Hit me again, you evil depraved coward." she sneered through her gritted teeth.

"What?" The Accommodant was stunned.

"Hit me again…or get out," she commanded.

For a moment the Accommodant actually considered striking her, but something in the room chilled his intentions with fear. He stood up, backpedaled clumsily and pounded on the door, demanding to be let out. The door cracked open and he slid through the opening as swiftly as he could. Outside, he recovered his authoritative demeanor and led the contingent back down the corridor.

Inside the cell, Panla could feel a warm blessed assurance salving the sting of her physical pain. It was the last time she would ever suffer the presence of her lost husband and there was a small celebration in her heart. As a smile formed on her lips, fatigue took her at last and she finally passed out in the cold dirty floor.

III.

The incandescent light in the room kept changing. Sometimes it was a thick magenta syrup. Then it would glow a fiery red gelatin. Then a blinding golden nova. Then it melted into a cool alien emerald green.

The modern techno-dance-pop music thunked, skipped and pounded against his brain stem, vibrating his consciousness into multiple levels of awareness. Gravity was fading. Up felt like down. His seat felt like it was against the ceiling. The walls looked like turning, spiraling, cone-shaped windows to the stars.

He could hear laughter, but only after the smiles subsided. People would speak to him, but their words, wouldn't connect to anything he understood. It was like a foreign dialect, jumbled with familiar words bouncing off the surface of his cognitive senses. He could barely piece together any language that was his own, no matter how hard he concentrated.

The thickening chemical smoke choking the atmosphere stung his eyes, but made love to his olfactory senses. The lurid aroma enveloped him like the double-jointed limbs of a seductive queen harlot. A succubi for the semi-conscious. It was a pleasurably disorienting misery he didn't want to end.

Mr. Pont was high.

He had refused everything offered to him. At least he was reasonably certain he had. But the smoke twisting from the round, warp-shaped glass "creature" in the center of the room, with all of its coiling rubbery appendages, kept billowing toward him like an enveloping gaseous kaleidoscope...until he lost track of everything but his ability to breathe.

He turned his head slowly and thought he saw Mr. Nil mounted by a topless Proptz Rotz on a fur sofa. She cackled, writhing in pleasure as she blew more smoke through her nostrils than it appeared her entire rail thin body could possibly contain. Mr. Nil licked her throat, then turned and smiled at Mr. Pont.

"But they hate each other." The confounding thought eddied and faded from his mind.

Yara Pique was sitting next to him, he was reasonably sure. Although he didn't immediately recognize the petite young woman until he concentrated on the texture of her hair. Her thick blonde mane was a swirling sculpture of symmetrical lines flowing around her head like shimmering tributaries of golden light. Perfect hair. Beautiful hair. And nice perfume. Expensive coastal perfume. Yes. This was Yara, the princess. Yara, the boss's niece.

In the seats across the shaggy rug, which appeared to sway like a sea of glowing anemone, sat Egs Bloyt whom he identified by her long black shins, her date, the diminutive Sving Schlonger, whom he vaguely recognized by the lubricated blonde spikes scattered about his head, and Yara's fiancé, whose muscular mass proudly bulged through his expensive dark suit as he aggressively gesticulated, physically attempting to dominate the conversation with the bulk of his body and the volume of his voice.

"The old religion's dead," Yara's fiancé loudly blustered. "I've been trying to tell my old man for years. The old religion's dead. That's why people don't want to follow it anymore. It's out of date, centuries out of date. The God we have today has nothing to do with the God people wrote about two-thousand-twin-moons ago. Values change. Society changes. Technology advances. Medicine advances. Philosophy evolves. How the hell can the same old religion apply?"

"But people haven't really changed." Egs leaned over to the giant glass vase and took a drag from one of its dangling rubberized nipples. "If you just look at people, nothing's changed. Males, females, mothers, fathers, sons, daughters...it hasn't changed."

"That's bullshit!" Yara's fiancé raised his voice and leaned forward threateningly. "How can a bunch of warlords who used to use their front lawns for a toilet begin to comprehend the world we have today? How can their rules apply to us? We've got the power of flight. We've got electronic media and communication. We've got more progressive sexual relationships that work just fine for everybody. And nobody's ideals are excluded. Those warlords want us to stay back in the Stone Age when we're ready to reach out to the stars and smack God on the ass!"

Yara yawned, leaned over and pinched up a smoky nipple. She puffed heavily and exhaled a cloud of azure blue smoke, hoping the deep conversation would dissipate into the wafting haze rising toward the ceiling.

"So you're saying the Break is...was...right?" Egs fell back and crossed her long legs. "There should be no God? No religion?"

"No, no!" Yara's fiancé threw up his hands. "No, fuck no! That's not what I mean at all! What I'm saying is that we need a new religion. A new way of relating to God that works for today, y'know? A way that incorporates the evolution of all sentient creatures. Otherwise, people are just going to say screw it...pretty much like they already are. I mean, even the Deliveress couldn't live up to her own code. What does that tell you?"

"That we're all sinners?" Egs exhaled an azure plume of smoke from her lips.

"No!" he slapped his knee. "That's that old outdated guilt bullshit! Those warlords knew they could control the masses through guilt. Why would a real God want us to feel guilty? What's the point of that? The God I believe in wants us to feel happy! Happy about ourselves. It doesn't matter who you are or what you do, we should all be happy. And we should respect each other's happiness and not judge what someone else is doing. That's what we need!"

Mr. Pont wanted to intercede on what he understood of the conversation, but his jumbled senses wouldn't allow him to construct a cohesive thought. He sensed that the young giant needed to be put in his place, but he was in no condition to take him to task.

He lost track of the conversation and felt something settle on his leg. Did someone sit on top of him? Why would they do that? Had he become invisible? Had he physically faded into the furniture where no one could see him?

Suddenly there were small delicate fingers in his hair, caressing his scalp. He couldn't see Egs across the room anymore. Something fleshy and white was blocking his view. Something that smelled randy, leathery, smoky and sweet. He reached out to touch the obstruction and it was flesh. Thin, lean, bony, flesh. Light and feminine to the touch, yet just a bit coarser than he cared for. He saw blurry little circles that looked like tiny breasts, but before he could be certain, he felt a small mouth attach itself to his and take away his breath. He was certain he would forget how to breathe now.

Gradually he felt the pelvis of a thin torso oscillate into his lap. It felt wrong. Horribly intrusive. It felt wonderful. But he needed to breathe. He reached up with his hands and groped clumsily for a pair of bare scrawny arms. When he found them, he pushed them back and the airless suction released his face. He heard a female curse. He looked up and saw long teeth and a hawking bobbed nose. He saw the sunken baggy eyes that were more drowsy than he remembered, framed by a black bowl haircut. It was Proptz.

Proptz Rotz. Apparently, she was making the rounds. He heard Mr. Nil snickering in the background.

"I hate you," Mr. Pont whispered, trying to catch his breath

"Good," Proptz voice droned emotionlessly, "show me how much."

Mr. Pont heard the room come alive with laughter. He wasn't certain the laughter was in response to him and Proptz or whether something else in the room had caused the sudden uproar.

"They can't even see me." His jumbled reason paused. "Or can they?"

"Shut up," Proptz sneered.

"This is bad," Mr. Nil snickered. "He's gonna hate us."

"Fuck him!" Yara's fiancé bellowed. "Who gives a shit? He should be glad he's finally gettin'…"

"Make her stop." Yara stood up and swatted her fiancé across the arm.

"This is wrong." Egs blew a thick stream of smoke through the side of her mouth and flipped her hair.

"What did you give him?" Egs' date frowned cluelessly.

"Shhhhh!" Mr. Nil quietly gestured with a frown. "Nothing. I gave him nothing. He's just drunk, that's all."

Mr. Pont heard the conversation. The word "drunk" slithered in and out of his consciousness. He remembered one half of one drink before his world grew thick and turbid. Mr. Nil must have given him "something". He hated all forms of medicines, prescribed or otherwise, and Mr. Nil knew it. His young reckless co-worker had slipped him "something" anyway. Perhaps it was supposed to be a prank. An idiotic, sophomoric joke whose poor taste and violation of his person was lost on Mr. Nil's amoral ignorance. He could hear the younger man snickering and whispering all around him like a mischievous demon taunting its victim from an imperceptible parallel dimension. But there was more cruelty than humor in Mr. Nil's delight. Mr. Pont sensed that much. Clearly their tenuous professional relationship had taken a turn for the worse. But what troubled him the most at the moment, was that his motor functions were not his own and he was totally helpless to do anything about it.

He felt the front of his trousers come unbuttoned as the damp smoky stench of Proptz's hot breath warmed his neck and polluted his nostrils. Under the pulsing music, he heard another female who might have been Yara start to cackle with appalled amazement. There was a loud guttural male belch. Then another "Shhhhhh" just behind his head from whom he was certain was the ringleader of his misery, Mr. Nil. Another female voice pronounced she was leaving. It wasn't Yara. It might have been Egs. He no longer could remember exactly who had been in the room to begin with.

Finally, Mr. Pont's body gave way to the pleasurable sensation of Proptz's light bony figure riding his lap. He disliked her, but it did not seem to matter. She smelled awful, but that did not seem to matter either. He was certain he hated everything that was happening, but his flesh had seized the reins of his impaired reason.

Mr. Nil snickered again, poured himself a drink and turned up the music.

IV.

"'Take care of my little Aami.'" Crilen recalled the day of his wedding. "I'll never forget the look on her father's face when he said that to me. Like he was handing over his life's treasure. It was the only time I was ever certain there was another man in the universe who loved my wife more than me. 'Take care of her', he kept saying all night. At the greeting altar. On the dance floor. Out on the terrace. 'Take care of her'. At one point, I almost thought he was trying to intimidate me. But I look back on it now and he was actually begging. Pleading with me not to forsake everything he'd done to make her the lady I fell in love with.

"When a man, a father, asks you to keep that kind of promise, you're not suppose to let him down. It's like a last request. A sacred covenant that seals the transaction between father and husband. When that happens, the father's not suppose to wind up at his daughter's funeral for something you did, or failed to do. A funeral where he can't even look at the remains and say good-bye because they're burned beyond recognition. A funeral caused by the selfish ambitions of a scientist husband who put notoriety and fortune ahead of love and devotion. If I had prioritized my life the way a man is supposed to, Aami would still be alive. We'd still be together, dealing with difficult adolescent kids staring back at us with her eyes.

"Instead I'm out here, traversing the stellar pathways, trying to save sentient souls from the corrupted civilizations they build. And she's with Him. With the Lord of the universe. That's the only peaceful thought I have. That my wife was as saintly a soul as I've ever known. And that He's looking out for her now…because I couldn't.

"Now it's Panla's turn. You'd think with fifteen years to figure it all out, I'd have gotten it right this time. But Panla's going to die. Panla wants to die. And there's nothing I can do to stop it."

Crilen stared through the tall warm glass of alien liquor sitting on the bar. The currents and streams of dark magenta liquid swirled around and around. A turbulent carbon reaction would build up at the bottom of the glass, swell up into a white froth that would rise to the top and spill over the sides onto the wooden surface. The drink would then bubble down again and settle for a short interval until the chemical reaction started all over again.

"You know what the problem is?" a gaunt pallid male in a tight silver suit slid onto the seat next to him.

"Excuse me?" Crilen's introspective trance was broken.

"With females." Juds signaled the bartender and lit the herbal cigarette flipping between his lips.

"Should I know you?" Crilen assessed the man with low regard.

"Should you?" Juds answered. "Probably not. But then again, it's all the same shit. We're all part of the brotherhood, you and me. We're brothers and we don't even fucking know each other. That's the beauty of it."

"How so?" Crilen's brows furrowed.

The bartender slid a short glass of liquid in front of Juds and lit it on fire. Juds lifted the glass, sniffed the fumes and then threw back the drink with one large gulp.

"Ohh yeah!" Juds smiled, smacking his lips. "You ever meet a chick who can down one of these, you run like a motherfucker, ya hear?"

"Sure." Crilen wasn't amused.

"So what's her name?" Juds scratched the pits of his jaws, then took a deep drag from his cigarette.

"Whose name?" Crilen grew quickly impatient.

"The girl who's had you staring at your drink for the last hour, that's who," Juds smirked.

"How do you know I'm thinking about a girl?" Crilen indulged him.

"Because we're brothers," Juds snickered, "and I know the look. When a guy's worried about money, he's got that pensive look. His eyes are jumpin' back and forth like abacus beads…tryin' to figure out all the angles. There's gotta be a way he can turn personal bankruptcy into all the coin he'll ever need for the rest of his life. He's just gotta figure out the angles. But with females, that's a totally different look. The eyes don't move at all. They just stare, replayin' the same scenes over and over again in your head, tryin' to figure out where it all went wrong. You keep telling yourself you did everything right. You said all the right things. You gave her everything she asked for and maybe a little bit more. And yet here you are, sittin' alone in a bar, wondering why she still said 'fuck you'."

Crilen snorted a polite chuckle at Juds's wayward insightfulness, but he was not in the mood for this particular conversation. He sipped from his glass and tried to silently sever their connection.

"I knew I was right." Juds smiled and signaled for another drink. "You offered her the whole goddamn world and she told you to go sit on a sharp stick! Don't ya hate that?"

"Look..." Crilen reflected on his last conversation with Panla.

"She lied to you too, I'll bet." Juds blew a ring of smoke over the bar.

"Actually, I wouldn't say she lied," Crilen responded inadvertently.

"You wouldn't, but everyone else would." Juds shook his head. "That's the problem with love. You know she fucking lied to you, but you're still holding out hope that she didn't. You still want her to be this statue of virtue to justify that knife wound in your gut. After all, you couldn't possibly have fallen for some worthless lying bitch, could you? Nah, you're too smart for that. We all are...brother."

Juds winked and nudged Crilen with his elbow. He took another deep drag from his herbal cigarette.

"She wasn't entirely truthful," Crilen finally confessed, "She didn't lie. But she kept some things from me."

"Hah! Hah!" Juds laughed out loud. "I knew it! That's even worse. She kept things from you that have the same effect as lying, but if you call her a liar, she can always say she didn't lie! Holy shit. That's why I don't date smart chicks. They'll skin you alive with that bullshit, and make it look like its all your fault! Have you sitting in a bar by yourself staring into space or talking ta' idiot strangers."

Crilen bowed his head and lifted his drink, trying not to smile.

"Well, listen, brother." Juds leaned in next to him. "I'm thirty-seven twin-moons old, and I've finally got the shit figured out. Took me three divorces, six arrests and two restraining notices, but I think I get it now. Listen to me and you'll never wind up alone in a bar talking to some fucked-up stranger again. First: A female is never going to tell you the entire truth no matter what they say. Only the stupid ones fully disclose. The intelligent to semi-intelligent ones always keep a few hidden grenades handy just in case they need to blow your ass out of the water. You think you know what they know, but they know what you think they know plus the bullshit they haven't told you about. So you get in an argument. You think you got her ass pinned in a corner. And then BOOM! She pulls the pin, stuffs the bomb in your crotch and blows your balls to hell with some shit you knew nothing about that she held back for just the right moment. She didn't lie. She just didn't tell you. So you're left laying on the battlefield of passion with your heart and testicles splattered all over the walls. Meanwhile, she's off scot-free, lookin' like a holy virgin church maid."

"Interesting." was all the response Crilen offered.

"Second." Juds looked at his new drink just in time to see the fire go out. "Shit. Anyway, second: When you're dealing with a female, you've got to remember that she's wired to do this."

Juds laid back on the bar and opened his legs. Some of the patrons nearby noticed but managed to remain engaged in their conversations as they watched him out of the corner of their eyes.

"Did you get that?" Juds sat upright.

"Yes." Crilen looked around to see if anyone noticed they were together.

"Males don't comprehend that," Juds continued. "We know about it, but we don't intellectualize it because it's totally the opposite of the way we think. Everything a female does is designed for her to wind up in that position. Dominated. Penetrated. Can you imagine? I mean, a guy spends his whole life thinking about getting on top and stickin' it in. What do you think they're thinking about? Just the opposite. I mean it works for me, but can you imagine what the whole thing looks like from their point of view? It's fucking crazy! Can you imagine living your whole life to have somebody bigger and stronger than you get on top of you and penetrate you?"

Crilen signaled for the bartender to square up his tab.

"That's why males don't understand females." Juds became animate. "Because we're thinking that they should be thinking like us. But they don't! They can't! They're living in a polar-opposite universe than we are. Up means down. In means out. Yes means no. Good is bad. Bad is good. And, then to top it all off, sometimes they use their language and sometimes they use ours. So you never really know where the fuck they're coming from. Are they speaking male or are they speaking female? Either way you lose. If they're speaking male and you assume it's more female shit, they want to know what your problem is because they're speaking your language, dummy. But just when you assume they're speaking your language, they revert back to their own language and they're still right and you're still wrong. They act like they're the bilingual geniuses and we're the dyslexic retards. It just ain't right, man."

Crilen tossed a large coin on the bar and slid off of his stool.

"So what's the answer?" Crilen couldn't resist asking for a conclusion.

"Sex is good. Love is bad." Juds's wry smile was sobering. "I mean, I love my kids, wherever they are. And I love good sex, wherever I can get it. But loving a female? Caring and all that shit? I prefer my sanity. When you love a female, sanity is the first thing you lose. No thanks."

Crilen extended his hand to Juds and nodded. "Good luck."

"Yeah, same to you." Juds fumbled with a lighter, trying to re-ignite his drink. "Whoever she is, don't let her kill ya. It ain't worth it."

Crilen exited the building with the memory of Aami and the plight of Panla indelibly etched into his heart.

V.

The ground was suddenly hard. The grass was terribly wet. The inside of his head felt like a large jagged stone was crowding his brain against the inside of his skull.

Mr. Pont lifted his face from the wet grass of Yolo's lawn and felt his limbs sprawled out as if he were set to be drawn and quartered. A tingling circulation gradually reawakened the numbness in his arms and legs. He rolled himself over to clear his head and suddenly noticed that the front of his pants were dry-stained and unbuttoned. Alarmed, he jumped up and re-buttoned himself. He looked out in the distance and saw the tall marble fountain statues surrounding the pool and the light emanating from the tall patio doors.

Gradually, it was all coming back to him. He was still at Yolo's party, although it appeared most of the guests had gone. The long formation of grills lining the golden patio walkways were cooling down with the smoky aroma of charred remnants of meats and vegetables, hours old. As he entered the courtyard, the servants were carefully plucking up abandoned china and crystal along with miscellaneous trash strewn about the vacated tables and chairs. The music was gone. And only sparse chattering and chuckling echoed from within the mansion, sounding predominantly like post-celebratory farewells.

Where had the time gone?

The sun had barely set when he and Mr. Nil had been standing in the center of a dense crowd of media luminaries and celebrities, watching for prospects of gossip, inspecting the female cleavages and waiting for Yara Pique and her fiancé to arrive with...

"Drugs," he muttered to himself.

Suddenly his memories grew imprecise. He remembered seeing Proptz Rotz arrive. He remembered an unpleasant conversation instigated by Mr. Nil. He remembered Proptz's, emaciated body, long teeth and sunken eyes accompanied by the stench of herbal smoke, new leather and a foul perfume that made him nauseous. He remembered someone saying that Yara had arrived, but he couldn't remember seeing her. He recalled the loud, pulsing music punching inside of his head. The thick smell of smoldering chemicals. The distorted colors whirling along the walls. He remembered a loud conversation about something that interested him, but he couldn't recall the subject.

Then there was the female. The sound of rubbing, stretching leather. The bony arms. The bare ribs. The small breasts. That perfume again. The stinking hot smoky breath. The thin legs straddling his waist. The hard little pelvis grinding into his lap.

"Proptz," he whispered under his breath in disbelief. "Oh god. How…?"

A servant walked past Mr. Pont and eyed his stained, rumpled appearance before quickly looking away. Mr. Pont looked down at himself and saw the spots on his trousers. He tried to pull his tunic down, but it wouldn't drop low enough. With a heavy sigh and a wince, he trudged forward until he reached the patio doors.

Inside, the plush chairs and sofas were almost empty. The marble floor was scuffed and lightly littered. More servants scurried about policing and straightening the ballroom. Yolo's throne was vacant, but he could hear the big man's voice presiding over a small court of party leftovers by the vestibule near the front entrance. In a nearer corner, to his left, was a gathering of more familiar faces.

Yara Pique and her fiancé sat on a burgundy velvet sofa. Across from the couple, Proptz Rotz sat quietly on a cushioned bone chair, smoking another cigarette, looking tired, dazed and worn, with her usually lean, hungry and assertive facade washed out by the long evening's festivities.

Mr. Pont slowly shuffled toward the group.

Yara was the first to notice him. She popped up with her hands clasped together bearing a remorseful gaze of sympathy. Her fiancé reached up with a giant paw and pulled her back down. He looked Mr. Pont up and down with a mocking smirk on his face.

Mr. Pont looked over at Proptz. She looked like the daughter of death. The rings around her tired sunken eyes were deep, dark and ashen. Her pale cheeks were drawn under her sharp protruding cheek bones. Her expression was almost lifeless, as if her animate soul had deserted her body. A thick stream of smoke billowed from her thin nostrils. She glanced at him carelessly, then coldly shrugged and looked away.

"Pont!" A friendly familiar voice came from behind his shoulder.

Before Mr. Pont could turn around, Mr. Nil had his arm around his colleague.

"Man, oh man." Mr. Nil smiled with a drink in his hand. "What a great night you had! I've never seen you like that, old man! And I thought you spent all your time hiding away in that cruddy apartment writing those crazy commentaries. You're a predator. A man about town and nobody knew it. I'm impressed!"

Mr. Pont violently shoved Mr. Nil away. Mr. Nil caught his balance partially spilling his drink on his suit.

"Whoa, whoa!" Mr. Nil brushed himself off and smiled. "What was that about?"

"You piece of shit!" Mr. Pont growled.

"What?" Mr. Nil gestured innocently.

"You piece of shit." Mr. Pont's anger intensified.

"Hey wait a minute." Mr. Nil grew defensive. "Is it my fault you can't handle your booze? I tried to look out for you."

Mr. Pont glared at Mr. Nil. He looked at Yara who was covering her mouth with her hands. Her fiancé sat forward, squaring his giant shoulders. Mr. Pont looked at Proptz once more. The woman merely leaned her head back, closed her eyes and exhaled another cloud of smoke.

"You drugged me." Mr. Pont returned his attention to Mr. Nil.

Mr. Nil tried to smile away the accusation, but a flash of guilt colored his expression.

"Look, man, I think you just had a rough night." Mr. Nil reached forward and tried to settle him down.

"You piece of shit!" Mr. Pont growled, yanked Mr. Nil by the sleeve and kneed him in the stomach. He followed with a barrage of wild blows glancing off the back of Mr. Nil's head and shoulders until the younger man buckled to the ground.

Mr. Pont tried to continue his assault, but found himself lifted off the ground by Yara's fiancé. The large male tossed Mr. Pont across a pillowed chair. Mr. Pont rolled to his feet and found Yara and her fiancé aiding Mr. Nil.

They helped Mr. Nil to his feet. He had a gash above his right eye that started to bleed profusely over his nose and into his mouth. When Mr. Nil gathered his bearings he pushed angrily against Yara's fiancé's restraint, acting as if he wanted to continue the fight. The larger man prevailed and dragged Mr. Nil back to the sofa.

Yara stalked up to Mr. Pont and stood directly in front of him. The young media princess stood nearly a half-meter shorter than him, but her authority was irrefutable in her uncle's home.

"Go." She pointed him toward the front door with the scowl of a little girl whose birthday party had been ruined.

Mr. Pont glared one last time at Mr. Nil, who held a cloth napkin over his bleeding head wound. Mr. Nil did not look back.

Mr. Pont turned and stalked toward the exit. As he did, his once proud theme of "Tolerance" mocked him. Tolerant amorality had brought him to this.

Across the room, near the main vestibule:

"What was that?" a middle aged gentleman reacted to the commotion across the ballroom.

Yolo sipped from his large glass, leaned over and witnessed the tail end of Mr. Nil and Mr. Pont's scuffle.

"Young people." Yolo chuckled. "Young people. They can't conclude a party without a spate of tears or violence, I'm afraid. A maladjustment to no longer having a proper bedtime. A pity. Now, you were saying?"

"Oh, yeah, okay." The short dark balding male reclaimed his anecdote. "So, this guy wouldn't give me an interview, so I wrecked him. I made every quote he ever gave sound like it came from Satan. I made every gift to charity look like he was lining his own pockets. People think he's the devil incarnate, thanks to me. I could have made him a saint, but now he's fighting for his public life!"

Yolo loosed a large flatulent howl, rolled his eyes and sipped his drink.

"So when are you going to let me come work for you?" The male ignored the wafting stench. "I'm tired of slugging it out in the minors!"

Yolo's body quaked with a chuckle rumbling beneath his girth.

"You can work for me the day you stop performing journalistic surgery with a sickle and hatchet." The large man lifted his thick brows. "Your work lacks guile. It lacks depth. It lacks the shadowy nuance that makes our craft so brilliant. You can't tell the audience what to think. You have to manipulate your audience into arriving at their own conclusion which just happens to neatly coincide with your agenda. They have to believe they've done all the arithmetic themselves, when, all the while, you've been dropping the crumbs along the path as they stoop and peck their way through the labyrinth. A labyrinth to them, mind you. To us, the longest route between two objects sitting side-by-side. For example, in the last three twinmoons, we've never uttered one negative remark about our dear fallen Deliveress. In fact, we've canonized her to the brink of total absurdity. How great now, then, her fall, in the wake of such vulgar scandals. The shock. The outrage. Had we sullied her all along, the impact of recent events would have been dulled.

As it stands now, the abrupt reversal of her image is having exactly the implosive effect I had hoped for. That is the art of the journalistic craft."

The short male smiled obsequiously, nudging the people next to him.

"So, uh, can we talk about that job?" the gentleman pressed on.

"No." Yolo's expression was affably cold and decisive.

"So, Mr. Pigue," a childish young woman's voice interceded.

Yolo turned and absorbed the vision of a slender young woman with fiery red hair and a deep black complexion. Her strapless golden gown shimmered like living sunlight under the vestibule lamps. Every movement of every muscle in her soft slender body was an excitable flirtation. She was the sexiest female he had come across in at least a month.

"Yes, my sweet lovely?" A sliver of drool spilled over his chin.

"A friend of mine told me that you've slept with every female in the studio." she swayed her small shoulders to and fro.

Yolo smiled a deep and lecherous smile, visualizing the consumption of so tender a tasty temptation as she.

"Why that's preposterous, my dear scarlet ingénue," the voluminous giant leaned over and whispered into the jewel dangling from her ear. "I sleep with most of them up at the villa."

The young woman giggled fiendishly and swatted him on the arm.

"You are so bad!" she smiled brightly, trying to seduce him with her innocent young gaze.

"Yes indeed," Yolo chuckled loudly, resting his large palm on her firm derrière.

"I'm…uh…doing an internship over at RATRAG Studios." She spoke in a soft breathy voice. "I graduate in the spring. Do you think…"

"Consider it done." Yolo's grasp firmed on her soft pliable buttocks. "I'm sure you're very talented. And we can always use more young talent."

The short older man frowned, yanked his overcoat over his shoulders and stormed out of the mansion unnoticed.

Just then, the disheveled Mr. Pont entered the vestibule.

"Sir." Mr. Pont spoke to Yolo's shoulder.

Yolo continued to exchange his flirtations with the young lady.

"Sir!" Mr. Pont raised his voice.

Yolo politely excused himself and turned to face Mr. Pont. The large man's warm and pleasant demeanor quickly dropped into a reprimanding scowl.

"Mr. Pont." Yolo looked him up and down. "You're a disgrace. Is there no dress code in that religious Text of yours?"

Mr. Pont's face softened. He looked down at himself. He looked back at the gathering of "friends" and "colleagues". He shook his head as if a liberating and illuminating chord had just rung through his conscience.

"Mr. Pigue." he spoke in a relaxed tone, "there is indeed no dress code in the Text. I apologize for my appearance, but there's more to the body than the clothing we wear and I'm not ashamed. The only thing I am ashamed of is that I've spent twenty twinmoons straddling the fence for you. Working for a person I loathe, in a job I've come to hate, going against every principle I hold dear. You're right about me. I'm the kind of person who cares way too much about what everyone else thinks. I do pray with one eye open to see if everyone else's eyes are closed. Just like I come to work and try to write columns that everyone will agree with. But I can't do it anymore. I can't serve you and them and God. I have to get off the fence and choose one master. Just one.

"So I quit, pig man. I fucking quit!"

"You can't quit." Yolo's voice became deep and firm. "You have a contract. I'll sue you out onto the curb and the only place you'll be writing is on the side of vacant buildings with a broken piece of glass. Don't be a fool."

"I've been a fool." Mr. Pont gathered himself and shuffled to the front door. "I'm not going to die one. Ladies. Gentlemen."

Mr. Pont left the mansion realizing he didn't have a ride back to his apartment. But his strides grew more assertive as he distanced himself from Yolo Pigue and the influence of his media monarchy. The walk ahead would be a long one but he had always heard that it would be.

VI.

The quiet man in the dark suit led her past the vociferous throng of daily demonstrators restrained by barricades and armed policers. The loud barrage of chants, threats and obscenities were more than her senses could absorb. The sea of dancing home-made signs graphically depicting images of Panla Jen as a demon, a whore, a sacrifice, an angel, a traitor and a murderess were as troubling to her as the circumstances which brought her to the Ponder Gulag that cold rainy morning.

Feebie covered her head with a large black beret to hide her strawberry-orange hair. Since her appearance on satellite, she had become a widely recognized and targeted public figure, against her will. There was no way to hide from the media who would certainly report on her visit, but she was even more afraid of random pedestrian acts of violence on her person. It had been more than a month since her revealing interview had appeared to a worldwide audience. The interview that told the entire planet of the secret life of Deliveress Panla Jen Tem. Her confessions had lit the fuse of the sequential munitions which detonated the foundations of the Break, the Cathedral and the lives of hundreds of millions of people. To some, she was a hero. To others she was little more than a co-conspirator turned traitor. The Cathedral's lawbookers had managed to construct a deal that would keep her from going to prison, so long as she continued to assist in Panla's prosecution. But this new role had become a personal prison all its own.

She had loved Panla more than anyone. She still did. Yet her detractors hated her for betraying Panla, and her defenders loved her for the same. Either way, the world had cast her as the enemy of she whom she loved most. More of an enemy than Yolo Pigue or the Accommodant. The crushing burden of this harsh public irony made her life nearly unbearable.

The iron gates slid open. Feebie and her government escort entered the stone prison. Her senses were accosted by the unnatural pungent smell of captivity. This was not the institutionally septic smell of a hospital or a nursing home where the sick were made well. This was the rotting odor of the damned. The forsaken. The condemned. A place where society defecated its living excrement. No one cared if anyone here lived or died. The only thing that mattered was that they were locked away from the rest of the world, never to do harm to society again. The best that would come of their incarceration would be their death notice to the law-abiding public. Notice that the good world had rid itself of one more sinful soul who would assuredly burn eternally in the molten rivers of Hell.

An iron gate slammed behind them. Then another. The loud metallic echoes, combined with the stifling stony walls, caused her already frazzled nerves to make her claustrophobically ill. She actually wanted to go somewhere and vomit to relieve her emotional discomfort. She wobbled on the dark stony staircase and felt as if she were going to pass out. Her escort steadied her and asked if she needed to go home. She swallowed decisively, gathered her equilibrium, and they continued their descent.

The warders they passed were frightening. They were a weather-worn crew of over-large, burly, and imposing male figures. Amoral sentries with deception shifting in their eyes, governed loosely by an authority that had no vested interest in the survival of its inmates. Every other warder looked Feebie over like a piece of raw meat. One even made an obscene wet sound with his mouth, but she was afraid to make eye contact and confront him. She shuddered at the notion that anything she had done had led Panla to so cruel a confinement. No crime, not even the murder of Rabbel Mennis, had earned her this. Not the female who had led her to the light of her faith. Not the friend and teacher who had shown her God.

What would she say to Panla? What would Panla say to her? Would Panla even speak to her after her abandonment and betrayal? She wasn't certain of the answers. She wasn't even certain of what she wanted the answers to be. All she knew was that she had to see her. She had to speak to her, even if it were unpleasant. Even if it were the last time they would see each other alive.

A grimy thistle-faced warder led Feebie and the government escort down the last dark corridor to Panla's cell. They stopped and the warder loudly ratcheted the ancient door open. She looked at her escort and he impassively gestured her inside. She gingerly took two steps forward into the dimly lit cell. The heavy door slammed behind her and the concussive impact felt as if it would crack through her sternum.

She looked around the cold, spartan cell and noted the empty unpadded iron bunk. Next to it was a cracked commode and a leaking sink. She searched along the walls for the cell's inhabitant, but didn't see anyone. Finally, she called out in a whisper.

"Mrs. Tem?" she spoke softly. "Mrs. Tem?"

There was a motion in the far shadows. A rustling sound revealed a head, then shoulders. The figure stood and moved forward.

Feebie became very afraid at the sound of heavy chains dragging along the stone floor. She wasn't sure of what she saw and was very frightened this might not even be the correct cell. Could the warder have played a cruel and deadly prank on her? What then?

She recoiled as the figure approached, but then she finally heard a comforting voice.

"Feebie?" The voice was gentle and inquisitive. "Feebie, is that you?"

Feebie focused on the approaching female figure. The hair was longer than she had ever seen it and woefully unkempt. Her left eye was bruised and swollen shut. Her garment was filthy and frayed. But the soothing sound was unmistakable. It was the voice of Panla Jen.

"Yes." Feebie found herself on the verge of tears. "Yes, it's me, Mrs. Tem. It's me."

Panla's bruised face broke into a broad smile. She dropped her blanket and embraced the taller, younger woman with a strong, loving hug.

The reception was nothing like Feebie had imagined. The embrace was firm and warm and assuring, just as their entire relationship had been. Feebie placed both of her arms tightly around Panla and started to sob.

"What is it?" Panla held her like a long-lost daughter. "What's the matter?"

Feebie could not believe the calm she was hearing in Panla's voice. It was Panla who was confined to prison, facing execution. Yet she was the one receiving consolation. Perhaps she needed it more. Still, Feebie fought to regain her composure. She hadn't come all this way merely to cry on Panla's shoulder.

"Your face." Feebie partially recovered herself with a sniff. "What have they been doing to you? They beat you up?"

"No." Panla smiled rubbing Feebie's arms. "No. They haven't done anything of the sort. I have a cold, you see."

"A cold?" Feebie was completely confused.

"Yes." Panla nodded her head and folded her lips. "That's the official line. That's what's holding up my trial."

"I don't get it." Feebie painfully inspected the bruised eye.

"Well, let's just say that the guards," Panla explained, "have been much gentler to me than my own husband."

"No!" Feebie gasped in disbelief. "He did this to you?"

"Hmm," Panla nodded affirmatively. "It wouldn't have been so bad if he'd taken off his ring. But it was kind of a spontaneous knock, so I'm sure he wasn't thinking of it at the time. So now the world thinks I have a cold. I can't have a public trial looking as if I'd been beaten all over the Gulag. So they'll wait for the swelling to go down, then try me, prosecute me and execute me."

"What?" Feebie whipped off her beret and stomped in frustration. "They can't!"

"I'm afraid they can." Panla sighed. "Even if they couldn't prove Rabbel's murder, the penalties for treason against the government and sedition by a high-ranking Cathedral officer are quite clear. I've read the Addendums myself."

"Did you kill Rabbel?" Feebie wanted to hear her say no.

"Yes."

Feebie leaned back against the wall and sank to the floor.

"I'm sorry." Panla could read Feebie's disappointment.

"It's all right." Feebie wiped away a tear. "I was just hoping they made it all up. But...I'm sure there had to be a good...reason."

"At the time I thought there was." Panla knelt down and placed her hand on the young woman's shoulder. "You saw how things were going. You probably saw better than the rest of us. You had the good sense to quit. I wish I'd have quit with you. But it got so out of control. Assassinations. Threats. I thought I had a handle on it, but everything fell apart and there was no turning back. So I killed him. Premeditated. Just like that. I guess that's what you become if swim in the muck long enough. I wanted them to become more like us, but I became more like them."

Feebie's expression fell deeper into recrimination and sorrow.

"Have you heard from Genna or Mr. Linnfeld?" Panla asked.

"I saw Genna while she was cleaning out her room at the Cathedral," the young woman responded. "She didn't speak to me. She wouldn't even look at me. That really hurt."

"Oh." Panla sounded remorseful. "What about Mr. Linnfeld?"

"I haven't seen him." Feebie stared at the ground. "I heard he just got out of medical last week. I think he's going to be fine. But our lawbookers say he and Genna are both going to be charged with sedition and treason also. They could wind up like Moll."

Panla looked away and shook her head.

"I'm sorry." Feebie sniffed.

"Sorry for what?" Panla asked.

"I'm sorry for going to the media." Tears ran down Feebie's freckled white cheeks. "I thought I was doing the right thing. I thought I could stop it if I told everyone what I knew. I…thought…I actually thought God would take better care of you if I told everyone the truth."

Feebie dropped her head and sobbed again. Panla nestled up next to her and held her with her chained hands.

"God *is* taking care of me. Don't you worry." Panla said softly. "And as far as going to the media is concerned, did you lie? Did you lie to anyone about anything? I saw the interview, and I was sick to my stomach hearing the truth about all the things I'd fallen into. But I was proud of you! I was proud that my student…my Feebie…had grown into such a wise and brave woman, that she could sit in that studio with the whole world bearing down on her and tell the truth. I had my chance the day before, in front of a world-wide audience, and I couldn't do it. But you did!"

"I betrayed you," Feebie cried and covered her face.

"To whom?" Panla rubbed her back. "To Yolo Pigue? The old hog will choke on the truth, I'll give him such a belly load of it. You didn't betray anything. You did what a loving servant of God is supposed to do. You believed in the truth. And you've left it all up to Him. That's all He could ever ask of you. I should be thanking you."

Panla kissed her on the forehead.

"Thanking me?" Feebie looked up sadly. "For this place? For the pain and suffering and humiliation and…death?"

"For freeing me." Panla smiled. "There are no more lies. There are no more truths untold. I am free. And when that trial begins, they will see what truth and freedom hath wrought in me!"

Feebie wiped her eyes and sat up against the wall. She took hold of Panla's fingers and held them tightly.

"I'm glad I came here today." Feebie smiled nervously. "I...might've killed myself if I hadn't. I didn't think I could live with everyone looking at me as the person who betrayed you. But you're still my teacher. My precious teacher."

"We teach each other." Panla met her eyes. "Now pray with me. I've gotten an uncommon amount of practice in this place. I think the Lord knew this would be a perfect sanctuary for prayers."

Feebie glanced around the cell at the dirty cracked walls and tried not to inhale the vile odor.

"That's a stretch." Feebie grimaced, wiping the tears from her eyes.

"Not as much as you think." A serene smile warmed Panla's face.

Panla and Feebie knelt down on the tattered blanket, clasped hands and prayed aloud for the next hour.

VII.

The flashing red information scrolling across the electronic chart on the baseboard of her bed told a large part of the story:
Name: Libbea S. Trullup
Sex: Female
Age: 34
Condition: Compound fracture of the left femur. Severed left leg artery. Compound fracture of the right collarbone. Crushed right fibula. Severed right ankle tendons. Multiple skull fractures. Collapsed lung. Spleen rupture. Partial left-side and facial paralysis. Neurological damage extensive/improving.

Libbi's former hairdresser quietly set the vase of flowers down on the nightstand next to her bed. Libbi looked ashen, bruised, puffy and lifeless, but her chest moved ever so slightly indicating that she remained among the living. The network of clear tubes ran into her arms, through her chest under the sheets and up into her nose. Her damaged arm and both legs were elevated and encased in clear plastic splints. But what he noticed most of all, was that her once shimmering dark mane had become a tangled frizzy mess.

"Girl, we're gonna have to do somethin' about this." He pinched up the strands of her hair with his fingertips. "Best damn medical in the city and they don't have any combs in this place?"

"The food sucks, too." Libbi groaned out of the side of her mouth as her eyes blinked open. "But the doctors are hot."

A broad white smile spread across the hairdresser's thin dark face. "I know which ones you're talkin' about. I wish I was sick."

Libbi coughed. Then the cough turned into a faint chuckle. "No, you don't. Not like this."

The hairdresser's smile faded and he touched the fingers of her free hand.

"I guess you're done with ballplayers and coaches," he offered.

"Not entirely," she responded. "Just the ones on medication. Especially the ones on medication who don't take their medication."

"That's what he's trying to plea at his pretrial," the hairdresser pouted. "He says he ran out of medication and didn't have time to buy more because he was preparing the game plan for the semi-finals."

"Bullshit." Libbi slurred out of the side of her mouth. "He quit taking his medication because it made his dick limp. He told me."

"Mmh." the hairdresser responded. "Well you better let your lawbookers know. That man needs to be in jail."

"They know." Libbi sighed and closed her eyes. "But YBS and the team are cutting a deal. Yolo's picking up my medical expenses which are probably going to be pretty high. Since his team won the championship, YBS is offering them more air time, but discounting their royalty for next season in exchange for div-vying up my medical bills and making the whole thing disappear. Neither YBS or the team wants the bad publicity so…"

"So he just keeps on coaching and beating up ladies on the side?" The hair-dresser threw up his hands.

"Always has, always will." Libbi winced ruefully. "I just should have known better, that's all. I should have learned from the last time we dated. A man who punches a woman in the face is not a gentleman. And a man who tosses a woman over a third-story balcony railing is definitely an asshole…no matter how good he is in bed."

"You should have stayed with that painter," the hairdresser offered. "I've found that artists are very gentle and creative."

"Oh yeah," Libbi snorted, "he was gentle all right. So gentle I started feeling like a lesbian. Besides, he kept wanting to take me to the cemetery so we could do it on his ex-wife's grave. Creepy! When I realized that our relationship was more about him and his ex than us, I was done shining my ass on cold headstones. I had to break it off."

"Eew!" The hairdresser's body tensed up.

They both wanted to laugh just as they always had, but the grim surroundings made it difficult this time.

"So, um, what are the sexy doctors telling you?" The hairdresser's expression became serious.

"Well," a sliver drool fell from the side of her drooping mouth, "they don't know if the seizures are permanent. If they are, I'll need medication. They don't know how well my spleen is going to heal, so I'm probably going to need medication. They think the paralysis will go away with rehab, but they're not sure. Assuming the paralysis goes away, I should be able walk. But I'll probably be a granny-dancer from here on out. Break out the oldies."

"Did they say anything about scars?" the hairdresser wondered.

"Um, well," Libbi swallowed, "I should be okay there, except where my femur broke the skin. They said there'll always be a mark. It's up to me whether I can deal with people seeing it. Guess I'll be shutting off those bedroom lights more than I use to."

"Well, just be glad you're alive, girl." He fanned his hand.

"I am." Libbi's eyes wandered. "But what gets me, the three-story fall wasn't so bad by itself. I landed on my head and shoulder. Cracked my head open...whatever. But the speeding traffic? I mean, if you suddenly saw an ass-naked female writhing in the middle of the street, don't you think it would occur to you not to run her over? I got hit three times! Shit! What the fuck are people thinking?"

"You're lucky it wasn't me," the hairdresser reflected. "I just can't drive. I'd have backed up and hit you again trying to see if you were okay."

A painful smile lifted the side of Libbi's face, then she started coughing again.

"Anyway, I brought something I thought you could use," he said reaching into his pocket and pulling out an amethyst/ruby stone.

"My healing stone!" Libbi's expression brightened. "I thought I'd lost it."

"I found it in Yara Pique's dressing room." the hairdresser said craftily. "She was using it for a paperweight. Ain't gonna be any healing for her."

He reached over and sat it next to her shoulder.

"My rock." She smiled and became teary-eyed. "Now I know why my luck has been so shitty. Now I know where my confidence went. I left it back in that old dressing room when I got fired. Thank you! Thank you! Now I know everything's going to be all right. I'm going to be back on the street and sexier than ever in no time!"

"And you might even have a doctor or two." He smiled.

"Or three or four," she chuckled and coughed. "You're a great friend. I don't know what I'd do without you."

"Obviously, you wouldn't get your hair combed." He plucked up a frizzy strand of her hair. "I'm gonna go find you a comb right now. It's bad enough they got you sittin' here with your arm and legs stuck up in the air. The least they could do is fix your hair. I ain't never seen a doctor out with a woman with bad lookin' hair. That's the truth!"

Her former hairdresser disappeared out of the room and she heard his sassy voice querying down the medical hallway. She smiled for a moment. Then she looked over her shoulder at the sparkling stone she had found among many like it on a sunny warm beach three twinmoons ago. She wondered soberly whether the ministrations of the doctors, her part-time friend, and her lucky stone could deliver the healing she coveted. And, if not…what then?

VII.

EB: Good afternoon. I'm Egs Bloyt. And here's the latest news on the imminent trial of former Deliveress and First Lady, Panla Jen Tem.

Earlier this week, Mrs. Tem received an unexpected visit from her husband, Accommodant Klin Tem, at the Ponder Gulag where she is being held under tight security. The Accommodant is said to have met with his wife for a little over an hour. Today a contingent of media greeted him on the front lawn of the Accommodant Mansion. Here's an excerpt of what he had to say:

Video:

"Sir, how is your wife?" the question was raised off-camera.

"She seemed to be doing well under the circumstances," A grim-faced Accommodant answered flatly. "She seemed healthy. Maybe a little anxious. I think she wants to get on with the trial so that she can finally air her side of the story."

"And what is her side of the story?" another question came blurting from out of view.

"Well," the Accommodant offered his practiced pensive gaze, "obviously, I know a whole lot more than I can talk about now. The best I can tell you is that it's better if you hear her side of the story from her."

"Was she glad to see you?"

"Um yes. We were very glad to see each other. She'd been through a lot and I was very worried. It was good to see her safe and sound."

"What did you say to her?"

"Well, I told her I was glad to see her alive and well, and I told her that I love her very much."

"What did she say?"

"She uh…well…I think that's kind of private. We were very happy to see each other."

"Did you gain any insight into why she allegedly did the things she did?"

"Again, I can't comment on much, but I'd say she explained her side of things very well. She always does."

"How do you think the trial is going to go?"

"I can't speculate on that. I think we have to trust our judicial system and live with whatever they decide."

"Right now she's facing execution if she's found guilty. Can you live with that?"

"I guess I'd have to, but we're a long way from anything like that right now. I think we just need to keep Mrs. Tem in our prayers and hope for a favorable outcome."

"Do you still love your wife, despite the allegations?"

The Accommodant's face appeared to well up with emotion. "Of course I do. I always will."

EB: With that, the Accommodant was escorted to his transport and departed. Observers say he was clearly emotionally shaken and frankly, didn't appear very optimistic about Mrs. Tem's predicament.

This morning, Mrs. Tem received another visitor: Feebie Bleik, her former attendant turned key witness, who sold her story to YBS studios and was instrumental in the events which led to Mrs. Tem's capture. No one seems to have offered any insight as to the nature of her visit. There is some speculation that, because they were once close, Ms. Bleik may have been used by the government prosecution to offer Mrs. Tem a deal. Again, that's all speculative. But its hard to imagine that the two females had very much pleasant to say to one another considering all that's transpired.

As far as the trial date is concerned, government leaks have stated that Mrs. Tem's trial will be delayed a week because Mrs. Tem is a little under the weather at the moment.

In other news, while authorities continue to search for the assailants who stole actor, Finx Melder's body, there are signs indicating that while Finx Melder may be dead, his legacy may only be gaining momentum. Proptz Rotz, has this report:

PR: Who are these people lined up along the wall in beards and robes and sandals? A casting call for a new play? No. These are the fans of Finx Melder, lined up outside a theatre, waiting to view the re-release of Finx's seminal *Bius II*. During these religiously uncertain times and in the shadow of Finx's recent death, the studios thought it would be an excellent idea to re-release what may be the most powerful performance of the most popular and talented actor in our history. It appears their idea has taken hold. Hundreds of thousands of Finxphiles around the globe are lining up to get another larger-than-life viewing of *Bius II*, the story of the world's most powerful and pivotal Deliverer in history.

I spoke with one young male who stated that this was the only alternative. 'The Deliveress has let us down. The Cathedral is nothing but a sham,' he said. 'Finx is the only reality we have left. It's probably the closest any of us will really ever get to Heaven. If Finx taught us anything, it was that we need to stop believing in God and start believing in ourselves.' Not a bad piece of advice. In addition to the re-release of this incredible film, we've received word that Finx's widow, Yanga Blas and singer Lesandra Diik are organizing a star-studded tribute concert in honor of this fallen icon. YBS studios is negotiating the satellite rights to air this momentous event that promises to be a powerful evening of world-changing entertainment. It should be a night to cherish.

This is Proptz Rotz, Eastern Bureau Chief, for YBS news.

VIII.

"I have great news," the dark, shifty-eyed, lawbooker flung open his monogrammed leather satchel and spread his pages of notes across the table, "all of the material witnesses for the murder charge against you are dead. The only proof they have is purely circumstantial and/or hearsay. When its all said and done, you didn't kill anybody. If you did, where's the proof?"

Panla closed her eyes and stretched forth her arms, attempting to negotiate the gnarled tension from her limbs. This lawbooker had come highly recommended by her husband. That was bad enough. But his casino hustler confidence coupled with the thick musty stench of his generously applied after-shave made him and the cold dank Ponder Gulag conference room even more claustrophobic than her dirty, dim prison cell.

She poked under her right eye where the swelling from the Accommodant's blow had receded significantly. Since the opening date of her trial would be scheduled by the health of her appearance rather than the preparedness of her defense, the degree of swelling became her measurement of time. Thus, she saw no point to this farcical legal exercise. She knew the outcome of her trial would be scripted by secular forces far flung from anything which would transpire in this room. By right, she had to be publicly defended, but since the conclusion was not in question, she found the machinations of a mendacious judicial charade little more than devilishly vacuous tedium which siphoned energy from her soul.

"Are you listening?" The lawbooker placed his palms down on the table and tilted his head.

"Yes, Mr. Cockcorn." She wound her neck wearily. "I hear you."

"Well, don't you think this is good news?" He sounded pleased with himself. "No material witnesses mean they have no case. If they have no case, then they can't prosecute. And if they can't prosecute, then they can't execute. If I were you I'd take that as a sign that fate is on our side."

Panla's eyes popped open with sudden and pointed anger. She stared through Mr. Cockcorn as if he were the lowest amoral vermin, ignorant of all virtue other than the basest instinct to survive at any cost. She was not far from the truth.

"What?" He flipped up his hands.

"You're forgetting one very important thing, Mr. Cockcorn," Panla addressed him firmly.

"What's that?" he answered curtly as if she were trespassing upon his legal expertise.

"I'm guilty," Panla stated plainly. "I killed Rabbel Mennis. I conspired against the Cathedral. I..."

"Whoa, whoa, whoa, whoa, whoa!" Mr. Cockcorn placed his hands over his ears. "Whoa! Shhh! Shhh! Shhh! You can't tell me that!"

"But..." Panla tried to continue.

"Whoa!" He held up his hands.

"I..."

"Shhh!"

"But..."

"No!"

"Mr. Cockcorn...!"

"Whoa!" he closed his eyes and shook his head. "Shhh!"

Panla pounded her fist on the table, fell back in her chair and folded her arms.

"Okay." The lawbooker raised his brows and stroked his chin. "Listen. Mrs. Tem, I do not believe in guilty clients. I do not defend guilty clients. The first thing you've got to do is stop thinking like a convict and start thinking like an innocent person who's been wrongly accused."

"But..."

"Shhh!" Mr. Cockcorn held a finger to his lips. "The key to victory is to erase the facts in your mind and bring forward the image you wish to portray. If you want to be an innocent person, you've got to act like an innocent person. When someone mentions the word 'murder', you've got to act like that's a concept as foreign to you as the dark sides of the twinmoons. You have to treat it like a ten-eyed monster from another planet. Something so distant and inconceivable, it even frightens you. The judicator and jury have to see a person so ideologically removed from the crime that they can't even fathom why you're on trial. They have to see you as an innocent victim of circumstance, wrongly accused of a heinous act that can't possibly have happened anywhere within your pious, pristine little world. You have to portray yourself as the Deliveress in her robes, conducting services, blessing children, defending the faith….all that stuff…in contrast to the filthy, immoral, low-life Break members who would just as soon kill their own mothers as kill their leader during some kind of organizational coup. Do you understand what I'm saying?"

"I think so," Panla answered him quietly.

"Were you at the tavern the night Rabbel was killed?" Mr. Cockcorn continued. "Hell no! Why would you be? You don't even know how to get there. You don't even want to know how to get there. Those people were your sworn enemies."

"So where was I?" Panla glumly played along.

"Anywhere you want to be," he continued confidently. "Anywhere you can convince yourself you were, where you don't need someone to corroborate your alibi. Private meditation in your Cathedral study. Prayer. That could take hours. And no one would've seen you."

"And how did I wind up at Father Rouan's Cathedral?" Panla egged him on.

"The Lord Regent got assassinated," Mr. Cockcorn brainstormed, "you got scared. You took off for someplace where you knew no one could find you. Somewhere you'd be safe until things settled down. I'd believe that. Don't you?"

"And what about Feebie's testimony?" she added another element.

"Jealous, backstabbing, conniving opportunist looking to coin-in on hearsay." He smiled. "Half the people already believe that. We just have to convince the other half!"

"And Genna and Mr. Linnfeld?" she continued.

"Traitors, trying implicate you to save their own necks." he gestured dismissively

Panla's expression grew sullen and rueful.

"And God?"

Mr. Cockcorn's face went blank. His eyes appeared to be processing a variable that did not register on any real or relevant plane in his realm of thinking. It was an abstract intrusion on his reason. A concept which fouled his clarity of purpose. Finally, his face broke into a nervous, condescending smile.

"I don't think the government prosecutors will be calling God in as a material witness." he chuckled. "Besides, we don't need God on our side. All we need is to convince that judicator and jury..."

"Mr. Cockcorn," Panla interrupted sternly, "God is my judge. God is my witness. I don't need to lie to a judicator or jury to save myself."

The lawbooker's mouth opened, but for the first time he, hesitated.

"Mrs. Tem," he spoke respectfully, "we are not talking about lying. In a courtroom there are no lies. There are no truths. There are only acquittals, convictions and what everyone in that room believes. If you believe you are innocent, we move that much closer to convincing everyone else that you're innocent. But if you believe you're guilty, everyone else is going to believe that you're guilty, and they'll convict you and you will die. Now if we stick to the plan..."

"Plan?" Panla scoffed. "Is that what you call this? This transparent veil of convolution? I would rather they find me guilty of the truth than to have an entire world watch me try to dissemble my neck from out of the hangman's noose. I would much rather they see that their former Deliveress fell deeply into sin and was willing to earnestly atone for her transgressions than to squirm and twist and cheat her way to freedom."

"Mrs. Tem, I don't cheat." Mr. Cockcorn became indignant. "I play by the rules and I win by the rules. I win! I've gotten dozens of clients freed that no one believed were innocent."

"Were they?" Panla questioned.

"Were they what? Innocent?" He grew annoyed. "What difference does that make? I know how to play and I know who to play. And I win! My clients win. And it's all legal!"

"Well, then, so long as it's legal and we win, there should be no more to it than that," she concluded, just above a whisper.

"You're goddamned right!" He thumped his forefinger into the table. "That's all that matters!"

"Well," Panla sighed, "clearly that's all that matters to you."

"And it doesn't matter to you?" Mr. Cockcorn leaned forward, glaring into her eyes. "It should. It's your life, Mrs. Tem, not mine. I only work here."

There was a part of Panla which grew increasingly outraged by the tone of the conversation. A blistering sermon welled up inside of her that might have singed the neatly manicured mustache from his arrogant upper lip, but then she considered the futility of casting pearls amongst the swine. She knew her time was short. But there would still be time for one last mortar round before the enemy closed in on her bunker and finished the battle. She would not waste any ammunition here.

"You're right, Mr. Cockcorn." Panla held up her hands. "It's not your life. But it isn't mine either. It's the life God gave me and I intend to give it back to Him in as repentant a condition as I can pray for. That's what matters to me."

The lawbooker frowned as if he were taking in the ramblings of a madwoman. He tried, once more, to bring the dialogue to a level he could comprehend.

"Do you want to die, Mrs. Tem?" He feebly conjured compassion in his voice.

"If the government wants to unlock these iron gates and set me free, I certainly will not dally," Panla said softly. "A day hasn't gone by when I haven't thought about a warm bath, clean underwear and a meal that wasn't stale or moldy. But free or imprisoned, I am accountable. And I will not betray the Lord in Heaven by resorting to lies and deceit to save my own skin. You can tell my husband or Yolo Pigue or whomever sent you, that I will not discredit my faith by flailing through some humiliatingly hopeless defense. I'm sure they'd have enjoyed it immensely, but I owe the world much more than that."

Mr. Cockcorn pushed his papers together, tucked them neatly back into his leather satchel and snapped it shut.

"Mrs. Tem, I'll do what I can for you." He pushed away from the table and stood. "But things would go much smoother if you'd cooperate."

"In case you haven't noticed, I'm not much for things going smoothly." a glint of PJ's wit colored her expression. "Let's both do our best and see what comes."

Mr. Cockcorn's personal com caller chirped loudly. He reached into the breast pocket of his pin-striped jacket, plucked out the device, and started rambling confidently into the receiver about an entirely different case. He was still in the room, but he had already left Panla Jen and everything else in the Ponder Gulag far behind him.

Panla quietly rose from her chair and excused herself to return to the relative sanctity of her dark, filthy cell. Mr. Cockcorn never noticed her departure.

XIX.

The News:

EB: Good afternoon, everyone. I'm Egs Bloyt. We've learned from our leaking sources that the trial date for the former Deliveress, Panla Jen Tem, has been set for early next week. Mrs. Tem had been battling a virus of some sort, but we're told that she is recovering nicely and should be sufficiently healthy to stand trial by that time. Mrs. Tem is accused of the murder of Rabbel Mennis, the late leader of the now defunct anti-religious movement known as The Break. Mrs. Tem is also accused of sedition and high treason against the Cathedral, where she has served as Deliveress for the past five twinmoons. She has also been indicted on numerous other conspiracy charges involving terrorist plots and the assassination of the Lord Regent. If Mrs. Tem is found guilty of any of these charges, because she held the highest position in the Cathedral, her sentence can be no less than death.

As for her co-conspirators, Feebie Bleik, one of Mrs. Tem's former attendants, is expected to avoid any prison time thanks to her cooperation with YBS Studios and government authorities. However, Lindell Linnfeld and Genna Klos, two of Mrs. Tem's closest associates, will also stand trial for similar crimes and face life in the Ponder Gulag if convicted.

Meanwhile, high-profile lawbooker Conn Cockcorn has announced that he has turned over the responsibilities for Mrs. Tem's case to his lawbooking partners. He says it has nothing to do with his assertions of Mrs. Tem's innocence or guilt, but rather with a personal conflict over his religious beliefs.

Shortly after this announcement, Mr. Cockcorn dropped another bombshell on the media stating that he would take the lead in defending Muus Durn, the man accused of assassinating the Lord Regent last month.. Our correspondent Miks Faks sat down with Mr. Durn and we have a sample of that interview for you right now:

MF: Mr. Durn, did you kill the Lord Regent?

D: Hell no. I don't even know how to get to the Bius Basilica.

MF: Were you a member of the Break?

D: Hell no. I was a bartender at the tavern where Rabbel Mennis held some meetings. That's how I was privy to some of the goings on between him and the Deliveress. But I was never a member.

MF: How did you get caught up in the policer chase that led to the deaths of hundreds of innocent bystanders after the Lord Regent's assassination?

D: Hell n…I mean…I have been advised by my lawbooker not to answer that question at this time.

EB: You can see the entire Miks Faks interview with accused killer Muus Durn later tonight on this YBS station.

In other news, the widow of late actor Finx Melder, Yanga Blas, wants a statue erected of the man she once had jailed for spousal abuse. Ms. Blas has joined forces with fellow actors and musicians who want a fifty-meter statue to be the centerpiece of a 1,000-acre park dedicated to Finx Melder's career. Tol Bulchette has this report:

TB: Yanga Blas, actress and widow of the late Finx Melder, wants to build a shrine in memory of her husband. "In today's world where so many of our heroes are turning out not to be what they're supposed to be," Ms. Blas stated, "my husband served as a shining example of greatness right up to the very end. The world should have a place to come and celebrate his life." The park, tentatively named Golden Icon Six, after Finx's Golden Icon awards, will be funded by a series of gala events and benefit concerts in honor of Finx Melder, the wonderful life he led and his innumerable contributions to our world's culture. When asked why funding for the park wasn't coming directly from Finx Melder's estate, Ms. Blas informed us that her late husband's assets were tied up in lawbooker battles between her, three of his surviving former wives and his seven children. Ms. Blas says she is optimistic about the estate settlement because she and Finx Melder were never divorced. Stay tuned.

EB: Thank you, Tol. World, we'll be back in just a moment.

X.

Panla was afraid. The end was very near.

Her trial date was set. In thirty-nine hours, she would stand in the Bius Basilica sanctuary before government judiciaries, Cathedral regents and Yolo Pigue's planetwide satellite audience. In symphony, this secular oligarchic trinity would play forth its composition of evidence, intone passionately the severity of carnage wrought by her wanton trails of treachery, and bewail the deservedness of her mortal fate for the greater good of the future of the world.

They would flay and impugn every jot of her character. They would excoriate and dismember every instance of her life. What flawed upbringing brought one so highly bred to the pit of a well, so tainted? By what deception did she ascend? By what lies did she extol corruption under the veil of her specious sermons? O'er what corpses did she build her influences of evil? Shall the silenced truths of those innumerable victims e'er be known?

History would be cruel to her. She was sure of it. The proceedings would lay the place setting and Yolo Pigue would dish up the feast. As for the world, the Accommodancy and the media would divide the spoils. They would make certain that everyone everywhere would always get exactly what they asked for.

Meanwhile, the Cathedral would be left a withering ransacked edifice representing two millennia of false promises, politicized clergy and a dubious conduit to Heaven. Oddly, this fraction of her original plan would succeed. The influence of the secularized, bastardized religious institution would finally be neutralized. Hundreds of millions would turn away. But turn away to what? The infinite maze of art, literature and philosophy spawned by the imperfections of mortal intellects? Mad spiritual anarchy tethered to nothing God ever intended? Millions upon millions of souls would be lost to chaos, ripened for the devil's harvest.

This is what she feared. Not the loss of her reputation or legacy. Not the loss of her life. But the loss of generations of immortal souls she herself had sent scurrying into the cankered bosom of the enemy. God could forgive her for this. But could she forgive herself for leaving the world in a lesser state than she had found it?

Panla prayed.

She prayed for one last opportunity to undo all the wrong she had done. To reverse, by some miracle, the errors which led this planet to the precipice of a dark age from which it might never emerge.

Her public repentance would be a beginning. Her willing execution would be her atonement. But she would also be permitted a statement before her sentencing. With the mouth of a convict, she would try to deliver a final message to the world that would leave some lasting remnant of God's truth on the fractured consciences of those who might still believe. Perhaps it would be the seedling for another sort of underground movement. A movement where believers would gather in small places, not to drink and profane the institutions of the world, but to profess their faith and commit their souls to evangelize the Text anew. They would always put God's words first and render all other influences of their own thoughts and desires to no affect. From this seed His truth would spring forth into the world of aimless souls and save those who would still hear Him. This was her final hope.

Panla tried to compose and memorize the words she would speak at her sentencing. She was given no implements with which to write, so she relied solely upon the organization of her thoughts and whatever God would choose to send through her when the time finally came.

She concentrated, but her cell had grown uncharacteristically warm.

She perspired under the tattered blanket as she sat in the corner with her eyes tightly closed. She tossed it aside, but the heat seemed to intensify. Finally, through her eyelids, she sensed a growing light. She was almost afraid to see what new unpleasantness the warders were visiting upon her now, but she had to look up and confront whatever it was.

The sight was a luminescent standing figure framed in the dim cell light. She recognized the fiery scarlet alien eyes peering down at her. This vision would have been positively chilling two months ago. But this evening it was a welcomed sight indeed.

"Mr. Len," she brightened. "I was hoping I'd see you again."

Crilen knelt down and inspected her. He lifted her chin with his forefinger and turned her face from side to side. The swelling of her eye had gone away, but the bruise was still evident. The muscles in his face tensed with anger.

"Who did this?" he said flatly.

"It doesn't matter." She smiled wearily. "It really doesn't matter at all. I'm so glad to see you again."

"Who did this?" he insisted as if she hadn't spoken a word.

Panla's smile dimmed. Her chest heaved with a deep and remorseful sigh. She was thrilled to see him again, but immediately realized he was taking her back into a world of emotions she had striven so hard to purge from her heart. What did loving any male mean to her now? What did regretting her marriage to the Accommodant matter any longer? She wouldn't be carrying the burdens of these relationships beyond this life, so why dwell upon them?

Crilen reached down and touched her hand. Instinctively, she reached up with her chained hand and touched his grey alien face. Her fingers traced the curvature of his pointed ears. Suddenly, she was a female again…flesh and blood and vulnerable to the emotions of her mortality.

"What a wonderful man I married," she finally answered him in an audible whisper. "He tried to hurt me any way he could. Fortunately for me, he doesn't know me well enough to cause me pain. He hasn't a clue. He never did. Before he resorted to violence, he tried to say something cruel about my parents, about how ashamed they'd be to see their daughter in jail. But the truth is, my father raised me to be a person of conviction. My husband doesn't know what that means, so how could he possibly hurt me? He thinks the world is about perception and popularity. He's a politician, you see. A politician trained in the law-booking chambers of winning and losing. There, it never matters what you believe so long as you win. Beliefs? Convictions? Those words are as alien to my husband as…wherever you're from, I suppose. No, my father wouldn't be ashamed. He might be a bit troubled to see his daughter in prison, but he wouldn't be ashamed."

"The Accommodant." Crilen drew his conclusion regarding her injury.

Panla didn't respond, instead continuing along her own train of reflection.

"Before my father died," her voice quaked sorrowfully, "he took my hand, looked into my eyes and begged me: 'Don't waste a second of your life. Cherish it as I do.' I was so shaken by his love. The love of a dying father still caring for his daughter.

"You see, there are two types of love we need from other people. One is the love of someone who loves us for who we are. The love of someone who knows us and appreciates us and understands us. The love of a person who needs us and fulfills our needs. A person who shares tender moments with us; shares our thoughts and desires and fears. That person who adores how we move; how we think; what we say; how we say it! The love of the person who appreciates God's artistry in constructing the summation of all that we become.

"But there is another love. A love nearly as pure as the love in Heaven. The love of a parent. The love of someone who loves us in spite of who we are. The love of someone who loves us simply because we are. Because we live and breathe. It doesn't matter how ugly, how foolish, how unaccomplished, how much a failure. They love us no matter how high we soar, or how far we fall. They love us no matter what. No matter…anything. It's like a safety net we take for granted, or even forsake altogether because its always there. But we need it, that mortal assurance. To know that someone really, really cares for you; cares that you're all right for no other reason than that they're your father. I used to get angry with him because he never seemed to care enough when I made perfect grades or received my first parish or even became a Regent. It seemed as though it didn't matter to him, all of my 'great' accomplishments. But the beauty was that his love was unconditional. He'd have loved me all the same if I hadn't accomplished a damned thing. My accomplishments made him proud, but they didn't make him love me any more than he already did."

Panla's large moistened eyes peered lovingly into the past. "I miss my father, Mr. Len."

Crilen's expression softened as he inspected the rest of her through the fraying white gown.

"Oh, don't look so sad, Mr. Len." Her voice became oddly optimistic "I'm finally getting my rest. Isn't that what you always told me? That I needed to slow down?"

Panla seemed slightly gaunt and malnourished, though she tried to smile through her discomfort. Her white flesh appeared dry and dinged by the rough-hewn surroundings. Crilen dreaded seeing her in this condition, which was partly why he had stayed away. The other reason he had not come sooner was her roundly predictable answer to his next query.

"Why won't you let me save you?" He clutched her hand and shook it.

"I am saved, Mr. Len," she answered with unwavering clarity.

"You don't have to die."

Panla closed her eyes and tilted her head back. He had almost convinced her to run away to the stars with him on the stairs of Father Rouan's cathedral. Thoughts of love and freedom flashed through her mind again. Then, the crushing force of logic and reality obliterated the notion.

"What would it say to the people of this world if I simply...escaped...ran away." she lectured. "What would the message be? That no matter what wrong you do, there's always a back door? That if you know the right people in the right places, outer space or otherwise, that there is no accountability? No. They need to know that in life, you answer to the law. And in death, you answer to God."

Crilen lowered his head and looked away.

"Remember when we first met?" Panla ran her hand over his neck and shoulder. "Our dance in Rabbel's tavern? I'd never met anyone who made me feel the way you did. And the longer you were around, it only became worse for me. But the timing was all wrong. It still is. I told you then that sometimes our obligations get in the way of our romances. Well, I have a big obligation here. Bigger than you or I. Hundreds of millions of souls are still depending on what I do next. You of all people should understand that."

"I do." Crilen's reserves neared empty. "But I also choose to err on the side of life."

"Temporal or eternal?" Panla challenged him.

No enemy's parry had struck him so bluntly.

"Do you really love God this much?" Crilen forced the issue.

"I can only love Him today more than I did yesterday." Her eyes grew moist and serene. "And tomorrow, more than today."

A haunting inertia of deja vu struck Crilen squarely. It was his wife's voice again. Her assuring sentiment. But then a loud heavy "klunking" noise rattled the door.

Panla's expression became startled.

"The guards," she whispered urgently. "They can't see you here!"

Crilen wondered why the warders should not see him. He felt that a mild singeing might actually do them some good. But he stood, backed into the far corner of the cell and faded into the shadow.

Panla rose up and stepped forward, hoping to divert the warders' attention from Crilen's presence.

The door creaked open and the entrance filled with the large burly warder who had made so many lewd taunts toward her over the past month. This evening, the expression behind his unkempt growth of beard was particularly confident and menacing as he swaggered into the cell and leered at her with a deep, lustful grin.

Panla glanced behind him, looking for the other warder who always accompanied him. Through the opening, there was only the empty corridor and the haunting moan of the cold wind. She felt her heart begin to pound heavily.

"Wh...where is the other guard?" She poorly masked her mounting fear.

He smiled hideously through his crooked, plaquened teeth and slowly approached her.

"What do you want?" Her breath became short.

His chuckle was a succession of deep guttural grunts. "I've been telling you what I want." He stalked closer, herding her into a corner. "Now I've got permission. They want you in the right spirit for your trial. I told them I can do that."

"I'll call out!" She tensed against the wall.

"They all call out." he snickered and settled his large paw on her bare shoulder.

"Please don't!" Panla begged him. "Can't you see this is wrong?"

He pressed his large stomach against her, pinning her body next to the cold damp wall. His thick, callused fingers groped for the hem of her gown as he reached for the opening of his trousers and fumbled with the buttons.

"Hmm!" he fussed clumsily.

"I can help you with that." A deep dark voice spoke from behind.

The warder froze, then tried to look over his shoulder. But before he could turn his head, something which felt like a hot mechanical vice gripped the back of his neck. In another instant, he found his bulk lifted toward the ceiling, then hurtled across the cell, head first, into the far stone wall. His skull cracked loudly against the solid stone. His body bounced backward and rolled over like a giant, lumpy burlap sack of potatoes.

Surprisingly, the large male was still conscious as he scrambled to gather himself on the dirty floor. Clearly, this was not the first time the grizzled warder had suffered such a hard and violent fall, but what he witnessed next was a first for all but a few on this world.

Crilen stood over the warder's sprawled figure, eyes blazing red; flames fluttering from the crown of his head; fists ablaze like golden torches.

The warder's face contorted with disbelief.

Crilen slowly moved toward him.

Instinctively, the warder crawled and staggered to his feet. But before he could fully gather his bearings, Crilen clutched the large man by his dirty leather tabard and pinned him against the wall with his smoking hands.

"You will never touch her again as long as you live!" Crilen snarled with a tongue that glowed like molten metal in his throat.

The warder struggled weakly against Crilen's iron hold, however the burly male bore no fear.

"Who sent you to do this?" Crilen demanded with a penetrating glare.

The warder growled defiantly, then spit into Crilen's face. The wad of green saliva sizzled and evaporated against Crilen's hot flesh. The warder responded by growling and struggling again.

Crilen lifted him from his feet and slammed him against the stone wall.

"Who sent you?" Crilen sneered. "Tell me now or I'll burn you into a pile of ashes."

"Hrrrh!" the warder snorted. "You don't scare me, whatever you are."

Crilen felt a sudden sharp piercing pain in his abdomen. He looked down and saw a half-meter blade in the warder's hand, buried into his side and protruding through his back. The wound was far from fatal for his pyrogenic physiology, but the abruptness of the injury screeched agony through his nerves and only made him angrier.

The entire corner of the cell burst into a ball of fire. There was a loud gargling death wail that quickly died away into the sound of crackling flames and the smell of roasted flesh.

In the opposite corner of the cell, Panla dropped to her backside with her teary eyes fixed upon the horror.

The flames receded into the form of a man again. Crilen's fiery figure turned to her. His rage-filled red eyes made him look positively demonic in the shadows. He started toward her, but she peered beyond him, through the smoke. She could see the hissing blackened, twisted, contorted skeletal remains of the prison warder, partially melted into the stone wall. It's burned skull bore the horrified yawning expression of his final dying scream.

She glanced at Crilen as he drew nearer to her. There was no evidence of the wound the warder had inflicted upon him. She looked to the smoking remains once more.

"Are you...?" Crilen started to extend his hand toward her.

But Panla lurched backward in revulsion, the sound of her chains dragging against the stone floor.

"It's all right." Crilen offered to her.

"All right?" She tearfully eyed the warder's remains. "Is this what you meant? Is this what you offered me, out there...in space...with you?"

"Panla..." Crilen tried to explain.

"More death?" she continued. "More revenge? More hate? More murder?"

"Sometimes..." he knelt down and tried to capture her eyes.

"No!" She looked at him with sadness and regret. "No! On this planet, it will stop right here, right now, with me!"

"Panla..." Crilen could feel the sudden chasm between them roaring wide and deep.

"Go, Mr. Len." Tears rolled down the sides of her nose. "I thank you for your service and your protection. I won't be needing you anymore. Please go."

Crilen searched her face for something that would allow them to continue, but she closed her eyes and covered her head with her chained wrists, wishing him gone.

He suddenly found himself abandoned in uncharted emotional territory. He had infrequently quarreled with his wife, but he had never experienced a cross-road of irreconcilable separation. Crilen and Aami had been deeply in love to the very end. But as he had failed to remind himself so many times, this was not his wife. This was Panla Jen. And now, abruptly...tragically...by his own actions, she could have nothing more to do with him.

Perhaps, this might have been the final movement of his marriage to Aami had she lived to see what he became. He never explored what she would think of him now. He had only dwelt mercilessly upon his failure to preserve what they had. Beyond the fire, there had been only missions and fading dreams of the life he had lost.

Crilen walked to the far outer wall, burned a small opening with his hands and flew out. He resealed the hole from the outside and quietly departed.

He was gone for good.

Heartbroken, Panla slumped over and wept.

XI.

The Accommodant lifted a ladle of steaming hot honey. It smelled so sweet, it delighted his senses. He tilted the ladle very gently and dripped the golden syrup down the crevice of the young female's bare back.

"Ow!" She giggled and arched her lean body. "That feels really...good!"

"I know it does." His smile grew as the honey welled in the small of her back.

"So...um, are you going to the trial?" she asked carelessly.

"What trial?" The Accommodant started streaming a honeyed hieroglyph across her shoulders.

"The uh…trial of your wife?" She tensed slightly and dug her nails into a pillow.

"Oh." The Accommodant smirked without losing focus on his work. "Well, I plan to be there for the sentencing. But my people and I decided it wouldn't look right for me to set aside all of the planet's affairs for my own personal interests, so, I won't be going to the trial. I'll issue some statements instead. Frankly, I don't think the trial's going to be all that long anyway."

"Why do you say that?" She wondered what her back was starting to look like.

"Just a hunch, baby doll." He trickled a stream of honey over her neck. "Just a hunch."

"Wow. OWW!" Her body tensed up again.

"Don't move." The Accommodant commanded her. "I'm allllllmost finished."

"Okay." She swept her hair around her neck so no strands stuck to her back. "It just feels yicky."

"You haven't felt anything yet." His face spread into a lascivious grin.

"Y'know," she embarked upon a vacuous thought, "I can't believe you and your wife had so much trouble. I mean, you're so creative."

"Well," the Accommodant nodded his head in agreement, "some ladies just can't appreciate what they've got until it's gone. You should have heard her begging me to get back together when I visited the gulag."

"Really?" The young woman's mouth fell open.

"It was sad." He set the hot pitcher of honey down on the dresser. "What can I say? I tried for twinmoons, but she wanted to control everything."

"What a witch." The young woman frowned.

"You don't know the half of it." He removed his silk monogrammed robe. "And then she'd beat me over the head with all that religious crap she didn't even believe herself while she was having an affair with that Rabbel Mennis character. It's been rough."

"You poor thing," she pouted.

"I know." He sighed. "That's why I'm glad you're here."

"You're so sweet." The young woman giggled.

"No." The Accommodant eyed the pattern of honey swirling across her back. "Actually, you're the one who's sweet!"

The young woman giggled once more as she felt the tip of the Accommodant's tongue touch her back, but the sensation did not last very long. She waited for him to touch her again, but all she could hear was the light undercurrent of music playing on the com system.

"Baby?" she called. "Sir?"

The room grew very hot. She could feel the honey melting and streaking on her back again. Thus far the game had been rapturously titillating, but she now sensed a more dangerous element entering into the mix.

She rolled over just in time to see someone or some thing clutching the Accommodant by the throat. Its eyes flashed a molten red. That was the last thing she saw. It grabbed the edge of the bedspread and twirled it over her head, spinning her body into a tightly woven cocoon. She felt herself helplessly roll onto the floor. She tried to struggle loose but her arms were pinned and her honey-covered body was glued to the material. She gasped for breath and was thankful she could at least breathe. Still, it was very apparent, even to her, that the game was over.

Crilen sneered into the face of the Accommodant with a violent molten rage which colored his grey features with a crimson glow.

"You like to hit women?" Crilen snarled through his teeth.

"Who...who...are you?" The Accommodant quaked.

Crilen did not answer immediately. With two pronged fingers, he thumped the Accommodant squarely in the nose and sent his soft, naked middle-aged body hurtling backward into the dresser mirror.

The Accommodant's body crashed into the mirror and collapsed on top of the dresser, covered in shards of broken glass. Before he could recover enough to determine whether he was alive, Crilen reappeared over his lacerated, bleeding body.

"Who am I?" Crilen leaned into the Accommodant's bloodied face. "That's a very stupid question coming from a very powerful man. You should be embarrassed. You hired me to protect your wife, remember?"

The Accommodant's eyes bulged bright white through the thick streams of red blood across his face.

"Mr. Len?" He blinked and squinted.

"I left some things off of my résumé." Crilen grabbed him by his hair and shoved him onto the floor.

The Accommodant screamed in agony as the shards of mirror cut through his flesh.

"But you hired me to protect your wife, so that's what I'm doing." Crilen stood over him.

The Accommodant cringed and covered his head with his arms.

"This is really sad." Crilen knelt down and grabbed his quivering arms. "Powerful people like you are like greedy little children who cower at the first sign of a real fight they haven't rigged."

"I….I'm not powerful," the Accommodant whimpered in an unrecognizable voice.

"Oh really?" Crilen snorted. "You destroyed the Break. You killed a child while 'capturing' the Deliveress. You even managed to pummel your own wife while her hands were chained. What would you call that?"

"Nothing," the Accommodant whispered.

"I didn't hear you." Crilen smacked the Accommodant across the side of his head.

"Nothing!" the Accommodant shouted. "Nothing! Nothing! Nothing! I give the people what they want! That's all I do!"

Crilen simmered at the irony. Throughout the cosmos, he had battled despots and dictators and religious demagogues who had withheld rights and freedoms from the masses. Now, he beheld an evil no less vile: an enabler of vice. An enemy of virtue. A monger of secular pleasures, severing all ties to the creator of the universe. What could be worse?

"Well," Crilen's eyes crackled with fire, "now you're going to give me something that I want."

"Anything! Name it!" the Accommodant bargained madly. "Women?"

"Woman," Crilen countered. "Just one woman. Your wife. I want Panla freed. I want her life spared. You have the power…"

"No," the Accommodant whimpered, "I don't have the power. Not anymore. She already signed the confessions. I tried to get her to play along. I could have used her. But she wouldn't cooperate. Now she's already confessed to everything. The trial won't last more than a few hours. Her sentence is already drawn up. I've seen it. There's nothing I can do!"

Crilen felt his stomach sink. It was as if Panla, herself, were rooking him at every move, to prevent him from saving her life. He finally understood the difficulty of the assignment It had prescribed to him on the asteroid. This road had no turns or exits. He had been sent to rescue someone who did not wish to be rescued. And, moreover, her compelling argument for her own demise made more sense to him than his heart was allowing him to accept.

He snatched up the Accommodant by the hair and stood. Some of the shards of mirror fell from the Accommodant's body while others remained firmly depressed into his flesh.

Crilen noted a bubbling massage pool filled with steaming oils and perfumes on the other side of the room. He marched the Accommodant's scarred, bleeding body across the room and tossed him in with an oblong splash.

The Accommodant shrieked and convulsed in agony as the normally soothing chemicals entered his stinging wounds.

Crilen crossed back to the bedroom window, ignited himself and flew out into the sky in a ball of golden flames.

XII.

Mid-morning.

The transformation of Panla's prison cell was astonishing.

Long colorful religious tapestries depicting historical scenes from the Text decorated the cracked and pitted walls. A large thick spacious rug covered over the cold stone floor. A heavily cushioned king-sized mattress had been hauled in and laid over two iron bed frames pushed together. Down-filled comforters, pillows and blankets were piled up high.

A small iron pot-bellied stove was brought in for warmth. An assortment of lamps were stationed in each corner of the cell and connected to a long thick cord which wound its way from her open cell door.

A folding partition was erected around the sink and toilet providing her with a humane measure of privacy. A small marble sitting-tub had even been brought in along with an odd array of floral soaps and shampoos.

A crude wooden desk and chair was set up in a corner with paper, writing implements and a large gold leaf version of the Text placed next to a reading lamp.

In the center of the room sat a triangular serving table filled with fresh fruits, vegetables, cold meats and an assortment of juices. It was more than she could consume on her best day, let alone after having spent nearly seven weeks conserving her strength on helpings of rotted gristle and gruel.

Sustenance was an invigorating idea, but at the moment, she was standing on a low platform in front of a tall mirror as a tailor fussed with the sizing of a dark plum, long-sleeved velour dress embroidered with swirls of golden fruits and curved vines. The lush, shimmering garment hung loosely from her thinned figure as the tailor busied himself marking adjustments.

"He said you'd probably lost weight," the tailor fussed and pulled on the waist.

"You said Mr. Linnfeld sent this dress?" Panla watched the bustle of warders moving in and out of the door, hauling additional amenities into her cell.

"He said it's from your designer," the short man said as he pinched, tucked and pinned. "Mr. Jivenché sends his regards."

A warder, pushing a wheelbarrow filled with satin sacks, stopped in front of her and dumped the load into the middle of the floor.

"What is that?" she addressed the warder curiously.

The warder paused and appeared nervous. He wouldn't raise his eyes.

"Shoes," his deep gravelly voice droned.

"Shoes?" Panla stared at the small hill of satin bundles. "These are more shoes than I've owned in my life!"

"Shoes," the warder repeated with his head bowed as he hastened toward the exit.

"No, wait!" Panla gestured vehemently.

The tailor, slightly annoyed, grabbed her arm and pulled it back.

The warder continued toward the exit.

"Guard, wait!" Panla commanded with authority.

The warder froze in the doorway. Slowly, he turned back toward her but never lifted his head.

"Guard...sir...you have a name?" Panla addressed him.

"Thoob," the warder answered with the shyness of an overgrown school child.

"Thoob," Panla said to him, "that's a very good name for a very good man. It's southern, isn't it?"

"Yes," he answered nervously.

"I knew a Churchlord named Thoob, who came from the southeast." Panla softened her tone. "He was a very good man, just as you seem to be."

Thoob remained silent and submissive as if he didn't know how to respond.

"Thoob," Panla spoke kindly, "I do appreciate everything that all of you are doing for me now. It's all very sudden and a bit of a shock really. I wish I could have had a better relationship with all of you earlier. It certainly would have made my stay here less difficult. I want you and everyone else here to know that I deeply appreciate their...belated consideration for my well being. But please, is there any way I can convince one of you to remove...that?"

Panla gestured to the far corner of the cell where the hideously burned and twisted corpse of the warder who had nearly assaulted her remained enshrined by a circle of Cathedral symbols, flowers and religious jewelry discarded by her jailers.

The tailor paused and glanced up at the macabre scene. He winced, shook his head and returned to his work.

"Blasphemy," the warder mumbled.

"I beg your pardon?" Panla thought she heard him incorrectly.

"Blasphemy," Thoob repeated with graveled clarity.

"Blasphemy?" Panla's expression became confused. "It's a corpse. A smelly, burned, rotting corpse."

"Wrath," Thoob cringed and recoiled from the burned figure. "Your wrath."

"My wrath?" Panla shook her head. "How many times do I have to explain to all of you that I didn't do this? I don't have any special powers. This wasn't some sign from Heaven. It was...an accident."

"God's wrath," the warder quaked and sounded as if he were going to cry. "No accident here. We all have been very bad. He was the worst. Your wrath. God's wrath. Forgive us."

Panla blew a huff of exasperation that flipped up the bangs on her forehead. In the eyes of the Ponder Gulag warder staff, she had gone from precious raw meat to sacred anointed deity in one wildly disturbing evening. Neither role was comfortable for her. But how could she even begin to explain to them what had really happened? Where would she start? With the attempted rape by the warder? Or with her fiery alien benefactor from another time and place who had come to her rescue?

"I'd leave it alone if I were you, Queen Mother." the tailor whispered. "I'm not a physician, but from what I can tell, you've endured weeks of terror and neglect and only a half-day of pampering. Considering what lies ahead, what difference does it make what the guards think?"

"And what do you think?" Panla asked him.

The warder scurried away.

"I think that God is still with you." The tailor patted her on the hip. "And tomorrow, I think this dress is going to make you a saint. Now take it off and go eat something."

The tailor unhooked the back of the dress. Panla stepped down and grabbed two pieces of fruit before she headed for her makeshift changing area behind the partition.

There came a hush in the cell. All of the warders stopped what they were doing and dropped to one knee with their heads bowed.

"What did I do now?" Panla thought. She looked over at the tailor who was staring at the doorway. She followed the tailor's gaze until she found a tall robed figure filling the entrance. She immediately recognized his dark face, his deep-set eyes, his thick grey beard and his large jeweled toque. This was the new acting Deliverer, the Holy Inquisitor.

The tall stately man gestured for his two attendants to remain out in the corridor. Without looking at Panla, he spoke to the room.

"I would have some privacy with Deliveress Jen," he said in a deep authoritative voice.

The warders stood, abandoned their chores and hastily exited the cell. The tailor glanced at Panla. More specifically, he glanced at the dress he needed to take with him. Panla shrugged. The tailor tossed his hands at his sides and shuffled out into the corridor to wait.

The Holy Inquisitor turned and looked out into the hallway at the crowd of faces comprised of the warders, the tailor and his own attendants.

"I said privacy." He commanded one of the warders, "Close it."

Quickly, one of the large, heavily muscled warders pushed the door closed. The Holy Inquisitor stood in silence and peered sternly through the peephole. The peephole slid shut and the cell was sealed at last.

Panla did not know what to make of this visit. Tomorrow, the Holy Inquisitor would sit alongside the newly appointed Lord Regent and the Supreme Judicator at her trial. When it was over, they would conjointly pronounce sentence upon her. And that would be the end.

She had no previous relationship with the Inquisitor other than a professional one. He had always been a dark, mysterious and shadowy figure, quietly monitoring the Cathedral's proceedings as he walked the Basilica hallways. She was leery of him and often wondered why he never questioned any of the subtle changes she implemented in the rituals of Cathedral business. In the back of her mind she thought he might be building a case against her that he would unveil when all the evidence was solid. Yet, she would often test him with blatant omissions of ritual and he would always carry on with a demeanor of indifference. She never figured out how to read him. She simply prayed he would never become a foe.

"I was told that the conditions for prisoners at the Ponder Gulag were rather severe," the Holy Inquisitor said as he took in all of the new amenities adorning Panla's cell.

"They have been." Panla met his eyes. "What you see here is the result of a recent revelation."

The Inquisitor looked down at the shrine comprised of the hideously burned corpse of the deceased warder along with notes, signs, jewelry and miscellaneous religious artifacts. He gazed up at Panla with a calm quizzical expression.

"An…accident," Panla gestured awkwardly. "They believe that I…"

"No explanation is needed, Queen Mother." he held up a hand.

Panla was surprised that he addressed her by her former title.

"King Father, I no longer bear that title," she addressed him respectfully.

"If I am the King Father and I choose to address you in that title, then you will not correct me," he spoke sternly. "Your title remains until you are found guilty."

"Yes, King Father." She bowed her head.

The Holy Inquisitor slowly stepped toward her. He reached forward, touched her cheek lightly and dropped to one knee.

"Queen Mother, I need your prayers and forgiveness," he said in a reverent whisper.

Panla looked down at him, taken aback by his abrupt penitence.

"I'm afraid you've got it the wrong way around." She reached down and touched his clasped hands. "I'm the one who's on trial tomorrow. You're the one who'll sit in judgment. I need your prayers, King Father."

"No, Queen Mother." the Holy Inquisitor reached up and clutched her hand. "I need your prayers and forgiveness. In my eyes you will never be unseated. Though I sit in farcical judgment of your transgressions tomorrow, I am the wrongdoer here."

"King Father, you're not making any sense." Panla shook her head. "You haven't done anything but your job. And that's what you'll have to do tomorrow. Don't..."

"No, Queen Mother." the elder man's face became a portrait of recrimination. "You don't understand. It was my sin which begat your sin."

"What do you mean?" She was lost in his distress.

"The Lord Regent," he said in a sorrowful whisper. "The Lord Regent was killed because of me."

Panla froze on the Holy Inquisitor's assertion. The Lord Regent was assassinated by Durn and Reza on the orders of Rabbel Mennis. Those facts were clear. This sudden admission of a nonexistent guilt seemed totally incongruous.

"King Father," Panla spoke softly and deliberately, "Rabbel Mennis had the Lord Regent killed."

"I know," the Holy Inquisitor answered painfully. "I know better than anyone. I'm the one who told Rabbel that the Lord Regent had found you out. And I knew that the Lord Regent had found you out because I'm the one who set him onto you."

Panla's body went numb.

"I knew about you and the Break," the elder man confessed. "I knew about you and the Break before your husband's security arrested Moll. I've known for a very long time and I believed in everything you were trying to do. Everything!

You can't know as much as I know about our faith and not realize that all of the truth lies within the Text...God's Word...not ourselves. Not our empty titles and our blind rituals, but the Word taken into our hearts. It is all we will ever need. It and He is all He ever intended for us to hold and cherish and worship.

"So I vowed to protect you. But the Lord Regent was fraught with jealousy and hatred and rue. I prayed sinfully that the old demon would die a natural death before he finally discovered your elaborate plan for the restoration of our faith. But he was dogged and determined, and he was getting too close. So I decided to hand him the keys to his coveted treasure trough hoping that it would consume him whole. I knew full well that if the Lord Regent became a viable threat to you, Rabbel Mennis would seal his fate. So, anonymously, I informed Rabbel thusly, and the Lord Regent's murder came to pass. And I was so horribly elated, until you disappeared. Then came the news that you had killed Rabbel. Avenged the deed I had done to protect you. And, in so doing, undid your-self...and all the rest of our faithless world. What hideous irony."

Panla collapsed to her knees in disbelief.

"I am so sorry, Queen Mother." tears filled the old man's eyes. "I needed to tell you in person, before I make my own sin known to the world."

"No!" Panla whispered as her eyes grew wide. "No, you will not."

"But I am as guilty as you," the Holy Inquisitor confessed.

"To God, yes!" Panla shook his hands. "But to this world you cannot be. In two days, I will be dead."

"That is not certain," the elder male lamented.

"You know it is." Panla met his eyes. "Tomorrow you'll be the one to pro-nounce it."

"I will be judged at your side," the Holy Inquisitor vowed.

"For what purpose?" she pleaded. "One traitorous martyr can be shredded more cleanly than two. And someone must remain to ensure that the faith of this world does not die. The devil has his sacrifice. Don't double the measure. Repent your sin. Accept the Lord's forgiveness. Then go on about His work! I'm begging you."

The pain and regret in the Holy Inquisitor's anguished eyes was evident, but there was also a powerful undertow of faith, logic and devotion which colored his sorrow.

"Your father raised you too wise," his voice grieved. "Our Father uses you beyond our ken. You are my Queen Mother. I will do, against my heart, as you wish."

Panla embraced him and kissed him on the cheek.

"Lord's Glory," the Holy Inquisitor spoke.

"Pray He will use me well." Panla clutched his fingers.

XIII.

Early evening:

"Mr. Pigue, you're going to love this!"

The room was completely dark. Then a large rectangular image filled the far wall:

Voiceover: YBS Productions presents, *The Lust of the Deliveress*, starring Yanga Blas as Deliveress Panla Jen Tem, the scheming religious vixen who betrayed the world!

The scene shifts to a pale thin semi-nude female figure straddling an oily massively muscled black-skinned body builder.

Yanga Blas (breathless): Oh, Rabbel, you hulk of writhing manhood! You are my god! You are my savior! Let us rule the world together!

Body Builder (snatches her by the throat): You spoiled, arrogant little horny waif! What can you know of my pain? What can you know of my people? I will rule alone or snap your scrawny little neck!

YB: Yes! Oh yes, my strapping hunk of maleness! (swings her bony leg around his wide neck and licks the sweat from his bald scalp).

Voiceover: But how could anyone foresee the treachery that lay ahead?

YB (covered in feather boas, fixing her make-up in a gold-framed mirror): God? Goddess? What difference will it make when I am queen of the world? I am the most beautiful creature who has ever lived! My believers would follow me to Hell! Hah! Hah! To Hell! (leans forward and kisses her reflection)

Voiceover: And whom did she truly love besides herself?

YB (wrapping her arms around an innocent-looking young woman): You love me, don't you? Don't you? (twirls her tongue in the young woman's ear).

Voiceover: But even she could not cover all of her crimes.

Body Builder: Panla, put that weapon away. I love you!

YB (pointing a large triple-barreled blaster): You pitiful fool! The world is mine! Mine, goddamn you! (A special-effects explosion blasts the body builder into chunks of flying meat. Covered in blood, she smiles).

Voiceover: But humanity knows that all evil must come to an end.

YB (being led to a large mechanical shredder): Oh God! Why hast thou forsaken me? Whyyyyy?

Voiceover: The Lust of the Deliveress. Soon, everyone will know the terrible truth. Thank God she's gone! Coming to theaters this summer!

The images on the screen faded and the room went dark. In another instant, soft lights illuminated the small conference room. A thick cloud of red smoke ascended toward the ceiling.

"Well?" A smiling and eager Mr. Nil obsequiously lobbied his employer for an affirmative response. "We outbid Avarice Studios for the script."

Yolo Pigue sat at the center of his personal swirling cloud of cigar smoke with an uncharacteristically blank and speechless expression. The muscles under his heavy hanging jowls worked curiously under the copious rolls of flesh sitting on his rounded shoulders. His thickly puffed fingers tapped, with thoughtful agitation, against the marble conference room table. The big man grimly processed the visual he had just witnessed.

Mr. Nil grew anxious for a response.

Finally, Yolo's bushy brows crawled up his forehead. His gargantuan girth expanded and contracted with a mammoth exhalation of wind. His eyes narrowed and tiredly rolled ruefully in his subordinate's direction.

"Is this what the theatrical arts have come to?" His piercing, aggravated stare struck like an interrogation flood light. "Is this what all of our knowledge and technology has been created to convey?"

Mr. Nil fought to make his own lips move.

"Y...Yanga Blas's last film was the third highest grossing film in the world last twinmoon." Mr. Nil swallowed hard.

"Yes." Yolo's lips smacked and folded. "I can see that she's gross. Does the girl ever eat anything besides sex partners?"

"Not recently," Mr. Nil grimaced. "She's been under a lot of pressure lately. Everyone's comparing her career to her late husband Finx Melder's. And the whole Melder estate thing has got her popping pills like..."

"...a junkie." Yolo filled in.

"Yes." Mr. Nil continued, "and she's in love with her co-star..."

"...the body builder," Yolo answered.

"Yes, sir," Mr. Nil responded. "But she's still sleeping with her oldest stepson..."

"...because of the estate." Yolo suppressed a yawn.

"Because of the estate," Mr. Nil confirmed. "And she just found out that her cosmetic surgery..."

"Stop." Yolo held up a hand. "I have an appetite to sustain."

"Yes, sir." The younger man nodded and settled back in his chair.

Yolo lifted his fat cigar to his lips. The smoldering end of it flushed an ashen orange. He removed the cigar and exhaled another rolling haze of crimson smoke. His body started to quake with a chuckle as the layers of his fleshy face lifted with a haughty smirk of irony.

"And so it is," Yolo smirked. "They shall crucify the martyr who sought to save their souls. And they'll canonize the vacuous thespian whore who defames her. How consistent, the masses. How reliable they are for us to manipulate."

"Uh, yeah." Mr. Nil smiled cautiously. "That's what I was just saying to…"

"Tell them to finish producing their 'drama'." Yolo laboriously hoisted himself to his feet. "When all of this nonsense has concluded, we'll let the mindless maw catch its collective breath. Then we'll restart the whole matter and begin peddling our theatrical incarnation as fact. It's so utterly absurd and unbelievable, they'll be clamoring to believe every word. That should come as no surprise from a world which chooses to consume more fiction than it does fact. With no luck at all, Ms. Blas's gross performance will be the top-grossing performance of the season. See to it!"

"Yes, sir." Mr. Nil wasn't certain whether he should smile.

With another slow revolution of the media giant's massive body, Mr. Nil's reaction no longer mattered. Yolo Pigue had given the matter all of the attention it was due. Propelled by a flatulent roar, he tottered out of the conference room and set a course for his private dinner buffet.

XIV.

Midnight.

"Does she have a chance, Mr. Linnfeld?" Genna sipped from her steaming mug, clutched in both hands as she leaned forward in her wooden kitchenette chair.

Mr. Linnfeld tried to prop himself up on the old sagging couch she had appropriated from Cathedral storage. He realized he had been slouching during most of their discussion regarding Mrs. Tem, the Break and everything which had transpired over the past several months. Hope was the one thing Panla had always instilled in her followers. Only now, he realized that the only true hope for anyone lay in life beyond this life. The present seemed a very grim and hopeless place indeed.

"Of course she has a chance." Mr. Linnfeld's round cheeks lifted with faint optimism. "She's done some wrong things. We all have. But they don't necessarily have to put her to death. She'll be excommunicated. That's for certain. And she may be forced to spend a great deal of time behind bars, but…"

"You think they're going to kill her, don't you?" Genna read through his conjugation of remote possibilities.

Mr. Linnfeld's expressive face drooped.

"Yes," he admitted, "I'm afraid it's probable."

"But why?" Genna shook her head with exasperation. "Can't anyone see what she was trying to do? Can't anyone see what went wrong? Doesn't she get any credit for trying to save this world?"

"In Heaven," Mr. Linnfeld nodded resignedly, "it will all even itself out there. As for this world, there are laws. And we broke a great many of them in hopes of trying to change the death spiral of our civilization. You only get away with breaking laws if you succeed in winning the day. We failed, and so now we all have to pay the consequences."

"She's better than all of them." Genna set her cup on the kitchenette counter. "Better than the Accommodant. Better than the Holy Inquisitor. Better than Yolo Pigue. Why should they be allowed to judge her? Why should they be allowed to take her life?"

"Because it's the law of the land," he grudgingly conceded. "You don't betray the government by throwing in your lot with known terrorists. You don't willfully compromise the integrity of God's highest office by consorting with rabid atheists to overthrow the institution you've sworn to protect. And you don't commit premeditated murder, under any circumstances."

"I don't accept that she committed murder!" The girl's dark face became angry. "Everyone's calling it murder because Rabbel Mennis wound up dead. You and I were there. You saw Rabbel haul her back to his office. We don't know what happened once the door closed. He might have had his hands around her throat. It might have been self-defense. Why isn't anyone talking about that?"

"Because Mrs. Tem isn't talking about it," Mr. Linnfeld answered. "If there's one thing we know about her, it's that she holds the truth in higher esteem than her own life. If it were self-defense she would say so. But you and I were there that night and we saw how she nearly insisted upon allowing Rabbel to take her back to his office. We thought she was sacrificing herself. In a way, she was. But she was going to take that devil with her. Then Mr. Len interceded…"

"Mr. Len," Genna interrupted. "Where is he now? He told us he was here to protect her, but he's letting her rot in the Ponder Gulag. He saves us, but he's going to let her die. What sense does that make? Crazy alien demon. I haven't said a word to anyone about him being on fire, have you?"

"I never actually saw him on fire," Mr. Linnfeld said with a light chuckle. "I was too busy gushing blood, remember? I wish I had seen it. Then they could cart me off to the crazy bin instead of the Ponder Gulag. I hear the company's a bit odd, but the recreational facilities are excellent and the meals are lice and mag-got-free. On fire, did you say? Oh, yes, I remember now, like a big flying slab of molten lava with big fangs."

"Stop it." Genna tried not to smile. "You're too austere to be a very convinc-ing loon. What we should have done is turned traitor like Feebie. Sold our souls to YBS Studios for a plea bargain. You think she's slept with him yet?"

"That's not fair," Mr. Linnfeld reprimanded.

"No?" her voice rose. "Why couldn't she have stuck it out like the rest of us? You got your head busted open. I got assaulted by that disgusting Leesla. Mrs. Tem's going to lose her life. We're both going to rot in prison for the rest of our lives! We all made sacrifices! Where was her faith in….?"

"…in God or in ourselves?" He finished her thought with a question. "If you're angry because she lost faith in our cause, don't be. She had the foresight to realize that things were falling apart and she left. It was her right. We all sided with Mrs. Tem because we believed in her. But more importantly, we sided with Mrs. Tem because we believed in God. Unfortunately, when God abandoned our cause, or perhaps we abandoned His, we forged onward when we should have had the good sense to shut the whole bloody mess down."

"Easier said than done," Genna countered. "Any of us could have walked away, but Mrs. Tem was stuck. Rabbel wasn't going to let her just walk away. Look what happened to the Lord Regent! Mrs. Tem had no way out. She needed us!"

"I know." Mr. Linnfeld leaned back. "So, here we are."

"And there she is," Genna concluded, "all alone in a cold cell, waiting to be executed by a planet full of hypocrites whose souls she'd have died for."

"Perhaps." He wearily rubbed the side of his head. "But I know she's not alone. She never has been. And neither are we, no matter what happens."

Genna looked at the tired old gentleman nestled uncomfortably on her used warped couch and thoughtfully folded her lips. She stood, removed her cup from the kitchenette counter and flipped on the water to the sink. As she rinsed the cup, she stared into infinity and prayed God would not abandon the world before the end came.

Meanwhile, thirty kilometers away, Crilen sat on a hill under the golden twin-moon light staring into the outer courtyard of the Ponder Gulag. The construction of the ancient machinery for Panla's execution, with all of its rusted iron spikes and twisted roped pulleys, was well underway.

XV.

Morning.

Every space in the ornately majestic Bius Basilica sanctuary was filled with media and dignitaries who had come to witness an historic and grim spectacle: The Deliverancy brought to disgrace through subversion, treachery and murder by the bearer of its title. In nearly two millennia, only one other Deliverer had ever been excommunicated from the high pulpit. That was Mongor I, the Deliverer from the tenth century who raised his own army and imposed a brutal theocratic dictatorship on the world for thirty twinmoons. When Mongor declared himself king, a splinter faction of the Cathedral voted to rescind his divine appointment to the Deliverancy. Mongor did not acknowledge the loss of the Deliverer title, but once he was captured and executed by his enemies, the splinter faction's decision was upheld and the divine lineage was passed on to another.

Over the centuries, however, historians and literati were exceedingly kind to Mongor's attempt to establish a purified and Godly planet by way of the sword. Literary reincarnations cast him as a brash and noble rogue. The hundreds of thousands whom he burned and beheaded in the name of God gradually faded into the footnotes of history. The Cathedral could not have been more pleased.

But the legacy of crimes committed by Mongor were never recorded by a technologically advanced media which could instantaneously beam the actual events into every home on the planet. This day, no cell or molecule of the events to follow would be disintegrated by the omissions or embellishments of fables and tales. It would all be captured and preserved electronically, diminished only by the arbitrary edits and deletions of media curators. For all future generations, everything and everyone would always appear as they were…until the world itself meets its end.

The upper triforiums were packed with reporters, cameras and audio equipment. The pews were filled with Regents from around the globe, parliamentarians, miscellaneous government officials and socially prominent laymen. The outer walls were lined with a blend of Cathedral security, government security and local policers in their formal dress uniforms.

Beams of sunlight shone through the crystal skylights and onto the large triangular altar at the center of the vast, ancient hall. There, on golden thrones, sat the Supreme Judicator, the Holy Inquisitor as the acting Deliverer, and the newly appointed Lord Regent. In front of them were two dark wooden podiums placed opposite one another for the defense and the prosecution. A burgundy velvet-cushioned stool was placed in the very center of the altar for the accused.

All of the players were in their places except for Panla Jen. Her arrival was imminent. The dense din of murmurs electrified the air with a churning collective anxiety.

Yolo Pigue had transformed his seating area in the upper triforiums into a makeshift luxury suite. He and Mr. Nil sat in high-backed leather chairs with a large serving table set between them. The triforium to the left functioned as the YBS control room operated by a crew of media technicians. The triforium to the right functioned as a miniature kitchen where one of his personal chefs diced up cold meat and vegetable hors d'oeuvres, and poured their goblets full of wine.

"This is going to be great." Mr. Nil rubbed his hands together.

"You think so?" Yolo glared over his shoulder at the chef who was taking too long to serve them. "This is the part I dread. The sentencing should be rather dramatic fare. It always is. There's such a profound sense of finality that accompanies a sentencing, especially when the sentence is death."

"We know that?" Mr. Nil spoke hesitantly.

"Of course we know that," Yolo snorted. "we're journalists. It's our job to know everything that's going to happen before it does. How else can we manipulate what the audience ingests? Unfortunately, there's one variable we have very little control over. That's the queen hag's final harangue. No doubt it will be some rambling spiritual sermon overwrought with references to heavenly Hell, the wrath of God, the salvation of our souls and all such insipidly delusional rubbish."

"It's all rubbish," Mr. Nil echoed.

"Indeed." Yolo's mouth twitched with a tickle of annoyance. "Unfortunately, she's made a life out of shredding rubbish and sprinkling the remnants about like fresh flower petals with a sweet alluring scent. She's a hideously adept virtuoso in the expressions of spiritual charm. She'll sing the song of angels with the hangman's knot around her delicate throat and make one last desperate lunge at martyrdom. There will be a foolish few who will celebrate her execution as some sort of sign and try to turn it into an excuse to fashion an all new delusion or religion, if you will. The good news is, while we're forced to air this proceeding in its entirety the first time through, the world will never hear whatever she has to say in its entirety ever again. I'll see to that. We'll put the queen hag's death wail on heavy rotation, but her words today will be evaporated by the passage of time and memory. Then we'll roll out the new entertainment season and that will be the end of that. A pity. Under the proper banner she might have made quite an entertainment icon. Her gamine-sage charisma is undeniable. But she's chosen the losing hand, so we must make short work of her and everything she represents."

The bustle of bodies on the Basilica floor below suddenly rippled into a chevron pattern. Bright media lights illuminated the epicenter of the disturbance. A black wall of government security officers pushed into the crowd. Behind them, entered Panla Jen.

Her short dark hair was, again, neatly cropped about her ears and neck as it had been before her imprisonment. Her bright face was smooth, fresh and effulgent with pensive conviction as she stared forward, oblivious to the energy charging the grand hall. She eyed the altar where she had presided over so many services. The altar from which she had ministered to literally hundreds of millions of souls. It had once been her home, but today, it bore all of the appearances of a former residence redecorated by new owners. She was now merely a passing guest.

The security detail wedged its way to the altar, then parted for Panla to ascend. As she climbed the short staircase, a hush came over the assembly as they took in the long beautiful plum velour dress and its elaborate, swirling vine pattern. In her hands was the large, thick, leather-bound volume of the Text which had been brought to her cell the night before.

Panla's eyes locked with the Holy Inquisitor who now wore the tall two-meter headdress of the Deliverancy. He appeared outwardly firm, but she could see the fatigue and regret behind his eyes. She glanced at the Supreme Judicator whose gaze was intentionally elusive; he searched for distractions to draw away his attention. It was as if he did not wish to look on her any sooner or longer than he had to. In many ways, the old man acted guiltier than she. Finally, Panla met the respectful gaze of the new Lord Regent. Under the jeweled toque was the dark familiar face of a young Regent from the northwest. For some reason, his name eluded her. Perhaps because the names of acquaintances mattered very little at this late hour.

She noted the junior lawbooking partner from Mr. Cockcorn's office standing in her defense, behind a podium. He might as well have been a mail room clerk or doorstop for all that there was for him to do. Everything was already decided. What followed would be an obligatory formality, but this did not keep the appointed prosecutor from clutching his podium as if a great battle were about to ensue. Panla glanced up at the sea of cameras and media in the triforiums and immediately understood the reason for his pose. Her own husband had clumsily parlayed posing pretty for the media into a popular Accommodancy term. One never knew when a political career might invent itself.

Panla inspected the stool where she was supposed to sit, but she chose to disdain its passive subjugation. She opted to stand tall, regal and straight before her judges. In her hands, she firmly held the Text as if it were her last possession in the universe.

Yolo glowered disapprovingly at the scene unfolding below.

"What's this?" A clump of partially chewed sandwich fell from his lips. "You said she looked awful. Worn down. Haggard."

"She…did, sir." Mr. Nil inspected Panla's refined and invigorated appearance on a side monitor.

"The Ponder Gulag is supposed to be a living hell!" Yolo belched. "It should have broken her in half; beaten her into a whimpering lump of flesh slinking to be put out of its misery. She looks as if she's been vacationing at some private coastal resort!"

"I…I…" Mr. Nil stammered.

"She's a demon," Yolo sneered. "They can't execute that Text-toting termagant soon enough."

The Cathedral trumpets sounded. The grand hall faded to silence.

Finally, the venerable Supreme Judicator turned his cold ancient gaze upon Panla and spoke:

"On this date, under authority of the governing laws of our planet and the laws of the Cathedral, Deliveress and Mrs. Panla Jen Tem you have entered a plea of guilty to the charges of high treason against the presiding government, sedition and heresy against the body of the Cathedral and the willful murder of Mr. Rabbel B. Mennis. By entering this plea of guilty to the aforementioned charges, you have waived your right to a trial by your peers. Do you concur?"

"I do," Panla answered clearly.

A low murmur groaned through the audience. The rumor of her admission of guilt was now confirmed.

"Then, before we pronounce sentence, we would allow you to address the proceeding." the Supreme Judicator commanded.

Panla could feel the anxiety building in her heart and lungs.

"If it should please this proceeding," she stated firmly, "I request that my statement be withheld until after my sentence has been pronounced. I would not have my final words construed as a veiled plea for my life."

The Supreme Judicator leaned back, eyeing her as he would a shrewd adversary. Clearly this request did not sit well with the agenda. He quietly consulted with the acting Deliverer and the new Lord Regent. They both appeared to nod affirmatively. The Supreme Judicator acquiesced.

"Very well," he said in a dry tone. "We will begin the sentencing now."

"Damn," Yolo cursed under his breath.

Panla bowed her head thankfully to the three who sat in judgment. However, the moment of reprieve was not allowed to linger.

"By your admission of guilt," the Holy Inquisitor and acting Deliverer said, "in accordance with the holy Addendums of Cathedral laws, your title of Deliveress is now rescinded."

Panla swallowed bitterly. She had borne the title with more grace, truth and dignity than any Deliverer in two centuries. Yet, in her heart, she had disdained the office and all of its secular encumbrances. Losing the title in this way brought upon her a concurrent surge of shame, indignation and relief.

"Mrs. Panla Jen Tem," the new Lord Regent said in a light tenor, "by your admission of guilt to the charges of sedition and heresy, you are hereby excommunicated from the body of the Holy Cathedral."

"Mrs. Panla Jen Tem," the Supreme Judicator continued, "by your admission of guilt to the charge of high treason against the Accommodant government of this planet, you are hereby sentenced to life imprisonment at the Ponder Gulag without possibility of commutation."

"What?" Mr. Nil whispered aside to Yolo. "I thought..."

Yolo held up his hand and silenced his subordinate. He massaged the folds of his jowls with anticipation.

"Mrs. Panla Jen Tem," the Supreme Judicator said, "by your admission of guilt to the charge of the murder of Mr. Rabbel B. Mennis, you are hereby sentenced to life imprisonment at the Ponder Gulag without possibility of commutation."

"This isn't right." Mr. Nil was unsettled. "She's not going to be executed. She'll be an icon in prison. She'll be..."

"Shhhh." Yolo held up a finger confidently. "Patience, dear lad."

"Mrs. Panla Jen Tem," the acting Deliverer said in a grave tone, "on the matter of your position as Deliveress of this planet and the responsibility you bore, you held greater duty in this world than any other to ensure that the Addendums of the Cathedral were upheld. You swore a solemn oath to the CDR: Complicity, Duty & Reverence. Complicity to the law, the Cathedral, the Deliverancy lineage, and the legacy of Addendums. Duty to the giver of life to the people of this planet. Reverence for the miracle of life, for the wisdom of the Nine, for the legacy of the Deliverers. This solemn oath you swore on your life. Therefore, by your admission of guilt to the charges of sedition, heresy and murder, you are hereby sentenced to death. Tomorrow you will be executed in the outer court of the Ponder Gulag in accordance with ancient Cathedral custom...by Addendum."

An inertia of profundity struck the entire Basilica sanctuary to silence.

Yolo had to restrain himself from clapping.

Panla felt her limbs grow cold.

Death...tomorrow. The end of her life. There it was.

This condemnation was no surprise. She knew the Addendums better than anyone, even though she despised them. She had anticipated this very moment for weeks. But the reality of this final pronouncement crashed through her resolve like a cast-iron wrecking ball. Her stomach felt as if it had plunged into her colon. Her heart pulsed violently. Her brain felt as if it were swelling against the inside of her skull. She became momentarily light-headed and swayed as though she would lose consciousness. A hushed murmur buzzed through the audience.

None of the government security men moved to aid her, but a Cathedral security officer in royal garb stepped up and held her steady until she gathered herself and restored her equilibrium.

"My apologies," she cleared her throat and spoke respectfully. "I thank you for your expediency. For the benefit of the world and our faith, I should not like to linger much longer under these circumstances."

The Supreme Judicator nodded solemnly, but she could also see he was swallowing a smile. The acting Deliverer appeared outwardly austere, but his countenance was ashen and drained. The young Lord Regent was stone-faced and impassive.

"If it would please these proceedings," Panla regained the steadiness in her voice, "I would like to offer my final statement now."

The momentary glow in the Supreme Judicator's face dimmed. It was as if he had already forgotten Panla's request to delay her address until after the sentencing. He glanced at the acting Deliverer and Lord Regent, but they did not return his gaze. The decision had already been made and they were all bound by it.

The Supreme Judicator returned to his evasive eye contact.

"Very well, Mrs. Tem. You may proceed." He lowered his eyes as if he would search for something to read until she was finished.

Panla gracefully pirouetted 180 degrees from the three who sat in judgment of her. She looked out over the pews at all of the legislators and dignitaries. She gazed up into the triforiums at the collection of media and satellite equipment. Finality caused her scalp to tingle. This one last time, the entire world was her audience. She cradled the large volume of the Text in her arms and held it passionately to her bosom.

Panla whispered a silent prayer, spread her soul upon the breath of God and let fly what may.

"I'm certain the question troubling most of the world is: Why did I do the things that led me to this? I pray those of you in positions of spiritual leadership will understand and take heed. Having full knowledge through the Text of the path to eternal life in Heaven, yet having no power to impart this knowledge to those whose very salvation depended upon it became unacceptable to me. The Cathedral? The Break? Take your pick. In the end, the only difference was that the Break never pretended anything other than to be in league with the devil. I wish I could say that the Cathedral has been so forthright. The Cathedral hierarchy has made of itself the devil's leach, sucking the life blood from God's Holy Word and leading, far astray, generations of innocent souls to their eternal damnation."

There was a hushed gasp that whisked through the audience. A murmur of discontent started to build. The acting Deliverer stood and gestured for silence. Quickly, the voices died down.

"Every day my job was to nurture the collective pains and anguish of a billion souls," Panla continued. "So many lost souls aching for answers to life and salvation. Drug addicted souls. Sex addicted souls. Souls addicted to money and power and social status. Souls who couldn't distinguish between the will of God and a sin that simply made them happy for a short time. I listened to it day after day after day…for twinmoons…as a Churchlord, a Regent, and, finally, as the Deliveress. It hurt so much. They were coming to me for answers, yet because of un-Godly Cathedral Addendums I could only give them a fraction of what they needed. Enough to keep them alive, but not nearly enough to salvage their souls. It hurt. To watch waves and waves of souls toppling over the cliff every day, falling into the abyss of the damned…it hurt. Listening to the devil laugh in my dreams every night as he harvested his crop from my land. It was an agonizing burden. Yet as the Deliveress I was helpless.

"By secular Addendums, I was forced into a sinful, idolatrous life. I was drowning in an ocean of mortal paganism which tortured and infected my loving relationship with God in Heaven. I enforced rules which were not His rules. I practiced rituals which were not His will. I had an office and an image to uphold about which He cared nothing. Try as I did, I knew I was not serving Him. I served mortality. Flesh and bone and blood. I served the edifices of silk and gold and stone. I did not serve God, but the secularized gate which bars us from Him.

I served the noise which fills our ears. I served the doctrine which clouds our understanding of truth. I served a flawed mortal legacy which had strayed from the clear path of righteousness written in our Text by the nine chieftains who actually met and knew God. Taunted mercilessly by this blatant blasphemous legacy, evil begat evil in me. Through vanity in knowledge, I faithlessly came to believe I could fix centuries of secular rot by myself. Instead of trusting God to shepherd the stray, I sought to clumsily corral the lost with my own two hands. I tried to bear the yoke of the Lord, but I actually bore a secular burden which darkened my heart under its shifting, cumbersome weight. I was a fool. And only in these final days, seeing myself a fool, have I truly become wise for the first time in my life.

"Because of centuries of Addendums to the true living Word, I couldn't break rank and show the world that the first, original living Word was all that they needed. I couldn't tell them that the truth wasn't in the institution or its leaders, but in the Text itself. Salvation through God's Word was at their finger tips, if they would only read it for themselves. This is what the world needed to know. And it was worth my life to unshackle this truth.

"When I started to act, I felt like I was finally doing something besides crucifying my conscience on the suffering of the world. My plan, I thought, was flawless. It didn't matter that I became trapped by a circle of mad ironies. The Cathedral's secularist ritual fed the discontent which fueled the Break. But once the Break had brought down the Cathedral, the rootless irrationality of the Break would nurture the Text-based reformation of our faith! The Break would collapse like a silly iniquitous fad. And the true living God of the Text would still be there for all of us. It was a noble and horribly flawed vision. I honestly thought my alliance with the Break was the wrong thing to do for all the right reasons. But no good can come of evil. Thank God, it all fell apart.

"I prayed and prayed that my plan for reformation would succeed. But today, I thank God He does not give us what we ask for when we petition our Father in Heaven with our puny mortal intellects. Thank God He gives us what we need instead of what we desire. For when we ask our Heavenly Father for the things of this world that we think we need, we are like ignorant children in a toy store, yammering to our parents for meaningless baubles. If God had given me what I asked for, today I would be the leader of a fractured religious movement. I would be like all of our politicians, a leader soiled with vulgar hidden secrets, depraved double lives, vomiting hypocrisies into our history, while I cast my soul adrift farther and farther from the purity of the truth which only resides on our Father's golden throne. I would be the queen of lies and deceit. Little more. I would be dead to the Lord. But fortunately, my Heavenly Father has rescued me from myself. He has broken my wayward secular dreams of presiding over that which only He can preside. He has revealed in my mirror the reflection of a foolish sinful child who threatened to consume herself playing with the fires of Heaven. Oh, thank you, my Lord, thank you! For today, I am not what I would be but what you would make me. There is no greater gift in Heaven or the world than to be what thou hast willed me be to become.

"Today, it is said that I have fallen from a hallowed place. It is said that I have fallen into the pit of sin. But I tell you now, confessed and convicted of these crimes, that I have not fallen into sin, but fallen from it. I thought I was serving God. I thought I loved Him. But my faith was in myself. My faith was in my own wisdom and my knowledge of the Text. If I had trusted Him…loved Him as we all should…I never would have tried to do what I thought was His will…without Him. My acts were faithless. I didn't trust Him enough. I thought I needed to do it all myself. And, in so believing, I destroyed everything that was important to me. I was the bearer of a cold heart. A heart that could endure no more of this planet's self-inflicted torment by its own ignorant secularism. A heart turned to rock by the corrupters of God's church. A heart turned to murder by the haters of Him that I serve. In my hatred I was lost. In my hatred I tried to do that which only our Lord in Heaven can make manifest. I hated the church. I hated the Break. And evil took my hatred and used it to spark the fires of my own undoing. For as long I remained mired in hatred toward the least of God's children, I could not serve Him. I could only undo myself. And so I have.

"In my hatred I dwelled in pitch blackness where Heaven's light ne'er shone. Only through my love for Him could illumination blot away the blindness of my deeds. Only through my love for Him have I rediscovered my true love for all the souls who reside in this world, good and evil alike. Hatred is an unbridled expression of emotional weakness. It is the expression of love in the most difficult circumstances which requires our greatest strength.

"So to my husband…my lying, lecherous, adulterous, corrupted husband who believes in nothing but personal glory and gratification…I love you. To Yolo Pigue and your lost, prevaricating minions who, with no repentance, slaughter billions of souls through distortions of truth and misappropriation of facts…I love you. You are my enemies in this world and the next, but God bids that I should love you all the same. I do not trust you, but I do love you. God will never tolerate the wanton indulgence of your sins, but I can no longer hate the sinner. For hatred is the fuel of evil and that is *your* calling; to soil my immortal soul with the hatred of you who sew the seeds of hatred. But God would not have it so. For hating you would be as hating He who created you and I shall always love my Father in Heaven and pray that He loves me. There is divine purpose in your iniquity and only God can comprehend it. So I leave it to Him. I am commanded to love you. For any depraved fool can love a friend, but only a person who loves God can love his enemies...even when those enemies are the enemies of God. And so I love you. Forgive me, you workers of evil. For unto my death and into eternal life I shall love you forever. Amen.

"Of course, some of you may ask how I can love my enemies? Well my wise father taught me to look upon iniquity as infirmity. To look upon the weaknesses of the flesh and mind as afflictions borne of each individual's inability to resist the physical or intellectual temptations which lead us astray. Not that I discount the harm that evil can do to a living soul, but I've come to know that a person may perform evil acts, but the person is not evil. The person is lost. The person requires forgiveness, compassion and love. Nothing less. It is easy to discount the people who do evil in this world, but would we want God to discount us? We all do evil in this world even when we're not conscious of it. Should we expect God, with his infinite wisdom and notions of righteousness, to condemn all of us for the wrongs that we do? If so, there would be no hope for any living soul that ever lived. With his dying breath, Muntor forgave the pillagers who murdered his family. He did this because he knew that the only way he could ever be forgiven by God for his own transgressions was to forgive those who transgressed against him. For how could he ask God to do for him what he was unwilling to do for others? I'm ashamed to admit that, in the midst of everything that went on with Rabbel Mennis, I totally forgot all of that. I allowed myself to become *of the world* and act as someone outside the arc of true faith.

"As for our institutions, be wary of a Deliverancy which elevates its secular Addendums above the Word of God. Any path to which a mere mortal Deliverer should lead you which does not shepherd us in the truth of holy scripture...the Text...is a path which will certainly lead to the destruction of our civilization and the damnation of our souls.

"And be wary of an Accommodancy which promises to give you what you want. With avarice and selfishness in our hearts, we elect the Accommodant to accommodate our carnal desires. We don't care who he is or what he stands for so long as he accommodates. If the devil were to offer us our streets lined with gold, our beds filled with sex partners, our cabinets stocked with intoxicating liquors, our iceboxes bulged with culinary delights, our monitors abuzz with an endless stream of mindless entertainment, our bank holdings profitable beyond measure, would we laud him and praise him and love him and make him our Accommodant, even if he were...the devil? A liar? A deceiver? A vile, cankered, beguiling demon contemptuous of all truth or morality? Would we love him and praise him, though he undermines the salvation of our souls? I fear we would. I fear we have. He tells us what we wish to hear. He fills us with all of our selfish heart's desires. He blunts our guilt and our sin with the complicitous embrace of his immoral fellowship. He poisons our conscience and tells us that it's good medicine. Then he harvests the spoiled crop of our dead souls and casts us into the fires of Hell. Fires stoked by our own material lusts.

"By contrast, God could never be an Accommodant. For when He snatches away our worldly fixations...our covetous greed, our insatiable secular musings, our nurtured ignorance of all truth, we would selfishly decry his righteous hand the intrusion of a dictator. How dare He, who created all, knows all and loves all, interfere with our pleasure. We are like children who push away their loving parents and yearn for the clown. Children who would rather rot their teeth on sweet candy than be filled and nurtured by a warm balanced meal.

"You can chase the treasures of this world if you like. But I've come to know that those who are blessed are cursed and those who are cursed are blessed. In the Text, it says that no man shall have greater difficulty entering into the kingdom of Heaven than a man who is wealthy. Wealthy in material possessions. Wealthy in intellect. Wealthy in skill or talent. Wealthy in physical beauty. For the man who is wealthy becomes so preoccupied with his blessings, his gifts if you will, that he forgets, altogether, from whence those blessings came. His money is his virtue. His talent is the altar at which he worships. His mirror becomes his idol. His mind becomes his scripture. His life becomes the only Heaven he will ever know. Meanwhile, the cursed...The poor, the afflicted, the sickly, the ugly, the meek...they have no such earthen treasures upon which to foolishly stake their souls. They know that there must be a greater glory in this universe than the spiritual dearth of wretched, ephemeral possessions. Blessed in life, snared in the undertow of Hell. Cursed in life, sanctified by the ascension to Heaven. Praise be to God.

"Aside from the spectacle of myself, I have noted the death of one of our most prominent entertainers has become quite a public obsession. I beg you, be wary of the worship of mere entertainers. There was a time when people's lives were ruled by books and family and community and the Church. Modern mass entertainment has changed all of that. Now we're ruled by the exportation of the entertainment culture. A culture built upon excess and fiction. A culture we've made wealthy beyond its worth. Because we've made the entertainers rich, they, in turn, bankroll the seduction of our sanity with the lure of their Godless, hedonistic, self-destructive lifestyles. They lure us into the drugs and alcohol that seem so fun. Lure us into those fluid sexual relationships that cover over with tempting flesh the spiritual rot they engender. They beg us to love their corruption. Love their addiction to narcissism. Love their perverted androgyny. Love their material greed. All veiled behind the auspices of an allegedly benign freedom the Text reveals as wantonness. We elevate these addled demons above ourselves. We worship these mortal cankers above God almighty. And all because they have reruns and replays and recordings broadcast worldwide. Just because something is large, loud and beautiful doesn't give it lasting value. More is often less. To God, these unrepentant narcissists are less than nothing. God doesn't care about their performances, or their scripts or the crowds they drew or the coins they amassed. All he cares about is the soul's relationship with Him. In the end…the very end…its all we have.

"Many of you who worship the Deliverancy and were foolhardy enough to worship me, now say 'How could she do this to us?' The answer is, because I'm not from Heaven. No Deliverer ever has been. I'm simply one of you. I know that so many of you put your love in me and your faith in me and I thank you. But your love and faith were misplaced. Your love and faith should always be in God alone, for He is the only perfection in the universe. Be wary of anyone who seeks to usurp His authority. Be wary of all the things of this world.

"Faith cannot lie in the things of this world. Not a person. Not a collective of persons. Not a government or institution. I am certainly living proof of the fallibility of a mortal leader. A person can be a leader, but God alone is the only perfect shepherd worthy of our souls. Follow no mortal leader unless you know your leader follows God's Word. And if that leader should falter, pass him over, take up God's Word and lead your leader. A rational mind must fortify itself with the wisdom to carry on, recognizing who the true leader is and never lose sight of Him. Your faith and trust must lie in nothing of this world but the creator of it all, God Himself. And the only way you can begin to understand Him is through the scriptures of the Text. Through the history of His relationship with our planet. Through the undeniable truth of His Word. You may think you know God, but without personal knowledge, all you know is rumor, opinion and hearsay. Hundreds of millions stake the fate of their souls on their ignorance. Many of you don't even have a sound basis for what you claim not to believe in. Perhaps you think that God is your enemy. Perhaps you think that God is your friend. Perhaps you think He is a mere observer. Perhaps you think he is an arbiter of good fortunes and bad. Perhaps you think He is a judge who approves of the laws you make up in your own head. Perhaps you think that He is the keeper of worldly treasures you must strive to earn. Perhaps you believe that He is a she. Perhaps He is cruel and merciless. Perhaps He loves us. Perhaps He forgives us. Perhaps He may yet save our souls from an eternity in Hell if we simply ask Him to.

"Some of you believe that right or wrong is measured in the caprice of ballots and votes. Yet, how many times in the history of our world has a visionary of justice been put down by the majority? More often than we care to admit. Even the purest democracy can underscore the flaws in collective mortal wisdom. We are inherently finite and linear in our reason. How can living creatures begin to understand what exists beyond the plane of our comprehension? Beyond flesh and bone and blood? Beyond the planets and the stars? It defies reason for us to defer to ourselves when there is a greater truth governing infinity than we can ever know. God's truth, that fraction which we are meant to comprehend, is written here for us! But unless you know the Text, you know nothing. God is real. The evidence is all around you. His Word is true. From the beginning of sentient history He has spoken to us. The nine Chieftains are not characters from a fairytale. They are our lineage. God spoke to them. And through them He gave us the Text. And through the Text is our guide which will lead us back to Him and the salvation of our immortal souls.

"Unless you believe that there is no supreme power in the universe, you cannot deny that the Text is true and that the application of God's Word in our daily lives will grant us peace. Look around you. We all know who those blessedly assured people are in our lives who wear their faith like a soft warm comforter. We envy them, yet we all have the same chance to be like them if we would only put away our worldly desires and take up his guiding, loving hand to live as He beckons.

"God tells us to take up his yoke for his burden is light. God cares nothing of material things. And God cares nothing for the lusts of the flesh. Imagine how light our burdens would be if we could curb our avarice. Harness our sexual thirsts. Imagine how light. Imagine how cleansed.

"What I would ask every living being who is tempted by some evil to do is take your faith in God in one hand and take that temptation in the other hand, and ask yourselves if you would trade all of God's love and all of God's eternal promises for that secular thing that you covet. If you would trade away a personal loving relationship with God for career or wealth or sex or drugs...or even family...then Heaven can never be yours. You only worship the world. You only worship your world.

"So should you now forsake me? By all means. I am prepared to fade into secular oblivion. But I beg you, do not forsake Him. Do not forsake your souls. God's truth is no secret. It's been right here in the Text for two millennia. For the eternal salvation of all that you are, read it. For the salvation of the souls of children yet to be born, read it. Know Him. Love Him. Because in spite of ourselves, our Father in Heaven has always loved us...and always will."

The giant hall was silent.

Panla stepped back, pirouetted again and faced the three who sat in judgment of her.

"Have you finished, Mrs. Tem?" The Supreme Judicator did not meet her eyes.

Panla's mind raced through every last light of truth that flickered in her soul. She felt a warm and blessed assurance caress her spirit.

"Yes," she responded breathlessly, like a nervous school child affirming her last answer to a grueling final examination.

"Very well." the Supreme Judicator leaned forward with a cold, vindictive scowl. "Mrs. Panla Jen Tem, you have chosen to use your final words to scurrilously condemn our good and free society. You have chosen to flaunt your unrepentant treachery and hatred for our world, its faith and its people. Fortunately, your way is not our way. May whatever powers that be have mercy on your soul."

Panla was stunned. She opened her mouth to respond, but the Supreme Judicator held up his hand and the government security personnel stepped up to the altar, seized the Text from her hands and bound her. To the confounded murmur of the audience, she was quickly led away.

XVI.

The News:

EB: Good evening, everyone. I'm Egs Bloyt. In a scene that can only be described as bizarre and sad, the First Lady and former Deliveress, Panla Jen Tem, was sentenced to death this afternoon. Miks Faks is outside the Bius Basilica this evening with more details. Miks?

MF: Well bizarre probably would describe what the world saw today as hundreds of millions around the world tuned in to watch the short-lived trial of the former Deliveress, Panla Jen Tem. Mrs. Tem kept the packed Bius Basilica waiting, arriving fashionably late to her date with justice. She made a dramatic entrance flaunting one of her gaudy signature outfits...a dark purple dress with a wild pattern splashed around the skirt and back. Defiantly, she tried to stare down the Supreme Judicator, but our most powerful sovereign of the court was in no mood for games. She also made several attempts to seduce the acting Deliverer with long gazes, but he was all business as well. Sadly, she appeared as a woman who really didn't have a friend left in the world.

As had been rumored Mrs. Tem pled guilty to all charges. Based upon the overwhelming evidence stacked against her, she really had no choice. This certainly explains why renowned lawbooker Conn Cockcorn deferred her case to a junior partner. The former Deliveress was literally indefensible.

Still, Mrs. Tem made what can only be characterized as a mad, desperate lunge for martyrdom as she launched into a rambling tirade of conflicting ideologies which certainly underscored the reasons why Cathedral patronage has plummeted over the last several decades. We should all be thankful that people are finally thinking for themselves. Here are some of the highlights of what she had to say:

(A poorly lit recorded image of Panla appears on the screen)

"You are my enemies in this world and the next."

(Jump clip)

"I did not serve God…"

(Jump clip)

"I hated the church. I hated the Break."

(Jump clip)

"God could never be an Accommodant."

(Jump clip)

"The Cathedral hierarchy has made of itself the devil's leach."

MF (bearing a look of pity): She even took a swipe at her husband who has publicly stood by her throughout this heart-breaking, world-shattering scandal.

(The poorly lit image of Panla returns bearing a scowl)

"My lying, lecherous, corrupted husband who believes in nothing but personal glory and gratification…"

MF (voiceover clip): But in the end, the Supreme Judicator had the final word.

(Grand wide angle image of the Supreme Judicator glaring down from his perch)

"Mrs. Panla Jen Tem, you have chosen to use your final words to scurrilously condemn our good and free society. You have chosen to flaunt your unrepentant treachery and hatred for our world, its faith and its people. Fortunately, your way is not our way. May the powers that be, have mercy on your soul."

MF (looking relieved): With that, Mrs. Tem was returned to the Ponder Gulag where she will be executed tomorrow morning.

EB: How sad. So many people thought she was such a great lady.

MF: The clothes don't make the woman, I'm afraid.

EB: They never do. Miks, regarding Mrs. Tem's final statement, she spoke at length. Was there anything of substance to it?

MF: Reactions I've gotten from the general public have been somewhat mixed. Most seem to have concluded that it was a preachy hypocritical sermon essentially saying "Do as I say, not as I do." A few religious extremists seemed to feel there was some merit to it, but they couldn't readily explain her crimes any more than anyone else. I think the hardcore religious contingent wanted to see something in her that just wasn't there. She's not God. She never was. Overall, I think the collective feeling is that she really wasn't sorry for any of the things she did. She tried to justify them. Fortunately, the law had the final say and tomorrow, it will be over.

EB: Amen. It will be over indeed. Thanks, Miks.

Tomorrow, YBS News will be up bright and early to provide you with full coverage of "The Execution of Panla Jen" live from the outer courtyard of the Ponder Gulag. Our pre-execution coverage of "The Execution of Panla Jen" will begin at dawn. That will be followed by the execution itself. And then our staff of journalists will provide you with detailed post-execution analysis of "The Execution of Panla Jen" including reactions from the acting Deliverer, the Supreme Judicator, Mrs. Tem's former associate Feebie Bleik, and a few words from Mrs. Tem's husband, Accommodant Klin Tem, who has been nursing a small laceration suffered in a kitchen accident.

Right now, we're going to take a break. When we come back, I'll be talking to Mrs. Tem's personal clothing designer, Ubert Jivenché. Also, the Bius Basilica cook will be joining us to tell us what he saw and knew before the rest of us. And be sure to stay with us later tonight as Yara Pique will be discussing today's trial with some of your favorite parliamentarians on the all new *Nailing the Newsmaker*. Then, later, we'll be joined by our staff of veteran journalists who can tell us all what we saw today on *The Disseminators*. So stay with us. We'll be right back!

XVII.

The cell door opened and Panla was forcefully shoved inside.

She stumbled to keep her balance and quickly noticed all of the amenities which had been brought to her cell by the Ponder Gulag warders were gone. Only a few flower petals remained littered in the corner where the burned remains of the guard who attacked her had been enshrined. The air was, again, very cold and damp. She could see her own breath in the dim light.

The three government security officers who had manhandled her through the corridors stood in the doorway with inscrutable stone faces.

Panla folded her arms and rubbed her shoulders, waiting for them to depart. It was apparent her final evening of life was going to be a very uncomfortable one.

"Well?" she addressed the three officers who stood in silence.

As if prompted by her cue, two of the officers strode toward her and seized her arms, pulling and tearing at the velour dress she had worn to her trial. She struggled against their strength, but they easily wound and twisted her limbs as if she were a child. They pushed her to the ground and ripped the fabric away from her body.

One officer collected the ball of torn fabric and stepped away. The other officer turned her on her stomach, buried his knee in her back and cut away her undergarments with a sharp implement. The second officer pulled away the undergarments and flipped her onto her back. Angrily, Panla kicked into his groin. The officer's pasty white face finally revealed an emotion. He cocked his fist to punch her, but the third officer grabbed him by the arm and shook his head. The second officer regained his composure, stood and walked away with the small wad of clothing. The first officer reappeared, walked behind her and seized her arms again. Panla tried to fight him, but his hold was like flesh-covered iron. She glanced up at the third officer and saw a long dripping syringe.

"No!" she shouted, remembering what the one warder had said before he attempted to rape her. "They all call out," he had snickered.

Helplessly, she was flipped onto her stomach against the cold concrete floor. She felt a sharp stabbing penetration against the cheek of her buttocks and a disquieting paralysis rapidly spread through her body. The first security officer released her arms and they bounced lifelessly to the floor.

Panla heard their footsteps march toward the exit, but could not lift her head to see them. There was a pause. She saw the tattered dingy gown she had worn during her entire incarceration flop to the ground by her face.

The cell door slammed shut with a violent echo.

Panla closed her eyes and searched for her prayers in the frozen darkness.

XVIII.

Dawn.

From the hill overlooking the Ponder Gulag, Crilen watched the twinmoons fade into the dusky horizon.

He had observed the government security carry Panla to her trial. He had witnessed them bring her back. It would all be over very soon now. She had confessed and she was going to die.

A small herd of media transports surrounded the outer walls as technicians and reporters scurried about, hooking up their cameras and equipment and scouting the best vantage points from which to broadcast the execution.

Security checkpoints were everywhere. Outside the gulag gates, a small battalion of policers clad in armored riot gear prepped and tested their equipment as if preparing for a war. Inside the courtyard, dark clothed government security men prowled the prison grounds seeking any potential source for disruption of the proceedings.

Just above the ground floor of the courtyard, a succession of seven stony arches, several meters apart, straddled an elevated walkway. It was two stories high and led from the main building, bordering the open court, and dead-ended at the archaically monstrous and sadistic machinery which would grind Panla's living body into bloody, pasty refuse. Surrounding the spiked metal and wooden apparatus were tiered rows of bleachers reserved for the same dignitaries, parliamentarians and laymen who had witnessed the sentencing. It was a grim and desolate amphitheater fashioned for no other purpose than to optimize the viewing pleasure of a death-thirsty contingent.

Building their legions outside the erected barricades were the sign-waving sea of conflicting protesters who had remained outside the Ponder Gulag since Panla Jen's imprisonment. "GOOD RIDDANCE, BITCH" read one sign bearing a ghastly drawing of a sunken shriveled corpse soaking in a pool of its own blood. "PANLA JEN IS GOD" read another sign with a colorful depiction of a pious Panla floating above a throng of worshippers, ministering to their prayers.

A cluster of young adults practiced a chant which intensified as their numbers swelled: "Get next! Get next! Get next to the Text! Get next! Get next! Get next to the Text!" Many angry stragglers cursed the young adults and made obscene gestures toward them. The chanters' response was to chant even louder.

The scene below played out before Crilen like a theatrical performance from which his character's part had been written out of the drama. He'd been at the very heart of this show for months and done his bit. He'd stared fiercely into the eyes of all the players and conversed with them in scene after volatile scene. He'd interceded heroically to rescue a passionate life which doggedly refused to be rescued. He'd even fallen in love with the heavenly heroine whom he could not dissuade from her cosmic predestiny. But now, he was finished. His role was concluded. All that remained was for the final scene of the final act to culminate.

At last, the curtain would be drawn shut and he would finally be on his way to another planet...another stage...in the present.

Crilen's stomach churned as he watched an insect navigate the end of his boot. A spark flickered at the toe and the insect popped into a plume of smoke. He gazed out over the grassy hill on which he sat and watched the bluish blades flicker in the breeze. This could be a beautiful world, he thought. It was unfortunate that the selfish, ignorant ambitions of sentients marred its splendor.

The wind rustled the leaves of the nearby trees. Crilen released an indolent breath.

Then, he heard the crunch of footsteps approach from behind. Before he could completely turn his head, Crilen caught only a glimpse of the sharp hoof that kicked him squarely at the base of the skull. The impact sent him toppling head over heels down a rocky slope that felt nothing like the grassy hill upon which he sat.

Crilen landed, shoulders first, in a cloud of grey dust at the base of a craggy stone cliff. He quickly righted himself, stood and looked out over the suddenly altered landscape. Surrounding him were coarse grey spires of iron rock. Above him was the infinite void lit with stars and floating interstellar debris. Under his feet, was the metallic dust he remembered from what now felt like mere hours ago rather than months.

He was back on the asteroid.

"WHAT...ARE...YOU...DOING??" a familiar voice screamed in his head.

Crilen poked his fingers into his temples, looked up and saw his long lost-host glowering from a rocky perch. It's twelve-point antlers appeared even broader than he remembered. Its gnarled, twisted grey torso seemed coarser and drier. Its black eyes appeared to bulge forth like smooth dark angry marbles crackling with cosmic energy. Behind It hovered a large three-dimensional cube with the moving scenery of the Ponder Gulag showing through its clear flat surfaces like multi-dimensional viewing screens.

"What are you doing?" It repeated intensely with a venomous rage that rattled Crilen's cerebrum.

"What are you talking about?" Crilen responded.

It leapt from its perch and landed a meter in front of him. It's snout struggled to cover its fangs. But the anger in its brows and gestures was unmistakable.

"SAVE HER, you interstellar ignoramus!" It pointed a thin needle-point finger toward the floating cube. "Save her, goddamn you!"

"Why?" Crilen folded his arms and responded with dumbfounding indifference.

"Why?" It gesticulated its sinewy extremities madly. "Why? Because she's about to die you moribund, melancholy, moron! You've got to save her!"

"But she is saved," Crilen answered calmly.

"What?" It threw its head backward and kicked the metallic sand. "What are you talking about? That...that...religious nonsense she spews? It's myth! It's legend! Gargled history interspersed with lies and coincidences! She's not saved! She's going to die unless you do something!"

"Is that so?" Crilen looked up at the floating cube.

"Yes!" It stretched out its wiry arms. "Yes, yes, yes!"

"So are we talking about a temporal death or an eternal death?" Crilen quizzed It.

"Temp...?" It's frustration mounted. "We're talking about dead death. We're talking about the kind of death where the person dies and never comes back. Dead...gone...forever...like your wife! Remember her? I can take you through it again if you like!"

The inference struck a nerve. Crilen's eyes flickered like crimson coals.

"You love Panla, don't you?" It cajoled with a begging gesture.

"I do love her." Crilen lifted his brows. "But this is all much bigger than one being's love for another, isn't it? What happens when I rescue her? Or should I ask, what doesn't happen?"

"I've told you!" It gestured to the asteroid debris floating over head. "The entire world will be restored! Your loving wife will be restored! Just as I promised! Now go and save her as we bargained!"

"No," Crilen replied flatly.

"What did you say?" It's snouted jaw dropped open.

"I said no,." Crilen responded.

"If you renege on our bargain, this world will die and you will never have your wife again!" It vowed.

"My wife is dead." Crilen met its eyes. "And so is this world. I can never go back to the life I had. And neither can this planet."

"But I've shown you..." It pointed toward the cube.

"Time travel?" Crilen interrupted. "Interdimensional transcendence? Very impressive. But it doesn't change the physical realities of the present, does it?"

"The people of this planet destroyed their world," It stated firmly. "Panla Jen is the key!"

"Where are the twinmoons?" Crilen asked out of the blue. "Where are they, right now?"

Its snout wrinkled with frustration and its antlers started to quiver.

"The twinmoons broke away from their orbit when the planet was destroyed," It affirmed.

"Did they?" Crilen questioned. "I thought they were still here amidst all this orbiting rubble."

"Th…that's ridiculous," It stammered. "I was here. This is my world. I know what happened."

"I don't question that you do," Crilen replied. "The problem is, you're a big fat intergalactic liar!"

Its black orbs narrowed with anger.

"The twinmoons were in a decaying elliptical orbit," Crilen continued. "Within a thousand years of Panla's time, the first twinmoon would have collided with the planet, obliterating every living thing on it. A second impact from the other twinmoon would have completely destroyed the lifeless husk of that world, resulting in this orbiting debris field of asteroids and other matter. I found lunar remnants in this belt days before you and I ever met. But I wasn't able to put it all together until I observed the twinmoon orbits from the planet's surface.

"So the people of this world did not destroy themselves. They were the victims of a natural galactic disaster. Which brings me back to the conclusion that you didn't bring me here to rescue a doomed planet from its destruction. You brought me here to rescue Panla. Or, to put it another way, you brought me here to stop her."

"Do tell." It fell back and leaned against the base of its craggy shelf.

"This world was trapped in a mounting vortex of conflicting ideologies," Crilen continued. "Ideologies that were taking them farther and farther away from God. The Deliverers covered over the true meaning of the Text with so many of their own ideals and whims that God's original word became totally obscured…lost. And, along with the lost word, came generations of lost souls. Panla was obsessed with re-establishing the truth of God's Word. She was obsessed with the salvation of souls."

"That's right, you imbecile." It's brow wrinkled. "And now you're going to let her die."

"As if rescuing her life were really the answer," Crilen charged. "*For whosoever shall save his life shall lose it: but whosoever will lose his life for my sake, the same shall save it.*"

"Hah!" It scoffed with a wave of his metallic talons. "The ramblings of a suicide cult from a dead planet! Those people failed."

"'Those people' didn't fail." Crilen met his eyes.

"They literally crucified the Son of God." It shook its antlers sarcastically. "What would you call that?"

"The gateway to redemption," Crilen answered evenly.

"Yes," It smiled darkly. "If only they'd seen it that way."

"It was the people who didn't believe God's words who brought their world to destruction," Crilen concluded.

"God's words?" It sneered. "Are you mad? Words from the almighty? Speeches? Rhetoric? It's all myth! It's all made up by sentient beings who refuse to believe there is no supreme creator watching every move of every creature in the universe. I can't believe you're really this stupid."

"Of course you can," Crilen responded. "You've been counting on it. You've been counting on my faith in God to lure Panla away from her own world. You knew I'd fall in love with her and you were certain she'd fall in love with me. Only her faith in God was so strong, she refused to abandon her people, no matter what I said or did."

"'Faith in God." It's face twisted into a mask of contempt. "You think it makes you better than those who know better. I think I'd like to see the cowering insecure little vermin you'd become without it!"

Before Crilen could respond, It gestured with a sweep of its arm. Crilen felt a cold blast of energy rip through his molecules that sent him collapsing to his hands and knees. The sensation was jolting. Some veil had been lifted. Some inner restraint of reason had been stripped away. It was liberating. Suddenly, there were no moral barriers. Joyfully, there were no ethical restraints. It was a bare and selfish freedom he had not sensed since he'd been a child. Only now the urges were mature.

He found himself on a sun-soaked beach full of taut, oily, sweating, nude golden bodies. Everyone was laughing, dancing, wading or copulating in plain view...males with females, males with males, females with females and a beast or two. It was all erotically arousing and he wanted so much to be a part of it. A young couple holding hands walked by. The female slyly winked and smiled at him. Her legs were long and smooth. Her large breasts were bulbous and pointed. Her dark shimmering hair swung like a satin cape above her perfectly curved and bouncing buttocks. He reached out and grabbed her by the arm. She was surprised and shaken.

The male who was with her confronted Crilen. Crilen opened his mouth wide and screamed a raging torrent of fire into the young male's face that burned and ripped all of the flesh from his skull until his neckbone snapped and his sizzling, smoking head rolled away. The young male's convulsing, cauterized, decapitated corpse spasmed to the ground. The female screamed in horror. Crilen slapped her, threw her to the sand and mounted her. The female continued to scream and struggle. It wasn't going at all as he had planned. So he punched her in the throat causing a thick stream of blood to eject from her mouth and splatter across his savagely enraged countenance. She died instantly.

A crowd of partly angered and partly frightened people surrounded him. He growled a bone-chilling wail and released a searing wall of fire that broiled every living body in the circle, three persons deep. He ignited himself and flew toward the planet's largest city. There, he met the leaders of this world and told them lies. Eventually he murdered most of those he had taken into his confidence because they made him jealous or afraid. He stole their wealth and their land and made himself king. For a time, he lied to the people for sport, but grew weary of sport and openly degraded, coerced and executed everyone who opposed him. Though he would often murder a loyalist for the sheer joy of treacherous irony. He satiated his voracious appetite for females, subjecting them to his maiming sadistic perversions, impregnating those who pleased him and killing those who did not. He murdered the offspring who displeased him and oppressed those who showed promise. He experimented on his own body with chemicals which created new sensations and altered perceptions and he tarried in illusionary realms for recreation. Still, he grew bored with it all and decided to destroy the entire planet. With his pyrogenic power, he destabilized the planetary core and ruptured its gravitational field, causing the planet to implode as he flew from it and watched its destruction from a distant moon.

This was fun. This was amazing. The power and joy of unrelenting cruelty filled him with a rapturous cosmic ecstasy which was insatiable. He searched out a new world where a new game would be played. He pretended to be good for a longer period of time. So long that he earned the world's trust. So well that they paid him homage with idols to his goodness. Then he betrayed them to their enemies and watched the males, females and children, weakened by their trust, savagely butchered and devoured by their cannibalistic rivals from a neighboring planet.

One glimpse of a half-eaten, slaughtered corpse of a young female child actually made him sad. There was something wrong with what he had done, but he couldn't define what wrong was. He set about constructing a moral code that would make sense to him. A moral code that would not trouble his conscience. But there were too many variables to account for. Too many contingencies to consider. Too many exceptions which would always apply. His tortured tautology of logical morality swirled about his reason until the confusion angered him.

Finally, he concluded that nothing so complex should torment so passionate a creature as he. The vexing moral arguments were like a cage threatening to steal away his boundless freedom. Crilen rationalized the dead young female's corpse and smiled upon the notion that he would have to live for himself. What other logic could there be?

"New game," he thought.

"Stop!" He heard a voice in his head.

"More deceit. More death. More sensual exploitation! How delicious!" Crilen thought.

"Stop!" The voice rang through his skull again. "Stop!"

Crilen tried to envision the rapturous swath of destruction he would cut through the universe, but the vibrations inside his head became disorienting. He covered his ears as the pressure mounted in his skull. An initially unwelcome shower of warmth and assurance crashed through his soul. He fell to his knees and clutched his shoulders. He rocked and swayed and frowned despondently over the horror of his own most recent thoughts.

"I'm impressed," It's voice chortled inside of Crilen's head. "Too impressed. A soul to rival the master of all evil bundled up neatly into that hypocritically heroic bosom of yours. It's a good thing God holds you prisoner. The universe wouldn't last a year."

Crilen dropped his arms to his sides and lifted his head. He was back on the asteroid again.

"It's a good thing God holds me," Crilen's crimson eyes intensified. "Otherwise, you'd be a burned etching on the face of that iron stalagmite."

"If you say so." It dismissed the threat.

"Those things I saw and did," Crilen staggered to his feet. "they didn't happen, right?"

"Of course they did," It smirked, "but don't worry. You didn't leave any witnesses and I really don't think God was there."

"You made me kill billions for no reason?" Crilen's chest heaved with anger.

"I didn't make you." It's snout broadened into a vile, sharp-toothed grin. "I let you. And who needs a reason? What a grand time you had, eh? Without your theological delusion you were free. Wasn't it exhilarating to only worry about your own wants, your own desires?"

"It was horrifying," Crilen responded.

"Granted." It tilted it's antlers. "But that wasn't the question, was it?"

"No." Crilen sneered. "You were attempting to prove that faith is a cover for weakness. But true weakness is giving in to every urge, relenting to vice. Strength and heroism lies in restraint. Carrying faith through a universe which has little requires more strength, suffering, agony and heroism than you can ever know."

"Then why bother?" It shrugged. "Look at the fun you had."

Crilen was about to launch into another angry rebuttal. But then something struck him solid and it was his turn to smile.

"Because it's not about me or my wife. And it's not about Panla Jen." He gazed starward. "It's not about yesterday, today or tomorrow. It's about eternity, the only thing in the universe that really endures…and you know it!"

Crilen's flickering crimson gaze lowered from the star-laden heavens and peered directly through It's cold black eyes.

It folded its arms and its thin needle-like fingers ticked tensely against its hard dry torso. It had nothing to rebut.

"Why do you want me to stop Panla's execution?" Crilen continued. "So the world won't see her make the ultimate sacrifice by holding to her belief and paying for her crimes?"

It turned its back to Crilen. It pointed toward the hovering cube of images and the cube slowly started to descend upon them. The sounds and sights surrounding the Ponder Gulag reverberated more richly and deeply as the cube appeared to expand over the asteroid's horizons and envelop them.

"No," It finally replied. "I'm afraid it's much worse than that."

The cube twirled into a disorienting blur of light, then smashed over the top of them like a square kilometer mass of solid concrete.

XIX.

Crilen quickly doused his flames as he found himself rolling through the tall blue grass on the hill overlooking the Ponder Gulag. He sat up and looked skyward. A thickening of clouds filtered the dull daylight.

He peered down toward the Ponder Gulag and was alarmed by the sudden time shift. The smattering of pedestrian protesters and onlookers had swelled to a dense sea of animate bodies which flooded around the barricades and media transports, and rolled over the near horizons. The enormity of noise and chants and songs swayed in chaotic rhythm to the dancing signs and banners which depicted a dizzying myriad of social, religious and political views.

The bleachers inside the Gulag courtyard were nearly filled. The government security men stood rigidly at attention in their strategically mapped places. All of the heavily equipped media snipers staked their claims along the inner perimeters. Some hawked from the upper turrets of the watch towers. Others slithered and crawled alongside the bleachers in the dirt. A few huddled in the tight corners of the elevated walkway. One transmitting technician even crouched onto the very spot where the rotating columns would eventually crush and dismember the prisoner's bones.

Crilen suddenly realized that the hours had moved ahead. The execution was not due to begin later. Later had accelerated to right now.

In the courtyard, a preamble of traditional music played by a small military band blared over the din of anticipation. Everyone seated upon the bleachers respectfully rose to their feet.

Crilen looked for Panla to appear from behind the far wooden door of the elevated walkway just before the first stone arch. But two stories below, another door swung open. A pair of dark-suited security men entered, then flanked the narrow opening. The Accommodant strolled onto the grounds with a young female assistant clinging to his arm. Obseq, his advisor, trailed closely behind them carrying a large black satchel filled with important matters the Accommodant was too important to be concerned with.

Crilen wasn't close enough to appreciate the liquid skin patches dotting the Accommodant's face as a result of their final "discussion." All he could discern from the hill were the condescending nods of approval and applause for the highest-ranking politician in the world as he was escorted to his reserved seat, front and center. Parliamentarians, politicians and dignitaries leaned over each other and their spouses to pat him on the back or shake his hand. Clearly, the popularity polls remained heavily in his favor.

"Yeesh. You'd think the guy would at least wait until his wife's corpse was cold to go gallivanting around with his new hotty," Mr. Nil commented from his seat in the master YBS control transport.

Yolo Pigue walked the large master control room as a great sea admiral would bestride the decks of a mighty battleship before its final triumphant engagement. The air was thick with the reddish haze of his giant cigar and rank with the steady roar of his flatulence which he had loosed liberally upon his own charges since his early morning breakfast.

"It's never stopped him before, if you think about it." Yolo eyed the Accommodant's image on a broad monitor. "In the public eye, his soon-to-be former wife is more of an adulterer than he. After all, he never laid claim to a false fidelity. The world hates a moralizing hypocrite. An admitted scoundrel carries a bit of flair. But a hypocrite? Compared to her treachery, he's become the sentimental cuckold in their eyes. Thus, he now carries what's referred to in the northeast as carte blanche.

"And from the looks of things," he eyed the female assistant's oversized breasts, "Mr. Accommodant knows exactly how the public grace applies."

"What a guy." Mr. Nil admired the Accommodant, shaking hands and greeting his fellow politicians.

"So it seems." Yolo exhaled another thick cloud of smoke. "Look how they honor him before our cameras. I've dined with most of the legislative lice and they despise the Accommodant. Yet his duplicitous charms con the masses like a schoolmaster charms an adolescent young girl out of her panties. So they flock to his side, competing to parade their false adoration, knowing that we'll project their mendacious loyalties back to their dull-witted constituents. It's all such a vulgar symbiosis. No creature of any integrity should wish to sustain a seat so desperately. But then we are talking about politicians, aren't we? To them, integrity is as disposable as toilet tissue, though in less abundance."

"You've got all the answers, don't you?" a familiar voice chimed in.

"Yes." Yolo chuckled without turning his head. "Yes, I certainly do. So how are things over at the RATRAG, Mr. Pont? I've heard next to nothing of you since you stumbled out my home covered in secretions."

Mr. Nil turned away and pretended his former colleague was less than a stranger.

"Well, that's because over at the RATRAG they do an interesting thing." Mr. Pont folded his arms.

"Do tell, dear boy." Yolo finally looked toward him. "I'd love to know what the sponsors are unwilling to support."

"Well, at RATRAG they insist on something I hadn't heard of since I graduated school twenty twinmoons ago." Mr. Pont met the media giant's confident gaze. "They insist that we report the story exactly as it is and let the viewers and readers determine what it means. No slanting. No hedging. No fudging. No planting of seeds. No creative editing or omissions. Just the story, exactly the way it happened. If you haven't heard from me, that's because you haven't been listening for that big loud sigh of relief I let out every morning. Now I know that when I take a shower, I won't need another one by noon because of how filthy my job makes me feel."

"Yes, yes. You're happy, poor and ignored." Yolo's expression went flat with annoyance. "Just don't come calling here when the rent to your dingy little hovel is overdue. Now, I believe you've interloped on my property for a reason?"

"RATRAG wants grounds rights to the execution," Mr. Pont stated seriously. "No images of Panla Jen. Just the right to air interviews and reactions from the grounds after today."

"And why would I do that?" Yolo scoffed. "Free gristle sandwiches at the drive-by of my choice for the next twinmoon? We have exclusive rights to the entire execution archive. Anything related to the execution can only be aired by us once the twenty-six hour grace period has expired. Roll your cameras all you like. Record everything you wish for personal posterity, but once the day has run full cycle, YBS will have sole rights to all related execution footage within a square kilometer radius. That includes the grounds rights, which we have no intention of relinquishing. Now you may stay or go. I leave it to you. But please don't waste any more of my precious time. It's a glorious day and I intend to enjoy every 'bloody' moment of it."

Yolo turned away and hoisted himself up into his giant leather command chair which overlooked the entire transport staff.

Mr. Nil snickered audibly, but never looked in Mr. Pont's direction.

Mr. Pont felt the old disgust rise up in his gut, but he wasn't prepared to leave just yet. RATRAG didn't own a transport. And all of the RATRAG reporters had already scurried away to their places inside the Ponder Gulag courtyard. He decided that this pit of asps might actually be the best venue from which to endure the painful end of Panla Jen's life. He calmly leaned against the wall and watched the omniscient collective of monitors gather images for the latest revision of history.

"Da, why do I have to watch this stupid execution?" Fembletun's oldest daughter whined.

Fembletun glanced over at his wife who'd grown far too weary of the topic. She tossed up her hands, gathered a bundle of reading material and trudged up the spiral staircase to escape this never-ending father-daughter debate.

"Because..." Fembletun watched his wife hastily disappear, "because the Deliveress is going to atone for her sins. That's what a person does when they've done wrong. They confess and atone."

"She's going to be slaughtered and it's going to be gross." His daughter rolled her eyes. "Besides, she's a hypocrite. She does what she feels like doing until she gets caught. Then she gives some flowery speech about not following her but following God...do dah do dah day. What...ever."

Fembletun could feel the veins across his smooth black scalp tighten.

"Now you listen to me, girl." He wagged his finger in her face. "We never had this problem until that skinny, horny, buck-toothed punk with the droopy drawers and the wild hair started coming around here."

"This isn't about Dev." The girl folded her arms in a huff.

"No?" Fembletun's eyes widened. "Your grades are down a full point. You walk out of here every morning dressed like a half-coin prostitute. Every other word out of your mouth is that damn boy's name and it's not about him?"

His daughter rolled her eyes and frowned.

"Maybe it's about you," she responded disrespectfully. "You spent our whole lives jamming your religious junk down our throats and suddenly it isn't worth a broken stick. I know what I'm about. You're the one who seems lost all of a sudden."

Fembletun swallowed his rage and counted very slowly to himself.

"My father would have gone upside my head if I had talked to him that way." Fembletun leaned forward with a dark angry scowl. "You better curb that tone before you find yourself picking your teeth out of the floor tile, young lady."

The girl lowered her eyes and pouted.

"Now did you hear Deliveress Jen's speech?" he continued in a level tone.

"Some of it," his daughter answered wearily.

"Did you understand 'some of it'?" He tried to capture her eyes.

"Not really." She turned her head away.

"Well, that's too bad." Fembletun poked her chin with his forefinger. "Because if you had, I wouldn't be making you stay here and watch the execution. Now you're going sit on that sofa with your religious old dad and we're going to watch this thing together. And if you don't want to do that, you can call up your stupid boyfriend and ask him if he's ready to put a roof over your head because I'll stop."

"Da...!" her brows furrowed with frustration.

"Call him...or sit!" Fembletun pointed to the couch.

Angrily, his daughter stomped toward the couch and plopped herself down in front of the monitor. Fembletun grabbed a large triangular glass full of juice from the kitchen counter, returned to the living room, and eased himself onto the couch, nestling uncomfortably close to his daughter. She squirmed away from him. He poked her in the ribs. She defiantly forced herself not to smile and tilted her head sideways impatiently.

For a fleeting moment, they were close again, but Fembletun could feel his daughter's soul pulling away. He found himself running thinner and thinner on ideals that would protect her from becoming another parcel of meat for the world's grinder.

Panla could feel them dressing her. She sensed the worn white gown being tossed over her hanging head. She could feel her numbed tingling arms, which had been twisted under her listless body against the frozen stone floor overnight, being pulled carelessly through the sleeves. What little sense of gravity she perceived indicated she was probably standing, but she could not feel her feet below the calves, either because of the deadening drug they had forced into her fifteen hours ago or the cold hard unconscious night she had spent lying naked in the chilly draft.

She attempted to lift her head, but it was like trying to hoist a boulder with the drugged, jellied muscles in her unresponsive neck. She searched her memory for the time. She scoured her recollections for the date. She mentally groped for the edge of some cognitive anchor that would tell her when or where she was.

Then, gradually, it seeped back to her: The soul-wrenching ache to reset the world upon God's scriptural path. The alliance with the Break. The failed reformation. Rabbel's murder. Hopelessness. Repentance. Reconciliation. Mr. Len's loving embrace. Surrender. Imprisonment. Prayer. Condemnation. Her final speech. Stifling rejection. Abandonment. Death.

Death. Today was the day she was going to die. Today was the day she would see God.

Blessed relief and a dogged restlessness grappled for her conscience. She was relieved that this painful, unperfected journey through life would finally come to an end. Battling with the legions of evil for the souls of this world had worn her to the quick. Wading against the tide of ignorant and selfish choices inherent to secular sentience left her lamenting whether the souls she had fought so tirelessly to win for Heaven cared less for their own salvation than did she. But ministry had been her charge. Ministry had been her passion. Winning souls to Heaven. Snatching the damned from the bloodied jowls of the devil. There was no greater work than this, but the work had taken its toll. Once she had put it upon herself to balance the spiritual burden of the entire world upon her own shoulders, she painfully collapsed under the immeasurable weight. For all of her love and knowledge and energy for God, she was only one living creature. Her resolve had run its course. Now she wanted nothing more than to finally rest at the foot of Heaven's throne.

But a nagging mortal uncertainty dogged her dream of eternal peace. What would become of this world once she was gone? Would the Accommodant, Yolo Pigue and all those who railed in opposition to God reign supreme? Would the circumstances of her execution mar the influence of her life's labor with the cankers and sores of her sins? Would her legacy in this world fail to glorify God and instead fortify the evil she had fought to eradicate? Perhaps, again, she placed more worldly relevance on her deeds than was warranted. Perhaps, in the end, the Lord would intervene and cleanse the trail of her abject failure.

The drug they had given her left her weakened, addled and disoriented. But beneath the fugue, she searched for her prayers, the Lord's forgiveness, the Lord's truth and the salvation of the world.

She heard the heavy chains clamp over her wrists and her ankles, but she could not feel them. There was a painful tug on her right arm and another painful tug on her left. She vaguely heard the door to her cell creak open. Sluggishly, she realized she was being led out into the corridor.

The cold, howling wind burned raw against her bare neck and shoulders. The wicked morning air cut through her thin garment and caused the surfaces of her flesh to sting. The muscles in her torso quaked and spasmed involuntarily as they rejected the icy intemperate assault.

She still could not feel her wobbly legs, but they were moving slowly, barefooting unsteadily, up the long winding stone staircases. A few times, her knees wanted to buckle, but the security officers would tug the heavy chains again and she would recover her steps just well enough to continue her unsteady climb.

She tried once more to lift her head but her neck was like a dead boneless limb. Her head hung and bounced from shoulder to shoulder, dizzying her ability to focus upon anything.

Finally, she sensed a light. She painfully squinted her eyes open and could see the daylight against the stone floor. Just outside the doorway, she could hear the murmuring anticipation of a large throng. A large throng who had come to see her die in disgrace so that they could comfortably sever all ties to Heaven and guiltlessly do as they willed for themselves henceforth.

"No," her thoughts struggled to order themselves, "not like this my Lord. Your child will not leave this world a broken disgrace in her service to You. Not broken by the devil's mocking minions who sit on the edge of their seats waiting for the yawning gates of Hell to burst forth and beckon a billion untethered souls to their doom. Let them rend this body. Let them crush it. Let them burn it. Let them scatter the ashes of everything I ever was into the lost memories of the swirling winds. But do not let them bear witness to the death of your soldier as a lost, faithless perversion of all of your loving promises to us. Let them see You in me as I walk to my death. Let the burning gates of Hell freeze shut upon this crystal shining moment where your glory and grace and righteousness stand strong and fast and true for all this world to regain its path to eternal salvation. Let the joyful shouts of You in this world drown the anguished howls of the devil as he is driven from our hearts, dragged from the shadows of lies and deceit and consumed by the blinding glare of Heaven's light. Reign supreme, my Heavenly Father. Reign supreme today…and forever."

With all the effort she could muster against the drug and the cold, Panla slowly, miraculously, lifted her head.

The pair of government security officers chained to her wrists tugged on her bonds, but it seemed only to rouse her to raise her head even higher. The two men looked at each other, then continued toward the open door leading to the elevated walkway of the Ponder Gulag courtyard.

Panla halted. The two security men jerked to a surprised stop. They turned back to look at her and she still appeared frail and unsteady, except for her eyes. The large brown eyes were filled with a sudden lucidity and clarity. Again, the two men looked at each other.

Panla worked her jaws and lips, raking up the thick phlegm which had built up inside of her throat from the cold air. She snapped her head sideways and spat a large thick azure clot against the stone wall. She raised her long slender neck even higher, closed her eyes…and calmly started to sing.

Crilen's scalp flashed hot at the first glimpse of Panla in the doorway of the elevated walk. His hands smoldered and crackled against the blue grass of the hill where he sat.

For the umpteenth time, he riffled through all of the pros and cons of this moment. His most rational conclusion was to sit and do nothing. Yet seeing her vulnerable and alone, chained to the government security officers, caused his heart to ache. Knowing she would be dead in a matter of minutes bludgeoned his intellect with sorrow.

A rescue would be so easy. Just as it had been in Rabbel's tavern. Ignite, fly across the courtyard, sever the chains and carry her off to safety. Let the world make of it what they will. Panla would live. The woman who held his heart would live. Why couldn't God's universe be any simpler than that?

The answer vexed his soul.

"Where is camera twenty-seven?" Yolo bellowed from his command chair.

"Coming around, sir," Mr. Nil responded nervously.

"What the hell is camera forty-one doing?" Yolo's heavy voice boomed. "I want a ground shot of her stepping into the grinding chamber! Tell him to get it right! And if he misses another frame, he's fired!"

"Yes, sir." Mr. Nil relayed the commands through his headset.

Yolo reached down to the breakfast tray next to his chair and clanged his thick fingertips against the empty platter. He looked down and saw only the large doily, a smattering of icing crumbs and a few smears of fruit preserves.

"Gone?" His mouth fell open.

Angrily, he pounded his fist against the tray, sending it flipping wildly across the broadcast transport until it loudly caromed off the forehead of a young marketing assistant who was prepping cues for the first commercial break.

"Has the goddamned world gone incompetent?" Yolo watched the marketing assistant crumple to the floor covered in icing crumbs and a large stained doily.

Mr. Pont quickly moved to the marketing assistant's aid.

Yolo observed the act of kindness with a callused disdain.

"I guess the world has gone incompetent after all," the media giant observed. "Compassion and journalism don't mix. It doesn't sell. Remind your soon-to-be unemployed friends at RATRAG when they come whoring for work at YBS."

Mr. Pont ignored the comment. He could afford to now. He was joyously free and clear of any dependence upon Yolo Pigue. Privately, he promised himself that no matter how destitute he became, he would never serve the ilk of this particular master ever again.

The scene was both ethereal and eerie to the enormous crowd who witnessed Panla, chained to the government security officers, marching slowly along the elevated stone walkway. The two males in dark suits locked to their female prisoner wearing white projected a symbolism that the audience could neither fully grasp nor totally ignore.

The wind swirled around the chained trio as they crossed under the second arch. Panla's powerful singing voice sounded to polyphonically harmonize over the flowing currents of nature. It's warm resonant tone poured over the Ponder Gulag walls with a rich supernatural clarity which defied the physical limitations of a single living being. Even the fervent protesters behind the outer barricades were dumbed like curious beasts upon the hearing of so beautiful a voice which they knew would soon be silenced forever. The momentary serenity which calmed this vast gathering of conflicted beings was awe-inspiring.

Panla's voice was so piercingly strong and clear as it soared into the heavens that the vibrations pained the eardrums of her government escorts. Discreetly, one officer would pull on her left wrist to quiet her resolve. Then the other officer would tug on her right wrist and she would stumble, but never fall or lose the crest of her intonations.

From below, the Accommodant watched his condemned wife pass under the fourth arch, moving closer to the ancient execution machinery with its rusted iron-spiked columns and the manually operated pulleys. Aware of the cameras, he clutched the hand of his mistress while bearing a melancholic expression of pain and impending loss. Inwardly, however, the sound of Panla's voice was the harsh convicting screech of the antithesis of his entire life. He longed to hear her silenced once and for all and to see her blood gush down the chute of the execution apparatus and into the pit of roasting coals.

Crilen's heart pounded as he listened to Panla's song and watched her pass under the fifth arch. Two more to go. It still was not too late to do exactly what It had asked: Save her. Save her and be rewarded with some transdimensional life in the arms of his reborn dead wife. There were so many times when that very delusion appeared preferable to his reality, but Crilen knew that no delusion could forestall the irrevocability of truth. His wife was dead and he was forever changed. There was no sound reason to take up residence in the past when...

Crilen's cosmic senses abruptly skidded off the chart. He snapped his gaze skyward and scanned the heavens for an alien spacecraft or some interstellar anomaly. He couldn't confirm if what he sensed was corporeal, mechanical or astronomical in nature. All he could be certain of was that the galactic inertia was enormous in range and scope. Larger than the entire world. Rippling through the solar system. Headed for this planet

There was a slight tremor which mounted into a substantial quake.

Inside and outside the Ponder Gulag, there were yelps and squeals as the ground thunder shook everyone and everything.

Panla's voice could still be heard over the rumbling and panic.

Inside the Ponder Gulag walls, the parliamentarians and dignitaries on the bleachers noted the arches over the walkway crumbling and collapsing; Many herded off of the bleachers and onto solid ground for their own safety.

The echo of Panla's voice hung in the air as the sixth arch collapsed and the government security officers hastened past the falling rubble pulling on their chains.

The quake gradually subsided and the rumbling died away.

The people in and around the Ponder Gulag regathered themselves with relieved chatter and nervous laughter.

Crilen's gaze remained fixed skyward. Whatever had caused the disturbance had departed the solar system as quickly as it had come. Gradually, everyone's eyes returned to the elevated walkway where five of the seven stone arches had collapsed into piles of rock and dust.

Still standing were the two government security officers in their chains. The first officer pulled on the chained right wrist of the other. The second officer pulled on the chained left wrist of his counterpart. They tugged simultaneously on the chains, then stared into each other's bewildered gaze. They turned back and looked at the crumbled sixth arch from which they'd narrowly escaped. They walked back, scanned the rubble and kicked the rocks. The first security officer dropped to his knees in the dust, pulling the second officer down with him, and started to sweep the dust with the forearm of his dark suit until both men were covered in grey dust. The second officer pulled the first officer up by the chain and ran to the edge of the walkway's outer wall. They looked over it and saw nothing but a steep hundred-meter drop onto an incline of jagged rocks below.

The two security officers looked at each in shocked disbelief. They slowly walked back to the edge of the walkway facing the courtyard and held up their chained wrists to the crowd below.

A nervous murmur rolled through the audience. Dignitaries and politicians whispered the unspeakable conclusion in broken sentences, over and over again; they simply could not accept what they witnessed with their own eyes.

Panla Jen was gone.

XX.

"Gone?" The smoldering cigar fell from Yolo's lips.

"Can't find her," a technician said from his terminal.

"Not here," another technician called into the air.

"I don't have her." A third technician scanned his row of monitors.

"Excuse me, you dumb shits!" Mr. Nil yelled into his headset. "We've got forty-six cameras out there! Someone find the fucking Deliveress, please!"

"Gone." Yolo's stunned, horrified expression remained fixated upon the image of the chained security officers standing next to the rubble of the sixth arch without their captive.

"Okay, forget it!" Mr. Nil yelled. "We need a time-out here. Cut to commercial! Cut to commercial right now!"

"Gone." Yolo's bottom lip quivered. All at once the media giant felt the moorings of his entire existence snap loose. He felt himself toppling head over heels into a bottomless abyss where he controlled absolutely nothing. It was a nauseatingly helpless sensation which made his bowels quiver and his fleshy neck tighten.

"NO!" Yolo pushed himself up from his command chair and swatted the burning cigar from his lap.

Everyone turned and faced the media giant who looked suddenly ashen and gasping for breath.

"No!" Yolo repeated, propping himself against the chair. "No goddamn commercials! Stay on the air! Keep recording! Record everything! How many goddamn cameras does it take to find one fleeing female? It's a hoax, don't you see? She's been planning this for months! Planning her escape! She planned the goddamn earthquake for all we know! But she's not far, I tell you! She can't be far at all! Now find her! Find her now!"

On the elevated walkway, one of the government security officers who had been chained to Panla dropped to his knees and broke into weeping prayer. The other security officer hastily fumbled for his electronic key, unlocked himself from the tangle of chains, and ran away as fast as he could.

"Aschen~exol," a shaken baritone voice said from the edge of the bleachers.

"Aschen~exol?" an elderly parliamentarian asked. "What is that?"

The former Holy Inquisitor and acting Deliverer lowered his teary eyes from the heavens and met the parliamentarian's query.

"Aschen~exol," he repeated. "The Exalted Ascent. The ultimate grace for the repentance of sin. According to the Text, it's only occurred one other time in recorded history, nearly two thousand twinmoons ago. Similar events have been reported through the centuries, but all of them were eventually proven false. The only time it really occurred was to the last of the nine Chieftains. The Text says that there were thousands of witnesses, but as with most of the ancient miracles, time has diminished fact into legend and legend into myth. Today most Text scholars have trivialized the Aschen~exol into a metaphor for something easier for us to grasp. But according to scripture, it was...amazingly similar to what we've all just witnessed."

"Hmm," the parliamentarian responded uncomfortably, "that's very interesting. But until we get all the facts, I'm not sure I'm ready to accept that Panla Jen made an exalted ascent anywhere."

The Holy Inquisitor barely heard the tail end of the parliamentarians skepticism. His eyes returned skyward and the tears continued to fall.

Confessed of her sins, Panla Jen had offered herself as a living sacrifice to the world for the restoration of God's Word...and, before the entire planet, God trumped all mortal measures.

Egs Bloyt, the YBS anchor, stood on the elevated walkway clutching her earpiece. Mr. Nil had been yelling a barrage of uncohesive instructions to the coverage staff from the instant Panla had disappeared.

"Stop," Egs said into her headset. "Stop! Will you listen to me? Stop! I've got one of the two security officers with me and he's ready to go."

There was a pause. Mr. Nil had to get permission from Yolo.

"Okay," his frantic voice finally came back, "but under no circumstances is the word miracle or God to be mentioned, is that clear?"

Egs's jaw dropped.

"Are you kidding?" she shouted above the din rising from the Ponder Gulag courtyard. "What the hell do you think this is about?"

"The boss says we are to treat this as a hoax, an escape." Mr. Nil's blaring voice vibrated in her ear.

"An escape?" Egs yelled back into her headset. "Is that fat bastard out of his fucking mind? Did he see what just happened? Panla Jen was chained to two government security officers. The woman could barely stand, for god's sake! We all saw it. She did not escape. This is not a hoax. It's the biggest thing to happen to our planet since…"

"Those are your orders, Egs," Mr. Nil snapped back. "Take 'em or leave 'em."

Her mind flashed over her meteoric rise to become one of the leading anchors for YBS News. The money, glamour and notoriety had been staggering and gratifying over the past few years. So staggering that she never bothered to search too closely for the truth in anything she ever did. The truth was not convenient. The ascent of her career was all that mattered. But this morning, a bold and garish truth had stalked her down and cornered her. As she had hunched down into a stony corner of the elevated walkway and watched the security officers emerge from the sixth arch without their prisoner, she didn't need anyone to tell her what she had witnessed with her own eyes. As she held on to the security officer's sleeve, preparing for a worldwide interview, the raw naked truth suddenly mattered more than anything.

"Put us on," Egs spoke resignedly.

"Good girl," Mr. Nil responded. "Ten seconds…

"…five seconds…

"go!"

"Hello, this is Egs Bloyt here at the Ponder Gulag." She met the camera with an unrehearsed candor. "I'm standing here with one of the security officers who was assigned to escort Panla Jen Tem to her execution. Sir, can you tell us your account of what happened?"

The security officer's impassive stoicism was completely wiped away. He looked like any other humbled civilian who had found himself stunned by complete astonishment.

"First, I want to praise our Lord and Savior for delivering this day to our world." The security officer's voice shook. "I never believed it. Never believed any of it. Never read the Text. Turned away from my parents. Thought it was all a bunch of nonsense. I'm so sorry..."

"I understand all of that," Egs tried to keep him focused, "but exactly what happened?"

The security officer covered his face with his hands, rocked back and forth, and looked as if he were about to break down and cry again. Then he pulled his hands away and shook his head clear with what little military resolve remained in him.

"Well, my partner and I were taking Mrs. Tem to the execution chamber," he began. "She was singing really loud, which was a miracle in and of itself. Mrs. Tem could barely stand. My partner and I were basically holding her up and pulling her along with the chains. Then the quake hit and the whole walkway started shaking like it was going to collapse. The Ponder Gulag's a very old structure and as soon we felt that shake, we thought we might be going down. We heard some rock and masonry crumbling as we walked under the arch. Some gravel actually hit us on the head and shoulders, so we jumped through just before the whole thing fell.

"It was weird when we jumped through though. We could hear Mrs. Tem's voice, but it was like she wasn't with us anymore. When we jumped through, it was suddenly just the two of us...chained together...like Mrs. Tem had never been there at all. It was impossible! Absolutely impossible! She didn't slip through the chains. She couldn't have. Those things were tight. And how did my partner and I wind up chained to each other in a split second? Nobody could have done that. Standing still, it would have taken us several minutes. Jumping for our lives, there's no way! We looked through the rubble of the arch, but there was nothing. No blood. No body. No clothing. No hole she could have fallen through. We looked over the outside of the walkway and that's a hundred-meter drop straight down onto jagged rocks. There's no way! She just disappeared. Flat out disappeared. By the grace of God she disappeared. Praise our Lord and Savior!"

"Are you saying, then, that you believe that divine intervention was the only explanation for this?" Egs questioned.

"I don't believe anything." The security officer shook his head as if his brain were about to explode. "I know. I know that the only thing that could have gotten Mrs. Tem out of those chains and out of the Ponder Gulag was God in Heaven."

"So what do you say to the people who believe it was an elaborate escape or a hoax?" Egs asked.

"Well," the security officer looked into the camera, shaking his head, "I'm here to tell you that anybody who claims to believe this is some hoax is either a fool, an idiot or a liar! You can't get any closer to what happened than I was. They have no idea what they're talking about."

Egs swallowed hard as she read the earnest conviction in everything about the security officer's demeanor. He seemed like a man liberated from the chains of his own personal imprisonment. A recessed corner of her own heart envied the invigoration of his newfound freedom.

"Sir, thank you." Egs grabbed his hand and held it up to the camera. "That's all we have from here. From everything we can gather this morning, it certainly looks like...a miracle!

"Back to the studio now."

Egs gazed into the camera, exhaling her own leap to liberation. The cost would be high, but the reward was immeasurable.

"Egs, the old man says you're fired!" Mr. Nil's voice blared through her headset.

At first, Egs felt a curse build on her lips. But then, she quietly pulled off her headset, tossed it to the cameraman and walked away with her arm locked solemnly around the elbow of the security officer.

Fembletun's daughter sat forward on the couch with her eyes widened and her mouth agape as she stared into the satellite monitor.

Fembletun gently ran his fingers along his daughter's spine as he attempted to retain his composure. He always promised himself that none of the members of this female household would ever see tears in his eyes. This morning, as his spirit swelled with joy, that challenge was greater than any felon or murderer he had ever had to face down.

He blinked and blinked. Then he bit his bottom lip. He looked toward the ceiling to dry his eyes and tried to catch his breath. Finally, he thought a prayer of thanks as his mind raced through the conjugations of what Panla Jen's miraculous disappearance meant to the faith and salvation of his family.

He leaned forward and placed his arm around his daughter's shoulder. He searched for his strong commanding voice, but it was still choked up in the emotional well of his throat. He released a short breath and spoke just above a whisper.

"This is why you trust God, baby girl." He lovingly jostled her. "This is why. Because you never know how or when He's going to come through. You just have to know that He always does."

The caress of her father's hand suddenly transformed into a welcomed pillar of assurance, although she wasn't prepared to admit as much to him. She could feel all of the priorities in her life gradually attempting to realign themselves. The tense confusion of her youth eased just a little. Deep down, she was very, very thankful to realize that her loving father was right after all.

Meanwhile, with world opinion and political influence teetering in the balance, the Accommodant hastily contrived his own leap of faith.

"Praise God Almighty!" the Accommodant blustered before the reporters and satellite cameras as his constituents jammed into view to be seen with him. "Praise God! My wife is saved! Hallelujah! Hallelujah! My wife is saved!"

The dense cluster of lights, cameras and arms holding microphones leaned toward him.

"Are you saying that you believe that this was an act of God this morning and not some sort of escape or hoax?" the diminutive Yara Pique elbowed for position against her peers and rivals.

The Accommodant spun around, cocked his head and whipped the tail of his pressed jacket behind him with a sweep of his hand. The parliamentarians and dignitaries standing behind him forced broad smiles upon their faces and prompted each other to applaud their approval.

"What I'm saying, my dear sweet little lamb, is that God's word is true!" The Accommodant jigged and pointed toward the sky. "My wife is with the creator, praise the Lord! She would not be brought low by the powers of the devil! When God saw my wife needed a helping hand, He reached down and plucked her from Hell's midst and shined glory upon this world. Hallelujah!"

The parliamentarians glanced at one another with dubious bewilderment as they continued to clap and smile upon the Accommodant's every word.

"And where were you when your wife needed a helping hand?" shouted a voice from the wall of reporters.

"I was on my knees, praying to God!" The Accommodant didn't miss a beat. "I was praying that my wife's words would ring true and reverberate over the hills, under the oceans and into the hearts of every living creature on this planet. Now, I knew that taking the religious high road wasn't the most popular avenue for me to take, but I've never been worried about what's popular. All of you who know me know that I only care about what's right! That's why I married such a righteous woman!"

None of the cameras noticed the government security officers quietly escorting the Accommodant's mistress from the grounds.

"Today is the dawn of a new day," he continued, preaching above the mounting applause of his constituents. "Those of us who believe in God no longer have to hide behind our false selves. We can stand up and be counted. God knows who his children are and we will all be counted when the day of reckoning comes. Rabbel Mennis and the Break tried to bring down the Cathedral, but in the end, God brought them down instead. And while my wife faced persecution for her noble cause I never lost faith. I never stopped believing. And today she is saved! She is saved by the grace of God. Oh glory! Hallelujah! And those of you who do not think that God is real, you've seen it with your own eyes. He is real! He is real! He is real!"

"So does this mean that you've turned over a new leaf as well?" Another question was raised.

"I am the leaf from the branch of the tree of life!" The Accommodant spread his arms open wide.

Everyone surrounding the bleachers looked at each other with confused expressions.

"Listen." He held up his hands. "I've got to go now. But all of you go home and pray tonight. Praise him! Praise him! Praise him! Hallelujah! See ya later!"

The applauding parliamentarians parted their ranks and the Accommodant was escorted from the Ponder Gulag courtyard by his security team. His assistant Obseq hastened quickly to catch up.

"That was brilliant sir," The young male assistant ran alongside the Accommodant.

"That was bullshit." The Accommodant's smile collapsed into a grimace as they entered the dark tunnel which would lead them to his private transport. "The goddamn things a person's got to say to survive in this world."

The Accommodant paused and gazed skyward through a narrow window opening.

"You bitch," he sneered coldly to the heavens. "You fucking bitch."

The master YBS control transport continued to buzz with technicians swiveling in their chairs, flipping switches and relaying information to one another through their headsets. Hundreds of monitors displayed hundreds of images of the biggest story to hit the planet in two millennia.

Yolo slovenly slumped in his large leather command chair like a large frozen dessert melting under a hot kitchen lamp. Each recording of Panla Jen's disappearance was more disconcerting than the preceding.

She was gone.

Gone.

Gone in a cloud of dust.

Sucked from the air by an imploding cosmic vacuum.

Whipped from existence in a spinning ball of white cloth.

Absorbed into the metal chains which bound her.

Morphed into molecules of thin air.

Every image from every camera angle showed a different incarnation of what transpired, yet they all funneled to the same maddening supernatural conclusion.

Yolo's eyes bulged; his mouth puckered and drooped. It was a mind-scorching nightmare screeching outward from the subconscious pit of his darkest fears.

"Cheer up, old man." A hand slapped Yolo on the shoulder.

Yolo's befuddled eyes darted to clarity as he shifted his weight and looked up into the smiling face of Mr. Pont.

"I believe you once told me, 'You mustn't dwell fiendishly on issues you haven't the power to affect.'" The former employee met the media giant's eyes. "I suggest you take your own advice. It's all out of your control. It's time to give it up."

Yolo's eyes narrowed hatefully. He drummed his large fingers on the arm of his command chair. His body started to quake as he broke into a disdainful chuckle.

"Confidence ill-suits an invertebrate, Mr. Pont." The media giant rolled his eyes. "None of what appears on these screens is of any consequence. The world will never see any of it. The earthquake damaged our equipment. All of the feeds to our cameras went unrecorded. How embarrassing, I must confess. So the only things that will ever be said about this nonevent will be reduced to the level of hearsay. And I will play an imperious part in what is heard and said henceforth. This entire matter is some hoax perpetrated by the queen hag and her delusional clique of religious cronies. An escape orchestrated by a prevaricating charlatan who sought glory for herself by the malpractice of her outdated, secularized theology. That's what the conclusion will be. Because I do have the power to affect this issue, and affect it, I will."

"You're going to destroy these recordings?" Mr. Pont was aghast.

"What recordings, dear boy?" Yolo grinned. "As I said, they never existed."

"And what about our recordings?" Mr. Pont asked.

Yolo smiled and quaked another chuckle.

"I believe you answered your own question earlier this morning, dear lad," the old man spoke confidently. "YBS owns all the rights to this execution. You and your guttersnipe brethren own nothing. If any of what's occurred here today appears on satellite, I'll sue the lot of you into an early grave. You'll spend so much time pleading in front of judicatories you'll have to wear diapers to defecate. If you don't believe me, ask the last woebegone do-gooder who tried to cross me."

Mr. Pont gazed upon his former employer with a blend of pity and contempt. There was no shred of truth in Yolo Pigue's heart, only the basest survival instinct which knew no moral boundaries. Fortunately, there was one final piece to be played.

"You're right, sir," Mr. Pont relented. "YBS does own exclusive rights to the execution. The only problem is that there was no execution."

Yolo lifted his head with an irritated expression.

"I beg your pardon?" Yolo spoke in a squelched whisper

"There was a hoax," Mr. Pont continued, "or maybe an escape. Or perhaps a miraculous act of God. But one thing we do know is that there was no execution, unless you're planning to climb up on the Ponder Gulag walkway and take one for the team."

Yolo's arrogance simmered.

"Don't be a fool," the large man blustered angrily. "My lawbookers will grind your vacantly semantic claims into hash and you along with it."

"Doubtful," Mr. Pont responded. "We've got lawbookers, too. Only being less educated and sharp as your lawbookers, they take forever to get their paperwork and arguments in order. Months if not twinmoons. In the meantime, we can show the world what YBS 'didn't record'. By the time you win, if you win, the truth will be stored in every personal record library on the planet. You can sue us into atoms, but you'll never delete the truth from the hearts and minds of a billion people. Of course I wouldn't put it past you to try."

Yolo's thin veil of confidence slowly receded. A wilted desperation appeared in his eyes for the very first time.

"Mr. Pont." Yolo grinned unevenly. "Must it come to that? Surely there must be some arrangement which would be agreeable to all parties concerned. Legal proceedings are so messy. Of course I have the means and resources to survive such a bloody encounter, but think of the livelihoods which would be ruined.

You and your comrades would be indigent and unemployed when all is said and done. A savage waste of talent. I'd spend you into the ground. And for what? A bundle of bizarre images which can't be explained by the rational mind? Come, come. You know I've always been fond of your work. Very fond, indeed. So much so that before that unseemly episode in my home, I was prepared to offer you your own division. Journalism just the way you like it, with unlimited funds to tell the world the truth in your own inimitable fashion. Think of the fame and profit. Your name would become synonymous with our profession. The plebiscites would swear by your every word. You'd wield a power which would rival all but my own."

Mr. Pont sighed and glanced up at the ceiling.

"There's only one power in the universe that matters to me, Mr. Pigue," he started, "and you don't have it. You never did. And the sad thing is, I think you know what I'm talking about. You just refuse to accept it. No matter how many times you look at those replays, you still refuse to accept it. Power. A person can wield power over information and perception, but nothing compares to the power we witnessed today. If I'm going serve anyone now, it's going to be a power that lasts, not the flavor of the month."

Yolo was jolted by the insult.

"Out!" the media giant's deep voice reverberated against the walls. "Get out!"

Every head in the control transport snapped around. Two technicians abandoned their console posts and seized Mr. Pont by the arms.

"A pity," Mr. Pont mocked him. "*He taketh the wise in his own craftiness*'. Good luck, Mr. Pigue."

Yolo rose from his chair with wild rage carved into his fleshy features.

The technicians escorted Mr. Pont from the transport.

Yolo released a loud wheezing flatulence that oddly felt very damp.

Crilen waded against the sea of bodies outside the Ponder Gulag which danced, sung, chanted and cheered all around him. The roaring chorus of "Get Next to the Text" was deafening. And there was an audible undercurrent of a song in an ancient language which repeated the words Aschen~exol. Still, there were many others who had come to celebrate Panla Jen's execution who now shuffled silently through the loud celebration with bewilderment blanking their expressions and dejection draining their limbs.

Crilen observed dozens of joyful believers embracing each other in large tearful huddles of abounding happiness. He walked by an elderly couple on their knees, prayerfully gesturing toward the heavens.

"It's all true!" The husband held up his Text and shook it skyward. "It's all true! Thank God almighty!"

Crilen continued onward toward the front gate where he witnessed another gathering. It seemed harmless enough at first, but then he heard something which was troubling.

"Panla Jen is God and God is Panla Jen." A shirtless male in a long greying beard shook his tall crooked staff.

Some of the people surrounding him appeared to consider the possibility.

"What do you base that upon?" Crilen interceded in a strong voice.

The people turned around and made nothing of Crilen's alien appearance.

"I base it upon the miracle we witnessed today!" The male pointed his staff vindictively.

"Panla Jen disappeared." Crilen met his eyes. "And God seems to have had a hand in it. But she was just a person. She never claimed to be anything else."

"Blasphemer!" the male's voice howled as his beard whipped in the wind. "I quote from the scriptures!"

The crowd appeared uncertain of what to think.

"Well, then you'd better learn how to read," Crilen scowled. "Because if you're lying to these people on purpose, the real God is going to impale your blaspheming carcass on a flaming skewer in the bowels of Hell."

The bearded man extended his arms as if to speak, but nothing came out. He clumsily fumbled his staff to the ground.

Everyone started to laugh.

"People," Crilen addressed the gathering, "if you really wish to honor Panla Jen, don't hand yourselves over to liars and pretenders. Do as she said: Pick up the Text and read it. Learn the truth for yourselves, then you'll always know God's voice when you hear it. And you'll always be able to tell when someone else is trying trip you down the wrong path."

The people muttered and milled around for a moment, then they slowly separated and went their own ways. The shirtless male in the beard eyed Crilen warily, then quickly scurried into the dense thicket of demonstrators.

XXI.

Crilen turned to enter the Ponder Gulag gates. He wanted to inspect the upper walkway for himself to satisfy the scientific aspect of his curiosity. He considered flying there, but did not wish to unwittingly undermine the incredibly miraculous event with everyone's eyes already fixed upon the heavens. The last thing he wanted was to find himself worshipped as the flaming deity borne of the aftermath of Panla's disappearance. He had been in such a position before on other worlds and had no desire to spend months untangling the ideological chaos it would cause.

So he remained on foot. He took two steps forward but found a wall of people blocking his path. They stared directly at him as they smiled, then they all broke into polite applause. It did not make any sense. The sky started to darken. The walls of the Gulag started to fade. The reddish soil beneath his feet kicked up in a whirl of dust and turned metallic grey. The natural sky dissipated into mist and was replaced by a familiar procession of floating rocky debris with bright distant stars flickering in the background. The applauding people faded into craggy stone stalagmites. All except one thin adolescent male who eerily continued to clap his approval for no apparent reason.

A familiar pair of antlers sprung from the young male's scalp. His mouth sloped and extended forward into a snout. His arms thinned into tight sinewy spindles. And his torso twisted into a dry grey stem.

"Bravo." It's voice entered Crilen's head. "Congratulations. It is finished. For all of your cosmic insight and pyrogenic abilities, you've completely flunked your assignment. A masterful exhibition of unparalleled incompetence. With the exception of your raggedly unconsummated romantic foray, you changed virtually nothing. You couldn't have had less impact on this world's events had you been a drowning insect floating in the middle of the ocean. Well done."

"Under the circumstances, I can only say thank you." Crilen wore a wry expression. "This was quite a cosmic con job you rigged up. I'm proud that I let you down. This was never about saving a person's life. This was never about saving a planet from destruction. This was about a harvest of souls. Panla's Aschen~exol was the catalyst for the salvation of hundreds of generations before this world died a natural death. If Panla had put her faith in something or someone other than God, the miracle would never have happened. If she had fallen for me as I fell for her, billions of souls would never have found their way to Heaven."

It's black eyes receded into its head with a respectful contempt for its adversary.

"You are absolutely, positively, one thousand percent correct, I'm afraid," It responded.

"So fill in the blanks for me," Crilen requested. "Tell me why you couldn't alter the variables yourself...Rabbel."

It's long angular limbs dropped to its sides. Its snout twisted sideways before a tongue appeared and licked the outer rims of its mouth. Its dry torso inhaled, then exhaled a deep, airless sigh of mounting annoyance.

"Hmh." It responded, "not so ignorant, after all. Very good. You're right: I was Rabbel Mennis. A fleshly guise for my *au naturel*. I convinced an entire gullible planet that I was one of them. How did you know?"

"I didn't until you 'died'," Crilen confided. "In my travels, I've seen enough creatures and entities expire to recognize a fake. Your death wasn't convincing at all. The body looked dead, but there's always a disquieting aura when a soul is wrenched from the flesh. I didn't sense anything like that from Rabbel. I wasn't sure what I sensed, but it wasn't death. It was very odd, but I had to rescue Panla from Leesla's armed thugs, so there wasn't any time for me to beat my theory out of a dormant carcass."

It's antlered, snouted head slowly metamorphasized into the black bald likeness of Rabbel Mennis, but It's mischievously reflective smile wasn't Rabbel's at all.

"I came to this planet 4,000 years ago to Enable the souls of this world for my master's harvest," It relayed in the sound of Rabbel's strong voice. "The work wasn't new to me. I'd been Enabling for countless millennia on countless worlds, maneuvering the ids and egos of self-centered civilizations as far from God and Heaven as eternally possible. On this world, Rabbel Mennis was my indigenous cover.

"When I met Panla for the first time I was enraptured. I viewed her spiritual purity as the crowning jewel for my legacy of corruption. But a foolish thing happened to me on my way to the destruction of her soul: I fell in love with her. Up and down the centuries no mortal sentience had ever touched my heart. But she moved my spirit like nothing in the universe ever had. As I probed for her weaknesses, her godliness bled into mine. Because of her, I actually grew to hate my own life's work. I finally resolved to forsake my duty to the master. Like some lovesick adolescent, I was actually going to ask her go away with me, much like you did. I was going to offer her eternal beauty and the rapture of our romance for the rest of time.

"But she shot me. I couldn't believe it. From nowhere, an explosion ripped right through my Rabbel torso. Suddenly, there I stood with a big bleeding hole in my gut with my stupid childish dreams splattered all over the walls. The wound from the weapon didn't hurt nearly as much as her rejection did. My mind raced in a million directions, weighing a million options as I stood there, but I didn't know what to do next. So I just keeled over and 'died'. What was I going to do? Pretend she missed me with my entrails spilling out onto the floor? I couldn't very well sweep her off her feet right after she'd killed me, could I? And, somehow, I didn't think she was using murder as a way of getting me to prove how much I cared. So it was over. I was out.

"What choice did I have? I'd been rooked out of my own game. Everyone had seen me die. And who was going to suddenly listen to some odd alien if I'd revealed myself? An antlered alien would have sent everyone bolting back to cathedral for certain! So my only hope was that I'd already done enough damage to Panla and the Cathedral that the world's faith in God would crumble apart on its own. I could still harvest a billion souls for the master if everything fell just right."

"But everything went wrong after that," Crilen conjectured.

"Ha!" It's laugh was incongruous with Rabbel's stoic features. "You saw. You were there. It took Leesla all of twenty-six hours to completely demolish the organization I'd spent twinmoons building up. Meanwhile, Panla completely recouped her faith. In fact, the corrupting adversity only made her stronger. Still, I thought I had put her into a totally unworkable situation which would lead to her inevitable execution. With her death, the Cathedral would have imploded and the secular rise to power would have accelerated exponentially. Her hideously painful execution would have served notice to the vast majority that faith, atonement and all of that nonsense wouldn't save you from a very nasty, agonizing death. Mortals hate that sort of thing, you know.

"But then the bloody God of the universe stepped in and turned what would have been a very tasty demise into one of the grandest miracles this corner of the universe has witnessed since God resurrected himself on some misbegotten planet I can barely remember. Why me?

"Needless to say, my master, whom I'd betrayed, was not pleased with the results. What few souls we were able to harvest for our cause over the next several hundred years were barely worth all the effort. So in a hellish rage, he abandoned me to fix the problem. Undo my mess. So, for the past 4,000 years, I've been stuck here, recruiting transdimensional mercenaries to re-enter the continuum and correct my mistakes. Unfortunately, each and every one of them has failed miserably."

"Why use mercenaries?" Crilen wondered. "Why not go back yourself?"

"Simple physics, Lenny. I'm disappointed in you." It's antlers grew out of Rabbel's head and its snout gradually returned. "Across the continuum at that particular juncture in time, I'm Rabbel. I can't occupy two spaces within the same dimension without shredding the balance of space and causing a chain reac-

THE PLANET OF MORTAL WORSHIP

tion which would collapse the entire universe. We're in the business of souls. Genocide would be killing the bird that lays the eggs. So my stupid rendition of Rabbel the romantic dissident has to remain a constant."

"So, you're telling me that in 4,000 years, you couldn't find anyone who could've simply killed Panla before the miracle?" Crilen questioned.

"You are so dumb." It shook its antlers and rolled its black eyes. "Panla's premature death would have prevented the miracle, but we needed Panla's living hypocrisy to drive the masses to us. She couldn't die the death of a princess saint. She had to die the death of a swine. If she was going to die, she had to die with her hand in the till. Otherwise, she'd have simply become another religious martyr. And God's martyrs always yield far more salvation for the enemy than my master can stomach."

"So you needed her to be corrupted," Crilen concluded.

"Led astray." It raised a needle finger. "Astray is a more appropriate term. I have Rabbel's bloody carcass as evidence that corrupting her wasn't going to work. But she could be distracted. Reasoned out of the equation. Led astray by someone like yourself."

"But I failed, too." Crilen's brows furrowed.

"I know." It sighed. "In fact I can tell you exactly when you failed. During your fumbling foreplay you told her that you could only love a woman who loves God more than she could love any man. I should have pulled the plug right there. You see, that's the woman she's always been, and you had to remind her. Just when she might have fallen for you and followed you to the ends of the cosmos, you realigned her heart with Heaven and she never lost sight of it again."

Crilen reflected upon that moment in Panla's bedroom at Father Rouan's when they had almost consummated their lusts. Upon reflection, it was the fondest missed opportunity he could remember.

"I really thought you had her." It appeared to be reading his thoughts. "But you blew it. I'd have thought that a man as well-traveled as you knows that on most planets a female means yes when she says no."

Crilen frowned and tried to erase his private thoughts on the matter from It's telepathic intrusion.

"You told me she was in league with the devil," Crilen reflected. "You warned me not to fall in love with her."

"Because you didn't trust me." It revealed the underwoven pattern in its tapestry. "If I told you not to fall in love with her, I considered it very likely that you would."

Crilen paused upon the simplicity with which he had been manipulated. He had come within a lover's heartbeat of whisking Panla away, and pitching a billion souls into the fiery pits of Hell as a consequence.

"So what happened before me, the first time?" Crilen questioned. "Who protected her originally?"

It conjured a large sphere in its palm and a dark female face appeared at the center of it.

"Moll." It answered simply. "Moll Shen was frightfully tenacious. You should have seen her and Leesla go at it. Leesla actually had a thing for her, but Moll was nearly as ridiculously obtuse about God as Panla. Personally, I hated the woman. She was always whispering the truth about me in Panla's ear. I'm reasonably sure it was she who got Panla to shoot me the first time. If there's been one sliver of satisfaction I've enjoyed over the past 4,000 years, it's been repeatedly causing Moll to get carted off to a dark sadistic dungeon in the bowels of the Ponder Gulag so that I could replace her with my succession of ineffectual mercenaries."

"For all the good it's done," Crilen countered.

"For all the good, indeed." It's expression sobered.

"So what became of everyone else?" Crilen wondered. "What became of Yolo Pigue, the Accommodant and all the others?"

"Temporally or eternally?" It's brows lifted.

"Temporally." Crilen nodded.

"Well, eventually, they all died." It tilted its antlers.

"Eventually, everyone dies." Crilen's brow wrinkled. "You know what I meant."

With a stomp of its foot, the asteroid floor cracked open and a 10 meter wide monitor emerged from the ground.

"Hmm, let's see what's on." It waited for the picture to come into focus. "Destroyed planets get the worst reception."

The monitor whistled and shrieked as horizontal lines darted from left to right and right to left like battling laser lights. Finally a picture formed. The moving portrait was vaguely familiar.

"Feebie?" Crilen recognized the strawberry-orange hair under a black toque instructing a group of impoverished adolescents in ragged clothing.

"Feebie," It confirmed. "The ennobled betrayer of our lady love. After the miracle she tried to rejoin the new Cathedral, only the media still painted her as a traitor to Panla. With Panla's popularity higher than ever, she became the scourge of all that was considered holy. So she eventually left and started a Text-based missionary cathedral in the blighted southwest. She was murdered by thieves before they could finish building it, but it became the hub for a series of missionary cathedrals throughout the impoverished south. Over time, the media finally stopped bludgeoning her reputation. Her birthday became a legal south-western holiday."

The monitor screen skipped as if the channels were rotating in a slot machine. Finally, the frame stopped on a short stocky older male and a young woman appearing to bid one another *adieu*.

"Genna and Mr. Linnfeld." Crilen knew them immediately.

"The girl Genna did return to the new Cathedral and taught Text for the next sixty twinmoons," It reviewed. "Mr. Linnfeld retired from attendant work and bought himself a vineyard."

The leering pallid face of an unkempt male with a scraggly thin beard and wild hair appeared.

"Durn." Crilen frowned.

"Acquitted for the murder of the Lord Regent," It snickered. "His lawbooker, Conn Cockorn, systematically discredited seventy-three eyewitnesses to the assassination because none of them could definitively identify the hand weapon he 'allegedly' used. Ironically, he would have lived longer in prison. He died two twinmoons later in a bar fight over a prostitute. And this was my lieutenant. No wonder the Break was destined to fail."

A blood-spattered image of Durn writhing on a dirty barroom floor, gurgling his last breath melted into the robed, jewel-toqued image of the former Holy Inquisitor.

"Behold, the author of the New Text," It offered carelessly. "He ended the lineage of Deliverers and retitled himself the first Servant of the Word. The New Text, combined with the original Text, contained the public biography of Panla Jen, her final speech, and a complete recounting of her Aschen~exol. Of course he scrawls several hundred pages of his own 'divinely inspired' interpretations of what happened and even confessed his role in the Lord Regent's murder. The damned thing would have been a bestseller, only he instructed the Cathedral to give them away for free. He died destitute and revered. In the end, the hundreds of millions of souls he shepherded away from us was absolutely devastating."

A blizzard of multi-colored confetti burst from the monitor screen amidst a buzz of party horns. As the flakes of fluttering paper settled onto the asteroid surface, a smiling, waving visual of the Accommodant appeared with his arm neatly curled around the lean, expensively accoutered torso of a buxom young female half his age.

Crilen's expression contorted bitterly.

"Now him, I like." It folded its arms and tilted its head.

"What became of him?" Crilen hoped for a dark disturbing demise.

"He was re-elected, of course." It's furry brows rose in amusement. "Accommodant Klin Tem rode the religious resurgence like a blood worm rides the ass of a stallion. For his re-election campaign, he raided the cache of his wife's sermons and preached up one side of the planet and down the other. He declared himself living proof of God's power to cleanse a sinful soul, and the people believed him. He was so charismatic that he crushed his election opponent, a former Cathedral Regent, in public debates specifically targeted toward the Text. Morally miscarried? No question. A debauched, conniving political serpent? Proudly. Completely devoid of any ethical center? How could there be room for ethics at his center when power and lust already resided there? But let us speak of the mastery of craft. Let us speak of genius. Genius transcends the limited definitions of good or evil. And this gentleman was certainly a genius."

"So the people actually elected him again?" Crilen fretted. "When will the creatures of this universe stop empowering the lowest element of our societies with positions of leadership?"

"The first few twinmoons of his second term were outwardly exemplary," It continued. "He even commissioned a billion-coin library and Cathedral to be dedicated in Panla Jen's name. But eventually, a gaggle of jilted concubines joined forces against him and revealed to the media all of the things, figuratively, if not literally, he had done after his alleged conversion to faith. The public outrage over his indulgences in all manner of sexual perversions with females he employed forced the parliament to call for his resignation."

"So he was ruined," Crilen concluded.

"Hardly," It smirked. "In the undertow of morality lies the briny appeal of deviltry. He was forced to resign, but this only allowed him to devote one-hundred percent of his time to his lifelong avocation: the sensual arts. He sold his salacious memoirs for a small fortune. And he died at an overripe old age in the position he most enjoyed. His reputation was sullied by scandal, but he was one of those rare scoundrels who could brandish depravity like a diamond crown and be admired for it."

"It doesn't seem fair," Crilen observed. "People like him aren't forced to answer for the wrongs that they do. They get to die in their sleep surrounded by all the spoils of a lifetime of carnal lies and deceit. They get to..."

"Ah, ah!" It interrupted with a raised finger. "As I said before, we liked him. More to the point...we have him."

Crilen paused and fixated upon the nightmarish thought. He had only seen glimpses of the true raging inferno of Hell where souls bore eternal torment for their chosen ignorance and departure from the love of He who created all things. A perverse satisfaction tickled his sense of justice. But an overriding sorrow tainted any emotions of triumph. A lost soul, even the most rotten unrepentant soul, represents a loss to the power of creation.

Unfortunately, Crilen lamented, a majority of living creatures fail to conceive of a destiny for their immortal souls until the hour is at hand. In life, they care only for their secular salvation: That their transgressions are never revealed to the world; that their reputations remain intact. They never consider that God, the Lord of all things, sees all, knows all, and renders judgment irrespective of meaningless public opinion or earthly perceptions. He unerringly measures the raw, naked, irrefutable truth which colors every sentient immortal soul in the universe. A being may live a hundred years of bliss in the flesh, but what does a fleeting joy so temporal measure when the soul faces eternal damnation in the searing fires of perdition?

"Don't look so glum," It teased. "We won the skirmish. We lost the war. That's why I'm still here.

"But of course, there's this fellow."

It tossed a fistful of iron sand at the monitor and the screen faded into a portrait of a slightly pudgy, disheveled old man, sitting on a park bench with a crumpled hat pushed unevenly over his head. He appeared to be muttering to himself as he reached into a white sack and tossed out crumbs to a gathering of small primate creatures and a few fluttering birds. The old man broke into a mad chuckle as he repeatedly mumbled "gone" to his animal audience.

"I'm sorry, I don't recognize this one." Crilen concentrated on the image.

"A pity." It's snout twisted into a smirk. "Few did at the very end. But if you take a much closer look…"

The view cropped inward on the man's face.

"…you might just recognize the inimitable Yolo Pigue."

Crilen's jaw dropped. He slowly walked to the monitor and tried to touch the screen.

"It's called the public humiliation diet," It commented. "Most effective with worldly, egomaniacal atheist dictators of commerce when faced with supernatural anomalies they can't accept. Worry does wonders for the figure, doesn't it?"

Crilen could only stare in amazement. The man in the loose sloppy clothes sitting on the park bench must have been one-third Yolo's girth.

"After Panla's disappearance, Yolo Pigue broke one of his cardinal rules," It continued. "Rather than manipulate the truth, he declared war on it. The entire planet witnessed a miracle, but Yolo continued to insist that it was a hoax or a conspiracy or some other secular plot to entrap the world in a delusional union with a God that didn't exist. He ordered his staff to use every resource at their disposal to discredit Panla's Aschen~exol. So they quit. Mr. Nil bolted his master's sinking ship like the rat that he was. Even Yara Pique, Yolo's niece, joined RATRAG and became its leading anchor. Eventually, Yolo launched a series of prime-time programs which he hosted himself. Every week he offered a new theory to explain Panla Jen's 'escape'. Each hypothesis waned pitiably less plausible than the one before it. He became a laughing stock as viewership plummeted by the millions.

"Finally, he announced a ten-part series where he would travel to the remotest corners of the world and connect the dots leading to Panla Jen's secret hiding place. The world howled as they watched this desperate hobbling old fool huff and puff and wheeze his way around the globe, climbing mountains, stumbling through riverbeds, camping in blizzards, wading through tar bogs, caravanning across deserts, negotiating with remote farmers, jiving with urban street hustlers…chasing a mysterious hooded figure purported to be Panla Jen herself. The comedic conclusion climaxed with a live broadcast of Yolo arguing in an empty underground cave with an angry foul-mouthed young actress, posing as Panla Jen, demanding to be paid her travel expenses. That was the end of the empire.

"Draxford Wyel of the Citadel Group initiated a hostile takeover of Yolo's asset-depleted Yolo Media Enterprises and it was renamed the Citadel News Network. Because Yolo had been a friend, Wyel waited an entire month before he jettisoned Yolo from his own company with the usual Citadel concrete parachute severance package. Yolo converted his mansion into a gaudy bed & breakfast to sustain his remaining property. He was rarely seen or recognized in public henceforth. Although one disturbing evening at the B&B, frightened guests found him standing naked on his patio cursing the stars and mumbling "gone" over and over again. Six people attended his funeral That was that."

The monitor went blank and collapsed into a heap of iron sand.

"Four thousand years ago." Crilen considered, "Nothing left but you to recall that this world ever existed."

"So it would seem." It tilted its antlers and gestured resignedly. "But you have overlooked something. Something I'm afraid you'll like."

It gestured in a circular motion and Crilen felt the tingling of electricity tickle his skin. The asteroid belt disappeared before his eyes. Slowly, another landscape materialized all around him.

The sky was a rich navy blue with islands of golden clouds drifting lazily across the horizon. He stood in a lush green grassy field with wild flowers blossoming over a series of hills that rolled into the distance. He turned slowly until he was surprised by the large square base of a mammoth marble statue. The subject was a six-tentacled female which soared a hundred meters into the sky. Crilen read the inscription, then backed away to get a wider view of it. When he finally realized who it was, he gasped.

"I thought you'd like it," It's voice was audible for the first time. "Welcome to the fourth planet in this system. The inhabitants of the third planet were religious, but they weren't complete idiots. Like you, they eventually figured out that the twinmoons were going to destroy their planet, so they packed up their transports and moved here. Thanks to a bit of terraforming and strategically placed atmospheric reactors, this world has become more of a jewel than the one they left behind."

"This is Panla?" Crilen gazed upward at the swirling black and white edifice. "It looks nothing like her. Why the tentacles?"

"This is actually a very strong likeness," It commented. "And the tentacles are an indigenous trait to these beings. As I said before, you saw her as you chose to see her: a likeness of your wife. Your cognitive senses used your own world as the point of interpretation for how these people appeared to you. You should see how the sex organs really look on this world. Awfully impressive."

"She never wanted a statue." Crilen shook his head.

"Don't worry," It snickered. "There are thousands more, all shapes, sizes and colors."

The giant statue of Panla depicted her as she appeared at her trial, wearing the high-collared dress with the winding vines scrolling up from the hem. In her top tentacles was the giant volume of the Text she had carried with her that day. Her chin was lifted slightly with her eyes raised to the heavens.

The inscription at the base of the statue read:

PANLA JEN
ASCHEN~EXOL
055719
LOVE, GRACE, FORGIVENESS, REDEMPTION
THE WORD OF OUR LORD RESTORED

"Why statues?" Crilen lamented. "Idols. Sentient creatures always insist upon the things that wind up taking them farther and farther away from the faith they should have in the things they can't see."

"Mortal worship," It advised. "You can always expect the worship of mortals to worship mortality. In fact, my master counts on it."

"So there'll be a harvest for your master on this planet?" Crilen questioned.

"Four thousand years and they're still entrenched Maybe we should sabotage the economy." It sighed. "That usually works. Unfortunately, we don't expect their current population to suit our needs any time soon. Of course time is something we have plenty of. An eternity, in fact. We'll see. In the meantime, my charge is to undo the damage at its root. So I'll continue to solicit mercenaries such as yourself in the interim."

"Do you honestly think you'll ever get Panla to turn?" Crilen asked.

It's antlers quivered slightly. It looked down and away with an almost vulnerable glimmer of humanity.

"It's always good to see her again," It reflected. "It hurts, but somehow, it's always good to see her again, wearing that stupid ponytail."

Crilen understood.

"So you should be off." It gathered itself. "You've fouled up my world. Surely there must be other worlds in the universe that require your bungling bonfire brand of heroism."

Crilen looked up at the statue one last time.

"You're right." He admired her, tentacles and all. "But one last question. The people's faces, the colors. What did they mean? Black, white…it was virtually random. And no one seemed to care what color I was even when my security guise was stripped away."

It shook its head admonishingly and waggled a finger.

"Nothing," It answered solemnly. "Nothing at all. The devil's ruse. On some failed planets, beings have attempted to ascribe a value to their fellow creatures according to the color of their coat or flesh. On particularly gullible worlds it leads to all manner of luscious hate, oppression and discord. The souls come to Hell by the bushel from those worlds. All because of random pigmentation. Unfortunately, the people of this planet remained completely neutral. To them, the only color that mattered was the color of a person's soul. In the end, only God knows for sure. Alas, if you'd played your hands according to the peoples' colors, you'd have missed the entire point even worse than you did."

A slight smile lifted Crilen's features as his body immersed itself in flames. He slowly ascended parallel to Panla's statue until he reached her head. He hovered for a moment, wondering where he would travel next. He looked into Panla's sculpted gaze and followed her eyes heavenward.

"Statues." Crilen chided himself. "Idols. Mortal worship."

In an explosion of fire and light, he rocketed up through the planet's atmosphere. For no rational reason, Crilen followed the trajectory of Panla's gaze as far into the cosmos as it would guide him.

EPILOGUE

▼

"So what are we going to name him?" Crilen asked as they watched the light of the setting sun melt into the calm distant waves of the ocean.

"Him?" Aami lifted her head from his bare chest. "Him? What makes you so sure that him won't be a her?"

"Because I'm the kind of he who doesn't have a she." Crilen tickled the fine hairs on the back of his wife's long neck.

"And what kind of he is that?" Aami playfully wedged her knee uncomfortably into his groin.

"The kind of he that's me." He pinched and twisted the flesh on her ribcage.

"Ouch!" Aami pushed away from him and jumped to her feet. "That's going to leave a bruise!"

"Everything leaves a bruise." Crilen chuckled as he propped up his head on a rolled-up beach towel.

"You think that's funny?" She inspected her bare side below her halter with annoyance.

"In a few months you'll be so bloated and fat, bruises will be the least of your problems." he teased her.

Crilen broke into steady laughter as the pouting expression on his wife's face deepened. All was well in his private little world until a torrent of sand flew into his eyes, nose and mouth. Aami kicked waves of sand onto her husband until the laughter turned to surrender.

"Whoa, whoa, whoa!" Crilen held up his hands to shield his eyes.

"Better get used to it." Aami started to laugh now. "Your fat, bloated, pregnant wife is going to be pretty damn moody over the next several months. One day it may be sand in the face. The next day it may be your dinner dumped on your head. Or maybe I'll just show up at the lab on a whim and scream at you in front of your staff for no particular reason. And there'll be lots of crying, you can count on that. And I love how skilled you are at handling tears. Like a dumb zombie mime who's forgotten his routine, gesturing helplessly in the middle of the floor without a clue. I'm looking forward to that. Aren't you? After all, we will be in this together. There's no reason we can't share all the fat, bloated fun."

"Okay, okay," Crilen pleaded for a truce as he spit sand from his mouth and raked the grains from his eyes. "You're not even showing yet. And when you do, I'm sure you'll still be beautiful."

"Oh?" Aami folded her arms as her large brown eyes sparkled with more mischief. "And what if I'm not beautiful? What if I turn into a raging hog covered in spider veins and festering rashes? Will you still love me then? Or should I call our attorney now?"

Caked in sand, barely able to see and the inside of his mouth tasting like the gritty stairs of a seaside dock, Crilen dreaded trying to handle an outwardly light-hearted question from his wife when her intent was heavily mined with marital munitions.

Slowly, he stood. He tried to brush the sand from his arms and chest but it clung to his flesh and fingers. He walked toward her with a gentle hand extended. She looked down and turned away from him.

"Don't touch me. You're filthy." She kept her arms folded.

He reached around her with both arms and she did not protest. He caressed the side of her head with the bottom of his chin as he had done thousands of times before. Instinctively, she took hold of his hands and held them around her bare waist as she leaned her head back against his shoulder. Together they stood silently for the next several minutes as they watched the final remnants of sunlight disappear into the watery horizon.

"I'm filthy, but I'm glad you don't mind." His heavy voice vibrated through her body.

"That's because I love you, silly man," she responded. "No matter how or where or what you are, I'll always love you."

Crilen found her words oddly familiar, but this evening they carried a far richer meaning than all the other times she had spoken them.

"That's good to know." He sighed and held her tightly. "And you need to know that I will always love you...pregnant, fat, covered with lesions and sores..."

She started to giggle.

"…open wounds, festering diseases, no arms, no legs…"

"Okay." She tried to interrupt him.

"…cross-eyed, no teeth…"

"Okay, stop." She laughed as he held her.

"Forever, Aami." His voice lapsed into seriousness. "I will love the wife with whom I have been so blessed forever."

She turned in his arms, slipped her hands around his neck and kissed him. Her body was warm and soft against his flesh as her familiar scent roused his senses.

"Sir?"

Crilen heard a voice he recognized, but wondered who had come so far down the beach to interrupt their romantic solitude. He tried to ignore it.

"Sir?" the voice repeated respectfully.

A new smell wafted over the scent of his wife. A burning hellish sulfuric smell. Distant voices echoed over the faint sounds of explosions.

"Sir?" A hand touched his shoulder.

Aami faded from his grasp.

Crilen jerked awake in the damp mud of a dusklit battlefield. Standing over him was Basar, the reptilian freedom commander who had recruited Crilen's help to liberate his world from the grips of a demagogic dictatorship.

"Sorry to wake you, sir." Basar was urgently apologetic. "Our people have prayed. The scripture has been read. We're ready to go."

Crilen stood and looked over the dark, blood-soaked hill strewn with freshly dismembered reptilian torsos, limbs, severed heads and exposed organs. Across the valley, he witnessed a dense sea of the enemy's chanting, torchlit army marching on their position. As far as he could see to the horizon, their navy leather-clad soldiers covered kilometers of rolling hills. Their thunderous, inexorable march upon the land was daunting. The snap of their sharp gnashing teeth and their thrashing tails was frightening. The large glistening metallic firearms they clutched in their claws promised a swift and merciless extermination of anyone who opposed them.

Their scarlet banners bore the likeness of their crowned emperor with the emblazoned words "Saahd is God" in black block letters.

Crilen looked over his shoulder at the worn and depleted forces of the rebellion. There was fear in some of their reptilian eyes. Resignation in others. But all of them held up their heads and their weapons as if no other choice but to engage this vile enemy were possible.

"This appears as though it's going to be very difficult." Basar sounded pessimistic. "I'm sorry to have drawn you into this."

Crilen's eyes flashed like crimson coals as he knowingly smiled with the confidence of experience.

"No." He patted Basar on the shoulder. "This one is going to be easy. Difficult…is a lot more complicated than this. Trust me."

Crilen stepped back and his entire body burst into bright golden flames.

Then he spoke to the rebel force:

"Tomorrow, your world will be yours again. Always remember that there is no greater glory in this universe than for your souls to be what you know God has willed them to become. Never lose sight of that."

The ground exploded beneath Crilen's feet. His body rocketed up over the valley, then screamed down into the heart of the Emperor's army with the fiery interstellar force of an exploding star. The planet shook as the valley erupted into a massive fiery cauldron of death and destruction.

Hope and truth followed hard upon.

About the Author

Donald Templeman is the author of *The Last Champion of Earth,* a science fiction novel which examines a future Earth whose hollow paradise falters under humanity's lost relationship with God. Mr. Templeman is a student of Christianity who also enjoys science fiction, fantasy and horror. His writing incorporates all of these elements to challenge his readers to challenge themselves.

0-595-32512-2